Victoria Routledge was formerly an editor in a London publishing house and now writes full time as a novelist and journalist. She was born in the Lake District and now lives in London. *Kiss Him Goodbye* is her second novel.

Praise for her first novel *Friends Like These*:

'*Friends Like These* is utterly unputdownable. Anyone who's ever blindly wanted their college mates to approve of them, without knowing exactly *why*, will love this book. I adored it'

Cathy Kelly, author of *She's The One*

'A confident new writer with a gift for sparky, witty dialogue and characters with real emotions'

Daily Mirror

'An all too realistic lesson in the importance of knowing your enemies'

Company

'A very sparky debut'

Isabel Wolff, author of *The Trials of Tiffany Trott*

D0226657

Also by Victoria Routledge

FRIENDS LIKE THESE

kiss him goodbye

VICTORIA ROUTLEDGE

WARNER BOOKS

A *Warner* Book

First published in Great Britain
by Warner Books in 2000

Copyright © Victoria Routledge 2000

The moral right of the author has been asserted.

A CIP catalogue record for this book
is available from the British Library.

ISBN 0 7515 2969 9

Typeset in Berkeley by M Rules
Printed and bound in Great Britain by Clays Ltd, St Ives plc

Warner Books
A Division of
Little, Brown and Company (UK)
Brettenham House
Lancaster Place
London WC2E 7EN

acknowledgements

Before anyone reads a single word of this, it goes without saying that all the characters in this book are completely made-up and fictional. Completely. Especially the publishers. Honestly, I wouldn't dare. Not when everyone at Little, Brown and Headline have been so nice to me.

I would, though, like to thank David, Hugo, Harry, PierPaolo, Bill and Ingo for all the best throwaway lines (and for drawing my attention to them), my sister Alex for outlining some very convincing reasons not to live in London, and Shona for her expert support, both on the technical editorial side and the sympathetic coffee side.

Also thanks to Daryl, for chasing the coach through North London and looking after me so well at the other end. You were right all along.

And of course, thank you to James Hale, Imogen Taylor, Cassie Chadderton, Emma Gibb, Anna Telfer, and my fantastic parents – the best a girl could wish for.

For Dillon, for everything

chapter one

'. . . and I've said it more than once, I know, but I'll say it again, it was that cold last May, my Arthur's . . .' the lips pursed momentarily, '*haemorrhoids* . . . ended up playing merry Ada with my routine . . .'

Kate murmured polite surprise and shut her eyes, allowing her eyeballs to roll unseen towards the ceiling. The old lady carried on droning in time to the coach's engine, on the same note as she had been since roughly three miles out of Stratford-upon-Avon. It was almost impossible to tell where she was taking breaths.

'. . . do you?'

Kate's eyes snapped open and she felt inexplicably ashamed of herself. Without looking, she could feel a penetrating Old Lady stare drilling into her left cheek. What was the logical train of thought from piles? 'Oh, well . . .' She hazarded a guess. 'No?'

Ker-ching! The old lady's hands folded in triumph. 'Exactly what I said, not that you would know it from the response I got . . .'

Kate settled back into courteous semi-consciousness. The final, definitive sign of adulthood was that of feeling morally obliged to talk to old ladies on long journeys.

Not that it had always been like this. Kate's abiding childhood memory was of her mother standing over her in

Birmingham railway station, arming her with a 10p piece for the phone and a sheet of Basildon Bond paper with her name and address printed on it, drilling home the message, 'And *don't* talk to *people* you don't *know*!' with anxious prods to the shoulder. Brownie trips, school excursions to ice-rinks and museums, right up to Duke of Edinburgh Award advanced camping, had been as one to Kate's mother: risky jaunts haunted by potential child abductors and mutilators.

Not one of nature's sunbeams at the best of times, and certainly not a child to doubt the warnings of 'Charlie Says . . .', the Prophet Cat of Doom on ITV, Kate would no sooner have talked to a stranger than she would have splashed the grouting on the side of the bath, which apparently resulted in instant earthworm infestations. Death and creepy-crawlies had hovered constantly on the periphery of the Craig nursery.

But, suddenly, at the age of eighteen, it had all changed. Despatched to Durham University in October with a broad selection of dire warnings about personal safety, Kate had returned home in December with a free Student Union rape alarm and a freshly minted 'Reclaim the Night' attitude, only to be greeted at the door by, 'Did you meet anyone nice on the train, dear?'

To Kate's slack-jawed disbelief, Mrs Craig, now mysteriously enrolled for a series of GCSE night classes in subjects she had firmly steered Kate away from five years previously, then proceeded to tell her off for not being more amiable. That was the beginning of the end.

There had been another seventeen trips back and forth to Durham since – the final triumphant homecoming only two months ago – and Kate had never spoken to any of her fellow passengers. And she certainly wasn't going to start now on National Express coaches, despite her mother's parting comments about Trevor Howard and Celia Johnson.

Two hours into the journey and still a full Tesco carrier bag of provisions untouched. Certain traits of her mother's old personality were proving hard to shake off, and her packed lunches had always been on a biblical scale. Kate tried not to rustle the tightly wrapped greaseproof paper of the sandwich section.

For the best part of the two hours the old lady rammed into the seat next to her had been keeping up a relentless monologue on the subject of her son-in-law's suspiciously bungled attempt to fit gas central heating to their bungalow. Kate, trapped by the window, wedged in by two string bags full of knitting, paperback books and old copies of *Take a Break*, could only listen.

'. . . not that I would *want* to go to Jamaica, not when you see all these programmes on the television, but that's not the point, is— Ooooh, sandwiches, how lovely.'

Kate turned as much of her shoulder as the bags would allow. Since she had last looked round the old lady had removed her angora hat for ease of expression and there was a distinctive red rim around her forehead. She looked not unlike Mark Knopfler in full 'rockin' headband' mode.

'Would you like a sandwich, Mrs . . .?'

'Mrs Brown, dear. Don't mind if I do!' said the old lady, peering into the bag like a sparrow on the edge of a litter bin.

Oh, God, thought Kate, suddenly remembering the earlier gummy grin, now I have to listen to her eat it.

Kate hadn't had very high hopes for this trip from the beginning. Her mother had been nagging her for the past year to get something organised for the summer, preferably job-related and definitely not home-based. Mrs Craig now had more GCSEs than Kate did herself, and she suspected her mother was working up to something more dramatic. Requiring an empty house.

But whereas Kate had once protested hotly that wild horses wouldn't drag her to London, she realised now that she should have amended that to wild horses and tall blond men wearing cricket jumpers. Obviously she would have kept quiet about the cricket jumper. Her brother Mike, a fund manager in the City, was ruthless about information like that. Mike – and the prospect of sleeping on his marital floor in Clapham – being another reason she hadn't exactly been rushing down the M1. Mike had never been the model big brother: his specialities included hiding £500 notes under the board during *Monopoly*, changing the home address on Kate's emergency piece of Basildon Bond and, most terrifying of all, repeatedly telling her she was adopted.

Kate's much-anticipated moment of retaliation had finally presented itself on Mike's wedding day the previous year, on which she had trailed up the aisle in pistachio satin behind his long-suffering girlfriend Laura. Yet, on hearing Kate trot out all these stories at the reception – with an appropriate look of sisterly forgiveness at the ready should their mother appear – Laura, now incredibly Mike's wife, had just swatted him playfully with her tiny, very expensive hand-tied bouquet, and cooed, 'Oh, you! I hope our children aren't so naughty!' before flouncing off to reorganise the champagne pyramid. Kate never had understood why Laura had married Mike when her vocation was so clearly reorganising the EU into manageable divisions, colour-coded in pastel shades, and Mike's centred largely on flicking dry-roasted peanuts into his mouth straight from the packet.

So although Mike had lived in Clapham since he graduated, Kate hadn't felt compelled to overcome her instinctive loathing of London in order to visit him in his adopted city. There was something about the place that made her shy away: whether it was the size of the city, or the complexity of the Underground, or the potential for getting lost or mugged or eating something unhygienic, or the unfriendliness of the people. Kate couldn't put her finger on it. But it probably began with 'un-'.

And despite having a boyfriend who she knew lived in a big flat in Chelsea, she had avoided going to London – just – for the last two college vacations. Fortunately Giles liked long drives. *Un*fortunately he also spent his vacations perfecting his Euro-friendly CV in various far-flung Euro-states, while Kate chewed her nails in frustration, cursing herself for not trying harder at German GCSE.

But she thought she would quite happily never have gone to London at all, or at least would have put it off for a bit longer, if Giles hadn't invited her in his irresistible way to spend a week alone with him in Chelsea while his parents were in the Galápagos Islands.

Fair dos – she had been washing his back at the time (Kate shivered with pleasure as she summoned up the image – one of her favourites). And concentrating more on the exquisite muscles of his shoulders, built up subtly with year-round tennis practice at the Hurlingham Club, than on what he was actually saying. Giles had the sexiest, poshest voice Kate had ever heard outside the films of Merchant Ivory and she was quite happy to listen to it wander like liquid chocolate around such relatively uninteresting topics as Keynes' theories of economy and the fluctuating values of gold reserves, while she gave his flat stomach and long legs the more immediate attention they deserved. By the time he slipped a quick visit to London after term finished into the conversation, Kate had been in a trance-like state of suspended lust and would have agreed to a trial for the England cricket team.

She shut her eyes and concentrated on his face again. Even after twelve months Kate felt like giggling when she described Giles as her boyfriend. He was bright, casually wealthy, didn't own a single pair of embarrassing shoes, and was criminally gorgeous. What he was doing with the likes of her was beyond Kate's powers of logical reason, but she was deeply grateful for it, whatever it was. When she was with him, Kate felt as though she could take on anything and anyone, because she was standing next to the First Prize; all tanned, blond, sweet-smelling six feet of him. However, lingering thoughts of Giles's expensively tanned bits were all too quickly dispelled by the monologue which had started up again in her left ear.

'You not eating these, dear? Skinny girl like you wants some feeding up. I mean, look, you can see the bones in your elbow . . .'

Too right you can see the bones in my elbow, madam. Can you imagine the lengths I have gone to to satisfy my dangerously attractive boyfriend's preference for skinny girls? thought Kate. She didn't know much about the Naicer Gels she was up against in Giles's affections, not having ever skiied or reeled in her life, but Giles had sarcastically pointed out his sister Selina in the party pages of *Tatler*, and the combined weight of her and the two identikit blondes she was with looked to Kate to be about seven stones (including the wrappings). That, and the way Giles kept buying her very small, very silky underwear, meant that she could only ever eat mayonnaise sandwiches in the holidays. But it was worth it. Without knowing she was doing it, Kate smiled at her reflection in the window.

'Where do you get off?' Mrs Brown continued.

You tell me, thought Kate, but heard her polite voice reply, 'London.' It sounded quite sophisticated when it was just part of conversation, not a reality, she thought detachedly. There was a stray knitting needle from Mrs Brown's exploded net bag stuck through the webbing of her rucksack and Kate wondered which piece of glamorous underwear it was ruining.

'Are you going to see a young man?'

'Er, yes.' The bus turned a sharp corner and a dog-eared paperback skidded out of the bag and slid down behind Kate's seat. She was rammed in too tightly to retrieve it.

'What's he called?'

Kate always wished she could fib spontaneously in these situations. Concentrate on pretending to be one of her friends so all the answers came out straight, instead of grudgingly revealing bits of her own life so inconsistently that she ended up looking like a compulsive liar.

'Um, Bob.'

Why had she said that? No one under the age of forty was called Bob.

'Oooh, that's nice, my brother-in-law's called that. Is he a Robert or a Bob?'

Is she just playing me along? thought Kate, panicking. Does she realise that I'm lying and is trying to catch me out?

'Well, I call him Rob.' She blushed deeply. Actually I call him Giles.

'Lovely, dear. Oooh, look where we are. Well, I'll be getting my things together.'

Thank God, thought Kate. She wondered where they actually were. The view out of her window had been pretty much the same for the past hour.

'Actually,' she offered, suddenly a bit nervous in the face of London racing up the motorway to meet them, 'I'm not actually going all the way to London. I'm getting off at, um, early – my boyfriend's, um, Rob's meeting me for a day out and then he's taking me home.'

'Oooh, to meet his parents, I hope?' said Mrs Brown, her eyes narrowing in Old Woman Interrogation mode.

No, to frolic with wild abandon in his glamorous American mother's conversation pit while she's sunning herself on a beach-bound turtle.

'Um, yes. Sort of. I've not been to London much before and he's sort of . . . breaking me in . . . gently, if you know what I mean,' added Kate.

It had sounded, when Giles suggested it over the phone, a wonderful idea: to have a Pleasant Day Out, walking romantically round the grounds of some stately home well outside London, surrounded by enough green stuff to convince her that she was almost still at home, then a very quick blindfold trip in the plush interior of Giles's mum's car, right up to the door of the lovely flat in Chelsea. A spot of romantic threshold manoeuvring, supper and bed. Very early bed.

No panicking on a crowded Tube platform, no being transported unwittingly to Romford on a red bus, no getting trapped in a pack of Japanese tourists and swept away screaming to Madame Tussaud's.

Or at least that was the idea.

Giles had suggested a day out at Kenwood (Mrs Craig had oohed and aahed, supplied her with five facts about the history of the place, which Kate faintly remembered from her own history notes, and then pointed out that it wasn't National Trust so there was no point in her lending Kate the family membership card). He had told her to get off at Hanger Lane, where the bus definitely stopped, according to him. He had even written it down for her. He would bring a picnic, ice-creams, whatever she wanted: all she had to do was turn up.

Kate looked anxiously at her watch, and then at the timetable. She bit the corner off a salad sandwich nervously. She felt her throat close up.

'Aaaah, I expect you can't wait to see him, can you?' croaked a voice in her ear.

'Um, no, I can't,' agreed Kate, who had decided on a politeness compromise of replying minimally but staring out of the window.

Before she could comment further, the bus drew to a halt and with some difficulty the old lady hauled herself out of her seat, dropping her battered paperback book as she went.

Kate rose awkwardly to help with the bags on the floor and a cascade of unseen – and now largely molten – Rolos flowed from her lap. She looked down at her jeans with distress. In a spontaneous lie, she'd once told Giles she never ate chocolate and he'd looked so impressed Kate would subsequently have died rather than admit she was dependent on Giant Smarties. It didn't help that he boasted about her chocolate superiority to his mates at college, preventing her from ever having a Twix in the bar again, and worst of all, after her long lonely summer while he was in Zürich, all she got from the international Capital of Chocolate was a stupid fluffy St Bernard dog – because what would she want with a foot-long bar of Toblerone, after all?

And now the evidence to the contrary was all over her jeans. And they weren't even her Rolos!

'Oh, dear. You want to put those in the fridge and then go at them with an ice-cube,' observed the Rolos' owner over her shoulder as she shuffled down the aisle, laden with bags. She looked like a series winner on a WI Bring and Buy version of 'Double or Drop' and was already waving perkily through the window to someone.

'Um, thanks,' mumbled Kate. They were her best pair. Her prized size eight jeans that she suspected in her heart were really a mislabelled size ten. How she loved to leave them thrown carelessly over a chair, advertising her temporary triumph over the hereditary Craig child-bearing hips!

With a lurch, the coach pulled away and Kate sank back into her seat miserably. How had the chocolate got on to her lap? The packet must have been on the seat when she got on and been incubating underneath her since Birmingham. No wonder she'd felt so restless – and she'd thought all coaches had rods down the side to stop you getting too comfortable.

Mrs Brown was waving energetically at her from the pavement and Kate managed a smile and a token flap of her hand. She couldn't even assert herself with old women.

There was a spare pair of jeans in the travel bag above the seats, amongst the many permutations of skimpy clothing she'd brought with her. Why not go for the full school coach trip experience and try to change out of a pair of trousers without mooning at passing motorists?

Kate hauled down the bag, found her Walkman and wedged herself back into the seat with her knees up against the seat in front, knowing full well that after half an hour pins and needles would set in with a vengeance. The sun was very hot against the window. She shut her eyes and turned the Walkman up so she could hear the music over the engine noise – which was dangerously loud, she knew, but Kenickie temporarily drowned out small voices in her head, the result of panicking about the bigger picture suddenly spreading out before her.

Europe. What was going on in Europe at the moment? Giles was bound to want to talk about proper things, and not the frivolous trivialities she tended to pass off as conversation. Kate had once invented an entirely fictitious Andrew Lloyd Webber musical about golf carts just to divert him from explaining Third World Debt to her. Admittedly, it had been the accompanying back massage which had finally defeated his educative zeal, and he had laughed quite a lot, but he was bound to discover the terrifying extent of her ignorance one day. And although it was flattering that he seemed to think she was much cleverer than she actually was, it was going to be deeply embarrassing when it emerged that she couldn't begin to explain the Exchange Rate Mechanism. Kate had got an A grade in her French oral exam simply by murmuring suitably muffled Gallic agreements in the right places, and the same technique seemed to work with Giles *and* world politics. But now she wished, with all the remorse of a lapsed Catholic, that she'd stuck to her resolution to read the Business section of the newspaper every other day.

'*I'm in heaven, I've been told . . . Who told ya?*'

Was she really the only one from college without a job lined up for the autumn?

Hmm, short and sharp. But effective. Kate's eyelids flickered with nerves, but she forced herself to keep them shut. She let the soothing wave of guitars and harmonies sink into her body through her ears.

'*I'm in heaven, I'm too young to feel so old . . .*'

Do you have to go into teaching if you have a general Arts degree and feel faint at the sight of numbers?

'*Yeah, yeah, yeah, yeah, yeah, yeah, yeah . . .*'

Kate's eyes snapped open. Enough of that. It was like having her mum in her head. Clicking off the tape, she reached for the urchin book to take her mind off the voices. The urchin book that, if the truth be told, was actually what Mrs Brown had been signalling for so frantically from the pavement.

chapter two

Giles was already perspiring gently into his white Hackett polo shirt as he walked down the Fulham Road and rounded the corner where the BMW was parked under a tree. He beeped the alarm system off and, pulling open the door, threw the Saturday papers on the leather passenger seat: *The Times*, the *Daily Telegraph*, the *Guardian*, *Le Monde* and the *Financial Times*. He'd never known Kate to be punctual yet and he had a lot of reading to catch up on before the bank's induction week started.

There were usually three giveaway signs that Selina had borrowed the car and they were all present and correct. He immediately had to push the seat back to accommodate his long legs. And there were Tic-Tacs all over the foot well. In the interests of family relations Giles let that one go – she was only home for one more day while her flat was being redecorated. He started the engine and pulled out from the kerb.

'Doctor, Doctor Fox, dun-ner-ner-nerrrrrrr . . .'

And there's the third, thought Giles, and shoved a Fleetwood Mac tape into the player. Bloody Capital Radio. I don't know where she gets it from.

While Giles and his sister got on pretty well, up to a point, he didn't want her around this particular weekend. It had taken some persuading to get Kate down to London in the first place. Kate's vision of London was constructed largely from the writings of Charles Dickens and Oscar Wilde, her two preferred authors, lightly flavoured with *Police, Camera, Action*. Selina, on the other hand, represented the glossy sections of the Sunday papers Kate refused to read on the grounds of her blood pressure. Socially, and now indeed professionally. Selina had got to know the social correspondents so well that in the end one of them gave her a job on the magazine.

Not that he meant to put her down in any way, he thought, accelerating smoothly away from the pavement without bothering to indicate: Selina was a very good writer, in so far as she ever did any writing. Her job, straight out of college, was to go to restaurants with her boyfriend the food critic, surreptitiously eat the food for him and make notes. His job was to make a lot of noise and get photographed with the owner and any random celebrities who happened to be there. The waters of this happy arrangement had been muddied recently though by Justin's announcement that he was going gay for a year, which had partially prompted Selina's frenetic decorating and life reassessment.

'He's a hetero-gay, Dad!' she had protested hotly when their father had read out that week's column over supper in an unusual display of deadpan humour. 'It's very fashionable.'

'Were you aware that he's now taking Chris Evans out to do his eating for him?'

'Oh, he's never done any of the eating,' she huffed. 'He's always going on about the state of his waistline and how it ruins the cut of his suits. Ever since I've known him— Don't say anything, Giles!'

Giles had held up his hands and passed the cheeseboard.

It was a good job his parents were away though, he thought, as he swung into the Brompton Road, with scant regard for a furious woman on a bike. They were probably a bit much for Kate to cope with on their home ground.

Particularly since his mother had reinstated the 'French at mealtimes' rule. Selina at least could be kept out of the house as long as the shops were open. He suppressed a smile at the thought of what Kate would say about Selina's Louis Vuitton football, currently holding pride of place in the hall, secure in the knowledge that it would probably never be kicked by anything less chic than a Manolo Blahnik kitten-heel. Kate wasn't known for holding back with her opinions.

Or at least she wasn't in Durham. Giles frowned. In Durham, as far as he was concerned, Kate had disdained for Great Britain on account of her refusal to be impressed with anything she didn't think worth the hype. She had no idea about what was fashionable and didn't want to know; didn't need to know. She had a curious but instinctive sense of personal style. Not everyone could have carried off some of the things Kate wore around college, but she always looked just like a model from the magazines she never read. Even Selina had been impressed with the photograph Giles had in his wallet of Kate looking 'incredibly other-worldly' (Selina's words, not his – to him Kate looked perfectly real) with her cloud of coppery hair and clear green-eyed stare. This, he thought, would probably tickle Kate, who was wearing a pair of wellingtons just out of shot at the time and was staring so confrontationally at the camera because she had just lost a contact lens.

There was a long line of traffic waiting to turn right and Giles absently slipped the car into neutral, wondering where to take her for supper. Half the places he'd go with Selina would seem embarrassingly pretentious in Kate's company. Which is not a bad thing, he reminded himself, nervously checking for nose hairs in the rear-view mirror.

Kate was not like any girl he had ever met before, and Giles had met a lot. But unlike the majority of them, she was unimpressed by the gift wrapping of life; or the gift wrapping of anything, come to that. He liked to give her lots of presents, partly because he *wanted* to give her everything just to see what she would make of it, but mainly because she responded to whatever it was, and not to wherever it had come from. Most of all, Giles loved the fact that she was the same when she was with him as she was all the rest of the time.

He knew Kate didn't remember their first meeting in the college bar (or claimed not to, at any rate), but he had seen her systematically take apart the stridently sexist captain of the college debating society, and then, despite being five pints down and still nursing a thirst (an astounding capacity for beer being another fascinating accomplishment of Kate's), she had rebuilt Shagger Dave in the shape of a very sorry individual indeed. Unfortunately, her big exit meant she couldn't go back into the bar that night, but Giles had followed her out and the rest was history.

Giles accelerated away. Well, almost history. She had taken some persuading. The more he went down the usual channels, the more she seemed to think he was winding her up. Frankly, he sometimes wondered what *she* saw in *him*. She was funny, beautiful, could be outrageously rude, and did massages that made his internal organs turn to soup.

But outside Durham, for some reason he really didn't get, she shrank into herself like a tortoise with halitosis. Giles was a realist. He had a CV to make cabinet ministers wonder whether they shouldn't take up watercolours again. And he simply couldn't understand what it was that made Kate wilt so badly. She was obviously intelligent – her Finals grades were far better than his *and* her pub quiz team had won a local television knockout competition – but she wouldn't glitter if she carried on sitting in her bedroom in Stratford while the rest of the world moved on. If Kate didn't grit her teeth and move out soon, the puny shoots of her ambition would wither altogether, and that would be a tragic waste of so much potential. Not to mention the fact that a face like that was wasted on mobile libraries and coffee mornings.

Giles gripped the steering wheel hard. Kate was far too extraordinary to spend the rest of her life trailing about in the back of beyond, memorising the words to the Top 40. She needed to be introduced to London. And London needed to be introduced to the fabulous Kate Craig. As soon, and as painlessly, as possible.

'By God, Billy Wainwright, I swear you'll pay for this!' gasped Meg, as the breath rattled in her wizened old throat. She shook her fist at him helplessly and then, her eyes widening as if she could see Death himself approach her, she fell back into the ditch.

'Billy! You've . . . you've . . .' Tears were streaming from Nellie's eyes like rivulets of silver.

Billy Wainwright shook the child roughly from his arm. 'She deserved to die. She were a wicked old woman.' He dusted his gnarled miner's hands on his rough pit trousers and spat into the dust.

'But Billy Wainwright, she were our mam!' exclaimed Nellie, crossing herself devoutly. One of the seven children hanging on to her skirt began to cry.

Billy spat again and turned away. He threw a stone at a passing dog and it yelped in pain.

This is absolute rubbish, thought Kate, turning the page. I could write better than this. Why do they all call each other by their full names even though they're all related? Surely the pit towns of The Unspecified North weren't so formal, even – she looked at the lurid line on the front – in 'the brutal times of the early century'.

'I'll tell thee sommat for nowt,' he rasped, throwing Leandra, the youngest of the family, on to the cart which now carried all their worldly belongings. 'She weren't yer mam.'

Nellie's porcelain-smooth doll-like face creased in confusion and she shook back her mane of golden hair.

'But I don't understand, our Billy. How can that be? Aren't we the spitting image of our dad, with the golden Wainwright hair

that has marked us out for so many generations?'

Billy spat into the dust and hauled another child on to the cart. It began to sob, like a frightened cow.

'Stop yer fettling, Lisa-Marie,' he snarled, cuffing the child round the ear.

Now that is definitely made up, thought Kate scornfully. Fettling? Please. She turned the page and shifted her weight from one pins-and-needled buttock to the other. God. Page 126 and not a sign of travel sickness, she thought with some surprise.

'Don't shout at her. She's but a child.' Nellie pushed herself between her five other sisters and her brother, who was reddening with rage.

Billy turned to Nellie, his face twisted in anger and his scar standing out lividly against the bright gold of his hair. 'Aye, and our mother, our real mother, were little more than a child when she gave birth to us! Oh, you may look thraiped now, our Nellie, but have yer never wondered why yer hands are so white and soft and where that voice like an angel came from? Not from the likes of Meg Wainwright, I'll tell you that for nowt!'

Who could it be, wondered Kate, despite herself. Almost every other woman of child-bearing age in the village was deaf, deformed or a known witch. Was this a colossal plot cheat in the offing? Could there be some master/servant rape or incest coming up? There were two hundred-odd pages to go and presumably surly Billy and radiant Nellie would have to be reunited with some long-lost blood relation before the end. If they didn't end up succumbing to the temptations of their own golden flesh – having, of course, conveniently discovered they weren't really brother and sister first.

She had a quick look at the blurb on the back to see if incest was imminent, but it didn't help. There were more . . .'s appended to each telling sentence than in a Morse

Code handbook. In fact, the whole thing probably spelled 'Author very rich man in Leighton Buzzard' in dots and dashes.

Still, the miles were flashing past nicely, the batteries were lasting out well on her Walkman, she'd managed to wriggle out of and into her jeans and she hadn't so much as thought about hailing taxis or whether she would have to meet Giles's legendary sister.

Selina.

Erk.

Kate quickly buried herself in *The Lost Children of Corkickle* again.

It was 1.30. Ten minutes to wait for the coach. Giles switched off the car engine and relaxed in his seat. Perfect. He could see the approach road clearly from where he'd parked and when the coach came round the corner, he could stroll up to the station and the first thing Kate would see of London would be him and a big bunch of flowers.

The engine ticked as it cooled down. Were the flowers a bit *de trop*? Selina had given him the address of the florist she used and he'd picked them up from Veevers Carter on the way. They'd tied them rather . . . dramatically. Giles had ordered them over the phone and had never realised colours could be such a problem.

Red, naff.

White, bridal.

Pink, girlie. And Kate was certainly not girlie. In the end he'd settled for a marmalade colour, to match her hair, and told them to put a lot of other foliage-y stuff in. He looked at them doubtfully.

The picnic was in the boot, the flowers were on the seat and now all he had to do was wait for her to turn up. She had his mobile number and hadn't called to say she wasn't coming, so fingers crossed she would be here on time. It wasn't as though you could go far wrong on a coach, once you'd actually got on it, could you?

Giles sighed and shook out the Motoring section of the *Telegraph*. It would be quite strange seeing Kate in London: He had a nagging feeling of guilt that he should have made her come down before now and get over her stupid phobia, but it had been essential to do the Swiss placements last summer before the final-round interviews. And getting that job had made it all worthwhile – even Kate, who had threatened to dance on the bar when he took her out to celebrate, had conceded that.

Giles glanced up the road but the coach was nowhere in sight, despite the milling crowds coming in and out of the Tube station. Must be traffic on the M25. He shuffled the broadsheet expertly, but he couldn't concentrate on the columns. A thrill of tension buzzed pleasurably in his stomach.

Despite what Kate might think, he'd missed her while he'd been away. At the time, she'd pretended not to care about his placement in Zürich, but his mate Dan had mentioned to him later that she'd been looking rather peaky when he'd told the lads what great work experience it would be. Apparently Dan had seen her throw a pint glass an impressive distance outside the college bar when she thought no one was looking. She'd looked a bit hurt too when he'd come back, her eyes vaguely reproachful over the top of the giant fluffy St Bernard he'd brought her. Though she had at least acknowledged his embarrassment at bringing it under his arm through Customs, at which point he'd been surprised to realise exactly how much he'd missed her.

It had been lonely in Switzerland without Kate's giggles and acid commentaries. It had been lonely last Easter when he'd been in New York on work experience. And, yes, he had wondered whether other, local, men might feel the same breathless feeling he did when she smiled over the top of her reading glasses; whether they too were transfixed by her fascinating blend of diffidence and stroppiness.

But that was last summer. This summer he finally had the

job he'd been working towards for years, he had a really nice car, and he had his parents' flat until he moved out into the flatshare more or less lined up for September. And in five minutes, his gorgeous, acerbic girlfriend – the likes of whom, Giles was pretty confident, had never been seen previously in Redcliffe Square – would be getting off a coach and summer would begin properly.

Nellie's white hand trembled as she lifted the sneck of the church gate. Surely in here, Corkickle churchyard, she would find the answers to the questions her yearning soul quivered to know. She clambered over the broken stones and mossy banks to reach the untended gravestone she had seen in the distance. She brushed away the snow and read, 'Lady Vanessa Henrietta Constantina Tollington-Smyth. 22nd February 1854 to 31st August 1874. RIP.'

'Mother!' cried Nellie and sank to her knees in the snow, clutching at the headstone. 'Thank God that the evil Mr Hedgington taught me to read during my incarceration, so I can make out your name on your grave.'

Kate bit her lip and a tear wobbled down her face. She brushed it away with the back of her hand and wriggled her bottom to a more comfortable position. Pins and needles had taken over completely and she had had no sensation in either buttock for seven chapters, though she'd barely noticed.

Poor Nellie. After all she'd gone through to get so far with so little in the way of 'school-larning', it was the least the author could do to make up a handy plot dodge so she could correctly identify her long-lost mother's stone.

Page 357. Kate riffled through the remaining pages. That there was still a significant chunk of book to go suggested that poor Nellie's yearning soul had a few more questions outstanding. Kate sighed and conceded that she personally wouldn't marry the hunch-backed son of the local mine-owner to stop her brother being lynched by a rioting mob of farmers. Although, unlike the mean-tempered but ultimately noble Billy Wainwright, Mike would probably have done something to deserve it.

Giles folded up the business section of *The Times* and looked for a moment at the crossword in *Le Monde*. He'd made himself concentrate through the market reports to pass the time, but only five minutes had elapsed. Excitement was making his eyes skid across the lines. Maybe if he left the car and walked towards the stop, the coach would appear.

He opened the car door and got out, enjoying the rich thunk as he pushed it shut behind him. The sun was hotter now than when he'd left the flat and his black Ray-bans slid down his nose, slippery with sweat. He pushed them back up with the heel of his palm and ran his fingers nervously through his blond hair, checking his reflection self-consciously in the wing mirror.

There were one or two people hovering around the coach stop on the other side of the road and his heart quickened as a coach appeared over the crest of the hill. Giles reached into the car for the flowers, bleeped it locked and walked to the bus stop, running through what he would say in welcome.

'Hello, darling!' Too cutesy.

'Welcome to London!' Too naff.

This was as bad as the flowers. But Kate was so quick to pick up on the wrong tone, he wanted to get it right.

A couple of people stared at him as Giles loped towards the bus stop and he offered a half-smile for the flowers which he was carrying a little too casually behind his back, in the same way you might carry a false leg. They continued staring.

The coach was now so near he could see the faces of the passengers. His eyes ran along the windows until, at the back, Giles caught sight of Kate's familiar ginger hair, her long legs in jeans folded up against the seat in front. Her brow was creased in concentration – she must be checking the timetable to make sure this is the right place to get off, he thought with a rush of protectiveness.

'Kate!' he yelled, waving his arms. If she didn't start moving to the front soon the coach wouldn't stop. Giles was now very aware of the starers' gaze intensifying on him, and raised his voice to a firm dog-summoning call.

'Katie!'

High up in the coach, Giles thought he saw Kate wipe her eyes and turn the page of what he realised was not a timetable at all but in fact a paperback book. And then, as he stood staring, to his horror, the coach swept past in a haze of chemical exhaust fumes.

'Shit!' he hissed, not forgetting for a second how stupid he must look, standing outside a Tube station, dressed up like a Gant advert, clutching an outrageously camp bunch of orange roses. The family waiting for the next bus into town looked inquisitively at him but said nothing.

'Shit!' Giles hissed again. He was about to hurl the flowers in the nearby litter bin, but suddenly thought better of it. Then he spun on his heel, tucked the bouquet under his left arm like a rugby ball instead and sprinted as fast as he could for the car.

'So, although I might die here in this childbed, I will nonetheless grant my own daughter the birthright I had to suffer without: the honour of a name.' Nellie's fevered brow was still for a moment on the soft cotton pillows with their costly French lace edgings.

'Nellie!' gasped Billy, clutching her delicate white hand in his own calloused palm. 'No other woman will ever replace you in my heart. And I will bring up the child to be just like you.'

'Bless you, Billy Wainwright,' whispered Nellie, as a beatific smile lit up her beautiful face for the last time. Her journey was over.

*

Kate sniffed and shut the book. It had been absolute rubbish from start to finish: there were plot holes you could drive a Land-Rover through, Nellie had eight, six and five sisters at various stages in the story and it was never clear who the father of little Nellie was, possibly because the author had forgotten herself.

But Kate felt wrung out with emotion and had actually begun thinking in archaic Northern sentence structures. Heaving a big sigh, she stuffed the book into her rucksack and looked at her watch.

Allowing for the traffic jam on the motorway . . . with a sinking feeling, Kate realised that she didn't know where she was now the timetable wasn't relevant. Bolt upright, she put both her hands on the window and stared out in panic.

Shops were flashing by with increasing regularity: high street shops at that – Dixons, The Body Shop, Woolworths. Frantically she looked for road signs or directions, but they were obviously too far into the city for that now.

'Oh, no,' she breathed. Her heart was hammering. Where was she? How would she manage with a rucksack and a bag? She would look like a tourist and get jumped on immediately. Her hands slid down the window on trails of sweat.

Breathe deeply, breathe deeply, she thought. She managed one slowish breath and then grabbed her stuff and bumped her way to the front of the coach, banging her shins on someone's shopping.

'Have we gone past Hanger Lane?' she gasped to the driver.

'Yeah, miles ago,' he replied cheerfully. 'Almost there now, love. Just sit down and enjoy the sights of central London. You'd pay a small fortune for one of them tour bus rip-offs.'

'But I don't want to go to central London!' wailed Kate. 'My boyfriend's waiting for me at the station! Why didn't the bus stop?'

'Because you din't ask, did you?'

'But it's on the timetable!' Kate thought of the buses back

home, which stopped at every place indicated on the route, regardless of passengers, sometimes for upwards of ten minutes.

The driver looked at her kindly. She sank on to the nearest seat and looked up at him with welling eyes.

'Please let me off the bus.'

'Jus' hang on and we'll be at Victoria soon, love.'

Panic seized Kate. She was strangely comforted by the sight of a Gregg's bakery on the corner, with the familiar blue and white checks of the Durham bakers.

Doughnuts.

Durham.

Giles.

'No, look, let me off at these traffic lights. I'll phone him from that phone box.'

The driver stopped the coach at the red traffic lights. There was indeed a phone box by the side of the road. He wasn't meant to let passengers out before the official stops but . . . Kate looked pleadingly at him with wide panicky eyes.

He tipped his head to her as though she were a little dog and smiled paternally. The doors hissed open and Kate bolted out, catching the strap of her rucksack in the hinge. She tugged at it, loosened it and, just as the coach moved off, pulled it free, staggering into the kerb with the momentum. Nobody stopped to look at her, for which she was grateful.

Kate stumbled towards the phone box and dragged her diary out of her bag. Her fingers were trembling as she stuffed the phone card into the slot and waited for the dial tone. Comforted by the familiar sound – hadn't she spent half her life on the phone to Giles? – she drew a deep breath and glanced casually about her, trying hard to give the impression that she was just a Londoner making a casual call to someone she knew very well . . . from a phone box, with a rucksack.

Giles answered on the first ring. From the traffic sounds in the background she could tell he was in the car. Kate braced herself for a lecture about not following instructions properly. But his voice was full of concern, if a little bit resigned.

'OK, sweetie, where are you?'

'How did you know it was me?' Her chest tightened with the effort of trying not to cry.

'Who else would it be? Now, do you know where you are?'

Kate looked around her. There were no tell-tale signs on any of the shops along the street. No street names anywhere. Lost. She drew in a shuddering breath and squeezed her eyes shut.

'I'm in the car, Katie, I'm coming for you. I've been trying to follow the bus, but I lost you at some lights a while back. I'm nearly there though – you have to give me a clue, OK? London's a big place!'

Giles knew as soon as the words left his mouth that this was the wrong thing to say, because a wail of panic immediately pierced his ear.

'Look at the phone box, darling,' he managed over the sound of hyperventilation. 'Is the number 0181 or 0171?'

There was a brief pause and the sound of belongings hitting the floor. 'No, no, I'm fine, really,' came Kate's voice, muffled but urgent. 'Please leave me alone, I'm fine. Go away.'

'Katie, are you all right?'

'Yes, yes,' she croaked. 'There was someone . . . a policeman . . . um, the phone says 0171.' Her voice went up sharply. 'Is that bad?'

'You've just gone . . . a little bit further than I thought,' said Giles carefully. 'Stay where you are.'

With scant regard for the last lingering mother and pushchair on the crossing, he wedged the phone between his ear and shoulder and accelerated crookedly away from the lights. She could be anywhere between Highgate and Victoria – drawing attention to herself horribly by trying to look as inconspicuous as possible.

'Can you see a Tube station?'

'No.'

'Are you sure?'

'Yes!'

'OK, OK, I'm in Mum's car, so shout if I go past you, OK?'

There was a pause of about a minute and a half and then an excited shriek.

'Giles! Giles! I'm over here!'

Giles slammed his foot on the brake and looked up and down both sides of the road, trying to see her. What was it she was wearing?

'Oh, no, hang on, Giles, it wasn't yooooooou!' Kate's voice hiccupped ominously.

'Katie, don't cry.' He pulled away again, apologising to the despatch rider behind him who'd nearly lost his break-fast. At least Selina hadn't buggered the brakes up with her driving. 'Please don't start crying.'

'It's bee-ee-een a very long daa-aa-aay,' began Kate, sound-ing like the Queen Mother in her nasal efforts not to sob. She bit her lip and leaned her forehead on the dirty glass of the phone box.

Don't cry, don't cry. What with the journey down, and having to be polite to that nosy old bag, and trying not to scoff all that food her mother had packed, and then reading an entire book – and one with five murders, matricide, arson, illegitimacy and alleged goat-bothering . . . Don't be pathetic, the Mum voice in her head warned in worryingly *Lost Children of Corkickle* tones, he'll not respect you if you start snivelling now. Oh, God, how she wished she hadn't come. This was exactly what she had thought would happen in London – too big, too anonymous, too dangerous . . .

A hand descended on her shoulder and with a swift reflex reaction, she raised her right elbow to jab backwards. '*Giiiiiiiles!*' she screamed into the phone.

'Don't worry, Katie, I'm here,' said Giles. He stroked her back with a gentle, circular motion. It worked on his mother's cats, no reason why it shouldn't work on Kate. Instinctively she stopped shuddering and arched towards him, happy to block everything out with his polo shirt.

'We'll go and have some lunch on the King's Road now we're in town, and do some shopping if you want, and then have a walk in Hyde Park?' His mind raced, trying to compute the shopping hours in which Selina was unlikely to be home.

'All right,' said Kate, obediently. Her breathing was returning to normal and despite herself, her attention was straying to a summer three-for-two offer in the Our Price store opposite. 'I'm sorry,' she began again. 'I really am . . .'

'Don't worry about it,' said Giles, and laid a finger on her lips. 'Let's not mention it any more.'

'But your ribs . . .' Kate shrivelled inside again at the thought.

'I've had much worse on the rugby pitch.' He opened the car door for her and managed to conceal the twinge of pain up his side. So much for college self-defence classes, he thought ruefully. Kate might get on better in London than she imagined – she certainly wouldn't have any trouble getting through rush-hour platforms on the Underground.

Kate slipped into the leather passenger seat even though her jeans were now welded to her. Giles got in the other side, leaned over to the back seat and retrieved the slightly battered flowers. Two green Tic-Tacs fell out of the foliage. He smiled and handed the bunch to her.

Kate stared in surprise at the wild orange flowers, surrounded by lush, spiky foliage. They were so unlike anything she would have expected Giles to have chosen that she was momentarily lost for words. Pink rosebuds like ballet shoes, yes; tropical lilies and tigerish roses . . . well. And they must have cost a fortune!

She dipped her head to the fullest blown lily, closed her eyes and breathed in deeply. The heavy scent swept through her nose and seemed to expand and fill her whole head. And then, as always when she hadn't seen Giles for a while, nervousness marched over the language section of her brain and staged a go-slow.

Kate kept her eyes shut. Apart from his startling gorgeousness – having a boyfriend that anyone else would actually want to have still being a relatively new and exciting concept – Giles radiated a casual assurance that things would work out exactly as he planned that made her squirm inside with gleeful delight. Failure, which hung permanently around *her* psyche like a creepy lodger, was not on Giles's list and certainly wasn't coming into his shiny, confident, dynamic life. While this was thrilling, it did have the unfortunate side-effect of making her wonder exactly what it was he liked about her, and how she could carry on doing it for ever, without actually knowing what it was. So, rather than filling her with confidence, the adoration of this über-man tended to make her rather nervous, until familiarity returned and she could relax again.

Kate became aware of an expectant silence and said the first thing that crossed her mind.

'Mmmmm. I love the way you can almost taste proper roses, the fragrance is sort of edible.'

Oh God, she thought crossly, you're meant to be thinking skinny shoulders.

Giles smiled broadly and remembered how Kate always stopped to smell the flowers growing round the college. What a gorgeous reaction. Selina was so blasé about getting the most lavish bunches. 'Are you hungry?'

'Um, quite.'

'Well, how hungry?'

'How hungry are you?'

'We'll go anywhere you want.'

'Well, I don't mind. I don't know anywhere to go, do I?'

'OK.' Giles leaned over and traced Kate's lips with his finger. It was amazing to see her again. Why was it he always forgot how vivid she was when they were apart? And why bother with a restaurant? It would be roughly 2.30 by the time they got home; couple of hours to eat, walk in the park . . . 'Why don't we just go back home and you can freshen up and I'll make some lunch there?'

Kate stared back into Giles's blue eyes and imagined that he could see right into her mind. 'Fine,' she said, kissing his fingers with a shaky smile. 'Let's go.'

chapter three

Kate was woken by the strong beam of sunlight coming through the stylish but, in practical terms, useless linen Conran blinds. Blinking unattractively without her lenses in, she put out an arm without bothering to lever up her body from its comfortable reclining position and located her watch on the table. It was ten o'clock.

Ten o'clock.

Her eyes snapped open, old mascara still cementing a few tiny lashes painfully together. The whole room was glowing in the morning sun like a Sunday-supplement guide to Fresh Living. Swathing everything in pristine white Egyptian cotton was a good start. Kate knew what her mother would say about the practicalities of white cotton bed linen. Particularly for girls who didn't take off their eye make-up with the recommended care before falling asleep face-down in the snowy pillows.

Vases of white longii lilies, artfully arranged to catch the sun in the window, were also a giveaway that someone else did all the hard labour in the household laundry, leaving the lady of the house free to concentrate on the finer points of the ambience, rather than the ironing. Kate could also hear her mother's verdict on the stark bundles of oriental twigs on the chest of drawers. And white carpets. And the faintly rude green screen print above the fireplace.

She, on the other hand, was completely bowled over by Giles's house, the like of which she had thought existed only in the professional imaginations of *Elle Deco* journalists. It reminded her more and more of an extremely expensive hotel. She sank back in the soft pillows and gazed at the blind, now bulging and falling gently in the breeze. One of those hotels where you would feel compelled to make your own bed out of politeness.

It had looked daunting from the outside. Giles had been a little economical with the truth when he said he lived in a flat in Chelsea. What he actually meant was that his parents had a whole house in a pukka cream-paint-and-pillars square, the top flat of which was his, for tax reasons.

'Didn't want to make you feel . . . umm,' he had mumbled in reply to Kate's opening and shutting koi carp mouth. In the event it wouldn't have made much difference what he'd said – she wasn't prepared for anything like this at all. The last time she'd seen a house this majestic was in *Upstairs, Downstairs*.

Inside everything was minimal and predominantly white. 'It gives my mum something to do,' explained Giles, in tones which implied that his mother was more like an unreliable infant not yet ready for unsupervised play than a grown woman with impeccable taste in decorative pebbles. His tone didn't change when he added, 'And of course it's her job, so the house is really a showroom, I suppose.'

Kate looked for somewhere to put her bags down without leaving a mark. She felt dangerously grubby all of a sudden. It hadn't slipped her mind that Giles's mother was an interior designer, but for some reason she had been imagining stencilled ivy leaves and distressed urns. Rather than Doric columns and sheet glass.

'It's, um, beautiful.' Giles picked up Kate's rucksack before it could hit the ground and, hoisting it over his shoulder, he began marching up the wide staircase to his floor. 'Well, there's not much on when Dad's away. She's more your professional luncher. I suppose that's where Selina gets it from. Dad keeps telling her she should do some sort of food guide for thin women who don't actually want to eat any lunch. A sort of Good Plate Guide.' He snorted, but from three stairs behind Kate couldn't tell whether it was an amused snort or a dismissive snort and she didn't want to come out on the wrong side.

'Where is Selina?' she asked, her nerves returning.

'Out to lunch,' said Giles. 'Metaphorically and literally, as it happens.'

He pushed open a door on the top floor, and dropped her bags inside. Light flooded into a big room from three full-length sash windows. The view seemed to be composed entirely of blue sky, green tree and more wedding-cake white houses.

'Do you like it?' Giles seemed suddenly shy. Kate grinned. She loved to see him nervous – it wasn't something she experienced often.

'Yeah.' She shrugged, and wrinkled her lip. Her eyes sparkled mischievously. ''s OK.'

Giles did a double take, the first genuine one Kate had ever seen.

'Thank *you* very much!' Laughing, he grabbed her and lifted her up in his arms to carry her symbolically into his bedroom. The moment was somewhat marred by Kate's panic that Giles might put his back out, and subsequent terror of marking the paintwork with her DMs, but her protestations were quashed as he dumped her on the enormous white bed – from which they reluctantly emerged when the front door slammed and announced Selina's return three hours later.

Selina. Kate pulled the cover over her head.

It had been going pretty well up to Selina. Perhaps it was the scrambling into clothes and then being faced with crisp and miraculously uncreased linen. Or maybe it was the way that Selina fixed her with that 'I'm-looking-through-you' stare, in a face that was so like Giles's, but more terrifyingly Aryan. Or perhaps it was the impression Selina gave of being utterly and completely bored and faintly dismissive of her lunch date, the decorators at her flat, her parents' house, Giles, Kate . . .

Whatever it was brought out all the anti-urban spikiness Kate had been trying to keep under control; on her way back from the loo, she had mistakenly wandered past the double doors to the cavernous drawing room and heard Selina say to Giles, in a voice which Giles had later explained was more impressed than outraged, 'God, Giles! Talk about off-bloody-hand!'

Naturally this made Kate descend even further into herself and, knowing from past experience that she was unable to do feigned enthusiasm without sounding sarcastic, she allowed the temperature in the room to drop accordingly. So, what with all the gleaming surfaces, it began to take on the party atmosphere of a Fox's Glacier Mint.

Even now, safely beneath the duvet, Kate still couldn't decide whether she was horribly in awe of Selina for having outfits that actually required impossibly pale kitten heels, or whether she just despised her for making her feel so small about things that had never crossed her mind forty minutes previously. It had not escaped her notice at the time that Selina's piercingly blue stare had more than a hint of coloured contact lens about it. Nor that even a hick from the sticks like herself could have told Selina that the fake tan/halter-neck top combo required a degree of foresight at the application stage of said fake tan. She had almost said as much in an unguarded and heavily provoked moment. Minutes later Giles had propelled her out for a film and supper.

Great. What was the first thing the magazines said you had to do? Make friends with his sisters. And what had she done?

Kate buried her head in the pillow and tried to make a list of the Ten Dreadful Things She Could Have Said To Selina

But Hadn't. It was not as cheering as she'd hoped.

In the middle of the sub-duvet recrimination the door opened and Giles walked in with a breakfast tray.

'Kate?' he said, seeing the duvet squirming.

The duvet shot back and Kate's face emerged, wreathed in blushes.

'Didn't think you'd make it down for breakfast if I left it up to you,' he said. 'So I've made you some and brought it up.' He proffered the laden tray. In a bud vase was a white gerbera yanked from one of the downstairs arrangements.

'Ah, pet!' said Kate, bouncing herself into a sitting position. She then remembered that she wasn't wearing anything and self-consciously clutched the bedclothes to her chest.

Giles raised a sarcastic eyebrow at the unusual display of shyness, but calmly put down the tray on the bed – Kate suppressed an impulse to warn him about coffee stains on cotton – and threw her a fresh white T-shirt from his chest of drawers, which she hurriedly pulled over her head. More white. She felt as though she was about to disappear into it all, leaving only traces of smudged eye-liner and an imperceptible aroma of The Countryside.

'I've done you some French toast and syrup. It's about the only thing I can cook so you may well be eating it a lot. It's also the only thing most of our au pairs could cook, which is perhaps why I'm so good at it.' Giles helped himself to a large piece which he doused liberally in maple syrup, and reclined on the bed with his head on Kate's legs.

Kate poured herself a cup of coffee. Very carefully. She took a piece of dry toast and nibbled, trying not to make crumbs. Should she ask Giles to pass her her glasses which were somewhere in her overnight bag? They were a bit grim and she generally tried not to wear them when anyone might see her looking quite so much like Ronnie Barker. And she really did look like Ronnie Barker. Giles looked good enough in soft focus without them – all blond hair and faded blue jeans. Very sexy. And the tea tray was in reasonable focus.

She could identify the cream cups from this distance, if not the writing around the top of them. More to the point, Selina could walk in at any minute and catch her, semi-naked and bespectacled.

'Anything you want to do today?' asked Giles casually.

'No, just be with you.' Kate smiled down at him. That was true at least. It would be a real novelty to have him all to herself without needing to share him with the rest of college (termtime) or the world of international banking (vacation).

'I thought we might have a drive round town, see some sights. I can give you the full *Monopoly* tour of London – Pall Mall, the Strand, Fleet Street. Lunch at the Angel, Islington?'

'Isn't that one of the cheap ones?'

Giles laughed as though she had just said something very funny and Kate felt a bit stupid. 'No, not any more. Although Pentonville Road is still a bit scabby, I suppose. Don't think it's safe to go by the *Monopoly* board these days.'

'Well, that's about the nearest I've got so far,' said Kate. She pulled half a horn off a croissant.

'Great!' beamed Giles. He had an evangelical gleam in his eye. By the time he'd finished, one way or the other, she'd be begging to stay. 'It'll be your first proper day in London.'

'Ever,' added Kate. And not without reason, she thought, remembering the panic of being swallowed up by the city the previous day.

'Ever.'

There was a brief pause. Kate nibbled her toast nervously and wondered how bad she looked with yesterday's Blondie kohl-ringed eye make-up still smeared round her face.

'Can we go before Selina gets up, please?'

Giles drove the way Kate wished she could drive. Whereas she had learned most of her manoeuvres on a local housing estate blessed with many redundant mini-roundabouts and fortuitously clapped-out Fiestas to reverse park behind, Giles seemed to have done a fortnight's crash course at the New York Yellow Cab School of Driving.

'Selina says I drive like a cabbie,' he said proudly, burning up a black taxi on the inside lane round Trafalgar Square. The driver gesticulated angrily at him and Giles gave him the full benefit of his college education in swearing as he took the corner with his attention fixed firmly in his rear-view mirror.

'Is that Marble Arch?' asked Kate, marvelling at the sight of so many Japanese people all gathered in one place.

'No, it's Admiralty Arch.' Giles careered down Horse Guards Parade with a minimum of indicating. 'Admiralty Buildings, Army HQ, Cabinet Office, Foreign Office, Her Majesty's Treasury.'

Kate's neck was beginning to ache. Where did all these people come from? Why were they videoing the traffic lights? Her worst fear in life was looking like a tourist, though there was no chance of that, doing sixty miles an hour in a sports car and heading straight for Buckingham Palace. Which she did at least recognise from the Royal Wedding tea towel at home.

'Please can we stop?' Kate said at last, unable to absorb any more neo-Classical architecture. 'And have an ice-cream somewhere maybe,' she added, to keep Giles's party mood going. At this rate they would have exhausted central London by teatime and have moved on to Kent and environs by the end of the week.

Giles found a parking space by the river, next to an ice-cream seller, and they sat eating Magnums in the sun, watching boats and the odd canoe go up and down the Thames. Kate had lathered herself in her usual Factor 25 before coming out and was grateful for it now. She could feel her skin tingling and extra freckles were virtually appearing before her eyes. She didn't remember it getting this hot at home.

'Of all the places I've lived in, I think London's my favourite,' said Giles. 'Hamburg was good, but we weren't there for very long. Are you OK with that ice-cream, by the way? I'll eat the chocolate off it if you don't want it,' he added, suddenly solicitous.

'No, I'll manage,' said Kate, quickly. This could be the only chocolate she would be getting until she got home. She licked her fingers where the ice-cream was melting. 'I didn't know you'd lived in Hamburg. Is that where you learned your German? Did you not mind all the travelling?'

'Well, it was just normal, you know, Dad moving about. We were the new kids in class almost every other year until we were old enough to board in England. We just got very good at fitting in. All diplomatic kids are like that.'

'Poor you,' said Kate, thinking of her local school. She had been called The Carrot Girl from the age of five to eighteen, having spent her entire secondary education with the same people she had done finger-painting with at primary school.

'I suppose it was why Mum got into decorating, having to start again on a new house every two years,' Giles carried on, thoughtfully.

'Well, white is a fairly international colour,' offered Kate, wondering how his mother could have brought up three children and maintained her décor. Perhaps she Sellotaped Harrods bags over their hands and feet? Kate slurped up a precious chunk of Magnum chocolate.

Giles looked blank.

'What did she do before she got married?' asked Kate through a mouthful of ice-cream.

'Well, she was a researcher, but sort of gave it up when she met Dad,' said Giles. 'I think it was more like a year in Paris after, um, finishing school.' He looked embarrassed again and started fiddling with the bass controls on the radio. Kate wondered how much of the Lighthouse Family she would have to listen to before she could politely put the radio on. Getting information about his family out of Giles was like pulling nails at the best of times, but since she was staying in their house it did seem polite to drag out some details.

'Look, Giles, I don't *mind* that your mother went to finishing school,' she said. 'My entire family has a rather unfinished quality to it. Mike's barely started. But you never talk about your parents much, and you've met mine loads of times.'

He let out an embarrassed sigh. 'It's hardly very PC, though, is it? Especially next to what your mum's done in the last year.'

Kate stopped sucking her Magnum and turned to look at Giles in disbelief. 'What *has* she done in the past year? Apart from show me up in most educational bookshops in the West of England? Giles, you have *seen* my mother line dancing, haven't you? You know, I still go cold inside thinking about the night she made us all come with her. I thought I was going to die of shame and you were going to run back to London, thinking you'd stumbled into the Walton family reunion by mistake. Mind you, if you could bear that . . .'

Giles laughed and slapped the steering wheel at the memory, honking the horn by accident. 'God, no, how many times do I have to tell you I loved that evening! Your mum looks great in her cowboy boots. She has got *the* most amazing legs. And to pass GCSE Latin from scratch in a year, as well as all the other stuff . . .?'

'Yeah, well, I'd prefer it if she just stuck to the local operatic society and doing jam for bring and buys like she used to, and left ritual family humiliation to the experts.'

'Yes, but that's—'

'Giles, when other people's mothers go through mid-life crises, they start wearing too much make-up and borrowing their daughters' clothes. My mother, on the other hand, is hanging out with the adult education gang and borrowing my revision notes.'

Giles sighed and missed the furious gestures of a passing cyclist he'd cut up three miles back. 'OK, my mum now does some Feng Shui as well. See? That's retraining. Parents are allowed to evolve too, you know.'

Kate snorted. Evolving was not the word for her mother's bizarre personality change. Anyway, wasn't there some unwritten rule about remaining exactly the same reliable mother figure until your children were safely married off?

'What else can I tell you? She's American, from New York, as you know,' Giles went on, 'and Granna and Grandad are both lawyers, quite well off, so she has some money of her own, which she collects bits and pieces with. She likes to travel, you know.' Giles made 'and-so-on-and-so-on' gestures with his free hand while he neatly licked the drip off the ice-cream before it hit the leather seat. 'Pretty boring really.'

'Hardly,' said Kate, wondering exactly what the bits and pieces were.

They watched a police launch motor past, rippling the water up behind it, followed by a documentary camera crew in a speedboat.

'You didn't tell Selina about me missing the stop, please don't tell her, will you?' said Kate at last, all in a rush as the reason for Selina's barely suppressed amusement suddenly occurred to her. 'It's just that she'll think I'm so stupid. I mean, now she just thinks I'm rude, which is bad enough, but at least it looks as though I know what I'm doing, whereas if she finds out about yesterday, she'll just laugh at me, and I hate it when people laugh at me, especially when it's not my fault.'

She stopped and looked at Giles who had laughed a large portion of his ice-cream on to his shirt. 'Giles, you bastard, if you've told her, you have to buy me a pair of big – and I mean really big – sunglasses so I don't have to look her in the eye when we go home. Oh, God, and I thought it was just my poor high street jeans that were amusing her so much . . .'

'Oh, Katie, I'll miss you!' laughed Giles, leaning over and burying his nose in her neck.

'Miss me?' said Kate.

There was an infinitesimal pause, which may have been caused by Giles wiping his ice-creamy face on Kate's neck, before he said, 'When you go home.'

'Oh,' said Kate. She hadn't realised until that point that when she did indeed go home, it would be a long time before she saw him again.

The thought occurred simultaneously to Giles and Kate that for the first time in their relationship, there would be no college to go back to in October. It had not been discussed, in the general celebrations and drunken 'You're-my-besht-mate'-ness of the end of term, whether their relationship would also come to an end. Which was not to say that Kate hadn't thought about it. It was just another of the small but persistent crowd of thoughts that she had been drowning out with loud music ever since, along with 'Where am I going to get a job?', 'What kind of job do I want?' and 'Will my mother end up with better exam passes than me?'

An uneasy silence fell between them.

'You don't want to move down here?' said Giles lightly.

'Certainly not. Mum would make me live with Mike, and I don't want to live anywhere where beer costs this much.'

Giles started the engine and pulled on to Cheyne Walk. Conversations like this were much easier when there was an excuse not to look at the other person.

'What are you going to do at home all summer then?'

'Get under my mother's feet, take back her library books, write a novel, you know, the usual stuff.' Kate rummaged in the glove compartment and found a pair of Selina's sunglasses which she put on. If Giles wasn't going to meet her gaze, she certainly wasn't going to meet his. She undid her hair from the loose plait and it lifted in the breeze behind her.

Giles saw her reflection in the window of a van in front and was struck once again at how good they looked together. Kate appeared even more arresting through the third-person view. When he pulled away from the lights, the hairs on the back of his neck stood up with desire as the wind lifted the hair from the nape of her neck, and he had to force his attention back to the road ahead.

'I thought I might do one of those dreadful sagas,' Kate said carelessly. 'Urchins and stuff. Coal mines. Donkeys. One-legged blind clairvoyants.'

'Look, Kate, I don't want to spoil what is turning into a very good day, but don't you think you should put your mind to what you're going to do—'

'For the rest of my life,' she finished for him. 'Thanks, Dad. Yes, I have been to the Careers Service and you know as well as I do that I would make the world's worst solicitor. You probably didn't notice, being Mr Financial Careers, but if you have English anywhere in your degree it's like a red rag to a bull for that lot. As soon as you say the word "Literature" they make you this little pile, comprising the prospectus for the College of Law, the Civil Service Qualifying test dates, Voluntary Work Abroad leaflets, then if you're looking a bit dazed they say, "And have you thought of teaching?" like you're some kind of masochist.'

She drew breath and Giles tried to interrupt but was cut up on the inside by a courier on a moped, which distracted him momentarily.

'Oh, yeah,' added Kate, 'and if you try and demur like a polite girl, they say, "And there's always publishing, if you like books so much. Have you thought of that?" and wheel you off to the Graduate Job Network because there are never any leaflets on it in the careers office. So don't tell me that I haven't explored my possibilities. My possibilities blow goats.'

She ejected the Lighthouse Family with some force and returned the radio to the first station playing proper music.

'Please don't tell me I have to come and live in a city where the air feels suspiciously second-hand and where you have to drive like a homicidal maniac to get to where you're going in case the other million people going in the same direction get there before you. And where the radio is shockingly bad and celebrity East End crims have their own columns in the local papers. Giles, you are in severe danger of sounding like my mum. If you carry on like this, I can only assume that you're in closer contact with her than I want to imagine.'

Giles flinched and tried to reason that at least Kate was showing signs of being properly herself for the first time since she'd arrived. The wide-eyed Bambi version, though enticing in its own way, was not what he was used to. Kate Lite. Not the full-strength article.

'I'm sure that if you wanted to do some work experience on the paper, Selina could—'

Kate looked at him over the edge of her shades. 'I don't think so, Giles, do you?'

'But I don't think you've given the idea of London a fair trial, Katie,' he said stoutly. 'It's my own fault, I should have asked you to come down to stay earlier, but I've never been here long enough in the vacations. Whatever it is you're going to end up doing, I don't think you're going to find it in Stratford-upon-Avon. Unless you want to make a career out of tractor-balancing. Or set up some kind of lemon curd cottage industry.'

Kate shifted in her seat and put her hand on his thigh. Her mood turned over. 'Sorry, I'm on auto-pilot. I've had this conversation so many times at home since I got back from Durham. You're lucky I didn't give you my "Why I shouldn't have to do all the housework as a punishment" monologue.' She paused and took off the sunglasses. 'Giles, London is great for a holiday but it just . . . I can't put into words how I feel about it but it makes me feel uneasy, as though I could disappear and no one would know. Don't you find it impersonal? I don't think I could ever live here.'

'Now you're just being stubborn,' said Giles. He knew when to stop. And he had lots more ammunition. 'Do you want to go and see where my parents were married?'

'OK,' said Kate, caught off guard. She was unsettled that Giles had dropped the subject so quickly but parents and weddings in one breath could only be a good thing. She pushed on the shades again and sat back in her seat, as Giles pulled up outside a discreet little church on Cheyne Walk. However, her instinct told her that she would have to come up with something very convincing, very soon. At the moment, the summer options weren't looking good.

chapter four

On Monday morning Kate felt Giles get up very early – and not quite as quietly as he was evidently intending – and when she stumbled down to the kitchen, emboldened by Giles's assurance that Selina was incapable of getting up before ten, she found a note addressed to her on the kitchen table.

Have gone for one-off pre-induction session at work. Sorry! Won't be too long. Have booked you in for Day of Beauty at Harvey Nichols' Urban Retreat at eleven a.m. to pass the time (Selina's idea, actually); it's on my store card so don't worry about paying. I'll meet you there for tea at four-thirty in Fifth-Floor Café. (See map attached.)
If you get lost, ask a policeman.
Lots of love,
Giles

Kate had always thought Giles had really nice writing. And nice writing was a very sexy thing in a man. It didn't look like a man's scrawl, but it didn't have girlie flourishes either. Not an easy trick to pull off. Underneath a heavy American diner mug, still warm and half full of coffee, was a hand-drawn map which he'd annotated with shops rather than street names.

Kate snorted. 'Big white house here!' indeed. That was like giving someone a map of the Coast-to-Coast walk with directions along the lines of 'Biggish hill – turn right'.

She took his dirty cornflakes dish to the huge sink to wash up before realising that the faint buzzing noise was coming from a huge state-of-the-art dishwasher, but she rinsed it clean anyway. Then she leaned back against the work surface and gazed around the kitchen, wondering which one was the cereals cupboard. It wasn't the sort of kitchen where food was immediately obvious.

There was an ornamental arrangement of fresh fruit on the dresser, which Kate was reluctant to disturb, especially as she wasn't completely sure about half the fruit in it. Giles had left some croissants in their patisserie bag, an absence of grease marks indicating that they'd not been there for long. She poured herself a cup of coffee and smiled at the map. 'Chanel shop here (women's collection and accessories)'. Really.

She had found that there were times when it paid for people to think you were a little bit denser than you actually were, but getting lost in a maze of posh houses and feeling too socially inept to ask for directions to 'the big white house' wasn't part of her plan for today. It wasn't the sort of area, as far as Kate could see, sipping her coffee, where one admitted that one was not *au fait* with the street layout. She felt a bit cold imagining crowds of Selinas, all looking down their horsy noses at her. There must be an *A–Z* somewhere.

She strolled across to the fireplace which now housed an Aga and above it a long row of designer cookbooks from a catholic variety of smart restaurants. They looked untouched and most had smart matt jackets, which Kate thought confirmed them as being intended for readers who wouldn't actually attempt to cook anything from them. Matt covers would have lasted all of five minutes at home, thought Kate, before Dad had them whipped off and covered in sticky-backed plastic for practicality.

The battered *A–Z* sat at the end of the line like a Blackpool beach donkey at Ascot. She settled down with it and before she finished her coffee, Kate had worked out an easy route which would take her to Harvey Nichols via a much more interesting way than past Giles's succession of overpriced clothes stores.

Roughly an hour and a half later, Kate sank tentatively on a wall and let out a big, big sigh. She didn't dare look at her watch, because she didn't want to know what time it was by now.

It had taken nearly an hour to pare down her outfit to an artfully careless minimum of black jeans and black cap-sleeve T-shirt and to apply artfully minimal make-up, which the girl at Harvey Nichols would be sweeping off with a fist-ful of cotton wool on arrival. Despite what Giles interpreted as her admirable disdain for fashion, there was no way she was spending a whole day at Harvey Nichols being snig-gered at from behind the massage beds on account of her dress sense. Kate thanked God for making summer too hot to eat in and therefore relieving her a little of her savage battle with her hips, which usually raged out of control in the holidays, when Giles wasn't around to make a big thing about short skirts.

She sneaked a look at her watch. Half eleven. Shit. It was intimidating enough to have to go there in the first place and be improved – and yeah, sure that was Selina's idea – but to be late as well . . . Her feet throbbed in the new mules she'd brought with her to wear for 'evening' but which had looked so good with jeans in the mirror, and her heart sank a little further.

She eased a foot out, shook it and found it wouldn't go back in again. OK, so walking much longer was out of the question. There was no way she was hobbling in there like Toulouse-Lautrec. Kate got the *A–Z* out again and pushed her borrowed sunglasses up on to her head to get a clear view of it. No, nothing leaped out. She turned it upside down, trying to match some of the names with the rough direction she'd come in. How the hell were you meant to know where you were going when everything looked exactly the same? For fuck's sake. Maybe the 'big white house here' thing was Giles's little joke?

Kate thought of calling Giles on his mobile phone and letting him guide her, but that would be giving up and she didn't know whether he'd be able to speak. He hadn't mentioned work the day before and it had generated twinges of jealousy, though whether she was jealous of the job for having Giles or Giles for having the job, she couldn't say.

So help was out. Particularly after the débâcle of her arrival. Kate tried to keep her mind focused on the map, hating the feeling of having no landmarks to navigate herself by, nothing that felt familiar. And the silence in these chilly white streets was almost eerie: no one coming in or out of houses, no children making noises, certainly no cars.

She took a deeper breath. There was only one person she could look to for guidance in this and he wasn't here. So she would have to go for the next best thing: what would Selina do in a situation like this?

In a sort of divine answer a black cab turned the corner and, pushing the sunglasses down from her hair on to her nose, Kate waved at it, suddenly aware that she didn't actually know what to do with London taxis.

Fortunately it was empty, and trying to look as cool as possible, she opened the door and said, 'Harvey Nichols?' as she got in. Was that right? When were you meant to announce your destination?

'Just round the corner, my love,' said the cabbie. 'You sure you want takin' there?'

'Er, yes,' said Kate. 'My feet hurt.' She tried for a Selina pout.

'I don't know,' said the cabbie over his shoulder. 'You gels and your shoes, eh? You wanna get yourself a nice pair of them trainers. Mind you, us lads like to see a bit of heel, know what I mean?'

Kate bit back a retort and mumbled something indistinctly Sloaney.

It took the cab under five minutes to retrace her steps and pull up outside Harvey Nichols. With some relief, she fished around in her bag for her purse. But it wasn't there.

Cold panic swept over her. She picked out diary, A–Z, rape alarm, sun cream, until she couldn't hold everything in one hand. Where was her purse? Frantically, she tipped the whole thing upside down on the seat and scrabbled through the debris. It still wasn't there.

'You all right, love?'

'Oh, yes, fine!' stammered Kate, flicking through her diary in what she knew was a completely futile gesture although she was unable to stop herself doing it. Think Selina, think Selina. 'Just want to refresh my lipstick before I go in, you know!'

The driver laughed indulgently. 'Fine by me, I'll just keep the meter runnin'. Now, that Mick 'Ucknall, 'e's a quality singer, innee?' He turned up Magic FM, which only served to make Kate more stressed.

She stared in horror at the pile of rubbish on the seat, the blood hammering in her veins. Had she left her purse on the kitchen table? No, because she'd bought a can of Diet Coke at the unbelievably up-market corner shop near Giles's house. But that was with the pound coin she'd found in her jeans pocket anyway.

She could feel sweat prickling under her armpits. Had it been stolen by a pickpocket? Not unless he was invisible. Or disguised as a rich old lady – the only person she'd seen on her walk. Oh God, this was London for you: you could be robbed and not even know! Bastards! She'd make sure Giles got the full version of this when she saw him. Kate sank back into her seat and bit her lip.

How was she going to phrase the news that she had been

robbed en route to the taxi driver? Maybe they could go straight to the police station so he could dob her in for fare-dodging and she could report her purse missing at the same time. Handbag crime. Bloody hell. How many times had she listened to Nick Ross demonstrating how you should make your bag safe.

Realisation dawned hotly.

. . . by zipping your purse into the middle lipstick compartment of your bag.

Kate unzipped her bag with trembling fingers and there was her red purse, all fat and smug. How embarrassing. She quickly stuffed everything else back in and fished out a fiver, which she thrust through the partition. Thank God. And this was the first song in the Simply Red triple play too. It only took the first two bars of 'Holding Back the Years' to make her hyperactive and that had to be coming next.

Waving away the change, which was painful to her since there was only £1.90 on the meter, Kate stepped out of the cab with her shades firmly on. A small crowd of tourists on their way to Harrods had gathered at a discreet distance, in case she should turn out to be famous. She limped, head down, into the shop and saw the flash of a disposable camera reflected in the door glass.

Inside, she took off her shades, not wanting to look pretentious, but since everyone else seemed to be wearing them anyway, put them back on. Kate could see immediately she wasn't wearing enough make-up and felt painfully underdressed. What had seemed like easy Chrissie Hinde chic at home was just scruffy in the hard light of a hundred cosmetics concessions, and she could see herself in the mirror of every single one. Clutching Selina's personality to her like a shield and sneaking a casual glance at the store directory, Kate snooted her way up the escalators to the fourth floor.

At half four on the dot, Giles glided up the escalator to the food hall, still tingling with the excitement of the induction course. It was incredible to be starting properly on the career he'd been preparing for as long as he could remember, and in his first choice of city, too. That was a real bit of luck. After all the hard work and all the meetings and all the interviews, everything was falling into place. He bounced the flat of his hand happily on the rubber handrail, thinking of the discussion group he'd led on the long-term implications of monetary union.

Kate.

He stopped his hand mid-bounce and negotiated the step up into the darkened wine cellar area.

Kate.

There didn't seem to be any sign of her in the restaurant. Give her a few minutes to be late, thought Giles, browsing idly through the sparkling wines.

He wondered how she had got on in the Urban Retreat. Either very well or very badly, he predicted. He'd given her a fairly lavish beauty treatment voucher after her bad dose of measles last year, in the hope she'd have her hair tamed a bit, but instead Kate had emerged from the salon with silver pedicured toenails and a fresh hole in each ear, joking that they'd only just talked her out of a nose-ring. He prayed that she'd be in a good mood this time. And not fuming at the snootiness of the clientele. Or stinging from perceived condescension from the therapists. Or both.

Giles sighed.

'Giles?'

He spun round to see Nicole Kidman in dark shades flash him a smile as she rose elegantly up the escalator and then almost stumbled off the moving step at the top. Except it wasn't Nicole Kidman. It was Kate.

With her hair dried straight in a sleek fall of copper, and her pale skin beneath the Ray-bans translucent with expensive make-up, Kate looked . . . almost out of his league, thought Giles, caught off guard by an unusual ripple of panic. She looked incredible. They had painted her bee-stung lips bright matt red like a film star's and emphasised the tiny coffee-coloured mole on her cheekbone. It was as though the glow he thought only he could see had been switched on for general admiration. Giles swallowed.

'Well?' said Kate, lifting the shades. Her eyes sparkled with barely suppressed nervousness and the very latest runway highlighter. 'You know, this is the first time in our entire relationship that I've seen you at a loss for words. Have you eaten something funny?'

Giles said nothing, being too busy marvelling at how a scruffy black T-shirt and straight-leg jeans could suddenly look so right. His eyes travelled up and down, noticeably widening. And – oh, my God! – the mules! An old teenage Olivia Newton-John fantasy popped into his mind for the first time in ten years.

Kate slid the shades back down. 'They've turned me into Jessica Rabbit,' she said. 'Not bad for someone who's more Carol Decker in real life.' She moved haltingly towards the tables. Although she was trying not to put pressure on the blisters which had formed on the tender part of her instep, to Giles it looked like a paralysingly sexy wiggle.

He had chills. They were multiplying. And – yes – he was losing control . . .

He recovered himself sufficiently to attract the waiter's attention.

'Table for two? Name of Crawford?'

The waiter conducted him smoothly to a table in the centre of the room, despite both their gazes being fixed on Kate's undulating walk.

She slid into her seat, leaving the waiter and Giles hovering redundantly behind her chair, looking at each other. Kate gave the waiter a pleasant smile which he returned, and Giles gave him a slight grimace which made him retire swiftly to the bookings lectern.

'He must think I'm someone else,' observed Kate. 'As do you.'

Giles leaned over the table, gently pulled off Selina's shades and took her hand in his. 'Kate, I just want to say you look incredible. Just . . .' He struggled for the right word, one which would express the full force of his new desire and yet not suggest she looked like a moncking hooner the rest of the time.

She smiled and then frowned suddenly. 'Look, Giles, before you say anything else, I think I know how much this afternoon cost and I'm really mad that you spent that much money on me. It makes me feel . . . I don't know, small, somehow.'

'How do you know what it cost? It's on my chargecard.'

'Yeah, well, there are price lists all over the place and I can work some things out by myself. It's—'

'It's worth every penny,' said Giles. He was still mesmerised by her appearance. 'You look like a model. That guy thinks I'm having a clandestine meeting with a film star. He's probably about to call the *Sun*.'

'Yes, well,' said Kate again, studying a menu in the hope that there would be something she could order which would fulfil her sugar craving and Giles's image of her as a woman without a sweet tooth at the same time. There wasn't.

'Anyway,' Giles went on, graciously, 'it's only money. There've been a lot of times when I've been working away, leaving you here, it's only fair you should have treats.' His face went serious. 'Umm, that reminds me, Kate . . .'

'A coffee. Milky. A milky coffee.' Kate shut the menu to prevent further temptation and looked up at him. The red lips went into a heartbreaking pout. Giles smiled stupidly at her. She was making him feel drunk. 'I know it sounds silly when you obviously think I look so . . . um, but I don't feel like me, all done up like this. I feel like someone else. Don't you think so?'

'Of course you look like you. Just a more . . . polished version maybe. Kate, I need to—'

The waiter appeared at Kate's shoulder. Giles ran his eyes

quickly across the menu and said, 'A *latte*, a double espresso and one of those, er, chocolate truffle cakes for me.'

The waiter raised his eyebrows at Kate and she shrugged and shook her head. 'No, nothing for me.' Inwardly she seethed and tried to get maximum enjoyment from Giles's approving look. It reached the satisfaction level of a small macaroon. Sometimes she felt as though she should have 'Elegance is refusal' tattooed on the back of one hand for easy reference.

In order to stop herself thinking about the silver cake stand on the table opposite, Kate changed the subject. 'Did you have a good day at the training . . . um, day?'

It was the right thing to say. Giles beamed with delight and Kate experienced a weird stab of jealousy in her stomach. 'Absolutely. It's exactly what I've wanted to do all this time, you know, and the other chaps seem like good fun. A couple of mates from school I haven't seen in years were there.'

'Mmm?' said Kate as encouragingly as she could, without having much idea about – or interest in – anything Giles did involving the wearing of a suit and laptop carry-bag.

'Yes, it's going to be a lot of hard work to begin with, I can see that, but the work experience I had last summer at Morgan Stanley will come in very useful, once I . . .' He trailed off in mid-sentence as Kate popped a tiny white sugar lump in her mouth. Normally he would have told her off for eating sugar lumps, but there was something disturbingly erotic about the way her deep carmine lips moved as she chewed and crunched.

'Go on,' she said encouragingly. 'I'm listening.'

Giles swallowed. God, it was hard to talk about banking when Kate was sitting there, restyled in a version of herself he had often thought about, but never dared suggest. 'Ah, right, yes, the training is going to be very intensive . . .'

She met his eyes with a smile, then dropped them to fiddle with a silver teaspoon. She had sensed a shift in atmosphere since her arrival and had been running it back and forth across her mind in an attempt to snag what had caused it.

His voice ran on, and she picked up one word in five for reference. Today had been an unsettling experience altogether. Her stomach had churned all through the Day of Beauty, sometimes embarrassingly audibly. Though she could tell that the Urban Retreat was the height of fashion, she had felt anything but urban and there was certainly no retreat to be had from all the prodding and tweaking and silent assessment. In the end, pretending to be Selina during the nerve-wracking treatments had been a stroke of genius, and she had never realised how much irrelevant knowledge about exfoliation and non-transfer lipsticks she had absorbed over the years. Out it had poured, in a torrent of AHAs and Liposome Bs.

By the time Kate had worked her way round the salon to the hairdresser, she'd reached a state of chit-chat exhaustion and had just slumped in silence, which the stylist seemed to have taken pretty well. In fact it had probably confirmed her definitively as Someone So Important She Didn't Need To Talk to Hairdressers. But now, back here with Giles and on firm-ish ground, the new persona was just confusing – particularly since Giles also seemed to be pretending she was someone else.

As the surrounding tables filled up with well-groomed ladies wearing neck scarves and slightly too much blusher, the alarming sensation of things moving unannounced beneath her feet, which had begun in the middle of Chelsea this morning, returned with a vengeance.

Kate looked contemptuously at the straight-from-the-salon blonde helmets of hair around her and realised, with a jolt, that she must look just like them.

Giles renewed his grip on her hand and coughed. 'Um, Katie, there's something I have to tell you. And I need to say it all at once and in context, so please hear me out.'

Kate's eyes swivelled back to Giles and her heart plummeted. Was this it? Had he dragged her down to London, tarted her up like a rah's handbag, just to dump her, in Harvey Nichols? She blinked rapidly, running through all worst-case scenarios and smudging her mascara.

Giles was blinking nervously too. 'Er, part of the reason I hadn't mentioned the session this morning is that it's not the main training course. It's a preliminary thing.'

Kate breathed again. Fine, if it was only work . . .

'Well, what it is . . .' This had come out a lot easier in the cab on the way here, thought Giles, feeling the blood rush to his cheeks. The polished-up Kate with her newly arched eyebrows was more difficult to speak to. More like – well, more like Selina and her friends. It was unsettling to see her looking so confident on his home ground.

'Come on, Giles, spit it out.'

He looked up and Kate was surprised to see such an uncertain expression cross his normally self-confident face.

'The meeting today,' he began, 'was to announce who's been selected to do the first part of the training course in London and who's to go to Chicago. And I'm going to Chicago. For four months.'

She tried to pull the brave smile back despite the lead weight of her disappointment which was plummeting in her stomach. She knew that the reality of his words would sink in within roughly five minutes, which gave her five martyred minutes of enjoying the drama of the situation before she would want to curl up and die. 'Well, hey, I'm used to that, aren't I? So I won't see you for four months. That's OK. We can write. I'd be at home anyway.'

The tray arrived. Kate stared at the frothy coffee placed, on a white napkin, in front of her and picked up the cup by its ridiculously tiny handle.

'Not necessarily,' said Giles.

She ignored this and took the first sip, tasting the bitter coffee through the foam. Why did she suddenly feel so abandoned when it was at least the fourth time they had had this conversation? She *always* got to sit out the holidays with Mum, Carol Vorderman and Jerry Springer.

'You don't have to go home,' he repeated, hesitantly.

Kate put the cup down. 'Of course I have to go home,' she said majestically. 'I always have to go home. That's the deal, isn't it? You go away and pursue your career and I wait for you to come back. If you're coming back this time?' Perhaps it was the residue of the Selina personality that was making her talk like this. Or it could be the red lipstick making her more dynamic.

Giles thought it best not to tell her she had foam on her upper lip.

She stared at him with film star eyes and though he knew he was playing into her hands and virtually putting on the screen villain twiddly moustache, the time had come to lay things on the line. Giles summoned up every last thing he had been told on the management course and realised that none of it could possibly apply to temperamental girlfriends.

'Come on, Kate,' he said. 'You can't have it both ways. We both know you don't ever want to come with me because you'd rather be at home, and we both know you secretly go mad when you're stuck in the house feeling sorry for yourself when everyone's travelling. There's no holiday reading to fall back on this time. This is real life now. And you've got to face up to it.' He began paring the chocolate shell off his truffle cake.

'What on earth do you mean by that?' bridled Kate. She looked covetously at the cake and tried to remember all the nice things Giles had said about her skinny shoulders. 'Just because I don't want to do one of those stupid, tedious trainee paper-pushing courses doesn't mean that I don't know what I'm doing for the rest of my life. I just haven't made up my mind yet.'

But even as she tried to form arguments for going home to find work, she heard her mother's voice reciting the library opening hours, and she felt ill. Not quite as ill as at the thought of having to go on the Underground on a daily basis, but much iller than she had felt this time last year. And that was without the missing Giles bit. 'Why has this day gone so wrong?' she added under her breath.

'You don't have to take it as a criticism,' said Giles. 'I just think you should have an experiment, that's all. Spend the four months while I'm in Chicago here in London, get a temp job, then . . .' He hesitated. 'Then when I come back, we'll . . . take it from there.'

Quickly Kate looked up and then back down at her coffee cup. And what was that meant to mean? Moving in together? Splitting up? Her pulse thudded again.

'It's only sixteen Mondays,' added Giles. 'You can survive sixteen Mondays, surely?' It was his killer line and he was rather proud of it.

'What about Mum?' hazarded Kate. 'She thinks I'm going home. Now Mike's in London, I'm the only one left to test her on her history. She needs me to go to the library with.' Go for the emotional blackmail, can't hurt, she thought. Even though Mum's been dropping hints about chicks leaving nests on an hourly basis since the end of the second year.

Giles flushed. 'Well, I've spoken to her and she thinks it's a good idea, actually. She says you need to find your own feet and learn how washing machines work on their own.'

'She would,' muttered Kate. She beat the spoon against the table. Damn. Suddenly going home seemed very attractive now it was evidently no longer an option.

Giles took a sip of his coffee and grimaced.

'Is there . . .?' began Kate, but he shook his head at her and signalled to the waiter, who came gliding over, eyes firmly fixed on Kate.

'Sir?'

'Sorry, this espresso is lukewarm. Can I have a hot one?'

'But it was—'

Giles did his 'Polite but Firm' smile. Kate cringed in her chair and hoped no one could hear. 'Look, I don't want to argue about this. If it's not fresh, there's no *crema*, the whole flavour deteriorates and it just tastes bitter.'

The waiter inclined his head slightly and removed Giles's cup.

Giles smiled apologetically at Kate. 'Sorry about that. Proper espresso is like a good wine, but it can be filthy if it's not made correctly. Yes, your mother and I had a long chat about you having a few months in London and she said she was sure you'd take to it like a duck to water.'

Kate rolled her eyes. She could just imagine Mum talking to Giles, jacking up her accent a few notches, inventing bizarre facts about her relentlessly normal family – 'a duck to water', indeed!

'But where will I live? *Would* I live,' she corrected, hurriedly. A smile lit up her face and her own accent rose a couple of postcodes. 'I can't possibly stay at your flat while you're not there, can I? And no one from college has got a flatshare sorted out yet.' She shrugged prettily, hoping against hope that the most obvious answer had gone over Giles's head.

It hadn't. 'Um, when I spoke to your mum she said that now Mike and Laura have moved to Clapham they have a spare room.' His fresh coffee arrived and Kate thought she could detect a trace of spit in the yellow coffee head. She didn't blame the waiter, either.

Kate's brow darkened and she exhaled heavily through her nose. 'Oh, great. Have you got it all set up then, between you? Anything else I should know about? You haven't had my birth certificate and dental records faxed down yet, by any chance?'

'But, Kate . . .'

'Haven't you been listening to anything I've said since I've known you? I. Don't. Want. To. Live. In. London. OK?' Her jaw slid mutinously. 'And if there's one thing I hate, it's being organised by other people into doing things they know I don't want to do.'

Giles shifted uncomfortably in his chair, aware of some curious gazes coming their way. He had rather been banking on Kate not making a scene in a public place.

'All right, I realise that,' he tried. 'But you must see that whatever I do, I'm going to be based here in London—'

'Except when you're in Chicago, obviously. Or Toronto, or Tobago, or Moscow.' Her voice was rising.

Giles ignored her and carried on, 'And if I'm based here and you're determined to be on library duty two hundred miles away, it's going to be very hard for us, isn't it?' He placed a deliberate emphasis on the 'us' and squeezed her hand. 'You seem to think that it's just you who feels lonely while I'm away,' he added in a more intimate whisper. The big blue eyes made headway where the management consultancy techniques fell on stony ground and Kate, like a happy cod, allowed herself to be reeled in. Again.

'Katie, can't you just try it for these few months, for me?' He tried a smile. 'You never know, you might like it.'

She put her head in her hand and allowed the sheet of hair to hide her face. A variety of emotions were competing for precedence, none of them very grown-up. Part of her wanted to be with Giles – more than anything else in the world – but not if it meant having to live in this unfriendly, alien city, with the brother who still liked to torment her with plastic insects whenever he could get away with it and the sister-in-law with neo-Nazi organising skills and not one, but two, Alice bands. Kate felt her head silt up with inarticulate 'new school term' mutiny.

'I've been completely stitched, haven't I? I feel . . . ambushed!' she mumbled from under the hair. Her stomach was lurching all over the place. It didn't feel real at all, this week. The coach journey seemed another life away. A disaster movie away. But if Giles was offering something more, dangling this promise of . . . Of what? 'But I love you!' she

yelled inside her head. 'Can't you see how much I love you?'
But her lips wouldn't move.

'Best way to do it, plunging straight in,' said Giles cheerfully, glad that things seemed to be back on anticipated lines.
He began dividing his pared chocolate truffle cake into quarters.

At this sudden change in tone, Kate pushed her
Hollywood mane back and was embarrassed to meet the
gazes of several curious ladies-who-lunch on adjacent tables
before that of her boyfriend, who was fixedly intent on
making the sides of his cake equal. So that was it, was it?
Once she was back on side, doing what she was told, he
could drop all the concern?

'You're dangling me!' she said, banging her spoon ominously on the table.

As a final resort, Giles went for Plan D: Harsh but Fair. He
braced himself and focused once again on all the long-term,
character-building benefits she would reap after the initial
shock.

'Well, that's life, Katie, and I think it's about time you
grasped the nettle and went for it. You've had three years of
faffing about. If you really loved me, you'd make this effort
to sort your life out, and if you had any self-respect you'd
stop making feeble excuses about not understanding public
transport and show me what you can do without me here to
help you all the time. You can talk a good fight, but up to
now, that's all it's been.'

Kate recoiled as if he'd slapped her. 'Oh, suddenly it all
falls into place, that little lecture in the car yesterday.' She
glared at him. 'Did you think that you'd have a go at bribing
me with pro-vitamin B hair treatments, if grown-up reason
hadn't made any impact?'

Giles opened his mouth and shut it again.

'Well, it might work on Selina, but I'm sorry – liposomes
just don't mean that much to me. I'm just a jam-making
bumpkin, after all. What do I know about living in London?

What do I know about *living* at all? I am sick to death of being told what to do, by you, by my mother, by the university careers service. You are *not* my dad.'

Kate pushed back her chair and stood up. If a razor-like pain shot up both her tender insteps, she didn't let on. With a last haughty look at Giles, which her heart couldn't really afford, she stalked away from the table, eyes racing across the room to find the exit sign, so at least she would look as if she knew where she was going. Helpless? Her? Certainly not. Certainly bloody fucking not.

She heard Giles mutter, 'Katie!' under his breath, not so loud that people would begin to relish the scene – and not so loud that she might actually hear and come back, she noted miserably to herself. Through swimming eyes, all she could see was white everywhere – on the tables, on the walls, on the backs of the soignée women dining around them – and she forced her steps to keep regular, dignified pace as she wound her way out of the café and into the darkened area of the Food Hall.

Why was he acting like this? Kate almost bumped into a very chic sales assistant offering her minuscule bites of what looked like cat food on crackers, and blundered on.

This time she didn't stumble on the escalator, and stood pulling her spine up to its longest length behind an elegant blonde in knobbly orange Chanel-effect tweed. Kate watched their twin reflections descend to the fourth floor in the mirror ahead and barely recognised herself. So this was the kind of woman Giles wanted, was it? Sleek and proud and urban. Harvey Nichols woman.

She turned the corner to catch the next escalator down. Well, that wasn't her, was it? Her hair had started to curl again under the serum they'd slicked on it to make it shine and, pulling a dirty hanky out of her bag, Kate wiped off the red lipstick angrily. It left a bee-stung stain on her lips.

If she was being honest, it wasn't the first time she and Giles had clashed over her apparent lack of direction, but somehow at college she had felt on firmer ground to argue back, while they had both been equal in rooms, friends, degrees. In fact, *her* degree made her more than his equal. She could defend herself with plenty of time left to choose, vacations to think about things, other people to talk to. Here, where she was suddenly vulnerable, looking up uncomfortably to him in all sorts of new ways, this kind of interference felt pointed. It made her defensive. 'But I love you!' shouted the voice in her head, sounding very weak.

By the fifth escalator down to the brightly lit cosmetics hall, the enormity of the situation had cracked over Kate's head like a giant egg, and her initial tears of anger were giving way to something approaching panic. Although her legs continued to march towards the door, the warning voices in her head were beginning to mumble inarticulately and, finally, striding down the street outside, it dawned on Kate that she had no idea where she was going.

She pulled up short and sank on to a low wall. Shit. She eased her aching feet out of the black mules, which had started the day irritatingly loose and now of course were as tight as if they'd been spot-welded on to her. She felt nauseous with misery.

If she stayed at home, her mother would nag her into a state of partial catatonia, Giles would find someone new and she would be safe but suffocated.

Or she could hurl herself into the complete unknown and maybe die trying, but at least die with some dignity intact.

Great.

chapter five

In Kate's book, window-boxes were a sign of premature ageing and should be medically treated. It came as no surprise to find that Laura had cultivated a large terracotta specimen on each of the four available window-sills of the neat Clapham terraced two-up, two-down, and filled them with brave pink cyclamen and rather scratty-looking ivy.

Mike and Laura's place was a doll's house after Giles's parents' Chelsea ice palace. Sliding her bag from her aching shoulder on to a reproduction boot scraper, Kate wondered where on earth she was going to sleep. How could there be a spare room in such a teeny house? Perhaps they had a fold-down James Bond wall-bed in the bathroom. It dawned on her that in a house this size there would be no escape from nocturnal transmissions from the master bedroom, even if she lashed the Z-bed to the dinky wee chimney-pot and slept out there.

The door opened before she could wipe the horror off her face.

'*Hell-ooo*, Kate,' said the woman Kate had trouble remembering was now actually her sister-in-law. And even more troubling, Mike's wife. She had always imagined her brother would run to type and end up getting hitched to some larky primary school teacher with her own clapped-out Mini Metro, whereas Laura was a solicitor and made Mary

Poppins seem faintly anarchic. Very nice, in her own way – but very scary.

'Hi, Laura,' mumbled Kate. Something about Laura turned her back into a shy teenager. The wedding ring, perhaps. 'I'm really sorry about landing on you like this.'

'No trouble at all,' breezed Laura, bouncing the bag up the front steps. 'Mike's very into the idea of families at the moment. Oooh, this is very light! You haven't brought much, have you?'

'Didn't realise I was leaving home at the time.' Flimsy summer dresses, sheer underwear and tiny flirty T-shirts didn't take up much space. That was the whole point.

Kate trailed disconsolately into the house. The phone was ringing in the kitchen.

'Just let me get that,' said Laura. 'Make yourself at home.'

Kate listened to her running around trying to locate the cordless handset. The sitting room was done out in shades of terracotta, and there were pictures of Mike all over the place, disconcertingly in every guise except that of her brother: groom, rugby player, cricketer, Action Man. Kate felt anywhere but at home.

'Do excuse the mess,' Laura called unnecessarily as Kate looked round for somewhere to sit. There was no mess. There were three visible magazine racks and a blue glass bowl that housed all five remote controls. She sat and fidgeted while Laura conducted an animated conversation, of which the only words Kate could make out were 'tonight', 'supper', 'baby' and 'carrots'.

Eventually Laura emerged bearing a tray full of silver cafetiere, cups and a plate of biscuits. No doily. Kate hastily put down the Russian dolls she had been fiddling with.

'I see you've got Mike to put his *Top Gear* magazines in binders at last,' she said with grudging admiration.

'Well, that's the thing about having a small house,' said Laura, pressing down the plunger carefully. 'You have to work to keep the pigsty at bay.'

'Have you tried locking the pig in his room?'

Laura laughed politely and put coasters out on the glass side table. 'We wanted to buy a house,' she went on, apropos of nothing, 'even though this is probably much smaller than the flat I had before we got married. I'd had enough of flat-shares, although it did suit Mike, you know, living with a bunch of lads who only used the Hoover for party games.'

Kate nodded; in the space of one diary year, she had had four different addresses of four different flatshares for Mike, his mates and their primordial domestic habits.

'And anyway, it's so much nicer, having a whole house to yourself. Your own front door, your own address, no one to go through your post before you do,' Laura went on. 'Biscuit?'

'Er, yes, absolutely,' agreed Kate, who had never known anything other than houses big enough to accommodate four noisy people. Nervously she picked up a biscuit since Laura was waving them under her nose and then put it down, thinking of her unending quest for skinnier shoulders. Then picked it up, hearing her mother saying, 'Don't paw the produce!' Almost immediately she dropped crumbs on the sofa and tried unsuccessfully to flick them off without drawing attention to what she was doing.

'And London property prices!' Laura rolled her eyes. 'Unreal. We were *sooo* lucky to get this place at the price we paid. In the end I could even budget the mortgage to allow for a cleaner. Thank God we had a college friend on the Halifax graduate training scheme. Boring but useful.'

Kate registered the pause which was probably intended for her to insert a 'Go on, tell me how much you paid for the house' phrase. But she didn't. She had no idea what London property prices were like but had a strong suspicion that Laura could hold forth for some time on the topic. And right now she didn't dare get too knowledgeable about London, in case Giles mistook it on his return for 'settling in'.

'What time does Mike roll up from work?' she asked instead.

'A shadow of a frown passed across Laura's forehead.

Ooops, thought Kate, have I touched a nerve? Shouldn't have said 'roll up', maybe. Or 'work'.

'Well, it's a Wednesday, so he usually has cricket nets tonight, but we're having some friends round for supper. Our social life isn't ruled by Mike's cricket club yet.' A steely look crept into Laura's eyes. 'And anyway, he knows you're coming and I did put a Post-it note in his diary last night reminding him to pick up some wine. He should be back any time now.'

'Oh.' First time for everything, thought Kate.

'You don't mind sitting in on supper with Alex and George, do you?'

Kate shook her head.

'All arranged weeks ago, I'm afraid. I'm a bit of a planner like that. It's amazing how far you have to book ahead when you're organising two diaries.' Laura put her hand to her mouth in a 'What have I said?' gesture and then smiled sympathetically over the gold rim of her green bistro coffee cup. 'Poor you, by the way. Mike told me about Miles abandoning you here all on your own.'

Kate pressed her lips together and let the Giles/Miles thing go, in case her voice cracked when she said his name.

'Still, you must be very proud of him, getting on that scheme,' went on Laura, clearly impressed herself. She broke a biscuit neatly in half. 'Mike and I know so many people who wanted to work for that bank and never made it past the first round. And his going to Chicago straight away is very prestigious, you know. They only take the really outstanding trainees.'

'Mmmm,' said Kate, forcing herself to smile, although half of her was aching with a dull pain again and the other half was bridling at being spoken to like a halfwit Legal Aid client.

'So when are you starting work?'

'Work?' Kate looked stupidly at Laura, who tipped her head in an encouraging way. Her honey-blonde bob slid neatly to the side too, like a shampoo advert for very well-behaved hair.

'Well, what are you planning to do?'

Pause.

'What are you going to live on?'

Curious pause.

'What have you got lined up?'

A more nervous pause.

'Kate?'

This was a sore point. At the airport, while Giles was checking in his extensive collection of suit covers and bags, Kate had sat in the Coffee Republic concession with a milky coffee and a piece of paper ripped out of his Filofax. On it, Giles had told her to list ten occupations she could imagine doing for the sixteen Mondays. Failing that, ten things she thought were important to her in a job.

After half an hour of serious application, in which she had made a comprehensive list of ten famous redheads in pop – she was reluctant to let Giles think he'd worn her down too quickly – all Kate had come up with in terms of gainful employment preferences were:

1) Nothing which will involve buying new wardrobe from Next;

2) No telephone sales;

3) Not living with Mike and Laura;

4) Must not be surrounded by rahs and Sloanes.

She spent the remaining time doodling blankly around a splodge of milk froth that had fallen on the paper, and in the end had been too embarrassed to give him the list before he disappeared for ever into the waiting area. Kate didn't want Giles's last memory of her to be linked with telephone sales, and they had both been concentrating too hard on fitting all they wanted to say into a meaningful, gulping silence to discuss her CV.

But once Giles's plane had spiralled up and too far away to see, Kate realised she didn't even know how to get to Mike's on the Tube.

An afternoon flicking through the careers book section in

Dillons didn't help much either. It wasn't as though she didn't *want* to do something – anything to take her mind off the Giles space in her brain for the four months it would take to prove to him that she wasn't a helpless bimbo. She just didn't have a clue what it was she could do. And, Kate thought, miserably counting the silk scatter cushions while Laura fiddled with the coffee cups, she'd failed objective number three already.

'Um, so what are we actually going to . . .?' Laura was looking at her with schoolteacher eyes.

Kate stared back at her, annoyed at yet another compulsive organiser hijacking her personal tragedy, but at the last minute she lost her nerve and turned her scowl into a helpless shrug, unaware that Laura was already very familiar with this Craig family habit.

'But what about your long-term . . .?' Laura began again.

Fortunately the sound of a key being aimed at and yet not quite connecting with the lock diverted her. 'We'll talk about this later.' Laura scrambled to her feet with a quick 'Excuse me' at Kate and disappeared grimly into the hall.

Supper was not a great success. Kate only knew Mike's friends vaguely from the wedding and felt extremely gauche in the face of Laura in full-on homeowner mode. However, given plenty of listening time while the conversation bounced back and forth between discussion of other people she didn't know and parking fines in central London, Kate began to suspect that her presence might be disrupting more than just the seating plan.

For a start, the guest list had included a toddler, who, after much cooing and gurgling from all sides, was now safely stowed in the spare room – even smaller than Kate had feared: if she did the splits in bed she could kick each wall, and it was right next to the master bedroom.

Kate picked at a strand of rocket and chewed it like Ermintrude the Cow. She had finished her individual

Emmenthal and Red Onion Tartlette some time before anyone else, mainly because she had no burning opinion to impart on European Monetary Union, unlike Mike's very serious friend George. George was still wearing his suit from the office. He was still, thought Kate, wearing his office personality too. George's girlfriend Alex looked a better bet; since the conversation turned to the EU, her eyes had taken on a glassy sheen and now she couldn't have looked more glazed if someone had applied a light egg wash over her face.

There was a brief lull in the Economics lecture while Mike and George took a simultaneous swallow of wine.

'I'll just check on Tom,' Alex said quickly and got up from the table, leaving her red linen napkin crumpled on the seat.

Immediately Laura turned to Mike and said, 'You see? They're such hard work, babies. You're always having to make sure they're OK. No rest at all, is there, George? I expect you and Alex are worn out. Rather you than me.'

This was, Kate noted, much less subtle than the earlier 'Should we really be bringing kids into this uncertain fin-de-siècle society?' and 'I'm not sure I'd like any daughter of mine to inherit these thighs!' comments Laura had thrown into the conversation.

George made an uncertain mmm-ing noise and began rearranging the condiment set. Kate remembered that it was the one she had given them for a wedding present. She looked up to remark on this and caught Mike glaring at Laura across the candles. The comment died on her lips.

'So, erm, how old is he?' she asked George, trying to pretend she hadn't seen anything.

He looked embarrassed. 'About, er, eighteen months? Laura? Is that . . .?'

'Yes, about that,' agreed Laura, 'and they're into everything at that age, aren't they? I bet you've had your briefcase safely locked all weekend!' She shot a satisfied look at Mike, who scowled in response and poured himself some more wine.

How old were these people? wondered Kate, looking aghast between the two. Alex couldn't be more than about twenty-six, but the offhand way George was talking about his son . . . How could he not know how old he was? Did they have a nanny? It's a different world, she thought, feeling her loneliness rise another notch inside her.

Laura, spotting Kate's confusion, leaned over the table and said, 'Tom isn't George's son, Kate!'

Kate looked even more startled.

'God, no!' spluttered George, dribbling wine on his shirt. He mopped at it with a napkin, which Laura discreetly removed from him and took into the kitchen area to soak.

'*Durrrr!*' said Mike to Kate, twisting his finger into his forehead.

'*Durr* yourself!' retorted Kate. 'How am I meant to know?'

Mike stuck his tongue under his lower lip in reply.

'Don't talk to your sister like that!' snapped Laura from the kitchen.

Mike looked slightly chastened. 'Yeah, well, maybe should have said before, Tom isn't George's baby. He and Alex are just looking after him for the weekend. Bit of a dry run, eh, eh?' He nudged George matily. 'Grown up things,' he added for Kate's benefit.

'Certainly not,' said George.

'It's the first time Rachel and Fin have been able to get away for months and months!' came Laura's voice immediately from behind a knock-through partition. 'Rachel looks a wreck! She says she hasn't had her hair cut since before he was born! Isn't that dreadful, Kate? Poor her!'

'Er, yes,' said Kate, sipping her wine and feeling about ten. She had last had her hair cut in November, at a training night. It had cost about a fiver. But at least she didn't still say 'Durr!' to people.

'But I think Rachel looks *wonderful* since she had the baby,' said Mike. His face took on a Tony Blair-like sincerity which Kate had never seen on her brother. She wasn't sure it suited him. 'Anyway, Tom's such a quiet little chap. No fuss at all. And I think motherhood has . . . softened Rachel.'

'Softened her brain more like.' Laura had come back in with the main course in an orange Le Creuset casserole, which she dumped on to the table mat.

A faraway expression came over Mike's face. Kate was reminded of how much his stupid smile irritated her.

Laura crossly slopped the ragout on to the plates she had been warming in the oven. 'Can you pass that round to your sister, Michael?' she snapped.

'Certainly, darling*aaaaggggh*!' Mike dropped the plate on to the table and swore furiously, sucking his thumb.

'Let me,' said George, using his napkin as an oven glove.

'Oh, sorry, didn't I say the plates were hot?' said Laura, not looking sorry at all.

By 11.30, Kate's eyes were drooping, the table was covered in the white shards of wax Mike had been picking off the candlesticks and the conversation had only moved from Jeremy Paxman to Jeremy Clarkson.

'Anyone for coffee?' said Laura, getting up.

'Yes, please,' said Kate. 'Would you like a hand?' she added, safe in the knowledge that Laura wouldn't.

'No, no,' said Laura with a broad smile. 'I'll just pop up and check on Tom while the kettle boils. OK?' She bustled off.

'I've got a lot of time for anyone who wears jeans like that,' Mike was saying earnestly to George. 'Although they really can affect your sperm count if you're not careful— Why are you laughing?'

'Shall we clear the table?' Kate looked up to see Alex piling all the plates together.

'Oh, er, yes, of course.'

They stacked side plates on salad bowls on dinner plates on under plates – Laura liked to get as much use out of her tableware as possible – and ferried the whole lot into the kitchen while Mike opened a fifth bottle of wine.

'I'm sure Laura has been far too discreet to mention anything to you,' said Alex confidentially, as they loaded the dishwasher, 'but as you might have gathered, there is a certain . . . difference of opinion going on. Even I can't quite keep track of it sometimes. It's a bit delicate.'

'Er, just a bit,' said Kate. 'But Mike treats me like a five-year-old anyway.' She blushed. 'As you might have . . .'

Alex rolled her eyes in sympathy. 'Well, just so you know, for the last six months, Mike has been trying to persuade Laura to have a baby and give up her job. And Laura doesn't want to. It makes it rather difficult for the rest of us. Especially when Rachel's baby – you remember Rachel from their wedding? – is such a little charmer.'

'I don't imagine any child of Mike's would fall into that category,' said Kate, scraping salad into the bin.

'No, well, Mike's been going on a lot recently about how your mum had you two so young and still talks about how happy she was when you were little.'

Kate stopped scraping and looked incredulously at Alex. Mike was unbelievable. 'As opposed to how stressed she's been ever since. Have you met our mother? She's barking. Even admits it herself. And she swears the rot only set in once Mike and I learned enough words to wind each other up.'

'But then you can understand why Laura's reluctant to start a family, given the mad parents she's got. Miss Rank Starlet 1962 and the first man to direct an all-nude production of *Uncle Vanya*? Not exactly your average nuclear family.' Alex switched on the dishwasher and hoisted herself on to the kitchen unit. 'How long are you staying then?'

Kate groaned. 'Please don't start. I don't know. I don't know anyone in London. I don't even want to be in London. And God knows I certainly don't want to be in a house this small while my arsehole of a brother is rutting and my sister-in-law is fending him off like something from a Brian Rix farce. The one time I need Giles – my boyfriend – to be here, he's buggered off and if it wasn't for him, I wouldn't even . . . Oh, shit.' She sank on to a bar stool as the nerves trembled in her legs. 'Do you realise that this is the first normal conversation I've had since he—' A big lump welled up in her throat and trapped her voice. Kate covered her mouth with her hand to stop the sob coming out.

Alex crouched down next to her and squeezed her shoulders sympathetically. The sudden kindness from someone she didn't even know made Kate fill up again. 'You poor, poor thing. Look, go upstairs and splash your face with water so Mike doesn't see you looking upset and when you come down I promise you we'll work something out,' Alex said. She gave Kate a gentle shove. 'Go on.'

Kate ran gratefully up the stairs to adjust her make-up, knowing her mascara must be making her look like Robert Smith. Mike wouldn't hold back in pointing that out to her. Her mother had packed some Freshwipes in her enormous tuck bag, the remnants of which were in her rucksack in the spare room, but as she pushed the door open she saw Laura bent over the carry-cot, prodding the sleeping toddler with the sharp end of her toothbrush.

'Wake up, for God's sake!' she was hissing at him. 'Scream or something, you little sod! You're doing this on purpose! I am not ready for breast pumps and varicose veins! I don't want to turn into my mother!'

Kate coughed and Laura spun round, toothbrush in hand.

'Oh, er, hello!' She blushed. 'Isn't he lovely? Little Tom! Mmmm, sweetie!' She tickled his chin half-heartedly. Tom carried on snoring gently and dribbling. Kate noticed Laura's hand twitching to wipe the dribble off the sleepsuit.

And, for the second time in two days, Kate found herself voluntarily rejecting the familiar but terrifying, in favour of a leap into the complete unknown.

chapter six

'So,' asked the blonder of the two blonde ladies, 'where-abouts were you thinking of, roughly?'

'Zones one to three at the furthest,' said Laura firmly.

The other one standing by the big map of London began fiddling again with the pins stabbed into it. The pins were in different primary colours. Kate wondered if they stood for privately agreed gradations of pukkaness. 'Well, of course, we don't do much outside Zone Two anyway, do we, Leonie?'

'No, we don't. Just Islington really. What sort of price bracket are we looking at?'

Kate looked at Laura, who paused for a moment, exhaled resignedly through her nose and said, 'Between eighty and ninety pounds.'

Kate blanched.

'Righty-ho,' said Leonie, flicking through her card index. 'I've got a lovely place in Fulham, a violinist and her daughter. Spare room, own bathroom . . . seventy-five pounds a week,' she raised her eyes hopefully, 'in return for a little light housework?'

'I think not,' said Laura, in a voice that suggested to Leonie and Miranda of 'Rooms with a View' that manual labour was out of the question – and yet suggested to Kate that she was about as capable of keeping a house tidy as a bear would be capable of using a chemical toilet in a wood.

'And it would have to be available in the next few days. Or immediately,' Laura added.

Kate had to hand it to her sister-in-law. It had been a tough decision: use Kate and her sleeping bag as ammunition in the 'Families are for Life and Not Just for Christmas' argument, or free up the spare room so all arguing could be done properly at full pitch. In the end it had been no contest. Kate's own offer to bail out after thirty-six hours had been welcomed on all sides.

So Laura had heroically taken a day off work, driven her straight to the agency in Fulham that she'd used to find her first flatshare and promised to view all properties before the end of the day. The decision-making process had taken under a minute and the practical application of said decision didn't seem to be taking much longer. Kate's complete lack of involvement seemed to be speeding the whole thing up.

'No preferences as to area?' Leonie directed a question to Kate, as if noticing her for the first time.

Kate shuffled on her hands. 'Well . . .'

'No, she doesn't know London at all,' said Laura. 'This is her first time here.'

They all shared a sympathetic and smug smile, which was, after half an hour of discussing her school, college and social accomplishments over her dazed head, finally too much for Kate to bear.

'Actually, I do know Chelsea reasonably well,' she said. Erk. Where had that come from? And why had her voice gone all northern?

Heads swivelled. Laura's gimlet eyes fixed on her like a vole. The silence opened up like a void and she rushed to fill it, deeply regretting her inability to sustain stroppiness these days. 'I've been staying in Redcliffe Square for the past— quite recently. Beautiful streets, lots of, um, trees. It's . . . very nice round there,' she finished up lamely, but in a more credible drawl, borrowed once again from Selina.

'Rather out of the eighty to ninety pound league though,

dear,' said Leonie, returning to her card file. 'Now, wasn't there something in South Holland Park, Miranda . . .?'

The other woman gave Kate a pitying look and yanked a bright yellow pin out of the King's Road.

Kate sensed a certain *froideur* rise up next to her.

'Is South Holland Park not Shepherd's Bush?' asked Laura.

'No, it's just *south* of Holland *Park*,' emphasised Leonie, a steely tone entering her cut-glass enunciation.

Wow, thought Kate, just like Laura's Legal Aid voice but even posher.

There was a discreet cough from the pinboard. 'Leonie, this morning I had a call from that . . .' Miranda approached the maple wood desk and pushed a fax from a small pile in a chrome in-tray discreetly towards her partner. 'Place in West Ken,' she added, almost mouthing the words.

Leonie snapped her head up from her files and ran her eyes over the fax paper. 'Not again,' she murmured, but then turned her frown upside down into a beaming smile for Laura and Kate's benefit.

She needn't have bothered. Laura was staring round the office, assessing how much rent one paid for a second-floor place like this and whether the dreadful watercolours of Scottish lochs, possibly painted by a friend of the Mulberry-ed pair, were a tax fiddle. Kate meanwhile had been staring at Miranda's preternaturally smooth complexion and wondering if her skin was somehow stretched and attached to the enormous velvet Alice band she was wearing on top of her blonde flicks.

Neither Laura nor Kate noticed the glance that passed between the two women.

'I have something ideal,' said Leonie. 'Let me write down the details for you . . .'

Laura parked her Corsa outside the red brick mansion block, effectively boxing in the battered estate car in front of her. Kate stared intently at the map, just in case they'd come to completely the wrong street, the wrong area. They hadn't. This was Deauville Crescent, West Kensington, and there was no getting round it.

Laura swung her car door open and marched across the road to the portico. 'Kate, did I give you the piece of paper with the details on?' she yelled, searching through her handbag.

Kate silently regarded the business card embossed with the 'Rooms with a View' logo. On the back, Leonie had scrawled, 'Dant Grenfell, Flat 27, Pennington Mansions' and a phone number. Suddenly she understood how Doris, their labrador, must have felt every time they bunged her into kennels when the family went on holiday: forced to bunk up in an uncomfortable, unfamiliar place with a bunch of other dogs she didn't know, and expected to be all pleased when the family came back tanned and happy to collect her. Poor Doris. Poor Kate.

'Come on, Kate, we haven't got all day!' shouted Laura. 'Which flat?'

'Twenty-seven,' replied Kate. Since her departure was pretty much settled, she wondered whether it was really necessary for her to get out of the car and see inside – Laura would doubtless be taking notes and could bellow all the salient details out of the window. Did it matter much where she went?

Laura strode over to the car. 'Come on, Kate,' she said. Her eyes softened when she saw the misery written on Kate's face. 'You never know, he might be a bit of a dish.'

'With a name like Dant?' Kate said sarcastically. 'What's that short for, Kommandant? Or Abundant?'

Laura took a deep breath and muttered, 'I can see what Mike—' to herself.

Kate noticed that there was a long trail of curling ivy decorating one balcony, and for some reason this, and the first opportunity she'd had for spontaneous sarcasm in some time, cheered her up.

She opened the door and got out, pulling her bag out after her. In it was her *Rough Guide to London* which she had been committing to memory the previous night, so she wouldn't look stupid when Laura dragged her round the flat agencies. She realised now that she shouldn't have worried: there was no way Laura was going to contemplate her living somewhere less than appropriate, even if she – and theoretically, Mike – was offering to pay the first couple of months' rent for her. Word could get round.

Kate inspected the doorbells and, leaning against the door to reach them, pressed number twenty-seven. The speaker crackled unpromisingly.

'*Hellooo*,' bellowed Laura, stretching across her. 'Laura Craig for Dant Grenfell. We're here about the flat!'

The intercom crackled again.

'No one at home,' remarked Kate hopefully.

The door buzzed from inside and she lurched forward as the lock was released.

Laura strode into the dark hall, stepping over the piles of pizza delivery leaflets and minicab cards. Kate followed at a safe distance. The place smelled of fried onions. And something else she couldn't quite put her finger on.

Flat number twenty-seven was up four flights of stairs, covered with slippery carpet. Laura took them at a brisk pace, swinging her arms as if on a Stairmaster; out of breath after one and a half flights, Kate hung grimly on to the banisters, conscious that their progress was probably being observed from the open door of the flat above.

However, on reaching the top, they found that the door was shut, and there was no sign of life. Laura tsked with annoyance and started to pick flakes of paint off the doorframe.

'They knew we were coming.' She hammered on the door and the brass figure 2 slipped forty-five degrees. She tsked again. 'Hello!'

There were muted signs of life from inside. Kate and Laura both strained to hear something that would indicate an approaching landlord.

'Inatten-Dant?' offered Kate cheerfully.

Laura scowled at the leperous paintwork and sighed loudly enough to be heard in the next fare zone. 'All it takes is a quick sanding. You know, Kate, it makes me so mad when decent old places like this are just left to . . .'

At that moment, the front door was pulled open just far enough to accommodate half a tousled and unshaven face, which could have belonged to a shop-worn twenty-year-old or an angelic thirty-something. An eye squeezed tightly shut and reopened, as if in surprise at still finding them there.

'Yerp?' The eye focused on Kate's spiralling red curls with obvious appreciation. 'What?'

'Let me deal with this,' said Laura, putting a warning hand on Kate's bare arm. 'Dant?' She extended the other hand and simultaneously pushed her foot into the door, opening it sufficiently for her to march inside the flat. She was already in the large open-plan kitchen, sizing up the fitted cabinets, before Kate shyly shook hands with the owner of the unshaven face and followed her in.

Dant Grenfell in full view resembled a bad-tempered teddy bear woken up early after a year's heavy-duty debauchery. He shuffled into the kitchen, dark hair falling into bloodshot eyes, which he rubbed with both sets of knuckles. He wore a very old black T-shirt with a Def Jam logo peeling away on the front and a pair of crumpled tartan boxer shorts. There was a date stamp on the back of his right paw.

'Have we caught you at a bad time?' asked Kate politely, her previous chipperness evaporating fast. Something about Dant made her faintly nervous – he reminded her of the scary lads at college who had hung around the English faculty in long black wool coats and used the film society as their own private Italian porn channel.

Behind her, Laura opened a cupboard and slammed it shut before Kate had a chance to see inside.

'Er, nooo, one of my friends had an opening last night,' he mumbled. 'Bit of a late one.' His head sprang up abruptly and he fixed Laura with a narrowed eye. 'Hang on, who are you? Are you one of Cress's mates?'

'My name,' said Laura, reverting once again to her Legal Aid voice, 'is Laura Craig. This is my sister-in-law, Kate Craig. We were assured by Leonie at "Rooms with a View" that the rooms you're looking to let out would be fine to view this morning. She was meant to ring you. She said she *had* rung you.'

Dant looked automatically at the sink, where the phone sat drunkenly in a fish-tank, its curly lead coiled around a sunken goldfish palace. There were five cigarette butts, one crushed can of Red Bull, and a half-exposed roll of film floating in it but no fish.

'It's actually me who's wanting the room,' said Kate. She smiled hopefully in the manner of a sixth-form prefect and wondered who on earth she was borrowing this personality from.

'Good,' grunted Dant, and looked as if he were about to say more, but Laura's acidly raised eyebrow stopped him.

'Right,' said Laura, 'can we see it then?'

Dant gave her a black look and shuffled off. Kate followed him. Laura muttered something under her breath and looked at her watch.

As they passed two rooms with doors partly closed, Kate became aware that underneath the rather rank aroma of unwashed male, Dant smelled of oranges, something she found quite reassuring, despite his otherwise moody attitude. He also scratched himself frequently. Perhaps too frequently.

'This is it,' he said, pushing a door open. Kate stepped in. It was very dark inside, partly due to the deep blue wallpaper, and partly due to the view, a red brick wall opposite. She heaved the window open to let some air in and gave herself a splinter.

'Who else lives here?' asked Laura, opening and shutting the drawers of a tall chest. 'Feels like a boys' flat to me.' She said this in a reasonably innocuous tone, but Kate knew it wasn't intended as a compliment.

'The flat belongs to me, and one of my friends from school lives here too. Harry. He's a car dealer. At work at the moment.'

Dant and Harry. Kate sighed and, sucking her wounded thumb, mentally abandoned rule 4. So much for not living surrounded by rahs and Sloanes. Still, it looked like rules 3 – not living with Mike and Laura – and 4 were mutually exclusive.

'And the previous tenant . . .?'

'Moved out.' Dant's expression made it clear that this was not a topic for further discussion.

'I see.' Laura had finished her inspection of the storage facilities. 'Can we have a look at the bathroom?' She had gone before Dant had time to reply.

Kate walked around the room, sucking her thumb where she'd been splintered, and leaned out of the window, aware of Dant lounging against the door-frame, but not sure what she should say to him. She could hear Laura marching down the parquet tiles in her sensible court shoes which elevated her to exactly two inches below Mike's ear. The view outside was limited to the window-boxes of the flat opposite, red and pink busy lizzies squashed flat by the big tabby cat sleeping on them. Cars droned past on the main road and she could smell the kebab shop on the corner warming up for lunch. It wasn't quite as bad as it looked from the outside. Perhaps because you couldn't actually see the outside.

'Excuse *me*!' squawked Laura's voice from the bathroom; Kate turned her head and saw a brief flash of pale flesh as a skinny male body, barely covered by a green hand towel, stumbled out of the bathroom and past the door, banging painfully into the wall on the way.

'Er, yeah, that's Seth,' mumbled Dant by way of explanation.

Kate raised her eyebrows. He matched her challenging stare but caved in seconds before she did. Kate felt an odd kind of triumph.

'Better go and . . . yerp, right,' he said and shuffled off.

Kate turned slowly on her heel. The room itself wasn't bad. Quite big, not too much horrible furniture, slight lingering odour, but . . . If she was going to have to spend four months somewhere, it might as well be somewhere she could hide. And it might as well be somewhere Mike and Laura wouldn't feel compelled to come and visit with their raging maternity battles and their bloody careers advice.

Kate wandered out into the hall, decorated with artistically scraped black paintings in clip frames, and through to the sitting room, which was comfortingly messy; African pots and spine-broken paperbacks filled the wall-to-ceiling bookshelves, and a Playstation was strung across the floor. There was much evidence of a good night in lying around. It didn't feel like home, but at least it felt like someone's home. As opposed to Laura's house, which felt like a show home. For a start, here the remote controls weren't colour-coded and the magazines appeared to be stored in a pile next to the toilet. There was no evidence of a magazine rack.

Laura strode in, handbag clamped firmly under her arm. She had stopped her barrage of questions and set her lips in a tight white line, which looked pretty ominous to Kate. Dant trailed in behind her, sullen and panda-eyed. He had put on a pair of manky jeans – very possibly, she thought, at Laura's request.

'OK, Kate, I think we've seen all we need to,' she said, turning to Dant with hand extended. 'More than enough, in certain cases.'

'But, I . . .' began Kate, looking from one to the other.

Dant wrinkled his nose offensively and ignored both of them.

Laura withdrew her hand and made for the door. 'Thanks so much for letting us have a look round. Sorry to have got you out of bed.'

'No problemo,' said Dant. Meaning, sod off, you cow.

Kate cringed. 'Er, thank you,' she said, hoping for a twinkle of understanding in the deep-set eyes. She wanted to whisper, 'She's not my blood relation,' if it wasn't already obvious enough, or 'I like your scrapy paintings,' but Laura was already clumping down the stairs and Dant heading back to his room.

'Oh, OK,' she half-said to herself and walked to the door, hesitating slightly as to whether she should close it behind her or not. She could almost hear Giles sighing in her head at her timidity.

While she was looking around her for help, a skinny black cat dropped down from its hiding place on a hatstand and curled round her leg. Kate smiled and bent to stroke it.

'And shut the fucking door as you leave!' mumbled Dant's voice, apparently from under a duvet – but not loud enough to be clearly heard. Kate straightened up abruptly. With a surprisingly strong paw, the cat prised open the door to Dant's room and slunk inside.

'Oh, OK,' she said again and left.

'Oh. My. God.' Laura pulled the plastic top off her double espresso as she drove and downed it in one.

Kate stared at this unusually rock-'n'-roll behaviour.

'You know, I'd forgotten people live like that,' she went on, checking carefully in her rear-view mirror before dropping the empty cup in the carrier bag tied to the passenger seat. 'You do forget once you've got a place of your own. Did you see the state of the bathroom? I mean, once his friend had kindly vacated the bath.' Laura snorted in an 'And we won't go into *that*' manner. 'Well, you could have grown potatoes in the side of it. Either they don't have a cleaner or they all coat themselves in mud before getting in to it. It was full of unwashed clothes too. And the grouting is appalling.'

Having spent her final year in the sort of house which made you grateful for a toilet that flushed comprehensively first time, Kate thought this was a pretty trifling matter.

'So, anyway, where else have we got on the list?' Laura reached out for the notes.

Bite the bullet, Kate. Walk it like you talk it. 'Well, that last one was fine with me, actually. I wasn't too bothered about the bath. I rather liked all the tiling they had.'

'But, Kate, didn't you see the state of the sofa?'

Kate furrowed her brow trying to remember. 'It was a new one, wasn't it?'

Laura waited behind a bus, ignoring the hooting traffic behind her. 'Exactly. Exactly. No one that age has a new sofa. Which makes you think, what did they do to last one that they *require* a *replacement* sofa?'

Kate opened her mouth.

'And more to the point, what happened to the last tenant that he won't tell us why they left?' she finished triumphantly. 'I'm going to call "Rooms with a View" when we get home. It's evidently gone downhill rapidly since I used it.'

'But really, Laura, I rather liked that flat. They had a little cat.' Kate made a resolution to start her new self-sufficient personality regime right now. Things could not get worse, and if she had to suffer, she might as well go the whole hog and make it as bad as possible. Why, the weeks would simply fly by. She set her jaw. 'I want to live there.'

Laura was sufficiently amazed to take her eyes off the road but her response was lost as her mobile phone started ringing. It was set to 'Whistle While You Work'.

'Oh, for God's sake, I told Mike to change the bloody ringing tone on that . . . Can you get the phone out of my bag, please?'

Kate obediently searched through Laura's capacious handbag and brought it out, holding it as if it were coated in sick.

'Well, go on, answer it, I'm driving,' said Laura testily, negotiating a box junction.

Kate looked at the phone. The tune was paralysing her brain.

'I can't. I don't know how. How do they work?'

'Press the green button!'

Kate couldn't see a green button. The marching dwarves

were coming up to a second verse. 'Ohhhh, Laura, do something!' She waved the phone helplessly.

Laura heaved a sigh and, grabbing the phone, pulled in to the kerb, shooting Kate a look of pure disdain. 'Hello, Laura Craig. Yes, we've just left . . . and I wasn't very impressed . . . Oh, hello!' The icy note vanished. 'I see . . . right . . . oh, did you? How funny . . . No! . . .'

Kate stared out of the window while Laura rattled on. They were parked opposite another Greggs bakery and she seized on the familiar blue and white shopfront as a comforter. The fourth one she had seen since arrival. It was a good sign. If she saw a red car before Laura finished her conversation, the house would be OK; Laura, Mike and her mum would get off her back and Giles would be sent home early to run the London office.

'Right . . . OK, then, that's fine . . . no, really, it's very kind of you . . . OK, then, thanks so much. Bye now!' Laura pushed the aerial back into its socket, dumped the phone in her bag and restarted the engine.

'Well?'

'That was Cressida Grenfell, the owner of the flat. The charming Dante's sister. Most apologetic. Apparently she was stuck in traffic and missed us by about five minutes and then bounced her brother off the walls for the state of the place.' A smug grin spread over Laura's even features. 'A very nice woman, and very sorry the flat is such a mess, too. Not normally like that, apparently.'

Oh, good. As long as Laura's flat-procurers haven't gone downmarket, that's fine, thought Kate. She found herself feeling sorry for Dant, getting the rounds of the kitchen even as they spoke from his own biologically-inflicted Laura.

'She says she's convinced he was only doing it to put us off,' Laura went on.

'And to think he nearly succeeded!' exclaimed Kate ironically. 'So is it OK for me to live there now, please?' The sarcasm went over Laura's head.

'Mind you, she wouldn't tell me why the last girl left,' Laura pursed her lips, 'and I note that "Rooms with a View" did *not* mention the fact that she actually left the country, but it occurs to me that whoever it was must have had a job, which is presumably now also vacant . . .'

Kate felt suspiciously set up. However, having sorted the flat out with the minimum effort, another afternoon down the Job Centre with Laura – or worse, going through her little black book for contacts – was surely on the cards. And that she didn't really want to have to go through, just for the sake of proving a point to Giles for four lousy months. What was that thing about killing gift horses with one stone?

She settled back in her seat and into the pleasant warmth of a pit of self-pity with a deep end yet unexplored. 'Fine. Let me get my stuff and I'll be out of your hair.'

Laura stole a quick glance at her sister-in-law out of the corner of her eye. Kate was smiling like Joan of Arc on the way to the stake. Something of a turnaround from the nervous, miserable creature who had arrived so apologetically with barely a spare pair of pants in her bag. Laura experienced a twinge of guilt that she was turning her only sister-in-law over to the company of strangers before she had even got her sorted out with a decent *A–Z*.

But then she remembered how quickly Mike had reverted since Kate's arrival from the polite husband she had spent the past four and a half years training him up to be, into a squabbling, argumentative whiner who had, for the first time in ages, argued that morning about who should get the plastic toy out of the new cereal packet. She shuddered. Maybe charity didn't have to begin at home. It could just as easily be someone else's home.

'OK, then,' said Laura, brightly. 'Let's call in at the office on the way home and get all the paperwork sorted out.' She dismissed the chinking sound of twenty pieces of silver from her mind and Kate turned on the radio.

chapter seven

Mike and Laura drove her round to Pennington Mansions on Sunday morning, after a farewell supper at the Bread and Roses in Clapham the previous night. Mike had annoyed Laura by pointing out all the kids' facilities and Laura had annoyed Mike by pointing out that having spent the best part of twenty years getting her figure, she had no intention of waving it goodbye just yet. Mike annoyed Kate by acting loud and stupid and Kate annoyed Mike by systematically dismissing London as a place for sentient human beings to live. They were all pleased to leave by nine.

'So, where do you want this?' said Mike, heaving her rucksack out of the boot.

'In the house, maybe?' Kate replied sarcastically.

Laura had already gone to the front door with the key and Kate could see her in the hall, sorting the pizza delivery leaflets into piles.

'Look, Kate, I'm missing Sunday morning nets to bring you over here, so don't push it, OK? I mean, I can't believe we're paying the deposit and first month on this place for you anyway. You'd have been just as happy in Archway. My old flatshare there was basic but full of . . .'

'Mum still doesn't know why the dog was so ill last Christmas, you know, Mike,' Kate said casually while keeping her eye on Laura, who had stopped screwing up leaflets and was now sifting through post. 'Think she'd be a bit upset if she knew why Dad had to rush Doris to the vet's on Boxing Day.'

There was a choking sound in her right ear.

'How the hell did you . . .?'

Kate walked over the road, leaving Mike to bring her bags.

Laura waved some post at her. 'Gas bill, electricity bill, water rates, council tax . . . My God, some of these go back months!'

Kate peered at the brown envelopes. 'Whose name are they in?' The name on most of the bills, which was not Dant's, looked vaguely familiar, but then everything was starting to run together like a bad dream sequence.

'Don't let them put anything in your name, whatever you do!' Laura was rifling through the abandoned bills on the mat and slotting them efficiently into the pigeon-holes. 'And don't under any circumstances give them your home address. Or ours, for that matter.' She finally stopped on a white envelope, hand-addressed to Flat 27, and gazed at it thoughtfully, as if torn by inner debate.

Looking across the road, Kate saw Mike finish a conversation on his mobile, make a note on the back of his hand with a pen and hoist her rucksack on to his shoulder, nearly taking out a cyclist in the process. Catch me on a bike in London, she thought. No way.

Laura tapped the edge of the envelope on her teeth and, reaching a decision, opened it.

'Laura!' exclaimed Kate, shocked. 'That's someone else's post! You can't . . .'

'Chill,' said Laura, reading.

Chill? Chill? Who had Laura been talking to?

'But . . .'

'Look, I knew there would be something like this.' Laura waved the headed notepaper under Kate's nose. 'It's a formal letter and P45 from the publishing house that Dant Grenfell's ex-tenant worked for. All you have to do is phone up, er,' she peered at the signature, 'Jennifer Spencer, tell her you've heard there's a vacancy for a . . .'

Kate scanned the letter. '. . . an editorial assistant . . .'

'. . . and could you come in for an interview? I'll bet they haven't even got the advert in the papers yet. They'll be glad to save the money. Publishers always are, from what I've heard.'

'Is this ethical behaviour for a lawyer, Laura?'

'Not really. But you want a job, don't you?'

'Yeees, but I don't know anything about publishing.'

Laura resorted to her Legal Aid voice. 'You can read, I take it?'

'Well . . .'

'In which case, for four months you can make it up as you go along, by which time you can leave, or they'll have sacked you.'

'Oh, well, fine, that's OK then.'

Mike had arrived with all Kate's worldly goods, including the parcel of clothes her mother had sent down, care of Mike's office, following her Judas-like phone call with Giles. Kate hadn't dared open it up – her horror at the thought of the clothes her mother would have selected as appropriate was roughly equal with her horror at the thought of the clothes Laura would have pressed on her as alternatives. It was a pitiful amount of stuff, but Mike still managed an abused sigh as he dumped them with a glare at Kate's feet.

She responded by making 'sad doggy feet' with limp wrists.

Mike hissed something unintelligible but obscene at her.

Laura tapped him cheerfully on the head with a pile of envelopes. 'Third floor, please, Jeeves!'

Kate followed the pair of them up the stairs, trying hard to remember the last proper book she had read and when exactly she had abandoned her resistance to Laura's organising.

The flat was empty and now smelled strongly of onion bha-jees.

'Gor, this is just like my old place!' Mike dropped the bags at the door, leaving Kate to drag them into her new home.

'Sorry we can't stop,' said Laura, as Mike began to wander around the kitchen, picking at the half-empty takeaway cartons. 'We need to get to Ikea for some curtain rails and I don't want to leave it too late. I'll just unpack this shopping for you and we'll have to be off.'

'Oh, that's no problem,' said Kate, looking round with a sinking heart at the unfamiliar mess. Her own mess she liked, but this was depressingly alien. So much for a welcoming committee. She wished Mike and Laura would hurry up and leave, since the longer these last two contacts with the outside world remained, however unwelcome in normal circumstances, the nearer she was to bursting into tears and begging them to stay. And she really didn't want to do that.

Laura bustled round the kitchen, emptying bags of carrots and onions into improvised vegetable baskets. There was no other evidence of any fresh vitamin intake. 'I put some bits and pieces in a bag for you, in case you didn't have bedding and so on . . .'

Giles's white bed, like a big, crisp, sexy, elegant meringue, filled Kate's mind. She bit her lip. Every single thought that entered her head carried traces of him.

'Mike, did you bring in that big Habitat bag?' Laura called, signalling to him with her eyes while she stacked tins of soup on the work surface.

Mike was fiddling with the Playstation in the sitting room. 'They've got Gran Turismo 2 and TOCA 2 and analogue controllers, the bastards . . . Oh, right, um, we off then?'

Laura clasped Kate. 'Give that publishing woman a call on Monday, won't you? Otherwise I've got some friends who work in the City who might know some temp agencies. If you don't have any luck, you've got that list of people Alex made for you the other night, haven't you?'

'Bye, sis,' said Mike, with a brief hug. 'Don't do anything

I wouldn't,' he added, a touch wistfully.

Kate nodded. The parameters of what Mike could and couldn't do were no longer as flexible as they used to be, and they both knew it.

As she walked them to the door, Laura turned and, squeezing Kate's arm, said, 'I know it's hard, but just think how proud Miles will be when he finds out how well you've coped!'

'Gahhaahh,' mumbled Kate and shut the door on them. As she listened to them clatter down the stairs, squabbling indistinctly, she leaned her forehead on the door and allowed the tears to flow down her cheeks at last. Crying silently, she went to the big kitchen window and watched Mike and Laura arguing over who should drive, Laura finally wrenching the keys out of Mike's hand and barging into the front seat. Mike flicked a schoolboyish two fingers behind his wife's back and got in just as Laura pulled away from the kerb, narrowly missing denting the door on a lamppost.

Kate pushed a pile of old Sunday newspapers off the window-seat and knelt down, staring at the empty space where Mike's car had been. At least Mike and Laura had each other, however much they wished otherwise. The tears dripped off her nose. Why should they be allowed to be together, pissing each other off constantly, when she and Giles, who adored each other, had to be apart? She glossed over the fact that even had he been in London for the college vacations she would have been at home with a pile of illicit chocolate and her mother's incessant lectures on the joys of education.

Kate pulled a red and white spotted hanky out of her pocket and pressed it to her nose. It still smelled of Giles, just. He had given it to her silently at the airport, even though she hadn't been crying. At that point. By the time he had to go through the departure gate, even Giles had shining eyes. But then he had turned resolutely, as he'd said he would, and marched through without a backwards glance. 'I hate long goodbyes,' he said. Part of her hoped he had meant her to hold the hanky to her nose in bed and remember how he smelled; part of her wondered if it had just been in anticipation of embarrassing floods. Fat tears were now blotting new patches of deeper red on to it and even though her stomach was heavy with misery, the narcotic effects of unfettered crying were beginning to soothe her.

With the hanky still pressed to her nose, Kate got up and looked for the Peter Jones bag with Laura's spare duvet in it. She pulled it out of its case like a sausage and dragged it into her empty room, along with her Walkman and a dwarf-choking Toblerone she had put in the trolley when Laura had 'got some supplies in' for her and which she had hidden in her bag in case Mike snaffled it.

Ignoring the state of the bedroom, which somehow seemed irrelevant, Kate rolled herself up for comfort, plugged in her headphones and blotted out all conscious thought with Led Zeppelin.

When she woke up two hours later it was with the groggy feeling that comes with sleeping during the day, and the nasty taste that comes with eating chocolate before bed and not brushing your teeth. The room was too hot and smelled fusty. Kate pulled a face when she saw what time it was and swung her feet on to the floor. First things first: if she locked herself in the bathroom with her toilet bag, as with sleeping, no one could get her.

The room with which she would be becoming very familiar over the next 121 days was scarred with bits of old Blu-tack and oddments that the previous occupant hadn't bothered to pack: a Biro, a hairband, a book of matches from a dodgy-sounding club, a condom – still wrapped, she noted fastidiously. Kate cast her eyes around for any unwrapped ones. It was that sort of room. There were also stray socks and greying trunks hanging off a dilapidated clothes-horse – presumably she was now living in the laundry. How she could have missed all this the other day, she didn't know.

Perhaps it had been the exhilaration of finding a nice roaring fire from which to escape the Craig frying pan.

Laura's 'Through the Keyhole' comments on the bathroom returned with crystal clarity. Bad grouting, grimy bath, nude strangers . . . What kind of a pig lives in a house like this?

Me, now, thought Kate. She wrapped herself in her duvet and ventured out into the hall with her washbag.

The flat was still quiet and the cool, if grubby, parquet was rather nice against her hot feet. Which was the bathroom? Not the door with the 'Do Not Disturb – Muff Diving in Progress' sign on it, obviously. Kate grimaced. That must be Harry's room. Fantastic. A rugby rah with a sense of humour and a gur-reat spiel for the ladies. Just what she'd always wanted as a flat mate.

The door next to that was ajar, showing blue and white tiling. The bathroom. With a sigh, Kate pushed open the door and shut it behind her. It was filthy, no doubt about it. But the shower looked powerful and there was a *Psycho* shower curtain – evidence of some kind of sense of humour, at least.

An unopened squirty bottle of Flash bathroom cleaner lurked under the sink. Jesus, thought Kate, as she attacked the bath with it, Laura must have been playing those Hypnotise Yourself Houseproud While You Sleep tapes at me. She tried not to look too closely at the grouting.

Chin-deep in the foam from the sexy bubble bath she had brought for Giles's enjoyment – the irony of which didn't escape her – Kate shut her eyes and focused on the small things.

Phone the publishing woman or let Laura organise more interviews?

Phone the woman.

Live in squalor or clean the bedroom?

Clean the bedroom.

This was easy enough. As long as she kept her mind empty she'd be fine. And a quick visit to a nearby off-licence for more chocolate and a bottle of red wine would be just the next small step to take.

She soaked until the water cooled down to body temperature and then stood up in the bath, still covered in bubbles, and admired herself in the shaving mirror over the sink. A large blob of foam tastefully concealed her pale pink nipples and her stomach was nice and shiny. Kate twisted and turned unselfconsciously. She looked like one of those improbable women painted on the side of American World War Two bombers, albeit with much smaller breasts. Kate experimented with her sponge and face flannel for optimum effect and at that point the door she hadn't noticed on the other side of the room opened and Dant walked in.

'*Aaaarrrgghuuch!*' Kate dropped her props in surprise, realised she didn't have a towel, let alone a dressing gown, and sat down inelegantly in the bath, sloshing foam on the floor.

Dant turned his back but didn't leave.

'I suppose that gets your sister back for catching Seth in the nod when you inspected the property,' he said. 'As it were.'

Kate was speechless with embarrassment and sank down beneath the rapidly dispersing bubbles.

'What were you doing with those sponges anyway?' he went on. The amusement in his voice made Kate feel even more vulnerable than she thought already possible. 'Hope I didn't interrupt anything.'

'She's not my sister!' Kate managed. 'And if you don't mind I'd rather you left! You can see I'm . . .' She supposed that it was obvious that she wasn't wearing any clothes, being in the bath and all.

Dant shifted his weight from one leg to the other, and showed no signs of leaving. 'Feeling's mutual. It wasn't my idea to have anyone else living here, but as you'll discover for yourself, my sister isn't one for negotiation either.'

'Do you always supervise your tenants' baths or am I being singled out for special attention?' snapped Kate, her outrage now overriding her embarrassment. If he was trying to unsettle her, he couldn't have picked a more effective method. She wondered if the Gestapo had thought of it.

'Don't worry, I've seen it all before,' said Dant airily to the towel warmer, 'I went to a very progressive school. And I don't go for skinny girls anyway.'

'Then sod off!' The cheek of it, thought Kate, doubting whether he went for girls in any shape or form. She clutched her sponge tighter to her chest and glowered at his back.

'Well, now I'm here, I just thought I'd run through some house rules. I'm going out in a minute and I don't know when I'll be in again.'

Kate turned on the hot tap with her toe, trying to keep as much of her body under water level as possible, and swished the water with the other one. There was no more froth left in the bubble bath. She looked about for something to cover herself up with, but since she'd been kipping in her underwear, there wasn't much and the duvet was just too far away.

'Can you make it quick, then, please?' Kate added, 'You fucking weirdo,' in her head, but didn't say it aloud. If he wanted to upset her, she wasn't going to give him the satisfaction. And not showing evidence of being riled was something she had had twenty years of practice of, in the face of competition-level aggravation from Mike.

'Milk is in the fridge and is supplied by Cress, my sister, in with the rent. Full cream. It's to make sure I get some form of nutrition. Teresa the cleaner comes in on Thursdays and does what she can. She'll read your mail, by the way, so don't leave it out. All bills – phone, gas, electricity, water rates, et cetera, et cetera – are split between the three of us.'

'You two must have a lot of interesting post if the state of the bathroom's anything to go by.' Kate made a mental note to find out what the absent girl owed and not pay a single penny of it. But she didn't draw Dant's attention to this. 'That it?'

'Don't wake me up before lunch-time, even if the house is on fire, don't feed Ratcat the vile stuff Cress leaves for him, and if my mother rings I am never, ever, at home. OK?'

'Why, hasn't she given you permission to be out?'

Dant turned round and Kate slid further down the bath. Dant's eyes, which were fixed unsettlingly a foot above her head, were very dark, with long lashes, and a shiver went down her spine. He clearly wasn't joking.

'I don't speak to her,' he said. 'Ever.'

'Fine,' said Kate in a small voice. If only she could build up her insolence stamina. She had a horrible feeling in her lower intestine that she was about to do a fear fart into the bath water.

Dant made to leave, then stopped, walked three steps backwards and picked up the duvet, which was draped over a wicker chair. For a moment, Kate thought he was going to walk out with it, leaving her stranded, naked, in the bathroom.

Dant paused. Then taking another two steps backwards he offered it to her without turning round.

'Cheers,' said Kate sarcastically, and waited for him to go. He did.

She listened for the front door shutting, then leapt out of the bath, wrapped herself in the duvet and hopped across to the other door. There was no lock on the bathroom side. Peering round it into the gloom of Dant's room, she could see a bolt on the bedroom side. So he could get in regardless of whether the other main door bolt was shot. Very *Phantom of the Opera*. Kate began to understand why the previous girl had left. Well, it might work on London girlies, but – she yanked the plug out of the bath aggressively – she was made of tougher stuff.

Strangely rejuvenated at the thought of having someone to loathe so close to hand, Kate got dressed. There was a moment of wobbliness when she stopped, mid body lotion, and asked herself for whose benefit she was moisturising her buttocks, but she put that thought to one side in favour of rehearsing some better put-down lines for Dant than, 'That it?'.

Durrrr.

Kate screwed her finger into the side of her head. It felt good.

Her pile of belongings was still where she had left it in the hall and a small puddle was forming beneath the bag of frozen food which Laura had uncharacteristically forgotten to unpack. Must have been her rush to get Mike out of the flat before he started to remember what life was like before Flora, she thought.

Kate kicked the parcel of clothes along the corridor to her room and hauled the food bags on to the breakfast bar for immediate attention. The kitchen, or as much of it as she could see beneath piles of dirty washing and empty cartons, looked like something out of *The Young Ones*. Kate switched on the Sunday night Top 40 countdown and examined the contents of her designated cupboard: small dunes of rice and curry powder, with unidentified sticky circles and the odd dead fly. She turned up the radio. It still didn't look any better.

Teresa kept most of her cleaning equipment as pristine as the Flash in the bathroom. In fact, the J-cloths were so clean, they looked as though they'd never been used. Kate pulled a Mr Muscle spray out of the bucket and squirted the cupboard liberally.

'And if you think I'm doing this for the entire room, you're misled,' she muttered to herself. 'I'm doing it purely for Laura's quality foodstuffs.' She wiped angrily and began to fill the shelves. The chilli-oil-and-sun-dried-tomato-type produce was ridiculously Laura, who had filled her baskets with a guilty conscience.

By the time Dr Fox was running down the Capital Top

Ten, Kate had cleaned one shelf of the fridge, one ring of the hob and one end of the big kitchen table. She had filled one shelf of the freezer with a selection of M&S meals and Laura's home-made frozen offerings, and swept the floor. In an act of generosity she'd done the whole floor, since she couldn't decide which area she would like to claim as hers and wasn't sure she could make the point clearly anyway.

She had moved the fish-tank out of the sink, although she hadn't emptied it, and had made a cup of coffee in a mug decorated with a model more or less wearing a bikini, which vanished when hot water was poured in. To her surprise, given the huge pile of dirty plates on the breakfast bar, there was a dishwasher behind one of the pine panels, and since she could do most housework as long as the music was loud enough, Kate loaded it up. It smelled fetid, but she didn't feel obliged to explore that on her first day.

Now everything was swishing away in the dishwasher the onion bhajee room fragrance dissipated a little. Kate wiped her hands on an unironed shirt and wondered if she should ring her mother, who, after all, ought to be missing her little girl by now.

She wandered into the sitting room in search of the phone, presuming that the sorry-looking specimen in the fish-tank wasn't the only one, and eventually unearthed, from under a discarded rugby shirt, a transparent model with brightly wired innards: the kind of phone she had begged her mother for in 1988. It had a long walkabout lead and Kate walked it back into the kitchen, dialling her home number as she went.

It took a suspiciously long time for her mother to come to the phone.

'Hello, yes?' A doom-laden talk about malicious callers at the local school the previous year had transformed Mrs Craig's telephone manner to the extent that double-glazing salesmen now hung up in shock.

'Mum, it's Kate.'

There was a pause.

'Mum? Mum, are you there?'

'I'm just marking my page, dear.'

'In what?' Kate hoped that just for once, she could have caught her mother halfway through a nice Jilly Cooper novel. Like the old days.

'In *The Approach to Latin*.' Kate wondered whether she'd now run out of GCSEs and had volunteered to resit her O-levels. 'Are you calling from Laura's house?'

'No, I'm calling from this new flat she's found for me. And it's as much Mike's house as Laura's, Mum.' She wished her mother wouldn't automatically prefer the partners of her offspring to her own children – and make it so obvious.

'Yes, well. Did you get that parcel of clothes? I had ever such a nice conversation with Giles about his new job. He's such a clever lad, Kate, you want to keep hold of him if you can.'

'Not much chance of that with him in America, is there?' Kate knew from experience that there was no point looking for sympathy. At best, it would only lead to a whole new raft of previously unsuspected problems. 'And thank you very much for encouraging him to abandon me here in London. He was adamant that you didn't want me to come home. Very maternal of you.'

'Katherine, it's about time you flew the nest. Your father and I want our lives back too, you know! These four months will be the making of you, love. Your brother never so much as brought his washing back after he went up to Cambridge. Look at him now.'

Just because Laura took over as his mum as soon as the biological one left off. Kate picked up a pile of pizza boxes off a work surface and dumped them in the bin. She squirted, wiped and sat down.

'I didn't ring for careers advice, Mum, I just thought you might like to know where I am. Everything's happened rather quickly; Laura saw the flat, arranged the deposit and dumped me here before I had time to run out of pants. Shall I give you the address?'

'No need, dear, I spoke to Mike this afternoon. Laura phoned me to let me know how it had all gone.'

Kate annihilated an ailing cactus with Mr Muscle. 'Anything else you'd like to tell me, since you seem to be better informed than I am?'

'No need to take that tone with me.' There was an indiscriminate mumbling in the background, and Kate heard her mother hiss, 'Don't clear the table until I've finished my timeline, Philip! Those books are in order!'

'How's Dad?' asked Kate, hoping that he at least might be missing her around the house. She was the only one who would make him curries now Mike had left home.

'Not bad. He's going to start learning your trumpet. I told him there were some community classes starting at the school during the holidays and he dug it out from your wardrobe. We're playing in the recorder consort again too, this summer. Why don't you ever play your recorder any more? You were always a lovely player.'

Kate ignored this familiar gambit and though she couldn't think of anything she could usefully talk to her mother about, now the conversation might be coming to a close, she couldn't bear it to end. 'Mum,' she began, tentatively, 'if I can't find a job, you know, and if it's just . . .' she cast about frantically for something that would make her sound vulnerable and yet not weedy, '. . . just too much for me, all at once, I can still come home, can't I?'

'Oh dear, didn't Giles say?'

'No, he didn't,' said Kate heavily.

'We're letting the spare rooms out for the language students at the summer school. One of the teachers asked me if I wouldn't mind, as the school's overbooked. Very cunning idea, really, and we're using the money to pay for a season ticket at the RSC.'

'Oh, great.'

'Isn't it? I'm going to take them all line-dancing.'

Kate suddenly felt very tired. 'Mum, I should go. I have to

prepare to lie my way into a job in the morning and my room still needs to be fumigated before I can feel safe without shoes on.'

'For Heaven's sake, Philip, we can eat on our knees! Are you expecting the Queen? Leave it, just leave it!'

'I'll ring you later in the week, shall I?'

'Yes, dear, you do that.'

'Bye, Mum, love to Dad and Doris.'

Kate slid sadly off the work surface and opened the fridge for some supper. So it looked as if she had to stay then. Her own mother hiring out her bedroom before the sheets were cold on the bed. Turning into some scary 'I reinvented myself through Adult Education' chat-show guest. Kate shoved a tikka masala for one in the microwave and miserably remembered the time in her childhood when her mother had watched endless soap operas with her and told her not to worry if she came bottom in maths, because she made a lovely Madeira cake.

The sound of the front door opening, shutting and the shuffle of feet came from the hall. Kate straightened up in preparation to be rude or apologetic to Dant – she decided it would hinge on whether he was wearing a baseball cap or not. But the figure shuffling into the kitchen was taller, blonder, dressed in very grass-stained cricket whites and clutching a bottle of beer. It was Harry the Muff Diver.

'You th' new bird or 's Dant pulled at las'?' he said, very carefully. A pleased smile spread over his face.

'Neither,' snapped Kate. The microwave pinged. 'I'm your worst nightmare.' She pulled out her supper, trying not to wince at the nuclear temperature of the plastic, and dropped it on a plate. 'Careful I don't spill this on you now.'

Harry staggered back in alarm as Kate stalked out to her room. She had to return almost immediately to pick up the cleaning bucket, but by then he was preoccupied with the mechanics of peeing into the sink and didn't notice her.

chapter eight

The second she announced herself at Reception Kate began to regret not doing more research on Eclipse Publishing. Every flat surface in the waiting area was covered with books she didn't recognise and photos of pouting authors she hadn't heard of. And she had thought she was pretty well up on books with matt covers and shiny cut-outs of disembodied legs. Giles would have gone berserk if he had known that yesterday's preparation for the interview had consisted largely of going to the nearest Waterstones and browsing cursorily through the modern fiction section before settling down on a window-seat with the latest Princess Diana conspiracy theory book.

Kate scanned the shelves now in vain for something she recognised and, when nothing leapt out at her, she grabbed a catalogue and feverishly ran her eyes up and down the backlist. Who were all these people? How could they make a living as writers when no one had ever heard of them? She looked up guiltily at the receptionist who was despatching callers through the switchboard with the savage rapidity of an acupuncturist and taking no further notice of her.

Oh, God. Kate slumped in her seat. What was the point of going through with the interview? It had been easy enough to blag it on the phone; indeed the woman she had spoken to had sounded positively relieved to have someone call in for an interview so quickly. But whoever was doing the interviewing would soon realise that she was hopelessly ignorant. Kate stared unseeing at the list of names blurring on the catalogue in front of her, gripped by a powerful longing for Giles.

He would have been practice-grilling her all last night; he would have known someone in publishing she could have spoken to beforehand; he would have given her the proper proactive team-player jargon to slot into the conversation, the right names to drop – or suggested that she make some up. Instead she'd had a sleepless night listening to Radiohead through one wall and Gran Turismo through the other. She had barely spoken to a soul for thirty-eight hours. Kate dropped her head on to the open catalogue.

'Kate Craig?'

A small blonde girl had materialised in front of her. This couldn't possibly be the editor, could it? Or could it? Kate looked her up and down nervously, and couldn't think of a single thing to say that wouldn't be interpreted as either overly familiar or stupidly gauche in either case. She could only focus on the fact that capri pants apparently could suit some people after all and cursed her mother for the embarrassingly random selection of clothing she had sent down via Mike for use in her new business life.

'I'm Isobel McIntyre.' The girl had a soft Scottish accent and sounded friendly, if harrassed. Isobel held out her hand, around which was twisted a security pass on a long chain. The photograph on it had evidently been taken in happier times.

'Er, hello,' said Kate, rising awkwardly to her feet and shaking hands. She felt like a giraffe next to the petite Isobel, and tugged discreetly at her too-short-for-work skirt. Bloody Giles. She could have been wearing her new linen trousers – if her mother had thought to send them – and not looking like some bimbo Ally McBeal lookee-likee. Oh dear.

Isobel had already spun on her heel and was leading her

out of Reception towards the lifts, her long milky-tea-coloured plait bouncing with each step.

'Are you, um, Jennifer Spencer's secretary?' asked Kate, trying to make up for her earlier dumbness.

The smile that had begun to form on Isobel's lips vanished. 'No,' she replied through gritted teeth. 'I am Jennifer Spencer's *assistant*.' She looked on the verge of saying more but instead stabbed the call button for the lift with a little more force than was perhaps necessary.

Well done, Kate. Great start.

They stood in the lobby in silence, waiting for the lift to arrive. More authors that Kate didn't recognise gurned or gazed modestly from the walls in tasteful black frames. Isobel twisted the chain of her pass round her hand until bits of her fingers went white. Next to Isobel's reflection in the stainless-steel wall, Kate shifted her weight from one leg to another, trying to keep her skirt as far down as it would go, and racked her brains for some intelligent pre-interview small talk. Was it too cheeky to ask Isobel who Eclipse's authors actually were? Or would it really matter, given how things were going so far?

'These lifts are very European,' she commented brightly for want of anything non-incriminatory to say.

Doh . . . A vision of Giles in his smart Hugo Boss Euro-suit flooded painfully into her head again. Kate noted miserably that the mere thought of him now rendered her all wobbly and invertebrate, and wished the angry stage would come back again. Would she ever be able to talk about the European Union without filling up like a . . . like a . . .

'Er, yes, I suppose so.' Isobel stared at her, then looked at her watch.

'I'm not late, am I? Oh, God, has my watch stopped? I'm so hopeless at being on time . . .'

Anything else you'd like to reveal, dimblebrain? thought Kate, mentally slapping her head. I'm very bad at spelling and I've only ever read the seven books that were on the reading list?

'No, not at all,' said Isobel. 'I just heard—' she seemed on the verge of saying something and then changed her mind. 'I just heard Jennifer on the phone before I came downstairs arranging a fitting in town for eleven-thirty – which only leaves you about fifteen minutes for your interview. Still, I did put it in her diary, so she must know you're coming.'

'A dress fitting?'

Isobel shut eyes deliberately and opened them again slowly. 'No, a shoe fitting. She has all her shoes hand made. In Jermyn Street. Many, many pairs. She has more shoes than Imelda Marcos and Barbie put together. All the better for trampling—' Her lips tightened as though she were deliberately reining herself in from further comment.

'Bloody hell!' said Kate, temporarily forgetting her interviewee status. She stared at Isobel, who was breathing deeply through her nose.

Isobel suddenly noticed Kate's curious gaze reflected in the mirrored sides of the lift and shook herself. Her plait twitched.

'Oh, sorry, it's been a very long morning. Already.' Isobel shrugged and then giggled. 'Dearie me, not giving you a very good impression of Eclipse Publishing Ltd, am I?'

They arrived with a slight bump at the fourth floor. As the doors parted, the lift was disconcertingly still three inches below floor level.

'We're part of a bigger company,' explained Isobel, as Kate's eyes skated frantically around the walls, searching in vain for an author she could claim to have heard of, should Jennifer Spencer demand an Eclipse bookshelf favourite. 'We do the mainstream fiction list, with some non-fiction – well, you'll know all this already, won't you?' She swiped the main door open with her security tag.

'Er, yeah,' said Kate.

Isobel bounced down a corridor of semi-open plan

office pods which reminded Kate of lab experiments to teach rats how to negotiate mazes. Everyone was on the phone. Two or three people were playing Minesweeper at the same time; seeing it was Isobel clumping past, they didn't bother to hide the grid behind the spreadsheet open next to it. Kate's eye was caught by one woman speaking very sweetly into her phone whilst using the WindowArt facility to scribble violently on an open document in red spray-can.

'Jennifer's office is just here. Would you like to wait out-side,' Isobel gestured to a leather and chrome chair and peered through the smoked-glass wall, 'while she finishes her phone call?'

Kate smiled politely and arranged herself on the edge of the seat. Was it possible to see up her skirt from any of the desks? Why didn't they provide slippery seats in changing rooms so you could check these things before you parted with your Switch card? Why did men always tell you to wear skirts to interviews?

'I'll bring you a coffee,' said Isobel. 'She might be some time.'

'No problem,' said Kate breezily. She now had potentially less than ten minutes' worth of interview remaining. As soon as Isobel disappeared round a grey rat partition, Kate seized the book of press cuttings lying on the table next to the seat and flipped through it.

There were several pages devoted to a very serious-looking young man, whom Kate hadn't heard of, called Warwick Barlett. His latest novel, *After Long Discourse*, had been reviewed in all the literary papers that she'd given up ploughing through in her first year at college and which she now realised, three years too late, were largely written by her lecturers. She tucked that self-recrimination away for later and concentrated on committing to short-term memory as many salient facts about Warwick Barlett as she could. If she was going to be exposed as a hopelessly ill-prepared bimbo, she might at least chuck in a few casually tasteful observations on the way down.

Although the office door was ajar, Jennifer Spencer was not making any gesture towards confidentiality and Kate soon began finding it hard to keep herself focused on *After Long Discourse*'s impeccable prose style.

'. . . no, you listen to me! Do you have any idea how long I've been buying hand-crafted shoes from your company?' shrieked a voice somewhere between Joanna Lumley and Joyce Grenfell. 'I have my own last in your workshops!'

Kate realised she had read the same sentence four times and her subconscious was considerably more interested in Jennifer Spencer's sandal-acquiring habits than in Warwick Barlett's diachronic layering. She couldn't ever remember hearing the word 'last' used aloud in that sense before.

'Over twenty years! Yes, that's right! I could have bought a small house in Chelsea for the amount I've spent with you! Which, frankly, makes the amount you have the imper-tinence to charge for the simple task of restructuring a pair of these shoes quite . . .'

Isobel returned with a small espresso cup, which she handed to Kate with an apologetic smile, and closed the door properly, shooting an acid look towards the opaque glass as she left.

Kate raised her eyebrows to herself and gave up on Warwick Barlett. Wasn't there someone easier? A nice fluffy girlie author who might have been on television? Or a celebrity chef? She downed the coffee in one and, being unused to anything stronger than milky Nescafé, was making a '*Gahhgg!*' grimace as Jennifer Spencer's office door opened and she strode out.

'Isobel!'

Kate's attention was now transfixed by the very pointy pair of authentic-looking crocodile-skin mules about two metres away from her own slightly scuffed black court shoes.

'Is this Kate Craig?' Kate sensed that she was being pointed at.

'Yes, it is,' choked Kate, rising to her feet and trying to find somewhere to put the coffee cup.

'Yes, it is.' Isobel had appeared out of nowhere again. 'Shall I transfer your calls?'

'Yup,' said Jennifer Spencer snappily, and turning 45 degrees purred, '*Hellooo*,' to Kate. She was obviously now leaning further towards Joanna Lumley. 'Do come in.'

The office was surprisingly light and the slatted blinds offered a green and un-London-like view of a park. Any shelf not prominently displaying paperback books was prominently displaying a variety of aggressively spiked plants in Baroque pots. Kate looked for somewhere to sit and saw with dismay that her choice was between a spindly designer chair and a very low tapestry stool. Or was it a high footrest? One of Giles's threatened corporate pre-interview tests. She went reluctantly for the chair and sat with her knees very close together. The resulting strain on her stomach muscles after a minute did not bode well for the rest of the interview.

'So, Kate,' said Jennifer Spencer, leaning forward on her desk with her fingers steepled and the long red nails extending some way over her fingertips, 'why do you want to work in publishing?' She asked the question with what Kate interpreted as an ironic smile.

'Because I am a pedant for punctuation,' said Kate. She added an ironic smile of her own in case this was the wrong answer.

'Thank Christ for that. If I hear one more person tweet, "Becauth I love bookth," I will scream,' drawled Jennifer Spencer. She leaned backwards and picked up a paperback at random, holding it face out between her palms. A small galaxy of jewels glittered on either side of the book. 'What do you think looks good about this cover?'

Kate stared at it. *The Satin Dress* by Andrea Cartwright.

She hoped it was safe to presume it was an Eclipse book, although this could be another of those devious pre-preparation tests. She craned her neck subtly to see the book's spine, but there was a beringed finger clamped where the imprint symbol would be. 'Well, the, er, "satin dress" on the front has got a nice . . . satiny texture?' she offered. Jennifer Spencer raised her eyebrows encouragingly. 'And, um, it's very grabby, the colour. Red, very appealing. To women. In supermarkets.' Was that where she'd seen it?

'And what's *wrong* with it?'

A-ha, a variation on that old Careers Service chestnut, 'What would you say are your faults?' Now this one, I've done. Careful, now, not too critical. Just enough to show initiative, thought Kate, looking pensively at the book cover. 'Um, I don't like the writing on the front. The bit underneath the title? It breaks up the image.'

Jennifer Spencer froze slightly. 'That's the shoutline. All books have them, if you haven't noticed.'

Kate flushed and looked closer at the writing. *When he undressed her with his eyes he was surprised at what he found underneath* . . . Thank God she hadn't got as far as reading that bit.

The book was dropped into an in-tray, presumably for Isobel to pick out and replace on the shelf behind the desk. 'Right then, tell me about yourself, Kate.'

'I'm twenty-one, I graduated from Durham with a 2:1 in Combined Arts in June – English, Art History and Classics – and—'

'Do you have any secretarial skills?'

'Yes.'

What?!

Jennifer Spencer was doing eyebrow prompting again.

'Er, I've got word processing skills and a typing speed of –' Kate tried to remember what a creditable – and credible – number would be, '– forty words a minute? And I was the secretary of the student union.'

Hello?!

'Now that's the sort of experience that will be very useful to you here. I'm afraid the early years of being an editor are rather secretarially based.' Jennifer Spencer settled back in her swivel chair and looked as though she were about to start dispensing Maundy money. 'It's not all lunching people and making multimillion-pound offers over the phone. To begin with,' she added as an afterthought. Kate assumed this was a joke and did a polite interview laugh.

'So, who's your favourite Eclipse author?'

Was this an interview or *Twenty Questions* or what? Kate forced herself to keep smiling and replied, 'Ooooh, um, I suppose . . . Warwick Barlett. I read *After Long Discourse* in two days. It was just brilliant.'

This was evidently the right answer, but there wasn't much more of the *Literary Review* to quote.

'He's a great prose stylist, isn't he?' said Jennifer Spencer.

Damn! thought Kate as her last pertinent observation floated out of her grasp. 'Mmmm,' she said, smiling hopefully.

Moving on, moving on!

'Shame we're just about to lose him to HarperCollins.' The acid look was back. Kate saw another big *Family Fortunes*-style cross appear on her interview score-sheet. 'Favourite book?'

Kate's gaze roved helplessly round the office, as she made noncommittal 'oooh, let me think,' noises, until her eye snagged on a strangely familiar image behind a cutesy framed photo of a tot on a potty. No! Could it . . .?

'*The Lost Children of Corkickle*!' she exclaimed triumphantly. 'I loved that book!'

Well, it was all relative, wasn't it?

'Really?' Jennifer Spencer's face came alive for the first time beneath the improbable Princess Margaret hairstyle. 'Why?'

'Well, I don't know exactly,' said Kate honestly. 'But I just couldn't stop reading it once I started. It was sort of addictive. I mean, compelling,' she corrected herself.

'Rose Ann Barton is one of our best sellers. We've sold over half a million copies of *The Lost Children* now, you know. I think it's very good that you can see the literary potential of sagas,' said Jennifer Spencer, leaning further forward. 'So many people look down their noses at a jolly good saga, but really Charles Dickens was a saga writer. As was Shakespeare, although the novel form hadn't been invented in those days, of course.'

Kate nodded sagely but imagined that Dickens would probably have been able to keep track of how many brothers and sisters his heroine had. Or whether the heroine's mother was dead or not.

'So, as I'm sure Isobel mentioned on the phone yesterday, we need to get someone in as soon as possible. I understand that you can start without any notice period?'

Was that it? Interview over? Kate tried not to let relief show too obviously on her face. 'Oh, yes, the sooner the better really.'

'Excellent. Well, I have a meeting with an agent that I must dash off to now, so I'm going to hand you over to the editor in question.' Jennifer Spencer buzzed her phone and Isobel appeared in the doorway. 'Could you take Kate along to Elaine for a chat? And while I'm out, can you book lunches for next month? There's a list in my in-tray.' With this she rose, and Kate sprang to her feet, her thighs aching in protest. She started to do her, 'Thank you so much for seeing me,' speech, but somehow Jennifer Spencer's regal smile dismissed any further contribution and she allowed herself to be guided out of the room by Isobel.

'Agent lunch, my arse,' muttered Isobel as they clumped down some more corridors. 'Here's Elaine. Try not to upset her, she's having one of her bad days.' And she disappeared again.

Kate was surprised to see the woman in the office Isobel had led her to, head in hands, apparently shredding a tissue into a cup of herbal tea. The desk was covered with piles and piles of loose-leaf paper, all weighted down with half-empty cups of foul-smelling liquid.

'Excuse me,' Kate began hesitantly, 'my name's Kate Craig, I'm here for interview . . .'

The woman's head sprang up, flipping her mousy corkscrew perm into a frenzy. Her eyes looked bloodshot, but to be fair, thought Kate, the lighting was of the unflattering fluorescent strip variety.

'Oh, God, right, yes, yes . . .' The woman began shuffling the papers frantically. 'I've just got some rewrites in and Mandy didn't exactly leave with . . .' She clapped her hand over her mouth and widened her eyes. 'Oh, damn, sorry, I shouldn't . . .'

Fearing she could be standing there all day, Kate moved a pile of paper off the other chair and sat down. The woman's eyes anxiously followed the pile, as if she were trying to fix its whereabouts in her mind.

'So . . .?' Kate prompted.

'Yes, well, right, I'm Elaine,' she extended a cold and bony hand, 'and I'm a senior fiction editor.' Her gaze returned by reflex to the script and with some effort flicked back up to Kate.

'Is it something good?' asked Kate, abandoning all attempts at interview technique.

'Oh, well, yes, naturally, but it's actually very late – well, more than late, really, virtually out of schedule, to be honest – which is a problem. We discovered that Mandy hadn't exactly been up-to-date with her Production work before she . . . before she left us.' The phone rang and she jabbed at the buttons until it stopped ringing. By the look on her face, Kate guessed the caller was after the manuscript.

Elaine fiddled spasmodically with an elastic band. 'Turned out she'd just been putting things under her desk. She was using February's lead saga as a footrest while I assumed it was with the author. No wonder her tray was always empty,' she burst out, and then bit her lip.

An uneasy silence descended.

'Is there anything you want to ask me?' prompted Kate.

'Can you type?' Elaine's voice came out more shrilly than she perhaps intended. 'Can you read and write clearly in pencil?'

'Er, yes,' said Kate.

'Can you start in the next twenty minutes?'

'Why not?' said Kate.

'Fantastic, we'll call it a trial period.' Elaine thrust a pile of paper at her and pointed to the desk outside her office, knocking a cup of camomile tea over in the process.

chapter nine

It took a surprisingly short time for Kate to clear a space on the desk, which, going on what she knew so far about her predecessor, probably meant that half the stuff that should have been there was filling unmarked files all over the place. Once Elaine had placed the two stacks of paper in front of her, explained that one was the pencil-edited original and the other the author's rewrites and that the two should be combined, and then established that Kate had a sharp pencil and a pencil sharpener, she promptly flew out of the office, 'to Boots'.

That had been an hour ago, and there was no sign of her or Jennifer Spencer. Kate had transcribed all the yellow Post-it notes decorating Mandy's in-tray on to a notepad and put everything marked 'File' in a folder. So far, she had ignored the phone. She was now at the end of her office skills and could put the manuscript problem off no longer.

She stared at the top page of the first stack of papers. Then she looked at the top page of the other pile. They weren't the same. Not even vaguely. She contemplated slipping out quietly and just going home.

'Having trouble reading Rose Ann's writing?' asked Isobel, materialising over her shoulder. 'Used to drive me mad.'

Kate jumped at this scary and unexpected piece of

mind-reading. 'Um, yeah,' she said, wondering how much of her ignorance it was safe to admit.

'When I first used to put in her rewrites,' continued Isobel, conversationally, 'I tried to edit them a bit. You know, take out all the obvious mistakes – wrong names, the bits she'd lifted from the problem pages in *Take a Break*. Didn't think she'd notice. But then I started to get the abusive faxes so I gave up. That's why Elaine's the way she is. A wee bit . . .' Isobel wiggled her hand. 'You know.'

'So,' Kate tried to look casual, 'what you're saying is just transfer all these notes in red in this pile, using a sharp pencil, on to this pile here?'

'The original copy-edited manuscript?' Isobel looked at her closely. 'That is the usual procedure, yes.'

Kate blushed. They both looked at the first page.

'Well, not that bit, obviously.' Isobel pointed to the phrase, '*Who is this fuckwit editor? Fucking Enid Blyton? How dare they fiddle with my fucking prose?*' which was scrawled in red across the third paragraph.

'Right.' Four months, thought Kate. Four months only.

Isobel pulled an unopened box of books over and perched on it. 'You might want to see who these books here were meant to go to, by the way. I think Mandy was in charge of entering prizes and, well, I think Jennifer will go spare if we've missed the Orange Prize. Not that that's your problem on your first day,' she added hurriedly.

'I wasn't expecting this to be my first day,' said Kate. 'I sort of thought there would be more . . . more discussion? No one even asked if I'd worked in publishing before.'

Isobel gave a wry snort. 'If you'd worked in publishing before you wouldn't be applying for this job in the first place.' She chewed the end of her plait. 'There I go again. I'm not trying to put you off, honest. God knows, I'm fed up of doing Mandy's job as well as my own. Did Elaine show you round before she ran away?'

Kate shook her head.

'Not even where the loos are?'

'She said something about free coffee in the kitchen but that's about it.'

'Aye, that'll be right.' Isobel stood up. 'Come with me, little girl.' The phone rang and she pressed the 'send call' button automatically.

'Um, is it fair for me to assume that I've got this job then?' Kate followed her down the corridor. 'I'm a bit new to the whole office thing.'

'Yeah, guess so. Elaine's been at her wits' end since Mandy walked out and it took so long to get Mandy in the first place I just don't think they can be bothered to go through the whole rigmarole again.'

'Oh,' said Kate. She wasn't sure if she actually wanted the job now she appeared to have got it, even if it did mean getting Mike and Irma Kurtz off her back.

Isobel marched into the kitchen and began fiddling expertly with a Gaggia coffee machine the size of a small car. 'You'll need to learn how to use this thing as part of your job description, along with photocopying and forging signatures. The idea is that when an author is invited in to the office to discuss something difficult, like being remaindered, or not getting a launch party or something, once you've collected them from Reception, you're promptly despatched to make them a "hot beverage". If you've got a very small cup of coffee in the author's hand within five minutes of arrival, so that they're busy concentrating on not spilling it, Jennifer or whoever can get the difficult bit over with first before the author's noticed you've brought it up.'

'Or failing that you can use the spillage as a diversionary tactic, I suppose?'

'Very good!' Isobel poured two very strong coffees into mugs decorated with the Eclipse logo. 'With an attitude like that you will go far. Milk?'

Kate looked at the fearsome milk-steaming arm and

decided she couldn't ask Isobel to go to all that trouble. 'No, I drink it black,' she lied.

'There you go then.' Isobel pushed one mug towards her, opened the fridge and decorated her own coffee with a tower of aerosol cream.

'Why did Mandy leave?' asked Kate, sipping her coffee. She blanched at the bitterness. Giles always drank espresso and she had tried for ages to like it too, without success.

Isobel's freckled forehead creased. 'Och, I don't think it's for me to . . .'

'Oh, sorry, forget I asked that, it's not any of my business, sorry, sorry . . .' Kate's face slipped. 'Maybe I should get on with my, um . . .' God, she didn't even know the proper name for what she was doing. Still, she thought, with a flash of her old belligerence, at no point had Jennifer or Elaine asked her if she'd done it before. And they'd seen her CV – albeit one which Giles had not so much made over as cosmetically enhanced.

'Let me show you round quickly first,' said Isobel. 'Just the people you need to know and maybe the publicity department – they get all the glossy mags. Bring your coffee.'

Covering the ground surprisingly quickly for such a small girl, Isobel took Kate on a lightning tour of the entire editorial department, which seemed to be half empty.

'Simon, the only male senior editor, sits there, but he's out. He does mainly literary fiction – whatever the rest of us don't understand, basically. That's Megan, his assistant . . . Megan, this is Kate, Elaine's new assistant.'

Megan looked up from her proofs and waved brightly. 'Hello, Kate. Can we go for a chocolate break soon, please, Isobel?'

'Half an hour, I've got to get a manuscript into Production, or they'll kill me.' Isobel rolled her eyes. 'One of their work experience girls phoned Jennifer to ask where it was – like she would know! – and Jennifer freaked because she didn't remember ever seeing it and took it out on me.'

'*God*,' said Megan. 'Still, at least you don't have to deal with all that nightmare stuff Mandy—' She covered her mouth with her hand and went red.

'Moving swiftly on,' said Isobel, steering Kate on to the next office, 'that's Alison's office, she does mainly feisty females but she's out at lunch too, her assistant Richard sits there, but he's out, probably skiving somewhere, that's Jo on the phone, she does a lot of American thrillers . . .' She stopped. 'Actually, I think she should be out at lunch with an American literary scout. I swapped her appointment with Jennifer's. Hang on a minute.'

Isobel darted into the office, scribbled something on a Post-it note and stuck it on the desk. Kate watched with interest as the editor stopped twisting her spiky blonde hair round her pen and slapped her forehead melodramatically. She mouthed 'Thanks!' at Isobel and tried unsuccessfully to wind up her phone conversation, waving her arms about in frustration.

'No problem,' Isobel mouthed back, muttering, 'Dizzy cow,' as soon as they were round the next corner. 'Assistant's on holiday, can't even find her own nail varnish. Phoned me to come round and switch on her computer this morning. You'd never guess she was an assistant herself this time last year. Amazing selective memory she has.'

They squeezed against the wall to allow a fraught woman with jet-black curly hair and John Lennon glasses to get past. She was bearing a tray full of coffee mugs and breathing through her nose.

'Ah, here's someone you should meet,' said Isobel. 'Sarah, this is Kate, Elaine's new assistant. Kate, this is Sarah, one of the production controllers. She's in charge of most of Elaine's books. In fact,' she added quickly, as Sarah opened her mouth to speak, 'she'll be the person to take that manuscript to, once you've finished adding the corrections. The one you're doing right now.'

Sarah gave them both a fierce sigh. 'I've told Elaine this

three times already this morning, if I don't get it by the end of the day, it doesn't go to the printers. It's as simple as that. No script, no books on time, no Christmas bonuses. What can I say? It's not as though I *like* shouting at people . . .'

'Fine, fine,' said Kate blithely. 'No problem.' She felt a slight dizziness at the thought of all that paper and clutched her coffee. Still, copying – how hard could it be? Last time she'd done copying she'd been using a purple crayon.

Sarah fixed her with penetrating blue eyes. Kate squirmed. 'And tell Elaine to take her phone off divert. She can run but she can't hide.'

'Anyway, better get back to it, eh?' Isobel gave Sarah a quick smile and pushed Kate along the corridor. They had come in a circle back to Elaine's office. A new row of vitamin bottles on the desk suggested that she had been and then gone again.

'I could show you a couple more people's desks, but as everyone's either on holiday or still at lunch I don't think there would be much point.'

Kate was still trying to fix those people she had seen in her head. The piles of paper were looming large on her desk and there were three new Post-it notes. 'Maybe I should get back to that manuscript?'

'OK,' said Isobel. 'But let me know if you want a hand with anything, and just ignore the phone – this is more urgent. I'll change the Voicemail message for you tomorrow, and we'll talk about how it all works then, too.'

If I'm still here, thought Kate.

'Rose Ann's rewrites are usually open to some interpretation,' Isobel went on, and then stopped. 'Oh, bugger, is that my phone ringing?' She trotted off.

Kate slugged back all her coffee at once and sat down at her desk.

Abraham Postlethwaite's frail, gnarled grip on his makeshift crutch loosened and the blind old beggar sank back into the

snowdrift with a faint curse. Had the squire of Postlethwaite
Hall and all its many surrounding areas of natural beauty come
to this? Why, happen not so long since, the tale had been a mite
different . . .

'Are you still here? You don't have to *read* the whole thing,
you know. Just put in the changes she's made. Elaine's been
going through those rewrites for the past ten days.'

Kate's head jerked up. Her eyes were almost crossed from
deciphering Rose Ann Barton's angry scrawl and her desk
was covered in the remains of two rubbers, which she had
employed to remove all the pencilled editorial corrections
Rose Ann felt were an infringement of her style. To begin
with she had left in editorial corrections which Rose Ann
had changed back to the original errors, but after three hours
(in which her only break was to ask Isobel how to work the
coffee machine), she had begun to doubt how to spell simple
words herself and, along with several warty and possibly
illegitimate characters, was rapidly losing the will to live – all
the while becoming reluctantly fascinated by the
labyrinthine plot. She had barely noticed the hours passing.

'What time is it?'

'It's nearly six o'clock,' said Isobel, sounding concerned.
'You can go home at five, you know.'

Kate sighed. 'I know, Elaine said when she left. But I'm
about fifty pages from the end and I know' – she glanced
quickly at the note on her phone – 'Sarah wanted this by the
end of the day, so . . .'

'There's nothing she can do with it now anyway. They've all
left. You can set your watch by the Production department.'

Kate was sorely tempted to go home, but natural stubbornness had set in around page 256, and she knew that if
she had to come in tomorrow morning and face all this again
she probably wouldn't make it to lunch-time. And she had to
make a good impression, if only to distract attention from
her lack of typing speed.

'No,' she said brightly, 'I'll finish it off and Sarah can have it first thing tomorrow.' She sharpened her pencil with more enthusiasm than she felt. Besides, what was there to go home to?

Isobel regarded her dubiously. 'I'll give you one thing: I never managed to do all Rose Ann's corrections in less than two days.'

Kate's sharpening hand froze.

'Well, I'll say goodnight then.' Isobel hoisted a huge rucksack onto her shoulder; it seemed incongruous next to her neat little embroidered cardigan.

'What are you taking home in that bag? The photocopier?' asked Kate, trying to sound cheery.

'Och, no, just some submissions,' said Isobel, pulling a face. 'Actually, Jennifer did say you could have some reading too. Hang on . . .' She opened up the bag and dumped a couple of manuscripts on to the other piles of paper on Kate's desk.

They both looked at the resulting paper nightmare for a few seconds and Isobel apologetically moved them on to the bookshelf.

'Just to have a quick look through in the next week or so. No big hurry.'

'Fine,' said Kate heavily, returning to the page she had been working on.

The first line, edited from, '"Happen as like as mebbe not the Good Lord'll be my judge, so help me God," croaked Karen, falling headfirst into the slag heap' to '"Aaaarrgh!" screamed Betsy as she plunged down the mine shaft', had been changed back to the original in Rose Ann's angry red pen.

'Isobel,' Kate called after her, as an afterthought, 'does it matter if Rose Ann changes the names of her . . .?'

Isobel was already shaking her head.

'Thought not,' said Kate, picking up her rubber.

*

Some time later, Kate turned over the last page of Rose Ann's rewrites, in which she revealed that the mother of the little mute boy was in fact his sister, and not, as the editor's complicated family tree proved, his cousin's wife. As well as the shredded remains of a further two rubbers, there were also five scrumpled-up tissues, into which Kate had snivelled during the accidental rat-poisoning deathbed scene, the sharpenings of three HB pencils, about a hundred pieces of coloured sticky tape which the editor had used to flag queries, and several pages of the editor's frenzied notes, across which Elaine had scribbled, 'Ignore!'

Kate let out a long breath. Thank God that was done. The office was quiet and the evening light streamed in through the big plate-glass windows. People were still filling the pavements below and Kate realised that she was hungry, not having had anything to eat since the coffee and chocolate bar she had grabbed to fill ten minutes before arriving at Eclipse for her interview. It seemed an unbelievably long time ago.

Enough, she thought, shuffling the papers into two neat piles. I'm going home.

chapter ten

Going home took nearly two hours.

The whole rush hour, people shoving, buskers, what the hell is that announcer trying to say, London Underground thing was easily the most claustrophobic experience Kate had ever had. Deeply suspicious of buses after her early coach disaster, she opted for the Underground on the basis that, for as long as she was actually on a train, she would know roughly where she was.

It had therefore come as something of a shock that, having safely got on the green line, in order to go to West Kensington, as carefully ringed in yellow on her pristine *A–Z*, Kate found herself terminating, without ever having sat down, at Wimbledon. Being squashed up against two lardy businessmen reading the *Evening Standard* hadn't helped her to follow the station map. Being informed that her ticket was subsequently out of zones and that she was liable to a ten-pound fine just put the tin lid on things. Losing a pound coin in the chocolate machine and weeping silently into her handbag for five minutes didn't really help as much as she'd hoped, and in the end she went back to Earl's Court, where the diverging branches seemed to have caused all the trouble, and walked home, ducking into every phone box on the way to check her map under the guise of making a call.

It was almost – not quite – a relief to recognise the turning to Deauville Crescent, scruffy though it was. Kate let herself in and looked hopefully in the pigeon-holes, in case Giles had somehow got hold of her address and written to say that he couldn't possibly allow her to live with two strange men and their mangy cat and that he was coming home on the next flight to get her. But there was only a red gas bill, some letters for the absent Mandy and a council tax bill addressed to some people she had never heard of. Kate dragged herself morosely up the stairs, trailing her bag with the submissions in behind her. It bounced sullenly on each of the sixty-eight steps.

The front door was wide open when she got to the top and clumsy activity was audible in the kitchen. Both boys were in. An attack of shyness gripped her and she wondered whether it would look antisocial to follow her instincts and go straight to her room. For the second time that day Kate was deeply conscious of her clothes: her tights felt clammy against her legs and she suspected she'd laddered them on the train coming home. She also knew for certain that her feet smelled rank. And her mother had selected a 100 per cent polyester blouse that had made her sweat profusely all day. Charming. The reflection in the hall mirror looked pretty sorry for itself.

'Hey, Dant, d'you think Scary Mary will mind if we use some of her truffle oil?'

Kate froze.

'Nah . . .' That was definitely Dant's sarky drawl. 'Shouldn't think she would know what to do with it anyway. Probably wonders why it doesn't taste of chocolate.'

Kate barged into the kitchen, pushing the door open so hard it banged on the wall behind it, dislodging a nude French maid plastic pinny hung on the back. Harry sprang back from her cupboard as though it was electrically wired to the door handle.

'Anything else you'd like to help yourself to?' she asked

sarcastically. 'If you have a look you might find some rather good olives – that's if you haven't already got them out.'

Behind her Dant spat out his last olive stone and slipped a tea towel over the bowl of discarded pips in front of him.

Harry was blushing furiously. 'Um, oh gosh, er, hello . . .'

'Thought you weren't coming home,' said Dant, putting his feet up on the kitchen table and lighting another Camel.

'Yes, well, I had to work late,' snapped Kate. 'I didn't realise that I should be at home guarding my kitchen cupboard.' She looked pointedly at the remains of some bread and pâté on the table. 'Was that mine too?'

Harry brushed his hand through his blond hair in a nervous gesture. 'Um, oh dear, I know it must look bad, but I was going to cook you some supper, to, er, apologise for last night.' He tried a puppyish smile. 'Don't think we quite got off on the right foot, did we?'

Kate gave him her best 'Oh, yeah?' stare, still fuming at the fact that he hadn't actually returned her, or to be accurate, Laura's truffle oil to the cupboard.

'Dant got some bread from the deli round the corner and as you were so . . . as you had to stay late at work, we started it.' He leaned against her cupboard in an attempt to close it discreetly.

Kate put her hands on her hips. Her initial anger was now sliding into embarrassment, particularly since she could feel Dant's amused gaze boring into her left buttock. She turned round to prevent him looking at her bum.

'Why don't you go and have a shower?' continued Harry persuasively. 'Won't take long and you'll feel much better.'

Dant raised his eyebrow. 'Yeah, you'll feel almost human again.' Kate glared at him, but he merely raised the other eyebrow in innocent surprise. 'Who knows?'

'At least I only need to have a shower,' she retorted.

For a horrible moment, Kate thought she had gone too far. The words had come out before she had had time to vet them for rudeness, although there was no doubt the smug pig deserved it. A black look crossed his face and behind her she heard Harry snort with laughter.

'Nice one!' he honked, in the manner of an amused duck.

Kate turned back to him. He was pointing at Dant and making strange hand gestures that evidently meant something to them both, judging from Dant's bilious expression.

'OK, I'll be five minutes.' She smiled uncertainly at Harry, not sure whether to consider him a potential ally or not.

'There mightn't be hot water to begin with, but if you let it run for a bit, some should come out eventually,' said Harry helpfully. 'If not, give the loo a flush. Seems to help, don't ask me why.'

'Thanks,' said Kate. 'Won't be long.'

'Wash off all that typist's grime,' murmured Dant as she left the room.

Kate stopped and almost turned back, but the exhaustion of the day was too much and she let it go. For the time being.

Shutting her bedroom door firmly behind her, Kate stripped off her work clothes, tied her hair into a thick top-knot and put on the fluffy white bathrobe Giles had given her when she'd admitted she didn't have one of her own. It had his initials embroidered on the left side, possibly to establish that it hadn't been nicked from an up-market hotel. Sadly, unlike the hanky, it didn't smell of him.

She gathered up her towel and shampoo – there was no way she was keeping toiletries in a communal bathroom, oh no – and padded down to the bathroom, straining her ears for any more witticisms from Bungle and Zippy. They had switched the radio on, to mask their conversation, no doubt, and all she could hear was Harry tunelessly 'diddle-iddle-eee'-ing the guitar solo from 'Layla' and the rhythmic clunk of the chopping knife. Probably playing the frying pan, she thought, peering round into the bathroom, and checking with long-suffering paranoia that there were no hilarious 'Let's scare the little lady'-style pranks in the bath. Aside from a smelly wet towel left on the floor and three pairs of comedy M&S boxer shorts drying on the radiator, there didn't seem to be anything deliberately unpleasant. She locked herself in and propped the chair up against Dant's side door.

Once she had stood under the powerful shower for a couple of minutes Kate felt a lot better, and was almost ashamed of her outburst. Until then she hadn't realised what a drain the day had been, all that concentrating for such a long period. Listening. Remembering not to say 'What?' when people spoke to you. Writing things down properly. Not going for a quick kip when you felt like it at three o'clock.

Kate soaped under her arms and the thought struck her that she would have to do today again, sixteen times. And she would have to do it all over again in about twelve hours, three times before the weekend. The soap slipped out of her hands with the physical shock of it. Mid-July, mid-August, mid-September, mid-October – that was what? Three bank holidays? She couldn't remember, never really having taken any notice of such corporate trivia before. She suddenly felt trapped. Tears sprang to her eyes and she blinked them back.

Giles, she thought. Giles, Giles, Giles.

In the kitchen Dant and Harry were debating what to do about the absence of any ingredients for the pasta sauce beyond Harry's onion and wrinkly courgette and Dant's copious supply of garlic.

'Not even any tomatoes?'

'You didn't tell me to get tomatoes. Anyway, it's years since I bought them. Mandy used to buy them in crates.'

'We need to do a Sainsbury's run,' said Harry, opening and shutting all the cupboards in case Teresa had moved anything around.

'You say that every other day,' muttered Dant, his, cigarette clamped precariously between his lips while he diced the onion with lightning strokes.

Harry sighed and opened Kate's packed cupboard. 'It's very bad, especially after last night, but . . .'

Dant looked up at him. 'Listen, she doesn't seem to know what's hers and what's not for some strange reason, so if she's that dizzy and you want to make her a nice meal, you'll just have to use all those shiny fresh vegetables of hers.' He blew out a stream of smoke. 'Don't know why she put them all in the laundry box though.'

Harry handed him two red peppers, an aubergine and a bunch of fresh basil.

Dant stubbed out his cigarette in the overflowing Bart Simpson ashtray and contemplated the vegetables critically. 'I seem to remember spotting some of that good oyster sauce when you were looking for coffee.'

'Dant . . .' said Harry warningly.

Dant gave him a disorientatingly winning smile. 'Do you want to make her feel at home or not?'

Kate towelled herself down in her room and put on some clean underwear. She didn't want to leave them alone too long just for Dant to be bitchy about her, but then again all she really wanted to do was to roll herself in her duvet and make 'Munch' faces all night. She pulled on her size ten jeans, slightly loose with all the stress, which cheered her up a bit, and found a white T-shirt. She didn't want to look like she'd made an effort.

Her black mules – now, it seemed, broken in, a week too bloody late – clacked on the hall tiles and gave the lads some warning of her arrival. Dant was still lolling in his chair, smoking, but there was now a large pile of diced vegetables in front of him. Harry was heating up a frying pan, which was also smoking. He turned and gestured to the table.

'Why don't you sit there and have that glass of wine I've poured . . .'

'Booze being one thing we do have in copious quantities in this house,' mumbled Dant, pushing his chair back and shuffling over to the hob with the brimming board of veg.

'. . . and supper will be ready in about ten minutes.'

Kate privately doubted this, given that they hadn't even started the pasta sauce, but decided not to point it out, in case they took her for an expert and made her cook the whole thing. She'd seen that one too many times before to fall for it again. Instead she sat down and sipped at the large glass of wine.

Harry came over and joined her.

'I thought you were cooking?' said Kate.

'God, no,' said Harry. He poured himself a large glass, then one for Dant. Kate noticed that he'd only got three glasses out of an entire bottle. 'No, no, no, Dante's the cook in the house. I can burn toast, me.'

Violent sizzling noises came from the hob. Kate twisted round in time to see Dant tip some alcohol into the pan and set it on fire. Clouds of smoke billowed around him.

'Is he OK?' she asked Harry nervously. 'That's not how I make spaghetti bolognese.'

'Hey, Dant, you OK there?' yelled Harry politely.

'Fucking fire alarm isn't working again,' replied Dant, waving his arms around his head. 'Tell Cress we'll have the inspectors in unless she reduces the rent.'

Harry turned back to Kate. 'He's fine. He did a cooking course at Prue Leith— Well, no, actually he did the first two days of a cooking course there. Their fire alarms worked rather better than ours. Fortunately for them.'

'Oh?' said Kate. 'Is Dant a chef then?'

Harry coughed over his wine. 'Er, no. His mum keeps sending him on these courses, hoping he'll find some kind of vocation. So far, he's done feng shui, cordon bleu cookery, interior design, target shooting, flowercraft . . .'

'Why? What does he do all day?'

'His mother's been asking him that for the last five years.' Harry's voice dropped to an undertone. 'She's a writer, you might have heard of her? She's called Anna Flail. Well, that's her pen-name, anyway.'

Kate nodded. The name rang a bell, which was more than the series of authors trotted past her at work had done, even though she had nodded and made, 'Ohhhh, right' noises at the time. Anna Flail's dog-eared horror-bonkbuster had been passed furtively round the class at school and Kate's mum had gone ballistic when she had found it in her gym bag. Not quite as ballistic as Carrie Jones – the owner of said book – had gone when Kate had to tell her that her mum had put it on the fire. After she'd read it herself, natch.

'She wrote *Roses of Death*? Wow!'

Harry made a warning face. 'Yarp, well, there's no love lost there so don't mention it.'

Dant strode across the room with two plates piled high with steaming stir-fry.

'I like to keep myself unfettered by the routine demands of working life, and besides, I know for a fact that it drives the old bag mad and winds my mad bitch of a sister up as a bonus.'

Kate blushed and wondered how he could have overheard. He was obviously more alert than his stoner appearance suggested. She felt strangely excited to be living with Anna Flail's son and stored the feeling up against the other, more evident drawbacks of Dant's personality.

'So what do you do?' she asked Harry. She guessed by his smart suit that he probably wasn't unfettered in the same way as Dant.

Dant hovered by her chair, glaring first at her, then at her plate.

'Er, thanks,' she said, looking up at him. 'It looks, er, great.'

'Not every day we have oyster sauce,' replied Dant, returning to pile up a plate of his own.

'I work in a sports car garage,' said Harry. 'Selling, driving, buying, the whole lot.' He fished around in the pocket of his suit jacket, which was slung across the back of the chair. 'Just got some new business cards today, actually, hang on.' He pulled out a thick card, embossed at the top with a golden wire wheel, of the smart 1950s racing car variety. Kate held it carefully by the edges and studied it: *Henry Harvey, Sales Consultant, Keyes of London.*

'I've always been into cars and I didn't really know what I wanted to do when I left college,' Harry went on, making free with the soy sauce. 'I did a bit of freelance programming – you know, internet sites and things – but I'm not really one of those computer geek types. I wanted to work with cars, Dad knew some people and I sort of fell into it.'

'Dad knew some people' – if only it was that easy for everyone, thought Kate in a Northern accent. These people didn't know they were born. She shovelled a forkful of stir-fry into her mouth and was surprised how tasty it was. She generally liked to know exactly what it was she was eating, and hadn't been convinced that she'd ever want to eat anything Dant had cooked. But this was really good.

'Have you sold anything recently?' she asked Harry, sliding the card in her jeans pocket.

His face dropped slightly. 'Er, not recently, no, I'm still learning a lot . . .'

'It must be great, though, to work with something you like so much,' Kate added, too polite to push home the point, though she felt privately vindicated. 'More like a hobby than a job, I suppose.'

'Oh, yes, it is.'

Dant plonked his plate down opposite her before Harry could go on. 'Speaking of hobbies, I hope you're better at Mandy's job than she was. Not that it's exactly a challenge.'

Kate was about to reply when she remembered that she hadn't actually told either of them what she did. 'How did you know that I had Mandy's job?' she demanded.

'Heard you on the phone blagging your way into the interview, recognised the manuscript you had to bring home to read tonight. Doesn't take Dr Watson to work it out.'

'Oh, very good,' said Kate, putting her fork down. Her appetite disappeared as adrenaline rushed through her body. 'So apart from bursting into the bathroom unannounced and eavesdropping on phone calls, is there anything else I should know? Would you like me to leave my bedroom door open at night so you can pop in? Or shall I leave my underwear lying about so you can give it the once-over before I wash it?'

Her heart thumped against her chest in anger and she had a nasty feeling that the tears she had managed to control in the shower were going to overflow. But she was really angry.

'Dant!' said Harry. 'Have you . . .?'

'Oh, for God's sake,' said Dant, glaring at her. 'I'm just joking. Can't you tell when someone's joking?'

'I don't think it's funny. I think it's an invasion of my privacy. And if you're trying to goad me into leaving by being an obstreperous arsehole, then forget it.' Kate bit her lip. 'Of course, if you're an obstreperous arsehole naturally, then I'm very sorry for you. But don't waste your time trying on my account.'

Harry stared hard into his stir-fry.

Dant looked thunderous. 'What is your problem?'

Kate knew she had reached the foothills of an argument from which there was no point in turning back. She might as well get it all out at once, and be done with it from the outset. She took a deep breath and tried to think Laura.

'Look, I don't know whether Mandy moved out because you boored her into submission, but I wouldn't blame her if this is what you're like all the time. And I've barely moved in! I'm not stupid, I can guess you want to live here with just the two of you and you'd prefer it if I went running home and you could have the place to yourselves. But I can't, so you're just going to have to get used to it.'

A vein in Dant's forehead was beginning to throb and his eyes were narrowing as she spoke. Kate swallowed.

'You gave me a list of house rules when you interrupted me in the bath. Fine. Here are mine: don't take things from my cupboard without asking me, don't ever come through that bathroom door again without knocking first and if I keep quiet about your whereabouts to your mother, you've got to do the same to my sister-in-law. OK?' She forked up some bean sprouts as casually as she could and spilled all except one, which she tried to eat in an offhand manner. 'This is delicious, by the way. You must tell me what you put in it.'

The pregnant silence was broken by a furious scratching at the door.

'Fucking thing,' said Dant, staring at Kate, and got up and let the skinny black cat in.

'Have you met Ratcat?' asked Harry conversationally, as though they had been discussing last night's television. 'He belonged to an old tenant of ours. Who also moved out.'

'Really,' said Kate. She was shivering inside, though she hoped it wasn't showing.

'Left that fish-tank too.'

'There's no catfood left,' said Dant over his shoulder. He banged some cupboard doors.

'There must be,' said Harry, scooping Ratcat onto his knee. He wriggled off immediately and returned to Dant's feet. 'Cress only brought a crate round last week when she dropped Kate's keys over.'

'Yeah, well, I'm not feeding him that shit.' Dant picked a holey blue jumper off the dirty laundry pile in front of the washing machine and pulled it over his head. 'I'm going down to the shops.'

He shuffled over to the table, shovelled three huge fork-fuls of stir-fry into his mouth and shuffled out of the flat. He tried to slam the front door, but Harry had hung some shirts to dry over it and the door bounced back apologetically.

Kate looked at Harry. 'Oh, dear.'

'What do you mean, "Oh, dear"?' he said, pouring Dant's wine into his own glass. 'Couldn't have put it better myself. As long as you stand up to the miserable bugger, you're fine. Haven't had a flatmate yet who could, but there you go.'

'Is he always like this? I mean, will he hate me now? Is my life going to be unbearable?'

'Nah. I've known him since school and he's always been a moody sod. Gets it from his mother. He only does it because people half-expect it and then let him get away with it. 'Sides, he's got nothing else to do all day.' Harry looked at the remains of Dant's stir-fry and after a brief moment's reflection scraped it on to his own plate. 'Shame to let that go to waste, eh?'

'I didn't mean to start something, honestly. I'm really not into arguments.' Kate sipped at her wine awkwardly. She wished she'd just gone straight to her room after all. Confrontations made her feel sick. 'It looked like I hit a nerve.'

'Well, you did a bit. Cress is Anna's legal landlady, and representative in the real world. She lets me and Dant live here on condition that there is a third flatmate, who has to be a woman – partly for the extra money and partly to stop the place looking like a bomb-site, I would guess.' Harry grinned. 'Not stupid is Cressida. She had a huge go at Dant after you came round to view the place and he hadn't cleared up after our football evening. Suppose that's still hurting. She didn't exactly hold back. Cress's a bit of a clean freak. She even pays for Teresa to come round.'

Kate wondered whether, by their standards, using Toilet Duck once a year made you a hygiene fascist. 'Why doesn't she live here then?'

'Live with Dant? Have you ever seen streetfighting at first hand?'

Kate smiled despite her sick feelings and shook her head.

'No, Cress lives in Soho. This flat is part of their mother's complicated legal divorce manoeuvring.' Harry waved his hands around dismissively. 'While poor little unemployable Dant is living here, she doesn't have to sell it for part of the settlement, or something. But obviously if poor little Dant was living here on his own and unsupervised the flat would soon have the market value of a shed in Auchtermuchty, so old Anna promised Cress the rent money to keep an eye on things in London, while she sits on her liposuctioned arse in Los Angeles having calf foetuses injected into her forehead and writing the odd film script.'

From what she remembered of *Roses of Death*, Kate assumed that the calf foetuses were for research purposes.

'So what does Cress do?' Her glass was nearly empty and she could feel the wine going straight to her head after the long day. She was almost beginning to feel relaxed.

Harry chased the last bean sprout round his plate. 'Have you met Cress?'

'Not yet. She sounded pretty scary when she talked to my sister-in-law on the phone last week. I mean, they seemed to get on pretty well.'

He looked up and Kate saw why Mandy might have moved in, even if Dant had made her move out. Harry's blond Sebastian Flyte fringe and cow-like brown eyes were classic English public schoolboy material; the sort of rugby-playing good looks she had always scoffed at until she met Giles. But Harry didn't have the spark that had made Giles so irresistible – whether it was Giles's ambition, or his worldliness, or the fact that he could talk dirty (after much prompting) in five European languages, she couldn't decide. Still, Kate thought dispassionately, if Giles was Premier Division, Harry was somewhere towards the top of the First.

'Cress is pretty scary, but she's very, very cool,' he said, after a pause in which he seemed to be weighing up various possible descriptions. 'She knows everyone. At the moment she's working as a, um, greeter in a rather fashionable bar in Clerkenwell.'

'Suppose that's more up-market than working as a waitress in a cocktail bar,' said Kate. She smothered a burp and looked suspiciously at her glass. How drunk was she? How drunk could she get? It was only ten to ten.

'You'll meet her soon enough,' said Harry, with a note of despondency creeping into his well-rounded vowels. He got up and went over to the fridge where he rooted around amongst the elderly vegetables and stray cans of duty-free lager, from when there was still duty-free lager to be had. 'Did you know there are six packs of butter substitute in here?' he called over his shoulder. 'I reckon that's how we keep track of how many flatmates we've had – they all, move in, stock up on Flora No-Fat and then move out.' He stood up, bearing a bottle of white wine and a Sainsbury's luxury cheese selection pack.

'Fancy a nibble of Stilton?'

Kate stared at the cheese pack. Was it familiar or not? God, she thought, I really must swallow my pride and get my eyes tested. 'That's mine, isn't it?'

Harry looked at it as if for the first time. 'Yarp, suppose it is, sorry.' He opened his own cupboard and fished out a battered box of Biscuits for Cheese which he waved triumphantly. 'Knew if I kept them long enough they'd come in useful. OK to use the same plates?'

Without warning, the warm-blanket feeling of belonging which had begun to settle on Kate disappeared, as the effects of the wine suddenly wore off. She just felt tired. The next day loomed before her and her eyes were sore and gritty. She missed her boyfriend. And she didn't want to make chit-chat any longer with someone whose casual array of social advantages would probably drive her mad on closer inspection. She wanted to be unconscious.

Pushing back her chair, she made to get up. 'No, thanks, I think I should really be getting off to bed. I'm worn out.' She leaned on the chair back, looking at the half-shut door and bit her lip. 'Look, are you sure I haven't offended Dant?'

Harry seemed to pick up on her mood swing and slid the cheese back into the fridge. 'No, no, he's fine. Honestly.'

'Well, then, goodnight,' said Kate. She began to lift her hand in a wave but stopped awkwardly at half mast. Do you wave good night to your flatmate? Or shake hands? The dynamics of sharing space were still unfamiliar, and she couldn't work out whether Harry's evident ease with the new situation was helpful to her or not.

'See you in the morning.' Harry was filling up the cafetiere.

'Coffee, at this time?' asked Kate, pausing on her way out.

He gave her a cheeky grin. 'Night is young, in case you hadn't noticed.'

She managed a laugh, and left, thinking miserably of the computerised wheel spins and high-speed crashes that would be going on until the night was finally deemed old. Back in her room she crossed off another day on the 'Four months to Giles' chart she had made for her wall.

chapter eleven

Kate hung tightly on to the sweaty handrail as the packed Tube carriage lurched towards the centre of London. Already it was rammed full of tourists, it being the height of the summer season, and already, at half past eight, the air was thick with morning-after breath and armpits.

She had partially shut herself off with her Walkman, which she had clamped to her waist before leaving the house, having spent ten minutes searching her rucksack for a tape that didn't remind her of Giles; the only eye contact she had seen made on a Tube train so far was when a scary-looking woman in a suit and a nose-ring glared at her to turn it down. Terrorvision at low volume was a contradiction in terms, but she had meekly complied and subsequently felt very conspicuous.

Kate looked over the shoulder of a Japanese couple who were studying an Underground map and checked she was going the right way. She had positioned herself this time so she could clearly see the station names as they stopped. Taking two hours to get home didn't matter, since she didn't really care how long she spent in the house with Dastardly and Mutley, but since she physically could not get up before 7.30, time was of the essence in the mornings.

She stood unselfconsciously by the open inter-carriage

window, letting the faint draught lift her hair off her neck, as the train rocked towards the centre of town. It was too hot, too airless, for her. And it wasn't even nine o'clock.

When she got into the office, a faint buzzing still ringing in her ears, Isobel was steaming milk in the kitchen. Her fierce expression suggested that had the milk been 'on' when she brought it up, it was probably 'off' now.

'Morning,' said Kate, as cheerfully as she dared.

Isobel responded with a grunt.

'Coffee?' asked Kate, rummaging for mugs.

'No,' hissed Isobel, pointing at the water dispenser. 'Hot skimmed milk.'

Kate banged her hip against an ugly water dispenser she didn't remember seeing there the previous day. 'Is that new?'

Someone – Megan? – appeared at the door, clutching a mug with Hot Babe written on it, looked at the coffee machine, sighed and filled the mug with filtered water.

'Yes, it is new,' Isobel spat. 'And do you know why? Because we're all detoxing. Apparently, there will be no more coffee until we have all completed the four-week detox plan.'

Jo, the temporarily assistantless thriller editor, appeared at the door with a mug. It was a small kitchen and Kate, Isobel and Isobel's mood were filling it.

'That's a bit draconian,' said Kate. 'Are Eclipse doing random employee drug testing too?'

Jo spun on the heel of her leather knee-high boot and vanished.

'No,' said Isobel, trying to enjoy her hot milk. 'Not yet. We're doing it because the non-fiction department wants to buy this fan-*taaast*-ic new diet book from some health expert on Richard and Judy and to prove our co-*mmit*-ment to publishing whoever this sadist is, it has been decreed that we are all detoxing until the date of the auction. There was a company e-mail this morning. Diet sheet included.' She held up the lead to the coffee machine. Someone had snipped off the plug. 'Bastards. I suppose if we were doing a book on Japanese Culture, they'd have us all binding our feet and leaping off the roof in funny headbands.'

Sarah the production manager came in with a tray full of coffee mugs, saw the notice on the kitchen board and the frayed ends of the coffee machine lead and swore loudly. Kate unconsciously shrank back against the notice-boards.

'Oh for God's . . . I hate editors! How do they think we can cope with all the shit they cause us without coffee? At the very least? Jesus . . .' She filled up six mugs of hot water, muttering to herself.

A tall woman with a sharply cut bob appeared in the doorway. She was tall and slim and dressed in floaty summer trousers that only tall slim people can get away with, albeit tall slim people ten years younger than she was. In her hand was a very big glass and a lemon.

'So who have we to thank for this outrage?' snarled Sarah to Isobel, slopping water on the floor.

'Wendy!' said Isobel.

'Jesus Christ, I might have—' began Sarah, but Isobel cut across her.

'Wendy, have you met Kate, Elaine's new assistant? This is Wendy, the non-fiction health and beauty editor.'

Wendy extended a bony hand with a lemon clutched in the palm. Kate shook it.

'Don't forget you can have as much water as you want,' she said, munificently. 'Delicious with some freshly squeezed lemon. You may find that for the first couple of days, while the toxins are being expelled, you have a bit of a bad head and a furry tongue. Some people do find that they have terrible mood swings, too.' She looked at Sarah. 'But you may just feel completely normal. It depends.'

Sarah stomped out, followed by Kate and Isobel.

'Freshly squeezed lemon, my arse,' she muttered. 'Sucks them for breakfast.'

Isobel raised her eyebrows. 'She's lovely really,' she said

when Sarah had disappeared round the corner, mugs rattling violently. 'Just gets very stressed when her books are late.'

'Well, she'll be thrilled when she sees the Rose Ann Barton on her desk,' said Kate. 'Tear stains, blood marks, sweat rashes and all.'

Isobel steered her over to the pigeon-holes. 'I hope so,' she said, levering out Jennifer Spencer's huge pile of post. 'That funny rash Elaine's got – all from Sarah's phone calls, you know. Had her sobbing into her camomile tea more than once last week because the manuscript was late for cast-off. And you should see Sarah out of the office – she's like a wee lamb, I'm telling you. A great girl to go to the pub with. It's scandalous what she has to put up with here.'

Elaine had almost as much post as Jennifer Spencer. Isobel looked critically through it and passed it to Kate.

'Don't worry, Elaine doesn't normally have that much. She just hasn't been opening any since Mandy upped and left.'

'Right . . .' said Kate doubtfully. How long had Mandy been gone?

'I'll come and change your Voicemail message for you,' Isobel went on, herding her down the corridor to her desk, against a stream of people coming away from the kitchen with glasses of water and green faces.

Kate sat down and sorted through her in-tray while Isobel dealt expertly with her phone, then fiddled with the computer, which Kate had so far avoided switching on – mainly because she couldn't see the 'on' button. Isobel booted it up, ran through various passwords, opened up a Word document and pointed to the screen.

'OK, this is the template I made for myself. Just read that when I say now,' she said. 'Now.'

'Hello, this is Kate Craig in the Eclipse Fiction department, sorry I can't take your call at the moment but please do leave a short message after the tone and I will get back to you as soon as I can, alternatively please dial zero to be returned to the switchboard and ask to speak to Elaine

Bridges senior fiction editor thank you for calling,' said Kate in one confused breath.

'Excellent,' said Isobel, pressing some more buttons. 'This is the "send" button,' she added, pointing to the one button without a label. 'Sends the caller straight to your Voicemail message when you're in the middle of something complicated, or if you can't bear the thought of talking to them.' She straightened up and brushed some imaginary fluff from her spotless bias-cut miniskirt. 'You'll see Mandy wore the print off it. Well, things to do, manuscripts to salvage. Give me a buzz if you need me.'

Isobel left her as Elaine arrived, bowed down under the weight of a large Mulberry Gladstone bag. Everyone, Kate noticed, seemed to have them.

'Hello, Elaine,' said Kate, spinning round on her chair and giving it as much 'happy secretary' as she could manage.

'Ah, Kate, hello,' replied Elaine. 'Sorry we didn't get much time to chat yesterday, but, um . . .' She was producing manuscript after manuscript from her bag. It was Tardis-like in its capacity. 'These are all rejections – they've sort of been piling up since Mandy left and there was no one to do the cover letters.'

Kate inspected the top sheet of each. Elaine had scribbled notes in a baroque scrawl over the original letter from the agent, and judging from the crossings-out, it had taken her about as long to compose the rejection by hand as it would have done to have typed it out in the first place. Kate watched as Elaine piled up nine manuscripts and two dodgy-looking American books in search of an English second home.

'OK?' said Elaine. 'There's a courier that goes round all the main agencies at lunch-time, so if you could . . .?' She trailed into her office where she started shaking a cocktail of vitamin pills into her hand.

Kate swivelled back to her desk, looked at her computer screen and realised that she had forgotten how to make documents on a PC, all the computers at college having been user-friendly Apple Macs.

Shit. Her heart sank. Another hurdle. And she had been doing so well.

Kate turned on her chair to see if she could see Isobel, but she was nowhere in sight. Asking how to do something so basic when she was meant to have been the editor of the entire college newsletter (thanks, Giles, for the CV enhancement) was going to look highly suspect. She *could* ask Isobel, but there was a fine line between asking someone for help and just getting them to do your job for you. And, she had to admit to herself, Isobel was just a wee bit scary.

Kate thought hard about who she could phone.

Not Giles, since he hadn't provided her with a phone number yet. Didn't want to upset either of them with unnecessarily disruptive personal contact before they were safely settled in.

None of her college friends, since they were all abroad with their rucksacks and comedy phrase books.

Not Mike. He wouldn't know. She had listened to an hour's raving last Christmas about his fantastic new secretary and how she did everything for him – and the three hours' worth of muffled marital conflict in the spare room afterwards.

Laura would know, but then she would launch into an interrogation about Kate's job and the flat and everything else she couldn't possibly discuss on the phone on her second day.

Kate wriggled in her seat to dislodge the seam of her jeans from the wedgie it was forming. It just made things worse. What was the point of wearing G-strings now anyway? She stood up and put her hands in her pockets to yank the crotch down, when her fingers closed around something sharp.

And she pulled out Harry's business card he'd given her the previous night.

Perfect. He was bound to know how to sort out some files and folders and would hardly hold it against her that she didn't. And she wasn't worried about what he and Dant thought of her, since they weren't employing her on the basis of a made-up CV.

She dialled the number on the card and checked behind her in case anyone was hovering.

The phone rang seven times before a plummy voice said, 'Keyes, good morning?'

'Er,' said Kate, wondering where the Durham flatness came from when she was nervous, 'can I speak to Henry Harvey, please?'

'Speaking?'

'Oh, Harry,' said Kate bending down as if to look in a low drawer of her filing cabinet. 'It's me, Kate, sorry to call you at work but I wonder if you could do me a favour?'

'Kate? Oh, *Kate*, hello there.' Kate could hear an engine being revved over the *Four Seasons*. 'Want to buy a car?'

'Er, no,' Kate fiddled with the computer mouse as Elaine rushed past with a box of herbal teabags. 'Look, if you can just tell me, very quickly, how to set up files and new documents on a PC, you can have all that cheese in the fridge. I've only ever used a Mac and I'm a bit . . . er . . .'

There was the sound of a computer being switched on at the other end of the phone.

'Are you looking at the screen?'

'Yes,' said Kate. Nothing was leaping out at her so far, and if she didn't get some kind of document on the screen soon she was going to look a right bimbo.

'Go to File Manager . . .'

'To what?' She could feel her throat tightening. No wonder Giles thought she was hopeless. She had the office skills of a giraffe. A giraffe with a degree in finger-painting.

'Listen, don't panic. It's really very simple, just like a Mac really. Close everything down until all you have is that screen at the beginning with the little icons, pictures, whatever.' Harry's voice was reassuringly confident, probably born from ordering CCF squadrons of second years to advance over the cricket pitch.

Kate prayed she wasn't consigning anything significant to a cyber dustbin and closed everything.

'Can you see a little computer chap?'

She skated her eyes in panic over the screen, then spotted the computer icon in the corner. 'Yes! Yes, I can!'

'Click on it.'

Kate clicked on it.

'Select "new" from the File pull-down menu . . . OK? Call it Kate's dayfile . . . OK? And next time you want to save a document, just save it in there when you get your "save as" options box.'

'Oh, Harry, you have just saved my life,' said Kate, breathing out. 'Thanks very, very much.'

'No probs. But the cheese has gone, I'm afraid. Found Dant eating it at five this morning.'

Kate shut her eyes. 'I can't think about that, there's too much else to worry about.' She heard Harry laugh in a not unpleasant manner and had a brief, warm feeling, which could have been the caffeine from the milky coffee she'd bought at the station for breakfast kicking in.

'Okey-dokes, see you tonight then,' said Harry and put the phone down.

Kate settled back in her chair and realised, as she made a whole cabinet of files, that at no point had he asked her why she didn't know how to do something so simple, or why she had phoned him for instructions.

Quite nice under the unbearable rah-ness, then, she thought, and pulled Elaine's first rejection letter out from under the elastic band.

Kate was halfway through her second hot milk and Elaine's fifth letter ('So sorry we couldn't find a place on our list for "The Mystery of the Magistrate's Cow" but we do find that bestiality, however beautifully expressed, isn't a plus in the cosy crime market . . .') when someone coughed behind her, in the absence of a door to knock on.

Kate spun on her chair. A woman she hadn't met before was standing with her arms full of papers, all about to escape their various elastic bands.

'Hi, I'm Alison,' she said, extending a hand. 'You must be Kate? Great! You can minute, can't you?'

'Er, yes?' said Kate, not being quite sure what she meant by 'minute'. Alison, Alison . . . the 'feisty female' woman? Whatever *that* meant.

'Fantastic!' Alison tugged some loose paper out of her piles and thrust it into Kate's hands. 'Are you coming, Elaine?' she called into Elaine's office.

Kate looked at the paper and read 'Editorial Acquisition Meeting Minutes, July 19th' along the top.

She looked up to see Elaine and Alison comparing herbal teabags. Her hand was on the phone to call Isobel for emergency advice when they came sailing out of the office, armed with over-sized mugs, pens, paper, sheaves of manuscripts and, in Elaine's case, a tube of hand cream.

'Sorry to land this on you,' smiled Alison, not looking vaguely sorry, 'did Isobel not explain? All the assistants take turns to minute the editorial meeting, so you can see what goes on and learn about what we have on our list. The others are all tied up and Isobel mentioned that it was Mandy's go this week.'

'Come on, Kate, chop, chop,' said Elaine. 'Pen, paper . . .' She rubbed her forehead. 'I've got to bring up Rose Ann's new deal this week and Jennifer's not going to like it,' she added to Alison who grimaced in sympathy.

'What do I . . .?' began Kate, uncertainly.

'It's really very interesting,' said Alison. Kate wasn't sure which one of them Alison was addressing. They began to move towards the lifts and Kate felt herself being dragged along on the tide of Elaine's nerves. 'Just write down what everyone says and then cut out all the waffle. Well, nearly all the waffle.'

This sent Elaine into a stream of giggles which Alison joined in. They sounded like a pair of mobile phones.

'You'll soon get the hang of what's important and what's not,' said Elaine as the lift stopped at the third floor.

Alison pushed the door of the boardroom open. 'To be on the safe side, I would write down everything that Jennifer says.'

'So we have a witness,' muttered Elaine.

At one o'clock, Kate stumbled down the stairs and shut herself in the ladies' loos. She didn't bother looking in the mirror. She had a good idea what sheer panic looked like already.

With her head between her legs, the pounding in her brain could be passed off as just the blood rushing to her extremities. She opened an eye and looked at her notes, lying on the floor next to the sanitary bin. Her right hand felt as though she had just taken down *War and Peace* for dictation and squeezed in a three-hour lecture on Samuel Richardson's longer works.

To begin with, she had written down absolutely everything that was said, and seemed to keep up reasonably well, given that she had no idea who anyone sitting around the table was. Then Jennifer had marched in, at which point Kate realised that the meeting hadn't even begun and, on reading back over her notes, saw that they had been discussing the previous night's launch party and the impromptu striptease of one of the publicists in a vain attempt to get the party into a diary column. And she hadn't even got the publicist's name.

From that point the meeting had gone into orbit. With Jennifer leading it like a dog trainer putting her charges through flaming hoops, they had whipped round the table raising new projects, which Jennifer had either dismissed as being 'painfully 20th century' or had dissected relentlessly. Kate had scrawled entire phrases she didn't understand, written down every number thrown out and at one desperate stage even made notes of facial expressions to throw some light on proceedings.

The official nadir had been plumbed when the new projects pass-the-parcel reached Elaine. Kate had pricked up her ears at this point since Rose Ann Barton was the only author she had heard of and she felt the pricklings of team spirit rooting for Elaine in the gladiatorial atmosphere.

'Rose Ann Barton, as you know, is going to be out of contract now we have the new manuscript, of, erm . . .'

'*Beggars and Choosers*,' snapped Jennifer.

Kate scribbled this down.

Elaine shuffled her papers and flushed nervously. 'Absolutely. Well, I've put together some sales figures . . .' She pushed several sheets towards Jennifer who dispersed them round the table and squinted at them through the glasses on her nose. Holding them at a distance did not apparently improve the overall picture. Kate leaned over Alison's paper but didn't know what she was looking for in the mass of figures and columns.

'Her agent is looking for a substantial increase in the advance since the television adaptation of *Corkickle Urchins*,' Elaine began bravely.

Kate saw everyone look down at the sales figures and Alison helpfully pointed to a number so enormous she thought at first it had to be the annual company turnover.

Jennifer said nothing, which even Kate realised was a bad sign.

'And, um, it's not the money, so much as the . . .' Elaine swallowed. 'As the other things.'

Jennifer took off her glasses.

'Looking at these figures,' Elaine went on, massaging hand cream into her cuticles, 'it's clear that Rose Ann has moved into a class of her own in terms of sales and yet we're paying more for the editorial work on her books than we're paying in advances to some of my other authors. You of all people know, Jennifer, how extremely labour intensive those books are. I have had to coax this latest into a publishable state, and for the last week or so, without an assistant – not that Rose Ann and Mandy were exactly bosom pals, I will admit – it's been a real nightmare. And now she's contracted to producing three a year. So, perhaps, we've reached the level at which, er, she needs to be handled by someone with more time to spend dealing with—'

'Elaine,' interrupted Jennifer. There was an instant 'Dead Lions'-style freeze all round the table.

'You must realise that Rose Ann is the sole reason we are all revelling in the knowledge that Eclipse is topping the *Guardian* Fastseller list. She is the reason you have a Christmas bonus. When I gave you Rose Ann to look after it was a chance many other people here would have been happy to seize with both hands.'

Everyone nodded their heads vigorously whilst trying not to catch Jennifer's eye. Kate's pen hovered in mid-air as she debated whether or not to write this agreement down.

'If you' re telling me that Rose Ann needs more money to continue writing these fantastically successful novels for us, as opposed to, say, Random House or Headline, then we can find it. It's not a problem. If you're telling me however that you don't have enough time to spend getting the best from her,' Jennifer put her glasses back on and peered down them, 'then perhaps we should have a bit of a pruning session on your own list. And what you save by ditching some mid-list granny-stranglers we can put towards Rose Ann's expenses. Hmmm? Two birds with one stone. We'll discuss the level of your offer outside the meeting. I don't want it minuted until John's had a chance to massage the returns figures. Next?'

Elaine had wilted, from then on managing only token disapproval of Jo's new American 'chiller-killer-thriller' ('psychotic freezer salesmen bring terror to New York's late-night deli culture') which Jennifer had seized upon with glee. After whizzing through old projects, which Kate had just about followed in last week's minutes, with Alison's occasional pointer, Jennifer then swept out to another meeting.

Elaine had slumped on her elbows, exposing her mousy roots. 'Oh, God, my last chance!' she had moaned to Alison. 'Three more books!'

Around them, people gathered their papers and over-sized mugs together and left for lunch. Kate heard one editor mutter, 'Jesus, for one moment I thought Jennifer was going to land me with the old sod.' She looked down at her garbled notes and felt ill again. Then she left.

Looking at the Rose Ann Barton section of her notes now, slumped against the door in the loo, brought back horrible echoes of her interview and the blithe way she'd invented office experience. Was she completely stupid, for God's sake? Had she imagined she would never have to type a letter? Kate bunched up a section of hair in each hand. And she'd thought *The Lost Children of Corkickle* had been a good omen.

She couldn't remember the last time she had felt so humiliated. There was nothing else for it: she would have to resign on the pretty basic grounds that she couldn't do the job. It would have to be Laura's little black book of bollock-breakers after all. She levered herself to her feet, flushed the loo so as not to look suspicious and pulled open the door.

Isobel was dumping a huge hand-tied bunch of yellow flowers in a full wash-basin and muttering darkly.

'Isobel, um—' began Kate and stopped as her voice wavered.

Isobel gave her a straight look in the mirror. 'You're looking a wee bit peaky, there.'

'Isobel, I—' Kate stopped and held up the jumbled mess of notes. Reflected backwards they looked even worse, although the doodle of Jennifer Spencer with lightning bolts coming out of her head was still recognisable.

'I've fucked up the meeting minutes, no one can help me salvage them because no one else was there, I—' Kate wondered how much she should admit to Isobel and decided there was nothing to lose. 'I have about as much office experience as Tara Palmer-Tomkinson and when Elaine realises she will sack me,' she finished dramatically.

'Oh, God,' said Isobel, drying her hands on a paper towel. 'And I thought there was something the matter. No one really has office experience, you daftie. We all just make it up as we go along. Give me your notes and we'll knock this off while they're out at lunch.'

'Bad Perm, Red Jumper. Offered three K for next two Inspector Lovie mysteries; agent outraged by offer and threatening to move author unless we take author's "Diary of a Medieval Midwife"; rejected by meeting in April. Bad Perm to lunch author but not somewhere too expensive. Moschino Bag Woman to bodge up marketing plan for Lovie using whatever we used last for DCI Waters series. Nylon Paisley Tie to invent export figures.' Kate looked up. 'That's all I managed to get.'

'Right,' said Isobel, flexing her fingers over the keyboard. 'Red Jumper Woman will be Cynthia, who does most of the crime authors. And I use the word, "does" advisedly, if you're with me. Know what you mean about the perm, but then you don't want to intimidate crime writers by being too trendy-looking. Hmm.' She began typing. 'Nadine Brownlow, two untitled Inspector Lovine mysteries. CH offered £3,000 – did you get the rights?'

'The what?'

'The territorial rights. Where we're allowed to sell the book.'

'No.'

'OK, no problem.' Isobel scrolled down the screen on her computer. 'Well, the last book was world rights, and somehow I don't think the agent's managed to get an American sale, unless Isle of Man detectives have suddenly gone huge on CBS, so let's say £3,000 world rights. Agent keen to find home for non-series "Diary of a Medieval Midwife" (see April minutes) as part of deal. CH to reiterate original offer with marketing plan from DH – that's Diane, the marketing woman. EJ – that's Ewan the export sales guy, his boyfriend buys all his ties and I think someone once told me he's partially sighted, and we're all very PC here, so we don't say anything – to investigate export sales. Not that there'll be any, but you don't need to say that in the minutes. Next?'

Kate pulled a face. 'I didn't get any of this next project, they talked about it so quickly and mostly in whispers. It was as though they didn't want me to hear it.'

Isobel looked through the notes. 'Ah, I know what this is. God, they're awful. If they don't want it minuted they should just say so. Or this kind of thing happens . . .' She began typing.

'Emma Ball, untitled thrillbuster,' read Kate from the screen.

'Shh,' said Isobel. 'We're not meant to know about this.'

'JS has offered £500,000 plus £100,000 marketing spend for next two books from highly successful author, should she decide to leave current publishers in summer. EB to lunch author and agent next week; DH to prepare marketing plan. Bloody hell, five hundred grand! Is that Elaine, EB?'

'Oh, yes,' agreed Isobel. 'Jennifer's desperate to get some young talent on the list. Everyone is. Emma Ball is unusual because she doesn't write girlie romances, and she's created her own sort of niche. Psychotic London-based romances.'

'How do you know all this?' demanded Kate. 'I didn't even hear them say her name in the meeting.'

'Well, they wouldn't, would they?' Isobel lifted a splayed-out hardback thriller to reveal a can of contraband and caffeine-enriched Red Bull. 'Needs must when the devil drives,' she added by way of explanation as she cracked it open. 'You'll find that the sole advantage of working for people who can't type their own faxes or take their own phone calls is that sooner or later you do get to find out what they're not telling you when you do it all for them.'

'Oh,' said Kate, amazed at how much Isobel had extracted from her notes. Seven projects had emerged from the page and, reading from Isobel's screen, Kate was beginning to feel she'd been at a different meeting.

'Is that the lot?' Isobel poured the Red Bull into a mug and drank it down in one. She pulled a face. 'How long does it take for this to start working? Faster than an espresso?'

'Depends if you have it with vodka or not.' Kate picked up a little photo frame decorated with Liquorice Allsorts. Inside it was a picture of Isobel being cuddled by a broadly grinning man about twice her size. They were sitting in a giant funfair teacup. 'Is this your boyfriend?'

Isobel looked up and smiled at the photo. Her face melted into the expression women are biologically programmed to reserve for babies and kittens. 'Aaaah. Yes. That's me and Will in Florida last year. He's my lovely big bear.'

'He looks a real sweetie,' said Kate. Apart from the 'I've been to The Epcot Center' T-shirt, but she didn't point that out. 'Have you been together long?'

'Oh, we've been together for ages,' said Isobel, going back to her typing, but still smiling. 'If it wasn't for Will keeping me sane I'd have rammed Jennifer's head in the filing cabinet years ago.'

'My boyfriend's away in America – just when I need him,' said Kate, rolling her eyes in sitcom 'Men! What can you do with 'em?' amused despair. It was a tough call between desperately wanting to talk about Giles to keep him real in her life, and just shutting her heart up. Having to explain where he was didn't exactly present an image of eternal togetherness. She didn't even have anyone here who could give her a stern talking to when she initiated random topics of conversation purely so she could steer things round to Giles. Like she was now.

Kate kept her eyes fixed on the 'Critical Path' chart on Isobel's board, so she wouldn't see the mixture of emotions on her face.

'Oh, Kate, that's awful hard.' Kate looked down and saw Isobel gazing at her with real sympathy. 'And is this your first time in London too?'

'How did you know that?' asked Kate in wonderment.

Isobel looked up at her with the same warm, sad expression in her eyes. 'I saw your CV. Well, let me know if there's anything I can do to make it less of a nightmare. I thought only nuclear war in Dumfries would ever make me come to live in England, but here I am. Happens to the best of us.'

'Thanks.' Kate managed a tiny smile. 'That's really kind of you.'

'No problem,' said Isobel. 'Was this the lot for the meeting? They normally go on for hours, but you can condense what's actually relevant into a page and a half.'

'There's a few more notes on the next page, but I don't want to take up any more of your time.' Kate pulled herself together and thought it might be wise to be seen doing the minutes herself, rather than perching on Isobel's filing cabinets watching.

'Fine,' said Isobel, looking through the scrawl. 'I'll just go through . . . Tum-ti-tum . . . That's been bought, no matter what Alison said, I heard her on the phone this morning, agreeing the high discounts. She's just keeping Jennifer waiting so she'll look like a hero. Tum-ti-tum . . . God! Jo wasn't sent that Mafia fridge thriller first, it came in for Elaine and she passed it to her. And I know that for a fact since I logged in the submission. Jo's never had anything direct from an agency as big as that. What a . . . The American Slapper isn't a title, it's what we all call Marguerite DuCoyne – her new book is provisionally titled *Love's Sweet Embrace* . . .'

Kate scribbled furiously, blushing at the thought of the potential humiliations Isobel was diverting. It occurred to her that Isobel might be winding her up, but she pushed the thought out of her mind. That was the as-the-crow-flies route to complete hysteria.

'I'll put what I've done on disk and transfer it to your system. Don't worry, I'll come and do it now,' said Isobel, seeing Kate's grateful smile slip at the mention of her computer.

'Thanks for helping me, Isobel,' she said, clutching her notes. 'I really was on the verge of running right out and not coming back. You've saved all two days of my publishing career.'

Isobel twisted one of her plaits. 'No problem. I can remember my own first week. It was a nightmare. Jo, you know, with the kinky boots, was an assistant then, just as snotty as she is now, and she let me struggle on on my own. Didn't even tell me about Jennifer's afternoon power nap, the bitch. So when I saw Jennifer slumped on her desk, shoes off, with her head between her legs, naturally I tried to revive her and naturally Jennifer went into a panic attack and naturally she had to lash out with her elbows and give me a nosebleed. Two and a half years it's taken me to live that down.'

Kate could not imagine the vision of efficiency with a nosebleed. Or indeed Jennifer with her shoes off.

Isobel sniffed and ejected the disk with the minutes on. 'So, that and the fact that one more day helping Elaine to run her life would have driven me to smack addiction . . .' She swivelled on her chair and looked at Kate. 'If there's one thing this office lacks it's a sense of irony. And I can't do it all on my own.'

'Well, I can certainly make you look like the greatest assistant ever known to publishing,' Kate said.

Isobel pulled a wry face.

chapter twelve

London seemed to get hotter day by day. It didn't get much cooler at night, either. Kate had never been able to deal with summer at the best of times, and now all the heat seemed to rise up from the pavements and bounce down from the tall buildings, trapping itself in an unending hot spin cycle. In the evenings she worked as late as she could, since the office was air-conditioned and Dant's flat, full of unemptied bins and dirty socks, smelled like nothing on earth. Then she came home on a series of buses, unable to force herself underground, and wandered through whatever green spaces she could find.

Wednesday was a low point. The temperature hit 32 degrees and the overloaded air-conditioning at work broke down. Someone in Production fainted. When she got home, Kate went straight to her room and peeled off her sleeveless shirt, which was sticking to her back and yellowing with all the deodorant she'd sprayed on. The Magnum she'd eaten while walking back had dribbled down her arm, and rather than cooling her down, it had just made her a bit sick. She felt sticky and grubby and not in the mood for anything, least of all the stupid American hospital thriller Elaine had foisted on her as she left.

She dropped her bag on the bedside table, stripped off the rest of her clothes and put on the white fluffy dressing gown, now becoming distinctly stringy, then flung herself across her unmade bed. The 'days to Giles' chart on the wall by her head still had a pitifully long way to go and already it seemed that she had always had to dial 9 to get an outside line when she picked up the phone. Kate sighed and crossed off another day. Two more to the weekend. She tried not to look at the number of days until he came home.

Kate rolled over on her other side and picked up the photo of Giles from the bedside table. He was wearing a dinner jacket for a college ball and looked gorgeous. She was wearing a green halterneck sheath dress and looked hungry. She wasn't wearing any knickers either, although you couldn't tell from the photo. You could perhaps guess from the gleam in Giles's eye, Kate thought hopefully, but that might be more to do with the fifty quid in her clutch bag that he had just won on the casino.

She put the photo frame back on the table with another sigh and imagined all the tension draining out of her body into the bed, like greasy chips on a piece of kitchen towel. *London* was draining her. It was being with people that she missed most of all; people she could just be herself with. Eclipse didn't count: concentrating made her too shy to speak to most of the other assistants, and though Isobel was friendly, Kate didn't want to irritate her by hanging around all the time like Norah No-Mates.

When she got in moods like this, she didn't want to see anyone anyway. In fact, she went to some lengths to avoid seeing people; the last time Giles had announced he was off for a working vacation without her, Kate had become so miserable that a rumour went round halls that the reason she hadn't been seen for three days was because she was in the river, by now heading for the North Sea.

The front door of the flat banged shut. Kate inclined her head towards the sound, but didn't get up. Harry must be back from work. There was some shuffling around in the hall and the door banged again. Harry must have gone out for cricket nets. And he didn't even say hello, thought Kate peevishly, forgetting that he wouldn't know she was in, and that she didn't want to see him.

She looked around the room from her bed, noting every stain and crack in the walls. Three hooks were missing from the saggy curtains, and Kate thought longingly of Giles's billowing linen blinds. Outside, the cat next door, much fatter and glossier than Ratcat, was back on the window-box, stripy belly up in the sun. A car outside drove past playing drum and bass so loud the cat got up, arched its back and slid back in through the window.

'Oh, fuck it,' said Kate out loud, aware that she was in danger of turning into Dant. With an effort she hauled herself up and, collecting the three coffee mugs on the floor by the bed, she trailed out to the kitchen, dumped them in the sink and went into the bathroom for a cool shower. There were two black pubes on the soap and for a moment she thought she would burst into unreasonable tears. Instead she opened the window, dropped the soap out, and rooted around in a cardboard box full of toiletries (Teresa's gesture towards tidying the bathroom) for Dant's shampoo.

Kate had long suspected that Dant's shiny black mop was chemically assisted and the discovery of treatment shampoo for 'coloured, dry and damaged hair' just confirmed her suspicions. Liberally lathering her sticky armpits with aromatherapy blends and pro-Vitamin B, Kate estimated that she had about fifty pence worth of conditioning treatment on her armpit hair alone, and wondered if Ratcat fancied a makeover.

By 7.30, there was still some evening sun streaming into the sitting room, and with no sign of Dant, and Harry out, Kate made herself a banana milk shake in the underused Magimix and padded through in her bathrobe, clutching the bad hospital drama under one arm. She settled herself in the sunniest spot on the sofa and waved the CD control regally at Dant's hi-fi. The flat felt weird without background noise, and without anyone to make her nervous, Kate felt unusually at home. Dant had apparently been listening to Lloyd Cole before crashing off to bed early that morning. It didn't exactly fit with *Ward 9: Blood on the Beds*, but, flicking through the opening chapter, Kate couldn't imagine what would. After seventeen pages of spurting plasma and besplattered surgical masks, her milk shake began to lose its initial appeal.

The front door opened during an especially emotional Lloyd Cole moment, with which Kate was joining in heartily, discarding pages at the rate of three a minute, and she didn't hear the footsteps in the hall until Lloyd's wailing had faded out. When she did, temporarily intoxicated by feelings of power (realising for the first time that there was no need to read to the end of the manuscript) and of health (the shower and milk shake), Kate made no move to get up. Dant wouldn't notice if she wore a strait jacket around the place and since her legs were recently shaved, she didn't mind if Harry got a glimpse of them. The number of back issues of *FHM* piled up in the loo suggested that wet-look girls were the in-thing round here anyway.

The footsteps went into the kitchen, and cupboards started banging open and shut. Kate read unmoved to the end of chapter seven, which disposed of the chief medical examiner in a particularly nasty misuse of forceps, and replaced the elastic band on the manuscript. Homework over. This one would be going straight back in the same Jiffy bag it came in.

'Dant? Do you fancy a milk shake?' she called, picking up her sticky glass. There was no response from the kitchen other than the rattle of the dishwasher being slammed shut.

Kate padded through in bare feet, squeezing the remaining water out of her hair as she went.

'I said, do you want a . . .' She looked up and realised that it wasn't Dant or Harry or even Seth the stripper.

'Hi, I'm Cressida,' said the vision in black, extending a

hand which reminded Kate quite strongly of Morticia from the Addams Family.

'Oh, hello,' stammered Kate, wiping banana gunk off her hand on to her dressing gown. Her squeeze was a lot more enthusiastic than the fashionably limp hand she shook, and immediately Kate felt gaucheness descend on her shoulders again like false Heidi plaits.

Cressida was tall, and black and white in a kind of Guinness advert way. She looked like a Goth, except that it was obvious even to Kate that her oyster-white skin and Tarmac-shiny hair were not courtesy of Barry M. She was also willowy, in a black linen trouser suit – but where Kate had dieted madly and only achieved skinny at the best of times, Cressida was fashionably lissom and had moss-green fingernails and a thumb ring.

Kate felt unaccountably like a sumo wrestler in her dressing gown.

'I thought I'd drop in to see how you were settling in, and to have a word with my brother about various things, but I can see he's gracing somewhere else with his presence. I take it from this pigsty that the boys haven't got round to organising that washing-up rota they promised?' Cress arched her plucked eyebrow.

'Er, no, I mean, I've tried to do as much as I can, but there are some things . . .' Kate trailed off, as her instinct to please and her annoyance at the state of the kitchen reached equal levels. She shuffled her feet on the cold tiles and remembered too late her promise to keep up her pedicure.

Cress rolled her eyes. 'If I left Dant on his own, he would have the place looking like a travellers' protest site, the lazy little bollocks. Never mind . . .' She switched on the dishwasher and then the washing machine. 'I've put Dant's red bedsocks in with Harry's dirty cricket gear, which was *strewn* over the table, and I hope it teaches the pair of them a lesson.' She wiped her hands together, Lady Macbeth-style. 'Would you like an espresso?'

'No, I'll stick to the milk shakes,' said Kate, remembering Harry's attempt to clean the espresso machine. The resultant spare part was keeping the table from wobbling. 'I'm on a detox plan,' she added, for effect.

'Oh, *God*, I couldn't do that.' Cress fished in her handbag for a fresh bag of coffee, ripped it open with her teeth and filled the machine. Her cranberry-red lipstick didn't even smudge. 'There are more chemicals circulating in my system than in the Betty Ford Clinic loos. Get rid of one lot and my veins would collapse.'

'It's for work, really.' Kate didn't think she knew anyone who actually did proper drugs. She racked her brains for any details of Miriam Goode's detox plan that would sound remotely chic outside the office.

'Oh, right, Dant tells me you've swiped Mandy's old job at Eclipse?' Cress rammed the coffee filter attachment into place despite the missing piece. 'That must be interesting?'

'Sort of. It's a lot to pick up all at once, but I don't know how long I'll be doing it for. My boyfriend's . . .' As this came out of her mouth, Kate remembered that it wasn't perhaps the smartest move to tell her landlady that she was planning to tunnel her way out to freedom by the middle of November, a good two months short of the lease she'd signed. She changed midstream to, 'My boyfriend's pulling some strings for me in the bank he works for.' This was a lie, but Cress was giving her the same shrinking sensation of inferiority that she'd got at school from the Sun-In high-lights girls.

Cress poured a slug of whisky from Dant's cupboard into her coffee and knocked it back in one go. She pulled a face. 'Ugh, I'd stick to publishing if I were you. Bankers are so fucking dull. The bar used to be so full of them we had to introduce a no-office-attire policy. 'Course, most of them don't have any. Non-office attire, that is.'

She fished in her bag again and pulled out an American soft pack of Camels. She offered them to Kate, who refused and busied herself chopping up the banana for her milk shake which now seemed hopelessly goody-two-shoes, along with her make-up-free face and unisex dressing gown.

Cress settled herself on the work surface, crossing her slim ankles. Kate threw some ice-cubes into the Magimix and tried not to notice how Cress's thighs didn't spread when she sat down. Probably on speed, she thought crossly.

'So how are you settling in with Bill and Ben?' Cress asked, blowing smoke out of the corner of her mouth across to the window.

'Fine.' Kate whizzed the blender and, as usual, imagined for a second the agony of losing a finger in the slicing blades. 'They're a bit messy but I've got a brother so I'm used to it.'

'Dant is a pig. Harry is a little dog.'

Kate wondered what this made her. A little cow?

'Is that why Mandy left?' she asked.

'Oh, her.' Cress recrossed her legs, forcing Kate to notice that the immaculate pedicure peeking out from the pony-skin mules was moss-green to match the nails. 'She and Dant . . . well, they didn't really get on. Or maybe they did, I couldn't tell. Lots of shrieking and throwing things. Not enough space in the flat for two drama queens. I think the upshot eventually was that some boyfriend had a ticket to Australia and asked her to go. So she did. Bloody inconvenient for me – I had to come back from America to sort everything out.'

But she still hadn't taken a day off work to show her and Laura round the place, Kate noted to herself. 'No one at work will tell me why she left. It's like being a second wife – I speak to authors on the phone and when I say whose assistant I am, there's this funny silence, and then they say, "Mandy?" as though I've come back from the dead.'

Cress stubbed out her cigarette in the saucer of the espresso cup. 'She found her job a bit frustrating after a while, I think. She was quite pushy. And hacking your way through piles of Dant's dirty underpants to get to the bathroom isn't what you want after a hard day in the office.'

'Have you never lived here with them?'

'For one week. Research purposes only, I can assure you.' Cress slid off the counter and gathered her bags together. Kate pulled her spine to its longest extension and casually leaned, on her toes, against the fridge for extra height.

'We must go out for a drink and a chat, anyway,' said Cress, in a tone of finality, much to Kate's surprise. The whole experience had felt more like an interview than her frenetic half hour crouched at Jennifer Spencer's feet. 'Maybe I can tempt you to something stronger than a banana smoothie.' She smiled, as if to a toddler, and rummaged for her car keys.

Kate simpered instinctively and hated herself at once. She pulled the belt of her bathrobe tighter.

'Tell Dant I was in and that I'll call him tonight.' Cress didn't need to add the proposed topic of conversation. 'Tell Harry I said hello.' She moved towards the door, kicking bits of cricket kit and Ratcat's soggy mousy out of the way as she went, with her glossy mules.

'Bye!' said Kate.

Cress lifted her hand without turning round. 'I'll give you a call,' she said and let herself out.

chapter thirteen

Kate had agonised for some time over how she should let Giles know about her move from the bosom of the Craigs to the House of Idiot. She didn't have an address for him in America; amidst the enormity of his departure she had asked for some point of contact in the foreign place, some way of holding him in her mind in surroundings she couldn't imagine, and he had told her she should write to Redcliffe Square, since Selina had been instructed to forward all his mail to the bank until he had somewhere definite sorted out.

Giles had made it clear at the airport, in his best firm-but-gentle voice, that it would help them both 'get on with things' if they didn't have any contact for the first few weeks. No letters, and definitely no phone calls. Although he didn't say as much, Kate imagined the thought of her snivelling down his office phone was clearly at odds with the new international banking image, which Kate could see creeping over him even at the check-in desk. Briskness and confidence were spreading upwards and outwards, like some heifer in Ovid being randomly metamorphosed into a tree from the hooves up.

Giles had always been much better at partings than her. 'Short and sweet, Katie,' he used to say at the end of term, as she leaned into the car window for a final teary kiss before he drove back to London. He'd been just as gentle, and just as relentlessly firm this time; so gentle in fact that she only felt the complete sting of his leaving her much later.

It had been on the numb Tube journey back into the centre of town that she remembered that he hadn't at any point apologised for going, or for leaving her to deal with a situation she clearly didn't want. Fat tears had rolled unseen down her face as she clung to the ceiling strap and swayed between a gaggle of American tourists. He simply hadn't seen anything to feel sorry about.

Kate's first impulse, on entering Mike and Laura's Clapham war zone, had been to write Giles a long and passionate letter, even if it did have to go via the supercilious Selina, whom she didn't put above steaming and resealing. Having scrawled eight tragic pages, intoxicated with self-pity, and closeted in the guest room while Mike and Laura squabbled through *Brookside*, she made the fatal error of reading some of it back in the morning. Disgusted at her own helplessness and use of the phrase 'emotional void' she thrust it to the bottom of her rucksack.

But now that she was stuck in Deauville Crescent, reinvigorated by righteous anger and Harry's Alanis Morissette tape whining through her bedroom wall most mornings, Kate had scaled herself down to a terse 'I'm fine' postcard format, but hadn't been able to get them quite terse enough. Not wanting to look needy by writing more than two abrupt sentences – one to cover her news and one enquiring offhandedly after his – she wrote and ripped up several cards, the tone of which ranged from casual to positively distant, until the symbolism of whatever was on the reverse of the postcard started to obsess her, and she gave up.

Through all this there was no word from Giles. Kate had included her new address in a thank-you-for-having-me note to his parents, and although dull longing continued to settle in the base of her stomach, she promised herself that she wouldn't get in touch until he did, no matter what it cost her. It was the same kind of stubbornness that her mother used to call her 'Spiteful Nose Complex' but which, when rigorously applied to chocolate, had nonetheless won her a pair of size ten jeans and Giles's admiration.

Kate was lying on her bed renewing her old acquaintance with Mr Yorkie – being unable to sustain her silence towards Giles *and* her chocolate ban – reading the Arts section of the Saturday paper, when the front door intercom rang. She waited a moment to see whether one of the boys would go, registered the fact that it was only eleven o'clock and therefore still the middle of the night for them, sighed heavily, and dumped all the papers on the floor.

There was a trail of chips leading along the hall and into Harry's room, and the kitchen table was littered with playing cards, overflowing ashtrays and empty ice-trays dripping on to the floor. Kate pulled the kitchen door shut and started undoing all the locks on the front door, only to find that whoever had come in last hadn't been at all preoccupied with home security. One twist of the Yale lock and the door swung open.

The front doorbell buzzed again and Kate shouted, 'I'm coming!' into the intercom. It struck her that it could be the postman with a registered delivery parcel from Giles, and she galloped down the stairs in her bare feet. Four flights suddenly seemed endless and she prayed the postman wouldn't have left before she got to the bottom.

Kate flung open the door. Standing at the front porch, holding a large box, was Selina. Behind her Giles's BMW was parked next to the abandoned Citroën, with what looked like Jamie Theakston in the passenger seat.

Selina couldn't disguise her flinch at Kate's Kill Rock Stars T-shirt and scruffy weekend jeans. Kate suddenly noticed that the red nail varnish pedicure applied so carefully and so recently at the Urban Retreat had started to chip in the manner of a trailer-park slut.

Kate clung to the door-frame and tried to look as though she was living opposite a Cypriot off-licence for style reasons.

'Hi, Selina!' she beamed. 'How nice to see you!'

Selina managed a tight smile and thrust the box at her. 'I was speaking to Giles last night and he suggested that I brought his stereo round for you while he's away. To keep you company.'

Like the animated Locket in the advert, Kate's heart split in two and poured warm feelings all through her body. 'Did he? That's so kind of him – I really miss not having my stereo here, and it didn't seem worth getting my mum to send mine down.' She held out her arms for the box.

Selina passed it on reluctantly. 'He said he couldn't imagine you without some kind of ear-splitting soundtrack in the background. I hope it's still under warranty,' she said in an ambiguous tone.

'Did Giles send any other message?' Kate asked, remembering a little late that she was meant to be being cool about the lack of communication. She bent her right leg behind her, trying to look casual.

Selina put her head on one side in an irritatingly Laura-esque gesture of coyness. 'Oh, just that he's loving the new job and hopes that you're not missing him too much. He's got a new address, which I've put in the box.'

Kate fought down an impulse to open it up straight away and scrabble around in the foam chippings. 'Oh good. Good. We decided it would be best not to write too much until we were both settled in, you know.' She forced out a shrug but Selina was already looking back to her car. Family chit-chat evidently wasn't part of Selina's Saturday agenda.

'Great,' she said, flicking her hair out from under the collar of her tennis shirt. 'Look, we've managed to get a court for half eleven, so I won't keep you, OK?'

'Selina,' called Kate, as she turned to go. 'Did Giles say he was . . . he was missing me?' She pinched the back of her calf with her toes, to prepare herself for the pain of being told he didn't.

Selina stared at her as though Kate had just asked why

her car was blue. 'Um, sort of. He said he was too busy to be homesick much.'

'Oh, yes, I suppose he must be,' said Kate quickly. 'He must be used to settling in to new places by now.' She wished Selina would take her smug self off somewhere, preferably a landmine area.

But she was already halfway back to her car and Kate felt her last link with Giles slipping out of her reach, just as she realised even Selina made him feel closer to her.

She returned Selina's airy wave as the BMW pulled out on to the main road. 'Don't drive into a lorry, will you?' she yelled but still watched until it disappeared from sight. Then she turned back to the smelly stairs with a heavy heart and began lugging Giles's stereo up to Flat 27.

Harry was up and frying bacon in his boxer shorts, oblivious to the squalor around him, when she reached the top of the stairs. Gran Turismo noises were screeching from the sitting room.

'Morning!' he said. 'Fancy a bacon butty?'

Kate tried not to notice the fine blond hair on his legs. 'No, I think I've just turned vegetarian. That cannot be hygienic. You want to watch out for spitting fat, frying bacon in your pants. Ever had a leg wax?'

He pointed his fish slice towards her box. 'What's that?'

'This?' said Kate, as if surprised to see it in her arms. 'Oh, my boyfriend sent me a present.'

The word 'boyfriend' sounded chocolatey as it left her mouth, filling the space around her with a warm feeling of belonging, even if the person she belonged to wasn't actually here. She had only made scant reference to Giles, or indeed any personal details about herself, until now, not wanting to give the impression he had abandoned her or that she had no other friends to save her from flatshare hell. But random boasting was safe enough, surely?

Harry raised his eyebrows and flicked bacon on to a plate.

'Boyfriend, eh? Just when Dant was hoping you were a lesbian.'

'Yeah, right.' Kate suppressed any outward sign of her deep internal horror. 'He's working in America for a while and sent me this as a surprise.'

'Nice,' said Harry, cracking an egg into the pan.

'Right then,' said Kate, remembering the address hidden in the box. 'I'll get it set up.'

She put the stereo unit on the bedside table and the speakers on either side of the bed. That was how Giles had had it in his room at college. She stood back and admired the subtle but expensive effect. The room looked instantly improved. He'd bought it with his summer holiday pay from Schroeders and she'd gone with him to HMV to help him buy new CDs. He'd raised his eyebrows at the till about some of her selections but rather than have an argument in the shop he'd just handed over his Visa card. Elvis Costello would still have been in his protective cellophane if Kate hadn't rescued him for her own collection.

Kate switched on the plug and began retuning the stations. Being fully equipped with modern devices, the radio retuned itself automatically to a lot of stations she'd never heard before, and, when she put it on long wave, mainly to jungle music that was apparently being broadcast from a coal scuttle in Dagenham.

What should she christen it with? All the music she had brought with her for her Walkman reminded her of the summer she had just left in Durham. Was that a good thing or a bad thing? Kate turned her rucksack upside down and emptied all the tapes out, then lay back on the bed and let Sergeant Pepper and Giles fill her mind.

Kate's trance-like state was broken by the click of the tape finishing and the sound of men regressing in the sitting room. For forty minutes the music had levitated her to the same place she had gone to at college when she lay on her bed and listened to it, somewhere disconnected and greenish. But now she was back in London. For a brief moment, she forgot where she was, but then she remembered and loneliness swilled around her chest. She wondered how she had been able to block out the barking for so long.

'You are shit!' bellowed a voice.

'Brake! Brake, you wanker!' yelled Harry. 'The grey area is the racetrack, for God's sake! Didn't I explain that bit?'

Despite herself, Kate swung her legs off the bed, wandered to the door and looked in.

Dant and Seth, the streaker from Laura's unfortunate bathroom experience, just about recognisable with his clothes on, were hunched over the Playstation, lurching and leaning as though they were actually in the cars on the screen. Harry was lying on the floor in his dressing gown with a can of lager, disparaging loudly. The remains of his fry-up were all over the table.

Dant took a corner too quickly and turned his car over. Even his compensatory 90-degree lean on the sofa didn't help.

Harry punched his shoulder and grabbed the controls off him. 'Watch me, you big fairy.'

'It's not fair, this is your job!' Dant complained as Harry righted the car and began to burn off Seth on the straight. He took a swig out of the orange juice carton and noticed Kate standing by the door. 'Oh, morning.'

There was a faint amusement in his voice which made Kate wonder if they'd been talking about her earlier. She forced a crooked smile, and tried not to let her intimidation show.

'Decided to join us then, have you?' Harry was now about to lap Seth, who had more or less given up and was trying to light a cigarette while steering his car into the spectators to see if they would die on impact. Kate deduced from Seth's dishevelled boxer shorts and crumpled T-shirt that he had spent the night on the sofa. His hairy spider's legs were still half-wrapped in a sleeping bag. She wondered whether he had slept there or in Dant's room and blushed, despite herself.

'Your sister rang,' said Dant. 'I told her you were out.'

'And she left it at that?'

'Well, eventually.'

'Cheers.' Kate wondered what Dant's tactics had been, given that she hadn't ever escaped after less than half an hour of intensive grilling. Laura might not deign to come round, but she wasn't going to let her remote control slip that easily.

She pulled herself off the door-frame and walked self-consciously to the unoccupied sofa, where she could watch the action on the television, their heads only partially block-ing the view. The room was a complete dump, even by their standards, and was littered with the remains of breakfast, overlaying the residual debris of the previous night. She picked bits of bacon off the sofa cushions and flicked them on to a nearby plate in disgust.

On screen, Seth drove his car into the grandstand and the windscreen shattered dramatically.

'Are you OK in there? What the hell's going on?' asked the concerned pre-recorded voice of Tiff Needell through the in-car radio.

'Seth, even allowing for the fact that you're a non-driver, you really are unbelievably bad at this,' remarked Harry.

'Yeah, how many times have you taken your test now?' Dant, in frayed jeans and an unironed shirt, buttoned twice at the navel, was cutting his toenails on to an old *Melody Maker*.

'Five.' Seth did a three-point turn into the path of an oncoming sports car and was spun back into the crowd.

'You'd better come into the pits,' said Tiff Needell testily.

Harry made scoffing noises. 'Have you tried taking it on the Isle of Skye yet? There's only about seven cars on the road there and no dual carriageways.'

He turned to Kate. 'Seth failed his last driving test because—'

'Fuck off, Harry,' Seth protested, throwing a fork at him.

'Seth failed his last test for going too slow on a dual carriageway *and* . . .'

'I'd had a bad night,' Seth mumbled.

'. . . and for buying a copy of the *Evening Standard* from one of those traffic light vendors during the test, then arguing about the change while the lights had gone green.'

'The guy was trying it on . . .'

'There are reasons for making people take the test in the first place,' said Kate, drily. It was a little known fact that Mike had failed first time round for exceeding the speed limit on four separate occasions, once outside a school for disabled children. In Kate's opinion, he should have started out with six points on his licence just to give other road users a sporting chance.

'Have it back then, you big Malcolm,' said Harry, lobbing the controller to Dant. With a grunt, he levered himself up from the floor and adjusted his boxer shorts. 'Who wants some tea?' He looked round, raising his eyebrows.

Kate nodded, trying not to notice that a crucial button was missing off his flies.

'And some toast.' Dant's eyes didn't leave the screen.

'Can't we play Tombraider now?' whinged Seth.

Kate found an empty Tesco's bag behind the sofa and started stuffing empty crisps packets and beer cans into it. She forced herself to look behind the cushions, but still couldn't bring herself to risk a hand down the side of the sofa.

Under last weekend's *Sunday Times* were four packets of photographs still in their Truprint envelope. Kate looked up to check Dant and Seth were still crashing into each other and pulled open the flap.

They were obviously holiday photos, and the location looked like somewhere in France. Someone's holiday cottage, thought Kate, with a disapproving shudder, as she flipped past Dant in the garden, Dant making omelettes with bloodshot eyes and hangover hair, Dant in an open-top VW Beetle, Dant shirtless in a fountain, Dant asleep on the table surrounded by a crowd of out-of-focus wine bottles.

The next packet had more group shots: Harry, Dant, Seth and Cressida she recognised, with lots more of the same sort of people. From the state of them, it must either have been a holiday near a vineyard, or they had won a trolley dash in the hypermarché on the way out. Not that any of them looked capable of dashing anywhere. A sequence of pre-dinner pictures followed: girls with shoulders even skinnier than Kate's in strappy summer dresses and cherry-red lipstick, men in chinos and jackets. Dant, amazingly enough in black linen drawstring pants, looking like a surly model from *Dazed and Confused*. Harry, with a white T-shirt under his shirt, towering over a couple of girls and smiling angelically. Tables loaded with wineglasses glinting in candlelight.

After this formality everything went blurry: lots of pictures of lights, people's ankles and unfocused close-ups of puckered kissy-kissy lips. Dant with red lipstick smeared accusingly over his neck. Harry apparently naked, sitting in a fountain, laughing hysterically. Cress, impervious and unsmudged.

Kate expelled air through her nose and went on to the third packet. That it was the morning after was obvious. Crowded round a kitchen table, everyone was wearing shades, except one girl, seemingly unaware that she was wearing a black eye. Much orange juice and coffee was in evidence. More interior shots of the sun-streaked cottage followed two pictures of Cress giving a weary V-sign to the camera and then partially covering the lens with her hand.

Kate flipped on until people came in again. One picture, taken from in front of the Beetle, featured Harry at the wheel, wearing a white T-shirt and cricket hat, with three girls (blonde, giggly) squashed in the back and Cress an ice maiden in black shades and black Grace Kelly cotton shirt, in the front. Harry, unaware of the camera, was gazing unselfconsciously at Cress, who was glaring through her sunglasses at the photographer.

Hmm, thought Kate, tucking it to the back. Interesting.

The rest of the photos all seemed to be of Cress: Cress rubbing sun cream into her legs; Cress drinking wine and dangling her feet in a river; Cress on a bike; Cress reading Philip Roth under a tree. In each one she looked cool and somehow remote, protected from the sun with a big hat and loose linen trousers, protected from everyone else with her Jackie O shades and a 'bugger off' expression. The other girls who sometimes flitted into shot seemed very gauche next to her black and white glamour, and despite their short skirts and cobwebby cardigans, which revealed, Kate noted enviously, expanses of full-time toned tanned flesh, Cress in her flowing layers still seemed to be wearing less than they were.

Harry came back in with a teapot and four mugs in one hand and a plate of toast and Marmite in the other. 'Oh, yeah, the holiday snaps,' he said, putting the teapot on a pizza box. 'I'd forgotten you'd sent those to be developed.'

'They're not bad,' said Dant, folding a piece of toast in two and stuffing it in his mouth. 'No visual evidence for anyone's divorce lawyer though.'

'Thank God,' said Harry. 'Kate, do you have milk? Or sugar?'

'Milk, thanks,' said Kate, absently. She flipped past Cress reclining on a sofa, Cress looking very un-Cress-like in a hammock, and was brought up short by a photograph of Cress, stretched out like a white cat in the shadow of a tree, sunbathing almost naked, a red and white sarong wrapped carelessly round her slim hips like a bloody bandage. Kate blinked in shock and her skin prickled with embarrassment. She felt a blush creep over her cheeks as she stared inevitably at Cress's round, ivory breasts and her tiny, perfect nipples, like two palest pink Jelly Tots. The long arched legs, naked apart from a daisy-chain around one slim ankle, were exactly as she had imagined under the flowing clothes, and though Cress was slender, there wasn't a muscle in sight. This was not a body that went to the gym. She was impossibly porcelain and cool in such blazing, unforgiving sun. Had Cress known she was being photographed? The eyes were hidden behind her omnipresent sunglasses.

Harry leaned over with the tea, and Kate hastily shoved the photos back in their envelope. If there were more she didn't want to see them.

'Thanks,' she said, taking the mug. It was the one with the model and her disappearing bikini.

Harry noticed the expression on her face and immediately gave her his own mug, which had a couple of Guide Dogs on it. 'Sorry, not very PC,' he said apologetically. 'Can I have a look at the pictures?'

'Oh, yes, of course,' said Kate, passing him all four packets.

'This is shit,' announced Seth and switched off Touring Cars 2. 'Let's have a go with Lara.' He began fiddling with the Playstation.

'I put all the films in to be developed,' said Dant through another mouthful of toast. 'You can work out how much you owe me when her Ladyship comes to pick up her set.'

Harry was engrossed in the first packet. 'You still owe me for the beers last night so let's call that quits. We all went to stay with a friend in Brittany in July,' he added for Kate's benefit. 'Fantastic time.'

She smiled politely.

'Apart from our married friends who split up during a boating expedition,' said Seth darkly. 'Dant.'

Dant pushed his unbrushed dark hair off his face with his fingers. 'Yeah, well, whatever. Have you saved— Oh, you anus, have you saved on this memory card? You have, haven't you? Oh for fuck's sake, what's the point in— Look, you can't save there . . .'

A boulder appeared from nowhere and flattened Lara Croft, pointy breasts and all, in a shower of blood. Dant wrestled with Seth for the controls.

'Nice one of you,' said Harry, holding up a picture of Dant looking miserable in a French hypermarché, pushing a trolley full of wine and cheese. 'Not.'

'Yeah, yeah,' said Dant, giving Seth a Chinese burn. Seth yelped and dropped the controller.

Kate got up and walked over to the window. She pulled the curtain aside, ignoring the protests, and let some of the fresh sunlight into the room. It was a gorgeous day outside. She sipped her hot tea and noted that Harry had used the Earl Grey teabags Laura had so generously provided.

A Jeep drove past, playing 'Walking on Sunshine': one of the songs that reminded her most of college and Durham. Just as she was beginning to rock her foot back and forth to the beat in a comforting way, it struck Kate like a slap that it *was* a memory, a sensation that would only get further and further away from now on. She was on a conveyor belt, being irrevocably drawn away from that part of her life, just as even now eighteen-year-olds were sitting at home with their reading lists preparing to take her place. She stayed looking out into the road long after the Jeep had gone past, not seeing anything, until a church clock a long way away struck the hour and the door to the flat opened.

'What do you want?' Kate heard the tension in Dant's voice and knew it must be Cress. She had her own keys and didn't bother knocking. She usually caught at least one of them doing something embarrassing.

'Hello, boys!' No trace of irony.

'Morning.' Harry and Seth.

Kate's first impulse to hide and not see her, having seen far too much of her already that morning, was swept away by a desire to have things smoothed out – to see Cressida behaving perfectly normally. Or what, Kate had conceded, passed as normal for her.

'Hi, Cressida,' she said, making herself turn away from the comfort of her window.

Cress was wearing a little silky summer dress that probably came from somewhere disproportionately expensive to its size and general appearance. More importantly, she was wearing the 'I don't care where this old thing came from' attitude which accessorised it perfectly. She looked unfairly gorgeous. For a dark-haired girl she had absolutely no visible body hair. Kate noticed that Seth and Harry were staring at her back view with undisguised admiration. Dant was cutting his toenails again with increased vigour.

'I came to see the holiday photos and take you out for a milk shake,' said Cress, stroking her long black hair into a pony-tail. 'Well, you can have the milk shake, I might have something a bit stronger.' She plaited her hair deftly behind her back, displaying perfectly toned upper arms, and sniffed theatrically. 'Bit smelly in here isn't it?'

'Great!' Kate hated the playground eagerness in her voice, but couldn't help it. Cress had the same kind of unsettling magnetism as Dant (she cringed at herself, but there was no other way of putting it), but in a much nicer way. And she needed to get out of the house, to blank the memories the stereo was spreading of happier times when it had been in Giles's room. Next to Giles's bed.

'I haven't finished with the photos,' snapped Dant without looking up from his dirty toes.

'No problem. It'll take a while for you to pick out all the ones of you looking like a werewolf. We can see them when we come back, can't we?' Cress looked at Kate with a friendly smile.

Kate smiled back automatically. There was no trace of Cress's imperiousness towards her as at their previous meeting, and she felt pathetically grateful.

Cress jingled her car keys. 'OK, let's go.'

'Oh, do you have to? So soon?' muttered Dant.

Kate picked a cardigan off the top of the laundry pile and wished she'd had time to iron.

'Is it, er, girls only?' asked Harry, too casually. He was sitting in a knot to disguise his boxer shorts but had only succeeded in making himself look completely naked instead.

' 'Fraid so. We couldn't talk about you lot if you were there, could we?'

'Doesn't usually stop you.' Dant tipped his nail clippings onto the carpet.

'See you later!' said Kate, following Cress out of the flat. She wondered if she had a lipstick in her bag and smiled at Ratcat as he ran in between their legs.

'Right, that's enough Tombraider,' said Dant suddenly, snatching the controls from Seth, who was still staring after Cressida. 'Where's Resident Evil? As if I didn't know already.'

chapter fourteen

Sooner than she had thought possible, Kate's days slumped into a routine. At 7.30 her alarm would go off and she would lie groggily listening to Capital Radio, trying to bring herself round to the idea of getting up, and hoping against hope for a bomb alert which might have sealed off the District line. The last possible moment for surfacing was the travel report after the news at eight; leave it later than that and there was no way of making up the five minutes lost.

Honed down to a bare minimum, this routine now allowed her ten minutes to wash, two for underarm deodorant to dry, five for rudimentary make-up, five to search the room for clean underwear, another five to iron a selection of crispy clothing from the tumble-drier, and whatever time was left was spent on breakfast. She hadn't eaten a whole bowl of cereal since she moved out of Mike and Laura's.

But this morning was bad, even for a Monday. She had dozed off for a critical four minutes after the news. Then Harry had thrown her plans by getting up twenty minutes early and having a loud bath during the essential 8.05 to 8.15 bathroom slot. Kate was shocked to hear herself whining with frustration outside the bathroom, as the Reservoir Dogs soundtrack blared away within.

'Harry! Harry!'

'Bom. Bom bom bom bom bom. Bom bom bom.'

Kate hammered on the door with her fist.

'Harry! I need to get in or I'm going to be late.' She looked at her watch. By this stage she should have had her underwear on at least, and the washing machine was still full of wet clothes from last night. 'I *am* late. Can you hurry up, please?'

There was a muted splashing, which she hoped was the sound of Harry levering himself out of the bath. The music stopped and then started again on the next song in the soundtrack. The second splash sounded like Harry settling himself back in the water. The 8.20 Eye in the Sky Roadwatch Update filtered through like a reproach from her bedroom.

Kate hopped from foot to foot. 'Harry!' How loud did music have to be in bathrooms, for God's sake? All three of them played music at festival volume, but this was mainly to be heard over the competition. After a couple of weeks Kate had stopped noticing Dant's stereo go on when he shambled home in the middle of the night, although she had been dreaming about Zodiac Mindwarp a lot recently.

Kate was rattling the door handle when it suddenly struck her that she *hadn't* heard Dant come in last night, and although a faint concern about his whereabouts did cross her mind, she was seized by more immediate matters. Marching as crossly as she could on cold tiles in bare feet, she took a deep breath and let herself into Dant's room, trying to keep her eye fixed on the door in front of her. Skewering herself on something unpleasant would finish her off. Noticing he was in fact tucked up in bed watching her would be even worse.

She strode across the room holding her breath but, two strides in, a sudden stabbing pain up her left sole made her shriek in agony.

There was a splash from the bathroom.

'Fuck, fuck, fuck,' Kate gasped to herself, hopping on one foot while she tried to bend the other up far enough to see if she had lacerated her sole. There didn't seem to be any blood. She felt about on the floor to see what the hell she'd trodden on.

Her hand fell on what felt like a dead mouse. Ratcat did spend a lot of time in Dant's room, and for an urban cat who existed mainly on line-caught tuna fish he was remarkably predatory. With a supreme effort Kate made herself lift the offending article close enough to her face to see it in the murky darkness. Where was the spiky bit on a dead mouse? She had a sudden horrible vision of a dead mouse *impaled* on something.

When her eyes adjusted, it was almost an anticlimax. The thing was a bright pink maribou mule, the kind Kate had seen in 1950s sex comedies and, more recently, in the windows of dodgy shops on the way home from work. Who had Dant had in his room who wore those? She turned it over in her hand. Quite big. Even bigger than her own feet which were the bane of her life.

Maybe it was Dant's.

Kate dropped the shoe hastily and, limping slightly, carried on her mission to the bathroom door.

Apart from the screen-saver scrolling across his computer monitor (currently reading, Kate noticed, 'The Drugs Don't Work, They Just Make You Burp') the room was in complete darkness, through which she could just see that the adjoining door to the bathroom was decorated with a full-length poster of Marilyn Monroe playing a ukelele in fishnet tights. Kate shielded her eyes with her hands and pushed it open.

There was a violent splashing from the bath and some splutterings only partially masked by the sound of recorded gunfire.

'Harry, I'm sorry to do this but I am in danger of being extremely late if I don't use the bathroom now.' It occurred to Kate that, having got into the bathroom, she wasn't sure what she wanted him to do. Embarrassment began to clutch at her stomach. 'I need to use the shower.'

There was a rushing of water as Harry got up. Why wasn't

he shouting? Did public schools have communal bathrooms? Did he and Dant share baths? Kate blushed beneath
her hands.

'Okey-dokey. You can open your eyes now, I'm all covered
up.'

Kate removed one hand uncertainly. Harry was standing up
in the bath, wrapped in a towel, festooned with clumps of
bubble bath, looking remarkably chirpy for someone who
didn't normally surface until long after she was out of the
house. The plug gurgled as the water ran out. Kate dropped her
eyes to the bath mat so as not to notice the bits of Harry visible
beneath the bubble bath. How could he be so unfazed? Maybe
this was how people like Dant got away with being really rude.

'I'm going to be so late for work now,' she said, unable to
keep the churlishness out of her voice.

'Hop in the shower, get dressed and I'll take you in to the
office. It's on my way,' he said, climbing out and drying his
hair with another towel.

Kate looked at the wall clock from beneath the one hand
over her eyes. Thirty minutes left to get from shower to photocopier.

'Well?' said Harry, throwing her his spare towel. 'Get a
move on.'

Ten minutes later they were cruising down North End Road
in his old blue Rover. Kate's wet hair dripped into the bowl
of cornflakes clamped between her knees.

'Why do you drive to work when it's only about a fifteen-
minute walk from the flat?' she asked, peeling a banana. 'It's
hardly eco-friendly.'

'Because I can't afford the residents' permit for our street.
Oh, ta.' Harry leaned over and ate half the banana in one go.
'Easier to park it outside overnight then move it before the
parking wardens come round. And I can keep an eye on any
little sods trying to nick my radio.' He pushed the rest of the
banana into his mouth.

'Lovely.'

'Are you having some kind of special day?' Harry squeezed some hair gel onto the back of his hand and ran it through his floppy fringe as he drove with his knees.

'No. It's Monday,' said Kate. 'Worst day of my week. Twice as much post as usual and authors phoning up with burning irrelevant queries they've been hatching all weekend. Everyone's in a foul mood and there's still no coffee until we've bought the fucking detox book.'

'Oh,' said Harry. He wiped his sticky hands on the cricket jumper on the back seat and ran his hands round the big wooden steering wheel like a man in love. The car, like a big boat, had barely deviated from its original course. 'Why are you wearing that nice outfit then?'

Kate looked down at her floral slip – one of Giles's favourites which she'd tried to dress down for office wear by adding a machine-shrunk purple cardigan. It had been an unusual style selection for an office day, influenced largely by the fact that she had no clean pop socks to wear with trousers, no black underwear or T-shirts left, and this was the only dress she could wear with her plimsolls without looking like Little Orphan Annie. It did look nice, but she had had some trouble getting the buttons done up over her premenstrually enhanced bosom.

'Because I can't wash any of my own clothes until you and Dant get round to emptying the washing machine,' she retorted. Then, since he was taking her out of his way to work, she bit her lip and added, 'And if you can't look nice on Monday . . .'

'That's the spirit!' said Harry, winding down his window so he could lean his elbow out. 'Keep 'em guessing, that's what I say.'

'Why are you up so early anyway?' she asked, carefully manoeuvring a spoonful of cornflakes to her mouth while they waited for the traffic to move on.

'Oh, you know . . .' said Harry vaguely. 'Some new cars

coming in at work. I've made a resolution to be more dynamic from now on. Can't end up like Dante. Doesn't impress the girls, does it?'

Kate thought of dynamic Giles, whose career focus was so impressive that she was prepared to sit back and watch it go into orbit from a distance of 1,000 miles. Or should that be kilometres?

'*Weeell*, I'm not sure girls are that bothered . . . Oh, fuck it.' A puddle of milk tidal-waved on to her skirt as he accelerated away from the lights. She mopped it up with the tea towel Harry had wrapped his toast in. When she looked up again she realised that they weren't far from the office.

'Do you want to drop me here?' she said, checking her watch. She was going to squeak in before Elaine – just – as long as the school run had been congested.

'I can take you to the back door, I know where it is.' Harry forced his way across a stream of traffic and overtook a post van before stopping on a double red line outside the couriers' entrance to the office block.

Kate gathered her bags together awkwardly while trying to keep the milk level in the cereal bowl. A taxi honked behind them.

'Cheers, Harry, that was really kind of you,' she said, conscious that a graceful exit would be desirable but near impossible to achieve. She still couldn't quite put the recent image of him decorated in bubble bath out of her mind. Quite apart from the fact that she had done to Harry exactly what Dant had done to her on her first night, it suggested an intimacy she wasn't altogether comfortable with.

Harry, on the other hand, seemed perfectly relaxed. 'No probs. I'll see you tonight.' He leaned over and opened the door for her as she fumbled to put all her things in one hand. The gesture made her blush, and she stumbled out on to the pavement. Harry roared away with a wave, which she returned, leaving her standing by the revolving doors with a handbag, a gym bag, an Oddbins bag full of manuscripts and a bowl of cornflakes.

The question of how she would engage herself with the revolving doors was solved when Elaine arrived at the same time. She didn't offer to unburden Kate of anything, but created enough motion on the door to allow Kate to follow behind, pushing the glass with her forehead.

The lift journey was silent and they both stared at their Monday expressions in the mirrored sides. Kate suspected that Elaine wanted to draw attention to her three-minute-late arrival but couldn't do so without drawing attention to her own. She made no comment about the cornflakes either.

When the lift arrived at the third floor, there was a small crowd of people all scrabbling in their bags for the electronic pass that would let them in.

'Kate,' said Elaine, 'have you got your pass?'

Everyone turned to look at her.

'I think it's in my handbag,' said Kate, 'but I don't have a free hand to check.'

Elaine gave her a reproachful look.

Kate walked up to the electronic scanner on the door and, swinging her bag round to the front of her body, thrust her hip at it. The door clicked open and the crowd of people surged past. One of the publicists, wearing a dress similar to Kate's but with a visible purple bra strap, held the door open for her, the last to go through.

Bloody manners, thought Kate, stomping towards her desk. Elaine was already picking up her Voicemail messages. Talk about contrast – from Harry's gallantry to serfdom at work. She threw her bags under her chair and took her soggy breakfast to the kitchen.

Kate realised from the smell of contraband coffee that something was wrong and was not surprised to find Isobel standing by the noticeboard, staring unseeingly at the poster encouraging them all to buy independent pensions, while the coffee machine hissed away on the side.

'Isobel?' Kate touched her arm and followed her gaze to see what was so interesting – whether someone from Personnel had put up a memo about long lunches, as threatened darkly by Jennifer in a curious pot-and-kettle e-mail to the department the previous week. But there was nothing other than the jolly man in the lump-sum sports car smiling back from his leather seat. It was obvious that whatever he had done before retiring so happily, it was unlikely to have been publishing.

'Isobel?' said Kate again, dumping her bowl in the sink. Isobel must have rewired the plug in her need for caffeine. She put a tentative arm around the neat shoulders. 'Is there something . . .?'

'The bastarrrrrd.' Kate had to lean closer to hear the faint whisper. Isobel gulped and drew in a deep breath, in the way babies do immediately before throwing back their heads and roaring. Kate grabbed her arm and shepherded her out of the kitchen, bumping into Jo at the door.

'Oh dear,' said Jo, peering nosily at Isobel's dishevelled plait. 'Is everything OK?'

'Un-neutralised contact lens,' explained Kate. Isobel, with surprising presence of mind, rubbed at her eye.

Jo looked unconvinced and seemed about to probe further.

'I've just seen Jim from the post room with some flowers,' said Kate desperately. 'Were you expecting any?'

Jo spun on her wedge heel and raced back down the corridor, throwing only one curious look over her shoulder. Kate noticed with a twinge of satisfaction that Jo had a Batman shape of peeling skin above the low back of her dress where she hadn't been able to reach with the sun cream.

They shuffled to the main door and Kate remembered that her electronic tag was in her handbag under her desk.

Without looking up, Isobel swung her tag from round her neck and the door opened for them to shuffle through. Kate led Isobel, whose shoulders were now shaking with suppressed sobs, like a bee in a paper bag, up to the fourth floor where the accounts department was, thinking that the loos would be freer of editorial informants. She pushed her into the biggest cubicle and locked the door.

Isobel sank on to the loo with her head in her hands, got up, put the loo seat down and burst into tears.

Kate hitched herself on to the cistern and waited for Isobel to stop crying. She wished she'd remembered to switch on her computer beforehand. At least her coat was hanging up by her desk, so Jennifer wouldn't think she was skiving. How would *Jennifer* switch on her computer if Isobel was hysterical in the loo and not even within shrieking range?

Eventually Isobel raised her bloodshot eyes and with her Scottish accent enhanced by misery said, 'He's goooone.'

Kate frowned. 'Will?' Isobel now had two photographs of Will on her desk and phoned him at least twice a day. 'But weren't you . . .'

'About to get engaged?' Isobel's face crumpled again. 'Yes, we were-er-er-er-er-er-er-er-ere.'

'So what happened?'

There was a pause while Isobel tried to collect herself. Twice she opened her mouth to begin and covered it again with her hand, squeezing her eyes shut. Eventually, Isobel gripped her plait in one hand and began unravelling it ferociously. 'Och, this is *soooo* stupid. Why do big rows always happen over stupid little things?'

'Mmmmm,' agreed Kate, who couldn't recall having a proper row with Giles – squabbles, yes, but everyone had those, didn't they? – mainly because he hadn't been in one place long enough to engage in a good all-out slanging match. Her brow creased. Had they really never had a row? Wasn't that a good thing?

'God.' Isobel divided her hair into three sections and hic-cupped. 'I'll tell you how it happened. I took some magazines home on Friday – the publicity department chuck them out every so often, you know – and I'd been reading one in the bath Friday night while Will was out with the lads. He crashes in God knows when, all smelly and horri-ble, saying he's my little hubbie, and I'm his wee wifie, all that rubbish. Anyway, next thing I know, it's Saturday morn-ing, he's standing there, unshaven, with a copy of *Company* in one hand, yelling blue murder and saying he's packing his bags.'

Her hiccupping sobs returned.

'Why?' asked Kate. 'Is *Company* that bad? There's much worse in *Marie Claire*, never mind what he probably reads in *Loaded*. And it's not for him to tell you what to read, is it?'

'Noooo,' said Isobel. 'He'd got up in the morning with a dreadful hangover and what he likes to call a funny tummy, but what is really the post-boozing shits, and while he was sitting there relieving himself of twelve pints and a kebab, he started reading my magazine.' She put a hand to her mouth. 'He only opened it at the "How Faithful Are You?" quiz, didn't he?'

'But you're about to get engaged!' said Kate. 'How faithful is that?'

Isobel pulled a face. 'Yes, well, *I'm* as faithful as they come, but *I* didn't fill in the quiz, did I? Julie and Maria did.'

The significance of this dawned slowly on Kate, as she tried to match the names to the summer party pictures Isobel had stashed in her drawer 'for safe-keeping'.

'"Your partner always goes out on Fridays with the boys,"' recited Isobel. '"Do you a) give yourself a facial and wait for him to come home? b) get the girls round for a boozy night in with George Clooney? or c) get the George Clooney lookalike from work round for a boozy night of passion?"'

'Oh dear.' Kate slid off the cistern.

'It didn't help matters that Julie had ticked b) *and* c).'

Isobel reached the end of her hair, which was now tightly replaited into a thick rope. There were a couple of shredded tissues in there too, but Kate didn't draw attention to them. 'Of course, once we got going we ended up dragging in all sorts – his socks lying around, me not being able to afford big bills, the mess I let the cat make of the garden, you know . . . the whole lot. He left the house by lunch-time and I haven't eaten or done anything since. I'm just . . .'

She trailed off but Kate knew exactly what she meant. It was the same feeling she had had when Giles went through the check-in gates: a dislocating suspicion that the world was going on with her outside it, like a ghost. She had felt numb and confused, recognising things but seeing only their incompleteness without him there to see them too. She squeezed Isobel's hand.

This seemed to bring Isobel back from wherever she had momentarily gone. 'The fecking sod,' she snapped. 'How dare he storm out like we're in some bloody Shakespearean tragedy? God, we've been living together since we left college. I think if I'd been having George Clooney lookalikes round every time he goes out drinking he'd have noticed be now. For one thing, I havenae got the time with all the proof-reading I have to do!'

Kate tried to keep her mind on Isobel and Will but was struck by the sinking feeling returning to her stomach with a vengeance. She could almost smell Giles's aftershave. For some reason she could picture the back of his neck much better than his face.

'I feel so much better for telling someone, mind,' Isobel went on, wiping off the mascara smears in the mirror. 'I can't tell my Mum and Dad because they think the sun shines out of his arse.'

'Isobel, he'll be back by the middle of the week.'

'I know that. He'll be back as soon as he runs out of clean pants. It's not the storming out that bothers me, really, it's the implication that he doesn't trust me, you know? And now

I've told someone how stupid this row was, I feel a lot better about it. At least I didn't allow myself to sink to criticising *his* parents' choice of car.'

Kate thought she would hate to be up against Isobel in a row. She looked demure but probably gave as good as she got. What was Giles like in a row? She wasn't sure she'd ever heard him express a passionate opinion.

'Let's go and pick up the post in case Jennifer asks where we've been.' Isobel pushed the last wisps of hair into her plait and smoothed down her parting. She turned and smiled at Kate. Only the red eyes gave away her earlier tears. 'You're a very good listener, Kate,' she said. 'Thanks.'

'That's OK,' said Kate abstractedly. Giles was crowding all other thoughts from her mind.

The rest of the day passed reasonably quickly. Wearing her best dress gave Kate the strange expectation that something festive was about to happen, although nothing did. She dutifully stationed herself at the filing cabinets and did all the filing that had accumulated in her tray, mainly so she could keep an eye on Isobel, who had several heated phone calls, conducted in an urgent whisper, and then put her Voicemail on.

At 5.30 Kate switched off her computer and went to see if Isobel wanted to go for a drink, but Isobel's cardigan had gone from the back of her chair and her screen was blank. Kate felt relieved but a bit hurt at the same time; hearing someone else missing their boyfriend gave her a comforting sense that it wasn't just her who was so easily abandoned, when Giles was still sitting around in her head being international and dynamic and absent. It was also nice that Isobel felt she could confide in her. Kate felt a twinge of guilt that her sense of warm friendship was coming out of Isobel's misery. It would have been nice to have got some wine and sat in a park and talked about things. Still, Isobel would work it out best on her own. Like she herself was having to.

For the first time since she'd arrived at Deauville Crescent, Kate got on the right train without needing to think too hard about it, and although she was reading a book from work on the journey, she instinctively closed it and got off at the right stop. As she walked down the street before the Crescent she actually enjoyed the sensation of the hot pavement through the rubber soles of her plimmies. So it came as a relief to find that she hadn't accidentally started to enjoy living in London when she got to the front door and remembered that her keys were inside on the kitchen table. From where she would have picked them up before leaving to catch the Tube to work. If Harry hadn't taken her.

'Oh, fuck it,' she spat. It was six o'clock. Harry wouldn't be back yet. As for Dant's whereabouts, he could be repre- senting Britain in the TT Races for all she knew. Hopefully, she rang the buzzer but there was no reply and with a certain inevitability she realised that she needed the loo badly.

Kate acknowledged the voice of reason that suggested she could go out for supper, browse round a few bookshops, maybe even stroll down to Kensington Gardens, then come back and see if anyone had turned up. This would disguise her ineptitude, but if Harry were going out with his mates after work, it could be midnight at the earliest before she got in.

There was a phone box across the road. Kate hoisted her bag over her shoulder with a sigh and trudged over to it.

'Harry, it's your girlfriend again,' yelled a very posh voice without bothering to cover the phone.

Kate flushed and waited. 'Harry? It's Kate again, sorry.' She hadn't yet stopped averting her eyes from the various prostitutes' cards Blu-tacked to the walls of the phone box.

'Oh, it's *Kate*, hello, sorry, I thought . . . Am I meant to be doing a home run now?' Kate hoped she could hear a jokey tone in his voice.

'Erm, no, I'm, er, locked out, actually.'

There was some guffawing on the other end.

Kate tried to muster some dignity. 'I just wanted to know when you were going to be home tonight. I can always call the police and get them to break the door down. A couple of choice hints about what might be in Dant's sock drawer? Or there's always the TV detector van. And I can do a good Irish accent, you know.'

She was down to eight pence and counting. A quick search of her pocket brought up a pound coin she was saving for an ice-cream. Reluctantly she shoved it in.

'Look, why don't you walk round to the garages and meet me? It's not that far, as you so kindly pointed out this morning. I'll be finished by the time you get here. You're lucky – I was meant to be going out this evening but they've cancelled, so we could go and get something to eat, if you want.'

Kate pulled all the cards that advertised girls under 21 off the walls and piled them on the shelf. She couldn't decide whether she really liked Harry enough to agree to have supper with him, since that would necessitate a proper conversation and would change things in the house: she couldn't just march straight to her room without speaking, as she had been doing. Not that lying face down on her pillow, reconstructing her last hours in London with Giles, was much fun, but there was a sort of obligation in it. And she knew from a visit to the cashpoint at lunch-time that she had roughly a Tube pass and four meals' worth of money left to last to the end of the month. Harry was unlikely to be thinking of McDonald's.

On the other hand, she was quite hungry and didn't much fancy the idea of hanging around Deauville Crescent. It would also be nice to get some wear out of her good dress before it went back in the wash and disappeared into the laundry pile for ever.

All this went through her mind in the time it took to remove four cards and push them down behind the phone unit.

'OK, I've got your card with the address on, haven't I?' she said, staring at the udder-like breasts of a Busty Brazilian Beauty.

'Good girl, see you in half an hour or so.'

Harry hung up before Kate could take offence at the 'good girl'.

In the event, Kate didn't need to find the little mews where Keyes of London were based, as she met Harry walking up the road towards her. From a distance, she thought, he could almost pass for Giles, if he didn't have that stupid walk. Giles strode. Harry, half a head taller, with darker blond hair, shuffled.

He raised a hand in greeting. 'Thought we'd go to Ed's.'

Kate wondered if this was yet another posh mate with a little flat off the King's Road.

'Ed's Diner,' expanded Harry, reading her face. 'Burgers, milk shakes – that kind of thing? OK?'

'Fine,' said Kate, doing quick addition in her head.

'Not far from here. Do you want me to take that?' he said, gesturing towards her manuscript bag.

Kate offered it thankfully. 'A saga set in Depression-era Bolton and a Canadian apple pie murderer.'

He pretended to stagger under the weight but slung it over his shoulder as if it weighed nothing. 'Good day at work?'

She found it easy to talk while they walked alongside each other down the broad pavements, and once she got going, told him about Isobel's disaster with the magazines and about Elaine's latest unreasonable demands on her time.

'. . . and then she left all this stuff on my desk with a yellow Post-it note, just saying "File". So rude!'

'Good God, Kate, anyone would think you were her assistant.'

Harry looked across at her. Striding next to him, Kate's pony-tail was bobbing up and down at his shoulder level, even though she was wearing flat plimsolls. In high heels, he thought with surprise, she wouldn't be that much shorter than him. With her Ray-bans and flowery, flippy-hemmed dress, she could pass for one of the artfully dishevelled locals, though he sensed Kate wouldn't take that as a compliment. She wasn't like most of the girls he knew. It was rather beyond his limited understanding of women, he thought ruefully, to work out whether she was going to be spiky or charming at any given moment.

'Yes, well, there's a fine line between having an assistant and acting like you're paralysed from the waist down. Thank you,' said Kate as Harry pushed open the door of the diner for her.

The diner looked like the set of *Happy Days* and smelled of proper chips, and the waiters waved at Harry who cheerfully waved back. He was obviously a regular. Kate hovered uncertainly until he hoisted himself on to one of the red-leather-covered stools at the bar that ran down one side of the room, behind which a chef was flipping burgers on a hotplate. She was relieved he hadn't opted for the cosiness of a leatherette booth. That would be a *little* too close.

Harry gave the menu a cursory glance and passed it to Kate.

'So you're not really getting into this assistant thing?' he said, leaning on the counter, with his head resting in his folded arms.

'No. In a word. What are you having?'

'I wouldn't worry about it. Mandy hated it too. And she wasn't as . . .' Harry trailed off. 'I'm having what I always have: burger, fries, atomic onion rings, chocolate malt.'

Kate looked at the menu with startled eyes and wondered whether all burgers cost this much in London. Giles had always told her that you could work out the cost of living in any city in the world according to the price of a Big Mac. At this rate, she was on the cheeseburger poverty line.

She put the laminated card on the counter and affected casualness as the waiter approached. 'I'm not that hungry actually. Hot weather makes me lose my appetite. Um, I'll have a Diet Coke and a, er, a small Caesar salad.'

Harry gave her a curious look. 'OK, then, I'll have a Big Bubba, well done, with extra bacon, large fries, atomic onion rings, a chocolate malt. And two coffees while we're waiting? Thanks.' He handed the menu back.

The waiter disappeared. Kate's stomach growled accusingly.

Harry fished in his pocket and brought out a handful of coins which he dumped on the counter and began sorting through for twenty pences. Kate counted about ten pounds' worth of change.

'For the jukebox,' said Harry, nodding towards the miniature jukeboxes gleaming along the bar.

She flipped through the selection, counting, with a rush of pleasure, songs she hadn't heard since she left home for university.

'"Let's Jump The Broomstick"!' she exclaimed. 'Oh, I love that! It's my dad's favourite.'

Harry divided the pile of coins in half and pushed them towards her. 'Off you go then.' The waiter placed white diner mugs of coffee in front of each of them, but Kate was already punching in her selections on the heavy melamine buttons.

'A8 "Great Balls of Fire"; B7, "God Only Knows"; A2, "Lipstick On Your Collar"; C9, "Mr Sandman"; E6, "Pretty Woman" . . .' She paused. 'Or E3, "Why Do Fools Fall In Love?". Which do you prefer?'

Harry poured milk in his coffee and drank half in one go. 'I'm not really an expert. Though it looks like you are.' He pushed one of his twenty pences over to her pile. 'Do both.'

Kate smiled and drank her coffee. The first piano chords of 'Great Balls of Fire' hammered from the speakers and she shut her eyes in a sugar rush of happiness. It always made her feel happy. Either the simplicity of the beat, or the urgency of the vocals, or perhaps it was the lingering association with her early childhood, when her mother and father had played them in the garage for her to dance to. For them to dance together. Her father used to laugh, as he whirled her round his head and swung her beneath each armpit, that she was a much lighter dancer than her mother.

She opened her eyes and realised Harry was looking at her. Their food had arrived. His variety of plates made her salad look rather paltry.

'Sorry,' she said, spearing a lettuce leaf without much enthusiasm as he tucked into his dripping burger. 'I love this kind of music. My boyfriend is more into Pink Floyd. Embarrassing, really.'

A silence fell as Harry chewed his burger and Kate wondered where her dad went to have moments on his own now her mum had filled the house with language students and Lett's revision guides.

'Try some of that,' said Harry eventually, pushing his milk shake towards her. The straw was sticking straight up like Excalibur in a lake of chocolate. Kate dutifully slurped, surprised at how much effort was required to move the liquid ice-cream up the straw.

'Wow! I never allow myself things like this,' she said, licking her lips. 'Too nice. It's just something else I'll get addicted to and then have to give up for the sake of my jeans.'

'You have to have one.' Harry waved at the waiter.

'OK,' said Kate. What a pushover. 'Pass the menu. What other flavours do they have?'

Harry looked at her with serious eyes. 'No, you have to have a chocolate one. It's the best.'

Kate frowned at the menu. 'What about peanut butter and banana? That sounds fabulous.'

'Chocolate.'

'Have you had the others? Strawberry, mmmm.'

'No. Why bother trying the others? I know which one's the best.'

'But how can you know if you haven't . . . Hello?' said

Kate to Harry. But he was looking at the waiter, who was hovering, waiting for an answer.

'Another chocolate malt, please,' said Harry.

'Sorry, that's a peanut butter and banana. Malt.' Kate glared at Harry.

'You tell him, darling,' said the waiter. 'Get him under the thumb now, save yourself time later.'

'He's *not* my boyfriend,' said Kate, trying hard to keep any offence out of her voice. If you could see my *real* boyfriend, she thought, with a pang of fresh misery.

Harry said nothing, and Kate was grateful.

When the malt came, it was not as nice as the chocolate one, although Kate faked near hysterics over it. Only a small hole in her stomach had been filled by the salad and she couldn't help picking at the substantial amount of leftover onion rings Harry seemed to have abandoned near her plate.

'I was right about the chocolate malt, wasn't I?' said Harry. He dipped an onion ring ritualistically first in ketchup and then American mustard.

'No,' said Kate, automatically. 'How can you be so sure about something when you haven't even tried the alternatives?'

'You know Dant's mother thinks he's gay?'

'Sorry?' Kate blushed and tried to forget Laura's embarrassingly swift interpretation of Seth's streaking. 'Er, does she?'

'Well, he's not, as far as I know, and I've known him since we were eight. The only reason she thinks that is because he hasn't had a girlfriend she's met. She keeps phoning him up, suggesting all these nice gay friends of hers he should "go out for a drink with". According to her, there's nothing wrong with Dant that a few family therapy workshops and some Broadway musicals wouldn't sort out.'

Harry's face was very serious. Kate squirmed a little and wondered if he should really be telling her this. Or, indeed, whether she actually wanted to know. Being accused of having a lovers' tiff had evidently moved their friendship on a few stages.

'Maybe he is gay?' suggested Kate, since he'd brought it up. 'Nothing wrong with that. Maybe he's not met the right *man* yet?'

Harry shrugged. 'I don't think so. I think it's just Anna trying to make herself look fashionable by having a sexually diverse family.' He pushed his fringe back out of his eyes. 'Anyway, what I'm trying to say is, sometimes you know what you want straight away and it's just not worth wasting time on the rest. Dant hasn't met the right girl, so he's not interested in wasting time with girls he knows aren't going to work out.'

'But isn't that the fun bit?' Kate thought of the boyfriends she'd had before Giles. Bastards, to a man, but temporarily diverting even at the worst of times. And they had proved conclusively, for a while at least, that there was life after Carrot Girl jokes. 'Anyway, how do you know when someone's right for you if there's nothing to judge against?'

'I know I'd prefer to save it for the right girl. Why sleep around in the meantime, and make yourself look cheap when that's the last thing . . .' Harry stared at his empty milk shake in a manner that suggested he had now gone beyond theoretical argument.

'For a twenty-seven-year-old bloke, you're doing a very good impression of a 1959 women's magazine problem page,' observed Kate. First Isobel, and now Harry. Loneliness must be infectious, or else she was starting to look like a maiden agony aunt.

'Sometimes it's so hard to work out when someone is difficult to get to know, or just not interested. I may be being very old-fashioned here, but tell me why it's OK for a woman to assume a chap's gay if he doesn't have a girlfriend, when women go berserk if you suggest they're frigid because they won't sleep with you?'

Kate couldn't think of a good answer to this and put 'Stupid Cupid' on the jukebox. The waiter came round with coffee refills. They sat sipping their coffee and listened to the lyrics.

Harry went pink beneath his tan. 'Kate, you're a girl. Why are women so crap?'

'Because men positively encouraged it for the past five hundred years and it's a hard habit to break.'

'Well, there are women and women.' Harry stared into the remains of his chocolate malt.

Kate thought of the photographs under the sofa: Cress in shades; Cress in the front seat of the Beetle; the sneaky one of Cress topless in a sarong looking like Morticia Addams on holiday. She wondered if there was another reason why Harry had been up early this morning. Or who his cancelled evening had been with.

'I assume the object of your affections is worth all this agonising?' she tried tentatively.

'Maybe.' He paused. 'Yes. I've waited about ten years already. Couple more can't hurt.'

'Ten years!' Kate was about to say more but stopped herself when she saw the look on Harry's face. It was not unlike the eyes-to-heaven expression worn by the plaster representation of John the Baptist in her grandmother's front room. 'It *must* be love,' she added instead, though she wasn't sure she meant it.

'I think it is. Dant doesn't think so, but then he's refused to discuss it for about a year.'

'Cressida?'

Harry nodded resignedly. 'Yes, Cressida. She's my ideal woman.' He blushed ironically. 'My chocolate malt. I've known her since I was at pre-prep school with Dant. I don't know what I would do if she started seeing someone else. That's about the only thing that keeps me going, the fact that I've never seen her with another man.' He smiled sadly. 'Which isn't much, since she's made it clear that she's not interested.'

Kate felt touched that he was telling her this, but couldn't really see how the glacially cool Cressida she knew inspired such tender devotion.

'I'm sure she's very fond of you though,' she said, racking her brains for something Cress might have said to her about Harry. The only thing that stood out was Cress calling him a little dog and she wasn't sure it was intended as a compliment.

Harry snorted at the 'fond'. Even as she said it, Kate wished she hadn't: 'fond', as she knew from her own sorry experiences, didn't just translate as 'I don't fancy you' but had overtones of 'I don't fancy you *and I feel sorry for you.*' She bit her lip.

'You've been seeing quite a lot of her, haven't you?'

Kate nodded. She and Cress had ended up in Hoxton Square and after a couple of glasses of wine (milk shakes not being on the bar menu), they'd had a good chat about flat-shares Cress had been in, what the boys were like to live with, how to get on the right side of Teresa the cleaner. In fact, after a bottle and a half, Cress had become quite confiding and had told Kate about Mandy's bizarre obsession with candles.

Kate duly responded with the story of her first evening in the flat – Cress had been so dismissive of Dant and Harry that she was sure she wasn't being indiscreet – and Cressida had shrieked with laughter in a very fashionable way. Though she hadn't felt completely at ease at any point, Kate had noticed a vaguely reprehensible smugness at being out in the company of someone so obviously cool. Since then she'd been round to Cress's bar a few times after work, or Cress had dropped in at the flat and carted her off to supper somewhere. And like being drunk, afterwards Kate knew she'd had a great time, but couldn't remember anything they'd talked about.

'Well, I wouldn't say we were best friends or anything, but we've had a couple of funny evenings, yes. She's . . . full of interesting stories.' Kate made a private resolution to drop a few casual references to Harry's charming offer of a lift to work and his good cooking into the next conversation.

'Gets it from her mother. Along with all the other problems she's been working out in psychotherapy for the past twenty years.'

'Really?' said Kate, not knowing how much concern she should blend with her obvious interest.

'Oh, dear,' said Harry. He squeezed his forehead. 'I suppose you need to know the whole story, so you won't put your foot in it with her. Um, well. OK, where to start? You know Dant and Cress's mum's book was pretty near the knuckle, all the bits about the twins and what they did?'

A large chunk of *Roses of Death* suddenly fell into place with a crash: the pyromaniac twins, the telepathic messages on the walls, the dodgy incest bits which had required a special 'What You Need To Know' lecture from the school nurse when the book was found in the possession of one of the teachers' sons.

'No!' said Kate, her eyes round with prurient horror.

Harry also appeared horrified when he looked up from his drink. 'No! Oh, gosh, no, nothing like that! No, I think Dant once set fire to a waste-paper basket, but that was about it on the pyro front. And they've always known what the other is up to, but I think that's more of a "Takes one to know one" thing. No, what I was going to say,' he continued, as Kate tried to hide her disappointment, 'was that Anna didn't bother to disguise the twins physically, if you remember – the dark-haired girl and the blond boy. People used to read it aloud in the dorm to Dant after lights out, and apparently they were just as bad to Cress. It broke her.'

'Er,' said Kate, 'I think you've lost me here. Dant was a blond?'

'Oh, shit,' said Harry, blushing. 'I'm such an *arse*. No, er, keep it to yourself but Dant actually dyes his hair.'

'No!'

'Mmm,' Harry nodded, rather embarrassed to have to pass on such personal information. 'The book went round the dorm at the weekend and by Wednesday he'd gone from being a baby Sting to more like . . .' He struggled for a comparison.

'Bob Geldof?' offered Kate.

'Er, yes, I suppose so. Well, anyway, that was bad enough but then the film came out.'

Kate hadn't been allowed to see the film. By then the parent-teacher association were on the case. She held out her coffee cup for a refill, and Harry waited until the waiter had gone down the other end of the counter before continuing.

'Anna went to the States to help with the casting, so it was all her fault really. You can't imagine what it was like for Dant and Cress to go along to the première with their famous screenwriter mother, who had made them a total laughing-stock at school already, and then see themselves on screen, played by a fat little girl with a squinty eye and some notoriously psychotic brat with an off-screen coke habit at the age of twelve.'

'Oh, God,' said Kate. It was hard enough to imagine the famous mother bit, although she could certainly empathise with the skewed parental vision. Albeit on a much smaller scale.

Harry sighed and cradled his hands round his mug. 'Poor Cress suddenly lost a lot of weight overnight and Dant dyed his hair and went off the rails. I suppose it was a case of "If that's how you see me anyway, why shouldn't I?"'

'Are they both OK now?' asked Kate, feeling guilty for envying Cress's skinny thighs.

'More or less. Well, no, actually. They've had a lot of therapy, the financing of which Anna claims forces her to stay in Hollywood writing absolute shit for cable TV. I mean, that would be ironic if Anna could see beyond her own surgically enhanced arsehole. But they're both pretty damaged. I've known Cress since before all this happened,' he looked up with a smile, 'since she was a little girl, and she was never exactly the easiest person to get on with even then, but, um,' he fixed his eyes on his coffee again, 'she needs someone to put her back together. I know I could be very happy with her. I could make her very happy again.'

Kate looked at him with a sharp tug of sympathy. Her eyes were almost filling up with the pathos of it all. She knew what it was like to feel you could make someone whole with your love: she was just lucky to have found Giles at college. Not that he had much damage requiring her attention. Harry looked so tender and serious, like a big Labrador. It was all she could do not to hug him. There had to be something still very wrong with Cressida if she wasn't crawling inside Harry's cricket jumper.

Then she remembered what Cressida was like in real life.

'Gosh,' said Harry, his voice bright with fake cheeriness. 'Let's not talk about me and Cress, it's really very dull. God knows, Dant has threatened to leave enough times rather than discuss my tragedy. What about you? Where's your man?'

'Oh, well, compared with you and Isobel it's all very straightforward,' said Kate, trying to match up the two visions of Cress. The Cress she was getting to know was a woman who probably wouldn't have sex lying down in case she got static in her hair. Painfully stylish, but *so* not his type. Harry, though deeply affectionate, evidently had the mating instincts of a panda. She dragged her mind back to the conversation.

'My boyfriend – Giles – works in banking and is doing his initial summer training over in Chicago. We've been together,' Kate hesitated over the inappropriateness of the word, given his multi-stamped passport, 'about a year.'

'Quite serious then?'

'Yes, I suppose so.' Kate remembered the vague hint about moving in together which she *thought* she had picked up at the airport as he left. It was getting more tenuous each time she thought of it, and she thought about it a lot.

'Lucky you,' said Harry. He pulled on his jacket and his whole demeanour changed back to the usual heartiness. 'Shall we make a move?'

Kate scrabbled in her bag for her purse.

'No, it's on me, since you were polite enough to hear my tales of woe without honking over my burger,' said Harry. He took out a couple of notes and left them on the stainless-steel counter, waving at the chefs again as they left.

Kate followed him out into the street, still fiddling with her mental pictures of Dant and Cress like a Rubik's Cube, trying to twist some sense into the fractured impressions.

chapter fifteen

The first letter from Giles arrived on the same morning as two fresh spots, the final demand for the gas bill and the worst period pain Kate had ever known.

So much for purging my body of toxins, she thought, squeezing one spot in the gunged-up shaving mirror while her internal organs knotted themselves into a passable impression of a balloon dog. At least, she reasoned, when regular sex is on the agenda, painful periods can be rationalised on the grounds that it's better to have your feet up with a stiff gin than to have them up in stirrups. She squeezed her chin harder to divert the pain from her lower abdomen. The spot wouldn't budge and now glowed red on her pale skin. She slapped her usual layer of Factor 25 sun cream on top and it retreated a little.

Harry banged on the bathroom door.

'Yeah, yeah.' And the other useful thing about periods was that they measured out time, whether you noticed it passing or not. It didn't feel like eight weeks since she'd come to London, but it apparently was. The city was enjoying what the weather forecasters called 'a spell of glorious Indian summer', and what Kate called an unnecessary prolonging of an unpleasant heatwave.

She let herself out, passing Harry in the corridor. He was dragging a brush through his tangled blond hair, his eyes still sealed shut with sleep. A freebie Guinness T-shirt was visible beneath the stripy dressing gown.

Kate could go through her morning routine with her eyes similarly closed, and it worried her when she thought about it. She had even abandoned the five minutes' rudimentary make-up, since the Indian summer and bad air-conditioning left her shiny-faced by lunch-time anyway. This did free some time for breakfast though, and for her new *Terry and June* habit of reading the post – and Harry's *Evening Standard* from the previous night – over cornflakes. She shuffled down the stairs, letting Ratcat out as she went.

In the pigeon-hole there was the usual sheaf of bills: some red, some ominously thin, some addressed to people who no longer lived in the house. Harry had printed some labels with Cress's other address on and left them by the door where the post piled up; out of habit now, Kate redirected all but the gas bill.

There was an *Autocar* for Harry and the NFT September programme for Dant. And tucked beneath that there was a letter in a thick Conqueror envelope, with her name flowing across it in Giles's lovely writing.

Kate's heart beat faster and she woke up properly. At bloody last. She held the letter in a shaking hand, just looking at it. There must have been a moment, as he wrote my name, when I was the only thing in his mind, she thought. And she ran upstairs.

She saved the letter until lunch-time.

There had been two postcards since July, which she knew off by heart; one of the World Trade Center and one of an ice-cream. The first said, 'Having the most amazing time meeting all sorts of people from all over the world! Weather is unbelievable – you would hate it! Hope London isn't too unbearable! See you soon, love Giles.' No kiss. The second said, 'So much to tell you! The bank is fabulous and I am learning all the time. It's so hot and sunny here –

my tan is fantastic but you would be suffering! Quite glad you're not here but looking forward to seeing you in November, Giles x.'

Being a law student equips you with skills to practise law, Kate thought, as she squeezed her knees together on the Tube to prevent the leery man opposite seeing up her skirt. A degree in French gives you the ability to chat merrily with French people, and even some Canadians. But an English degree just sets you up for a lifetime of paranoia. What, she pondered, was better? 'Love' and no kiss, or a hasty 'x' when he was running out of space? And what was the significance of the fact that he had mentioned her inability to tan twice? Was he being thoughtful, or was her whining about sun cream the most memorable thing about her? As for 'Quite glad you're not here' . . . She hugged her bag containing the letter closer to her.

Kate had wondered whether he had used the same rationale as she had about postcards: that they were too small and too public to contain any meaningful communication. Also Giles's lovely writing was quite large and limited him to approximately twenty words. But here was a whole letter, which must surely include a proper Selina-free address at last, and some indication of how he was missing her which she could read over and over again.

She kept her handbag close by her feet all day and at lunch-time walked to Hyde Park where she found a bench under a tree and stretched her legs out along it, unwrapping her almond Magnum. Magnums had taken on a reassuring personality of their own, tasting of the morning she and Giles had sat in his car by the Thames and talked about their mothers. Magnums, of all flavours, were now her friends. The letter felt long, at least two A4 pages.

She fished around in her bag for her purse, took out the little photo of Giles, a spare passport photo from the set he'd had done for his visa, and tucked it into the strap of her sandal so she could see him as she read. Licking her fingers clean, she opened the envelope carefully, resisting the temptation to skim straight to the end where the paragraph about how much he was missing her should be.

'*Dear Katie,*' he wrote.

Katie, thought Kate, rolling the sound of his voice round her mind. No one else calls me Katie but him.

'*Sorry that it has taken me so long to write to you, but I'm sure you will understand how mad it has all been. In fact, I'm sure you've been just as busy as me and probably understand better than I do how offices are only as efficient as their secretaries!*'

Kate bridled at the use of the word secretary. So that was what Selina had told him she was, was it? The cow. This was what came from relying on short postcards with insufficient explanations. The edge of excitement was blunted and she couldn't quite get it back.

'*Working here really is amazing and though I do miss you and being in London, things here are moving so fast that I feel like I'm at the epicenter of everything. I'm picking it all up very quickly . . . IT revolution . . . useful experience at Microsoft . . . international frontiers . . . monetary union . . .*'

Kate's eyes began to skate across the page and she pulled herself up and made her eyes read the technical bits about Giles's training, which seemed to be very practical, and which he described in some detail. He obviously found it all fascinating, and she should try to share that interest. Her stomach cramps began to throb again.

'*I'm sharing a company flat with a couple of other graduate trainees, Jurgen who is from Munich and Benedict from Paris, so I'm getting some good practise* (Kate mentally checked the misspelling without thinking) *in my other languages every time we do the shopping. Our flat is amazing and looks out over one of the busiest streets in the city. I hope your flatshare is working out OK – I had a look on my A–Z to see where you're living now, but can't quite picture Deauville Crescent itself.*'

Good, thought Kate.

Giles rambled about the courses he was doing and what he was expected to achieve in his four months. He seemed to have covered just about everything in half the expected time and suddenly Kate felt a strange twinge of resentment pierce her pride at his success.

She put the letter down on her knee and pulled off her sun-hat. Her head was aching where the band was too tight. If only *her* office could take her out for dinner as a reward for being Trainee of the Week. The closest she got to that was Elaine sending her out to pick up Rescue Remedy from Boots before crime strategy meetings. But Giles is different, she reasoned. He's always wanted to do this. You've only got to put up with Jo's photocopying politics for another eight weeks.

Kate pushed the fact that she was only halfway through her prison sentence out of her mind and picked up the letter again. She couldn't help feeling disappointed that, after the interminable wait for this communication, there was quite so much about the bank, not really very much about Giles, and not nearly enough about her. She decided her resentment must be a hormonal thing.

'*Banking exams next summer . . . blah, blah, blah . . . line-dancing society like your mother! . . . blah, blah, blah . . .*'

Kate skimmed the page. She could read it all later in her room, but what she needed now, before returning to an afternoon of typing replies to Rose Ann Barton's moronic fan mail, was something concrete, and preferably saucy with it, to look forward to.

Giles didn't let her down.

'*It won't be long before I'm back in England and the first night I'm back, I'm taking you for supper at The Ivy. I booked the table before I left, to be sure of getting a reservation, so put it in your diary for November 10th, and make sure that green dress I bought you in Newcastle is ironed.*'

Kate knew the one. It was smaller and tighter than a hippo's G-string. The last time she'd been able to get into it had been after a protracted bout of food poisoning. She would have to look up The Ivy in Harry's restaurant guide when she got home, though using her skills in reading between the lines she could guess it was bound to be expensive.

'*I know you must be very busy, as it's not like you to send a postcard where an eight-page letter will do, so hope this means you're settling in and making new friends. Although I miss you very much, work takes my mind off things during the day; but at night I feel lonely without you, and wonder whether you miss me as much as I'm missing you. Is this very selfish of me?*'

Not when you compare it to buggering off and leaving me here in the first place, said the sarky voice in her head.

Poor Giles, he must be lonely, said the other.

'*Anyway, think how much we'll have to talk about when I see you in November! Until then, lots of love, Giles.*'

Kate turned the page over in case he had added a PS. He hadn't. She reread the last paragraph. It seemed rather abrupt, but perhaps he'd run out of time to catch the post. She turned the envelope over. It had been franked by the office mail. Kate wondered whether he'd got his secretary to send it Swiftair, or whatever the equivalent was in America.

The streams of people mooching towards the park gates indicated that lunch-time was over. Kate carefully replaced the letter in its envelope, settled her hat back on her head and picked up her bag. She noticed, as she walked back up the path, a nanny with a couple of children feeding the ducks on the edge of the lake. No rushing back anywhere for them. This was the afternoon, a long sunny expanse of it, with tea at the end. Kate experienced a sudden longing for home, with the summer vacation parade of afternoon quiz shows, all-in-family-war talk shows, *Countdown*, and the ongoing bickering with her mother about the quality of Carol Vorderman's degree.

I'll phone Mum tonight, she thought, letting an old lady through the gates first. If she's in.

*

'Thank God you're back,' said Elaine, as Kate hung her hat on the peg.

Kate looked at her watch, which only made it five past two, and thought this was pretty rich coming from someone who generally came back late from lunch twenty minutes before Jennifer Spencer left an hour early.

'Is there a problem?' asked Kate. Her desk looked the same as it had done when she went out. Admittedly she had hidden some urgent letters in a file in her stationery drawer (Isobel's Office Management Tip number 8), but Elaine wouldn't have found them.

'I need you to go out and buy a case of brandy, some bright red knitting wool, and a *Cluedo* set,' said Elaine. She was slipping her right shoe on and off nervously, which made her height go up and down like someone on a very small trampoline. 'And some geranium oil, though that can wait.'

'What kind of brandy?' Kate picked up a notebook out of habit, though she had no idea what Elaine was on about.

Elaine's eyes widened. 'I don't know! Courvoisier, Remy Martin, it's in here somewhere!' She thrust a manuscript at Kate and nodded at it.

'Er . . .' Kate furrowed her brow in desperation.

'I need the whole lot biked over to her agent's by three, to coordinate with our faxed offer letter, so hurry up, please!' Elaine waved her bony hands helplessly and skittered off to join the queue of people lined up outside Jennifer Spencer's closed door.

Kate took the manuscript round to Isobel's office for interpretation.

'Elaine's gone mad.'

'". . . *pass your letter on to the author who will, I am sure, be fascinated to hear your real-life experiences of ferret-breeding in East Anglia. Best, Jennifer Spencer.*"' Isobel banged the 'enter' key and sent her last letter to print. 'Sorry, is this about the offer on Emma Ball?'

Kate shrugged elaborately.

'I gather,' Isobel said, rooting in her desk for an envelope, 'that Elaine's last lunch with Emma Ball's agent was so successful that we're offering the half mill promised at the editorial meeting that you minuted all those weeks ago, remember, plus a crate of brandy and the other assorted rubbish, which, PS, is how the heroine kills the various murderers in the book.'

'Shades of Richard III.' Kate looked down at the manuscript in her hands. It was a good 700 pages long. 'Have you read this?'

Isobel pulled the letter from the printer and demurred modestly. 'Weeeeell,' she murmured, dashing off Jennifer's signature, 'I may have had a quick flick through, though I wasn't strictly supposed . . .'

A twinge of pain shot up Kate's back and she squeezed her spine like an old woman. 'Have you got any painkillers, Isobel?' She narrowed her eyes at Elaine's head, which she could see bobbing up and down in line over the filing cabinets. 'Does Elaine seriously want me to get this brandy? It's, what? Twenty quid a bottle? Times nine?'

'At least.' Isobel pulled open a desk drawer filled with pharmaceuticals and deodorants and handed her some Nurofen Extra.

'But I can't pay for it! I've only got fifty quid in the world!' Kate sank on to a low filing cabinet and swallowed the tablets with a mouthful of Isobel's contraband Red Bull. That couldn't be good for you. 'What am I meant to do? Does this happen a lot?'

'All the time, I'm afraid,' said Isobel, raking through a file for something. 'You weren't here when Jo sent half a stone of Turkish Delight and a photograph of the editorial team posing in belly-dancers' yashmaks to an agent touting a novel called *Turkey, My Turkey* Turned out on closer inspection of the script that she'd have been a wee bit more topical had she biked a family pack of cranberry sauce over . . . Ah, here it is.'

She passed a requisition form over to Kate, with a wine merchants' brochure. Kate flipped through to the spirits section and blanched at the prices.

'*Gaaaaaahhh.*'

'Good God, woman, the amount Elaine's spent on lunching the agent alone would pay for a couple of crime novels,' said Isobel dismissively, scribbling on the pad. 'Now get Elaine to sign that bit and take the form over to Berry Brothers and Rudd. It'll be a nice walk for you.'

'You haven't filled in the price on this.'

'I know,' said Isobel. 'It's on our very expensive and not common knowledge wine account. No one knows about it, or we'd be bankrupted by some scam Simon would set up with some agent to refill his wine cellar. But if you were paying for it, it would be a case of Ribena, wouldn't it?'

'What about the rest of the stuff?'

'Hmmm,' said Isobel, turning back to her fan letters. 'I'm afraid you're on your own with petty cash and John Lewis there. Get fifty quid and take a cab. Elaine would.'

To her own surprise, Kate had the knitting wool and the *Cluedo* set on a bike to the agency within the hour. That the brandy was coming separately was a detail she didn't bother to furnish Elaine with. For someone generally assumed to be office-phobic, Kate thought she'd done pretty well on the organisation front. She was even able to synchronise the arrival times down to the last minute, using the fax Elaine gave her to send, which, following Isobel's example, she read as it went through.

It was so interesting that she took it round to Isobel so she could have a look too.

'Can you believe that amount of money?' Kate pulled an incredulous face. 'That's more than all of the assistants earn in five years put together. For two "thrillbusters" set in the cosmetics hall of Harrods.'

Isobel was silent, then grabbed the fax and stared at it.

'Have you sent this?'

'Yes, you can tell by the little blue dot on the . . .'

'Did you type this?'

'No, actually,' said Kate, beginning a sarcastic monologue. 'I just do the dull stuff. When it's something interesting, she types it and I just have to stand here like a lemon . . .'

'Shit, shit, shit,' Isobel muttered, then said, 'Get me the *Writers' and Artists' Yearbook* quickly.'

'Why?' asked Kate. 'Is there something . . .'

'Yes, you've sent it to the wrong fecking place.' Isobel dialled with one hand and flipped through her card index file at the same time with the other. 'That's another publisher, and I bet they're in the auction too.'

Kate's balloon dog insides immediately stopped knotting themselves and deflated. 'Oh, my God.'

'It's not your fault – Elaine got the fax number wrong on her template, silly cow . . . Oh, hello, is that Diane? Hi, Diane, it's Isobel here. Yes, I'm fine, how are you? Really? How fantastic! Oooh, congratulations . . .'

Kate wondered how much geranium oil it would take to poison a fully-grown woman. Or how exactly murder by *Cluedo* set could be achieved.

'No, listen, Diane, you might just be able to save my life. Oooh, yes,' Isobel went into girly shrieks of laughter which did not match the grim expression on her face, 'just like in the Yellow Pages ad, yes . . . Now, listen, someone has sent a fax through to Carol which wasn't meant to go to her at all and it's a wee bit delicate, so I was wondering . . . Oh, you can? Okey-dokey, I'll hang on . . .'

She covered the receiver and rolled her eyes at Kate. 'Don't bite your nails.'

Kate realised she had her right hand and a strong taste of nail varnish in her mouth.

Isobel waved at the fax, which, now that Kate looked at it, had 'PRIVATE AND CONFIDENTIAL' scrawled across it in Elaine's wonky handwriting. 'Send *that* to *this* number.' She pointed at the right page with a sugar-pink nail. 'As quickly as possible – they haven't had it yet and when was the deadline? Three o'clock?'

'Should I cross the original out, so Elaine knows she made the mistake?' said Kate, searching for a way of absolving herself from the impending slaughter. Elaine's head was still bobbing in the queue for Jennifer. Jennifer's door was still shut.

'No!' said Isobel emphatically. 'Oh, gosh, Diane, you are a life-saver and no mistake! It was already in her tray?' Her face dropped. 'But you don't know if she read it. *Riiight.* OK, well, we'll just have to hope, won't we?'

Kate shut her eyes and prayed as the fax went through the machine. She would have to hope Elaine didn't notice the second dot. Or she could say that she'd sent it twice, to be sure. How could Isobel know all the fax numbers off by heart?

'Well, the drinks are on me at the next SYP meeting!' Isobel was getting more girly and Scottish. 'Thanks so much, Diane, you're a star. OK, now, bye!'

Kate pushed the door shut and leaned on it as Isobel put the phone down with a heavy sigh. 'That's all we can do, I'm afraid.'

'Oh, shit.' Kate covered her mouth with her hand: an old habit she thought she had broken. 'Oh. Shit.'

chapter sixteen

Elaine did not get the Emma Ball book. A black mood descended on the department, culminating on the Friday when copies of *The Bookseller* circulated in the office, featuring, on page four, a large photo of Emma Ball and her bloated but smug agent being embraced by the managing director of Another Publishing House, over an inflatable bottle of brandy and a silver-painted lawnmower. An embarrassed assistant stood in the background, painted silver ('Death by asphixiation, à la *Goldfinger*'), apparently not wearing much more than her vest and pants.

'There but for the grace of God,' said Isobel darkly.

With shaking hands, Elaine added three more bottles of essential oils to the collection on her window-sill, and asked Kate to book her an appointment at the hairdresser's.

Kate had pencilled Giles's return date in her desk diary and frequently flipped back and forth to it, counting the days in between. It seemed like a lot of pages, but office weeks slipped by far more quickly than the endless summers at home. Once you got past 11, it was almost lunch, then an hour for that, then after 3.30 came by, it was virtually home time. Mondays she spent in a near trance, once Tuesday was over it was mid-week, Wednesdays she went to an aqua aerobics class in the council pool round the corner after work, then by Thursday it was almost the weekend again.

She also kept a photo of Giles in his dinner jacket in her desk drawer. Not on her desk, as she didn't want to have to explain where he was, and therefore give away any clue as to her plans to bail out when he got back, but tucked away next to her reduced-fat chocolate drinks, which she had bought in a fit of guilt from Sainsbury's and not touched since. A quick look at Giles before tackling Elaine's out-tray helped Kate's morale immensely. She tried not to think whether he might have a matching picture of her in his desk.

Kate's phone rang as she was logging the latest bunch of hopeless manuscripts from the morning post into the submissions database – she was now so adept at phone balancing that she didn't have to break off her typing.

'Eclipse Editorial Department,' she said automatically, signing off 'Murder In A Modern Manner' into the 'Manuscripts Received' column. Kate could now type 'murder', 'death', 'tomorrow' and 'American' without looking at the keys.

'Kate, this is Jennifer. I want you to come into my office for a chat.'

Kate's blood froze, in the style of a bad crime novel. Jennifer must have found out about the fax.

'Fine,' she squeaked and hung up, since Jennifer had already done so.

When she peered round the door of Jennifer's office she found Isobel, Richard and Megan already occupying the available seating. They all looked up at her as she came in. Megan was holding a box of tissues and her eyes were crimson.

Kate felt the blood rush to her face – just one of the Classic Signs of Guilt series her body language was running through. For good measure she crossed her arms and began chewing her lip. Was Jennifer about to bollock her in front of the other assistants as an example to them all? When it was Elaine's fault? The injustice of it filled her with wobbly-kneed anger.

'Ah, Kate.' Jennifer smiled down her long nose like an Afghan hound with a roller set. 'That's everyone then. Do shut the door.'

Kate shut the door and leaned casually against it. There was only the footstool left for her to sit on, and simple geometry suggested that, if she sat down, her knees would end up higher than her bum, providing Jennifer, and Richard if he looked round, with a view straight up her flippy short skirt.

'You will all know by now that we didn't get the Emma Ball book,' said Jennifer, steepling her fingers.

Kate tried to catch Isobel's eye for help, but Isobel was apparently transfixed by Jennifer's twinkly earrings.

'And you will also know that I am very disappointed, *very* disappointed *indeed*,' she went on. Richard pushed his spectacles up on his spiny nose and scribbled industriously on his notepad. Kate shut her eyes.

Jennifer's voice tightened. 'In fact, I am *livid* that we lost out on that book, because it has an angle that we're missing badly. I am very much aware of that. What we need on the list is young, upbeat, sexy fiction. Fiction which will look fantastic on the supermarket shelves, but will compete with the best in the literary awards. Authors we can put in the Style section of *The Sunday Times* and have quoted in the *TLS*. Books that will make the twenty-something market go, "Hey, that's me, that's my life."'

Kate looked up. Jennifer had now shut her own eyes and appeared to be talking in jacket copy. Isobel steepled her own hands in mock-reverence, then folded them away with precision timing as Jennifer opened her eyes again.

'Now this is where you come in.'

Richard stopped writing in surprise. A sticky hanky fell unnoticed off Megan's knee.

'I want *you* to find these new writers. Writers who don't have agents yet – undiscovered, unrepresented talent. I'm sure you've got friends from college who always threatened to write books about you all. Well, go out there and make them do it. Get those books and drag them back here.' An evangelical gleam was lighting up her face.

Richard and Megan opened their mouths simultaneously but Jennifer raised her hand. Megan sneezed anyway. 'We'll discuss all the details in the next strategy meeting, but I wanted to brief you before I leave the office for a fortnight's holiday. Kate, can you stay behind for a minute, please? There's something we need to talk about.'

The others filed out. Kate moved rigidly away from the door.

'Tissue!' barked Jennifer, pointing at the floor.

'Oh, God, sorry, Jennifer.' Megan spun round and picked up the stray tissue, then sneezed into it.

Jennifer winced.

Kate sat down in Megan's chair and held on to the sides. 'Door!'

'Oh, right, yes,' said Megan and closed the door behind her.

Jennifer waited until the door clicked and Megan's flip-flops were audible slapping along the corridor, then said, 'Kate, you've been here for over two months now, haven't you?'

She was smiling, though Kate wasn't sure how she should interpret it. Jennifer's smiles had a rather sinister quality. 'Yes, that's right,' she replied cautiously.

'And you're getting the hang of things, you think?'

'Pretty much.' Kate tried to look modest but competent. 'I'm learning quite quickly, I hope.' If she was going to be sacked over the fax, there was no way she'd be shielding Elaine's ineptitude on the way down.

'Yeeeeees,' said Jennifer. 'Apart from one or two little hiccups? Well, I wanted to talk to you about—'

The phone rang and Kate recognised Isobel's voice. 'Jennifer, Reception say that Rose Ann Barton's agent's phoned to say Rose Ann's coming into the office and wants to meet you for lunch.'

To her surprise, Kate saw Jennifer's face pale. 'Fine, tell

them to tell her I'll be outside the building in five minutes. No need to come in.' She put the phone down. 'Oh dear,' she said to Kate, pulling the smile back on. 'Sorry about that. It looks as though we'll have to have our little chat when I'm back from holiday.'

Kate breathed out and let her shoulders sag. 'OK, then.' She got up and dared herself to say, 'Have a good time.'

'Martha's Vineyard is always lovely once the day-trippers have gone,' said Jennifer as she stuffed books and pens in her Tanner Krolle bag, then added darkly, as Kate had her hand on the door, 'But we do need to touch base about a few things. Rather important things. I'll get Isobel to put a time in the diary. Liaise with her.'

Kate fled.

Isobel had three diaries on her desk. Her own desk diary, with proof dates, publication dates, launch dates all in different colours; Jennifer's desk diary, with lunches, launches and lynchings in Jennifer and Isobel's very different hands; and Jennifer's home diary, which had school trips, nanny assessments and Neighbourhood Watch meetings.

Megan was sitting on Isobel's low filing cabinet, whining.

'All she wants us to do is get inexperienced people to exploit for no money at all, and Richard will get all his revolting mates to write books about *Star Trek* and goblins so he can edit them and . . . Oh, hi, Kate.' Megan didn't meet her eye, which made Kate think Isobel had told her about the fax.

'Did you make up that call to save me from death by shouting?' Kate said, rummaging in Isobel's desk for a can of Red Bull.

'No. Rose Ann never comes in the building, Jennifer has to go out to her. Always at short notice too.' Isobel ripped open a bag of Giant Smarties and began sorting them into colours. 'Still, she's away for a fortnight now. I can't see her bothering to come back in after lunch.'

'And it's the weekend!' Megan sneaked an orange Smartie and had it in her mouth before Isobel could protest.

'Going anywhere nice?'

Isobel opened her diary and smiled like a cat at it. 'Well, if it's Friday, that'll be John. The doctor.'

'Oooh,' said Megan. 'Doctor John.'

Kate sighed disapprovingly. 'Isobel, far be it from me to sound like Claire Rayner, but going out with all these different men isn't going to persuade Will you're missing him and want him to come back. It just makes it look as if you really *are* the mad unfaithful type.'

Isobel tossed her plait. 'It's fun. I like it. You can get to know the contents of one man's sock drawer a wee bit too well over the course of three years, believe me.'

'What about you, Kate?' said Megan.

'She'll be sitting at home missing one man by chatting up two others,' Isobel replied tartly, uncapping a pen.

Kate tsked. 'Will not. I'll be reading my manuscripts like a good girl and worrying about whatever it is Jennifer wants to discuss with me when she gets back.'

'At ten-thirty on Monday fortnight,' added Isobel. She made a note in Jennifer's diary and copied the details on to a Post-it for Kate to take away with her.

'"Whatever it is",' mouthed Megan satirically. 'Not coming out for Sarah's birthday lunch with the Production department?'

They shook their heads and she shrugged. 'Suit yourselves.' Megan slipped off the filing cabinet and flip-flopped down the corridor, recruiting lunch companions on the way back to her desk.

'Don't worry about her,' said Isobel, seeing Kate narrow her eyes at Megan's retreating back. 'The little madam. She's not so great as she thinks; I had to type up her last appraisal. You're not the one who sent inappropriately jolly publication day flowers to a *very* recent widower. Not a lot of people know that.'

'Did you ever interview for MI6, Isobel?' Kate asked in wonder.

Kate loved Friday nights because both lads were out and she could pretend the house had been transported somewhere else, somewhere she actually wanted to be. It was also a Teresa day, so it was even clean.

She began by throwing all the manuscripts she'd brought home behind the table in the hall where the post accumulated and making herself a powerful espresso which she downed in one. In her room she took off all her clothes, enjoying the coolness of air on her skin after the dirty warmth of the Tube and the office, and walked through to the bathroom, where she ran a bath and smeared a thin layer of purifying clay mask over her face. Then she lay in the bath for half an hour, playing on Harry's Gameboy and listening to the Friday night *Wheels of Steel* on Virgin Radio.

What bliss, thought Kate, wiggling her toes above the foam as the espresso raced through her system. I should really think what I'm going to do for Giles's homecoming. November the tenth. Not so very long really. About the same time as the proofs will be coming back from the printers for Rose Ann's new book. Not long at all really, considering all the things that have to be done before then.

She ran some more hot water into the bath using her toe to turn on the tap. Over halfway through the sixteen Mondays. She thought of Giles. In all the vacations apart, she had never longed for him so much as here in this too hot, too busy city. She supposed this was partly brought on by the constant reminders of why she was here in the first place: waiting for him to come back. She was here because he wasn't.

She sank back under the bubbles until her nose was just above the waterline. The warm water was making her feel horny and she ran an experimental hand down her slippery thigh. Her skin was shiny and sleek, like a wet seal, and still surprisingly hairless after the waxing. It felt like years since Giles had last run his hand up her thigh to test the new Harvey Nichols smoothness, not nine weeks. Nine and a half weeks, to be precise.

The phone rang in the hall. Kate ran her hand over her stomach, thinking of strawberries. Strawberry ice-cream that Giles had once eaten off her stomach. How long was it since she had last kissed him? Even basic sensory memories faded so quickly.

The phone carried on ringing. The answering machine was still in several pieces in a box in Harry's room. Whoever it was was either very persistent, or had some bad news to impart. Kate weighed up how bad the news could be. It could also be Dant, off his face, requesting Harry to come and rescue him from some all-night party that had just finished. Practically no one called for her any more. Not even her mother, now night classes had started up again during the week.

The phone rang on. It had to be bad news. Dant would have lost patience by now. With a snort of annoyance, Kate ignored the dull ache of frustration spreading through her body and levered herself out of the bath. The towel she had draped on the heated rail hadn't warmed up and still felt damp from the morning as she wrapped it around herself and found her slippers with uncooperative feet.

The hall was cool after the steamy bathroom, and needly goosebumps rose on her arms.

'Hello?' she snapped, nearly yanking the phone off the wall.

'Katie?'

Kate gasped in excitement.

'Giles! Oh, my God, how wonderful to hear your voice! I was just thinking of you!' All her postcard promises about feigning distance evaporated in a caffeine rush of happiness. She shut her eyes to hear him better. It felt weird to hear his voice in this house he'd never seen.

'I'm calling from the office.' His measured tone warned her that he couldn't really talk freely, but Kate was too excited to care.

Dant and Harry had pretty posh voices, but over the phone Giles still made her feel naked just by talking to her. It was the way he could make the most innocuous comments sound positively erotic – when he wanted to – which usually reduced her to a quivering state of pliant inferiority, as much as what he actually said. And for someone calling from the office, he was certainly treating her to his best bedroom tones.

'It's about seven here, so it must be lunch-time with you?' Kate hugged her towel tighter. 'You got me out of the bath. I'm completely naked, apart from a towel.'

'Really?' The interest in Giles's voice was unmistakable. Kate smiled happily.

'Oh, yes. In fact,' she dropped the towel on the floor, 'oops, no towel.'

Giles laughed down the line, then coughed. 'Listen, Katie, much as I would love to talk about towels with you, I'll get to the point.'

So this wasn't a social call? A chill of vulnerability ran up Kate's spine. She tugged the towel nearer with her foot.

'I've just had some amazing news which I know you're *not* going to think is so amazing. But I wanted to tell you straight away. I only heard this morning.'

'Get away,' Kate said indulgently, stroking the goosebumps which had risen on her arm. 'I did read that letter, you know. I don't glaze over completely when you talk about international bond dealing and all that stuff.' She leaned against the wall and remembered how sexy he looked in his suit. Suits, she should say. He had lots. 'Go on then, what have you done?'

There was an infinitesimal pause on the line, and as soon as Kate heard the forced bright note in his voice, she knew something dreadful was about to spring up between them.

Someone else? Some disease? Dismissal? She felt acutely vulnerable, blind on the end of the phone line, unable to read his face, or hold his hands.

'I've been promoted off the immediate graduate pro-gramme.'

'Oh, but that's fantastic!' Kate let the breath out with some relief. Promotion. Just promotion. 'Of *course* I think that's amazing news. Well done! What a star!'

The pause again. 'Um. Yes, I've been moved on to a dif-ferent project. But it means I'm going to be staying on here until Christmas.'

The pause turned into a duet of silence. Kate's mouth widened in a silent scream. Christmas. That was – her mind spun – thirteen weeks away! Her face crinkled up like a little girl's.

'Katie? Are you still there?' Giles sounded concerned, guilty even.

'But I *need* you here!' said Kate, unable to stop herself. She wanted to take the words back immediately but couldn't. She opened her eyes and saw the remains of last night's supper encrusting the kitchen table and wanted to stamp her foot in childish frustration.

'I'm really sorry, but it's only really another few weeks extra and I just can't turn it down – it's such an amazing opportunity. Kate?'

Kate bit her lip. She was filled with a sullen silence, a desire to say nothing at all. She couldn't see Giles in her head any more, and the only thing filling her mind was the irritating chorus from 'Rock Me, Amadeus', the last song she'd heard on the radio before the phone rang. She wanted to think of some-thing gracious to say but the only words in her head were 'Amadeus, Amadeus, Amadeus', up and down on two notes.

'Kate?' Giles was more worried now. 'Kate, please say you're pleased for me. I thought you'd be pleased for me.'

'Of course I'm pleased,' said Kate automatically. Couldn't he tell she was lying? Did it matter? 'I just . . . I just hoped you'd be coming back sooner. I'd made plans,' she added, twisting the knife despite herself.

'But from your letter you sounded as though you were really settling in.' Giles was back on firmer ground. 'All that intrigue from work, that fabulous story about your flatmate, what's his name? Darius?'

'Dante.'

'Dante, yes. It was a wonderful letter. I loved it. It felt like you were speaking to me. I keep reading it over and over again.' Kate noticed with dismay that he had dropped his voice – as if he were ashamed of speaking to her from the office. He felt further away than ever.

They breathed quietly at each other for a few moments, unable to think of anything to say that wouldn't make things worse than they already were. In the silence it suddenly dawned on Kate that if Giles wasn't going to come and rescue her in November, she would have to face the music at work, not just for the remaining month after Jennifer Spencer came back from holiday, but for five additional weeks on top of that. She felt sick.

'Giles, I miss you so much, much more than I even thought I could.' He'd been right about not speaking to each other for a while: hearing his voice now was bringing it all back in spades. Tears wobbled in her throat.

'Please don't say that, Kate,' said Giles.

Kate could hear the despair in his voice and hated herself for being unable to behave like a grown-up. It was hard for him too, being alone there, working under such pressure. Yeah, *right*, said the sarcastic voice in her head.

'You're going to be fine. It's not that long until Christmas and we'll have the best Christmas ever. I promise. I'll bring you anything you want back from America. We'll go somewhere together on our own.' He sighed. 'I just wanted to tell you as soon as possible so you could get used to the idea, rather than spring it on you the week before I was meant to be coming home.'

Kate was torn between one powerful impulse to hurl the phone down and throw herself on the bed for a good sob and an equally powerful desire to hear his voice for as long as she could. She wouldn't start crying though. Not down the phone – it wouldn't be fair.

'Giles, I know I don't sound it but I'm really proud of you,' she managed in a tight voice. 'You're so clever, and you should just go ahead and do everything you can.' She wanted to say, 'I'll still be here when you come back' but it sounded too much like an epitaph.

'I knew you'd understand,' Giles said with audible relief. 'And I'm really glad that you're finding your feet on your own, without me there. Have you been out for a drink with Selina? She said she would give you a call and fix something up.'

Kick me while I'm down, why don't you, thought Kate. Sympathy drinkies from Selina? I'm not *that* desolate. 'No, she hasn't called, but she did bring— oh, I never said thank you for the stereo. It's made such a difference. I keep listening to . . .'

There was a muffled noise on the line. Giles was answering a question in a different language. French? Kate strained to hear.

'Kate, I'm really sorry, but I'm going to have to go. This deal I told you about in the letter, it's going postal and I have to speak to some people in Paris. I'm looking forward so much to seeing you again, really. Really, I am.'

'Me too,' said Kate, her voice very small. 'I love you, Giles.'

His voice dropped to a whisper. 'And I love you too. Put that towel back on or you'll get a chill.'

A shiver ran through her, despite everything.

'Bye,' she whispered. Hot tears ran down her cheeks and cut rivers through the face mask, now over-parched and tight on her skin. She imagined Doris being left at the kennels just because they wanted an extra month's holiday; her big sad doggy eyes not understanding. More tears welled up.

'Bye.' Firm but caring.

'Bye.'

Giles drew a sad breath. 'I'll write as soon as I get in tonight, OK?'

'Bye.' On an impulse Kate put the phone down before she could hear the click on the other end and immediately regretted it. The smell of dishes left too long in the sink came rushing up to her.

Like a zombie she walked back into the bathroom and looked at her face. Clay was flaking off in white shards, with deeper grey tracks where her tears had run. Elizabeth I meets Night of the Living Dead. It sounded like one of Jo's crap thriller pitches to the editorial meeting.

She rinsed it all off, let out the cooling bath, pulled on her oldest jeans and the first T-shirt that came to hand and went in search of a bottle of wine.

Kate heard the knocking on her bedroom door when the music stopped. For the past hour she had been working her way through every single song which reminded her of Giles, and when those ran out, of previous boyfriends, getting progressively more morbid and more drunk. She had cried until there was nothing left to cry. Which had taken a surprisingly long time.

'Kate?'

Knock, knock, knock.

Go away, I'm dying, thought Kate. She tipped what was left of the bottle of wine into the mug and was surprised at how little dribbled out. She downed it in one anyway.

'Kate?'

Knock, knock, knock.

Playing through various tragic scenarios in her head, Kate hovered between pretending she wasn't there, so she could hide away to pick at her misery in peace, or displaying it for some sympathy. She tried to sit up and found she was very dizzy all of a sudden. And her left foot had gone to sleep.

'Kate, I know you're in there. Dant says if he has to hear that tape you keep playing one more time he will come in and personally cut you loose, footloose with the bread knife.'

Harry's head appeared round the door. He screwed up his nose in disgust. 'Bloody hell. What have you been drinking?'

Kate looked up forlornly.

'Red wine,' diagnosed Harry. 'You've got a nice red wine moustache.' He came in and picked up the bottle. 'You drank all this yourself? It's only half eight!'

'Is it?' Kate was surprised. It felt much later.

'Look.' He put the bottle down. 'You can't stay in and drink on your own. It's antisocial, for one thing. Why don't you come out with us? Dant and I are going out into town with some mates.'

Kate looked dully at him. He was wearing a smart, blue, ironed shirt with a white T-shirt just visible underneath. He had also recently shaved, by the distinctive aroma of Eau de Horn which hung in the air. Harry looked strong and concerned and kind. She wanted to hug him but still had enough vague glimmerings of sobriety to know that this wouldn't be a good idea.

'Bit of dancing? Something to eat? You don't have to be happy if you don't want to.'

Kate nodded. 'Let me get changed,' she said carefully, in case he'd got the impression she was too drunk to speak.

'Jolly good.' Harry looked relieved. 'Sitting room in five minutes. That's a good girl.' His head disappeared.

Kate looked round her scruffy room, covered with reminders of Giles. But she wasn't going to let herself think of Giles any more tonight, otherwise she would find herself at Victoria Station at midnight with her rucksack and a ticket home. She leaned deliberately over to the countdown calendar and ripped it off the wall. Then she pulled her old T-shirt off over her head with some difficulty, rummaged in her drawer for a slightly sexier cut-off vest and automatically squirted herself with perfume.

Mid-squirt, it occurred to her that Harry, Dant and whoever they were carting along with them probably weren't worth too much effort. Knowing Dant and Harry, they were hardly likely to be going anywhere nice. But then, as long as they brought her home afterwards, in a state of oblivion, she didn't care where they went.

chapter seventeen

'So you're called Oscar?' shouted Kate over the sound of high-pitched screeching.

'No, *Tosca*,' said Tosca for the fifth time.

'Tosser?'

'*Tosca!*'

Kate rolled her eyes theatrically. 'Can't hear a word you're saying, sorry.'

The waitress finished taking Dant's order, which he was laboriously pointing out from the plastic menu, and leaned over the table, yelling to be heard. 'So you want mixed meze for seven to start, two carafes of red wine, one carafe of white wine for the lady, another round of ouzos and the set meal.'

Harry raised his thumbs in agreement. A Wonderbra flew out of nowhere and wrapped itself round the back of his head. Unbelievably, the level of screaming increased. With a huge grin, he checked the cup size and threw it back to the table it seemed to have come from – although with four groups of hysterical hen-night parties to choose from, it had to be a guess. The woman wearing the condom necklace and L-plate caught it and had to be restrained from coming over to congratulate him on his lucky night.

Kate had felt for a while that she was moving and speaking in slow motion, but had stopped caring after the first round of ouzos, which tasted like antiseptic and acted like anaesthetic.

'So, Tosser,' she tried again, 'you must be the lucky man?'

'Not as far as I know,' he replied, looking confused. Then a leer spread slowly across his pock-marked features. 'Unless you're going to tell me different?'

Kate flinched away and turned to Dant on her other side. 'What a creep,' she confided in a loud voice.

Dant laughed.

For the first time since she'd moved in, Kate thought Dant was looking passably attractive in a black polo neck and jeans. As usual, there was an expression of superior amusement in his eyes and he hadn't bothered to shave, but the scratchy shadow of dark stubble went with his dishevelled hair. Amazingly enough, in public, he seemed able to carry off the 'so rough it's nearly handsome' male model look. If she didn't know what he did with his takeaway cartons, thought Kate, he'd be almost fanciable. In theory.

Dant leaned nearer so he could whisper straight in her ear. 'Kate, your flies are undone. It's probably exciting Tosca.'

Kate looked down and realised that these weren't her button-fly jeans. She'd done up the button at the top when she last went to the loo and forgotten all about the zip. With an effort she held her breath and yanked it up. The zip snapped halfway. For some reason, this didn't matter as much as normal and she tucked her napkin in her waistband to hide the gap.

'Dant.' Long gaps seemed to be appearing in between each word. 'We're in this . . . place.'

'Tottenham Court Road,' supplied Dant, helpfully. 'It's a Greek restaurant called Kebabarama.'

'Surrounded by hen parties.' Kate's eyes focused on a woman removing her bra through the sleeve of her blouse and looking purposefully at their table.

'Yes.'

'Would I be right in thinking then that we are a . . . stag party?'

'Yes and no.' Dant stood up and caught the bra before it hit Harry again and gave it to Tosca, who began examining it eagerly.

Kate was impressed by Dant's unimpaired hand-eye co-ordination. 'Why aren't you . . . drunk?'

'Because, little girl, I'm far more used to it than you are and you did start before we even got home.'

Through the cotton wool, it registered somewhere in Kate's mind that this was the longest conversation she had ever had with Dant.

'Are you getting married?'

'Fuck, no.'

'Is Harry?'

Dant laughed nastily.

Kate looked slowly round the table. Harry was spitting olive stones into a bowl, apparently unaware of the gusset-wetting effect he was having on the table behind. Seth, she recognised; Oscar was a vile gawping accountant type; there was a ginger one called something like Igor or Agar who was in charge of the kitty and who had been to the loo more times than even Kate had; and a very tall one called Tom, whose name she remembered only because it was the first sensible one she had heard all evening. He'd then spoiled it by adding that he ran an art gallery – the one Dant floated in and out of during the day. None of them looked worth the effort of securing for life.

'So who *is* getting married?' Kate asked doggedly.

'OK.' Dant put a casual hand on her arm. She was too drunk to embark on a complicated insult but noticed how long his fingers were. 'Concentrate. The men you see in front of you couldn't pull if you gave them a convent school full of hormonal teenage girls and a tow-rope.'

Kate looked at them spitting olive stones at each other and was inclined to agree.

'So, every so often,' said Dant, removing his hand to light another Camel, 'when we are all hopelessly single, we have a stag night. Everyone puts fifty quid in the kitty, the bloke who hasn't had it for the longest is nominated to be the Fake Stag, we go out, get smashed in a specially selected venue, guaranteed to have a high ratio of women desperate to pull any grooms going, and let nature take its course.'

'Oh, my God, that's dreadful!' said Kate. The waitress came back with another tray of ouzos and Kate picked hers up before Tosca could drink it. 'Who's the groom tonight?'

'Tom. I wanted it to be Harry, but he's far too uptight about my sister. Arsehole. As we all know—'

'All apart from Harry,' interrupted Tosca, suddenly leaning in with the practised timing of someone who recognises a familiar anecdote.

Kate glared at him. 'Don't believe we were talking to you, Tosser.'

Tosca shrank visibly in his seat.

'As we all know,' Dant went on, 'the only person Cress fancies is herself – frankly, he's got about as much chance of shagging me as he has her. Anyway,' said Dant, waving his match out, 'even with all these women gagging for it, we're so crap no one ever manages to pull, so it's a bit academic.'

'That's one word for it.' Kate knocked back her ouzo without bothering with the water and slapped the hand that was wandering on to her thigh.

Tosca spilled red wine over his white linen trousers.

It was inevitable that when the female belly-dancer appeared, there would be audience demands for male accompaniment. Hopelessly pissed as she was, Kate slid down in her chair with embarrassment as four cross-eyed women, falling out of their Lycra, staggered over to their table. Harry immediately excused himself and escaped downstairs, which one woman seemed to take as an open invitation until the ginger one whose name Kate couldn't remember got up and went too. That left Tom and Tosca to be dragged 'unwillingly' on to the tiny dance floor. Kate couldn't watch the rest.

The toilets were down a scary flight of stairs and she felt a pressing need to have a sit down after the first flight. Kate covered her eyes with her palms. Everything was spinning. She hadn't been this drunk since her graduation dinner. At least she knew where everything was then. Small distant warning bells were ringing about finding herself unable to stand in a city she didn't know with a bunch of men she didn't know either ('With just one thing on their minds!' added the voice of her mother in her head). Or the ringing could just have been drunken tinnitus. Or a fire alarm.

She tried hard not to move, or make any sudden movements which might set the spinning off again. Half a line from a Kenickie song floated through her congested mind:

> *'There's stains on all my clothes, I don't remember,*
> *so now I walk with back to walls in front of friends'*

Glitter, PVC, loud music, sequined miniskirts, going out, having a laugh, the cool Geordie girls in the pubs they used to go to in Durham . . .

'God!' moaned Kate, her round green eyes widening with shock as the first cold hand of ageing panic gripped her heart, 'I'm too old to be a pop star!'

'Oh dear, looks like a bad case of the helicopters.' A hand settled on her shoulder. 'Kate? Are you OK?'

Kate looked up. It was Harry.

A wave of gratitude for his concern swept over her but the effort of looking up increased the spin speed to a dangerous new level.

'Harry, 'm never going t' be on *Top of the Pops*,' she said with tears in her eyes.

'Oh, honey!' said Harry, squatting down to put an arm round her.

Kate looked down again and was sick over his shoes.

Then there was a gap which she couldn't account for at all,

after which they were suddenly all in an Irish pub listening to a live band playing 'The Irish Rover'. Three pints of Guinness were lined up on the bar in front of her and the ginger bloke had disappeared. 'With all the fucking money,' Dant snarled. Tom had two tones of lipstick smeared all over one cheek, but that was the extent of their success with the hen night girls.

'You'll have to come with us again,' said Harry, sucking the froth off a pint of Guinness. A short man with no front teeth winked at Kate from the other side of the bar and Kate smiled back politely. 'You realise they think you're the most Irish girl they've ever seen? Just don't open your mouth. Especially if you feel there might be a build-up of vomit behind it.'

Kate had long passed through the invisibility barrier of drunkenness ('Doesn't matter how I'm dancing, no one's looking at me!'), the silence barrier ('Is that woman over there a prostitute? What do you mean, shut up? No one can hear me! I'm *whispering*!') and had now wandered into the complete short-term memory loss zone.

The noise in the pub was incredible.

'I'm fine,' she said, and picked up her next pint with an unsteady hand. Being sick certainly freed up stomach space.

'You weren't fine when I had to pull you off that girl in the Greek place.'

'*Wooooarrrrrrgggggh*,' crowed Tosca, who was standing behind them waiting for his pint. He waved his forearm suggestively. 'Nice bit of girl on girl action!'

'Shut ya head, ya t'ick ya, or I'll shut it for yiz,' spat Kate in a thick Dublin accent.

Tosca and Harry stared at her in amazement.

'Which girl?' Apparently back to normal, Kate concentrated on drinking her pint.

'The one you leapt on, yelling, "Isobel, don't do it!" just as she was about to snog Tom.' Harry tried to raise an eyebrow drunkenly. 'Don't you remember? She didn't seem to know you as well as you seemed to think you knew her.'

'No, don't remember.'

'I hope Tom remembers. She wrote her phone number up his leg with her lip thing. Why do you girls have so many lipsticks and no pens in your handbags?'

The band finished 'The Irish Rover' and started on a slow song they'd written themselves called 'The Bogs of County Galway'. There was a stampede to the bar.

Harry picked up all the remaining pints and took them to a table where Seth and Dant were setting fire to beer mats. The bells in Kate's head reminded her that she had about half an hour left until she collapsed in a heap, and that collapsing in a heap on any of the men here would be a very bad idea. She made a mental note to tell Cress about how nice Harry had been about his suede shoes. She'd appreciate that.

'Didn't like to ask before, but now we're both pissed, why are you so intent on drinking yourself into a coma tonight?' Harry sounded almost normal, apart from the way he was squinting at her ear as he spoke.

'My boyfriend has abandoned me,' said Kate. She knew she was speaking in whole – if short – sentences, but she couldn't remember further back than the previous one. 'He is a gorgeous shit. Who is more in love with his career than me. But I love him. And I hate London. And I hate my stupid job. But I can't go home. And I just want to forget all about it. Or else I will just cry.'

'Don't cry.' Harry didn't put an arm round her. Kate squinted at him but he still didn't offer an arm and she felt inexplicably put out. 'At least he's coming back eventually. At least he doesn't tell everyone you're gay to get himself off the hook rather than sleep with you.' His eyes unfocused.

'She doesn't do that,' began Kate but the pain in Harry's eyes made her stop. Maybe she did.

Dant put down his lighter. 'Just think. You could have any one of this lot. Seth's been waiting for a nice girl like you ever since school.'

Kate didn't need to raise her eyes from her pint. 'I'd rather die, cheers.'

'Who are you, anyway?' Tom looked at Kate as if seeing her for the first time that evening.

'You will never need to know.' Kate turned to Harry who was lost in his own miserable thoughts. 'Do you think it's hot in here?' She wriggled drunkenly out of her jacket which took longer than normal since she was sitting on the hem.

'*Wooooaaarrr*— Oh, er, sorry,' said Tosca.

'Are you Harry's chick?' continued Tom.

'No,' said Kate, though she noted through her drunkenness that Harry was polite enough not to leap to deny it.

Tom and Tosca conferred in whispers until Tom looked up again and tried to leer at Dant.

Kate banged her empty glass on the table. 'More beer!'

'I'll go,' said Harry, although his own pint was still half full. He got up carefully from the table.

'So, you must be . . .' a lecherous smile spread across Tosca's bright red face, '. . . Dant's bird!'

'No!' exclaimed Dant and Kate together, equally forcefully.

A dazed confusion hung over the table for a few seconds, while the band started tuning up their instruments for the third and final set.

'Oh, I get it!' Tosca pointed at Kate with a wobbly finger. 'This is a boys' night out, so if you're not Harry's bird, and you're not Dant's bird, you must be . . .' There was a pause while he licked his lips. '. . . the stripper!'

There was another silence while all the men looked expectantly at Kate.

'This one's called "My Irish Eyes Are Weeping for Waterford",' announced the singer and picked up his tin whistle.

'Come outside and say that.' Kate put her pint down.

Tosca's face lit up. There was a swell of manly stag noises from the lads as he got up and walked out, nodding cockily at the bouncers on the door as he went.

'Oh, shit,' said Harry, returning with five pints in his hands. He put them down as carefully as he was able to on the table and grabbed his coat.

'Leave it,' Seth pushed him back in his seat. 'Tos's pulled, mate.'

'I don't think so,' said Dant with a sardonic smile. 'Drink up, lads. It's time to go.'

Harry pushed past Tom and Seth in time to see Kate walk back through the swing doors. Outside, Tosca was stretched out full length on the pavement.

'I want to go home,' Kate slurred and staggered into the wall. 'But not before I've had a kebab.'

chapter eighteen

'Try this. It works wonders for me.'

Cress took the eye mask out of the freezer and draped it over Kate's inert face.

Kate groaned. She was lying on the sofa with a sheet thrown over her. Sun was streaming in through the blinds and her head was throbbing.

'God, I feel grim. I can't even be bothered to make up all those crap metaphors about how bad my hangover is.'

'I wouldn't worry.' Cress went back to the fridge and poured herself some orange juice. 'They're oh-so-familiar. Once you've had Satan and all his tribe of rag-rug makers working away on your tongue, you've had them all.'

'There are these whole segments of last night that I just can't remember. Like where that Irish pub was. Or how we got there.'

'Or how you've ended up wearing Harry's pyjama bottoms.'

'What?' Kate felt under the sheet and the sudden movement jarred her head painfully. She wasn't wearing anything on top half and, lifting a corner of the eye mask, saw that on the bottom half was an unfamiliar pair of green pyjamas. 'Oh, God.' Also in her immediate field of vision, next to the sofa, was Teresa's red bucket. Fortunately she was at the wrong angle to see the contents. 'Oh, *no*.'

Cress hitched herself up on the kitchen units and opened the window so that she could smoke out of it. 'Well, I say they're Harry's, but I really wouldn't know. I mean, I know they're not Dante's, so I assume . . .' She arched an eyebrow. 'No, seriously, he's far too gentlemanly to take advantage of a drunken woman. And from what you've told me about last night, you'd all have been completely incapable. That's if the vomiting on his shoes didn't put him off in the first place.'

'Yeah, thanks for bringing that one back.' Kate put a hand to her head. She knew she'd feel better if she could brush her teeth and wash some of the *smell* off herself but the thought of moving was impossible.

'It was a fake stag night?'

'Yes.'

'And, what? You assaulted some innocent by-stander you thought was someone from your office . . .'

'Yes, well, we haven't actually established that it *wasn't* her . . .'

'The boys got involved with a belly-dancer, you nearly got thrown out of a pub for yelling at the barman, Dant chased a taxi down Piccadilly because for some unexplained reason it wouldn't take you, Igor absconded with two hundred quid, you all ran off without paying at the restaurant . . .'

'Because there was a fire alarm, according to Harry . . .'

'And you decked Tosca for coming on to you in the street.'

Kate groaned and pressed the eye mask harder. White meteorites rushed towards her eyelids, not unlike the *Dr Who* credits. 'Let's just say I have selective memory loss. But I *do* remember that Harry was a complete gentleman while I was whining about Giles and honking on his shoes.'

'I just told you that. You can't remember him taking your pants off, can you?'

Kate slid a hand down the pyjamas. 'I'm still wearing them, actually.' Thank God. Out of gratitude for Harry's kindness, she made herself go on with the Harry Harvey sales pitch, even though complete sentences weren't coming naturally to her. 'And all he talked about all evening was how wonderful you were.'

Cress made a sympathetic noise from the window. Kate wasn't sure whether it was out of sympathy for her or for Harry. 'Harry is such a sweet guy, you know, Kate. He really is. I've known him since he was about eight and to be honest, that's how I still see him. This lanky little lad with the wrong kind of T-shirts who was the only one in Dant's class who'd talk to him.'

'Really? What do you mean by the wrong kind of . . .' Kate stopped herself, conscious that she too probably had the wrong kind of T-shirt at school and not wanting to know exactly what that meant. 'But—' she began again.

'Darling, I'm afraid that all the PR in the world couldn't make me consider Harry as anything more than a great big puppy. With no dress sense.' Cress blew smoke rings out of the window and Kate felt acid creep up her throat ominously. 'Although I do have the greatest respect for anyone who can stick living with that pig for as long as he has,' she added thoughtfully.

Through her hangover, Kate registered that this sounded like the introduction to one of Cress's long-playing anti-Dant whines. Top of the Deauville Crescent Pops was 'Why can't he get a proper job?', which had been aired frequently over the past week, 'Doesn't he ever tidy up?', to which Kate had been forced to reply in the negative, and her favourite, the unanswerable 'Where does he go when he's out?'

Cress had been coming over to the flat more than usual recently, and Kate had noticed a correlatory upswing in the number of shirts Harry was ironing before wearing. Aftershave use was also on-the-up, as was cricket practice – and wandering around the house afterwards looking athletic and hopeful.

Even though she still found Cress pretty scary, Kate had

to admit she was flattered by the attention Cress paid to her. She just wished she could pay a bit more to Harry.

If only she wasn't so hungover. Given the way Harry felt about Cress he really deserved an advocate whose tongue felt like it actually fitted her mouth.

'He kept on saying that you were a real lady, instead of all the pretend girls he met at school, and that . . .'

'Morning!' Dant shouted in her ear.

Kate clapped a hand to her mouth and lurched for the bucket. Nothing came up except a mouthful of acid bile which made her wish she *had* been sick.

'Dante!' snapped Cress from her perch. 'That's not sociable!'

'I hate you,' mumbled Kate. 'Water. Please, Cress, quickly.'

Cress grudgingly slipped off the kitchen unit and filled a pint glass at the tap.

'Thanks,' said Kate, stretching out a shaky hand. Half the water slopped on to her bare chest, which she made a half-hearted attempt to cover.

'That must have been a sacrifice of malice over personal cost,' remarked Cress as Dant staggered to the fridge. 'Even with that going on in her ear, Kate doesn't look as rough as you do. And before you ask, there's no orange juice, I finished it off.'

'Why don't you get back on your broomstick and piss off back to La-La Land?' Dant found nothing in the fridge except the can of mixed vegetable juice so old that neither he nor Harry could remember which flatmate had bought it. With a grimace, he cracked it open and emptied half the contents down his neck.

Kate squeezed her eyes shut and concentrated on not being sick again. So this was why they told you to drink water before you went to bed – so you would vomit up what was left of the alcohol swilling round your stomach. In the circumstances, she could think of nothing new to say in response to Dant, particularly when hangovers seemed to make him even more linguistically inventive than usual, and so she fell back on a phrase she had been saving up for some time.

'I am in hell,' she croaked.

'Not on *Top of The Pops*?'

'What?' She flicked one eye open.

'Nothing.'

'Dant, why don't you go back to bed?' said Cress. 'Kate and I were having a private conversation.'

'Without wishing to seem rude, Cressida, Kate isn't capable of holding a glass of water, let alone a private conversation. Or is that the way you prefer your co-conversationalists? Unable to contribute more than ten words an hour?' Dant finished off the can of vegetable juice and burped appreciatively.

Kate breathed in just as a gust of something unpleasant hit her nose and she felt her stomach lurch again. Hangovers always heightened her sense of smell to an inappropriately vivid level.

'Go away, Dant, you're making me sick,' she said before regurgitating the glass of water into the bucket.

'You heard her,' said Cressida. 'If you're so full of energy, why don't you go to the shops and get some orange juice and Dioralyte for your flatmates? You smug bastard.'

Kate wanted to ask how Harry was this morning, since the last time she had seen him – she suddenly remembered now in bad flashback – he was sitting on the sofa clutching the bottle of duty-free tequila someone had brought round before they'd set off for the evening, talking aggressively about how he and Cress would have 'beautif'l creat've ch'l-dren', all of which he would send to Bedales so they could 'be free an' spiritu'l like Cressida'. But her need to know wasn't so great that she was willing to risk opening her mouth or moving her head.

'And what about Harry?' demanded Cress. 'Is he OK this morning? Did he remember to drink a pint of water?'

Dant paused in putting his trainers on. 'No. In a word. He's asleep in the bath. I thought it would halve the number of rooms to clear up.'

'I must apologise for my brother, Kate,' said Cress, shooting Dant an icy look and lighting another cigarette. 'Thanks to my mother's refusal to moderate her bacchanalian lifestyle while we were gestating, we seem to have grown up with iron constitutions. Dant!' She yelled and Kate flinched. 'Get out and get the poor girl some orange juice.'

Dant flipped her a V-sign and shuffled out of the flat, banging the door too loud on his way downstairs. As he went, Ratcat slunk in, looking guilty, his fur matted and wet.

'So, go on,' said Cress, once she was sure Dant had left the building. 'What did Harry say?'

'I've told you,' said Kate. She wished her tongue would deflate. 'The man is in love with you and I just don't understand what is stopping you from having a fantastic life with him. He's lovely. Like a big dog.' She would have been more eloquent had the language section of her brain been working.

Cress sighed. 'Look, Kate. I can understand why you want to help him out. I *know* he's lovely. Even if he does . . . He's just . . .' She paused and screwed up her eyes against the light to see her better. 'Just . . . not for me. Sorry.'

Inexplicably, Kate felt as though she herself had been dumped and through her glue-like hangover was tempted to demand a reasonable explanation for this outrageous behaviour. 'But couldn't you . . .? He's so . . .' she started, not sure how to go on without sounding like Cilla Black.

'Kate, Harry is a very kind, very sweet boy,' said Cress, dismissively. 'And one day he will make someone a wonderful husband. I just don't think he could be happy with me. I don't think I could be the woman he wants.'

Cress said all this so graciously that Kate was reminded of a 1950s ladies' etiquette book her grandmother had given her – specifically the section on how to decline a proposal of marriage while giving the impression that the fault lay with you, rather than with the unreconstructed Leslie Phillips-style chauvinist in the bad houndstooth sports coat who was illustrated doing the proposing. No wonder Harry had been hanging on for years if this was how he got turned down, thought Kate, marvelling.

'Can you not remember anything he said?' Cress asked, with a touch of coyness in her voice.

Now her imagination was well and truly fired by the romantic possibilities, Kate wondered whether Cress was secretly more in love with Harry than she was able to let on, that she was guarding him from her own shortcomings – and possibly a family curse? – with a veneer of indifference. All the self-obsession might be an act to hide her broken heart, while she watched her brother's friend grow into a hand-some, successful businessman. The Rose Ann Barton plot potential was endless . . .

'Um, he said you and he would have beautiful, creative children,' she offered. The more immediate realisation that she was lying on something uncomfortable finally broke through the murky surface of her conscious mind, but she didn't want to move in case she was sick again. She put out an exploratory hand beneath the duvet.

Cress pulled a face which didn't quite go with Kate's pre-vious vision of Cress the selfless victim of love. 'God! And women are meant to be the hopeless romantic ones. Can you imagine?'

'I should think your children would be gorgeous,' said Kate stoutly. At least they would be if they took after Harry. She took a deep, careful breath. Something about Cress reminded her strongly of Ratcat: she was never sure how much either of them liked her, or when they might sud-denly put out their claws. And though she knew it was pathetic, she was constantly driven by a childish desire to please them both, which probably annoyed them as much as it did her. 'I think he'd be a great father.'

'Yes, well, that's not going to be necessary,' said Cress. 'Not just yet. Oh, speak of the devil.'

Kate twisted her head painfully and saw Harry emerging from the bathroom. He was obviously trying to sneak down the corridor to his own room without being seen, but his apparent lack of hand-eye coordination, as he felt his way along the wall, nudging books off the shelves, meant that sneaking was somewhat beyond his capabilities at the moment.

'Morning,' he muttered sheepishly.

'Morning!' said Cress. She bestowed a bright smile on him and Harry withered visibly.

Kate's hand closed on the foreign body that had been making the small of her back ache. Rather than bend her arm, she stuck it out at 90 degrees until the object emerged from the side of the duvet.

It was a tequila bottle. A tiny trickle of clear liquid ran on to the carpet. Almost empty.

Kate held her breath as the alcohol fumes hit her nose. She tried to breathe through her mouth but that seemed to make things worse. The helicopters came back in a Flying V formation.

'Bite the bullet and run through to the bathroom,' advised Cress. 'But do it all at once otherwise you'll hurl on the carpet.'

Kate nodded imperceptibly, regretted the sudden movement and then gathered all her strength and launched herself off the sofa, across the hall and into the bathroom, clutching her arms to her chest to disguise her bare breasts.

She lay curled around the loo for about ten minutes, enjoying the coolness of the bowl against her clammy forehead. In the sitting room, she could hear Harry and Cress talking away about a wine auction at Sotheby's. Kate wondered how Harry could even think about wine after last night. Greater love hath no man. Poor Harry. If Cress didn't want him, she should at least tell him properly, she thought protectively. 'Reluctant' but definite refusals like that only worked when the man was as equally apprised of fifties etiquette as the apparently regretful lady. It was strange that Cress, who was so modern in almost every other way, should be so old-fashioned about turning him down. Maybe she just liked the attention, Kate reasoned. But then, who wouldn't? If only Giles could be so attentive. If only Giles could be here. A fresh egg of misery broke somewhere inside her and temporarily displaced the sickness.

But not for long.

After another ten minutes of lying very still and trying to think of nothing but white expanses, the dizziness seemed to have abated enough for her to stand up, and Kate tentatively mountaineered her way up the basin until she was more or less upright.

Toothbrush.

She looked at herself in the shaving mirror and was repelled by what she saw: eyes as red as her hair, two new spots glowing on the deathly white skin and a greyish dusting of old mascara all over her eye sockets. Mmmm.

'Kate!'

She ignored Cress yelling from the kitchen. Give Harry another few minutes with her on her own.

'Kate!'

Kate clung on to the side of the basin as Cress's feet marched over the tiles in the hall. The bathroom door was edged open with no formalities.

'Kate, I'm shouting for Harry because he says he can't raise his voice.'

'Oh,' said Kate weakly. She knew she was weaving from side to side because she was having to cling on harder to the sink with alternating pressure on each hand. Now she knew how revolting she looked, she wasn't sure if she was happy for the spotless Cress to look at her. She supposed this was how Beauty and the Beast got going. Or was it Phantom of the Opera?

'He says Tosca is on the phone,' Cress went on, 'and he's wondering if . . . Oh, hang on . . . What was it Tosca said?' she shouted behind her.

Kate flinched, and angled the mirror so she wouldn't have to turn round to look at Cress. To her horror, she saw Harry appear at the crack in the door. He was covering his eyes politely with one hand. The need to talk to Cress had overcome his hangover, but he was looking unusually ropey.

'Tosca's just phoned and wondered if we'd like to go and watch him play cricket this afternoon. There's a barbecue and urrrr . . . lots of Pimm's.'

'He's playing cricket after last night?' asked Kate incredulously.

'Apparently so.'

'And you're all going?'

Kate saw Harry turn hopefully to Cress.

'Yes, I rather fancy a day out,' said Cress, breezily. 'And naturally I want to find out all the juicy gossip from last night. We should be able to patch something together from the little you all seem to recall.'

Kate saw Harry flinch and she took a deep breath. It made her feel queasy again, so she stuck to shallow ones.

'Well.' She chanced a quick glance at her own grey reflection. Could it get worse? No. Would Giles come back if she stayed in? No. Would it feel better to forget about him for a bit longer? Yes.

'Be rude not to, really, wouldn't it?'

chapter nineteen

By the time Kate came to be walking down the author-lined corridor to have her prearranged chat with Jennifer Spencer two weeks later, she found she didn't really care any longer about the possibility of being sacked. Her hangover was killing her. She hadn't meant to embark on a second weekend Pimm's fiesta, but the combination of Harry's concern, Dant's derision of 'shabby, lightweight chicks' and the promise of another twenty-two men in cricket whites had been persuasive. Unfortunately, the after-effects were proving as stubborn to shift as her debilitating longing for Giles.

On top of all this, Kate was also concerned about the fact that she was overdrawn by two hundred pounds for the first time in her whole life and hadn't bought a single magazine since she arrived in London. Desperate measures were now in force and if Harry didn't come home with an *Evening Standard* every night she would never read the papers at all. Shaking cocktails over her head wearing dark glasses in Cress's bar paid better than this. Isobel had told her only that morning that cleaners on the Underground were earning three times as much as they were. It was enough to drive a girl to writing sagas.

Despite her having returned from holiday only two hours earlier, Jennifer's office was full of pink Medusa lilies and purple Liberty carrier bags, and her desk was already covered with property magazines. Her out-tray was towering.

'Hello, Kate,' she said as Kate hovered by the door, feeling sympathy filing pains for Isobel. 'Do sit down.' Jennifer's smile looked whiter than ever. It was obvious that she had been somewhere extremely expensive, since she wasn't sporting anything so vulgar as a tan.

Kate perched on the uncomfortable chair and tried to psych herself up to defend her faxing skills, without dobbing Elaine in it too obviously.

'Now, I wanted to talk to you before I left about your probation period,' began Jennifer. Her hands formed their usual spiky steeples on the desk.

Kate blinked at her. 'Probation? I didn't know I was on probation.'

Jennifer laughed. 'Goodness, yes. Did you think we'd just forgotten to give you a contract?'

Kate didn't know she was meant to have one. She had obviously been unconscious during that bit of Laura's careers advice. Her brow furrowed. Was she not going to get one?

'Anyway,' Jennifer swept on, 'a few minor problems aside, I'm delighted to let you know that we've decided to keep you on as Elaine's assistant' – benevolent smile – 'and I want you to speak to Personnel about further training as soon as possible.'

Kate was so surprised by Jennifer's unfamiliar tone of friendliness that she heard herself speaking without even being aware that the accompanying thought had gone that far across her brain. 'Oh, that's wonderful,' she heard herself say.

Fair enough.

But then she heard the voice continue, 'I've been having a chat with a friend who works in publishing and she suggested that now my probationary period is over you might be reviewing my salary?'

Kate covered her mouth in her instinctive 'oh, shit' gesture but at the last minute managed to turn it into an inquisitive 'hand on cheek' gesture instead. It was true that

Laura had lectured her on the phone again about 'renegoti-ating' her 'abysmal and exploitative' salary, after an innocent call to discuss Christmas travel arrangements, but she had zoned out after ten minutes.

Jennifer's face returned to its more familiar expression of polite surprise. 'Well, that will, to a certain extent, be reflected in your contract, as you will see when you go through it.' She passed the spiral-bound contract over the desk.

Kate picked it up nervously. It looked official. Suddenly, her 'bailing out after four months as soon as Giles touches down' plan felt embarrassingly childish. For one thing, would they *let* her leave? Her brow furrowed. Would she have to do something so appallingly inefficient that they'd have to *sack* her? More to the point, would Elaine notice?

'Read it through, sign both and send one copy up to Personnel.' Jennifer paused, and added, 'And see if there's a typing course they can send you on, as well as the usual proofreading thing.'

Kate blushed at her 'forty words a minute' lie at interview which sprang into the silence. Jennifer's expression was not making it obvious that she was remembering it too, but she didn't need to. This was apparently the signal to leave and Kate rose to her feet. 'Um, thanks, Jennifer,' she said, feeling something was expected of her.

'Good to have you on board.' Jennifer flexed her fingers. The accompanying fixed smile provided the subtext, i.e., *now go away, please.*

Kate flinched at this. Surely no one said, 'Good to have you on board' in real life? Wasn't that just advert-speak? Before the unpredictable voice in her head could respond to this too, she pushed open the office door to leave.

'Oh, yes, before I forget,' said Jennifer as an afterthought. Kate turned round. 'That fax about Elaine's Emma Ball offer you sent to IPM instead of Phil Hill.'

A trickle of sweat formed in Kate's armpit and she didn't

even bother with an ingratiating expression. Panic gripped her on the upper arm and she let the door swing back shut behind her. Why had Jennifer waited until now to spring this one? There must have been repercussions even more serious than Elaine going on double vitamins that Isobel hadn't told her about.

'I know *all* about it.' Jennifer's face was completely unreadable beyond the cosmetically enhanced brows.

Kate clutched her contract. *How*, for God's sake?

'Fortunately, no one else does, and I think it's best if it stays that way,' Jennifer went on. 'You will find in your *particular* job that there are some . . . personal matters . . . which we rely on Elaine and her team to keep absolutely confidential.' She tilted her head in a 'significant' way, but Kate was none the wiser. Elaine's vitamin dependency? Jo's petty larceny? Was it something to do with Mandy and her mysterious departure?

'So as long as I can rely on you to remain discreet, I will keep this incident to myself, OK?' Jennifer breathed out through her nose in what passed for a mini-laugh. Kate expected fire to come forth. It was evidently inappropriate to ask exactly what she was meant to be being discreet about, and equally evident that Jennifer now had far more pressing matters to attend to, so, bemused, Kate nodded meekly and let herself out.

The confusion this raised in Kate's mind helpfully distracted her from the indignation that bubbled up when, back at her desk with water to flush through her sluggish system, Kate realised that she had not only taken the blame for Elaine's ineptitude once again, but had been effectively blackmailed because of it. For something she didn't even know about.

While she went over and over Jennifer's conversation in her mind Kate opened the file of readers' letters which had been sitting in her small filing cabinet for the past fortnight and began making piles of letters: delighted, critical and abusive.

Could she ask Isobel what Jennifer had been on about? A letter written on Fido Dido notepaper, pointing out the inaccurate training of homing pigeons in one of Elaine's author's crime novels, hovered over 'critical' and 'abusive'. A second shock struck her. Had *Isobel* told Jennifer about the fax in the first place?

Kate put the letter in the bin without thinking and colour flooded into her face, closely followed by hot flushes. If Isobel had told her that, what else did Jennifer know? Her mind went back to the 'minor hiccups' Jennifer had referred to.

How minor was minor? The minutes. The returning of manuscripts to the wrong agencies. She'd had to spend an hour sorting out couriers for that. There had been another small incident with an edited manuscript on which Elaine had scrawled some scarifying comments, with a note saying, 'Please write up polite note for author and pp. from me' – Kate had forgotten to remove Elaine's original note from the top copy of the manuscript before biking it back to the author, but Isobel had rescued it for her. Literally. Kate wouldn't have had the presence of mind to send a bike after a bike, but Isobel not only got the parcel back within an hour but even managed to pass off the double courier bill as 'initiative testing' for the courier company.

She sighed and swept the entire 'abusive' pile into the bin. There was a bottle of Vitamin C tablets by her computer, with only three tablets missing since Laura had sent them in August. Kate twisted it open and shook three into her palm. Dant's 'Resolve' and a pint of orange juice had barely made a dent in her grinding headache. And unless these were Willy Wonka's own-brand Magic Hasta La Vista Hangover Sweets . . . Kate looked at them sadly and swallowed them anyway with the dregs of some orange juice she'd found languishing in the office fridge. The resulting burp was not pleasant.

The initiator of the weekend-long hangover rose before her eyes. Drinking to forget Giles obviously wasn't working, since he was the only thing in her throbbing mind now. After sobering up from Saturday night's Pimm's binge (oh, what an enjoyable half hour that sobriety was), Seth had dragged the three of them out to a pub in Kingston for a roast lunch and it had all started up again, but with marginally more to line the stomach this time. Kate groaned. None of this office trivia seemed to matter against the bigger picture of Giles staying on in Chicago until Christmas. She might as well sign her life away to Eclipse – how else was she going to pay the rent until Christmas? Kate struggled to define the heavy, disorientated sensation occupying her entire body: it was more than a hangover – not unlike the miserable feeling of trying to go to sleep on a hot night, when your body is dozing off but your mind won't. If she could only work out exactly what this feeling was, there might be a chance she could dissolve it. Then again, it might just turn into saga jacket copy.

She picked up the top letter from the 'critical' pile. It was, as usual, for Rose Ann Barton. 'Dear Ms Barton,' it began frostily, 'I recently had the misfortune to be given "Angel in Clogs" whilst bed-ridden in hospital with a hip replacement, and I can honestly say that in all my eighty-one years I have never read such a badly spelled, incompetently proofread piece of shabby workmanship.' Was that all? thought Kate. No mention of the husband magically resurrected at the end after a fatal pit collapse? Perhaps the anaesthetic took some time to wear off. She opened up the 'Polite Letter' template on her computer to reply on behalf of Rose Ann, the shabby workman.

The phone rang. Elaine's extension was flashing on the display. Kate got up and took the five steps into Elaine's office. It was now one of her goals to get it down to four steps, although this did mean leaning into the office on the door-frame, rather than stepping right in front of the desk.

Elaine had her head in her hands as usual. Curls stood out in wiry clumps like a badly ripped mattress, and she was twisting individual chunks round and round a pencil. No wonder her hair looks like that, thought Kate. Split end central. And with all those vitamins she takes, too, you'd think she'd have better cuticles.

'Kate, I want you to photocopy Rose Ann's copy-edited manuscript,' she mumbled without taking her eyes off the manuscript she was making notes on. 'It needs to go today, before she leaves for the book tour in Scotland. And empty my out-tray too, please, it's getting beyond a joke.'

Kate looked at the out-tray which was indeed teetering ominously, partly because there was an Oxford English Dictionary at the bottom, elevating everything by roughly twenty centimetres. Kate's Oxford English Dictionary.

'Oh, *you've* got my dictionary. I wondered where this had gone,' she said, removing it. The pile dropped significantly.

Elaine either didn't rise to the bait, or didn't notice.

Kate shuffled the rest of the out-tray into some kind of order. Post-It notes covered in scribbled instructions were stuck together like filo pastry. Her head ached just looking at them, let alone working out what they meant.

'Oh, yes,' said Elaine, raising her head as Kate turned to leave, 'I hear that Megan has found an exciting new author for Simon.'

'Already?' Kate's furry tongue attempted to catch up with her brain.

'Yes,' Elaine gave her a meaningful look, 'and Jennifer is very keen to offer for it. It's a novel about a man trapped in a virtual-reality pet cemetery. The author is eighteen. And Irish. Jennifer thinks it could be a contender for various important literary prizes. It would be a lead title on the literary imprint.'

'Oh,' said Kate. 'Right.'

'So, where's your author for me then?' Elaine was trying for a light bantering tone, but it came out as more of a threat.

Kate blinked her gummy eyelids. Only ten o'clock and already she was in some nightmare *Supermarket Sweep* scenario, with Elaine yelling at her from the sidelines and Megan snatching the Mick-Lit goodies for Simon.

'I'm sure you must have some young friends from college who do some writing?' Elaine tilted her head to one side expectantly. 'Journalists? DJs? Drug dealers?'

'Accountants?' offered Kate. 'Or lawyers. Sorry. I went to Durham.'

Elaine considered this for a moment. 'Accountancy froth-busters . . . hmm. "Double entry romance?" "Stocks and sharing?"'

Kate gathered the filing and left.

The morning dragged by more slowly than any morning so far. Kate discovered that an ordinary, everyday hangover could be infinitely worsened by the simple addition of strip lighting and exposure to a constantly ringing phone.

Just before lunch, with no more simple letters left to deal with, Kate forced herself to photocopy Rose Ann's manuscript. It was 700 pages long and sometimes on both sides of the paper. Not always, but sometimes.

She stood over the photocopier feeding in ten pages at a time, while the flashing light burned white shapes on the back of her eyes.

'Come. Away. From the machine.' Kate spun round so fast she swallowed an orange juice and stale vodka hiccup.

'Put the paper down. Put your hands on your head. And walk into the kitchen.'

It was Isobel.

'Move it, move it, move it!' Kate felt the sharp point of a pencil jabbing in the small of her back.

She left the pile of paper on top of the photocopier, put her hands on her head and walked into the kitchen.

There was a bottle of chocolate milk on the counter.

'Oh, God, no, Isobel, I'll honk all over your new shoes,' she protested.

'You noticed!' Isobel beamed with pleasure and poured

the thick milk shake into her big water glass ('*You* drink two litres of water a day and *you'll* see the difference in your skin!'), displaying the chunky heels of her shiny red Minnie Mouse shoes as she went.

'Even I couldn't miss those.' Kate stretched her aching eyes with her fingers. 'Have your contact lenses ever dried up so much they've fallen out?'

Isobel ignored her and added a couple of ice-cubes to the glass. 'Well, when you're a single girl you have to treat yourself to nice shoes, don't you? It's amazing how much money gets freed up when you're not subsidising the local pizza delivery service.' She pushed the milk shake towards Kate. 'Drink all that up, it works miracles on a fuzzy head, believe me. I've had more chocolate milk in my time than a purple Milka cow.'

'How did you know I had a hangover?' Kate sipped cautiously.

Isobel rolled her eyes. 'Doooohh. You're wearing a blue top with a red and green skirt. Your whole outfit looks as though it was assembled in the dark by a blind Tibetan monk.'

Kate looked down at her skirt. She hadn't noticed what she'd dragged out of the tumble-drier. In fact, she couldn't remember whether she'd even managed to open her eyes by that stage. She'd never got pissed on a Sunday before. Not even at college. It was finally time to confess to Isobel.

'Giles isn't coming back until Christmas. He phoned on Friday night. He's been promoted, the bastard.' Kate took a bigger swig of milk shake, which seemed to be going down quite easily, unlike her earlier, unsuccessful attempt at cornflakes.

There was a pause.

'Oh, God, I'm so sorry, I didn't realise,' said Isobel, contritely patting her hand. 'I wouldn't even have mentioned . . .'

'Forget about it. I nearly have. I'm not even sure I'm a hundred per cent sober yet. I've drunk so much random alcohol this weekend that I'm a one-woman cocktail shaker. Last night Dant and I even finished off the bottle of Bailey's Mandy left in her cupboard.'

'Ooohh, "Dant and I",' said Isobel. She jiggled her eyebrows. 'So it's a bit schwings and roundabouts then?'

'Excuse me, did someone let Denise van Outen in? What *are* you like? You were with Will for how long? Five years? And now look at you. Talk about born-again singleton.'

Kate glared at Isobel and felt her contact lenses scrape dryly against her eyelid. There was no point carrying on with these lenses. She felt as though she had Copydex peeling off on her eyeballs. The thought of wearing her Ronnie Barker glasses around the office – and what Megan would say – only worsened her mood. She adjusted her glare and found it hurt less if she covered one eye with her hand.

Before Isobel could reply Richard appeared at the door with his Tolkien Society coffee mug. He was looking ratty and nervous, more so when he saw Isobel, and ran a hand through his lank fringe.

'Hello, Richard,' she cooed.

Kate stared at her in disbelief. Isobel was unstoppable.

'Oh, yeah, and what are you two cooking up in here?' said Richard suspiciously, filling his mug at the kettle. 'Planning the next auction of unrepresented fiction at knock-down prices? I suppose your little brother has scribbled some fantastic male/female touchy-feely novel on his Etch-a-sketch, has he? Or is it your cat who might just be the next big thing in Kitty-Lit, Isobel?'

'Oooh, raw nerve!' said Kate, cheered somewhat that she wasn't the only one lagging behind in the Jennifer Spencer Acquisition Handicap Stakes. 'So, not bitter at all about Megan's scoop, then?'

'Never mind, Richard, I'm sure there's plenty more where that came from,' said Isobel, admiring her ankles in the Minnie shoes. 'Hmmm?' She looked up from beneath her long lashes and flicked her plait over her shoulder.

Richard mashed his teabag as quickly as possible and left so abruptly his jumper caught on the door handle.

Kate turned to Isobel, who was making herself an espresso and playing with the steaming arm. 'Not only are you the world's worst flirt, but your quality control department seems to be on holiday.'

Isobel coyly whooshed the steamer into a glass of water.

'Have you ever thought what might happen if someone like Richard actually *fancied* you?'

'Ah, drink your milk shake and leave me to it,' said Isobel. 'You auld alkie.'

'Isobel, I've seen him wearing sandals,' persisted Kate.

'Look,' said Isobel patiently. 'I'm way ahead of you in the lost and abandoned stakes here. Don't you think I've been down the drinks cabinet road already? Well, it's like the North Circular – you could go round it for ever and it's pretty bloody tedious after the first time you pass Brent Cross, let me tell you.

'And, anyway, unlike you, I don't have any little male helpers to assist me in opening the bottles.'

Kate began to protest but Isobel held up her hand. 'I know what I'm doing, all right?' She squared her shoulders. 'A few months' idle flirting and I'll soon remember how wonderful it is to be single. Or to be in a permanent relationship. One or the other. I hope.'

'Stop it, you'll make me cry.'

Kate and Isobel stood in the kitchen and looked at each other.

'Stupid air-conditioning,' said Isobel, suddenly rubbing her eyes.

Eight weeks
One whole repeat run of Blackadder 2
Four nights getting mildly drunk in Clerkenwell with Cress
One night getting very drunk with Cress in Soho House
Fifteen nights getting drunk with Harry and Dant in front of the television
Two (bad) nights getting drunk alone in room
Thirty-one submissions read and rejected
Two brave soldier phone calls to Giles
One completed Tombraider 4 (with cheat book)
One hundred and thirty-nine espressos
Three packs of monthly disposable lenses (one set removed conscientiously but drunkenly in the kitchen and never subsequently found)
One haircut
Twelve aqua aerobics classes
Forty Magnums (twenty-one Almond, nine White Chocolate and ten Mint)
    later . . .

chapter twenty

'Take my car, for God's sake,' said Harry. He twisted the keys to his Rover off his key-ring and slid them across the table to Kate. 'But *please*, just get a move on.' He shook out the paper and went back to reading it.

Kate was stopped in her tracks. 'Your car? Your Rover?' Harry's lovingly polished, older than she was, leather bucket seats, midnight blue Rover P6? It would be like driving the Queen Mother.

He looked up. 'No, take my Audi quattro. Of course I mean the Rover. You think I have a fleet of cars? Where's the butter?'

Harry lifted and dropped bits of paper, opened letters and carrier bags but couldn't find the butter dish. The kitchen table was covered with newspapers, half-full mugs, discarded teabags, toast crumbs, milk cartons and five different packets of cereal. There was a thin layer of crumbs over everything. Breakfast had been going on for so long it was almost time for lunch.

'But I've never driven in London! What if I crash it?' Kate ran her fingers, with some difficulty, through her hair. It was damp from the shower and spiralled down her back like oiled copper wire. 'I can't *believe* I didn't notice the Tube strike in the papers! What a bunch of bandits! How often does this happen here? Oh, God, I'm going to be so late. There's so much still to do . . .'

'Ah, there it is.' Harry carefully picked off the strand of cheap tinsel which had attached itself to the surface of the butter. Kate's attempt to decorate the kitchen with festive colour had been on a strict budget. 'Go now and you'll be fine. Won't be much traffic on the road yet.' He lifted his eyes from buttering his toast. 'Is there any coffee left?'

'Have you lost the use of your legs, or something?'

'Sod off, the pair of you, making all this noise.' Dant slunk into the kitchen, rubbing his eyes. Kate noted that he was still wearing the previous night's clothes underneath his dressing gown. He shuffled over to the sink and turned down the radio, which was blaring away to disguise the sound of roadworks outside. Dant grimaced at the pneumatic drill which replaced the Spice Girls and turned them back up. 'Shouldn't you two be at work, anyway? It's not the weekend, is it?'

'Not that you would know,' said Kate, punctuating herself by frantically opening and shutting drawers, 'given that the rhythms of your life [slam] are governed by the changing of the displays in Marks and Spencer's food hall [slam], but the workers amongst us have finished for Christmas [slam].' She turned a tangerine box of washing upside down and began rummaging through Harry's sports socks and pants. 'Doesn't anyone but me ever put things back in the right place? And while we're at it, could someone please explain to me what exactly Teresa *does* that we pay her for?'

'Have you lost something?' asked Dant. He looked in the dishwasher for a bowl, but it was empty. On top of it stood six days' worth of washing-up. He tipped some cereal into a clean saucepan, in the absence of clean bowls, and inspected a couple of not clean, but not pasta-encrusted, spoons. 'If it's your sense of humour, I saw it leave in a taxi about three months ago.'

'Ho, ho.' Kate stood up. Her hair had begun to dry upside

down and it stood out in a halo of curls around her head. She looked like Crystal Tips. 'In case you'd forgotten, I'm meeting Giles off the plane at Heathrow in just over two hours, my hair is going mental, I can't find the necklace he gave me for my last birthday and now, apparently, there is a sodding forty-eight-hour Christmas Special all-out Tube strike!'

'How could we forget? Take my car,' repeated Harry. He put down the paper and scattered muesli on top of his corn-flakes. 'All the insurance is fine, because of work, and you can hardly miss the signs to Heathrow. Be quicker to drive anyway.'

'Everything about London blows goats,' Kate muttered, yanking her curls into a high pony-tail, twisting it into a French pleat, and then fastening it with a clip. She inspected herself in the reflection of the oven door. Not the sleek straight look Giles had left her with but it would have to do. Using some brown parcel tape she had unearthed from a drawer she roughly defluffed her short black skirt, which, like everything else in her wardrobe now, was covered in Ratcat's hairs.

'Do I look OK?' she asked Harry. 'I've only worn this skirt once and it looked much better in the shop.' She tugged it down nervously, so the hem came within three inches of her knees. It rode up again as soon as she reached for the car keys.

Harry put down his paper politely. 'Kate, you look fantastic. Have you done something with your hair?' He peered closer. 'There's something . . .? Something different?'

Kate rolled her eyes.

'You're not wearing glasses?'

'Harry, I never wear my glasses except first thing in the morning.'

'Aye, aye,' said Dant from behind the business section.

'You'll find there aren't any temp jobs in that paper,' said Kate acidly.

The paper bristled.

'Ermm . . .' Harry squinted at her and shrugged helplessly.

Kate put her hands over her eyes. 'God knows, I don't have enough time to start this bloody pantomime . . . What colour are my eyes, lads?'

Harry and Dant exchanged 'Who knows?' glances. Harry stole a quick look at the fake stag night photos pinned to the fridge with fruit magnets.

'Brown?'

Kate sighed deeply. 'How many redheads do you know with brown eyes? They're green, you anus.' She removed her hands to demonstrate.

'But they *are* brown,' said Harry, peering at her. He gave up and sat back in his chair with a shrug. 'No. Confused. Sorry.'

'At immense expense and as an early Christmas present to myself, I ordered some coloured contact lenses when I had my last eye test.' Kate took her compact out of her bag. 'I think I look rather good, actually.' She applied some brown lipstick too quickly.

'Oh, yeah,' said Harry, leaning closer. 'Now you mention it . . .'

'Dant? No *FT*, no comment?'

Dant put his paper down. 'You look like a myopic tabby cat. Let's say Bagpuss, if you want to be specific. Happy now?'

'Oh, fuck off.' Kate pulled her coat off the back of the door and rammed a manuscript in her shoulder bag. 'I won't be back this evening, since Giles is booking us into a sur- prise hotel for the night.'

Dant raised his sarcastic eyebrow. 'I thought you were meant to be going away somewhere *naice* for the weekend. Has Pan-Continental Loverboy let you down? Don't tell me he can't make time for you after you've waited here so patiently in this pigsty. Too much international wheeler- dealing to pick up a phone?'

'Yes, well,' said Kate, thinking of the French phrase books she had optimistically pocketed at work and then replaced yesterday. 'Things got a bit mad for Giles in the office and he couldn't organise it in time, so we're just going to have a luxury long weekend somewhere where I can forget that you even exist.'

Dant made a dismissive snorting noise.

Kate fixed him with a glare. 'Unless they're showing *Roses of Death* on the in-house TV movie channel.'

Dant got up and walked out.

'I might not be here when you get back,' said Harry. He didn't seem to register the spats between Kate and Dant any more, or at least gave no sign of doing so. 'I'm going up to my mum's in Northumberland for Christmas, so could you park the car in the mews behind the garage and put the keys in my room?'

'Won't you need the car yourself?' asked Kate, checking she had everything in her overnight bag. She frowned into her toilet bag. How many condoms was it decorous to have in there?

'No, not really. I'll be back for New Year.' He emptied the last of the milk into his tea and threw the empty carton in the direction of the bin. 'I think Dant and Cress might be going out to Los Angeles to see their mother, so don't be surprised if there's no one here when you get back.'

'I won't,' said Kate, hoisting her bag on to her shoulder.

'I've got a plant for Teresa as a Christmas present from us – I've done the card, so if you leave it well watered somewhere obvious, she'll find it when she comes in later today.' Harry paused. 'Well, maybe don't make it too obvious, going on the speed with which she killed off Dant's cactuses. Cacti. Might be nice if she got it home first before it turns into a bunch of dried herbs.'

Kate stopped making herself a quick toast sandwich and looked at him suspiciously. 'Dried herbs? What kind of a plant did you get her?'

'Oh, Dant and I went up to Colombia Road market.' Harry stared at her, taking in the overall impression of gingeriness – hair, eyes, jumper . . . 'You know, now you mention Bagpuss . . .'

His eyes met hers in undisguised appraisal and for a moment, Kate felt uncomfortable. She could sense a moment between his initial glance at her – to check her new lenses – and the gaze that held hers a fraction longer once he had seen them. She didn't know what he was looking for then, or what he was reading in her eyes other than brown plastic.

'Yeah, yeah,' she said, pushing the butter away and taking the keys off the table. 'And you're Rupert bloody Bear. Now, have you got a road map with Heathrow on it?'

'In the glove compartment.' Harry stood up. 'So, then. This'll be the last time I see you before Christmas, I suppose?'

Kate busied herself unnecessarily with her scarf. 'Unless Giles's flight's cancelled and I come back here tonight, I suppose so. Given his habit of staying on to do extra homework, you can't rule it out completely.'

'Stay there a sec.' He pushed his chair back from the table and loped off to his room, bare feet slapping on the cold hall tiles.

Christmas presents! Kate put a hand to her mouth. She had been so busy thinking of Giles that it had gone straight out of her head. She hadn't even shopped for her parents yet – everything that wasn't immediately Giles-related had been shoved back into the short time between the weekend and going up home with Mike and Laura.

She was thinking fast but unable to come up with a good excuse when Harry returned with a small parcel. 'Harry, I . . .'

He brushed away her apology with a shy hand. 'I know you've had other things to worry about. It's really a thank-you present, too, for being so . . . you know . . . In the past few months, I've . . . you know . . .' He blushed and dug his hands into the pockets of his sweatpants, rocking back and forth on his long toes.

Kate's heart thumped with embarrassment. What was he going to say? And what could be worse timing for what she *thought* he was going to say than just as she was about to pick up her boyfriend from the airport? 'So . . . you know . . .?' *what?* she wondered.

As if reading the question in her eyes, Harry said, 'You know, so understanding about all that stuff with Cress.' Once he had got it out, he lifted his head and smiled sheepishly. 'You have no idea how much it's helped, having a girl's point of view. Makes a change from Dant, anyway, the miserable old sod.'

Kate put the parcel in her bag to hide the faint wash of disappointment that she was sure was showing on her face. If she hadn't been policing herself for feelings of disappointment, she probably wouldn't have noticed it. 'Oh, Harry, it's nothing. I'm sure I've been just as—' She was about to say 'boring' but realised this wouldn't be polite, or true. Her relationship with Giles was nothing like Harry's big, hopeless crush on Cress. 'Just as lovelorn,' she finished lamely.

They stood smiling at each other for a few moments, until Kate impulsively leaned forward and kissed his cheek. She felt a faint prickle of morning stubble against her lips and he smelt of soap and Right Guard. A boys' changing-room smell. 'Have a great Christmas, and I'll see you in January,' she said, too aware of a defensive formal tone slipping into her voice. 'I don't know what our plans are for the New Year yet, but I think Giles and I will be in London.'

'Our' distracted her. It had a wonderful ring to it, thought Kate. 'Our plans.' It almost sounded as if she had some part in making them.

The workmen stopped outside for a mid-morning arse-scratching and leering break. As a festive gesture to the motorists caught in the traffic lights around the roadworks there were fairy lights on the cones they had used to section off most of the North End Road. In the sudden silence the radio was very loud and for some reason the limited rota of

Christmas records came round to 'In Dulce Jubilo' by Mike Oldfield, which Kate used to play on the recorder most carol services at school. The first flutterings of excitement, like those that used to begin at the end of term when the final assembly before Christmas was over and the holidays were half an hour away, rose up in her stomach and fluttered away excitedly. It occurred to her that in the general slide of one month into another at university, she had forgotten how to build up a sense of anticipation about things like Christmas and birthdays.

'Have a good time,' said Harry, kissing her other cheek. Kate, lost in thoughts of paper-chains, wasn't prepared for a second one. She was caught unawares, and it felt like a proper kiss. Colour flooded into her cheeks. 'No doubt we'll liaise about January. And don't trash my car in the Heathrow car park!'

'As if,' said Kate. She picked up her handbag with an unsteady hand and shouted, 'Merry Christmas, you lazy fecker!' as she went past Dant's room. There was a grunt and a volley of computer death sounds.

The stairs were more precipitous than usual because of the annual carpet cleaning service, and she had picked her way down to the bottom with great care when Ratcat came hurtling through the catflap, with something dangling from his mouth, and up the stairs, between her legs. Kate lost her balance and sat down with a thump. Her skirt made an ominous ripping noise.

'Oh, arse,' she said with feeling. A thought occurred to her and she said, 'Oh, *arse*,' again and, pulling herself up on the bannister, dumped the bags and took the stairs back up to the top two at a time.

She arrived, gasping for breath, at the front door in time to see Harry remove his jogging pants and place them in the machine along with everything else he had been wearing. Kate covered her eyes politely and bent double to try to get her breathing back to a less embarrassing rate. Oh, my God, that was a flat stomach to end all flat stomachs, she thought guiltily, between gasps. It put her own pathetic attempts at exercise to shame. Aqua aerobics evidently weren't enough to maintain even her low fitness level.

'Back so soon?' said Harry.

Kate threw out her spare arm in the direction of Ratcat's eating area, where he was now tucking into a bowl of festive tuna fish. 'Ratcat,' she gasped. 'Who's looking after him over Christmas?'

'Ah,' said Harry. 'Ah. Yes. I meant to talk to you about that.'

Getting to Heathrow was a doddle. If the road signs weren't enough, thought Kate, all you had to do was follow the ant army of black cabs heading west. She slowed to join the back of a traffic jam and checked the time. An hour before the flight came in. Well, that would be OK. He wouldn't come through immediately. The 'No Room at the Inn' Ratcat discussions had delayed her by twenty minutes – it would have been indefinitely if time had not intervened, causing her to roll over from her position of unilateral refusal and agree to take him home with her; otherwise they could have rowed on until the plane landed.

Ratcat will just have to stay in my room, thought Kate. She checked her contact lenses in the rear-view mirror. In a box.

Do these lenses make me look like a wolf? She inched the car forward a few metres and played her hands along the studs on the back of the thin wooden steering wheel.

Mind you, after the shock Doris had had last Christmas, courtesy of Mike, Ratcat would be like a little friend come to stay. She wondered what the chances were of persuading Laura to keep Mike in a box in her room for the duration of the festive period.

Now if Giles were coming home for Christmas I wouldn't let him *out* of my room, she thought. A wicked grin spread involuntarily over her face. How will he have changed? She hadn't let her mind play on the fragile possibilities of the next few months, for fear of a supposition becoming set in her mind and therefore potentially disappointing. She made herself look at the weekend with blinkers. Better not to know, not to hope. Just enjoy the time for what it is.

But once Giles sees me, he'll have to be impressed, thought Kate, overtaking a school minibus with some panache. Harry's Rover glided by with the understated power only a truly big, old-fashioned car commands. Here I am, I've passed his stupid test, plus overtime, I've found somewhere to live, I've found a job, albeit a ridiculous one. She smiled into the rear-view mirror. A job I can now pack in any time I want, now I've proved I can do it. He'll want me to.

The smile broadened as the thought of packing in Eclipse spread out in her mind. She imagined Jim from the post room arriving with a massive bouquet of flowers, sweeping past the disappointed faces and expectant open arms of Jennifer and Elaine – 'Mr Crawford says please can you come now, as the table is booked at The Ivy for one?' Then she saw herself handing the massive pile of press cuttings back to Elaine, dropping her copy-editing pencils casually into Jennifer's cleavage, strolling down the front stairs into the sunlight and hailing a taxi without checking in her purse first to see if she had her bus fare . . .

Kate drove through the endless industrial estate sur- roundings of Heathrow airport and instantly flew into a panic. Long-term or short-term car park? Her hands dithered on the steering wheel. What did they mean by short term and long term? The boyfriend she'd had before Giles at college had classed long term as 'the space between washing one set of match kit and the next' and short term as 'before the spin-drier finishes'.

The traffic was pushing her to a decision. Short term. The flight would be coming in very soon and they would be straight off to the mystery location. Car parks were terrifying enough in her own red Mini but a saloon the size of a tank with no power steering would take every ounce of nerve she had. She turned into the short-term lane and drove round until she found a space for Harry's car, squeezing it in between an S-class Mercedes and a brand new Golf VR6 with blacked-out windows. At least no one would try to burgle the Rover for its antiquated stereo next to those two.

With one last check in the mirror for hair and make-up, she got out, locked up, wrote down the registration number on a napkin in her bag in case she forgot it and marched off as fast as she could in her new knee boots towards the arrivals area.

This was only the second time Kate had ever been to Heathrow, the first being Giles's departure five months ago. Unlike her brother, who kept anti-malaria tablets in his 'ready-to-go' overnight bag, Kate had never been further than Lille, for her French exchanges, and had gone on the Hovercat both times. When she casually revealed to Giles that she had never been on a plane, he had reacted as if she had admitted that they had an outside loo and a bath with coal in it at home. Kate didn't think she was missing anything, and it had quickly turned into the usual 'You should come to London and see the world' argument. Perhaps it had been her mother's fiercely protective/pessimistic attitudes that had killed off any impetus to travel, but Kate had about as much wanderlust as a house brick.

According to her watch, the flight from Chicago should be landing in under five minutes. She was standing in roughly the right place. Butterflies started in Kate's stomach at the thought of seeing Giles walk through the gates, and she couldn't stop herself smiling at nothing.

Minutes ticked past and nothing seemed to happen. The cold air was whistling round her exposed legs and she began to debate the practicality of finding a Sock Shop which might sell thicker tights, buying them, finding somewhere to put them on and still making it back in time for the flight arriving. Wearing stockings for Giles had seemed sexy and thoughtful at home. Kate could feel goosebumps forming on her recently deforested upper thigh area.

The arrivals monitor above her head flickered and rearranged itself. She looked up and watched the list of flights come round to: *Flight XB3941 Chicago delayed for one hour due to weather conditions.*

'Oh, fuck it.' Kate let out an irritable sigh. One hour would make it two o'clock and she hadn't had breakfast or lunch. Her stomach rumbled and she looked about for a place to get something quick to eat and continue the inner tights debate.

Kate had never reached a state of caffeine frenzy. The sum total of her drug-taking at university had been one Pro-Plus tablet: facing a last-minute all-night History of Art project with minimal inspiration, she had gone into town for some Pro-Plus and taken one as a trial run on the way home; after an hour of surmising she was immune to them, since she didn't feel any more hyper than usual, she suddenly vomited all over a flower-bed on the way to the bar and suffered the indignity of being taken home by a Christian Union member who lectured her on the impropriety of drunken women and their colourful track record of biblical downfalls until she pretended to pass out. Not even Giles knew about that. Kate had never decided which was more embarrassing: being so pathetically sensitive to something her friends chewed like Smarties, or being known around college as a shandy lightweight.

However, now, after five *caffès lattes*, her pulse was racing in a mildly unpleasant way and she was feeling light-headed and sick. She was also desperate to go to the loo, but dared not leave her position in front of the arrivals gate in case the flight suddenly appeared and she missed the moment of seeing Giles come through. On the other hand, she didn't dare *not* drink a coffee every half hour in case she was asked to vacate her prime vantage point.

The plane was now well over four hours late and there was no explanation on the screen. In fact, it seemed to have disappeared entirely from the monitor in front of her, and the glamorous underwear Kate had wriggled into was losing its appeal by the minute. A family of five with more baggage than Billy Smart's Circus had been hovering around the full seating area with a tray of drinks and cakes for a while and when the red-faced father caught Kate's eye for the fifth time, guilt finally got the upper hand.

She stuffed everything into her bag, including the manuscript from work she had brought with her to read, paranoid that she would leave something vital, like Harry's car keys, in a paper cup. Then she made her way out of the crowded café, bumping several people on the head with her heavy bag as she went. The coffee was definitely affecting her coordination, she thought, as she almost fell over a small child and had to grab hold of someone's skis to steady herself.

Giles was flying with Delta Airlines and, surprising herself with a flash of Isobel's efficiency, Kate marched round the hall until she found the information desk. A smart woman in navy was dealing with a small line of people, all seemingly after the same information. Her smile never faltered.

'So, it's snow, then,' said Kate when she got to the front of the queue.

'I'm afraid so,' smiled the stewardess.

'How long?' Kate already knew the answer to this one too, having heard it repeated in increasingly incredulous tones by people in front of her.

'Well, we can't really say anything definite yet, because the airport is suffering adverse weather conditions and the flight *is* in a queuing system.'

Kate closed her eyes and was alarmed to see the Delta insignia on the woman's jacket dancing in front of her eyelids like a bad seventies-era *Top of the Pops* fractal. She opened them again quickly.

'We will be letting you know as soon as we have any information about the arrival time, and obviously we're very sorry for the delay.' The stewardess's voice was unbelievably soothing. 'Please do have a Christmas cookie while you're waiting.' She proffered a basket of biscuits, all the size of Laura's cork drinks coasters.

'Well,' said Kate, helping herself, 'I suppose mid-air runway crashes in snowstorms do tend to spoil the Xmas atmos, don't they?' She crunched her biscuit. The woman carried on smiling. 'So, being honest, you're saying that we all have to wait here until the flight does appear, which could be anything up to . . . what? Ten hours?'

The woman nodded and Kate took another biscuit, walked to Sock Shop and bought a ridiculously expensive pair of 70-denier tights out of the twenty pounds she had left to last her until New Year.

Any minute now someone from *London Tonight* is going to come up and interview me about sleeping rough in international airports, thought Kate. She gave her bag a token squeeze to redistribute the knickers and tried to get comfortable on the three seats welded together outside the Coffee Republic café and directly in front of the arrivals area. The suspender belt had been stuffed crossly into an outer pocket of her bag and the stockings, one laddered just above the knee, were in a bin outside WH Smiths.

Just as well, she thought, adjusting her skirt to protect her bum against the cold wall. The weather and her mood were far too frosty for stockings. It was now 70-denier opaques all the way. The Delta Airlines lady had been remarkably patient during her last (fourth) outburst and had given her a spare flight pack containing foot spray, a pair of bedsocks and an eye mask to make her go away.

'Do you know, it's the worst storm they have had in

Chicago for years?' she had said, nodding her French pleat reprovingly when Kate had shrieked on about lack of customer information and getting Anne Robinson on the phone. 'There are women having babies right there in 7–11s.'

In the end, Kate had' taken the flight pack and the remainder of the consolation biscuits and slunk back to her position. The delay had ceased to mean anything, the plane was now so late. Kate pulled off her boots which were hurting and put on the red bedsocks over her tights. Much better. She wiggled her toes. Her feet felt sleepy beneath two layers of fabric. At least with all that coffee on board the rest of her wasn't going to fall asleep before Giles arrived. Out of her skimpy long weekend with Giles, which she had longed for so much she had almost lived out the conversations, they had already lost half a day and a night. Only a whole Saturday remained, then on Sunday afternoon she would have to go round to Mike and Laura's house and be driven up home. And round the bend.

Kate shivered and folded her long legs up beneath her for warmth. At least if it snows here and we're staying somewhere log-firey, it'll be romantic, she thought, trying to take her mind off the paranoid suspicion that maybe Giles wasn't coming back at all. What if there was a message on the answering machine, saying he was staying over for Christmas?

She ran her fingers over the thick velvet of the padded eye mask. It was tempting. Just for ten minutes, thought Kate, slipping it over her eyes. It was like wrapping her head in black cotton wool, and Kate's whole body went limp with pathetic gratitude. I can still listen for the announcements, she thought, as the boom and glare of the airport retreated to a manageable distance. I am still listening . . .

The lady from Delta Airlines leaned over her with the same concerned look on her face. It now seemed positively sinister to Kate, who was aware that she violently wanted to change her mind about something but didn't know what.

'You'll be amazed what a difference it will make to your life,' the Delta lady said, in her lovely transatlantic tones, and produced a *Star Wars* light sabre from somewhere. She pulled an eye mask up over her nose and mouth like a surgeon.

'No more nasty glasses,' said Giles, looming up behind her with a Toblerone.

'Jolly good,' said Harry's disembodied voice. Kate searched frantically for him, but he wasn't there.

'Harry?' she yelled. 'What the hell's going on?'

'Corrective laser surgery,' smiled the Delta lady. 'Make those lovely eyes all better.' She wielded her laser and Kate felt surrounded by intense white light.

'Over here!' said a voice that sounded a bit like Dant. 'Jeez, would you look at those legs!'

The Delta lady leaned over her and began boring her eyes out with the laser.

Kate felt herself swimming up towards consciousness but the pain in her eyes wasn't going away and neither was the light. Had she missed Giles's flight?

'I don't want to be blind,' she mumbled and pushed the eye mask aside with a dopey hand. Her eyes blinked painfully in the light.

First of all she registered that the pain in her eyes was coming from her dried-out contact lenses, and secondly that the bright light was coming from a camera crew of eight people, one of whom was holding a strong light above her, and another in a baseball hat was pointing a camera at her legs. She twisted away from him with a glare. Somewhere in the background, the lady from the Delta Airlines desk was smiling fondly at her, as if she were on *Blind Date*.

'You know, she's been waiting here since two o'clock this afternoon,' she said to a woman holding a clipboard, nodding at Kate at the same time.

'*Ahh*. Did you get that, Steve?' A walkie-talkie crackled. 'Hi, yeah, we're with a story here by internal arrivals if you want to come over . . .' She scribbled on her clipboard as she spoke. 'Yeah, it looks rather cute. Nice Christmas story. Yeah, she's awake now . . .'

Kate sat up and struggled to see what the woman was writing down so furiously. It wasn't easy to maintain a level of dignity when her skirt was somewhere around her waist.

The man with a video camera moved round the bench to get a shot of her from the front and she stared mutely at him while the airline lady filled them in on the details.

Kate was very conscious of the camera pointed at her, and even more conscious of not looking at it. She badly wanted to rub her eyes but was aware that if she did, her expensive lenses would almost certainly fall out. She also wanted to say something, something very rude, but didn't necessarily want it to be captured on film before she had a chance to wake up properly and marshal her thoughts. Despite her crispy lenses, she managed a hard stare that would normally have sent most of the foreign rights department scuttling away in terror.

The situation was so surreal that Kate didn't have an instinctive verbal reaction, which took her by surprise, as she was usually pretty quick on her feet.

She looked at her watch. It was two in the morning, way past her normal bedtime, and she still didn't know if Giles's flight had come in. Reluctance to look stupid was preventing her from saying anything. The camera crew hung about expectantly, waiting for her to say something. The only good thing, as far as Kate could see, was that the late hour had at least spared her an audience of gurning nine-year-olds on a school trip.

'Has the Chicago flight arrived yet?' Kate asked the air stewardess, ignoring everyone else as best she could.

'Honey, we came over to tell you that it's due in in the next ten minutes!' She held up ten fingers for emphasis.

Now that she looked more closely at the woman, Kate could see that the lips forming the wide smile were suspiciously glossy and the nose was much less shiny than it had been before. There was a strong aroma of hairspray in the air.

'Oh, right.' Kate sat up and swung her legs on to the ground, noticing that she was still wearing the bedsocks on the end of her black legs. She looked like a horseshoe magnet. The camera crew adjusted themselves accordingly. Beneath the bench, the manuscript was scattered all over the floor around her.

'Are you filming this?' she asked, squinting into the light. 'Because I must look like a troll and I'd rather not . . .'

'Oh, no, no,' lied the cameraman, focusing on her dishevelled neckline.

'We're part of a bigger documentary about British airports,' explained the woman with the clipboard. 'Covering Heathrow over Christmas. Human interest, that sort of thing. Lost cats. Reunions. Babies born in the strip-search customs room. You know.'

'Right.' Kate looked hard at her, wondering what she could do to make herself unbroadcastable. Random advertising? Speech impediment?

'You've got a great story,' the researcher added, flipping through the notes.

Kate leaned over towards the Delta lady. Her skirt was all over the place as she stood up, and she pulled the socks off and the boots on as gracefully as she could manage, without exposing her crotch to the camera. Her legs were agonisingly stiff.

'So he'll just come through here then, will he?' she said awkwardly, gesturing towards the doors. The baggage belts had clanked into life and a lone red sports holdall was revolving. It registered in the back of Kate's mind that the holdall had been revolving unclaimed since about six o'clock and could quite possibly be a bomb. Would that be enough to distract them?

The cameraman moved and she pulled down her skirt.

'Why would he be coming through there?' asked the researcher, as if to a small child. She pointed to the monitor.

'This gate is for internal arrivals only, honey,' added the Delta lady. 'For people flying within the UK.'

'What?' Kate snapped. 'So UK arrivals doesn't mean people arriving in the UK? You let me wait here when I should have been— Hang on, where else is there?'

'*International* arrivals are downstairs, love,' explained the cameraman, and just to make sure he got a good reaction shot, 'Dearie me, he could have walked in hours ago and you'd have missed him altogether while you was kipping up here.'

Kate flung him a bad, bad look and dragged all her stuff to her.

'Can you just walk normally towards the lift?' said the woman, who seemed to be in charge of things. 'Just pretend we're not here. OK?' She did a schoolteacher 'Isn't this fun?' grin.

Kate tried to resurrect the butterflies of excitement. The prospect of Giles re-entering her life as a reality, rather than a voice on the phone or a photo, had preoccupied her constantly since he went away, but the more she woke up, all she could think of was how ridiculous she must look, as she clip-clopped through the airport in her new boots with a camera crew filming her from behind. That the highlight of her miserable time in London was being intruded upon in this way had only vaguely occurred to her so far.

The renovations at the international arrivals gate were still only half-finished, and the feeble attempts to make the building works look festive hadn't quite come off. A weary crowd of drivers hung about, all equipped with clipboards, bearing surnames, that looked rather like businessmen flashcards. They were eating Kit-Kats and leafing through yesterday's *Sun*. Kate had been expecting a setting a little more along the lines of Grand Central Station for her big reunion and felt like someone ushered into their *Home Front* transformation three hours too soon.

The first business-class passengers from the Chicago flight were already stumbling through the gates, most carrying a single piece of hand luggage and a general air of intense dissatisfaction.

It's not exactly *Brief Encounter*, is it? thought Kate, kicking the wheel of a luggage trolley with her new boots. Can't see Celia Johnson drinking endless cups of tea in the waiting room for six hours and then being desperate for the loo when Trevor Howard's train pulls in.

With her first faintly witty thought of the day on her lips, she looked up to impart it to the cameraman and, as a waddling man in a suit moved forward to meet the driver waiting for him, she saw Giles coming through the gates, wheeling a luggage trolley and looking handsome. So handsome her stomach lurched. How could she have thought she wouldn't get excited?

Kate wanted to hug the moment to herself: to crystallise the second before he saw her and their worlds reconnected; before she would have to condense the churning jumble of emotions and impulses into one tiny appropriate gesture – to remember for later the giddy feeling that was filling her mind: how intensely glad she was to see him. She forgot everything except how glad she was to see him.

Giles had almost wheeled his trolley past her and all of a sudden Kate was paralysed by incomprehensible shyness. She just wanted to look at him. He had existed in her mind for so long, in the photographs she had by her bed, that it was surreal to see him walking towards her. Like seeing a film star in Boots.

Fortunately, or unfortunately, the film crew made the first move.

'Over 'ere!' shouted the man with the camera.

Giles looked over his shoulder, expecting to see Julia

Roberts coming through in a mass of bodyguards. An embarrassing number of other travellers also began checking behind them, adjusting their jet-lagged expressions when they saw the camera crew at the barriers.

Kate pushed forward. 'Giles! Giles!' she shouted, waving her arms. Between self-consciousness and the weird feelings he was stirring up in her, she didn't know how she was meant to react. But her heart leaped inside her chest when she saw the smile breaking over his face.

'Kate,' he shouted, pushing his trolley faster. One of the researchers started moving people out of his way, so as not to spoil the shot, and Giles glared at him.

Oh, shit, thought Kate.

'Excuse me,' said Giles, in a bit of a 'Look here, my good man' voice, Kate noted nervously. 'Can you let me through, please? Whoever you're here to film has probably come through the back entrance.'

'Giles, they're not . . .' began Kate. Giles was glowering at the cameraman, and she tried to steer him away from the crew, so that she could explain in his ear what was going on.

But the more she tried to steer him into the main area, the closer the crew followed.

'Who the hell are those clowns?' said Giles testily, wheeling his trolley so fast that Kate had to jog to keep up. 'I don't know who they're waiting for, but we've all been on that plane for hours and hours, not to mention all the hanging around, and you'd think . . . Oh, will you just fuck *off*?'

He stopped and Kate turned round to see what he was looking at.

There was a boom microphone hanging over their heads.

He turned to her and her butterflies returned for real, but this time with air guns. 'What's going on?' He tried a weary smile, but Kate saw with a sinking heart that it didn't spread up to his eyes, which were bloodshot and cross.

'Um, I think they're some kind of outside broadcast crew,

doing something about Heathrow at Christmas? Emotional reunions, goats lost on planes from Namibia, that kind of . . . I'll tell them to go away now, shall I?' It's not my fault, she yelled in her head, but there was something about Giles's expression that made her feel personally responsible.

He closed his eyes. 'That would be nice, yes. I'm not really in the mood – sorry.' He opened one eye, and Kate was relieved to see a flicker of his normal humour, but he shut it again quickly.

She walked up to the woman with the clipboard, who pointed at the camera with an encouraging smile.

Kate flashed a brief and forced smile at the camera and, said, in as measured tones as she could, 'Hello, I don't know if the lady from the airline explained but my boyfriend has been on this flight for a very long time now and he's absolutely exhausted, as, of course, am I, and we haven't seen each other for over four months, so if you could stop filming . . .? So we can go home?'

Eight pairs of eyes trained on her. She tried another quick smile, but a titanic internal struggle was taking place inside her, between immense pride that this gorgeous man would be recorded on television as being hers, and a strong desire to get him on his own as soon as possible. There was also a fair amount of awkwardness, embarrassment, left-over irritation and caffeine swilling about.

'Of course,' oozed Clipboard Woman, 'but could we have some kind of hug, some reconciliation shot we can use for the footage?'

Kate stared at her. 'What?'

'Well, so far you've been a bit, well, stilted, haven't you?'

Kate ground her teeth. This was turning into a nightmare. 'As I mentioned, he has been on the flight for the best part of a day and I haven't seen him . . .'

Clipboard Woman looked at her with an extremely fake beseeching expression, then pointed to the camera which was still running. 'Just a quickie? Then you can go?'

'Right,' said Kate, exhaling through her nose, and turned on her heel and marched back to Giles.

He still had his eyes shut, and was leaning against his luggage trolley. Despite his hours on the plane, he didn't look the creased and crumpled wreck Kate thought she would have been. Instead she noticed proudly how his chinos were still fairly crisp and he had a new Ralph Lauren half-zip top. Kate felt a tug of possession – barely recognising how unusual it was for her to feel protective of him.

'Giles!' she said, coming up behind him, flinging her arms open wide and hugging him tightly to her. She could feel his spine through the soft material of his top. He smelled exactly of his old familiar smell, and Kate fought back tears of tired joy as she felt his warmth against her cheek.

He turned, hugging her back on reflex, and opened his eyes. They were bloodshot, but happy – ish.

'Let's go,' she said before he could open up the topic of who the camera crew were and what they were doing. 'Let me help you with that trolley.' She began pushing it towards the lifts, hoping that the rear view of them pushing the luggage into the sunset together would be enough 'reconciliation' for the camera crew. 'I drove here and left the car in the short-term car park,' she babbled on, repeatedly hitting the call button on the lift. It seemed stuck on the ground floor. Hurry up, hurry up, she thought, biting her lip.

'You seem in an awful rush,' said Giles. His voice was weary and amused and faintly American.

'Can't wait to get you on your own,' said Kate, punching the lift button a few more times for good measure.

The lift arrived and Kate shoved the trolley in as fast as she could, dragging Giles with her. Mercifully, the doors shut immediately and they were left looking at their reflections in the mirrored door. Kate's eyes skated across the familiar features, ticking them off against the list in her heart: the mole under the eye, the long lashes sweeping his

cheek, the heavy diver's watch, the light prickling of blond
stubble . . .

Funny, thought Kate as Giles's reflection turned to hers, I
thought he was taller than that.

'You've got no idea how much I've missed you,' he murmured in her ear as his arms snaked round her waist. Kate
turned her face up to his and shut her eyes, blocking out
everything except the first warm touch of his mouth on hers.
She could feel his breath on her face, and realised he was
looking down at her, holding the moment. Her stomach
flipped over again and she opened her eyes, and when she
saw the face that she had tried, night after night, to conjure
in her mind, finally real in front of her, she couldn't suppress
a gasp.

Giles's face came nearer, Kate's eyes shut again and her
lips parted as he kissed her. Her head was filled with soft,
dark dizziness.

Then the lights came on as the lift doors opened.

'Phew, just caught it. Mind if we squeeze in?' asked
Clipboard Woman, waving the rest of the crew over.

Since the lift was big enough to park a Vauxhall Corsa in,
Kate could hardly refuse.

They all filed silently into the lift. Kate crossly shoved the
furry boom microphone away from under her nose.

'Sorry.' There was a strained silence.

'I take it the privacy laws haven't got any better here then,'
said Giles.

This didn't help the strained silence.

Kate fixed her gaze on the floor numbers. It was a source
of perpetual misery to her that her splendid anger, which
could swell out of nothing like a tornado, nearly always collapsed in the manner of a souffle, into a soggy heap of
contrition and appeasement. TV images of her grumpiness
were now bouncing around her mind. Only famous people
could get away with that.

She rested her head on Giles's shoulder and tried to see if

the cameraman was still filming. In a triumph of Britishness over confined space, no one was looking at each other.

The lift doors opened and the crew came out backwards, filming Kate and Giles as they tried to overcome the left-hand steer on the trolley.

'Did you say you were in the short-term car park?' asked Giles, taking control and avoiding eye contact with anything except his hand luggage.

'Yes,' said Kate, at the last moment throwing in an 'I'm *so* pleased to have him back!' Hollywood wife-style gaze over her shoulder. Then she turned back, set her jaw and pushed the trolley as fast as she could towards the exit sign.

chapter twenty-one

Things didn't really improve in the car park: once they had located the car and found the right exit, Giles remembered to remind Kate that she had to pay for the ticket before leaving the car park. It was when she stumped back to the cashier that she realised exactly how much time she had lost, wandering the parallel universe that was Heathrow Airport.

'Sorry, can you repeat that, please?' she said to the man at the car park pay desk.

'You're in the twelve hours or more bracket now. So . . .' He pointed at the amount on the display board, as it was obvious from Kate's face that it was too painful an amount to be spoken aloud. In the background, his black-and-white TV was showing a rerun of a Morecambe and Wise Christmas Special. Kate wished she was anywhere but West London; even at home, watching TV with her parents.

'I'll have to write you a cheque, sorry,' she said, too tired to argue, or come up with any sarcastic remarks about being able to buy a car for that amount in Bristol. She *really* didn't have any spare money at all now until after Christmas. Everyone would have to have presents courtesy of her flexible little green friend, Mr Mark N. Spencer.

'Why did you park in the short-term car park, Katie?' asked Giles when she eventually stumbled back. He was wearing her Delta Airlines eye mask and had reclined his seat back.

'Because at one o'clock yesterday afternoon – *when I arrived* – I had no idea I would be starring in some kind of marathon airline disaster film,' she replied tersely, yanking on her seatbelt. In the great scheme of things, being organised enough to borrow a car was rapidly being counterbalanced by parking in the wrong place and not having enough money to get out. Kate: 1. London: 1.5.

She started the engine, which responded first time with a throaty un-PC roar that echoed through the empty car park, and they drove off into the snowy night. Little flakes skimmed in and out of the headlights, and aside from the odd truck, the roads were quiet. London stretched out towards them like an unrealistic cinema backdrop of dark massed houses dotted with the neon trademarks of out-of-town office blocks, strings of street lights like Christmas decorations leading them into town.

Kate put the radio on in case there were any major traffic problems ahead, which would round off the evening nicely. Some kindly soul in Blackheath had requested 'Sleigh Ride' by the Ronettes, which was always enough to restart her holiday mood.

'Ring-a-ding-a-dong-a-ding-dong-ding!'

Giles's hand stretched out and turned up the radio as soon as she started singing.

He always does that, thought Kate fondly. He must know I want it louder.

She came to a roundabout, and it occurred to her that she had no idea where she was going, or even if the hotel would let them check in at this time of night.

'Giles, where are we going for our mystery break?' she asked. 'Don't tell me exactly and spoil the surprise, but I need to know so I can get in the right lane if we're going far out of town.' Hertfordshire would be nice, for a start. Or somewhere in Surrey? Kate ran through the nicer parts of the newspaper 'Homes and Property' section in her head.

Giles sat bolt upright in the passenger seat and ripped off

the eye mask. 'Oh God, Kate, I'm so sorry,' he said. 'I meant to tell you at the airport.'

'Tell me what?' Her hands gripped the steering wheel tighter, until the skin around her rings went white. 'Tell me very quickly,' she added, 'unless you want to die in a traffic accident.'

Giles rubbed his eyes. 'Things got so mad in the office before Christmas, I just didn't have time to book anything, and then, well . . . Mum and Dad are away in Barbados until New Year, so I thought we could just . . . spend the weekend at my house,' he finished weakly.

'Right,' said Kate. 'Fine.' And she indicated her way into the Central London lane. The Ronettes carried on harmonising, but she left them to it. For the first time ever, since she had read that apparently you could hear Cher doing background vocals, Kate didn't bother trying to pick her out. She was too busy trying not to burst into irrational tears.

The record finished and the DJ came on with some travel news, none of which Kate thought applied to them, did some linking rubbish, gave the number for the phone-in and put on 'Christmas Wrapping' which only reminded Kate of all the shops she hadn't been in on behalf of her family and their need for seasonal tributes. Maybe Giles would take her Christmas shopping, she thought, trying hard to wring some pros out of staying in London. A very small pro dripped out: what had he brought her back from America? It wasn't enough.

Giles was rummaging in his bag. Kate wished he would say something spontaneously nice, but his exhaustion was only too obvious. It hung in the car like an old air freshener. She herself had reached the stage of tiredness at which she knew she could easily say exactly the wrong thing, and moreover, not be alert enough to rescue the situation.

Kate's eye was caught by something flashing on the instrument panel. She squinted through sticky contact lenses at the unfamiliar dials, and realised she was about to run out of petrol. Either that or the temperature of the engine was even lower than the air outside.

In Kate's first stroke of luck of the day, there was an all-night garage coming up on the left. As soon as she had flicked the indicator on, her bladder starting its singing and dancing number again.

'Giles, I'm just going in here to get some petrol,' she murmured, not sure if he was still awake or not. 'Won't be a minute.' She pulled up to the nearest pump and leaped out with her bag.

It was freezing outside. Shivering in her 'decorative, not practical' jumper, she unlocked the petrol cap and picked up the pump. God, petrol was expensive, she thought, as the numbers rattled up on the display. A Polo drove up to the pump opposite and a teenager got out. Kate pictured her bank account rattling further and further down into the red.

She glanced across at the other pump. Were they putting four-star unleaded into their car? Her hand twitched on the trigger, and a few drops of petrol slopped round the rim. Was Harry's car too old to take unleaded petrol? She didn't actually know what kind of petrol she was *meant* to be putting in.

This would be all she needed. Squeezing what she hoped were her internal bladder muscles (at last, she was doing pelvic floor exercises!), Kate rammed the nozzle back on to the petrol pump and yanked open Giles's door so she could rummage in the glove compartment. Crossly, she noted that he was sleeping with his mouth open and his breathing was approaching a definite snore.

Harry had a complete service history in his owner's manual (of course, thought Kate) and she flipped back and forth, trying to find the petrol details. It was probably too late now anyway, she decided. I've probably ruined the engine for ever. Well, what's another few thousand pounds? Fatigue was blurring the edges of her brain, and she couldn't concentrate on the paragraphs and diagrams. In the end she threw the manual back into the glove compartment, slammed it shut while concentrating on Giles's face beneath the eye mask (he didn't even flinch) and marched inside to pay.

The inside of the petrol station was very brightly lit and hummed quietly. Kate made a beeline for the toilet. Years of long car journeys to British holiday destinations had given her expert insight into finding the most carefully hidden petrol station loo. She could be in and out within five minutes of demanding that her dad stop the car, no matter how much the shop layout was designed to make desperate motorists give up and find a lay-by further on. Weeing in grass verges alongside Mike had lost its novelty value at the age of five. Not for her the nettles and ants and vestiges of Mike's last cream soda all over her shoes. Oh, no. The fact that Dad routinely sighed and said, 'We might as well stock up while we've stopped', allowing Kate to make free at the till with Maltesers and other essential car supplies, only enhanced the charms of her weak bladder to the whole family.

Kate tried to repair her make-up in the dirty mirror, but it was really too far gone for that. Her skin was shiny – but not in a fashionable sense. With a sigh, she undid her hair clip, turned her head upside down and ran her fingers through her clean hair. It fell around her face in glossy, cherubic curls. Always a good diversion.

She paid with a cheque, and out of childhood habit, picked up an Aero and a bag of Maltesers, which she remembered, on walking back to the car, she wasn't meant to like. All the same she managed to consume half of the evidence in three bites via a casual perusal of an air pressure chart.

'Chocolate?' said Giles, as she opened the driver's side door. He had taken the eye mask off, and also his shoes.

'No, Maltesers!' Kate ostentatiously opened the glove compartment again and dropped them in.

'Maltesers are chocolate, aren't they? I thought you . . .'

'No, it's an advertising slogan from the eighties.' Kate

looked affectionately at the confusion scampering across
Giles's face. 'You were probably abroad? It's just a surprise for
Harry, for lending me the car for the weekend,' she went on.
'It was really kind of him.'

'Harry – the flatmate?'

'One of them.' Kate checked her mirrors to pull out on to
the road and saw that she had a lump of Aero stuck to her
top lip. She hastily brushed it off with a finger, but couldn't
stop the reflex action of putting the crumb in her mouth. She
hoped Giles hadn't noticed.

'I'm so sorry not to have arranged something for this
weekend, sweetheart,' he said, putting a hand on her thigh as
she moved into the fast lane. The chocolate boost had been
just what she needed. Ha! she thought, take your expensive
social drugs and give me a family pack of Aeros.

'It's OK. Your parents' house is smarter than most hotels
anyway.' Did it really matter where they were as long as they
were alone? And she could show him all the places she had
found, the Appalling Towers Building where she worked,
the coffee bar by the office, the park where she went to feed
the ducks, her flat.

Maybe not her flat.

Giles smiled and squeezed her thigh. 'It's so wonderful to
see you!'

'And it's wonderful to be bringing you home,' said Kate,
glancing across at his tired but handsome face.

'Your hair's grown even longer.' He twisted a strand round
his fingers, bounced the resultant ringlet on his hand, then
massaged the soft short hairs at the base of her neck. A little
thrill of anticipation buzzed through her stomach.

Giles turned up the radio as she accelerated down the
empty fast lane, playing with the extra power in the engine,
which felt like a track car after her mum's apologetic Fiat.

'If you want to call in to Heart 106.2 with your late-night
Christmas requests,' the DJ was saying, 'our lines are open for
the rest of the night. And we're going up to the three-twenty

news with Mariah Carey, which we're playing for Kate out on the M4 . . .'

Kate didn't know the road numbers, not being a regular driver, and would have missed it if Giles hadn't caught her eye.

'. . . and it comes with love from Giles, who's been away for a while but says he's looking forward to catching up on lost time this evening!'

'Well, I didn't exactly say that,' said Giles. 'But you know what I mean.'

And all he wants for Christmas is you!

'But how did you . . .?' A faint blush of pleasure was creeping up Kate's cheeks.

'While you were in the garage.' Giles waved his mobile phone and leaned over to push his lips into the crook of her neck. Kate swerved but managed to keep reasonably straight. He nuzzled the soft skin underneath her ear as he had done a hundred times before at college and Kate was very lucky that some kindly Christmas policeman had forgotten to load the speed camera with film, as Harry's Rover flew down the A4 to Chelsea.

Redcliffe Square was silent and lit up with street lights outside and with several majestic trees in the tall windows inside.

'Double park next to Mum's Beamer,' said Giles, pointing to a badly parked car outside his house. 'Oh dear,' he added almost immediately.

'Why, "Oh dear"?' asked Kate, trying to remember which button on Harry's key-ring set the alarm and which one would set off the high-pitched screeching that had woken most of their block at least three times since he'd had it retuned.

'Um, oh dear, I think we have company,' said Giles, getting out of the car. He stopped, got back in and pulled Kate's face towards him. 'I think we're both a bit too tired to do this properly, aren't we?' He turned his head and kissed her gently, nibbling her lower lip with his teeth. A warm flood of pleasure spread over Kate, mingled with exquisite weariness. It felt wonderful to be shutting her eyes at last.

She wrapped an arm around his neck and pulled herself as near to him as she could over the gear stick. They sank back into the bucket seats, and she felt his hands tangle up her hair. The radio was still playing quietly in the background and it felt deliciously exciting to be here with Giles at last, parked outside his house while everyone slept. Behind her tired eyelids, everything was deep, deep red and even though this was hardly as she'd planned it, all she wanted to do was find a comfortable bed and sink into it with him.

It surprised her that the image in her mind was predominantly of the softness and fluffiness of duvet and pillows, rather than of Giles's nakedness, but she put it down to physical and mental exhaustion.

'I've been thinking about this moment for weeks,' said Giles, hoarsely, two inches from her mouth. His breath felt hot on her lips.

That was a terrible cliché, thought Kate, but again was too exhausted to pull him up on it. She just smiled up into his face and stroked the rough beginnings of stubble along his jawbone, running a fingertip over the bump of his chin.

'Shall we go in?' he said.

'No, let's stay here for a bit,' said Kate, drawing him back for another kiss.

After some minutes Giles broke off and said, 'Please don't take this personally, but if I keep my eyes shut any longer I'll fall asleep on you.'

'Fair enough.' Kate pulled the keys out of the ignition. 'Let me give you a hand with your bags.'

'No, it's OK, I haven't brought very much,' said Giles. He got out and opened the boot.

Kate looked hard at the key-ring, held her breath and made an educated guess. With a hiss, all the door locks went down and the side lights flashed on and off three times.

Giles hoisted a large rucksack over his shoulder and offered Kate a small computer bag to carry while he went through his keys to open the front door.

'Is that all you've brought?' asked Kate, following him up the white steps, with her own overnight bag on one shoulder. Surely he'd left with more than this? Was he getting the rest shipped back?

'It's only girls who like to travel with their entire wardrobes,' he replied, pushing the red door open with his back, so that he could drop a kiss on her forehead.

'But where are your suits?' asked Kate playfully, then, looking over his shoulder into the hall, said, 'Oh, hell,' before she could stop herself.

'. . . well, Lydia *knows* the rules about these white-tie bashes as well as *you* or *I* do, it's simply *declassée not* to wear knickers. Especially to *a Highland Ball*. Just *asking* for trouble, *as* I told her. Yes, and *everyone* there agreed with me . . .'

Kate groaned silently as she took in Selina lying with her long horsey legs up against the immaculate white wall, cordless phone clamped to her ear, with a full ashtray and an empty bottle of wine within reach of her French-manicured hands. As she spoke, one hand fluttered along the carpet in search of the packet of Marlboro Lights, made contact and flipped open the packet. She was obviously dissecting the party she'd just got back from, since she was dressed in a tight blue mini cheongsam, slashed to the very upper thigh, and her car keys were lying by her feet, next to a huge pair of strappy silver platforms.

'Happy Christmas, Selina!' said Giles, opening his arms.

'She didn't stay long after that, I can tell you . . . Oh God,' said Selina drunkenly into the phone, 'my big *bro* and his *girlfriend* have just pitched up, so I guess I'll have to *go*.'

Giles rolled his eyes affectionately at Kate, and she tried to return the expression without seeming too rude. Selina didn't get up.

'No, please don't get up for us,' said Giles.

'*Yeah*, I should be back in my *own* flat in a few *weeks*, once Mum and Dad are back from '*bados*, yeah . . .'

Giles gave up waiting for her and stepped over her legs, making his way down the short flight of stairs to the kitchen. Kate followed, as Selina moved her wine and cigarettes out of the way with an offended pout.

Giles opened the fridge door and was instantly surrounded by a spaceship-style pool of yellow light. The fridge was rammed full of food and, Kate noticed, there was no Flora anywhere. He poured two glasses of milk and from the chill section took half a Devil's Food Cake, the remains of a roast chicken and a whole wheel of runny Brie, and set them on the table with some plates, then started picking ravenously at the chicken.

Kate edged her way nervously into the room and wondered how much Devil's Food Cake she could get away with. She put a hand casually on her hip and felt that the zip on her skirt had been pulled half down by the pressure of her stomach acting on it. She tugged it up discreetly and, staring at the cake in an attempt to fool her brain into thinking she'd already eaten some, forced herself to go for a ridiculously out of season strawberry.

Selina appeared at the doorway, swaying on her platforms like an elm in a strong wind. 'I'm staying *here* while Mum and *Dad* are away,' she said. 'There's more *food* in the *fridge* than at mine.'

'I thought you'd see enough gourmet food in the course of your job,' said Kate brightly, to prove to Giles that she remembered what Selina did.

'Don't get to *eat* it!' replied Selina. She gave Kate an up-market '*Duuurrrhhh*' look.

'Right, fine,' mumbled Kate, but Selina had moved on and was now addressing Giles in the slightly too loud voice of someone trying to pretend they're not drunk.

'Lydia, Charlotte, Olivia, and Caroline are sleeping *over*

tomorrow, bit of a *girls'* night *in*, you *don't* mind, *do* you, that's *fantastic*.' She tottered off, and Giles and Kate listened to the irregular thumps as she made her way upstairs.

Giles finished his slice of cake and drank off his glass of milk, then put his arms round Kate. He kicked the door of the fridge shut so that they were standing in the darkness. 'Here at last,' he whispered.

Kate's heart sped up as she inhaled the familiar, intimate smell of his breath. She wasn't sure she could cope with any more atmosphere swings.

'And nearly all alone.' She wiped off his milk moustache with her little finger and kissed him, tasting the milk and chocolate on his tongue. Giles's arms tightened round her, pulling her against his long, hard thighs and she tried to remember how sturdy the kitchen table was, where it was, and what was on it.

A loud clunking echoed through the silent house as one of Selina's shoes slipped off her foot and bounced down a flight of stairs.

'Oh, let's give up, shall we?' said Giles, disengaging himself with a sigh. 'I'm so sorry. I thought Selina would be in her flat by now. I had no idea she would be recreating Christmas at Malory Towers here.'

'Bedtime,' said Kate as brightly as she could manage.

He held her arms and looked at her. As her eyes adjusted properly to the soft darkness, she could see the tenderness in his expression and the last vestiges of her irritation at the evening's fiasco melted away. 'I really have missed you, Katie,' he said seriously. 'I rather thought you might not be here when I came back.'

She shrugged, smiling up from beneath her eyelashes. 'How could I leave?'

Giles hugged her, then suddenly swept her up in his arms and carried her upstairs. This time she didn't care about kicking the walls, even if he had to change his grip to a fireman's lift for the second flight of stairs.

chapter twenty-two

Giles and Kate slept in the next morning until midday. Kate's body clock had grown used to being triggered by the many and various disturbances which she had come to take for granted in London: loud radios, roadworks, bad singing in the kitchen, her alarm clock, the distant rumble of Tube trains beneath the street, the early morning rows of the married couple in the flat below, etc., etc. The soporific peacefulness of Giles's house completely overrode her subconscious attempts to wake up.

Curled in a ball in the soft duvet, she was also pleasantly exhausted from Giles's early morning advances on her still half-asleep body. Being to all intents and purposes asleep had given her licence to murmur many things she wouldn't have murmured while awake without blushing to the roots of her hair, and as Giles's hands and lips covered her warm body, a variety of erotic semi-dreams had passed through her mind, including, to her surprise, one in which Giles had morphed into Ronan Keating from Boyzone.

Kate opened her eyes and blinked against the crisp December sunlight that was streaming through the useless linen blinds and bouncing mercilessly off every white surface in the room. She stretched an arm out and picked up Giles's chunky diver's watch from the table by the bed, bringing it close to her face, since her glasses were in her bag, and she intended to leave them there.

It was ten past twelve.

Kate rolled on to her side and kissed the bridge of Giles's nose. He looked much better for a night's sleep. In profile he was like a Greek statue: a classically handsome composition of high cheekbones, long nose, soft, full lips curving gently downwards. Kate wondered for the hundredth time what someone so gorgeous saw in her.

The eyelids flickered and opened. She allowed herself the usual ripple of amazement at the deep blueness of the eyes, more intense than any coloured contact lens could achieve. As the thought passed through her mind she remembered with a jerk that he hadn't noticed her own marmalade eyes, now sitting in lens-cleaning solution in the *en-suite* bathroom, but she rallied quickly on his behalf – it *had* been very late and she'd almost forgotten herself.

Giles noticed her sudden frown and sat up, pulling her on to his bare chest.

'What are we going to do today then?' he asked lasciviously, breathing kisses on to her neck.

'Whatever you want.' Kate slipped a hand beneath the duvet and ran it up the length of his lean thigh.

Downstairs the phone started ringing.

'Leave it,' murmured Kate, working her fingers in 'Insy-Winsy-Spider' movements up his leg, 'let Selina get it . . .'

The phone carried on ringing. Giles nuzzled his way up from Kate's neck to the skin behind her ear. Kate felt herself float blissfully off into suspended animation.

'Giles, phone!' yelled Selina's voice. She sounded a long way away.

'Well, get it then!' yelled Giles. Kate, her ear just beneath his mouth, flinched.

Selina screeched something incoherent, the only words of which Kate could make out were 'razor' and 'bikini'. Giles ignored her.

'Won't the answering machine pick it up?' said Kate, beginning to feel distracted.

'Depends whether she remembered to switch it on again this morning,' said Giles. 'And there's an extension in the bathroom anyway. *Selina!*'

There was a splash and the ringing stopped. After a few seconds, Selina yelled, 'Giles! The office!' up the stairs and slammed the bathroom door.

'Excuse me for a moment,' said Giles, pulling back the duvet and reaching for his dressing gown. He turned back to look appreciatively at Kate, lying naked at full stretch on the bed. 'And I do mean a moment.'

It wasn't a moment at all. It was more like fifteen minutes, and by the time Giles came back, he had gone distinctly office-y and was towelling off his wet hair. Although Kate was prepared to lie in the soft bed and make the most of Giles walking around in a small bath towel, opening and shutting drawers and pulling out crisply ironed clothes, when he announced that he had run her a bath, she reluctantly took that as a cue to get up.

After a brisk breakfast of coffee and croissants in the downstairs kitchen (no sign of the newly fuzz-free Selina), Giles and Kate took the Circle line into the City. It felt like skiving off school to Kate, sitting in the almost empty compartment with a couple of old ladies and a man listening to his Walkman. Someone had left the pink business section of the *Standard* lying around on the seat and Giles flicked through it to the shares.

Kate watched his eyes scan down the columns, with a sort of pride. That was the section she used to line the vegetable box at home. It would never occur to her to actually read it. She always had a warm sense of inclusion when she thought of Giles working away in his office – shouting on the phone, making deals, staring intently at computer screens, or whatever it was he did. It was a world she literally knew nothing about, and not one she particularly wanted to be part of herself, but she knew by association – and the fact that everyone at college (except her) wanted Giles's job – that it was desirable and glamorous. Somehow, in his company, London made sense. Kate pushed Eclipse and Elaine and Rose Ann to the back of her mind. Now Giles was back, she was happy enough to watch his reflection in the Tube train window opposite, and rejoice in the fact that the smug-looking woman sitting next to him was her.

They got out at Monument station and already Kate could feel the light draining out of the day. She glanced at her watch. It was twenty to three, but the pubs were still crowded with young people in suits, red-cheeked with the cold breeze coming off the river and with office party bonhomie.

'We can walk to the office from here,' said Giles, taking her hand. 'I bet you haven't been down into the City yet, have you?'

'No, I haven't. Would you credit it, but my power suit has been at the dry cleaners since August.' Giles's hand felt smooth but strong in hers, and she squeezed it proprietorially. The sky was leaden and lowering in between the buildings, and all the bright colours of Christmas decorations in the windows and shops took on a vivid intensity as the sunlight faded.

'This is "Magic Hour" light,' she told Giles. 'It's incredible. The whole of *Days of Heaven* was shot in the one hour of magic hour light you get in a day. They rehearsed all day, waiting for this amazing, clear light quality, and then had to race against time, to get the scenes down before it faded.'

He dropped a kiss on her head. 'All these things you teach me.'

'Hardly.' The crowds of people milling about were reminding Kate of all the things she didn't know about London: careers she was ignorant of; languages she couldn't be fluent in; clothes she would never wear. Self-pity made her put aside her prior commitment never to wear grey suits for work. Suddenly Kate felt a stab of resentment that these men and women would know a side of Giles she would never see, the efficient, knowledgeable banker at work.

Stupid and irrational. She shooed the thought away with a guilty flap of her hand and concentrated on the murky reflected light bouncing off the mirrored windows of the office buildings. When the towering office blocks parted, she caught glimpses of the gloomy grey Thames beyond, chopping and shifting with the gusting breeze, and the boats chugging up and down the river.

No one was rushing back to the office two days before the Christmas break, and crowds of lunch-time drinkers spilled out on to the narrow streets and down into the dark passages. Giles negotiated their way expertly through the throngs, cutting through the alleys until they arrived outside the glass foyer of his bank's London office.

'Stay here for two seconds while I drop some paperwork off,' said Giles, rummaging through the file in his leather document wallet to check everything was there. 'Won't be a minute.' He kissed her quickly and pushed his way in through the revolving doors.

Kate leaned against the white marble exterior of the bank and looked up and around her. If Giles had been doing his training here rather than in America, would things have been different? Would she have been part of this bustling, chrome-and-glass London, rather than the scruffy, more casual world she had found herself in?

A motor cycle courier pulled up, his radio crackling urgently, jumped off his bike and rushed into the building with a bag. Two women, dressed in sharply cut navy suits, walked up to the revolving doors and one gave her a curious look as they carried on their rapid conversation. Kate suddenly felt very conscious of her faded jeans, and pulled her streaming hair into a pony-tail with her hands.

No one at Eclipse wore suits, except when authors came

in, or unless they were going for an interview somewhere else. Isobel wore her red miniskirt suit every six weeks or so, just to keep Jennifer on her toes. Sporadically, when an agent sold a book for an obscene amount of money, one of the editors was filmed in the boardroom making some comment on the mad state of publishing today, for the benefit of *London Tonight*. Isobel had told her that when Jennifer had been called upon to contribute her thoughts on Rose Ann Barton's last deal, she had insisted on everyone wearing suits, which had resulted in the most embarrassing display of flared lapels and Joan Collins shoulders since the last episode of *Dynasty*.

'OK, all done,' said Giles in her ear. Kate jumped. 'Shall we grab something to eat? I'm ravenous.'

He put an arm around her shoulders as they walked away from the office, and they wandered back through the streets, which were beginning to empty and darken as dusk fell.

'You know what I really fancy?' said Kate.

'I can't imagine.'

'A Big Mac meal.'

'Oh, Katie, no! After all the nice places I've taken you to, has nothing rubbed off?' Giles laughed and tugged at her nose.

Kate pulled away, pretending to be offended. 'You can't possibly understand what it's like growing up in a town with a Wimpy, can you? You've no idea how exciting and urbane a Big Mac meal is to someone introduced to burgers with knives and forks. Can we go in here, please, please, can we, can we?' She pointed at a McDonald's over the road. 'Look, they're doing Happy Meals! Free Mister Men! *Pleasepleaseplease*?'

Reluctantly Giles allowed himself to be drawn in, and they stood in line behind a queue of men in suits who were trying to remember the meal specifications of the small children clinging to the hems of their Hugo Boss jackets.

Kate ordered a Quarter pounder with Cheese and no Gherkins ('It makes them cook a fresh one.'), and Giles had a Filet o Fish ('Because in the greater scheme of things it makes no difference to me how long it's been standing there.'). The upstairs was packed and noisy and in the absence of any proper seats downstairs, Kate and Giles settled themselves on plastic mini mushrooms in the family area.

'Chicago managing without you then?' asked Kate through a mouthful of lukewarm burger.

'Just about,' said Giles seriously. He removed the garnish from his Filet o Fish and put it in the box lid, wiping his fingers on the napkin. 'I had to fax over a couple of things I'd been working on right up to the last minute. As I told you in my last letter – I probably went on and on about it, sorry – I was asked to help out on a research project they've had going for a while, so as you can imagine, there's a lot of responsibility attached to that and I wasn't leaving the office until eleven most nights.'

'If you're trying to apologise for the lack of country house hotel minibreak, I've already told you you're forgiven.' Giles had the kind of innate confidence, thought Kate, that completely precluded false modesty. It was very American, very direct. Very unnerving, come to think of it.

'I've been pretty lucky,' he went on earnestly. 'Some chances have come up to really get a head start and, you know, I've just gone for them in a big way.'

'Mmm,' said Kate, getting a feeling that this was headed somewhere. The lurching sensation she had felt five months earlier in Harvey Nichols' Fifth Floor Café was making a surprise guest appearance in her stomach. 'Why did you bring me down to the City today? You could have faxed those pages from your dad's fax machine at home.'

Giles took a big swallow of his Sprite Light. 'I wanted you to see the kind of milieu I work in . . .'

Kate pulled a face. 'Oooh, *milieu*.'

He frowned at her in a half-serious way and Kate felt herself draw back a little, scalded.

'I knew you wouldn't have been down this part of town

and you have this trait of ignoring everything you don't know, so I thought it might give you an idea of why I love all the urgency and excitement of banking if you saw the places it all happens.'

Kate looked round the family area at all the fathers balanced uncomfortably on mushrooms. City Daddies trying to do pre-Christmas bonding with their scared-looking little girls in Alice bands – most of them were wearing trendy bead necklaces with Jemima spelled out on cubes. Handy.

'So you brought me to McDonald's?'

'No, *you* wanted to come to McDonald's.' Giles sounded exasperated, although it could just be nerves, thought Kate. She was developing an out-of-body perspective of the scene, and wished she could behave with a little more grace.

A little boy opposite them spilled his drink all over the table and started to cry loudly, his mouth a black letter-box of dismay.

'Let's go for a walk,' said Giles, getting up.

Darkness had fallen over the City and the street lights had come on. Kate and Giles walked over Blackfriars Bridge and stopped in the middle. Kate leaned on the wall and watched the reflection of the lights along the Embankment ripple and shimmer on the water. She was cold.

'I'm not saying I want to split up with you,' said Giles.

Kate continued to stare into the water, mute with shock. Her mind was racing with thoughts, all spinning wildly against each other like cogs out of gear, but she refused to speak. Why should she make it easy for him?

'But you have to see that . . .' His voice trailed off miserably. 'How did you know?' he asked.

'When you didn't have a suit carrier,' said Kate, mechanically. 'You wouldn't come back to work here without your suits.' She turned to look at him. 'I'm not stupid.'

He turned to face her and she saw real sadness in his eyes. The panicky tears that had been strangely absent until now started to well up in her throat.

'That's the last thing I think you are,' he said. He stretched out an arm to her, but dropped it at the last minute. Kate hoped it was to offer her some dignity, rather than because he didn't want to touch her any more. 'That's the very *last* thing I think.'

Giles shoved his hands in his pockets. 'You know, when I left in July, I thought you'd be back at home by August, leaving me a string of outraged excuses why you couldn't possibly live in London on your own. But you didn't, you stuck it out and found a job and a place of your own, and when I came back—'

'Eventually,' interrupted Kate, biting her lip.

'Yes, when I came back *eventually* you'd driven through the London traffic to pick me up. And you drove back as if you'd been driving here all your life.'

'It's the first time I've driven in London,' protested Kate. 'I mean, it's not as though I've been jazzing about enjoying myself!'

'Well, more credit to you then,' said Giles. 'It's an attitude thing. Six months ago you'd have refused to do it outright on principle. You'd have been scared. Now you just . . . do things.'

'If you're trying to make me feel grateful to you for forcing me to upgrade my personality, then please don't,' said Kate. A great tide of bitterness was washing through her, as deep and black as the river thirty feet below. How dare he move the goalposts like this!

Giles carried on, desperate to bridge the growing tension between them. 'When I said that we shouldn't write or phone for the first few weeks, it was as much for me as for you. I missed you so badly, but I didn't want to stop you settling in with your life in London by reminding you of your life in Durham. You had to move on.'

Kate bit back a sob, as her lovely simple life at Durham flashed before her eyes. She didn't want it to move on at all, but she was being dragged further and further away from what she actually wanted.

'Don't think I didn't lie awake at night on my own, working out what time it would be in your office and whether you'd be there if I called. I wanted to hear your voice so much.' Giles leaned over the bridge and stared at the water. 'But I knew how disruptive it would be for us both, so I didn't.'

Kate broke the silence. 'How long are you going back for?' she asked, then answered herself, 'Though I suppose it's all a bit irrelevant in the long run, isn't it? A month, four months, a year – it's all extendable.'

'They want me to stay and finish the project I've been working on,' he replied. She could hear the effort he was making to keep his voice level. 'It may take three months, maybe longer.'

'Oh, fine.' Kate saw the misery of dragging herself along the North End Road and into the office through the pouring winter months stretch out before her. She saw Dant's under-wear strewn all over the smelly flat, and Elaine's neurotic Post-its strewn all over her desk. She saw herself Sellotaping yet more photos of Giles to the inside of her food cupboard so the image of him in her head didn't solidify purely into the black-tie ball photo she had by her bed.

'Why didn't you tell me this before?'

'I didn't want to spoil these few days, our Christmas together. I told you about having to stay on until December as soon as I knew, in September, and you didn't write to me for three weeks.'

Kate bit back a retort. The temptation to lacerate him with sarcasm was almost overwhelming but she knew it wouldn't help. She wondered whether this was a step forward. Part of her new upgraded personality.

'And I was so jealous,' said Giles unexpectedly.

She was caught unawares by this and leaned on her elbow to look at him. 'Jealous? Of me?'

'In so many ways. Jealous of you discovering London for

the first time, of you doing a fun job instead of one where your every move is monitored . . .'

Kate was about to remind him that she was an editorial assistant in a publishing house and not a Chocolate Button tester, but stopped herself.

'. . . jealous of all the things you had to tell me last night and in your letters – the work intrigues, your new friends, the chaps in your flat—' He looked as though he were about to say something else, but went on, 'I suppose if I were being ultra-honest I'd say that I wanted you to be . . . less happy, so that I could come and rescue you. Or because I didn't want you to have a great time in London without me. But you've done really well, despite what you might think, and I'm really proud of you.'

Kate wanted to point out that she had only stuck it out for so long at Eclipse because she was counting off the days until his return like a convict. And that she hated living with Bill and Ben, and that as far as she was concerned, the London Underground and all its little buses blew goats. But Giles was away again.

'I know it's not fair of me to ask you to wait here for me—' He hesitated and looked embarrassed. 'Especially when we haven't even talked about *your* plans.' He looked at her. 'What *are* your plans? Are you going to go home now you've done your sixteen Mondays? Or are you . . .?'

'I think you'll find that it's nearer twenty Mondays now.' All of them Blue and none of them Happy. Kate averted her gaze back to the river. 'I hadn't thought about it, to be honest. I was just waiting for you.'

They stood in silence, leaning on the bridge. Behind them, Kate heard cars speeding past, leaving the city, and watched the slowly moving traffic mirrored in strings of red and white lights on the other bridges across the river.

Kate realised with a dull sensation that all the misery she had felt when he left her in July was going to start again, but this time without the numbness of shock to tide

her through. It was all too familiar. She remembered the
hopelessness she had felt in September, and the loneliness
that had washed over her when the hangover finally evaporated and she realised there was nothing she could do but
wait.

She was torn between a strong desire to tell Giles to get
lost and stop manipulating her life to suit his own CV and an
equally strong desire to throw her arms around him and beg
him not to go back. It had been hard enough for five
months, missing him, keeping his face fresh in her mind,
revolving the rest of her year around these precious
moments they would have together, never daring to ask
when he would be returning for fear of what he might say.
How long could she keep this up? How long could she
expect him to want her, while he was in Chicago, achieving,
growing up, getting on?

Kate covered her face with her hands and leaned her
elbows on the cold stone of the bridge. There was no point in
telling him not to go back. He had to. Never let it be said later
on that she stood in the way of Giles and his career – as if she
could. It had never really been so clear to her as now that, as
far as Giles saw things, it wasn't so much a case of his career
taking precedence, as there being no comparison between it
and anything else. He had seen his parents move all over the
globe without hesitation or apology. It was just a normal part
of working life. Her misery stretched up and away in front of
her, filling up her conscious mind like a granite wall too big
to see all at once and impossible to define.

She let out a sigh, punctuated by giveaway hiccups, and
pressed her fingertips into her temples. It wasn't as though
she could blame him – at least he *had* a career he was passionate about. The best she could do would be to let him go
with as good a grace as she could dredge up from some
hidden part of her character, and make his last image of her
a dignified one. There was no point in being a martyr, highly
tempting though it was.

'When are you going back?' she asked, like a brave little soldier.

'Boxing Day,' said Giles. 'It's the first flight I can make. That was another reason why I had to—'

Kate burst into tears. Four days. Three of which she had to spend with her family at home.

'I'm so sorry, Katie.' Giles pulled her into his arms and buried her head in his moleskin jacket. 'You've been so fantastic up to now, and I know it's a lot to ask. It's not so bad here, is it? I mean, can you bear to stay a little bit longer? For me? If you want to finish things I'll understand, but . . . I just can't bear the thought of being without you.'

All the tension of the past month flooded out of her in streams of tears as she shook her head weakly into his chest. What else was there she could do? Absolutely nothing. But even as she replayed the scene in her head, making herself braver, more dignified, more magnificently generous, she couldn't tell whether she was crying out of heartbreak, or anger, or frustration, or a miserable mixture of all three.

chapter twenty-three

Kate often imagined herself destroying things – hurling vases in department stores, stepping out in front of Tube trains, chucking bricks through shop windows, driving her car through fields of upright wheat and hearing the snapping of the stems. Sometimes she imagined looking at the debris through her own eyes, but more usually she was included in the daydream, as if her imagination was directing her from above. After a bad day at work, when she was left feeling that her presence in the Eclipse scheme of things was marginally less essential than the filing cabinet next to her desk, she would wander through a shop, imagining herself pushing over shelves of fragile wineglasses, just to feel the ease with which she could turn wholeness into fragments pound through her system. The exhilaration of touching the edge of that chaos and drawing back, walking on, containing the disaster safely within her, was enough.

She had always played with these fantasies of destruction but London brought them out even more in her, being so full of half-destroyed things already. The Underground in particular. Each rush of hot, dirty air blowing through the platform to announce the oncoming train triggered a vision of herself arching towards the hurtling square of metal: the simplicity with which she could step one foot-length too far across the white line on the platform, one foot-length too near the grubby mice that scuttled beneath and around the shining, slicing tracks. Would she really feel nothing? No final sense of guilt at the horror on the driver's face, or at the screams of the people on the platform, delayed for work and left with a bloody snapshot of her final moment sprayed on their minds for the rest of their lives? The determined anonymity of the London community would be sheared through the middle with a simple step too far across the white line.

Kate stared out of the train window at the passing fields, which were edged around the corners with a dusting of dirty snow. She imagined Boadicea blades on the wheels of the train, scything the hedges down to a uniform size as the train rushed past. She tried to make her mind go completely blank – something she used to practise on endless car journeys, bickering with Mike and therefore with her mother – but her mind wouldn't cooperate. Various lurid pictures of the Christmas she had left behind seeped through her concentration. Even the clicking wheels seemed to be going, 'Have you washed up? Have you washed up?'

The truth was that Kate was desperate to avoid the thought currently knocking in an irritating fashion on her subconscious: that she had actually *chosen* to come back to London, albeit in preference to spending one more day in The Craig Family Boot Camp. In fact, her dad, a co-sufferer, had slipped her a hundred pounds so that she could get back there more quickly on the train.

Ratcat hissed at something beneath her seat and she leaned over to check he was still in his cat box, and hadn't burrowed out in search of nutritional excitement. The brand new carry-box, purchased from Peter Jones at the last minute by Harry, out of guilt and on his mother's charge card, was taking up the seat next to her, much to the disapproval of the woman opposite. Fighting spirit must still have been hot in her veins since Christmas Day, as this time, Kate did not feel compelled to engage her fellow passenger in conversation, share her tuck box, or even enquire as to her reading matter.

Once she had come back from yet another wretched farewell with Giles (after lunch at the Pizza Express on the King's Road – an experience not enhanced by the screeching presence of no less than three office Christmas parties), she had driven home in silence, parked Harry's car in the garage mews and walked back to the flat. Even the empty roads and a full tank of petrol in Harry's beautiful, purring, V-8-engined Rover couldn't tempt her to stay out any longer. Every five steps, she would catch sight of Giles or hear his voice in a passing conversation and her heart would speed up, as the possibility that he hadn't got on the plane after all flashed through her mind, almost real – and then the man would turn round, insultingly unlike Giles, and fresh tears would fill her eyes, making her stride away even more quickly to try to dispel them. Seasonal jollity everywhere grated on her bad mood.

Fortunately, neither Harry nor Dant had been around when she let herself in, and she had phoned Laura to tell her she was ready to be picked up, rather than wait any longer. It only took a few minutes to stuff some more clothes into her bag – who at home would notice what she wore anyway? – and she dragged the contents of her laundry basket into a bin-liner for good measure.

It had taken her twenty minutes just to find the cat. The big new carry-case was sitting by Ratcat's food area. If Harry had put it there hoping Ratcat would learn to love it before spending the best part of a day trapped inside, listening to one of Laura's Jane Austen audiotapes, he'd been mistaken. Eventually Kate had tracked him down to Dant's box of clean underpants, but getting him into the box had been like stuffing a king-size duvet into a pillowcase. Every time she had him half in, a paw would shoot out and lever the lid open, or he would fix his lower jaw on her hand so she couldn't open the lid and hold him simultaneously.

In the end, Kate had lost her fragile grip on her temper and shouted at Ratcat so fiercely that he had slunk into the capacious box of his own accord. Once she had the catch down, Kate had realised she was shaking with frustration and it had scared her so much she had had to sit down and make an espresso to calm her nerves. She had waited at the window with her bag so that she could run downstairs as soon as she saw Mike and Laura's car. She didn't want either of them coming in. One quick lecture on home hygiene and Laura would be wearing Dant's household pet like a Davy Crockett hat.

Ratcat now glared out at her from between the bars of his carry-box. He looked livid. As well you might, thought Kate, given the lap of luxury I've just wrested you from. She picked at a roast beef sandwich and pushed a bit of meat through the wire.

Far from spending the holiday season (all six glorious days of it) shut in Kate's room, Ratcat, Doris, Dad and Kate had had quite a passable time – once they'd moved exactly half the drinks cabinet, the 'spare' Christmas cake and a radio into the outhouse at the far end of the garden. Not exactly a glamorous location she would be bragging about at Cress's bar, but the outhouse was reasonably companionable, warm, and blissfully free from the procreation debate raging in the house, where Mum, Mike, Laura, Carlo and Nina (the two Spanish students who had somehow 'forgotten' to organise flights home to Santander), two grandmothers and assorted relatives were competing, via home videos, in the 'All-comers' Happy House and Home' festival.

'Like *You've Been Framed* filmed by a pack of Mormons,' her dad had mumbled during the second Christmas Day episode of *EastEnders*, ineptly concealing the giant cracker of Maltesers under his jumper and making for the back door.

In just two days Laura had completely dehumanised Kate's bedroom. Or, rather, what was left of Kate's bedroom, after her mother had packed most of it into the attic. She'd come in from walking Doris one evening to discover that Laura had box-filed her entire *Smash Hits* collection, from 1985 to 1993, and cross-referenced them with her slightly smaller, secondary, *Number One* pile. While Kate was prepared to concede, with seasonal goodwill and all, that this ridiculous filing was possibly Laura's last-ditch attempt to hide from Mike and his rampant baby-fixation, it was one of several final straws. Coming home to her room after five long months away and realising that, to all intents and purposes, she'd been moved out by her own mother, was pretty hard, what with Giles and everything too.

Giles and his sodding international lifestyle. Kate stared out of the window and tried to work out how she could feel so sad and so angry at the same time. Of course he had to do what was right for his career, of *course* she wanted him to do well. He couldn't get her with that one. Hadn't she been the first to tell him he should accept the offer?

She shifted in her seat, trying to rearrange her pants. No glamorous undies for London this time, although having been through her mother's more rigorous washing programme, her everyday M&S knickers felt mysteriously cleaner than in Deauville Crescent – which was down to either hard London water or Harry's unsuccessful 'fixing' of the rinse cycle.

But, Kate thought, chewing her lip, hadn't she kept her side of the bargain? Hadn't she stuck out the four months, *plus* injury time, and even collected Giles from the airport? Surrounded all the while by idiots, authors and Dant's weird habits? Could he not take that into consideration?

Kate pushed the thoughts away and tried to flush her mind of circular arguments. Like a loo, her mind filled up again straight away.

Home wasn't home any more, and London, too busy and stupidly expensive as it was, was still a little nearer Giles. Even when he wasn't there. Kate thought of her room, the room she had had since she was four, drained of all her stuff and stripped back to a guest room bareness. How long had it been like that? Or was that just what it looked like when it was tidy? Her mother had made noises over the Christmas Eve mulled wine about going to IKEA and getting some shelving units to turn it into a study. This was the same mother who had been wearing contact lenses for the past twenty years ('Because men don't make passes, Kate'), but who was now sporting a pair of black Calvin Klein *glasses*.

The buffet trolley came past and since her dad had pressed an extra twenty quid into her hand at the station, Kate had a coffee out of habit, even though she had the regulation two bags of food and a Thermos of tea in her rucksack. Thank God her mother's desire to transform herself into a student hadn't affected her sandwich making instinct. Twenty years of treating Mike and Kate like *foie gras* children was a hard habit to break. The day Mum doesn't equip me with at least half a loaf and a packet of Penguins for a train journey, thought Kate, prising the lid off her coffee, will be the day I buy her a pair of 32-hole DMs.

When Kate had announced the previous night that her newly discovered intolerance to childbirth stories meant that she would be returning to London on the next available train, Mike hadn't bothered to hide his relief at not having to drive her back, but Kate had seen a brief look of panic flit across Laura's Elizabeth Arden porcelain visage. Kate was the best argument against starting families that Laura had.

Kate sipped at her coffee which was scalding hot and not as strong as she'd got used to. It had been interesting, in a kind of David Attenborough way, watching Laura's behaviour over Christmas: it was well known that the more tedious and predictable the Craigs were (fighting over the blue Quality Streets, arguing over the washing-up, unearthing horrible pictures of each other in flares), the more Laura squealed and cooed in delight at the suburban normality of it all. It was an undisputed fact that her family were all certifiable. Their idea of a quiet night in was not bothering with spot-lighting and make-up for a game of charades. So running *Scrabble* leagues and drying-up rotas was Laura's idea of heaven and she had certainly gone full out in honour of the season.

However, Mrs Craig's alleged yearning for grandchildren – which seemed to intensify in proportion to her Brandy Alexander intake – had driven something of a wedge between the mutual admiration society, and for six days Laura had ricocheted from Mike's Sid James to Mrs C's Hattie Jacques with ever-widening eyes and ever more tightly clamped knees. And to think, thought Kate, Mum used to be more like Barbara Windsor.

Kate played with the increasingly plausible idea that her mother was trying to dump her own position of family matriarch on to Laura so that she could concentrate better on doing her A-levels. No wonder Laura took to hiding in my room with half of W.H. Smith's stationery department, thought Kate, inspecting the cat-carrier with a twinge of guilt. Ratcat settled down once she had refilled the integrated water dispenser and catnip holder (Harry had obviously felt *very* guilty during his last-minute shopping) so she switched on her Walkman and stared out of the window again, trying to construct a fantasy in which Giles was waiting for her at the flat with a bottle of wine and a good apology.

Not having to maintain an alert ear for sounds of her sister-in-law approaching with yet more food was astonishingly liberating – so much so that she dozed off, and was only woken by a crackly announcement about the closure of the buffet car. Kate opened her eyes and shut them again in a reflex reaction.

The outskirts of London were arriving even more quickly on the train than they had done on the coach, and to her dismay she felt an old tightening of panic in her stomach as the fields turned into rows of houses and shops and road bridges. Around her, people were getting bags and coats down from the racks, which always increased her arrival anxiety.

When the train drew into the station Kate waited until everyone had got off before she gathered her own bags together, and lifted Ratcat off his seat.

'You must be dying for a pee, you poor creature,' she said, trying to spin some of her own nervousness on to him. She wondered if he'd had to pee in the box on the way and felt bad. Could you take a cat to the loo in a train?

Ratcat glared back at her with glinty green eyes and it occurred to Kate that five months living together probably meant that they could dispose of such polite niceties. From the look on his face, Ratcat was thinking more along the lines of: 'For Christ's sake, get me home before someone I know sees me in this revolting cat travel case.'

At least one of them was pleased to be back.

Kate considered taking the Tube to West Kensington for about thirty seconds – the thirty seconds between wheeling her luggage on a trolley to the arrivals hall and taking all her bags off it again. There was no way she could carry all her bags and a cat with a full bladder up and down escalators. Besides which, it was freezing cold, she hadn't ever been to this station before and therefore would have to check on the Underground map where she was going, and the station was full of women clutching their handbags with fixed 'Sales! Sales! Sales!' looks on their faces.

It would have to be a taxi.

Gritting her teeth against the expense, Kate stood with Ratcat in the taxi queue (at the back, as a result of Kate's laggardliness in getting off the train) and waited. Resignation sank into her, as the sounds of London became familiar again and she realised that, like it or not, she had become accustomed to this city. She had almost missed the constant drone of background noise (apart from that which Laura and Mike had supplied, anyway): the rumble of traffic, the hooting of cars, the general white noise of conversations carried on loudly in public and yet so instinctively ignored by everyone else that they were as good as private.

When they finally reached the head of the queue and got a cab, the journey to West Kensington took about half as long as the wait. The roads were quiet between Christmas and New Year, with no roadworks, and the driver picked up on Kate's sullen silence and didn't attempt to make conversation. Ratcat whirled round and round in his box – probably at the thought of some decent company, thought Kate.

Predictably, as soon as she let him out of his box, Ratcat disappeared downstairs, no doubt to make up for lost time with the fat tabby next door, and a wave of mild depression engulfed Kate. She wished the numbness would come back.

The Christmas Tidying-Up Fairy hadn't been. Tragically, it looked as though she must have been held up in the same Sleigh Strike as the Washing-Up Elf, and the Hoover-Bag Pixie.

Everything smelled.

Kate dumped her rucksack and bag on the kitchen table and opened as many windows as she could bear on such a cold day, then went to put the kettle on, noticing en route that the Dirty Washing Fairy *had* put in an appearance, but hadn't got round to emptying the machine. She opened the catch and the stench of mildew rushed out. She slammed it shut, then with a big resigned sigh, poured a double dose of Ariel Automatic into the dispenser and switched it on again.

At least there was no one here. At least she could tidy up a small corner of the flat and pretend that her life was under control. Starting with a nice cup of tea. The Dishwashing Fairy for one was reasonably reliable, thought Kate, opening a faintly foisty dishwasher full of mugs and hoiking out a non-offensive one.

The kettle boiled and she poured hot water on to the

teabag, remembering at the last moment that there wouldn't be any milk in the fridge. Or rather, that there *would* be milk in the fridge, along with many other perishable and smelly items that Dant and Harry would have happily left for her to discover, but the fridge was somewhere she couldn't face going yet.

Determined not to lose her fragile grip on good humour so soon, Kate pulled a face even though there was no one there to see it and poured the tea down the sink. It cut through the limescale in a not entirely pleasant way. Why, she had four days' famine rations in her bag! Mum wouldn't see her only daughter starve!

So Kate settled herself down on the sofa with two rounds of roast beef sandwiches and a large slab of Auntie Sheila's Christmas cake, which her mum had given her to take back to London to curry favour, Enid Blyton-style, with the boys. Since Mrs Craig's Christmas cakes were planned and made in August, it was also surplus to requirements. Laura had, of course, made her own, following an eighty-year-old family recipe handed down, naturally, from Ellen Terry.

Kate flicked on the television, which was showing a comforting and familiar selection of clips from Carry On films; some of which were bound to feature Laura's mother in a bikini. Excellent. While the canned laughter shrieked away in the background, Kate gazed round the flat and stroked the terracotta chenille throw Cressida had brought to cover the beer stains on the sofa. It was quiet and, with the lads not around to make her feel stupid, she felt as though she had come home to something pleasingly familiar.

Kate took a large bite out of a roast beef sandwich and the thought struck her that if there was ever a moment to have a good snoop round the flat it would be now. She'd never set foot in Dant's room again after using it to burst in on Harry's bath. The thought of the pink mule still made her wince. What else might be in there that she should know about? Dant looked the sort to have a lot of dodgy stuff just lying around. And, she thought, her heart rate quickening fractionally, this might be her one and only opportunity to have a look through some soft porn for research purposes.

She looked over towards his bedroom door, which was open and inviting. As if led on an invisible chain, Kate got up off the sofa, still eating her sandwich, and walked in, her ears straining for the sound of feet on the stairs.

Dant's room was extremely messy, to the point where there didn't seem to be any visible furniture. Clothes were piled up on top of more clothes which may or may not have disguised chairs beneath them. Kate trod carefully around the piles, in the small spaces of visible floor. The room smelled musky, with the faint scent of oranges that Dant seemed to carry around with him, despite his minimal vitamin C intake. Kate was suddenly reluctant to poke around, in case she found something she didn't want to know about. Her eye had already fallen on a crusty bottle of Insignia aftershave on the bedside table, next to a recent picture of Cress in her shades, sitting side-saddle on an enormous marble horse.

Apart from the (unmade) bed, there was a desk with his computer on it, surrounded by piles of disks and cables, and his Gothic stereo, against which were stacked three precarious towers of CDs, each about three feet high, and a massive pair of headphones, the like of which Kate had last seen in the Band Aid video. She noticed Dant had gone for separates. He obviously knew what he was doing.

This was more like it. Kate put her sandwich carefully on a small clear patch of desk and squatted down to scan the CD spines. She believed you could tell a lot about a man from the type of music he listened to. (Or, in Giles's case, even more from the still shrink-wrapped albums he'd bought and *not* listened to.) All Dant's CDs were open and seemed to have been chosen with surprising taste: classics like the Beatles and Bob Dylan mixed up with more modern classics – all the Blur backlist, early Verve,

Television, the Chemical Brothers, Portishead, Matthew Sweet . . .

Kate made herself more comfortable and turned her head on one side to read the spines better. There was a whole jazz section of people she'd never even heard of. This she found very attractive, knowledge being a much sexier proposition than blue eyes, or a flat stomach, in her opinion. She liked the possibility of being taught new things.

But she'd never have guessed this about Dant. He liked to project an air of mystery about his personality, which she thought *he* thought made him seem more interesting. But they could have been having the best conversations about music, her *own* favourite topic, if only he'd said. Kate thought grimly about the gigs she had missed because she'd been too miserable and scared to go alone in London. Not that Dant was the ideal companion, but . . .

By her rough estimate, Dant's CD collection must have cost about the same as Laura's nearly new Vauxhall Corsa. Kate scraped a fingernail down another column of CDs. His collection was like a kaleidoscope: seemingly random influences and styles all jumbled up, but somehow making sense taken all together. She'd always assumed Dant was a bit of a misogynist pig, but apparently he listened to Beth Orton, Dusty Springfleld, Julie London, Kate Bush, Patti Smith, Ella Fitzgerald, Aretha Franklin . . .

Even more impressive, in Kate's opinion, and what saved the collection from being an indiscriminate mish-mash of everything, were his omissions: no Alanis Morissette, no Celine Dion, no Levellers. He even had the early 'Now That's What I Call Music' collections on vinyl, propped up by the wall. Kate's fingernail stopped in surprise at both Kenickie albums – her favourites, which she had been playing in endless rotation since she arrived in London, to remind herself of being happy. Really? Her opinion of Dant wobbled around in her head. No one with such amazingly wide-ranging taste – and she really didn't think Dant worked on Giles's trolley-dash approach to music buying – could be reluctant to talk about music. So why did he never mention it?

Downstairs in the hall, the front door slammed and footsteps started on the stairs. Kate sprang up, her knees protesting sharply after four hours on the train, and scurried into the sitting room, where she arranged herself behind the Christmas edition of the *Radio Times*.

The footsteps came up to her floor, then continued up the stairs to the flat above. Kate's heartbeat carried on hammering in her chest, even as she remembered that with Dant in LA and Harry in Northumberland, she was hardly likely to be caught red-handed going through Dant's pants. Presumably both would be staying for New Year, or if they were coming back for New Year in London, wouldn't bother leaving until New Year's Eve. She lowered the *Radio Times*, noting that there wasn't much on that night after *EastEnders*, and breathed out hard.

Why not Harry's room too?

In comparison with Dant, Harry was meticulously tidy. His bedroom, with clothes on the bed and bedclothes on the floor, still gave the impression that a mild earth tremor had recently struck West London, with perhaps a collapsed Tube tunnel nearby, but clear areas of carpet were visible. His room smelled of the lemony aftershave he wore, which gave Kate the creepy sensation that he was in there with her. Like Dant, he had a computer and a stereo, but there the similarities ended.

Harry's computer looked neat and businesslike, with red boxes for his disks and blue filing trays for printing paper, and everything in a neat stacking system. His stereo was tiny and silver, and balanced on a bracket above his bed, with the speakers bookending a long shelf of Brit Lit Lad paperbacks. None by Eclipse, noted Kate approvingly, running her eye along them. Along the top of the bookshelf were various bits of random carved artifacts which he'd brought back from his travels: little giraffes, eggs made of volcanic rock, strange flute things. She stretched out a hand to touch a smooth round seal, made from black stone, and stopped herself just before her fingers made contact.

Self-consciously, she dropped her hand to her side and looked around some more. Next to the desk was a pile of magazines – *Classic and Sportscar*, *FHM*, *Esquire*, the usual suspects. She felt an impulse to run through them, to see if there was anything more interesting tucked away at the bottom of the pile, but part of the bargain she had made with her conscience was that she could look, but not move anything. That wouldn't be snooping; it would just be . . . the same as Teresa saw. Besides which, after the surprises in Dant's room, she wasn't sure how she would react to finding a complete collection of *Spunk Junkie* under Harry's bed.

Kate pushed the thought away and bent to examine Harry's musical taste. After the riches of Dant's collection, she was surprised to feel a murmur of disappointment run through her. Harry's CDs, most still bearing the 'Buy 3 for £21' stickers, were stacked in luminous green holders which waved up one wall like tentacles. None of the albums in his collection had racked up less than a gold disc's worth of sales: Oasis, Natalie Imbruglia, Kula Shaker, Madonna. She asked herself what she had expected him to have, and didn't wait for the answer.

Kate straightened her back, not wanting to see any more. Above his desk was a pinboard full of photos – Harry and Dant at school, Cress in wraparound shades, Harry in shorts on a camel, Harry wrapping his arm protectively around Cress dressed as a mermaid in a long silver sarong at a party, a blurry close-up of a middle finger (probably Cress's). Kate wondered whether Cress had ever gone snooping round the house while they were all out, and found this little shrine to herself.

Then Kate remembered the photos that she had found down behind the cushions and wondered if they were still there too. She flinched at the images which appeared at the back of her mind and stood up, coming face to face with a team photo of Harry's school fencing club. Harry's Golden Retriever good looks hadn't changed much in ten years, unlike Dant, who hovered anaemically at the back as though he had strayed into the picture by accident from The Cure's rehearsal rooms.

But Kate couldn't dispel the memory of the covertly snatched shot of Cress, lying ambiguously beneath the trees. It wasn't so much seeing her in a state of undress, thought Kate – though Cress was quite frosty, she also looked like someone who would whip off her kit at the drop of a hat, given enough tequila. It was – she probed her conscience hard to get a full answer out of it – it was realising that Harry had taken the pictures, and what he intended to do with them.

'Urgh,' she said aloud, and went back into the kitchen.

Kate felt she knew Harry pretty well now, after six months' close confinement with him and the Dark Man of West London. Dant was rarely about during the evenings and consequently she and Harry had spent quite a lot of time together, just watching television or cooking, growing to feel comfortable enough without talking. But despite now knowing all the sorry twists and turns of his feelings for Cressida, after many long cups of coffee and supermarket runs, it dawned on Kate – so many fresh thoughts in so short a time were beginning to unnerve her – that she hadn't really thought of Harry as having *real-life* lustful feelings for Cress. Perhaps because what they had actually talked about was all thoughts and possibilities. Or because he had such a knight in shining armour attitude to her it was all a bit mythical. Or, more to the point, because the gentlemanly longings he displayed tended, in Kate's mind, to be mutually exclusive of dirty photographs – shyness in a male being something quite unprecedented in her experience.

She sat down on the window-seat with a thump. Did Harry think the same about her and Giles? That their relationship was more theoretical than practical? He'd never seen them together. Although the bare facts of the Giles situation looked pretty bad (and once Kate had got beyond proud silence on the topic, she and Harry had gone well into angry denunciation of his behaviour over several burgers and malts), she knew the good bits – on the strength of which she was still waiting for him here in this horrible place. It was hard to explain them to someone else though. Maybe she hadn't done them justice.

Kate let out a peevish breath. An uncomfortable sense of bad-relationship competition was creeping over her. Was it because Harry's abstracted feelings for Cress had been easy to dismiss as way beneath her own personal tragedy, when they had seemed just that: abstract? She remembered Laura and Mike's cheerful dismissal of Giles's endless four-month absence, and how short the time had seemed to them. Suddenly she got a sympathetic blast of Harry's painfully unrequited lust and nearly groaned.

An advert for the Harrods Christmas sale came on the television and Kate waved the remote control at it. After a week of self-inflicted zombie-ism she felt dangerously close to a surprise attack of insight.

Was she disconcerted because finding those photos made the man she had been spending so much time with . . . a man? And not a floppy-haired, overgrown schoolboy?

Ker-ching! said something in her brain.

'No,' Kate said aloud.

Then she said, 'Surely I'd have noticed before now?'

She sat on that one for a while.

The voice in her head jiggled its hand from side to side and reminded her that she'd never noticed Laura looking vulnerable before now, either. But there had been a moment on Boxing Day when Kate, on behalf of the Shed Committee, had sneaked into the kitchen for supplies, and had discovered Laura slumped alone at the breakfast bar, while a row escalated in the sitting room about the respective merits of terry nappies against disposables. One hand had supported her bowed head, the other had clutched her stomach, as though the baby Mike was so keen on was already bouncing around in there. She looked utterly miserable. Kate had hesitated at the door, unsure as to whether she should go in and say something, but it was probably the first moment Laura had had alone all week, and she reckoned that she was the last person Laura would want to see. Apart from maybe her gynaecologist.

Before Kate could hesitate any longer, Laura had sighed, stuffed a handful of brazil nuts in her mouth and slid off the high stool, whereupon Kate had grabbed the two-kilogram paving slab of Dairy Milk her Aunt Gillian had parked temporarily on the hall sideboard and retreated to the outhouse. It had been a very brief peek into Laura's private world, but it had shifted something in Kate's mental image of her sister-in-law: she wasn't quite as armour-plated as previously imagined. In fact it was almost enough to . . .

Kate got up and sat down again. It wasn't *that* significant. And as far as her own situation went, it didn't change anything. In between dishing out advice on breast-feeding (Mr Craig being safely in the shed and out of earshot), her mother had shimmied effortlessly between her old favourite, 'There's plenty more fish in the sea . . . but probably not as good as [insert name of freshly detached boyfriend here]' and her new regular, 'You want to try to hang on to that Giles if you can – what's a few months when you're young?' Kate had hoped that the new lease of life issued by the four GNVQs her mother was steaming through between courses would have given her a more adolescent view of Young Love, but apparently not.

To add insult to injury, since there was a temporary lull in the feeding schedule, Carlo and Nina had thrown in their own two pesetas worth with, 'He issss han'some, yes?' and 'The slow rrrrabbit isss faster than the long pike.' Kate suspected this last may have lost something in the translation but, alas, her mother's GCSE Spanish was even more inept than Kate remembered her own being. She never thought she'd be telling her own mother that standards were obviously slipping in schools today. But whatever the Denise Robertson of Santander had meant by this was more than conveyed by the accompanying eyebrow wiggling and Latin shrugging, all of which only set Mrs Craig off into fits of girlish giggles and into a whole new debate with Mike about paternity leave in the European Union.

Mike had managed to avoid the whole ugly topic of Kate's love life, even during the long drive home for Christmas, during which Kate had sniffed pathetically in the icy silences between Mike and Laura's sniping. When forced into an opinion on the matter (his mother had pointed a butter knife at him over breakfast on Boxing Day and said, 'Mike, you're a young man, don't you think Kate should let Giles do what he likes?'), he had surprised Kate and indeed everyone at the table by saying, 'If he's out in the States having a good time, there's no reason why she should be sitting at home on her own. I wouldn't.'

Obviously Laura had blanched at this, and retorted, 'Well, that's funny, because you seem to expect me to,' for which diversion Kate was grateful, since it meant she could escape back to the outhouse with the rest of the toast and a dog-eared copy of *The Thorn Birds*.

Mike's comment leaped to the front of her mind now. Together with Isobel's exploits, it felt dangerously like permission – and she was feeling dangerous. It wasn't as though Giles going back to America put her on red alert for single men. And it wasn't as though she could imagine fancying anyone more than him. But why should she be bored and frustrated? Why should she be held to ransom by his career?

Kate checked herself. Watching her mother's old *Dynasty* tapes when she and her dad had run out of *Dad's Army* videos had evidently had a more subliminal effect that she'd thought. There was no point in flouncing around the flat now, for the simple reason that there was no one here to witness it. And anyway, being realistic, Giles would be coming back soon and if Christmas at home had proved anything, it was that she now had to make the best of a bad job here in London, because home was no longer an option. Giles's return would give her a day to work towards.

Again, said the voice.

She pleated the throw between her fingers. Anyway, wasn't all this gradually turning her into the independent woman he was always banging on about?

She found the remote control for the hi-fi under a cushion and put some music on before she could think of a reply. For some reason the theme from *Top Gear* blared out from the hidden speakers. Kate slid her hands down the sides of the sofa until she found the CD case: *Top Gear Driving Anthems* 2. That made sense – the Playstation was still strewn across the carpet and Harry had probably been using it for the full Tiff Needell effect. Kate pushed away an image she hadn't realised she'd retained, of Harry sprawled out on the floor in his boxers and not much else, playing Gran Turismo with Dant. Tiny details, like the tanned knots of his spine, and the faint tracing of hair on his back, made the picture disturbingly vivid. If only Cress could see his lovely spine, she wouldn't be so heartless, thought Kate loyally.

The best way to deal with Giles and his unspecified return date was to put him to the back of her mind, get on with her life, and when he came back it would be a wonderful surprise.

Yeah, right, said the voice. But you don't want to end up like Harry: in love with an idea, not a person.

A terrible craving for a bacon sandwich suddenly swept over Kate, so she got up and went out to see if there were any minimarkets open.

chapter twenty-four

After a bracing stroll around some of West London's finer scenic points, including Brompton Cemetery, Eel Brook Common and the outside of Queen's Club (locked), Kate made her way back down the North End Road, feeling pretty sorry for herself. There was a hungover atmosphere in town – she passed a few people who were back at work between the bank holidays, resentment written all over their faces, while some shops were closed until after the New Year. Hugely discounted wrapping paper and tinsel were everywhere.

As usual Kate wondered if there were some way she could give out all her Christmas presents on January 4th next year; perhaps by contracting some highly infectious illness which would prevent her from going home until well into the main January Sale period, thus killing two birds with one economical stone? Since most of the sales in London seemed to start on Christmas Eve, she wouldn't even have had to wait that long, if Giles had got his act together on the minibreak front: with a suitably exotic break rendering her unable to go home until the last minute, she could have had three days off her Christmas purgatory and still saved money.

Ratcat was sitting motionless on the step, staring up at the cat next door in its usual window-box. In honour of the season, the owners had placed a string of flashing reindeer along the edge. The tabby didn't seem to be bothered much by their presence, while Ratcat seemed to be hypnotised.

'Come in and I'll make you some tea,' said Kate. As far as company went, Ratcat was not exactly Bagpuss material, but since she had no idea when the boys were coming back, he would have to do.

Ratcat carried on staring upwards. Kate wondered if he had frozen there, and gave him a gentle nudge with her foot, at which he casually bit her leg and stalked in through the catflap.

She struggled up the stairs with her bags of shopping, which had swung and twisted themselves round her calves all the way back, tightening the handles round her fingers until they went white. Two flights away from the flat, Kate started hallucinating her bacon sandwich, but when she got to her floor, she realised that someone in the flat actually was frying bacon.

Harry must be back! A rush of gladness rose up in her chest, surprising her. Some intelligent conversation at last!

'Hi!' she called, pushing her way in through the open front door.

'Who's that?' Kate's gladness rush dropped. It was Dant.

'Who do you think it is?' she snapped back. 'Do many women have the front door key for this flat?' She dropped the bags by the fridge. 'No, please, for God's sake, don't give me a hand, I can see you're up to your eyes in it.'

Dant was standing by the hob, poking at a pan full of bacon with a wooden spoon.

'And a Merry Christmas to you too, Kate Craig,' he said, turning round with the spoon aloft. He gave her a critical up and down and turned back to the frying pan. 'I see Santa didn't bring you any new clothes this year.'

'Merry Christmas,' mumbled Kate, feeling quelled. Her immunity to Dant's sarcastic tone had worn off over six days at home. A man wearing a cardigan had no right to make personal comments about clothes, in any case. She began unpacking her shopping. 'Are you making one of those for me?'

'Can do,' said Dant. 'If you don't mind strange free-to-roam-and-shit-in-the-woods, happy-pig bacon.' He shook the pan at her. 'We're eating the contents of the Harvey Nichols hamper my father sent Cressida for Christmas. Touching, eh? It's that special, personal thought that makes the difference at this family time of year. Ah, I see you've remembered to buy some ketchup.'

'When did you get back from LA?' asked Kate, filling the toaster with thick sliced white bread.

Dant turned and frowned at her. 'From where? What would I be doing in LA? Do I look like a freak?'

'Harry told me you and Cress were going to see your mother.'

Dant levered some of the bacon out of the frying pan. 'I think it's safe to say that I would rather have spent Christmas in a tent in the middle of the Hammersmith flyover than pass a jolly Christmas with my mother. If that isn't a mutually exclusive idea.'

'Oh.' Kate wondered if she had made a terrible *faux pas*, but Dant was squirting huge haemorrhages of tomato sauce on to the toast happily enough. 'Did Cress go?'

'Of course not. She loathes our mother as much as I do.' He picked up some bacon and began arranging it over the toast. 'Although she might have gone, for all I know. She's less scrupulous about using the old hag for what she can get.' He sucked some ketchup off his thumb. 'I saw her for a couple of days after you left – she came round here once Harry was safely off up to the frozen North – gave me the third degree about the flat and what was going on.'

'Meaning?' asked Kate. She squashed a buttery piece of toast on some bacon and watched the ketchup ooze out of the side. Cress was extremely nosy about what went on when she wasn't there, and grilled her mercilessly about

Dant's habits. Sometimes Kate thought it might be wise to check with Dant that they were feeding her the same stories.

'Meaning, was I getting Teresa to dust the dado rails, was Harry still madly in love with her, were you enjoying your job, was I checking that everyone was only using two squares of toilet roll each time they went to the loo . . . You know. Random landlady-style nosiness.'

'She's probably just paranoid about what you say about her when she's not here. With good reason.'

'Yeah, well,' said Dant, making a pile of sandwiches. 'That would be my sister summed up rather neatly – a fragrant blend of paranoia and rampant egomania.'

'Well, there's twins for you.'

Dant put the hot frying pan in the sink and it sizzled as cold droplets from the dripping tap bounced on to the hot fat. 'She may have gone off to see Anna for Christmas. They both like a good row over the festive period. Maybe we should put the news on and see if there've been any riots on Rodeo Drive lately. Cress is pretty handy with a shotgun. Which is just as well, given her less than charming personality.'

'I don't know why you're so down on her,' said Kate defensively. Something in his tone made her take it personally. 'I've never seen this Dark Side you keep going on and on about. She's always been sweet to me.'

'Yeah, well.' Dant opened the fridge door in search of milk. Out of habit, he shook the bottle to make sure it was fresh and not halfway to cottage cheese. 'You have to remember that she's not like you. She's damaged.' He straightened up and Kate saw how serious his face had turned. 'Broken, and badly reassembled. We both are. Cress is inherently as much of a selfish arsehole as I am, only she's a lot better at covering it up. I can't be bothered, as you know.'

Kate grimaced. 'Spare me the Catherine Cookson clichés. I get enough of that at work.' As soon as the words were out of her mouth, and hanging in the air between them, she realised she had completely misjudged the tone. He actually meant it. But then Dant was so rarely serious, she argued to herself, how was she meant to know when to spot it?

There was a pause while he examined her face. Kate blushed. Sudden, raw glimpses of other people's souls made her flinch. She was painfully aware that Dant could probably see straight into hers whether she wanted him to or not.

He let out a tetchy sigh. 'Oh, Christ, not another member of the Cressida Grenfell Appreciation Society. Harry's bad enough. What does she do? Brainwash you? Cash hand-outs? Drugs in the coffee?'

Kate said nothing. She was remembering the eye mask Cress had gently put on her hungover head after the fake stag night. Then she remembered the way Harry had looked in the pub that night. Then she remembered the photos. As soon as she thought she was getting Cress sorted out in her head, her personality twisted like a kaleidoscope. 'She—' she began, and stopped.

'Jesus wept,' said Dant, slamming the fridge door but keeping his eyes fixed on her. 'And I had you down for something brighter. Well, don't say I didn't warn you.'

'Your trouble is that you think everyone is as cynical and morally decayed as you are.' Kate recovered herself and poured some milk into the only clean glass left in the cupboard.

'And?'

'And nothing.' She pointedly put the milk back in the fridge and carried her plate through to the sitting room. Dant followed her with a cafetiere of coffee and a tray full of food. 'Why did Harry think you were going to America?'

Dant switched on the television and arranged himself into one corner of the sofa, a pillow clutched to his chest while he flicked through the channels. 'Don't know. He may have spoken to Cress about it, he may even have answered the phone to Anna, I really have no idea.' He wedged an entire bacon sandwich in his mouth to indicate that that was as much as he wanted to say.

They sat in surprisingly companionable silence, watching the *Countdown* Christmas special, drinking Dant's coffee with whisky in it and eating their sandwiches. Kate felt a strange new impulse to get on better with Dant now she knew he liked Kenickie, although she was equally happy to attribute this goodwill either to guilt at going through his room or to drinking whisky in the afternoon.

Dant put the rest of Cress's hamper on the coffee table and soon they were picking away listlessly at bottled apricots and chocolate-covered espresso beans in the traditional post-Christmas manner. It felt more like home than home had done. Even Ratcat deigned to join them, curling up on Dant's leg in a convincing impression of a family pet.

Typically, the point at which they stopped taking the piss out of Richard Whiteley's seasonal tie and began low-key competition occurred in the middle of the second round of letters. By the commercial break they had pieces of scribbling paper out. To Kate's annoyance, Dant was astonishingly good at the numbers round and even beat Carol at one point.

'I realise this is quite late in the day to be asking you this, in terms of our acquaintance,' said Kate, emboldened by the throat-cloying effects of several cherry liqueurs, 'but why haven't you got a job? You're not stupid and as far as I know you don't have a criminal record.'

'Apart from my literary reputation as a convicted pyromaniac child killer.'

'Well, putting that aside for a minute.' Kate realised too late that the question that had come flippantly to her lips was actually rather personal, but Dant seemed to be taking it seriously.

'I assume you won't accept the simple reason that I don't want to slog my guts out for other people who would take me for granted and drive me round the bend with their endless bovinity?'

'If I had a pound for every time I've heard someone say that on the District line in the morning . . .' said Kate, lightly.

They both stared at an appeal for blood donors, and though their eyes were fixed straight ahead, a strange sense of intimacy vibrated between them. Kate wasn't sure if she was entirely comfortable with it. In the back of her imagination, she thought she was reminded of reading *Dracula*, although she had a guilty feeling she might be mixing it up with *Roses of Death*.

'If you really want to know,' said Dant, 'since this seems to be family counselling evening, it's because, as long as I am idle and give off the general air of artistic failure, I'm not destroying anyone's opinions of me. I'm not letting down my mother, who always said I would be a hopeless wastrel – which was hardly ambitious of her, since she gave me a career as a psychopathic pyromaniac stockbroker in her third sequel – and I'm not disappointing my father, who always said that my mother ruined me and Cress right from the beginning. Correctly, as it happens.'

'But you're so . . .' said Kate, and trailed off. Onscreen, Carol started selecting vowels for some speccy woman from Wakefield. She was wearing a pixie hat in honour of the season.

'So what?' said Dant.

'So . . . complicated.' Kate would have liked to have said less, and was sure Dant would have made her say more when the front door slammed and a familiar tuneless whistling of the theme from *The A-Team* floated up from the hall.

There was some thumping of stairs being taken two at a time, and a minute later Harry crashed through the hall and into the kitchen. Ratcat slid traitorously off Dant's knee and slithered towards the sound of food.

'Hi!' yelled Kate.

Dant said nothing, concentrating on his circle of letters.

Harry put his head round the door. 'Hello, all.' He looked tanned and well fed, and was wearing a new red jumper, which had a distinct hand-knit look about it.

'Hello,' said Kate.

'Gastric,' said Dant.

Harry ignored him. 'Does anyone fancy some tea? I'm going to make some toast.'

Kate looked at the empty box of Matchmakers on the sofa between her and Dant and suddenly felt sick, which was strange, since she had felt fine while she was stuffing them in her mouth five at a time.

'No, thanks, I'm trying to get drunk and sick at the same time,' said Dant. 'The whole Xmas experience in one afternoon.'

'You antisocial arsebadger,' said Harry cheerfully, putting the kettle on in the kitchen.

'Arsebadger?' said Kate to no one in particular.

Dant leaned back on the sofa and shouted through, 'Not antisocial at all – I'm being excellent company and you wouldn't suspect a thing about this coffee unless you tried to ignite it.' He picked up the whisky and sloshed in another shot to his cup. It was an oversized blue china number – one of a set Cress had bought for use when she came over, in protest at the stripper mugs.

'Very Prohibition – nice touch,' said Kate. 'Garish. Oh, shit, that's just six letters.'

Harry came back in with his tea and toast and plonked himself in the carefully maintained space between Dant and Kate on the sofa. Kate, who was sitting with her back against the arm, suddenly found her toes feeling the firmness of Harry's upper thigh through his jeans.

'Oooh, cold feet,' said Harry. He put his plate on the coffee table and rubbed Kate's feet briskly between his hands. 'Didn't you get any slippers for Christmas?'

'Yes, but I left them at home.' Kate's feet tingled appreciatively. Every year, she and Mike got a pair of sheepskin slippers and a paving slab of Dairy Milk from their Aunt Gillian: the Dairy Milk was gratefully received, but Mike's slippers were always the size of tennis racquets and Kate's were the size of her Sindy doll's. Mike's suggestion that his would fit her better had resulted in their third major row of the holiday. Despite the fact that it made perfect sense.

Harry stopped rubbing and picked up a piece of toast.

'Oh, don't stop,' pleaded Kate, at the same time as Dant said, 'Urgh! I can't believe you're not washing your hands! You have no idea where her feet have been!'

'Is there nothing on television?' asked Harry, flipping through the channels once *Countdown* had finished, with Dant beating both contestants, Carol and Martin Jarvis put together.

Dant threw him the *Radio Times* and got up to go to the loo. 'James Bond film at eight.' He weaved slightly when he reached the door. 'The one with the lezzie bint. The Girl with the Golden Tits or something.'

'It's like I've never been away,' said Kate.

'Did you have a good Christmas with Giles?' asked Harry.

Kate bit the inside of her lip. 'Yes, we had a wonderful time,' she said.

The echoes of Dant peeing ricocheted through the flat. 'Sometimes I wonder if he has a microphone hidden in the seat,' said Harry, turning the television up to mask the water-fall effect. He turned back to Kate. 'So where did he take you in the end? Babington House? Somewhere in Brighton?'

Various spontaneous fibs sprang to Kate's lips, but the genuine expression of interest on Harry's face shamed her into telling the truth. Ish. 'We decided to stay in London,' she said. 'He took me out for dinner' – which was true, they had gone to the Bluebird – 'and we just spent the rest of the time . . . going around town, you know.' Going around in a daze more like.

'That sounds nice,' said Harry encouragingly. 'Rather romantic, London at Christmas, with all the lights and the window displays.'

'Mmm.' Would that she had had time to get to any shops, thought Kate. It might have saved some strained thank yous at home when everyone received a variation on tights, pants and pop socks – the local M&S not having quite the range of Marble Arch at the best of times, and especially not on Christmas Eve. There would have been no presents at all if she hadn't volunteered to go into town for last-minute nuts, and diverted past the shopping centre. Home-made fudge might have been Valerie Singleton's solution to a penniless Christmas, but Kate knew from experience that unless it had a bar-code, it cut no ice with the Craigs.

'Giles showed me the Lloyds Building,' she added, in case 'Mmm' didn't sound enthusiastic enough.

'Well, I suppose you wouldn't really be concentrating on your surroundings,' said Harry, slapping her thigh with the remote control. 'I'm surprised you went out at all, after five months apart!'

Kate opened her mouth to comment, but stopped herself as Dant came in.

'Looks like one of us had a romantic Christmas, eh?' said Harry jovially. 'Unless you surpassed previous years?'

Dant wedged himself into the corner of the sofa and studied the TV guide. 'Oh, yeah, Love's Young Transatlantic Dream.'

'We had a wonderful . . . few days,' said Kate, irked.

'Nice present?'

'Yes, of course.' Giles had presented her with a very large bottle of Amarige and a bright red Chanel lipstick. He might as well have left the 200 duty-free Marlboro Lights he'd got for Selina in the same bag. The reasonable part of Kate's brain repeated the 'He's been very busy' arguments over and over again as she placed the delicately wrapped travel clock she'd racked her brains and her current account to find for him into his hands. It was tiny and shiny gold and had two separate faces: one for the time in Chicago and one for London.

'I won't ask what it was!' said Harry, nudging her again with the remote control.

Thank God he's being a prat, thought Kate, chewing a chocolate-covered cherry that she hadn't wanted even when she started eating it. It makes it a lot more difficult to imagine him having sex with anyone, let alone Cress.

'Switch over to BBC1,' said Dant. 'There's a Christmas special of that docusoap we were watching after the news.'

'Excellent,' crowed Harry. He settled himself into the sofa, one cushion behind him, another on his lap. 'Pass me a chocolate brazil nut, Kate, there's a girl. No, save yourself the bother, pass me the box.'

Kate finished her cherry, spat the stone out into her hand, dropped it into the half empty box of brazil nuts and passed it up without comment. She wondered at what point they had all moved into 'squashing up on the sofa together' territory. Probably when they had felt the tiny worm of relief at being back in the flat and safe in their own lives again burrowing around in the back of their minds.

'I'm going to the loo,' she said, heaving herself off the sofa, 'and don't think you can have my space while I'm gone.' The effects of Dant's Irish coffees hit her as she stood up and she had to walk carefully to the bathroom.

'Does anyone want a drink?' she yelled from the kitchen. Oh, God, that's my mother talking, she thought, looking for the milk in the fridge behind jars of cranberry sauce and Tupperware boxes which Harry must have brought back.

There was no response from the sitting room, apart from Dant's dirty laugh.

'I said . . .' began Kate in a louder voice, and then muttered, 'Would you listen to you?' to herself. She walked through with her own coffee and found Harry had stretched his legs over her space on the sofa. She hoisted them up and sat down. He stretched them over her lap.

'You don't mind, do you?' he asked with a winningly puppyish expression. 'I have terrible discs.'

'I know,' said Kate, thinking of his CD collection. 'What's this?'

'Oh, God, it's just dreadful.' The ultimate Dant and Harry docusoap accolade. 'It's Christmas at Heathrow.'

A flutter of panic rose up in Kate's throat; the same kind of panic that used to sweep her when the French teacher would go round the class asking for volunteers to translate unseens. Surely they wouldn't have used her piece with Giles? There wasn't enough material there. Not after she had spoiled it with all that glaring.

As the camera swooped round in the wake of a choir trip to Vienna making its way through Departures, the setting looked horribly familiar: white walls everywhere, echoing announcements, shops with 'Christmas in New York' displays, freezing weather, endless paper coffee cups.

An over-made-up steward was leaning confidentially into the camera as he strolled through the green channel with a very chi-chi pushalong suitcase. 'Of course, what makes this time of year so very special are the family moments. It gives Heathrow a lovely atmosphere and, you know, makes us all feel like one big happy family.'

'Yeah, right,' snorted Harry.

'It's going to be a very special Christmas for one little girl,' went the voiceover. 'Sascha has been suffering from leukaemia and hasn't seen her daddy for two whole years . . .'

Thank God, thought Kate, with relief. Sick kids in documentaries override virtually anything, apart from tormented donkeys. They won't bother with us, especially not with all the dirty looks Giles was giving them. She tried a piece of candied peel from Cress's hamper and wished she hadn't bothered.

'If her daddy is going to be that shagaholic flight attendant, I think she's going to wish she'd stayed in,' said Dant.

'God, you're so cynical,' protested Kate, her eyes filling up instinctively as the tiny little girl was swung around by her ecstatic father, while the mother hugged them both from behind. The little girl's Santa hat fell off and a crowd of technicians rushed to pick it up for her. 'It's just what you want at Christmas . . .'

They sat through some more large families from Antigua

being reunited with long-lost relatives in the passport control area, and the shock discovery of four kilos of cocaine in a box of chocolate snowballs. Five girls from Newcastle en route to Christmas in Rio de Janeiro were lost and then found by the chief stewardess (who was releasing her version of 'Leaving on a Jet Plane' on Christmas Eve, following her triumph at the staff karaoke night in November). They were chatting up the park-and-ride driver in the short-term car park. A dachshund, which had flown over from Tenerife to be with its elderly mistress, and had inadvertently been flown back again, was reunited with his owner. He was also wearing a small Santa hat. Kate, on to her fourth Irish coffee and feeling deeply philanthropic, had tears running down her face.

'Not all reunions are so happy though,' said the voiceover. Kate's face froze as a large picture of herself, recumbent on the bench outside Coffee Republic, filled the screen. Her head, with the eye mask on, was out of shot. Maybe they'll leave it at that, she thought desperately.

'Bloody hell,' said Harry, leaning forward for a better view. 'Would you look at the legs on that! Phwooaaar!'

'Kate,' said Dant, over Harry's craning neck, 'isn't that . . .?'

She nodded.

'Oh,' he said, a smile lighting up the dark circles under his eyes.

'This young lady has been waiting for several hours to welcome her boyfriend back from Chicago. Unfortunately, what began as a romantic afternoon has rapidly turned into a nightmare.'

'Jesus, no!' exclaimed Harry, jerking back in his seat. 'That's . . .'

'Shut up, Haz,' said Dant. 'According to Kate's version, the nightmare is about to blossom into a fantastic weekend of Lurve.' They both leaned nearer the television.

Kate felt sick, as the camera homed in on her legs. They looked so long and gangly and her hair was everywhere.

Huge long curls hanging over her bag and round her face, all wild and tendrilly, and about as far from the glossy perfection of the Harvey Nichols hair creation as you could get. No wonder Giles had looked so shocked when he saw her.

'Unbeknownst to her, Chicago is under feet of snow in one of its worst snowstorms of recent years, and the airport is in chaos.'

'They could have told me that at the time,' protested Kate, as the shiny stewardess lady was filmed dealing with her stream of stressed-out passengers, her smile and her eyeshadow brighter than ever. She was behaving with the manic normality of the docusoap victim, overenunciating, and automatically flicking her eyes towards the unseen camera every forty seconds.

'Meanwhile, Leanne and Karen are still in danger of missing the flight to Rio . . .'

Kate sank back in her seat. Thank God that was it.

'Why didn't you phone home?' asked Harry. 'We'd have come and got you, or come out and kept you company. You looked wrecked.'

'Oh, it wasn't as bad as they made out,' said Kate, knowing full well that the only thing able to drag them out of a warm flat and miles away to Heathrow would have to involve the Royal Mint and a fleet of Lotus Elises being driven by the Corrs. 'Giles came back almost immediately and then we had a fabulous time.'

'Must have been great to see him again.'

'Absolutely,' agreed Kate, warming to her role now the danger was over. She checked the television out of the corner of her eye, but the crew were filming the two girls from Newcastle who had locked themselves in the toilets at Harry Ramsden's fish restaurant. There was only another five minutes to go – they couldn't have used any more footage of her and Giles. A few white lies wouldn't hurt. 'It was so romantic – just like something out of *Brief Encounter*.'

Harry nodded and smiled sympathetically. 'Absolutely.'

'NB, Harry, not "Briefs Encounter", which I know for a fact you have under your bed,' said Dant. 'Oh, hello, here you are again.'

Kate dragged her eyes back to the screen in horror as the crew focused on her waking up.

'You look amazing, Kate,' said Harry, as the onscreen version pushed her hair off her face and fixed the camera with a searing stare. 'So photogenic.' Her eyes looked like marmalade in her translucent skin – so that's what the lenses looked like in, thought Kate. *Creeeeepy*. 'A real Sleeping Beauty.'

'All right, Harry, let's not have any accidents,' said Dant.

'I do not look amazing.' She inspected her pale face critically. 'I look like I've just had a night of passion with a vampire.'

'After delays lasting the best part of twelve hours, the scheduled flight from Chicago has finally arrived,' went the voiceover, covering the footage of Kate being sarcastic to the researcher. Though her words were inaudible, the expression on her face was clear enough.

'Oh to be able to lip-read,' said Dant, drily.

'Is the flight from Chicago in yet?' she said on screen. Her voice sounded small and sleepy.

'*Aaaaahh*, bless!' chorused Dant and Harry.

The onscreen Kate unfolded herself from her sleeping position, dragged her scattered possessions from around the bench and hauled on her boots, offering the viewers of BBC1 the best display of quality leg since Royal Ascot.

Harry was politely, and noticeably, silent.

'Oh, right, yes,' said Kate, hurriedly. 'This is the bit where I meet Giles off the plane and he's really jet-lagged and the camera crew told him to play it a bit grumpy because of the delays and the appalling danger involved in flying from that airport to begin with, and . . .'

She stopped as Giles emerged from the arrivals area, pushing his trolley. He looked pretty grim, now she saw him again, without the benefit of the butterflies in her stomach.

'Oh, so *this* is the Captain of Industry,' said Dant, sarcastically. 'How nice to meet him for the first time through the medium of television.'

'He doesn't look all that pleased to see you,' observed Harry, 'given that you waited for hours and hours to meet him and even borrowed my car.'

'Yes, thank you very much, thank you very much, I thought I'd done all the gratitude for that.' Kate swigged at her cold coffee, through which the whisky suddenly tasted too strong. 'If you use your imagination, you will realise that you don't normally see your girlfriend surrounded by a camera crew.'

'Unless you're going out with Geri Halliwell,' said Dant.

'Or Cress, actually, she had someone from *London Tonight* filming in her bar over Christmas and . . .'

'Shut up, Harry,' said Dant. 'I want to hear what Our Hero is saying to Kate.'

There was a close-up of Giles wheeling his trolley away, leaving Kate trotting along behind. The extended microphone clearly picked up Giles snapping, 'Who the hell are those clowns?' as Kate put a consolatory hand on his arm. He shook it off crossly.

'The brute!' said Dant, theatrically.

Kate bit her lip in surprise. She hadn't remembered him doing that.

'But now the wait is over, the holiday can begin for Katherine and Giles.'

'How did they get my name?' cried Kate. 'That's invasion of privacy!'

'Probably took it off the passenger list,' said Harry. 'And did you tell the flight steward what you were called in case they had to page you about the flight?'

'Oh, arse,' said Kate, 'I did. God, I'm so stupid. They've bodged the editing here, haven't they?' she added as the camera fixed on a lift door. 'They should have cut this out, because all we do now is leave. Should this bit be . . .?'

The doors opened to reveal Kate and Giles kissing passionately over his luggage.

'Oh,' she said weakly. 'That.'

Dant and Harry did ironic cheers, then stopped at Giles's thunderous expression and did ironic 'Ooohs' of fear instead.

'They've cut out all the nice bits,' protested Kate. 'There was a lovely bit where I gave him a hug and he sort of picked me up, and . . .'

'And then there was the bit where he came through the doors looking delighted to see you, with a big cuddly toy and a bunch of flowers, and you sort of rushed up to him in slow motion in a nice dress, and he went down on one knee and said, "Kate, I've missed you so much, I want us to get married!" Except they cut that bit, because the footage of him looking like a grumpy arsehole and you looking like someone about to be lashed to a stake and barbecued for your beliefs was so much better television?'

'Dant!' said Harry. 'I'm sure that's not what . . .' He looked at Kate, and she was deeply annoyed to see a soft expression of pity in his eyes.

'And from the snow of Chicago, Katherine and Giles are off into the snow of London to celebrate Christmas together at last,' said the voiceover, as Kate and Giles pushed his luggage out of the automatic door. Kate's triumphant backward glance, which she had intended to look like something from a film, had more panic in it than she would have liked. It was strange seeing herself on television: she seemed taller than in real life, almost as tall as Giles in her new boots.

The videotape froze on her coppery curls being thrown back, and her unusually brown eyes smiling shyly at the camera, against the swirling flakes of snow picked up in the dark open doorway into the car park. The credits rolled. Kate tried to remember some names in case she ever got a chance for revenge. A curious feeling of flatness was creeping over her.

'Well, it's not often you see your flatmates on telly!' said Harry.

'You never let an obvious moment go by unheralded, do you?' said Dant, stretching his legs off the sofa.

'I thought you looked rather dramatic, Kate,' said Harry, turning to her. 'Very photogenic.'

Kate blushed and pushed his legs off her lap.

'Yeah, but, as we used to say at school, don't fancy yours much,' said Dant.

'I'm sorry?' said Kate. 'I don't speak Public School.'

'Come on, Dant, the guy was jet-lagged!' said Harry, looking back and forth between Dant and Kate, in case there was a fight to disperse.

But Kate threw up her hands. 'I'm not going down this road, because it's not worth it.'

Because you don't want to hear what Dant has to say, said the voice in her head.

'So where's the International Bright Young Thing now?' asked Dant, ignoring Harry.

Kate looked up and met his eyes. They were blackly challenging. 'He's in Chicago.'

'Of course.'

Dant raised his eyebrows, and anger surged up Kate's chest and into her throat.

'Of course he's in Chicago! I knew he was going back! He's in the middle of a very demanding training course, at the end of which he will have a fantastic job—'

'In Chicago,' finished Dant.

'Shut up!' Kate flashed back. 'Just . . shut up!'

'All I'm saying,' said Dant, in an unusually gentle tone, 'is that you're obviously very involved with this guy and it seems rather unfair that you get to spend so little time with him. That's all. No need for hysterics. Defensive hysterics,' he added more quietly.

'What the hell do *you* know about how *I* feel about him?'

'Come on, Kate,' interrupted Harry, 'you wear his clothes

round the house, you talk about him constantly, you go on about not phoning him even though you want to, your kitchen cupboard is full of pictures of him—'

Kate gave him a glare.

'Yes, all right,' Harry raised his hands, 'I had those olives, I'm sorry, I'll replace them when the shops open again . . . But, you know, either he's a very lucky man to have such an accommodating girlfriend, or he's . . .' He trailed off, uncomfortably.

'Taking the piss,' finished Dant for him.

They both met her eyes. Dant looked questioning, Harry looked worried.

'What is this?' demanded Kate. 'Ricki Lake? Or Morecambe and Wise?'

'Forget it,' said Dant, throwing up his hands. 'Let's just . . . forget it and go out and get properly drunk. Call it warming up for tomorrow night. We'll get Cress to let us into her place. Then the four of us can have a proper big brawl in Old Street and get arrested. I've always wanted to spend New Year's Eve in the cells.'

'Come on, let's go out,' said Harry, rubbing Kate's leg, as he would one of his mother's Labradors, she thought. 'Ignore him,' he added as Dant strode out to find his shoes. 'He's just . . . you know.'

Kate didn't think she wanted to know what Dant was. The whisky was making her Confused, and after Confused, she knew from experience, came Maudlin. Seeing the docusoap – seeing herself and Giles through a dispassionate eye – had stirred up a wide variety of emotions, most of which she felt too drunk to pin down, and that made her feel angry. Kate hated feeling out of control, which was why she'd never wanted to try drugs. And now not only was she drunk (partly, to her shame, on horrible Christmas liqueurs), but the entire nation had witnessed her difficult reunion with Giles. Which hadn't even been entertaining for her, let alone prime viewing for them. People all over the country would be speculating about them. About her. Hot bands of embarrassment squeezed her head.

'It's not what it looks like,' she muttered.

' 'Course not,' said Harry reassuringly, ruffling the loose curls on the top of her head. She pulled her head away instinctively. 'Let's go out.'

chapter twenty-five

Kate's phone rang again for the fourth time in ten minutes and she knew without looking at the caller display who it was.

It was Thursday morning and the collated proofs for *Death in the Drawing Room* were two days late already. Kate hadn't been able to face them before today and they would still have been at the bottom of her 'To Do' pile if she hadn't had a brief but to-the-point call from Sarah in Production.

In the moments since Will had last phoned she had only managed to transfer three corrections from the author's heavily annotated set of proofs to the scantily adorned set proofread by Megan for extra buttons. So far, Kate hadn't seen much evidence of the twenty-three hours Megan alleged she had spent on them: there was one instance of 'a rare pubic appearance' and a 'discarded pair of crotches'. It was a 'cosy crime' novel: the pacemaker factor of the readership was too high for such risky typos. It was also too soon after Christmas for Kate to whip through the pages on her usual autopilot, and she was getting heavily involved in the plot as it was. Perhaps it was just as well, she thought, spotting the blue-rinsed detective 'peddling' furiously on her bicycle.

She could really do without the phone pest. Kate tried to ignore the ringing but it didn't stop. She put down the red Biro and the blue Biro she was holding in her teeth and picked up the phone.

'Will, please will you leave me *alone*,' she said firmly. 'Even if I *did* know what Isobel is doing at this very moment I wouldn't tell you . . .'

There was some impassioned mumbling on the other end.

Kate rolled her eyes and started doodling on the margins of the proofs she was collating – big spiders on top of other big spiders.

'OK, I imagine she's probably doing some photocopying, all right? She's probably standing by the copier right now in her tartan wool trousers and her red jumper, talking to one of the all-female workforce about knitting patterns and babies and certainly not regaling them with tales of what we got up to at the office Christmas party with the post room boys.'

Kate gently put the phone down on a pile of filing while Will ranted on the other end, and stirred her coffee with the blue Biro. When she had drunk enough coffee to fortify her for the rest of the conversation she picked up the phone again and said, 'Haven't you got any work to do? Much as I would love to spend my first week back in the office discussing Isobel's underwear preferences, there are one or two more pressing matters requiring my attention. Like where Rose Ann Barton's new manuscript has got to.'

This provoked a squawk of anguish.

'Try flowers,' said Kate, 'or a kitten,' and hung up, seeing Isobel stagger past her office behind a three-foot stack of Jiffy bags.

'Isobel, can you phone Will, please? If only to tell him I've left the company and can't be contacted on this number any more.'

'Noooo, is he bothering you now?' Isobel tipped half the envelopes on to the depleted pile by Kate's desk. 'He plagued my family over Christmas, I'm telling you. My poor mother. He spent thirty-five minutes confessing how much he missed me and how he'd never leave his socks on the settee again before she could get a word in to say she'd have to get me from the kitchen. She missed the entire Queen's Speech. Mind you, he didn't phone back for at least two hours.'

'Well, it's been nearly six months now, hasn't it?' Kate gave her a closer look. 'Although if you didn't keep "nearly" getting back together, the poor man might get over it a bit quicker. That is, if you *want* him to. Did you not miss him a little over New Year?'

'Kate,' said Isobel in surprise, 'I did *tell* you that my folks live in Edinburgh, didn't I?'

Kate gave her a searching look and put an internal call from Elaine's office on to 'send'.

Isobel cracked after two minutes. 'OK, so I did miss him a little bit,' she confessed. 'Well, quite a lot, actually. But, you know, this is the first Hogmanay I've had in years where I've been allowed to go out on the Royal Mile and snog policemen and what have you. I know it's not what you want me to say, but being able to lech at random lads in kilts is a right laugh after five years of pretending I don't even see other men.'

'Isobel!'

'Well, you know what I mean. Joseph Fiennes.' Isobel leaned forward confidentially and stopped herself just in time. A blush spread upwards through her face. 'No. OK. Maybe I'll just keep that to myself for the time being. I just can't quite bring myself to give up the fun of being single now I've remembered what it's like.' She looked pensive for a moment. 'I mean, I care a lot for Will – I've lived with him since university and I still want things to work out, but sometimes it *scares* me how much I like being single . . .'

'I know what you mean about Joseph Fiennes though,' said Kate mournfully. 'Call me sad, if you will, and many people have, but I've developed this powerful thing for Ronan Keating. I even—' she held up her hand to carry on as Isobel protested, '—no, I have to tell someone, I even bought the *Boyzone Greatest Hits* video with the token I got for

Christmas. It's a strange obsession. I've watched it seven times all the way through already.'

'PS, Kate Craig is twenty-two.'

'Yes, but he's so blonde so responsible, so Irish . . .'

'Three-second warning.' Isobel twitched and Elaine strode into Kate's office.

Kate had suspected from the first hour back in the office that Elaine had been given a course of beauty treatments for Christmas by her husband, since her straggly mouse hair had been fluffed into a shaggy bob and her nails were an immaculate shade of peach. The fact that Elaine had come in wearing open-toed mules despite the four-inch deep puddles of rainwater surrounding the building was a bit of a pedicure giveaway – although the pale shade of blue on her toenails was rapidly being overshadowed by the deeper shade of blue which the rest of her foot was turning.

'I might have known you two would be in here gossiping,' she said with an abortive attempt at lightness. Her eyebrows had been tweezed and waxed into a state of polite interest, as though there were a plate of suspect canapés permanently beneath her nose.

'Did you have a good rest over the holiday, Elaine?' asked Isobel sweetly.

Elaine scowled. Kate reminded herself that the effects of a makeover could only last so long, and didn't extend to light personality brushing. As Giles could have told her. 'A rest? God, no, what with all the reading I had to do it felt as though I hadn't left the office. The kids didn't stop once, Sainsbury's wouldn't deliver over the New Year and the nanny went home to Killiney for five days. And I had this lot to get through.' She gestured to a huge pile of rejection letters which Kate realised with a sinking heart Elaine had actually asked her to type up and send out with their accompanying manuscripts before the courier came round yesterday lunch-time. 'Which reminds me, Kate, where's that thriller I gave you? The agent's been on the phone chasing it up.'

Isobel slunk out of the office, impersonating Elaine's eyebrows.

The manuscript was in Kate's reading bag, and as she hauled it out she tried feverishly to remember three salient facts about it. She'd only read another sixty pages after starting it in Heathrow, then dumped it in her room with the reassuring thought that if it had been any good she would have been gripped harder.

'I don't think it's something I'd go mad to offer for, myself,' she said cautiously. 'It's quite . . . American in tone.'

'Heroine?'

'In an Irvine Welsh sense or an Amelia Earhart sense?'

'In a strong female lead sense.' Elaine evidently wasn't in a comedy mood. Or didn't know who Amelia Earhart was, maybe, thought Kate hopefully.

'No, I got the impression that the narrator was a horse,' said Kate.

Elaine's eyebrows went from tweezed surprise to genuine confusion.

'You can read it if you want to,' offered Kate. 'I don't think I really understood it. I must be thick. Maybe you'd get it more than I did.'

Safety in ignorance. With a back-up team in flattery.

Elaine weighed it up, full desk stress struggling with the chance to snatch a piece of literary fiction so esoteric her assistant couldn't understand it from under the nose of the official literary editor, Simon. Kate's phone rang and she diverted the call to Megan.

'Oh, arse, you'd think I'd have the run of these phones by now, wouldn't you – sorry, Megan,' she shouted unconvincingly over the partition.

Elaine was doing her nervous tic of slipping her shoe on and off. Up and down. Up and down. 'After we lost that Emma Ball book, I did—'

Jennifer Spencer's number flashed up on Kate's phone. Jennifer was undivertable.

'Hello?' said Kate.

'Kate, tell Elaine I need to speak to her immediately about Rose Ann. In my office.'

'Right,' said Kate to the dialling tone. 'Elaine, can you pop into Jennifer's office? It's about Rose Ann.'

Elaine's shoulders sagged.

Kate suppressed a desire to shout, 'Didn't the ayurvedic masseur warn you about your posture?' at her.

'Do a nice rejection letter,' Elaine said, flicking her eyes nervously down the corridor to Jennifer's office. 'From me. Recycle everything he said about the author on his covering letter – you know, "great potential", "unique new voice", all that lot – but make out we've got too many like this already. Just don't make it sound as if you didn't understand it.'

Elaine was in Jennifer's office for over an hour and then the pair of them went straight out for lunch. Kate finished *Death in the Drawing Room* and handed it over to Sarah, who informed her that her New Year's Resolution was to introduce a 'tough love' policy to the editorial department.

Since Jennifer had phoned Isobel from the restaurant to let her know that she and Elaine would be "working from home" for the rest of the day, Kate and Isobel slipped out half an hour early, under the guise of buying books for cover research purposes. They wandered around Dillons with takeaway cappuccinos, moving all the Eclipse books to the top of the table piles and generally commenting on the dire state of publishing.

'You know the new Rose Ann Barton's late?' said Isobel in a hushed tone.

'Is she the only author Eclipse has, or something?' replied Kate, trying to work out from the prelim pages what reprint *Bridget Jones's Diary* was on. 'Elaine's got twenty other books on the go, but you'd think that Rose Ann . . .'

'I'm just telling you,' said Isobel ominously.

Kate looked up and saw Isobel perform one of her mean-ingful nods. Perform was an accurate word. Through the big display window behind her, rush-hour cars swished past on the wet road, their lights reflecting stickily in the puddles.

London looked horrible in the wet, thought Kate. There was no freshness to rise into the air after rain as there was at home, just a sense of grimy relief that it wasn't raining any longer. Was it really settled that she had to stay here? Wasn't her place at home, helping her mum with her homework? Hadn't even Giles himself acknowledged that it was a lot to ask her to stay here any longer?

And now Elaine's nervous tension was about to go off the scale. Kate looked at her friend. Isobel's brows dropped and her small nose crinkled up, in the adorable manner of a Rose Ann Barton heroine.

'Still, nice bit of atmos in the office – it'll take your mind off Giles, won't it?' she continued cheerfully.

'Oh, yeah, him,' said Kate, her mood suddenly as damp as the grey street outside the bright lights of the shop.

They meandered around for another ten minutes and then Isobel went off to have supper with Will, at which they were meant to be discussing their future. Again.

'He never used to buy me supper when we were living together,' remarked Isobel, peering at her reflection in the window and redoing her pink lipstick. 'Might as well make the most of it.' She gave Kate a quick kiss on the cheek and clip-clopped off to the bus stop.

Kate wandered through the streets looking half-heartedly at the sales, then since she was still in debt from Christmas, walked to the Tube station.

There were delays on the District line and Kate found her-self eating a Crunchie from the chocolate dispenser before she realised what she was doing. She looked at the empty wrapper in horror, as the honeycomb stuck to her molars and twanged her fillings. That was the worst thing – not just lovely empty calories, but calories consumed without even tasting them. They'd barely bounced off the sides of her throat on the way down, cackling to each other as they went about the effect this would have on her best jeans.

She walked along North End Road twice as fast as normal to try to burn some of the Crunchie off before it all settled down to a happy life of permanent residence on her thighs, but she merely ended up treading on the Jack Russell belonging to the *Big Issue* seller outside the off licence. Kate then felt so guilty she made him sell her a copy, even though he was finished for the night and just popping into Victoria Wine for some beer.

At least the cover story is Ronan Keating, thought Kate, taking the stairs two at a time and flipping through the magazine for the interview pictures. And it is for a good cause. It's not like buying *Top of the Pops* magazine so I can look for pictures of Ronan. Or *Smash Hits*.

She reached the door of number 27, out of breath.

Smash Hits. When she had been a regular reader, how sad had she considered anyone over the age of sixteen buying *Smash Hits*?

Or anyone over the age of sixteen, full stop?

'Oh, God, I'm old,' she said, pushing open the door.

'Would you say Harry had a GSOH?' Dant was lying on the sofa, surrounded by newspapers and swilling down a can of Coke. He was wearing Harry's rugby shirt and the pair of track suit bottoms Kate had bought from the sale rail at Gap when she thought she might start running again.

'I don't know – is that what you had at your posh boys' school instead of GCSEs?' Kate looked hard at Dant, unable to decide whether she felt more mad with him for taking her joggers or more guilty at herself that the beautiful unworn bargain joggers still had the price label swinging from the pocket.

'It's an acronym. Shall I spell that for you? Good sense of humour.'

Actually, now she applied her mind to it, Kate thought

she was more despairing that Dant could fit so easily into her clothes, the skinny malinky. She kicked off her office shoes which didn't keep out the wet very well.

'Harry, good sense of humour? He lives here, doesn't he?' Kate opened the fridge to see what was available for supper and noticed that even the Flora stocks were down. In fact even the four small bottles of gnat's piss French lager which had been there since Kate moved in ('Worked out at twenty-three pence a bottle once we'd loaded the car up!') had gone. Kate pulled out the entire salad tray, which made an unpromising slopping noise, and dumped the contents in the bin without looking at it. 'Well, he has that T-shirt – the "Rowers Like Firm Strokes" one.'

Dant chewed his pen. 'I don't think that kind of humour is valid with *Guardian* readers.'

Kate inspected the current selection of takeaway menus, attached to the fridge with Tetley Tea magnets. She could murder a pizza, if she didn't require a degree in maths and a Venn diagram to work out which was the best offer to go for. 'What have *Guardian* readers got to do with it? Harry only ever reads the *Standard*, *Private Eye* and Pizza Hut weekly.'

'Yes, well, that's the idea. We're going to widen his social circle for him.' Dant drained the Coke, rinsing it round his teeth appreciatively, and smacked the cap off the last bottle of French lager.

If Dant was drinking that lager, thought Kate, then there really was a post-Xmas grocery crisis. She put her hands on her hips without realising it.

'Dant, what are you doing?'

Dant stopped fiddling with the pen and directed a sarcastic glare at her. 'I'm dissolving my wisdom teeth with Coca-Cola, what do you think I'm doing?'

'You expect me to believe you have wisdom teeth?'

Dant pulled a face which indicated he couldn't be bothered to reply, and threw the newspaper he was studying at her.

'Kate, I cannot stand the whingeing any longer. After you bailed out last night, I had to listen to him until one, mumbling on and on about what love meant and will we ever find the right person, nuh ner, nuh ner . . . All I'm going to do is provide him with a small selection of hopefuls and let them get on with demonstrating what love means in the practical sense, and he can work out the theory later. What he needs is a nice normal girl with her own Alice band and VW Polo, who'll take him off to the Pitcher and Piano for Sunday lunch and make him realise what a total waste of time Cress is.'

Kate bridled. Typical arsey London attitude. Living here must be getting to her – sometimes she forgot what a pair of snobs Dant and Harry were. 'Oh, that's right, saddle him with some useless Sloane who can only talk about Peter Jones and how much it costs to fill up the Range Rover. Either leave him to work things out with Cressida, or find him someone *normal*, for God's sake.'

Dant shrugged in reply. He had smudges of blue ink on his right cheek from chewing the Biro.

'If you know anyone normal,' she added spikily, and looked down at the paper. Dant had ringed some of the ads he thought worth copying. Or worth following up, maybe.

'Honestly. I've known Harry for a long time, it's what he needs. And these Lonely Hearts things are the way forward. All you have to do is make Harry sound like a catch in twenty words or less, including his age, occupation, compulsory good sense of humour and some improbable claim about his penis.' He threw her the Biro. 'Oh, and it has to sound like he wrote it too. Off you go, thirty seconds on the clock, starting from now.'

Dant had come up with *Rev my engine! Sexy 20sthg, W14, seeks wild Riverdance babe with own teeth to drive to Heaven and back. Hotwiring a speciality*.

'That's revolting,' said Kate. 'And where did the Riverdance bit come from?'

'I don't know, I thought it might be nice to have some Irish chicks round the place.'

'Own teeth?'

'Better than saying "No over thirties", isn't it? Anyway, it's written in the style of the *Guardian* Soulmates column,' said Dant, lighting up and lying back on the sofa. 'They're all like that.'

'Are they meant to be ironic?'

'Well, given that they're all either actuaries or students . . .'

Kate skimmed over three columns of 'Reluctant accountants' and 'Bosomy Kate Winslet-a-likes'. If Giles found someone else in Chicago, she would probably be reduced to this. How else would she meet another man in a city full of people she didn't know? Panic gripped her stomach, commented on the fact that it could pinch more than an inch, and gave it a bit of a jiggle around.

'I think you're being unnecessarily cynical,' she said. Paranoia made her sound more po-faced than she intended, and she tried to relax her voice. It didn't work. 'These are all just people who . . . who . . . just want to meet new people.'

'You mean they've shagged all their shaggable friends and find themselves considering shagging the unshaggable ones?'

'And *your* last girlfriend was called . . .?'

Dant's brow darkened, in a Heathcliffian – though not the Cliff Richard version – way and Kate swallowed, remembering just too late that now she was in London, she shouldn't assume that someone's partner was automatically of the opposite sex.

'Write something good or I send in my version.'

She opened her mouth to protest or apologise. Visions of Dant auditioning rah-rah hopefuls via the intercom fought with visions of Dant in Elvis Vegas Comeback biker leathers hanging around Soho (mental picture courtesy of *Time Out* Eating Guide and Mike Craig's *Guide to Parts of London We Don't Go To*).

'Whatever happens, I'm sending something in. It's my New Year's Resolution on behalf of Harry. If he says, "If someone's special, she's worth waiting for" one more time I'll throw every single thing he owns into the street.'

'Dant . . .!'

'Including his computer. Anyway, in purely practical terms he'll have to shut up about Cress if there's someone else sitting on his face,' finished Dant cheerfully.

Kate struggled for something to say, but couldn't think of anything quickly enough. The visions of Dant's private life were getting worse and she hadn't even got her coat off.

Dant threw the empty lager bottle into the old fish-tank. Since it had been refilled with water, if not goldfish, and replaced in the living room, it was looking more like an installation than ever. Teresa ignored it. Kate wished Dant had never mentioned the 'installation' joke to Teresa, since there were now self-installed outsider artworks of dust and beer cans going on all round the house.

'It'll all work out like a dream, I promise you. *I'll* phone up to confirm the details and say I'm Harry, so as not to draw suspicion, I'll give them a code name, so that when the girls phone up in their droves, I'll take the call and pretend it's someone he met at a party when he was pissed who took his number, *he* doesn't realise he's being set up, meets a nice girl, *Cress* can stop coming over here and creating rows so she looks like a horrible bitch, and we can all live happily ever after. I'm going to Tesco's with Cress's house credit card, so if there's anything you want?'

Kate shook her head. She didn't think that Cress's behaviour was entirely for Harry's benefit. Or at least it looked pretty natural from where she was standing.

'Excellent.' Dant pulled on his fisherman's sweater and pushed his bare feet into an ancient pair of Green Flash trainers, which were so old they were probably still calling themselves 'pumps'. 'I'll leave you to it then.'

Kate pulled a loose piece of paper out of her reading bag

and sat down at the kitchen table. She knew Dant would send in his version if she didn't write a better one and his was so horrible that the only women who could possibly respond to it would have to be Jeremy Clarkson's ex-girl-friends.

What were Harry's best features? She started out with all the obvious ones.

Male, 27, graduate, blond, tall, sense of humour.

She crossed that out and wrote *GSOH*.

Well-travelled. If the collection of artifacts in his room was anything to go by.

Kate blushed and realised that she wouldn't have known about the collection if she hadn't had a snoop round. Still, he was always on about his years out, and there were photos all over the flat of Harry in travel sandals, looking tanned, astride a variety of exotic-looking pack animals.

She chewed Dant's pen, remembered the woad effect on his face and took it out of her mouth. Her eye fell on a pile of Harry's gym washing.

Sporty.

Was that appealing enough? She crossed it out and wrote *fit*. Despite herself, the fifth-year implications of the word leaped into her mind. Kate blushed. Except that Harry *was* fit in the 'blue eyes, blond floppy fringe, long legs' common room sense – he'd have had three-quarters of her class at school lying on the floor forming the words 'Shag me, please' in human letters. There would probably have been enough available bodies to run to 'Deflower me now, if you don't mind'. And it was a co-educational school.

Not that he was the type she'd have gone for at school. One look at his CD collection had confirmed that.

'Tsk,' said Kate, remembering that that was something else she shouldn't know about. Still, what was the betting that the pair of them hadn't had a good look round her room when she wasn't there?

Moving swiftly on from that unwelcome thought, she

scanned the previous week's ads and decided that it was safest to play it straight.

Blond-haired, blue-eyed, generally happy, grad M, 27, seeks girl to enjoy London life with. Must understand cricket, rugby and why DB5s are worth it. No Carolines, whiners or in-line skaters.

There. She could go for someone like that. Kate looked at this and crossed out the last part. Not fair to allow her own pet-hates to govern Harry's love-life. Although it was for their own good, given that they'd all have to go through Dant first, and despite Kate's suspicion that Laura secretly enjoyed Dant's horrible phone manner, it wasn't really on to subject more unsuspecting 'naice' girls to it.

Dant's probably only doing this so he can cream off the best contenders for himself, thought Kate in a sudden flash of inspiration. The arsehole. He gets me to do all the work, Harry to take out all the rejects while he finds himself a nice Irish girl with long legs and millions of pairs of opaque tights.

Right, she thought, chewing the pen again. Right, you beggar.

Heathcliff, dark eyes and heart, seeks Cathy to run wild on emotional moors. Must be dangerous, acquiescent, nubile and telepathic. All offers considered.

That'll teach him to have the *Best of Kate Bush* on CD, thought Kate. She copied out both versions on to the forms, stuffing both into the envelope Dant had thoughtfully provided and licked the flap.

She put a hand to her head. Oops, Kate Bush. She just wasn't bright enough to keep her cat-burgling to herself.

Still, it could have been worse, she thought, as she ratched through her bag for a stamp. Harry had more than his share of Meatloaf albums.

chapter twenty-six

It amazed Kate how quickly the Christmas holidays vanished into memory after only a few weeks back at the office.

The photographs from the office party, which the publicity department had arranged into an attractive and unilaterally embarrassing collage by the toilets, so that everyone would see them, fell daily like unseasonal autumn leaves as people surreptitiously removed evidence of themselves drunk, dancing or pointing at items of furniture. By the end of the second week there was only a handful left, mostly the flattering pictures which the publicists had taken of themselves before leaving the office, and one of Isobel and Kate, surprised mid-gossip, looking wild-eyed and dangerous. Apart from Skinny Wendy the Beauty Editor's failed attempt to make everyone follow a new detox plan (even Jennifer put her foot down and claimed to have a wheatgrass allergy), it was as though New Year had never happened, and that they had always been stuck some unspecified time into the Current Year.

Will and Isobel officially resumed their relationship on January 28th. It was a day Kate wasn't likely to forget in a hurry, since January 28th was also the day she was meant to put the new Rose Ann Barton book into Production, all edited and tweaked, ready to hit the shelves for the big Mother's Day promotion.

Rose Ann, as Elaine patiently explained to her, was more of a brand name than an author, and the production of her three books a year ran like a well-oiled sausage machine. On Jennifer's specific instructions, Kate had had the copy editor booked since before Christmas, the cover had been designed and approved and even Elaine's copy had been ready for weeks, despite the big mystery about what the story was to be.

Despite, in fact, the big mystery about the actual where-abouts of the manuscript.

The effects of Elaine's Christmas makeover had now worn off completely. She no longer summoned Kate to her office by phone, she just shrieked 'Kate!' from her desk and banged her mug when she required her ginseng teabags replenish-ing. Kate had her journey from chair to office down to three big steps and a lean. She didn't want to be completely inside Elaine's office any more. She was beginning to understand why Mandy had just hidden things.

Now she stood in front of her boss's desk with a notepad, scribbling frantically as Elaine rattled through all the impending crises they had to conceal from Jennifer, while twisting a pencil in her hair. She was so stressed that she hadn't noticed she still had a Biro tangled up over her left ear.

'. . . you'll have to make up some copy for the new Maureen Murphy since Production need to proof the jacket tomorrow – Sarah left the most *abusive* message on my Voicemail . . .'

'Maureen Murphy is . . .?' In five months Kate had picked up the background for most of Elaine's authors, but every now and again something would appear out of the blue, usually late, or presumed dead.

'Saga, Irish, Edwardian, potatoes, the Auld Mammy, shamrock, Guinness, sailing to the old country, whatever . . .' Elaine scanned up and down her production list. 'Then you'll have to get on to Sales about Jan Connor. She's been going into bookshops again.'

Jan Connor (gritty crime, Northern, ex-prison warder) was a serial 'Why is my book not on your shelves?' stock policeman.

'Well, she's keeping the rep on his toes, I suppose.'

Elaine looked up witheringly. 'Even I don't expect Bob to get Jan's books into Christian Scientist bookshops.'

Kate watched Isobel sail past her window with an armful of bright red carnations. From the beatific expression on her face, it seemed that they were hers, rather than Jennifer's.

'. . . and can you phone Alan Spires, Diana Wilmsley and Lizzie Lahinche and tell them that I've read the scripts they've delivered, loved them, real breakthrough, etc., etc., but I'll need some time to get my notes together. You can pay the delivery advance on Diana's, but, er, leave the others until I see how much work they'll need.'

Kate grimaced. She hated phoning authors about work she hadn't read. They always wanted detailed breakdowns of what you thought the best bits were and, unlike Isobel, she hadn't yet learned how to tease that out from what they said themselves.

Elaine rested her head in her hands. 'They all have far too much *time* over Christmas, it's always the same . . . I *tell* them not to deliver until I say, but . . . And I don't dare start anything until Rose Ann produces her new manuscript.'

For once, Kate felt sorry for Elaine. She looked raddled and on the verge of tears, possibly because Jennifer was phoning her on the hour to see what the Rose Ann update was, and Sarah was phoning her on the half hour. From her office Kate could hear Elaine's side of the conversations, and it sounded like police brutality. Sort of bad cop / bad cop.

'Is there anything I can do, Elaine?' asked Kate, meaning, apart from the immense amount of what Elaine liked to call 'spadework' now filling up three pages of her shorthand pad.

'Oh, God, no, it's all stuff I'll have to do myself, it's all such a nightmare,' Elaine replied automatically.

Oh, good, thought Kate.

'But actually, now you mention it, I haven't had a chance to go through the submissions since we came back . . .' Elaine leaped up from her desk and went over to the pile of manuscripts that had come in from agencies. Her energy would have passed as enthusiasm to a layman, but Kate recognised it as a potent combination of buck-passing and immediate crisis avoidance.

Elaine was tossing folder after folder on to the floor. 'You could have a look at this one . . .' she peered inside, 'American dachshund detective, I suspect not one for us, and this one . . . thirtysomething biological clock woman becomes man-eater, literally . . . Oh, buggeration, I was meant to have read this. Oh, Christ, I can't believe I didn't take this home!'

She clutched the manuscript, an expression of aghast disbelief stretching her face.

'Is it something important?' asked Kate innocently.

Elaine gave her a hard look, as if sizing up the abilities of a small horse. 'You remember the Emma Ball book?'

'Yes,' said Kate. Like I remember my smear test appointments, you stupid woman.

'Well, this came in from her agent last week. Phil Hill.'

I know who Phil Hill is, thought Kate, biting back a retort. *I* wasn't the one who mixed him up with IPM on the fax header.

Elaine gave the pencil in her hair a nervous twist and went on, 'We talked about it over lunch when I was trying to get the Emma Ball book, and because we'd got on so well, even though Emma decided to go somewhere else, the silly bitch, Phil biked this over specially to let me have first look at it.' She studied the covering letter again and looked back at Kate, then back to the letter. Then back at Kate.

'What's it about?' asked Kate, bridling at having her critical faculties sized up so obviously.

'It's a modern twentysomething London thriller,' said Elaine. '*Lock Stock* meets *South Park* in the flat from *Shallow*

Grave but in London. Phil is very excited about the author – he wouldn't tell me who it is and went into all that ridiculous agentspeak about pseudonyms and amazing new talent and fabulous connections.'

'It sounds exactly what you're looking for,' said Kate, determined to say the right thing. Or at least say enough to get to read it. Megan was making much of the fact that Simon had bought the weird virtual pet cemetery novel she had found, although Isobel was putting feelers out to discover the truth about who the author really was. It couldn't hurt to be the first to read something that actually sounded quite good.

'I don't mind doing some extra reading,' she added, which was true – after all the stress of Christmas, filling up the hours that she might spend thinking about Giles with ostensibly career-enhancing homework might just persuade all concerned that she had better things to do with her time.

Elaine considered this rare burst of enthusiasm. 'OK, well, why don't you get it photocopied and we'll read it at the same time. You do some spadework on it and if it's good I'll take over from there.' She caught Kate's eyes narrowing automatically and amended herself to, 'I'll have a closer look and we'll talk about it.'

'OK,' said Kate, holding out her arms for the pile of manuscripts.

'It's just the kind of thing Jennifer wanted *you* to look for,' Elaine pointed out as Kate staggered a little under the weight of five people's hopes and dreams. 'Shame you couldn't have intercepted this one before Phil Hill stepped in.'

'Elaine, I don't *know* any authors.' I just know a lot of characters, thought Kate. And they're all short of a plot.

'Well,' said Elaine, stepping back to admire the light now filling her office in the space where the towering pile of submissions had been, 'that feels a lot better.' She brushed the dust off her grey jersey trousers. 'Can you get me a taxi to Bertorelli's? I'm lunching someone from ICM at one.

Excellent.' She rubbed her hands together, sat down at her desk and resumed looking at the phone.

Kate carried the manuscripts back to her desk and dumped them by her printer. Quite how she was going to get all that lot back on the Tube she didn't know. She briefly considered bagging them all up and having them biked over to her house, but Jennifer went through the courier accounts with a fine-tooth comb, and anyway, as far as she knew, Dant hadn't come back to the flat after his encounter with the third would-be Cathy the previous night, so there would be no one to sign for the package.

At half past twelve Elaine sailed out for lunch and Kate took out from her secret drawer a pile of typing she had assured Elaine she had already done.

The phone rang and she answered it, tucking the receiver under her ear as she squinted at Elaine's handwriting.

'Hello, Kate, it's Harry.'

'Oh, hello.' Kate stopped writing and held the phone with both hands. He hadn't phoned her at work since before Christmas – before her worrying slide into inappropriate thrillseeking. She tried to ignore the fluttering in her stomach. Ronan Keating, now Harry – where was this going to end?

'Cress is wondering whether you'd like to come out for supper this evening? About eight-ish?'

Cress? Kate experienced a stab of jealousy. 'Who's going?' If it was a cosy threesome then she certainly wasn't interested, keen enough as she was to see either Cress or Harry individually.

'Cress, Dant, me, you, I think.'

Me, you . . . that was better. Kate shook herself. 'Er, where's she thinking of going? Only I've got a lot of stuff to carry home.'

'Listen, I'll come and pick you up, if you don't mind staying on a bit?'

'Have I ever left early?' Her heart rate had speeded up.

This was ridiculous. 'Give me a ring when you want me to come out, OK?'

There was a cough behind her and she turned round to see Isobel looking coyly out of the window. She had her hand extended behind her back, the fingers of her left hand spread out like a starfish.

A starfish with a diamond ring on. 'Isobel!' exclaimed Kate involuntarily. 'Harry, I'm so sorry, I have to go, I'll speak to you later.'

Kate spun on her chair. 'Oh my God, Isobel? Is that what I think it is?'

Isobel beamed. Her whole face was full of light. She looked like a blonde angel. 'We had supper last night and before we had time to kick off another row, Will put this little box on the table in front of me, and there it was!'

'Let me see, let me see!' Kate inspected the diamond solitaire which sparkled lavishly beneath the strip lighting. She held Isobel's hand and looked up at her. 'Is this definitely it then? Definitely engaged?'

'Yes,' said Isobel, a deeply satisfied smile breaking out on her face. 'He said that the last six months had been the most miserable of his life and that he couldn't bear the thought of being without me.'

'So, he really is a romantic then,' said Kate. She seemed to remember Giles coming out with something similar on the bridge, but for all his many qualities, he had a chronic irony deficiency. Most men who claimed they couldn't bear the thought of being without their girlfriends didn't generally get on the next plane back to the other side of the world.

Isobel took her hand back to admire the diamond. 'Well, he probably means that he's sick of washing his own socks and has run out of mates to bunk up with, but it'll do. I know things aren't going to get better than Will, and you know . . .' She shrugged. 'We've an awful lot of kitchenware to argue over if we did call it a day.'

'So what happened to Young, Free, and Single Isobel?'

Kate probed her tingling conscience and realised she was experiencing slight resentment that Isobel wasn't following the script: just as she herself had begun to entertain the possibility, as recommended by Isobel, of having some fun while Giles was scaling the dizzy heights of work experience, here was Isobel now turning Laura on her.

Well, Kate corrected herself, not so much *seriously* entertaining thoughts of finishing it with Giles. Just, sort of, inviting them over for coffee. If they were in the area.

'Ah, well, that,' laughed Isobel, in what Kate narkily thought was a *very* Laura-ish manner, 'it got it all out of my system, you know? All my doubts about what I'd be giving up. It was a lot of fun and all in a good cause. But now I know what I want.'

Kate wondered what Will had been up to in *his* time off, and how much charity Isobel would be willing to offer that good cause, should it turn up heartbroken on their doorstep in the next few weeks.

'You should try it,' Isobel added as an afterthought, but just as Kate's conscience seized gratefully on the words said, 'But then, what with Giles being in America and all, maybe it's better to wait until he comes back to have the big row in person. Else it would just be cheating on him, wouldn't it?'

'But I don't want to have a big row! Giles and I don't *have* rows,' protested Kate. 'I just want—'

'Then what's the problem?' smiled Isobel.

Before Kate could wade any further into the murky waters of what she did want, Martin the receptionist buzzed her extension.

'Hello?' said Kate, glaring at Isobel, who was looking irksomely joyful, veiling her head in Kate's white silk devoré scarf, her bridesmaid's present from Mike and Laura's wedding, and the only grown-up accessory she owned.

'Kate, there's a man here in Reception for Elaine.' Martin sounded stressed. 'He says he has a package and he won't give it to anyone but her. He's rather . . . over-excited?'

'Oh,' said Kate, confused. She could hear someone talking stridently in the background. 'Elaine's gone for lunch, but I'll be right along.'

'Who was that?' asked Isobel beadily when she put the phone down.

'Someone in Reception for Elaine.' Kate slipped her shoes back on underneath her desk.

'Well, just remember to find out who they are,' said Isobel. 'Check the name badge security makes them wear if they won't tell you.'

Eclipse's reception area was small, with several large chairs and a wide variety of Eclipse reading matter to occupy waiting visitors. The thin, well-dressed man standing by the desk haranguing Martin was not availing himself of either. Martin, wearing his telephone headpiece and still attempting to operate the switchboard while the man ranted on, looked like a harrassed pilot being assaulted by a mad runaway passenger.

'It's just not good enough, when all the little men come at once,' the man was saying, jabbing his finger at the manuscript on the front desk. 'I just can't cope! I just. Can't. Cope.'

Martin saw Kate and threw up his hands up in despair.

She took a deep breath and stepped forward. 'Hello, can I help you?'

The man swivelled round and stared at her. Kate shrank back instinctively from his unnaturally shining eyes and sudden flash of halitosis.

'Maybe, maybe not. Where's Elaine?'

'She's having a lunch meeting.'

The man started cracking his knuckles and muttered to himself. Kate strained to catch what he was saying but it was too rapid and generally mad-sounding. One of the publicists from the non-fiction department walked in with a couple of footballers, saw the racket going on and virtually ran them through to the lifts.

Martin was now answering calls as though nothing at all was happening and Kate realised that she was on her own.

'Um, I'm Kate, Elaine's assistant.' She offered her hand, he looked at it and she quickly withdrew it. 'Perhaps I can help you?' Rule number one of dealing with authors, Isobel had told her, was never admit you don't know who they are. Just waffle in a friendly manner until they give themselves away. Kate had spoken to most of Elaine's authors, and this one wasn't ringing any bells. Loonies she generally remembered.

He was in his mid-forties, she reckoned, maybe younger. It was hard to tell when he was so deranged-looking. His navy suit was rather smart though. Was he one of her City thriller writers?

'I *have* to speak to Elaine, or Jennifer.'

'Well, I'm afraid they're both out at lunch, but I'm sure I can sort out whatever it is you need,' said Kate, more confidently than she felt. A surprising number of unpublished authors phoned up claiming to be Jennifer's best friend from school and could they speak to her about a manuscript she would love . . .?

The man clicked his teeth in a scary Hannibal Lecter way. 'It's all there,' he said, pointing at the desk. 'All there, every last piece of it. All there. All there.'

'*Riiight*,' said Kate, moving slowly towards the desk, keeping her eye on him the whole time.

'Tell Elaine I want to speak to her as soon as she comes back.' He flipped a lank chunk of dark hair out of his eyes. 'As soon as she comes back. And I want to see Jennifer. I will call Jennifer. I will communicate with Jennifer. You understand that?'

'Yeees,' said Kate, wondering if she should call the police. Her hand connected with the manuscript on the desk. The man let out a series of strange clicking noises and walked to the security door. Kate was relieved to see that at least he walked like a normal human being. Martin, apparently deep in a phone call, buzzed the door to let him out, but not before the man had banged it with the flat of his hands like a condemned man, a couple of times.

Martin and Kate watched him leave, mesmerised.

'What a steaming weirdo,' breathed Martin.

'Absolutely,' agreed Kate. 'Who the hell *was* he?' And they looked down at the manuscript in case he had written a covering letter to explain. Or in case it was ticking.

Written in large black letters on the front of the script were the words, '*Cobblestone Tinkers*, by Rose Ann Barton'.

'No!' said Martin.

'Don't tell a soul,' said Kate as several things fell into place in her head, then, as her brain worked on a bit further, she added, in a tone of wonderment, 'Shit.'

While it was obviously a matter of top security that no one should know that the apple-cheeked saviour of Eclipse was in fact a man on the verge of a nervous breakdown, Kate didn't for a moment hesitate to tell Isobel.

Isobel gave her Jennifer's secret mobile phone number.

'I can't believe you're not on full outside broadcast mode!' said Kate as she dialled the number which would ruin Jennifer's nice lunch at the Caprice.

'Some information is too precious to pass on,' replied Isobel mysteriously, and tweaked the mammoth array of red carnations on her filing cabinet.

Half an hour later, Elaine was locked in the boardroom with the manuscript, Kate was sitting on the uncomfortable chair in Jennifer's office and Jennifer was wearing the grim expression of someone about to cut a deal for ownership of their grandma.

'You realise the immense importance of this, don't you, Kate?'

Kate smiled nervously. If Jennifer had not been looking quite so fierce, she might have tried a bit of maneouvring at this point, perhaps see if her new-found knowledge might not have some effect on her salary, but frankly Jennifer was scaring her in a whole new way.

'It means that we can all get started on Rose Ann's manuscript, now it's finally been delivered,' Kate said, as if she had known all along that Rose Ann was not the twinkly-eyed granny she appeared on her publicity material.

'Quite,' said Jennifer. Kate didn't think she had blinked once so far in the course of their tense interview.

'Of course, you may be jumping entirely to the wrong assumptions, you realise, Kate,' she went on. 'As you know, Rose Ann has four grown-up sons, all of whom work for her in some capacity. Who's to say that it wasn't Albert, Arthur, Alfred or Ernest dropping their mother's script in?'

Kate knew this was a hopeless throw in the dark, and she knew Jennifer knew she knew. By extrapolation, she also knew now that Albert, Arthur, Alfred and Ernest, all allegedly named after dark-eyed, high-spirited, tender-hearted, best-selling heroes created by their mother, were as fictional as their apparent namesakes.

Their eyes met and Kate could see a measure of panic in Jennifer's face. If this got out, Eclipse would be a laughing-stock. It was all useful information. But what Kate wanted to know now was, if the real Rose Ann was Norman Bates by any another name, who was the twinkly-eyed granny who turned up at hospital readings and supermarket signings all over the country?

'Jennifer,' said Kate, in her most charming voice, 'I think you can trust me to—'

Just then the door of Jennifer's office burst open and Elaine let herself in, shutting it tightly behind her. She didn't see Kate.

'God, Jennifer, he's really lost it this time! I knew we shouldn't have added the extra book to the schedule. There are talking donkeys, and the heroine is called David, and—'

Elaine registered Jennifer's poker face and followed her gaze down to where Kate was perched on the uncomfortable chair.

'Oh, God.' She wilted in the style of an Edvard Munch painting.

'Oh, come on,' said Kate. 'I'm not stupid, I can keep things confidential. There are all sorts of things I haven't . . .' She trailed off, realising that it probably wasn't a good idea to draw attention to various disasters Jennifer wasn't already aware of.

'It is of paramount importance that no one knows about this,' intoned Jennifer, her voice more imperious than ever. 'Not even the publicity department know Rose Ann's . . . real identity.'

'*Especially* not the publicity department,' muttered Elaine, picking at her fingernails with her teeth.

'You will have to remain completely, completely confidential about this matter,' said Jennifer, 'otherwise I will have no alternative but to terminate your employment with Eclipse.'

Kate blanched.

'And needless to say,' finished Jennifer, 'it would be for reasons which would prevent you from working in fiction publishing again. Are we clear about this?'

'Yes,' said Kate, unsure what else she could say.

'Excellent.' Jennifer gave her a wolfish smile. 'Because you really are coming along so well, and we'd hate to lose you, wouldn't we, Elaine?'

Elaine mumbled something into her cuticles, then looked up. 'Oh, God, left the door of the boardroom open!' She bolted out as quickly as she had come in, leaving a faint aroma of fresh sweat and lavender oil.

'Can I ask one question, please?' asked Kate. 'Because I'm amazed you've been so thorough in keeping it all quiet.'

Jennifer inclined her head.

'Who is it that goes round being Rose Ann? How do they know so much about the—'

'There's such a thing as too much information, Kate,' snapped Jennifer, rising to her feet. 'You'll need to spend the rest of the afternoon in the boardroom with Elaine, taking notes as she goes through the script. Tell Isobel she'll have to divert your phone to her extension.'

Kate scrambled to her feet. 'Um, fine, I'll get my notepad.'

'And Kate?'

Does Jennifer get *all* her management techniques from bad 1980s legal thrillers? Kate wondered. She nodded, resisting the temptation to reply, 'Yes, Jennifer?'

'Not a word to anyone. And that includes Isobel.'

'But of course,' said Kate, lying through her teeth.

'What did we decide the main heroine was called?' asked Elaine, tetchily.

Kate flipped back through her notes. 'On average? Marlene.' There were pages and pages of scribbled queries and so far they had only covered eight chapters. The heroine hadn't even got pregnant yet, which was a record for Rose Ann, who generally delivered at least one bastard per chapter, either of the fatherless baby variety, or the flashing-eyed seducer variety. Usually one led to another.

Elaine looked up from between the hands that supported her throbbing head. 'Do we think that's an OK name for a nineteenth-century chambermaid and part-time medium?'

They considered.

'Is she German?'

'No, she's from Wakefield.'

Kate pulled out one of the Post-It notes she had left to remind her of this very problem. 'Um, Elaine, if this is the chambermaid I'm thinking of, she was called Fionnuala when she left the poorhouse.'

Elaine dropped three pipette-fuls of Rescue Remedy on her tongue, picked up her pencil again and wrote, '"Thank God I changed my name after I left the poorhouse so Roderick would never find me here," gasped . . .' She paused and looked up at Kate for help.

'Fionnuala?' supplied Kate. 'Or would she think of herself as Marlene now?'

'Gasped the distressed young girl,' wrote Elaine, crossing out three lines of Rose Ann's manuscript. She put down her pencil and sighed deeply.

In the distance a phone rang in the empty office. Kate looked at her watch. It was ten past six. Ten past six! That was probably Harry phoning to say he was outside. How time flew when you were having fun.

'Oh, shit, er, sorry, Elaine, but I have a . . . dental appointment at six-thirty in Olympia, so can I . . .?'

Elaine's eyes narrowed, but it might have been with profound weariness as much as suspicion. 'You really do suffer with your teeth, don't you?'

Over the past four months, Kate had pleaded a scale and polish (girlie night out with Cress in Clerkenwell to 'cheer her up'), a dodgy filling (James Bond marathon night at the NFT with Harry, Dant, Seth and the slavering Tosca, who 'was rather keen on her', according to Harry) and a random examination (self-indulgent post-New Year night of nostalgic misery alone with bottle of wine and *Top Gun* video while the boys went out with two Riverdance hopefuls).

'It's not as though I *want* to go,' said Kate, unconvincingly. And she wasn't sure she *did* want to go out for dinner with Cress and Harry together, never mind Dant into the bargain. Small things she hadn't even noticed in the past were beginning to irritate her beyond reason, and she could hardly point out to Harry that she hated the way he held doors open for the oblivious Cress, when it now gave her an illicit thrill when he held doors open for *her*.

'Well, if you have to go, you have to go,' said Elaine, making an equally unconvincing show of putting down her pencil reluctantly and piling up the paper as if she had been keen to carry on all night. 'I'll need those notes typed up by the time we start again tomorrow though, so you'll have to come in a bit early. We have to have this at the copy editor's by the end of the week. Or Jennifer will kill us both.'

'Mmm,' said Kate, thinking what a good excuse that typing would be, not only to get out of dinner, but also to 'borrow' Harry's computer.

She gave Elaine a four-minute head start, while she listened to the message Harry had left on her answering machine at six.

He'll be long gone, she thought, looking out of the big automatic doors at the mist of rain in the air. It looked like fine hairspray. She pulled her scarf over her hair against the drizzle, and ran out of the building. No matter what she did to straighten her hair, this weather always turned her into a ginger poodle in the space of five minutes.

She slung the bag of manuscripts over her shoulder, like a hod carrier in the World's Strongest Man competition, and staggered a little under the weight. It dawned on her that Harry hadn't told her where Cress had booked the table for dinner, but before she could seize on the relief this thought suddenly offered, in the shape of going home and forgetting all about it, she heard the loud honk of a car horn. Harry's blue Rover was parked right outside, streams of rain running off the highly polished panels like puddles of mercury.

'You waited for me!' she exclaimed, pulling open the door and sliding into the passenger seat with her bag. He was listening to Oasis, but Kate politely resisted her instinct to turn the music off.

'Well, you know . . .' demurred Harry shyly.

'And you've been home and got changed!' she added. It would be hard not to notice the fresh T-shirt under his best V-neck jumper, the newly shaved chin and the fresh aroma of recently washed hair.

'Er, yes.' Harry blushed and started the engine. 'I wanted a bit of moral support, you know. Haven't seen Cress since before Christmas. Can't help feeling a bit . . . you know . . .'

Kate felt a small knife of jealousy twist in her stomach. It's all right, she reassured herself, it's just a normal panic reaction to Giles leaving, it won't last long, and the less you let it show the easier it'll be to forget all about it when the red mist lifts. Just be grateful it's not Dant.

Unable to bear any more Mancunian retro-whining, she ejected '(What's the Story) Morning Glory' from the cassette player and switched on the radio, tuning it to the first station she found playing chart music.

'Bad day in the office?'

'Yes, appalling. Rose Ann has delivered and it's my job to remember what all the talking donkeys are called.'

'Ah.' Harry stole a quick look across at her before the traffic moved on, but Kate was applying more powder to her face in an attempt to repair her minimal make-up. Looking good next to Cress was hard enough at the best of times, and near impossible when all she had in her bag was face powder and the red lippie Giles had given her for Christmas. She rubbed it on to her lips to stain them crimson. Trying to apply it properly while moving in the London rush hour was just asking for results more Coco the Clown than Coco Chanel.

'Where's Cress booked?' She smacked her lips together to even out the colour. The intense red stain looked quite good against her bare face.

'Some Italian place near the bar. Dant's already there.'

'Why does she want to see us for supper?'

'I don't know,' said Harry, suddenly going thoughtful. 'I had kind of thought she wanted to see us, you know, because she enjoyed our company, but now you mention it . . .'

'I'm sure she wants to see us,' said Kate, seeing his face fall. She added recklessly, 'Maybe Dant and I are just cover so she can see you.'

That wasn't fair, she thought, as the enthusiasm rushed back into his face. Some warped instinct in her had said it partly to make him happy, but partly so he would disagree with her – but of course it was exactly what he wanted to hear.

This is all too complicated for you to keep up with, and you don't have a clue what you're doing, her conscience pointed out, rapping hard on the inside of her head.

Mmm, agreed Kate.

'So I said, if you want to do *that* in *this* bar, Liam, you'll just have to make arrangements of your own!' finished Cress triumphantly. She banged her empty glass down on the table and dribbled the last of the wine in. 'Get some more wine, will you, Dante, lover?'

'I'll go,' said Harry, leaping up immediately and grabbing his wallet out of his jacket.

Kate watched his retreating back and sneaked a look at the enormous clock projected on to the far wall of the restaurant. Ten o'clock.

They had been there three hours and four bottles of wine and were still waiting for someone to make polite enquiries about pudding. Kate had caught a glimpse of someone else's meringue extravaganza being toted across the busy floor and was angling to get Harry to order it so she could tuck in without looking like a pig in front of Cress, who would dismiss the whole idea of further food with a wave of her cigarette and her usual expression of horror.

'You have to fancy Liam Gallagher, don't you, Kate?' said Cress. She tucked her newly cropped black hair behind her ears. The cap of dark hair emphasised her sharp cheekbones and made her skin look like porcelain in comparison. Kate felt a pang of envy for Cress's dramatic beauty. 'I think he's just about irresistible. He's got those fantastic dark eyes, and incredible hair . . .'

'And those amazing eyebrows that meet in the middle,' added Dant, sarcastically.

Cress ignored him. '. . . and that sulky smile. I love men like that. A bit dangerous. No, it has to be a dark-haired man every time,' she said, stubbing out her cigarette on a side plate. 'Blonds just don't do it for me. Too milky.'

Dant made some dismissive noise and elbowed his way through the frantically gesticulating throng by the loos to get more cigarettes from the machine.

'No, I have to disagree there,' said Kate, thinking of Giles's piercing blue eyes and golden stubble. And Harry's teddy bear good looks. 'And if you'd lived in the north of England you wouldn't find Liam Gallagher such a novelty, believe me. Most men up there look like that and half of them are in bands. The other half are on remand. Anyway, don't let Harry hear you say that about blond men,' she added as he returned from the bar with a fresh bottle of red wine and an over-piled dish of cashew nuts. She thought he looked more schoolboyish than ever, weaving his way apologetically through the tables of picture editors and designers.

'Oh, Harry,' said Cress, flashing Kate a confiding smile.

Kate blinked and her eyes went back to the tall blond figure coming towards them. She felt strangely guilty and strangely protective all at once.

'There you go, ladies.' Harry put the bottle and saucer on the table in front of them.

'Thanks, sweetheart,' said Cress, squeezing Harry's knee as he refilled their glasses before his own.

'No problem.' Kate watched the flush of pleasure creep up his face and felt a matching flush of confusion begin on hers. She violently wanted to go home. There was a reason why this type of embarrassing crush usually happened to teenage girls in the privacy of their own rooms with a huge pile of poster mags. She should know. The last time she'd gone through this it had been on behalf of Tom Cruise (Mark I). Much better to sit on your own in a locked bathroom and get it out of your system in a series of increasingly baroque fantasies than to try to cope with the embarrassing side-effects in real life.

'You're very bubbly tonight, Cress,' said Harry through a mouthful of nuts. 'Any reason?'

He looks so hopeful, thought Kate mournfully. God, it's like watching visiting time at Battersea Dogs' Home.

'Oooh, nothing in particular,' replied Cress, darting her eyes around the room.

If you hadn't visited the bathroom four times already this evening I might believe that, thought Kate. Only some kind of infection would explain it otherwise, and no one with cystitis could possibly look so cheerful.

Cress drummed her empty cigarette packet against the table. The noise in the restaurant was steadily increasing – or Kate's headache was getting worse. 'I haven't actually been to bed for about three days,' she explained. Harry's eyes widened in admiration. 'So many of my friends went away for New Year that they're all having their New Year parties now and it's just one thing after another.'

'You told me you'd barely been out,' said Dant, throwing a packet of Camel Lights across the table to Cressida. 'Your mate Khadija even called the flat one night trying to find you.'

'Oh, yeah, Khadija,' said Cress, sipping her wine. 'She found me in the end. *There's no big mystery*,' she added, widening her eyes at Dant, who was giving her the full benefit of his disbelieving look.

'Yeah, right,' said Dant, 'anyone would think that you were trying to hide something, or should I say some—'

'Can we get the waiter over here for some coffees?' asked Kate hurriedly, seeing Harry's eyebrows knit in hurt. Sometimes when Dant and Cress locked horns like this it was as though everyone else ceased to exist for them. Normal embarrassment levels didn't even register.

They continued glaring at each other over the table. Seeing Cress through Harry's eyes for once, Kate could understand the attraction: she and Dant together were like two androgynous Rossetti models, all black eyes and black hair and evidently black tempers, too bright for their mortal background.

'Absolutely. Great idea,' said Harry, twisting in his chair to look for a waitress. Kate turned too to avoid the savage mutterings going on across the table.

All the waitresses in this particular restaurant were still doing the heroin-chic look, and were accessorising it with real-life glazed expressions. It took ten minutes of furious eye-catching before one ambled over.

'Yerp?' she said, fishing in her trouser-skirt pocket for her order pad.

Hearing the word again reminded Kate that Harry no longer said 'Yerp' as much as he used to. Maybe it was just that, next to Jennifer Spencer, he sounded like a pupil from *Grange Hill*.

'I'll have a double espresso . . .' she said, trying to pretend to her whining brain that she'd already had the meringue.

'And so will I,' said Harry. He turned back to Cress and Dant. 'Coffee?'

'. . . think I won't find out because I will . . .' Dant was hissing to Cress, who was hissing, '. . . my own life now and if I want to see Mom I'll fucking do what . . .' over the top of him.

'*Do* you want *coffee?*' asked Kate in a louder, crosser voice. There was only so much she could take of places like this. The pretension irritated her at the best of times. It was one thing people talking in braying yells to make sure everyone else heard their second-hand *bons mots*, but when you had to yell to make yourself heard over them, they talked even louder and the end result was extremely wearing.

Dant and Cress broke off their snarling. 'Yes, please, two double espressos,' said Dant. He shot a contemptuous glare at his sister. 'Four sugars in hers, please. She's feeling a little tart this evening.'

'You wish,' snapped Cress. 'Ignore him,' she said to the waitress who was casting anxious glances all round the room for some back-up help. 'Doesn't normally come out with adults.'

'So four double espressos and can we have the bill too, please?' asked Kate, guessing that it would arrive some time after midnight if left to evolve by itself. She'd had about four glasses of the small lake of wine they'd consumed, knowing she had to sort out Elaine's notes, either later that night, or far too early the next morning, and much as a stiff drink would probably help things along, she didn't want one. Consequently she had reached the self-righteous stage of comparative sobriety, and an uncomfortable mood seemed to have settled over their table after the much wittier banter that had accompanied the North London cuisine mains.

'Did you have a good Christmas with Giles, Kate?' asked Cress.

Kate had the feeling she was being used as a conversational detour and couldn't reply with any enthusiasm. With Dant in the mood he seemed to be in, there was every chance he could provide an action replay of the docusoap horror, with added drama. 'Yes, very,' she said, forcing a smile. 'Have I not seen you since then?'

'I've been *extremely* busy running the bar over the holidays,' said Cress, looking challengingly at Dant, before Kate could retract the perceived criticism.

Harry shuffled in his seat. The coffees arrived, surprisingly quickly.

'I'm sure you have,' said Kate. 'No, I had a lovely time with him. We stayed in London and, you know . . .' She trailed off, realising that Cress wasn't listening to her.

After a few seconds of her silence, Cress's eyes slid back from Dant to her. 'I'm sorry, Kate, I'm just . . . Why don't we have lunch next week and catch up properly? When can you do?' She pulled out her diary. 'Next Monday? I'm flying out to Val d'Isere on Wednesday. Big secret, don't tell anyone.'

'Er,' Kate juggled potential office disasters in her head.

'I've got a bit of a crisis on at the moment, which should be over by the end of the week, and a lot of reading to do at home, but . . . Tuesday?'

'Fine.' Cress scribbled in her diary. 'Early, then I can make a yoga class at two. Really need to keep flexible.'

Harry made a small noise in the back of his throat as he sipped his espresso.

'Excellent.' Cress clicked the clasp on her tiny handbag. 'What sort of reading?'

'Oh, you know, manuscripts.' Kate rolled her eyes. 'Thrillers, sagas, detective dachshunds. Probably total rubbish, otherwise someone else would have them. Five to get through this week.'

'Sounds fantastic.' Cress ran a hand through her new spikes then smoothed them down again. 'Wish I had a job that was sitting around reading all day.'

'Mmm,' said Kate, wondering exactly how much further from the truth that description of Eclipse could be. She picked up the tiny but heavy cup full of thick black coffee, and shutting her eyes, tipped it all into her mouth at once. It ran through her tastebuds like an electric shock, and as always, she nearly grimaced at the mini explosion on her tongue. She had never been able to drink espressos before she moved to London, but now they felt like kisses.

When she opened her eyes, she saw that Dant, Harry and Cress were all looking at her. She dropped her gaze to the table to avoid meeting theirs and her eye fell on the bill in front of her. She grimaced. 'How are we splitting this?'

Though Kate had forgone a starter in the hope of getting a pudding, and Cress had just had a small sushi plate, Dant and Harry had both had the massive seared lamb and chips special as well as three starters between them, and, with all the wine, they had hiked up the bill to something approaching Kate's weekly wage.

'Because I really didn't have that much.' She usually protested like something from *Crown Court* when it came to splitting the pizza delivery bill, but with Cress there, she didn't want to harm what little reputation she had.

'Oh, don't worry, it's on me,' said Cress unexpectedly, throwing her Visa card on to the saucer.

'Hello?' said Dant at the same time as Harry fumbled in his jacket and said, 'No, really, let me.'

Cress lit another cigarette and waved her hand. 'Forget it. I picked the restaurant, only fair I should pay.'

The waitress, suddenly animated, swooped out of nowhere and took away the saucer.

'Skiing, meals out, new clothes . . . Come into money, have we?' said Dant. 'Or should that be "come into Mummy"?'

'It's what happens when you have a job,' sniped back Cress. 'You get this funny thing called a salary slip. It lets you buy things with *cash*.'

'That's very kind of you. Thanks, Cress,' said Kate, awkwardly. 'Why don't we leave the tip for the waitress?' This kind of casual largesse made her feel more of an interloper than ever. It just wasn't a circle she could feel comfortable in – or even part of. She scrabbled in her purse for some pound coins. The tip alone would come to more than the cost of her food.

'Great idea!' said Harry. He dug a hand into his pocket and came up with the usual fistful of change.

Between them they left about fifteen pounds on the table, which was removed as quickly as the credit card slip. 'And can we have another bottle of wine?' Cress asked the waitress, as she took the two empty bottles away.

Kate could see the others were settling in for the night, which only increased her own weariness. 'I think I'll head off, actually,' she said. 'I've got an early start.' It was too late now to borrow Harry's computer to type up the notes, and the alternative was getting into the office before Elaine. Which wasn't that hard, come to think of it. Still . . .

'Oh, do you really have to go?' wheedled Cress, unconvincingly.

'Can't you stay another ten minutes?' said Harry. He gave her a B-grade Labrador look. 'I'll run you home?'

'I don't think you'll be running anyone anywhere, the amount you've had to drink,' said Kate, shrugging on her big winter coat.

'But you can't go home on your own,' said Cress. 'Dant, why don't you take Kate back?'

Harry's eyes flashed with delight at the thought of being alone with Cress, and Kate felt the coffee curdling the risotto in her stomach.

'Sorry, I can't possibly leave my friend here to get drunk on his own with the likes of you,' drawled Dant.

'Why not?' demanded Harry, turning to him.

'Little boy, one day you will thank me . . .'

'Shut up, the lot of you,' said Kate. 'Why should I need anyone to take me home? I'm not a sugar mouse.' The fact that she now desperately wanted Harry to pull on his fleece and take her back on the bus was beside the point. And since she was leaving with her martyr's hat on, all of a sudden she badly wanted to stay.

'Well, be careful, won't you?' said Harry.

'Don't talk to strange men on the Tube.' Cress giggled.

'Isn't that where you get your best dates?' Dant flicked a sharp sideways look at her.

The giggle evaporated from her face and they glared at each other.

'Phone me on my mobile when you get in, so we know you got back safely,' said Harry, seriously. 'OK?'

'OK.' Kate pulled her scarf round her head and slipped her bag over her shoulder. 'See you all later. See you on Tuesday, Cress?'

'Bye,' they chorused and resumed their bickering.

Kate pushed her way through the crowds of trendy people, all wearing clothes she didn't understand and plastic-framed spectacles they didn't need. Outside the air was cold but clear and she saw to her relief that the bar was right opposite an Underground station. She'd had just too much wine to feel safe about getting the right bus, and still didn't trust them to stop in the right place.

All the way back, rocking back and forth in the nearly empty carriage, Kate wondered what they were arguing about now, whether they were talking about her, how Harry was looking at Cress. Harry would have to leave his car there and get a taxi home; would he get a taxi with Cress? Would he take her home – and stay? She looked at her reflection in the carriage window and pulled a face at herself.

Once she was back in the flat, which was freezing cold, the last dregs of her energy seeped away, and she just remembered to set her alarm clock an hour earlier before she got into bed. The duvet was cold and she lay as still as possible to conserve her body heat, running through all she had to do the next day. While she was floating off into slumbering unconsciousness, she felt Ratcat leap on the foot of her bed for the first time, and remembered too late that she had left all her manuscripts in the back of Harry's car.

chapter twenty-seven

The credits for *EastEnders* blared out too loud from the tele-vision, and since no one was watching it, Kate grabbed the remote control from the coffee table and irritably flicked off the set. It had been annoying her for the past half hour, but she'd done nothing about it on principle. At one point, the radio in the kitchen, the television, the sitting room hi-fi and the CD player in Harry's room had all been on at once. The lads couldn't seem to exist without a background of white noise.

'Oooh, touchy.'

'Are you going out?' said Kate, barely lifting her eyes from page 251 of *Bitch Rota: A Novel of Shame and Pride*.

'Like that,' said Dant.

Kate looked up. Dant and Harry were both fiddling with their hair in the mirror over the fireplace. She noted that Harry was wearing a new pair of trousers and Dant's cash-mere jumper, which gave him an almost grown-up appearance. Dant was wearing a deep green velvet jacket which gave him the appearance of a complete rake.

'Sorry?' she said.

'Are you going out like that. It's what you're meant to say to us in your role as stand-in Mum.'

Kate picked up her pages again in a pathetic show of indifference. 'I'm not your mum and I don't care where you're going. If I *were* your mother I would no doubt be handing you a brown envelope of drugs and checking you were off somewhere appropriately sordid. As I'm just me, I don't mind where you're going since it gives me a chance to get through some quality fiction without Lara Croft grunting away orgasmically in the background.'

She hoped this didn't sound like protesting too much.

'Suit yourself.'

'It's just one long social round with you lot, isn't it?' said Kate, pretending to read the pages she was flipping through at the rate of five per minute. 'Party after party after party. Are you off out to another of Cress's strange gallery views? Or is someone opening a club in the back of a Transit van in Hoxton Square?'

'Actually, we're going out on a date. So stop sneering.'

She looked up. 'What? You've found *the* two most indiscriminate women in London? Never.'

Much as she regretted to admit it, Kate's cunning plan to set up Dant with some dreadful women had backfired on her. She had told Dant that she had placed his horrible car-molesting personal ad *and* hers, so they could judge for themselves which one got the most replies (and, conveniently enough, so he wouldn't get confused when pretending to be Harry on the phone and arouse suspicion in those applying as would-be Cathys). He had then sorted out the necessary paperwork and sat back and waited for the letters and photos to flood in to their box numbers.

And they had flooded in. Up to ten a day. In the end – and faced with piles of romantic witterings about moors and storm-filled nights, which even Dant couldn't relate back to *Riverdance* – she had to tell him what she'd done, expecting a tirade of ranting and hair-tossing. To her surprise, Dant had taken it remarkably well. In fact, in the final count, he ended up with two candidates to every one of Harry's and even after 'vetting out all the mooses' had been operating a two-dates-per-week system to work his way through the backlog. He could have done more, but, typically, couldn't be bothered.

Remarkably, Harry still thought his dates were girls who'd got his number at a party.

Blind Date Night had become something of a weekly fixture, to Kate's creeping distress and resentment. It hadn't dawned on her until now how much she had grown used to being one of the lads – Dant and Harry assumed in a brotherly way that she was included in bowling or drinking with Seth and the Fake Stags – and her one attempt to follow their date night at a safe distance, to observe them in action, had just made her so miserable that she'd sneaked away after half a pint in the far corner, and gone home to snivel over her albums full of pictures of Giles. Cress, naturally, had required all the details and Kate had provided them, but with her own loneliness edited out under a gloss of ironic disdain.

'Have you got any, what do you call it? Hair wax?' asked Harry, tugging at a particularly wayward chunk of blond hair.

Kate put *Bitch Rota* down heavily on the sofa. 'What is this? Vidal Sassoon?'

'She's got some in the bathroom,' said Dant, helpfully. 'But it's nearly finished.'

'Cheers, matey,' said Harry, disappearing into the bathroom.

Kate snorted. It was some balm to her stinging heart that Harry wasn't throwing himself into this with the same predatory zeal as Dant. As far as he was concerned, he'd confided to her on the way to work, he was helping Dant out in a double-date situation, and was perfectly prepared to be charming to the jolly hockeysticks gels who seemed strange friends for the often rubber-clad vixens who usually wanted to talk to Dant about outdoor sex. He still spent at least half of the weekly trudge around Sainsbury's pushing Kate's trolley for her but talking about Cress. It was beginning to disturb Kate how much she enjoyed the masochistic twinges this provoked.

'It's not working,' Dant murmured at Kate. 'He keeps asking them if they've thought of dying their hair black. It's like *Vertigo* in reverse.'

Kate raised her hands. 'I don't want to know what you get up to. Really, really, really.'

'You won't be lonely on your own?' asked Harry, coming back in from the bathroom, smelling of almond oil and running his hands through his now much flatter hair. 'You could come with—'

'I *don't* think so,' said Kate, staring at her manuscript, 'and anyway I'm busy. Just go on out and don't make a racket when you get in.'

'See ya later,' said Dant, striding into the hall. 'I feel pretty, oh so pretty . . .' His voice trailed down the stairs.

'Laters,' said Harry. He smiled sadly.

'Go away and bring me back some chocolate if you're passing a garage,' said Kate. She wouldn't let herself look up from the page until the front door slammed downstairs.

Once she had heard the double lock crash safely into place, she put down the manuscript and wandered over to the window. Kneeling on the seat, she watched Harry and Dant lope down the road to the Tube station, pushing and shoving each other on and off the pavement. Her heart twanged (there was no other word for it) at the sight of Harry's blond head bobbing as he strode along. It was a delicious feeling of illicitness, like eating stolen sweets as quickly as possible, or drinking in the park at lunch-time. She knew it was wrong, but she also knew by the intensity of what she felt that it could only be a transitory thing. A crush made all the more intoxicating by its secretive lushness.

Kate sighed and slid down the wall to the floor. She leaned her head back against the warm radiator. It was impossible to pinpoint when she had begun to feel like this about Harry, but it had overwhelmed her like a cloud of gas.

In the midst of all her swirling hormones there was a lone voice of calm which told her that the only way to deal with something so potentially embarrassing was to ride it out in silence rather than try to fight it away. It was just a stage nearer reality than Ronan Keating.

But she wasn't going to torment herself over what Dant and Harry might be up to *again* tonight. She pushed herself up off the wall and went purposefully back to the submission she'd been reading.

It had taken four days in the end for her and Elaine to plough through the whole of Rose Ann's manuscript, and Elaine had spent a further week in virtual sentence-by-sentence contact as the copy editor 'tidied it up'. It would have been cheaper for her to have flown the copy editor down to London and holed up in The Ritz with a crate of Krug to steady the nerves. Elaine's near-hysterics in the meeting Kate had minuted right at the beginning of her Eclipse career (which was beginning to seem an awful long way away) made much more sense now.

Since the manuscript had arrived, Kate had been staying at work until eight most nights, despite Isobel's increasing concern. Even after they'd got rid of the bloody (lit.) thing, so much had been suspended pending Rose Ann's delivery (Kate still couldn't equate the name with the stubbly reality) that she had mountains of reader letters, advance copies of books and the like to work through – and that was just the stuff Elaine knew about. All the manuscripts she'd been given to read had fallen by the wayside, and now Elaine's vitamin fog was clearing, she was becoming more aware of Kate's furious activity – and what it might mean in terms of overdue spadework.

Since the boys were going to be out all night, Kate had resolved to get through *Bitch Rota* and start the twenty-something thriller from Phil Hill, before Elaine started asking difficult questions about the plot.

She settled herself along the length of the sofa, with the

phone and a mug of coffee beside her, and concentrated on the manuscript in front of her, trying to construct a convincing argument for buying it, or rejecting it. So far, *Bitch Rota*, a biting satire on the internal politics of a Victorian bordello in San Francisco (or perhaps not), had been morbidly fascinating for many reasons – none of them, sadly, ones she could bring up in an editorial meeting while keeping a straight face. The lurid descriptions of 'ro-mance' aside, Kate had become particularly absorbed in the hierarchical details of the lace-trimmed corsetry worn by the staff, and the seemingly endless variations on the farmyard-animal-based insults thrown around by all and sundry.

Unfortunately, that wasn't going to cut any ice in the meeting, she thought, flipping to the end in case May-Jo-Beth's dramatic appearance in the dock did affect her rich lover's combined divorce proceedings and murder trial. It didn't.

Right, that's your lot, thought Kate, bundling it all back together again. It was a shame, since she had grown fond, in a fairly disinterested way, of May-Jo-Beth's endlessly wide-eyed pronouncements and her frothy lace pants. But it was already ten to nine and she suspected that the Phil Hill submission wouldn't be so easy to dismiss. Given Elaine's 'discussions' with Phil just to see it before the rest of the publishers, she would have to read it all the way through in order to brief her on the plot. Elaine's own spadework was more like a gentle hoeing.

Kate looked longingly at the remote control and tried to pretend that if she switched on the television she would just watch the news and then turn it off again. As luck would have it, next to the remote control was a pile of Lonely Hearts photos, which Dant and Harry had been arranging into rank order – and that was enough to make her turn with a martyred heart to the task in hand.

Learning from past mistakes, Kate had photocopied the covering letter as well as the text this time, so that she would have a vague idea of what she was meant to be reading. No horse narrators this time. Phil Hill's letter was the usual liberal scattering of unsupported superlatives: startling new talent . . . dark side of London (tell me about it, thought Kate) . . . vivid characters . . . fabulously promotable author . . . yadda, yadda, yadda. She pulled out the front page.

'Guilt Trap' by R. A. Harper.

Great, thought Kate. They obviously want to be either A. L. Kennedy or E. M. Forster. She put a book mark in at page 150 (to make herself read that far) and was relieved to see that the typeface was quite big, which explained the daunting chunkiness of the script. To her surprise, most of the sentences had verbs in. She settled herself in to the corner of the sofa, checking the time. No more coffee before twenty to ten.

There is little natural light left in the evening by the time Cameron reaches his front door. Less when he finds the porch lamp has been vandalised again.

Shit.

He kicks over the mess of broken glass angrily. A child's giggle, warped with alcohol, floats down from the flats above. It cuts through the sticky darkness of the London night.

He fumbles for his keys and wonders again what he could do to get rid of Ariel. It couldn't go on.

Fuck, no.

Ariel had to go.

Oh no, thought Kate. This might be better than I thought . . .

Kate heard the phone ringing in the kitchen and was amazed to find it was 10.30. She'd been reading solidly for well over an hour. Her eyes flickered between the kitchen and the manuscript and she decided in an instant that if it were important the caller would leave a message. She didn't want to stop reading.

Kate had reluctantly conceded around the third chapter that *Guilt Trap* was actually quite good. It was set in a London she didn't really know – a hard East End being flooded out by yuppie developers (of whom Cameron's flatmate David was a prime and extremely flaccid example). It was also written in a dark, terse style she found rather pretentious. But the central setting of the claustrophobic flat was so well done she was drawn in despite herself. The tensions about bathroom hygiene, the shorthand rows, the brooding and unexplained violence existing in every exchange drew a sharp and merciless picture of male communal living. The only thing missing, in Kate's opinion, were the discarded dirty socks that appeared like chunks of dog poo in every corner.

The intimacy between the two men, in particular, brought about by their enforced closeness in the small flat, made her think uneasily of her guilty desire for Harry – perhaps it *was* just nature taking over. After all, she hadn't seen Giles with his top off until they'd been going out for ten days, whereas she regularly saw Harry wandering around the flat in his Boden boxers.

The story, as far as she could work it out, was about Cameron's unexplained need to dispose of Ariel, and to sleep with David. Kate couldn't work out whether Ariel was a man or a woman, since they hadn't been introduced yet, and whether she might just be imagining the whole Cameron/David thing. But it was that kind of book, and this obliqueness didn't worry her unduly. She had come to accept that with literary fiction you generally had to supply your own plot.

Kate tried to scribble notes on the back of the letter as she went along, working out what her spiel would be if she had to sit there and convince Jennifer to let her offer real money for it. Isobel had told her to do this, following her own experience of being told at the last minute to bring up a project when Jennifer's shoe fitting overrran; apparently, 'I like it . . .

it's quite good' hadn't been quite persuasive enough for the assembled meeting. Isobel had been reduced to feigning a nosebleed to escape the humiliation of Jo sniggering openly as she minuted.

Much as she was gripped by what was happening, Kate couldn't ignore the niggle at the back of her mind that what she was enjoying were the parallels between the novel and her own flatshare. She felt the writing was precious, but knew that that kind of thing went down well in certain quarters, and Cameron was a real dark-eyed sub-Dean Martin knicker-ripper of a hero. In fact, she was looking forward eagerly to the huge plot twist which would explain why gorgeous Cameron was living with the oceanically wet David, who was so limp he virtually needed support to make a cup of tea.

Well, if I'm reading it to get some insight into my flatmates, then other people will too, she thought. A sales point! Kate had never had a spontaneous sales point before and she wrote it down. After all, nearly everyone her age lived in flatshares (albeit not ones which harboured would-be murderers in the spare room) and the author had got the sordid lethargy of post-party comedowns, and filthy sinks down perfectly. 'Could be me!' she wrote, adding an extra exclamation mark.

What she really wanted to know now was what Ariel would be like. She picked up another four chapters. Using her best new urbane attitude Kate assumed Ariel would be a man, who would bring the unspoken sexual tension between Cameron and David boiling to the surface. David's ex-lover? Hence Cameron's murderous rage? Or Cameron's ex-lover who might spoil things between him and floppy Dave? Kate curled her feet up underneath her and read on.

Within four or five pages, the interesting similarities between Cameron and David's flat and her own had turned distinctly spooky, because Ariel turned up – and turned out to be a girl. No sooner had Ariel dumped her fluffy bedroom mules in Cameron's lap than the plot (which had been limp up to that point, to say the least) took off at a violent rate, with territorial rows between Ariel and David – though his rage was limited to flapping his hands at her – and passionate hate-filled rows between Ariel and Cameron, the first of which began over a pile of dirty clothes and ended stickily over the washing machine. All were delivered in the same brittle, ominous prose style, which constantly left Kate wondering if she was missing something more significant.

No wonder she has to go, thought Kate. Ariel was a Formula One bitch, and her savagely offhand remarks about David's prep school dress sense would have had an elephant squirming. She strode through the finely balanced homoerotic atmosphere in the flat like Germaine Greer in Gary Glitter's biggest boots, despite having little or no discernible sex appeal of her own. What Cameron saw in her was baffling to Kate – even more baffling was why wimpy Dave didn't want to stick her through the jugular with her own Gucci stiletto first.

A-ha! she thought, maybe that's the plot!

Her eyes were beginning to droop, but she felt that she couldn't stop until she found out what was going on with Ariel. Many things about the style were annoying her deeply, but it was a gruesomely addictive read. 'To the end of this chapter' turned into 'To the next round figure' and on and on . . . The nightmare goings-on (or rather, *not* goings-on, since all the action was perpetually hanging in the balance) were reminding her increasingly of the petty arguments and snipings that she put up with from Dant all the time, and Ariel had some fabulous one-liners, which could come in handy.

Kate's eye stopped short at the phrase, 'Cameron, your sense of humour blows goats. Or it would do if it could reach.' Her brow creased with confusion. 'Blowing goats' was one of her favourite phrases, one that Giles had tried and tried to get her to stop using, and she'd never heard anyone outside the Craig family use it. In fact, as far as she knew, Mike had made it up during their summer holiday to Wales and they had sniggered in the back of the car all round the Snowdonia National Park.

What a weird coincidence.

And that Ariel, the Bitch from Hormone Hell, should have used it.

It would be wrong to jump to conclusions, she told herself briskly, noting that it was now midnight and there was no sign of the boys coming back. Maybe they're 'staying over', she thought, relishing the wrench of jealousy the image caused her. You're just getting spooked because it's a dark wintery night and you're here on your own in a flat in a slightly rough part of London and your boyfriend has only sent you one letter since he got back to his loft-style apartment in the business heart of Chicago.

Remembering this depressed her so much she got up and went to the fridge. The contents were not inspiring; she made herself a bowl of Special K and took the bowl and the manuscript through to her bedroom. Beauty sleep was obviously not going to be any use for Dant and Harry, but she could do with some.

Kate put on her Portishead CD and got into bed, sitting cross-legged, with the pages and the bowl in the circle of her legs. She spooned cereal into her mouth and carried on reading, trying not to drip on the pages.

The whole thing was curiously vivid. The narrative fall-out from David's disastrous attempt to poison Ariel by squirting Immac into her facial moisturiser was hilarious, but barely enclosed by the terse style. Long bubbling sentences of sarcastic description of the boys' constant hangovers strained at the boundaries of the 'noun-verb-expletive' patterns set up earlier. It felt as though there was a much funnier story trying to get out from under the Martin Amis sunglasses.

Kate put down her cereal spoon and wrote some of this on the back of the covering letter – it had been a long time since she had thought in literary critical terms. She was quite proud of herself for making such professional observations about what passed for a serious work of literary *noir* – and was even more surprised to find that the next scene, set in a fashionable Thai-Moroccan fusion restaurant and featuring all Cameron and David's camp mates, was not a birthday party, as she had initially thought, but a stag night.

It took her several attempts at the two pages in question to work out what was going on – mainly because no one so far had even mentioned getting married.

And then the penny dropped. It was a fake stag night.

Kate blinked. Either these things were more common than she had thought or . . .

Or what?

She read on, chewing her lip furiously and not even noticing the blisters forming on the tender skin.

By the time she reached the bit with the four hen parties in the same Thai-Moroccan fusion bar, and Cameron's dodgy friend Marmaduke making off with the kitty while Ariel decked the bouncer with her Prada handbag, the pennies were dropping at roughly the same rate as Cameron and Co's trousers. The accompanying letter was covered in Kate's own questions, viz.:

1) Why is Cameron so very attractive?
2) Is David in love with Cameron?
3) Who is Ariel meant to be?
4) Why has no one tried to kill her properly?
5) How universal is the Fake Stag Concept?

She bit the top of her pencil and took some deep breaths. It could be a coincidence. Dant had a lot of friends who were arty writer types, all of whom had doubtless heard about the stag night, and any of whom could be – she checked the front page – R. A. Harper. It was a good dinner party story – even her own mother had been entertained with an edited version of it over Christmas – and Dant went to enough parties for it to do the rounds.

She breathed heavily through her nostrils and tried the old relaxation trick the college nurse had taught her. It didn't work. Questions and parallels piled up in her head, and the more she thought about it, the more one answer became increasingly plausible. The unbearably handsome and irresistible matinée idol hero, the grim flat, the purloining of her best put-downs, the misogynistic attitude, the latent homosexuality (she blushed at this and noted that Laura had spotted it first off), the pretentious prose style . . .

So this was what Dant had been up to all day when she and Harry were at work.

'Oh my God!' exclaimed Kate, upsetting her cereal bowl on to her duvet.

Then she said, 'Oh my *God*!' as it dawned on her how ruthlessly she and Harry had been stitched up. Particularly Harry.

Her heart twanged painfully again, as she tried to reconcile the limp property developer with Golden Retriever Boy.

Then a creepy thought entered her head: what if Dant really *was* trying to off her? And what had *really* happened to Mandy?

In the hall there was the sound of someone trying to fit a key in the lock. Except that it sounded more like someone trying to thread a javelin through a needle. If she hadn't been so furious, she would have been screaming her head off with B-movie fear. Kate looked at her alarm clock and saw that it was twenty to two. She threw back the duvet and stormed into the hall, as forcefully as she could in bare feet.

Dant and Harry were clinging to the door-frame.

Kate stood in front of the kitchen door with her arms folded across her chest, unconsciously doing her best impression of a Northern fishwife. Dant focused his eyes on her and frowned darkly.

'What the hell have you been doing all evening? Why didn't you answer the fucking phone?'

Anger leaped up in Kate's throat and almost took her breath away. 'What have I been doing all evening? Well, thank you for enabling me to introduce what might otherwise be a difficult matter of flatsharing etiquette.'

Harry looked from one to the other and shuffled towards Kate. ' 'M a little bit drunk as you can see, and 's'very late, but I did get you this, and now 'm going to bed.' He dug in his pocket and pulled out a Bounty bar which he pressed in to Kate's hand, then shuffled off to his room, banging the door shut. A muffled 'Sorry' floated through.

Dant and Kate remained glaring at each other in the cold hallway. Kate tightened her grip on her chest to disguise any inadvertent nipple visibility through her T-shirt, and wondered how she could open up the batting in the most devastating way possible.

'If you had bothered to answer the phone, instead of dribbling over that pathetic Boyzone video,' spat Dant, looking every inch the flatmate-murderer, 'you would have heard a message from me and Harry. We were calling from Islington police station. You might know it. *Very* accommodating staff. The reason we were calling from Islington police station was that the two charming young ladies we had met for drinks at the Angel turned out to be not *quite* so charming as we had been led to believe by their letters, and in fact relieved us of both our wallets, and in a particularly spiteful touch, my travel card as well.'

'Oh dear,' said Kate, trying to make it come out sarcastic.

'So we have *walked* back from Islington, which is why we are so late home. I don't suppose in your *extensive* travels around London you have got as far north as Islington, but let me assure you it is a *long* way away.' Dant's brow darkened even further. 'I have incredibly sensitive arches, you know. Had you answered our call, you could have driven down and picked us up. But no. Ronan Keating's gain is *our loss.*' Tiny speckles of spit flew out of his mouth.

Kate allowed for a couple of beats of silence just to unnerve him. 'Shall I tell you what gripped me so much I barely noticed the phone ringing?'

'The unification of Ireland? The Pope on drugs charges? Or has Elvis appeared on *Police, Camera, Action*?' Billy Idol rode again in Dant's sneer.

Kate lost it completely at that. 'You manipulative arse-hole!' she yelled into his face, not caring whether Harry woke up or not. 'Did you think it would be funny to get me to read your disgusting and . . . and . . . pretentious stitch-up? Did you? That would be just typical though, wouldn't it, you self-centred wanker? And to be so horrible about your own best friend as well! I mean, I don't care what you say about me, because I know you're a complete lowlife, but poor Harry . . .'

Kate only realised her arms were flailing around when Dant caught her by the wrists. 'Hey, hey . . .'

'And don't take that patronising tone with me either,' she hissed impotently.

Dant yanked up her wrists so that she had to look him in the eye. He was wearing his irritating amused look. She felt like spitting in his face, then remembered with a shock that this scene was straight out of *Bitch Rota.* Am I going *totally* mad? she wondered. Am I only existing in Eclipse novels?

'Listen, Pussy,' Dant said in a Sean Connery voice, 'I don't know what you're talking about, but for a little lady, you sure have a man's temper on you. How about you tell me what's on your mind?'

'You know exactly what I'm talking about.' Kate turned her face away from his. 'And put me down. You pathetic cliché.'

Dant dropped her arms and she shook herself angrily.

'All I want to do is take off my shoes and go to bed,' he said, as if talking to a small fractious child. 'Is this your time of the month, by any chance?'

'No, you make me feel sick week in, week out,' snapped Kate. Dant was walking towards his room and short of following him in and demanding to examine his computer, there wasn't much she could do. Besides which, the usual post-scene embarrassment was coming over her and doubts were creeping into the back of her mind. It was late, she was going submission-crazy, lots of people had flatshares in London . . .

'And don't think you can write that one down and use it!' she shouted at his back.

'I haven't a clue what you mean,' said Dant and shut his bedroom door.

'You fucking . . . arsebadger,' said Kate into the suddenly silent flat. Then she turned on her heel and went back to her soggy duvet.

chapter twenty-eight

'So, then, Dr McIntyre, tell me, am I going mad?' Kate asked Isobel.

Isobel looked at her over the rim of her coffee mug. They were sitting in a Starbucks near the office, Kate having called an emergency lunch as soon as Isobel had got her coat and hat off. 'Weeell, you have been working awful late, and . . .' She shrugged.

'Oh, cheers.' Kate licked the froth off her coffee spoon disconsolately.

'Let me tell you a story,' said Isobel. She put down her mug and steepled her fingers on the table, like Jennifer.

'Is this another of your elaborate but thinly disguised morality fibs?'

Isobel widened her eyes. 'Do I ever tell you fibs?'

'Let's just call them unprovable suppositions.'

'You are a very suspicious woman.' Isobel pretended to be offended but she could never quite pull it off, out of the office. 'Anyway this one's about me, so. When I started working at Eclipse, Jennifer's bought a lot of saga authors and all I'm doing all day is checking clogs per page, regional dialect in the right place, was this type of warship built at the time of the Second World War, you know the kind of thing. Anyway, I got really into them, you know, couldn't stop reading them, so—'

'To cut a long story short,' interjected Kate.

'To cut a long story short,' said Isobel with a glare, 'I start reading this one set in Glasgow after the end of the last war. All about the art college and stuff, really good, but the more I read, the more I'm thinking, "Hey, my mum was at the art college round about then." And then Oor Brave Wee Heroine marries a man from the Highlands – who looks uncannily like my dad – and before you know it they're shotgun married, she loses the baby in a tram accident and then ends up having terrible problems conceiving more children. Before you know it, she's stealing Wee Bairns, as she calls them in her quaint Glasgow accent, out of prams and the like.'

'No!' said Kate. 'Can you get to the point, please? Elaine wants me back at my desk by three.'

'The *point is* that I got myself so convinced that this was all about my mum – don't forget I hadn't been in publishing long enough to get the whole fact/fiction thing straight in ma head – that I actually confronted her with it and basically accused her of being a child-snatcher, which didn't go down at all well, and my dad went mad and I found out loads of things I didn't really need to know about my parents' malfunctioning reproductive systems, and I've only just lived the whole kerfuffle down. So don't go stirring things up, is what I'm telling you.'

There was a significant pause while Isobel scraped the remaining cappuccino foam off her mug.

'It wasn't your mum's book, then?'

Isobel gave her a dirty look. 'No.'

'OK, just wanted to get it straight in my head.' Kate finished off the last crumbs of her muffin. 'Fine, you're saying I'm just being paranoid.'

'You're just doing what we all do. Trying to make your life more exciting than it really is.'

'Thanks, Isobel,' said Kate. 'You really know how to make me feel better.' She slid off the high stool and picked up her handbag. 'Can you hang on a second while I get a takeaway espresso?'

'Sure.' Isobel followed her to the counter. 'You're drinking an awful lot of that stuff at the moment.'

'Good girl's speed,' said Kate. 'Cheaper too. And I need it, with all the work Elaine's doing now that Rose Ann is into Production. Suddenly all her other thirty authors have stepped forward and made themselves known. Thank you,' she said to the barista and twisted the plastic lid off the little espresso cup.

They made their way into the street where Kate tipped the coffee down her throat in one easy motion, dropping the still steaming cup into a litter bin as she walked past.

'No word from Giles?' asked Isobel.

'No.'

'And the horn is still in the house for Harry?'

'Yep.'

They strolled through the small park to the Eclipse office in reflective silence. Where there had been luscious banks of blowsy pink tea roses when Kate arrived at Eclipse for the first time, there were now empty beds and the first green prickings of crocus nibs. Kate nipped a stem of lavender off a bush and rubbed it between her fingers to release the smell. It was still very cold for February.

'And you're sure you don't fancy—'

'*Yes*,' said Kate, pushing Isobel into the revolving door.

'Eclipse editorial,' said Kate into the phone without taking her eyes off the list of publication-day flowers to be sent. In two instances it was going to be a very tight squeeze if they were to make it to the author before the advance copies of the book arrived.

'Ah, hello, editorial, it's R. A. Harper here.'

'Dante,' said Kate heavily. 'Make it quick, some of us are working.'

'You left . . .' there was the sound of fluttering pages,

'*Guilt Trap* at home. Aren't you going to make me an offer for it?'

'Ho ho ho,' said Kate. 'Are you trying to tell me it's *not* yours?'

'Well . . .'

'Dant, there's an incontinent black cat in it, for fuck's sake. Limp David drives a Simon Templar Volvo. Cameron dyes his hair!'

There was a minuscule offended pause at the other end, and then Dant went on, 'I've been having a read through this manuscript of mine, and I have to say it's not bad. Rather pretentious in places, but very funny, all the same.'

'I was under the impression it was a modern London *noir*.'

Dant laughed. 'Would *like* to be modern *noir*. It's a modern *noir* in the same way that *Spinal Tap* is an incisive study of modern rock music.'

Kate's attitude softened slightly at the reminder of Dant's 'Not Nearly As Bad As She'd Have Thought' CD collection. 'Can we cut this short, please, Tom Paulin?'

'I thought I came out of it pretty well,' Dant said, ignoring her urgency and continuing in the same languorous tone, 'although I didn't realise I cut such a sex god figure about the house. Poor Harry gets a regular stitching, and as for Mandy – she should consult her lawyers. Not even those repellent tart's slippers were spared. It's so accurate, it's pure libel. And of course, we did want to kill her, in many different horrible ways.'

Kate put her elbows on the desk and shut her eyes. Mandy's slippers? Dant and Mandy? She pressed the heels of her hand into her eye sockets. It had been easier somehow to imagine that they were Dant's. 'Dant, I'm having a bad day for endless fairy stories and I'm still tired after last night's excitement, so can you *please* get to the point?'

'Well, you were absolutely right about one thing,' he said, 'it *is* our flat.'

'No!' said Kate. 'Really? I'm not just imagining it?' And

you're sure I'm not really in it, she wanted to ask, but felt she couldn't for fear of exposing her own paranoid need to be liked at all times.

'I hope for the sake of modern civilisation that there aren't two flats like ours in the world. We'd be on television otherwise. People would follow us round with cameras. Oh, sorry, I forgot they do that already to you.'

'So . . .' said Kate, not sure how to go on. 'Who's, um, R. A. Harper?' Was it Harry pulling a massive double bluff? Could he be that sneaky? Did he have enough time?

Dant snorted down the phone. 'Oh, come on, Kate, I'd credited you with more intelligence. Who has access to all the gossip in the flat, knew Mandy, has the spare time to write this kind of up-its-own-arse drivel . . .?'

Kate's mind raced. 'Teresa?' It would explain the state of the sinks and there *were* two computers in the flat.

'For fuck's sake! It's that stupid bitch Cressida!' There was the sound of a lighter clicking and Dant exhaled heavily down the phone. 'This is just like her – completely shallow and meaningless guff, dressed up in trendy stylistic bollocks! I'm going to kill her when I can find her.'

Kate slumped back in her chair while this news sank in.

Cress. It made perfect sense. Hadn't she herself given her every single detail of the fake stag night, as well as a lot of other gossip Cress had wheedled out of her, all in the name of 'getting to know her'? Kate's skin tingled with shame. It was all her fault. She had given Cress every piece of ammunition she had wanted to shoot them all in the back.

Her cheeks burned as she remembered her attempts to push Harry's cause, even when her own feelings for him had made it more of a martyrdom than a pleasure – if she'd known what shameless use Cress was going to make of him, she'd have refused to say a word. Poor Harry! She bit her lip, remembering David's shabby Snoopy dog he carried around with him. All Harry's little gentlemanly habits blown up to parodic feyness, and worst of all, the implication that he had some kind of crush on Dant! Not that there was any-thing wrong with that, *per se*, she corrected herself, but . . .

Kate's stomach turned over as she realised how much anger and hurt suddenly swept through her. She felt physi-cally shaken by the force of her outrage. Just thinking about the pain Harry would feel when he found out what Cressida, the woman he'd idolised for so long, had done with his devo-tion made her feel sick. She felt worse than she did for herself.

'What can we do?' she whispered down the phone.

'We can stick pins in her, for a start,' offered Dant. 'Then we can move on to the hard stuff. I always knew she'd do something like this. You'd have thought she'd be the last person to appropriate real people for cheap fiction after what Anna did to us. The silly, silly bitch. You know what I really want to—'

There was the anxious sound of an empty mug being banged up and down in Elaine's office. Kate turned towards it, and then turned back to the phone. 'No, hang on a minute,' she said, as the wheels started turning in her mind. 'I can think of something much more cunning than that.'

'It's ringing, it's ringing.' Kate cupped her hand over the phone in the sitting room. She was hunched on the sofa with a notebook in front of her on the coffee table, in case she forgot anything.

'Bloody well should be,' muttered Dant, riffling through the final pages of the manuscript. 'Costs a fucking fortune to phone mobiles abroad. Even at this time of night.'

'Don't put me off.' Kate shut her eyes, and tried to get the tone right in her head. *Hello*, Cress! Hell-*oooo*, Cress. *Cress! Hi!*

'If it's after eight, she'll be well stuck into the *après-ski*. You may as well ring the Accident and Emergency Unit, see if they've got any stomach-pump candidates. Bloody hell, she's got a whole paragraph here on my—'

'Hi?' said a weary voice.

Kate swallowed. 'Cress, how are you, it's me, Kate.'

'Kate?'

Dant put the script down and pressed the speaker button on the telephone. Cress's permanently exhausted drawl boomed out of the machine, the borrowed North London vowels accented by the crackly reception.

'Oh, God, *Kate*, I'm sorry about lunch, I just went totally out of my head when I was in the queue at Thomas Cook, and I bumped into this designer I knew at college and he asked me if I'd been to the Nu Bar where the old R Bar used to be and . . .'

Dant rolled his eyes.

'No, look, it's not a problem, honestly, Cress.' Kate tried to keep her voice measured and professional, while imagining Cress covered in boiling oil and ants. 'Listen, we need to have a chat about . . .' her eyes skated around the room for inspiration, '. . . about your novel.'

There was a noticeable silence on the end of the line.

Oh, shit, thought Kate, widening her eyes at Dant, we've got this totally, totally wrong. It must be Harry after all. She raised her eyebrows at him in a 'What now, Superman?' expression. He shrugged helpfully.

There was a cough. Kate and Dant transferred their gazes to the phone.

'Yeeeess? What about it?'

Dant gave her a thumbs up.

'Cress, let's not be coy about this,' Kate plunged in, relief pounding in her chest. 'I've read the manuscript and I just wanted to tell you that it's brilliant. I know for a fact that the editor I work for wants to buy exactly this kind of novel and she'll probably give you a ridiculous amount of money for it. I'm so excited for you!'

'You are?' said Cress. There was more than a hint of suspicion in her voice. 'Has Dante read it?'

Dant leered angrily at the phone and threw two V-signs at it.

'Er, no, just me,' said Kate hurriedly. There was no point pretending Dant had read it and liked it. 'It came in on sub-mission at work and I was asked to have a look, you know, as a target audience member. I was just . . . hooked right from the beginning! If I didn't know Mandy to begin with, I certainly do now!' If it *is* Mandy, you bitch, she thought to herself.

'Mandy? Oh, um, God, that's wonderful. I'm so pleased you enjoyed it. I found it a real challenge to write in that style . . .'

'Really?' said Kate. In case that sounded too incredulous, she changed it to a noncommittal, 'Mmmm?'

'. . . I wanted it to read like Elmore Leonard, if he'd been born a woman in Highbury around 1970.'

'Well, it's certainly very . . . distinctive.' Kate tried for a matey, confidential tone. 'I had no idea you were writing a novel – you kept it very quiet.'

Dant muttered something under his breath and Kate shoved him away from the phone.

'Well, I knew Dant would take the piss if he knew, so I just, you know, sat on it,' admitted Cress.

Kate leaned over and clamped her hand over his mouth before he could say anything.

'The thing is, Cress, it's not finished, is it? I couldn't believe it last night, when I got to that bit where Ariel meets up with Cameron and David and the loan sharks, and it just ended.' This wasn't strictly true – Kate had speedread the rest of the book as soon as she got in from work, with Dant pacing around the sitting room, spitting out the occasional threat. As luck would have it, Harry was out at a rugby prac-tice, and missed the whole pantomime.

'No, it's not finished.' Cress let out a half sigh, half groan. 'I wanted to give it to an agent to see if they could sell it on what was there, and Phil whizzed it out to publishers before we really had a chance to talk much about how I would finish. He's Mum's agent, you know. Really amazing. I've known him for years.'

'Mmmm,' said Kate. She consulted her notes. It was so important to get this right first time. 'Thing is, Elaine's just had her fingers burned really badly by this It-Girl who signed her contract on the basis of three chapters, spent the lot on shoes and still hasn't delivered the book. Everyone at work went absolutely berserk at Elaine for wasting their time – she had marketing, sales, publicity, editorial, the lot on the case – and I know she just won't offer for your novel until it's finished. The basic problem is that this type of fiction is so "of the moment" that you have to move immediately, so I was—'

'Oh, God!' wailed Cress over Kate's careful explanation. 'And now I can't finish it! Phil will go ballistic! Oh, shit!'

Kate ground to a halt and she and Dant looked at each other over the phone.

'Oh, come on, Cress, it can't be that hard. I mean, I don't mind giving you a hand and lots of authors take a while to tie up all—'

'Kate, I'm in hospital, for fuck's sake! I'm in fucking traction! I'm only talking to you now because the nurses propped my mobile up by my right arm plaster cast!'

Dant leaped up from his seat on the arm of the sofa and started dancing round the room, punching the air and generally carrying on like someone from Madness.

'Oh, *no*!' said Kate. This couldn't be more perfect – although it was a little hard on Cressida. 'You poor thing! What happened?'

'I'm not meant to be here,' said Cress, bitterly. 'Phil told me to stay put in England while he sent the book out on submission, but a friend of mine from college was going out to Val d'Isere with a group of mates and asked me to come along, and I was so excited by all Phil's hype that I just decided to go. I'd had two good runs when some arsehole on a quadbike ran me over outside a bar.'

'Oh *dear*,' said Kate, holding her breath.

'*Then*, when they winched me into the nearest hospital the bloody Nazi nurses decided that my blood wasn't absolutely clean, so I had the third-degree from some police-men as well.'

Dant stopped dancing and looked at the phone, thumbs suspended aloft for a moment.

'Turned out the miserable little Aussie bastard joyriding the quadbike wanted to press charges against me, but then they bloodtested *him* and found out he was stoned in charge of a four-wheeler,' finished Cress, triumphantly. 'But basically, I'm stuck here until everything stabilises and I can't even go to the loo. It's so depressing. I mean, it's not as seri-ous as it sounds and I am in a private ward, but everything is *so* seventies. I thought it was retro until the painkillers wore off properly.'

Dant resumed his joyous dancing.

'Oh, no, and with your fabulous début novel about to happen and everything!' Kate commiserated, hoping she wasn't laying it on too thick.

Cress made a strangled noise.

Dant came round to lean on the back of the sofa as Kate moved in with their masterstroke.

'Cress!' she exclaimed, as if it had just occurred to her. 'Listen, maybe I can help!'

'Really?' said Cress doubtfully. 'Do you have a degree in physiotherapy?'

'No, I mean, maybe I can help finish your book. You've made notes and things, haven't you? Or you can Fedex dic-tation tapes to me, if you want. I'll just type it up for you. Take me no time at all.'

There was a pause. Kate held her breath. Maybe she'd been over-optimistic to hope that Cress would go along with this. It was a bit of a Scooby-Doo plan when you thought about it.

Dant scribbled on the back of one of Cress's finished

pages and held it up. Three pound signs in a row, followed by an exclamation mark.

Kate stared, uncomprehending.

Dant took it back, added two more exclamation marks and waved it up and down.

'It would be a real shame to wait until you get back to normal,' said Kate, suddenly understanding. 'Elaine's just missed one of these London *noir* thrillers and she's desperate to find another one before the trend moves on. I wouldn't like to say how much she'd be willing to pay, but I guess it would be somewhere between a four-bed flat in West Kensington and a three-bed in Notting Hill.' She looked down at her notepad to check she'd got that bit right.

Dant gave her a thumbs up.

Cress squeaked in frustration, a most un-Cress-like sound.

'It would just have to be rough, to finish it,' Kate improvised. 'You could change it all at copy-editing stage. Most authors do.' She crossed her fingers at Dant.

'There are notes in my flat,' said Cress finally. 'I wrote most of it out longhand and there are notes on my laptop too. For Christ's sake, don't show Dant. Or Harry. They're rather . . . sensitive. I'll get someone to get me dictation tapes and talk you through the rest of it. There's really not much left to write.'

'Oh, but go on, Cress, tell me,' said Kate, managing a sugary tone through her gritted teeth, '*do* they kill Ariel in the end?'

'Kate, it's not the kind of novel that has an "end".' This sounded more like the normal Cress. 'That's a very Thatcherite expectation. It's up to the readers to take away what they will.'

'Riiight,' said Kate. It crossed her mind that Cress probably had no idea *how* to end it, having created three characters all equally killable. Perhaps there was going to be a massacre. Or a gas leak.

'It's all in the notes and I'll dictate some stuff too,' said Cress. She paused and then said, 'How are we going to get this round Phil? If he finds out where I am he'll go mad. If he finds out what you're doing he'll go *berserk*.'

'Well, I've had a think about this,' said Kate, 'because I do think it's very important that the final version seems to be coming from you, so we thought—'

'We?' said Cress suspiciously.

Kate glanced at Dant. 'Um, sorry, that was a corporate we, there, I meant I thought, so as to save as much time as possible, I could finish it off and send a copy to you and Phil simultaneously, so he can bike it round to Elaine, and you can have a copy by your side to read through if he phones you up to talk about it.'

'Mmm,' said Cress dubiously, 'he did say that he just wanted me to get on and finish it. I mean, there weren't any major changes he wanted to make . . .'

Dant did another thumbs up and tapped his watch in an amateur dramatic style.

'God, Cress, you're breaking up a bit now, are you sure, your phone is OK?'

Dant leaned nearer and went, 'Kkkkkrrrrrrcccccchhhhhh' into the receiver.

'Kate, you're breaking up. Kate! Phone me when—'

Dant put his finger on the cradle and disconnected the phone. He looked at Kate with undisguised pleasure all over his face. 'Couldn't have done it better myself. Now, where did I put those spare keys to her flat?'

chapter twenty-nine

'. . . No, really?' Kate looked surreptitiously at her watch. It was quite incredible how conversations with Laura really did seem to slow down the passage of time. And this one was a corker. From an ostensible sisterly chat over sandwiches, it had sharply taken a turn for the unexpected. 'No, I can see that . . .'

'I'm not saying that I don't love him—' said Laura and broke off. She had obviously said more than she meant to and an uneasy silence fell between them. The ducks on the other side of the small lake quacked hysterically as an old lady hurled half a Mighty White in their direction.

Not for the first time in the past forty minutes, Kate was at a loss for something to say. Even with her limited experience of adult relationships, she could work out that Laura hadn't really wanted to meet her for lunch to check that she had registered for council tax. Three arbitrary minutes into the conversation and Laura had desperately hauled the subject round to child benefit and supervised crèches in the Clapham/Balham area. What she wanted, obviously, was to be reassured that bearing Mike's child was a normal and natural thing to do, and that a few stretch marks were a small price to pay for carrying on the Craig name.

Except that even Kate could tell, listening to Laura's pauses and hesitations where the rest of her family tended to fill up such gaps with enthusiastic baby-talk, that she was worried about more than stretch marks and never being able to wear Agnès B again without a splashguard. It was a pretty sad state of affairs, Kate thought, if the only person to whom Laura was able to hint at the shortcomings of her marriage was her immature little sister-in-law.

'I'm sure you do love him,' said Kate, feeling hopelessly inadequate and not a little embarrassed. She threw the last bit of her baguette to the lone brown duck at the edge of the pond. 'But having a baby is such a big thing, isn't it? You can't take them back if they don't work out.'

She wasn't looking at Laura as she said this, but thought she could hear a faint sob. Kate turned and saw her sister-in-law staring out over the pond with her big chenille scarf pressed up against her nose. 'Laura? Are you OK? Laura?' Oh, God, this was all she needed.

'I'm fine,' said Laura bravely. 'It's just hormones and things and . . .'

'How long have you and Mike been together?'

Laura huffed an ironic snort of air into her scarf. 'A hundred years? Two hundred?'

Kate searched around for something truthful but not wildly pessimistic to say. 'Laura, I know Mike isn't perfect, and there have been *many* times when I've thought he doesn't deserve you, but all marriages go through rocky bits, don't they? I mean, my mum and dad—'

Laura held up her hand. 'Kate, please don't let's go down that road. It's one of Mike's favourites.' She snorted. 'It's virtually a four-lane motorway. How your mother gave up work to have kids and never looked back, how your dad has loved having children around the place—'

Kate put her cold hand over Laura's. It was weird sometimes how things only occurred to you when you were trying to be deep for someone else's benefit. 'Laura, my mother gave up work at twenty-four to have me and Mike and since we left school she's spent the rest of her life frantically trying to catch up on all the things she felt she missed out on. When I was a little girl, she was a lovely finger-painting mum who liked shopping and making pasta dragons. Now she's like some terrifying knowledge junkie who knows more about the Internet than I do. She goes line-dancing, for God's sake! I feel I hardly know her—'

Kate grappled with her own conscience. 'I feel that she's trying to turn herself into me. I mean, I love my dad more than anyone else, but even he was under stress, having us both so young. And they've always adored each other.' Kate stopped herself, not wanting to fall into commenting on Mike and Laura's rowing. Being rude about their marriage was such a standard comedy routine that it was hard to hold back the wisecracks, but she felt horribly close to the truth here, and she didn't want to hurt Laura. 'It's not that easy.'

Laura pulled her knees up on to the bench and hugged them. She had obviously taken a day off work, since she was wearing fresh DKNY jeans, instead of her usual pea-green business suit. 'Sometimes I feel the reason your mother is so keen on me reproducing is so that someone else can play Mum for a change. Don't you think that?'

She looked at Kate, who had to nod in agreement. They sat in silence, and the bareness of the situation resonated between them on the scuffed park bench.

'I just feel . . .' began Laura, then paused for a breath but, as she'd started, she carried on, 'that having a baby will trap me into a life I'm not sure I want yet. I don't know if I really *want* to be a mother. I used to think all I wanted was to be married – when I *wasn't* married – and now . . .'

She looked at Kate, who blushed beneath the weight of the unexpected confidences. Laura blushed in return but set her sharp little jaw determinedly.

'When you're going out with someone, you're prepared to make allowances for the fact that they won't put their socks in the laundry basket, and they don't ever change the sheets. You have the escape route of splitting up, so you give them, say, a twenty per cent irritation allowance. Then when you get engaged, and you're facing the prospect of living with them for ever—' Laura turned to Kate and looked her straight in the eye. '—and believe me, that's a scary prospect, that irritation allowance goes down to about one per cent. But by then you're so excited and amazed that someone can want you so much they're prepared to give it all up for you, you don't care. And if you stop to think too hard about what's happening, you get mown down by the wedding wagon gathering speed behind you, and before you know it, you're married.'

Kate opened her mouth, couldn't think of anything help-ful to say and shut it again.

'Now, I know all about compromise,' Laura went on des-olately. 'And sometimes I think my parents' marriage worked purely because one or both of them was on tour at any given time and we were all at boarding school. But when you have a child involved . . .' She looked at Kate and Kate impulsively squeezed the hand in hers. 'When I'm cov-ered in baby sick and I've had three hours' sleep in a week, how am I going to cope with the demands of the other baby I'm married to?'

'I don't know,' said Kate simply. 'But it's about time he grew up.'

'I know.' Laura stared out at the ducks on the pond, then turned back to Kate, drawing in her breath and stretching up her spine as far as it would go. 'Kate, I'm really sorry to burden you with all this, but, to be honest, you're the only person I know who doesn't think the sun shines out of Mike's arse.'

'Thank you,' said Kate automatically. 'I mean,' she cor-rected herself, hastily, 'I know what you mean. It's . . . hard when everyone thinks your relationship is perfect, because you've told them so.' Like me and Giles, she thought. Who could I really tell about Harry, when, according to my own publicity, I'm meant to be going out with a god amongst men? 'Still, I'm sure you love Mike,' she went on, 'or else you would have killed him by now, wouldn't you?'

Laura squeezed her eyes tightly shut and stretched her arms out above her head. When she opened them, she looked at Kate and Kate wondered if Laura had pretended to yawn to hide the tears now glistening in her eyes.

'When I remember how glib and self-assured I used to be, I could cry. I used to think I knew what love was,' she said sadly, 'but now I'm meant to have it, I'm not sure if it's the same thing I had in mind.'

The resignation in her voice struck Kate like a punch, and she put an arm round her sister-in-law, something she would never have seen herself doing six months earlier. Laura leaned her head briefly against Kate's shoulder, and Kate stared out at the ducks circling the pond. It was so cold the park was emptier than usual of lunch-break escapees, and when Kate shut her eyes, and listened to the ducks and the birds and the wind humming gently in the background, she could pretend that she wasn't in London at all. How easy it would be to slip out from the scene via a trapdoor, leaving everything exactly as it was.

But where would she go? Where could Laura go? Kate's arm was starting to get pins and needles and she moved it gently. Only six months in London and already she was bound to the place like some unwilling mythological sacrifice.

Laura let out a long breath and unwound Kate's arm from her shoulder. She gave her a brief awkward hug and stood up, rearranging her scarf over her jumper, and searching through her big handbag for a tissue.

'Better get back,' she said. 'I'm meant to be working from home today. And you need to get back to the office.'

Kate got to her feet. 'I never said thank you for blagging my way in to Eclipse.'

Laura smiled. 'Yes, well, I'm usually quite resourceful on other people's behalf.' She leaned forward and gave Kate a kiss on the cheek. 'Please don't tell Mike I—'

'If he asks,' interrupted Kate, 'I'll tell him that we met for lunch, which we did. Nothing wrong with that.'

'OK.' Laura touched her arm. 'I'm going back to the Tube station . . .'

Kate pointed her in the right direction. 'The office is . . .' she gestured across the park the other way.

They stood and looked at each other for a few seconds. Kate felt a trickle of guilt that she hadn't bothered to look beyond Laura's bossy Habitat exterior before now – and how lonely Laura must be, she thought, if that image was now pinning her down instead of propping her up.

Then Laura's phone rang and she delved into her bag to answer it. 'Mike! Hello, darling!' she cooed into the phone.

Kate lifted her hand in a silent wave and let Laura turn and walk down the path to the station, clenching and unclenching her spare hand as she went.

Kate left her piles of editing and sheaves of Elaine's typing notes on the dot of five and by six o'clock was in Dant's room with a whole new set of pages. They worked mainly in silence, with Dant chain-smoking and Kate reading out the occasional pretentious paragraph in a sarcastic voice so that Dant could argue about its literary significance. Kate ate a whole family-sized bar of Dairy Milk without noticing.

They broke off for supper at eight, so that Harry could come in from work, have a bowl of pasta and go back out to rugby practice without suspecting anything was amiss. Then they went back to work.

'We have to tell Harry at some point.' Kate crossed off another section from the photocopied page of Cress's notes. Her pen hovered over the next bullet point. 'You've done this bit with the loan shark being found in bite-sized chunks all over the Barbican?'

Dant grunted his assent and carried on typing.

'I mean, hasn't he wondered what you're getting up to all day?' Her eye fell on Cress's outstandingly harsh description of Harry/David's attempts to make a Caesar salad, and she scrubbed it out angrily with her red editing Biro. 'I think we'll forget the attempts to poison Ariel with the out-of-date Parmesan.'

They sat in the standard semi-darkness of Dant's room, with the curtains drawn and the halogen desk lights on to read the scattered reams of paper surrounding them. Pages of notes in Cress's angular scrawl covered the bed, the desk and the floor around their feet. Dant had insisted on photocopying everything, so as to have some evidence to keep back for himself. They had picked up the notes Cress had mentioned, and then, in the style of the best *noir* thrillers, Kate had tactfully stepped outside the door of Cress's loft flat while Dant had a rifle through her belongings for himself. She hadn't asked what had been in the bulging Joseph carrier bag he had brought out.

'What you have yet to learn about Harry is that unless he is made *aware* that he doesn't know something, he really doesn't mind not knowing it,' said Dant without taking his eyes off the monitor screen. 'If you cut him in half with a chainsaw – which I noticed Cress has jotted down as a possible means of disposing of the cleaning lady – you would find he has "Ignorance is Bliss" running through him like Blackpool rock.'

'How handy for him, given your "progressive" education. Yes, well, on reflection I suppose it *would* be difficult to get suspicious about you apparently staying in your room all day, fiddling with yourself.'

'How do you know I'm just fiddling with myself? I've had several very good offers recently from young ladies who would like nothing more than to fiddle with me.'

'Quite. Meaning they'd like to do nothing, more.'

'Oh, ho ho ho. Give me the editorial verdict on the stabbing scene.'

As soon as they'd got hold of the necessary materials, Dant and Kate had fallen into a surprisingly efficient working pattern, given that Dant was a self-confessed idler and Kate would normally rather stick pins in her tongue than do one sentence more editing than she had to. When they had opened up the files on Cress's laptop Kate's eyes had widened in disbelief at the merciless observations about the flat and its inhabitants, but without saying a word Dant had completed various bits of technological wizardry and transferred the whole book as written by Cress so far on to his computer.

And then they started changing it.

For a whole week, Dant sat smoking heavily in his room during the day with the notes, rewriting whole sections – he kept the events the same, but transformed the over-serious, darkly stylised prose into the kind of thriller Jilly Cooper might write if she was chairing a creative writing collective with Marian Keyes, Harold Robbins and Elmore Leonard. Under Dant's skilful style, which hovered precisely on the knife edge between parody and brilliance, fey David turned into a Bertie Wooster-ish lovable idiot, Cameron into a lupine gay predator and Ariel became Cressida herself, right down to her estate agent's eyes, constantly assessing the worth of everything and everyone in the room. It was no wonder David, Cameron and Ariel all wanted to kill each other. And as they now attempted to do so every three pages, it was a farcical triumph that they weren't all ex-flatmates by the end of the first chapter.

Kate left work on the stroke of five every night and came home to edit what Dant had written during the day. Although she didn't mention it to him, even as she edited his words onscreen she was taken aback at how even-handed he'd been, making his 'own' character scarifyingly horrible, while gently removing the sting from Cress's character assassination of Harry. His style was perfect, hitting pastiche dead on with a lightness of touch she should have guessed at from his acid put-downs.

Sabotaging Cress's book to make it unbuyable would have been too easy, Dant had explained to her. Stealing her authorship, in the same way that she had stolen their personalities, and transforming *Guilt Trap* into a parody of its own genre so good that, in Kate's opinion, Elaine would be lucky to get it, was a stroke of warped genius worthy of Anna Flail herself. And if all went to plan, the first Cress would know about it would be when the offer was being made. At which point, Dant was certain, her pride and acquisitiveness would struggle for the upper hand – 'But if I know Cress, if someone tells her they love her *and* offer her money, she'll happily admit to being Naomi Campbell's ghostwriter.'

He even rubbed his hands while he said it.

Kate had a faint twinge of guilt at the long-term psychological effects of changing the product of someone else's imagination, but then reasoned she did this every day with Rose Ann, so she was hardly in a position to get moralistic about it. Besides which, the pace at which they were working left little time for agonising about ethics.

While all this feverish activity was happening, Cress managed to phone from her traction device once a day to check on Kate's progress, which meant that Dant had to create a second pretend story-line, to follow what *should* have been happening in the book. Once or twice Kate thought about hanging up on Cress, when she was being imperious and/or pretending to be friendly, which now sickened her, but Dant made her carry on talking. He said hearing Cress on the speakerphone gave him better inspiration, knowing what he was up against.

Kate observed with a morbid glee that her relationship with London had now reached its all-time nadir, but like a Jerry Springer Show guest, she was drawing a sick strength from delineating exactly how bad it had become. Her landlady, whom she had mistaken for a slightly supercilious but still fundamentally caring big-sister type, had turned out to be a cow of the first order and with hopeless delusions about the quality of her writing to boot.

Giles hadn't been in touch for ages, but she didn't really mind any more. It was better to put him right out of her mind than to keep on picking at the scab while being unable to do anything about healing it. Besides, thinking about Giles got in the way of her guilty but highly erotic fantasies of grappling over the washing machine with Harry, which showed no signs of abating after at least a month. If anything, Cress's book had made things worse, since her reactions to Harry's humiliation were so extreme that she was beginning to wonder whether she might be suffering from something more serious than a crush after all.

Work was mad, she was exhausted from staying up editing late (Dant gave her Cress's laptop so Harry wouldn't draw any conclusions from the amount of time she was spending in Dant's pit – although he did spare her blushes by handing it to her with the words, 'I can't stand being crowded, so take this and fuck off!'), working out how best to mastermind the R. A. Harper submission with Elaine was nerve-wracking, and just to add insult to injury, she knew she was putting on weight because the last time she had tried to pull on her size ten jeans, they had stuck at her knees and refused to go any further. They were now balled up in the corner of her wardrobe.

'Have you worked out how you're going to end this?' Kate asked Dant as she inserted some punctuation into his free-flowing dialogue. There was something rather satisfying about going through the text, neatening and straightening. That said, she had a feeling that he went through it all again as soon as she left the house, and took out all her changes.

'I was thinking about having Ariel storing some poison in the water filter, then have David make ice-cubes with it and inadvertently poison everyone, including her, at a wild cocktail party.'

'Mmmm,' said Kate. 'Has to be cleverer than that. And less probable.'

Dant leaned back on his chair, swinging the front two

legs off the ground. 'The great beauty about this whole "genre", if you will, is that – and I'm quoting the great novelist, R. A. Harper herself – the idea of an ending *per se* is a bit bourgeois. I did think about having the narratorial eye panning around the flat for the final chapter, and noting no sign of life at all, just the faint humming of an overworked dishwasher and a stack of unpaid bills piled up behind the door.'

'And a funny smell coming from the bathroom?' suggested Kate.

'And another from the bedroom and an interestingly Pollock-influenced decoration on the kitchen wall. Yes, it could work.' Dant scribbled it down.

'And how far is that from the intended conclusion?'

Dant looked at the file in front of him. 'Quite a long way, actually. From what I can make out from these incoherent drunken ramblings, Cress intended to wrap things up with the sudden unexplained arrival of a very attractive yet glacial brunette, mysteriously working both sides of the law at once, natch, who would step over the dead bodies and claim all David's investments as her own, turning them into an internationally renowned chain of vodka bars.'

'Natch.'

'I think we can do without her though. Or . . .' Dant scribbled on a piece of printer paper, '. . . recast her as the confused bimbo detective inspector assigned to the case, who comes in at the end and hasn't the faintest idea what's been going on.' He drew a big circle around his notes. 'Yes, I rather like that image.'

Kate covered her mouth with the back of her hand to suppress a yawn. It was well after midnight. 'How much more have you got to do? Elaine's making vague noises at work about talking about the book, which I reckon means that Phil's assistant's chasing her for a reaction. I would imagine she hasn't read it yet. Which actually would make it easier for me to substitute the new version, wouldn't it?'

Dant did a quick word count on the entire document. 'Not much more. I reckon we could finish it by the end of tomorrow night, Acts of God and the sudden arrival of Cress in a full body cast permitting.'

'You have amazed me. I never knew you had it in you to be so efficient.' Kate picked up the piece of paper Dant had been writing on and started drawing a flow chart. 'OK. This is how we'll have to do it. Tomorrow I'm going to tell Elaine how much I love it, so that she starts getting excited about it.' She drew a square box, then added an arrow coming off it. 'But while I'm doing that I'll have to remind her about Araminta Fforsythe and how great *her* three chapters were meant to be, so the two ideas get lodged in her brain, for want of a better word, at the same time.'

'Meanwhile . . .' she started another box opposite, 'I'll have to tell Cress to phone Phil Hill, ask him how it's going, feign shock and surprise that he's sent the manuscript out, *find out where it's gone—*' she drew a double circle around the words, 'which is vital, and then tell him that she's finished the whole thing and wants to send an entirely new version to the publisher in question *directly from her.*'

'That's a lot for Cressida to remember,' said Dant.

Kate looked up at him. The big panda circles round his eyes were looking more exaggerated than ever, but he had a restless buzz of suppressed energy about him that she hadn't noticed before. Kate didn't think she'd ever seen him fidget. Now he was banging pencils and twiddling paper-clips like a sixty-a-day smoker going cold turkey. Except that his nicotine intake had actually increased. Whatever went on between him and Cress was just too bizarre to contemplate, she thought. 'We *are* talking about the woman who runs the seventh most fashionable bar in London, according to *Elle* magazine. I think she can steamroller Phil Hill without too much trouble.'

'Yeah, I guess she is about to make him quite a lot of money,' conceded Dant. 'And that is something of a motivating factor with her.'

'OK,' said Kate, joining up the boxes with long swirling purple arrows. 'We then send the manuscript to Cress in Val d'Isere . . .' She pulled a face at Dant. 'God knows how much that will cost.'

'Forget it, my mother gave us a Fedex account.' Dant stretched his long legs out on the desk and looked at Kate with a ruefully amused expression, as though he half didn't expect her to believe him. 'Last time she came out of rehab she set it up so we could send stuff out to LA, to keep her in touch with her "inner mother". Things we'd made for her, you know. Expressions of our love. I think she forgot we were a bit beyond the potato printing and toilet roll angel stage. Cress sent her some scary psycho child artwork made from razors and Mars Bar wrappers and I think that was it.'

'OK,' said Kate, pretending not to have heard the last bit. You couldn't make it up. 'One copy to Cress, one to Phil Hill, and I'll take one in to the office and pretend it came in with the post.' She bit her lower lip. 'All this has to be timed so Cress and Phil get their copies *after* Elaine, so there's nothing Cress can do about it when Elaine wants to make an offer.'

'You're really certain that Elaine will make an offer for this?' Dant stopped picking his cuticles with the paper-clip and looked at her very seriously.

'Positive. I've been reading the kind of scripts she's been offering for and this is just so much better. I mean, I think Elaine would have offered for the original, but this is . . . inspired.' Kate wasn't sure how far she could go with praising Dant. 'Not only have you got the *noir* pastiche exactly right, but the whole thing could have been written by a fluffy girlie fiction author. It's . . .' She shut her eyes to squeeze out the right phrase, 'it's old-fashioned boys' fiction, written by a modern girl, set in modern London with old-fashioned wit.'

Dant raised his eyebrows, impressed. 'Have you been thinking about that?'

'You're not the only one who can do spontaneous drivel.'

Kate flapped her hands at him. 'Go on, write that down. We're going to have to do a covering letter from Cress. Might as well give them a free shoutline into the bargain.'

'There's one other matter arising, since we're talking about it,' said Dant slowly, 'and that's money. Have you cut any kind of deal with Cress? You're doing all the work and she's getting all the cash.'

'Oh, that,' said Kate. 'That's a very Thatcherite expectation, isn't it? Well, to be honest, the expression on her face when she realises she's contracted herself to write another two spoof thrillers will be worth more than mere money but, I don't know, I thought ten per cent of the whole deal, in cash, when she signs, and then free rent as long as I want to live here? Does that sound reasonable? In return for total secrecy, of course.'

'Of course,' said Dant. He smiled grimly. 'It's about time she had a lesson on how to treat people properly.'

Kate put her hand to her mouth. 'God, it's just occurred to me,' she said. 'What do *you* get out of it? *You've* done all the work here and you still have to see Cress walk off with a whacking great cheque. God, Dant, I'm sorry. We can split the money, if you want. I could ask for fifteen per cent, to cover it?'

'Don't worry about it,' said Dant. 'We have ways.'

He turned back to the computer. '"Ariel takes the candlestick from the shelf. Weighs it thoughtfully in her hands . . ."'

'Isobel, have you got a minute?' asked Elaine, peering round Isobel's office door.

Isobel looked up from the letter she was typing and saw Kate standing behind Elaine, stretching her eyes into circles of intimated excitement. 'Of c—' she began.

'Good,' said Elaine, barging her way in. Once Elaine was out of the doorway, Isobel could see that Kate was leaning on the post room trolley, on which were stacked about twenty-five full-size manuscripts.

'Manuscript,' said Elaine, holding out her hand behind

her. Kate pulled the top manuscript off the stack and put it in her hands.

'Isobel,' she went on, 'I've just had the most amazing submission in from Phil Hill, and since you're part of the target market for this type of fiction, I want you to read it for me and report back tomorrow morning.'

'Tomorrow?' said Isobel before she could stop herself.

'Isobel,' said Elaine reprovingly. She started running her hands nervously through her dry curls. 'This is a major project. I will be asking the entire senior team to read it overnight, and I hardly think *you* can be busier than them.'

'OK then,' said Isobel. While Elaine turned her back she dropped the manuscript in a corner with a loud thump. Elaine spun round and Isobel smiled sweetly up at her.

'Come on, Kate, we need to get these out as soon as possible,' said Elaine, turning on her heel and tottering back down the corridor.

Isobel spread her hands wide in amazement, and did a silent scream. 'Oh my God, you've actually done it?' she whispered.

Elaine's high-pitched voice drifted back to them from the export manager's office. 'Ewan! I have something very special and exciting for you . . . Kate!'

'Tell you later,' said Kate and trundled her trolley down the corridor towards Elaine's excited sales patter.

chapter thirty

It didn't escape Kate's notice that the meeting she was minuting now could not be further from her first miserable attempt last year. For one thing, she knew everyone's names now, and only used the rude abbreviations for amusement value. For another, she probably knew more about what was really going on than they did.

Elaine had called an emergency meeting to talk about the revised and finished manuscript of *Guilt Trap* which had arrived by courier yesterday morning, and which everyone in the company had now read. Even Isobel had been called into the meeting to express her views on it. Megan, whose own opinion of her significance was currently far outstripping everyone else's on account of the cybernovel, had tried to stroll in casually with her notepad, but Jo, a Megan herself but for the all-important six-month head start, had spotted her and immediately asked her to make coffee for those on the circulated agenda.

'So, can we get on?' asked Jennifer. Today she was sporting an outfit that made her look like a very tall pea pod. 'I have a meeting at eleven.'

Isobel, sitting next to Kate, wrote 'Aromatherapy appt' on her notebook.

'Elaine?' The boardroom table was democratically circular, but Jennifer managed to make it clear where the head of it was. And despite it being Elaine's meeting, she had settled herself and her massive lead crystal goblet of mineral water right there.

'Yes, absolutely, yes,' said Elaine, shuffling her papers together in a businesslike manner. She coughed and instinctively reached up to shove her fingers in her hair but, perhaps in anticipation of her nervous twitch, it was all pinned back in a tight French pleat. Renegade strands were already escaping. She gave the impression of having been recently electrocuted.

Everyone sat around the table with matching manuscripts in front of them. Kate jotted down the initials of all the those present, noting as she went how far most of them had got with the manuscript. Ewan the export manager had read a derisory twenty pages, which meant he thought it was appalling or fabulous. Julie from publicity had dutifully read the lot. Or just taken out all the pages and shuffled them back together again unread.

'I want to be very bold about this,' said Elaine firmly.

Kate wrote 'First time for everything' on her notes.

'I think this is our major title for the autumn, if not *the* summer blockbuster. *Guilt Trap* is the cleverest treatment of a crime genre I have ever read and it works on all kinds of different levels.' Elaine injected a serious pause in which she gazed at them all from under her rabbity-pale eyelashes. 'This could be the first cross-over book from the American *noir* genre to the frothbuster market.'

'A heistbuster!' said Jo brightly.

'That said, I don't think we should ignore the deeper, more philosophical side of the novel,' said Elaine. 'There is a very real message about the implicit trauma of urban life within these pages and I honestly think, really, I honestly think that this could be our first serious contender for the Orange Prize.'

Simon the literary fiction editor felt professionally obliged to make some noises of polite demurral.

'Really?' said Jennifer. 'Do you think it's by a woman? I had rather thought it was a male author.'

Cynthia, the main crime editor, who clearly felt bypassed by the whole thing, made noises of surprised agreement, and nodded at Elaine.

'Well, that's the hook,' said Elaine, 'it could be by anyone. Phil won't tell me who it is but assures me that the contacts are so incredible that publication would be the media event of the year. I had thought it could be a DJ or perhaps a minor royal?'

'Naming no names, I notice,' said Cynthia, rather cattily. She stroked her perm and smiled fakely at Elaine.

'I don't think Phil would waste his time with a nobody,' snapped Elaine.

'OK,' said Jennifer briskly, 'let's garner some opinions. We all know what it's about, so, Julie, perhaps I can start with you?'

Julie had come to the meeting in her miniskirt suit to try to ward off some of the interdepartmental prejudice about publicity. 'Well, Jennifer,' she said. 'I thought it was fan-tas-tic.' She tipped her head on one side, sagely.

'A bit more specific?' prodded Jennifer.

Kate noticed that everyone was fixed on poor Julie, as she would be testing the waters for the rest of them, to see if the sharks were circling today, or whether it was the turn of Jennifer's piranha mood. When all flesh was stripped from the bone before the victim had time to realise what they'd said.

Julie's head slowly resumed an upright position as she searched for something enthusiastic but noncommittal to say. 'Urmmm, the manky flat is really great and there were some really wonderful insights into the very real squalor of flatsharing,' she offered, much to Kate's indignation. 'And the really inventive ways they come up with to kill each other off are really good. We could hang a lot of publicity angles on that,' she added more enthusiastically. 'And naturally it would be really fan-tas-tic to have someone really famous to work with.'

'Yes, good,' said Jennifer. 'Cynthia? You seem keen to contribute a thought.'

'To be honest, I really worry about the author of something like this,' said Cynthia. 'And what else they could write.'

Kate looked up from her notes.

'Oh?' said Elaine, before Jennifer could convert her raised eyebrow into a pithy epithet.

'Yes,' said Cynthia. 'Because he, or she, seems to have read every crime book going and forged something from all of them without bringing anything of him, or her, self.'

Kate drew three question marks and an exclamation on her pad. She looked over and saw that Isobel had done exactly the same.

'Yes, that's interpretation of influences,' interrupted Jennifer. 'Very Zeitgeist-y.'

'But if you really must sell crime through supermarkets, I suppose this is one which could break through,' Cynthia conceded sniffily.

'I think that's the major market for this novel.' Chris, the key accounts manager, had walked in late with a pile of sagas under his arm which Kate recognised as the advance copies that had disappeared off her shelves the previous week. 'And if you don't mind me saying so, it's pretty damned prehistoric to think otherwise.'

Kate's pen hovered over her pad as she innocently caught Elaine's eye. Elaine shook her head furiously.

'Myself, I loved it,' he went on, settling himself down and helping himself to an open prawn sandwich from the tray in front of Cynthia, who had been eyeing them hungrily, but had been politely waiting to be asked to start. 'You've got pace, you've got gory bits, you've got black humour, you've got a tits-out, in-yer-face bitch, you've got TV potential. Very sexy book altogether. Much better than the usual po-faced rubbish, all short sentences and no verbs. You're not going to get anything better all year, in my opinion.'

'Let's talk figures,' said Jennifer, her face illuminated.

Chris fiddled with his calculator. 'I'd be reckoning on two hundred all in.'

Kate swallowed hard. Her heart was hammering against her chest in a Rose Ann Barton manner.

'Maybe more with a good cover and if the author turns out to have babe potential. Get it into some promotions, decent marketing campaign . . .'

'Yes, where is Diane?' said Jennifer, noticing for the first time that Diane's assistant Fidelma had been sent in. Kate noticed she didn't actually address the question to Fidelma, who waited a moment for anyone else to have a guess before she muttered, 'In Oxford, Jennifer,' rather timidly. She looked up to see Jennifer's basilisk gaze directed at her, and elaborated, 'Checking they've got the main-line station advertising right.'

Jennifer blinked. 'Right. Sounds good to me.' She was now giving out strong signals that she was on the home stretch and with the aromatherapy couch in sight.

'What did you think, Isobel?' said Elaine, in a last-ditch attempt to stamp some of her own personality on the meeting before Jennifer banged the gavel on it. 'As one of the target market readers?'

Kate felt Isobel tense up next to her. She glanced across and saw Isobel looking distinctly uncomfortable.

Elaine gave her an encouraging nod.

'Um, to be honest, Elaine, I thought it was, um, pretty dreadful.'

Kate's head nearly spun, *Exorcist*-style, on her neck as she whipped round to glare at her friend, forgetting for a moment that *Guilt Trap* was *meant* to be dreadful.

'I mean, if it was meant to be a pastiche, then it was very clever, but if it was serious, then it was . . . pretty dreadful.' Isobel shrugged. 'Sorry, but . . .'

'Fine, well, that's one opinion,' said Jennifer briskly. 'Jo. You're about the right age for this sort of thing. What did you think?'

'I loved it,' said Jo immediately. 'I thought it had vigour, wit, great bravery, immense style and really summed up what it means to be a young person fighting through the urban jungle of London today. This is a major new talent, and Chris is right, we ab-sol-utely have to have whoever it is.' She smiled her Colgate smile at Jennifer. 'Whatever the cost.'

Kate craned her neck and noticed that Jo had made herself crib notes on the front of the manuscript. The creep.

'Ewan? Chris? Can you come with me, please?' Jennifer pushed back her chair and beckoned them out of the room.

Elaine fiddled importantly with her pen and paper but only succeeded in drawing attention to her continued presence in the boardroom while the movers and shakers had moved out of it.

'How could you say that?' Kate hissed to Isobel.

'Give me a break!' Isobel hissed back. 'It is awful and we all know it. I've my professional reputation to think of here! Besides, if someone says it's crap it'll make Jennifer even more determined to buy the bloody thing. Remember how we both hated the Emma Ball book?'

'Yeah, well, you want to watch out she doesn't have you dressing up as a bunny girl and skating over to Soho to deliver the offer.'

'That happens?'

'Cameron takes the ball-bearings out of Ariel's skates and puts them in her mouthwash in chapter twelve. Didn't you get that far?'

'Didn't need to.' Isobel broke off as Jennifer strode back in with her black leather file.

'OK. I've done some calculations and we've decided, Elaine, that you should make a pre-emptive offer of five hundred thousand pounds for this and one other, the same as for the Emma Ball book. I don't want this to go to auction.'

Kate farted with excitement. It echoed in the suddenly silent room. She slid down in her chair and looked accusingly at Jo.

No one spoke.

'*Why* is there all this silence?' demanded Jennifer, raking the table with her eyes.

Everyone stared at their typescripts.

'What we are all wondering, Jennifer,' said Andrew, the Production Director, at last, 'is whether this novel is meant to be funny.'

Jennifer arched her eyebrow at him. 'That's a very pre-scriptive attitude, Andrew. I think the only important interpretation is the one which the individual reader takes away with him or herself, don't you? And I think this book can be all things to all men.'

'Or women,' added Cynthia with a sideways glance at Elaine.

'And women,' confirmed Jennifer.

'Right,' said Elaine, shakily. 'I'll get on and make the offer then, shall I?'

Kate rushed to the kitchen to make herself a double espresso to calm down. Her hands were trembling so badly that she spilled coffee all over the machine and on the floor. She was searching jerkily in the sliding cupboards for a dustpan and brush when Isobel came in to refill her water glass. She took one look at Kate, banged it down on the work surface and put her hands on her hips.

'What the hell are you doing? Why aren't you earwigging on Elaine's phone call?'

Kate swept up the coffee and tried to breathe deeply through her nose. 'I can't think about doing anything until I've had a coffee. I know that sounds like something from a government health warning about the dangers of drugs, but when you don't smoke there's a limit to what you can do.'

'Have you tried snorting that stuff off the top of the fridge and cutting out the middleman? You could chop it out with your security pass.'

'That's not helpful.'

Isobel filled up her glass from the water cooler and took the spoon out of Kate's hands. 'I'll make you a coffee if you go and find out what on earth is going on with Elaine.'

'OK.' Kate steadied herself on the side of the cooler and walked out. She had gone three paces when she turned back, a stricken look on her face. 'Should I phone Dant and tell him, in case Cress phones home?'

'No.' Isobel twisted her finger into the side of her head. 'He's not meant to know anything about it anyway, is he? Go, go, go! We're losing precious seconds here!'

'Yes, you're right.' Kate turned back to go, then spun round again. 'What will Phil do when he finds out Cress is in traction?' she hissed urgently. 'He'll know she's done something dodgy.' Her hand flew up to her mouth. 'Shit, shit, shit.'

'You are the most hopeless liar I've ever met,' said Isobel in a low voice, turning the steaming arm on.

'Am not!'

'No, I mean you're hopeless at lying.' Isobel tsked. 'What's wrong with her asking someone else to write up her notes for her? She could be in hospital somewhere in England. Somewhere pretty inaccessible, though,' she added quickly. 'Dartmoor, or Cumbria or somewhere. Where he won't try and visit her with a bunch of grapes. But getting someone to finish the manuscript makes her look dedicated, doesn't it? Perfectly plausible. As long as she doesn't get hold of *your* manuscript until after she's accepted Elaine's offer, she won't know any different. And *until* she knows different, and presumably phones Phil to go berserk, he won't realise that the version he and Elaine have got isn't the one she wrote. And if she's just pocketed half a million pounds, I hardly think she'll be phoning up to protest, will she?'

' 'S'pose not,' said Kate.

'Jesus God, do I have to do all your thinking for you?' said Isobel. 'Now get into Elaine's office with some filing and pin back your ears.'

*

Kate walked slowly back down the corridor. She could hear from several metres away that her phone was ringing, and she broke into a gallop in case it was Dant.

'Hello?'

'Erm, hello? Is that Kate Craig?'

Kate sank to her chair. 'Yes, it is. Is that you, Harry?'

'You recognised my voice!' He sounded genuinely pleased.

'Well, it's a trick of the trade.' Kate picked up the whole phone and peered round the open door into Elaine's office. She was nowhere to be seen. 'Most authors phone up and just say, "Hi! It's me!" and you have to maintain the illusion that you're sat there all day just waiting for their call. All part of the service.'

Harry laughed, which made Kate's scalp tingle with pleasure. Harry nearly always laughed at her jokes. Recently it was getting tempting to talk in a series of one-liners, just to hear his fruity public school chuckle. Simple tasks such as making toast, which now required a running stand-up commentary, had never demanded such mental exertions before. In fact, being holed up in her room with Cress's book for the past week had been something of a break for her.

'I know you're probably rushed off your hooves,' said Harry, 'but I was wondering if you fancied a burger tonight? I managed to sell a car and I feel like a bit of a celebration.'

'Oh, God,' said Kate. *Aargh*. The only time in her entire life that she really couldn't appreciate a long bantering conversation with Harry. 'Um, I . . .'

Behind her, Elaine walked into her office carrying the shiatsu cushion she heated up in the microwave and applied to her neck at times of stress.

'Elaine?' Kate swivelled on her chair as she went past.

'Is this a bad time?' Harry's voice sounded cooler.

'Um, no, I'd love to, um . . .' Kate's eyes were fixed on Elaine as she sat down and began taking deep breaths, the cushion slung around her shoulders like a baggy snake. She was stretching out her fingers one by one. Ten seconds before she picked up the phone.

'If it's a problem, forget it, I just thought—'

Kate dragged her attention back to the fact that she was being asked out for (a very informal) dinner by the man who so obsessed her that she had even volunteered his shopping list for interpretation by non-fiction's recently acquired star graphologist.

'I'm sorry, things are a bit . . .' Her voice had risen an octave above its normal range. She cleared her throat and started again. 'That would be fantastic, Harry, I'd love to have a burger with you. And you've sold a car – that's so cool!' It would all be over bar the shouting in the next hour anyway. By which time she could in theory be quite a wealthy girl. 'Shall I meet you there?' After all, what could happen this evening? Cress was in *traction*, wasn't she?

'OK, let's say half six?'

'Fine, yeah.' Should she be having a drink with Dant to celebrate? Or was that tempting fate?

'Kate? Are you there?'

Kate was staring through her open office door at Elaine. 'Um, yeah, Harry, I'll call you . . . um, later . . .' Elaine looked up and beckoned her in. 'Later, bye!' Kate slammed down her phone and got into Elaine's office in two strides and a slide into the chair by her desk.

'Elaine?' she said brightly.

Elaine shut her eyes and pressed her fingers into her temples. 'I want you to write down everything I say and everything Phil says during this conversation,' she said. 'I find in my experience of dealing with him that you need to have some kind of second witness to everything.' Her eyes snapped open. 'Not that he isn't a completely reliable and trustworthy agent, of course.'

'Oh, no, no, no,' murmured Kate.

'But he is, by definition, an agent.'

'Quite.' Kate flipped open her pad and poised her pen.

She took careful pre-interview breaths but the blood was still banging round her veins.

'OK,' said Elaine to herself. She jabbed out the numbers on the phone and pressed the speaker button.

Kate experienced a strong sense of *déjà vu*.

They both listened to the phone ring out four times, and when a male voice answered they both jumped.

'Phil,' said Elaine.

'Elaine!' said Phil. 'R. A. Harper?'

'Absolutely!'

'You're well?'

'Fantastic. And you?'

'Wonderful!'

Well, now we've established who we all are, can we please get on with it, thought Kate, drawing nervous circles on her pad.

'OK, Elaine, let's not beat about the bush here.' Phil Hill had the kind of rich and faintly sleazy voice usually heard on voiceovers for special-blend instant coffee. 'I've worked with some damn fine authors in my time but R. A. Harper writes them all into a cocked hat. I mean, I thought the original manuscript was something else, but the rewrite is just something else again.'

Kate drew five tally marks for clichés and wiggled her pen ready for the next one. She jotted down Phil's remarks for irony value.

'Oh, yes, I couldn't agree more, Phil,' said Elaine. 'We're just over the moon to have snatched some advance time on it.'

Kate started a separate cliché tally for her. It could be tight.

'Down to business then. Can you give me some figures here, Elaine? I don't want to mess you around, but I'm looking for a most significant level of advance and I do have several other folks who are pretty much desperate to see this manuscript. Including some film people.'

Kate's head bounced up at this and she wrote down 'Film Rights!' The meeting had been funny but this was too surreal and, frankly, the whole thing was getting out of control. Elaine saw her interest and smiled patronisingly.

'Well, let me say that I've just come out of a project meeting, Phil, and I've never heard such unilateral enthusiasm for a script in all the time I've been editing here.' Elaine braced herself against the desk.

Kate knocked off another tally mark and noted the blatant lie for good measure.

'We'd like to offer five hundred thousand pounds for *Guilt Trap* and one other similar novel, British Commonwealth including Canada, with the usual bonuses for film adaptations, *Sunday Times* bestseller lists, positive discussion on the *Late Review*, et cetera, and all the standard sub rights splits and high discounts, as per the Emma Ball offer.'

Kate and Elaine held their breath as the line went quiet at Phil's end.

Oh my God, thought Kate, as it dawned on her properly for the first time. That's fifty thousand pounds!

'Right,' said Phil, as if Elaine had just offered to pick up his dry-cleaning. 'Right. Let me get back to the author about that, Elaine.'

'Ah, the mysterious author!' said Elaine, as if the dry-cleaning was on her way home and she had to pick up her own anyway. 'I hope the fact that I'm pretty much making a blind offer here isn't going unnoticed, Phil. Now I've put my cards on the table, can you at least tell me whether R. A. is a man or a woman?'

Kate longed to say, 'Both, actually.'

Phil laughed richly and smoothly. 'All I can tell you, Elaine, is that R. A. H. is a fabulous, fabulous talent, with more connections than you can shake a stick at and fabulous, fabulous potential for all those glossy mags. You will be looking at that five hundred thousand as a drop in the ocean in a year's time, believe you me.'

'In London?'

'At this very minute.'

Well, sort of, thought Kate.

'I suppose what we're all dying to know here,' wheedled Elaine, trying a final attempt at flirting, 'is whether R. A. is Cameron or Ariel?'

Oh, *please*.

Phil just laughed knowingly and ignored her. 'Elaine, I will try to get back to you as soon as possible, my sweet. I know you'll all be on tenterhooks, so I promise I won't keep you waiting a moment longer than I humanly can.'

Even Elaine scribbled 'Patronising git' on a Post-it note at this point and slapped it on Kate's notepad, while stretching her lower teeth over her top lip.

'Fine, OK,' she said. 'But I can't guarantee that the offer will remain on the table overnight.'

Oooh, tough cookie, thought Kate.

'No, understood. Give my love to Jenny, won't you?'

Jenny?? Did he mean Jennifer Spencer?

'Speak later,' cooed Elaine.

'Speak later, Elaine!'

They raced to put their handsets down first. Elaine slammed hers into the cradle and won by a microsecond.

She rested her hand on the receiver and looked at Kate. 'Well, that wasn't too bad, I suppose,' she said. 'I always feel as though I want to go and wash my hands after a phone call with Phil Hill.'

'Mmmm,' said Kate. She wondered whether she was in shock.

Elaine stretched out her hand for the notes Kate had been taking and Kate hugged them quickly to her chest. 'Oh, they're very rough, Elaine, I'll go and type them up for you.' She flashed a quick smile.

'Right,' said Elaine. 'You do that, then I need you to go to Culpepper for me. I'll make you a list.'

'So, the agent is phoning her now with the offer and she's got until this evening to make up her mind.' Kate looked over her shoulder in case Fidelma came back unexpectedly. Marketing was the only department empty enough to borrow a phone in without being overheard.

'Did you get anything on paper about that ten per cent?' asked Dant. Kate heard the click of his lighter again. It sounded as though he was smoking two cigarettes at once.

'No, but she knows I can dish the dirt on the whole thing, doesn't she?' Kate privately doubted whether this would be much of a deterrent to Cress in full stampede.

'Surely the agent will just accept on her behalf for that kind of money? He must know Cress well enough by now to know that she is seriously liable to fuck up any situation that good, purely out of habit.'

'He has to tell her. He's legally obliged. I just hope he doesn't start going on about how fantastic the new-look characters are, that's all. As long as Fedex don't manage to deliver early, we should be OK.'

'You're not having a laugh about the money, are you?'

'Nope.'

'Shit.'

Fidelma's blonde head bobbed past the partition. 'Dant, look, I have to go. I'll let you know as soon as Phil Hill rings back with Cress's response.'

'What are you doing in Diane's office?'

Fidelma was standing right behind her. Kate spun guiltily away from the phone. 'Elaine said Diane had mocked up some kind of marketing plan for the R. A. Harper offer. And I've come to look for it.' It had to be said, her improvisational lying had come on no end since leaving university.

'But I put it on Elaine's desk before the meeting.' Fidelma's eyes narrowed.

'Ooops, my mistake!' said Kate breezily. 'I'll go and tell her then.' She strolled out of the office, but not before noting, for Isobel's benefit, the projected sales figures for Cynthia's Mother's Day crime promotion.

*

By mid-afternoon, the full blissed-out after-effects of Kate's four double espressos had kicked in properly, and she was feeling remarkably at peace with the world. She had cleared the backlog of readers' letters which had been threatening to overflow the drawer, and authorised all the freelance editors' invoices, and was in the middle of writing some rather good copy for one of Elaine's historical romances.

Things were looking almost as rosy for her as for Lady Eglantine de Lacy de Montagne. Even though a moated castle and a life doing nothing more demanding than stitching endless tapestries and palpitating at the sound of approaching horses were out of the question, things weren't bad: she was about to make more money than she would earn in three and a half years here, Cress was about to get exactly what was coming to her and, for the icing on the cake, Harry was taking her out for dinner. Kate had even phoned up Fedex to check the arrival time on the parcel, and they had confirmed that it wouldn't reach the Hôpital du Sacré Coeur until the following afternoon.

She added her final 'dot, dot, dot' to the end of the copy and e-mailed it to Sarah in Production with a sense of a job well done.

Kate picked up her phone and speed-dialled Isobel's extension.

'Fancy a quick stroll to the sweetie shop for some four o'clock chocolate?'

'Give me five minutes,' said Isobel. 'I'm trying to think of some sales points for Dilys Richards and her collection of hairdressing short stories.'

'Right-o,' said Kate. Out of long habit, she glanced at the international time chart she kept in a small corner of her computer screen. Quarter past nine in Chicago. Giles would probably have been in the office for at least an hour.

To distract herself from the twinge of guilt, if not repentance, this thought gave her, she leaned back in her chair and looked through to Elaine's office.

Elaine was rattling away furiously at her computer, typing out the very complicated confirmation letter she would have to fax to Phil later that afternoon.

'Elaine, would you like some chocolate? I'm going to the Post Office.' Kate called through.

Elaine stopped, and without taking her eyes off the screen, pressed her lips together hard, then said, 'Yes, can you get me four Kit-Kats, please?'

'Four?' said Kate incredulously before she could filter out the rudeness from her voice. She couldn't actually imagine Elaine eating chocolate, let alone four Kit-Kats at once.

Elaine flushed. 'Nerves.'

Well, thought Kate, the things you learn about people at times like these.

She had one arm in her jacket when Elaine's phone rang. They both froze.

Elaine made herself wait four rings before answering, then affected a Jennifer-like lack of interest.

'Oh, hello, Phil!' she said.

Kate slipped her other arm into the sleeve and shrugged on the jacket. The Milky Bars were on her!

'Oh. Oh.'

Something in Elaine's voice made Kate take off her coat before she knew what she was doing. Without speaking she gravitated towards the door of the office and leaned on the door-jamb, her mouth half open.

'I see,' said Elaine tightly. 'As you say, it is the author's prerogative to ask for time to consider. If there is anything to consider. But, as I said, I don't think I can allow an offer of this magnitude to stay on the table overnight.'

Oh, God!

Kate's bladder sent a red hot pain through her lower body as she saw in a flash how everything was about to go horribly wrong. If Cress made everyone wait until the following day, just to be a prima donna, she would get Dant's manuscript, and go berserk, and maybe call the whole thing off altogether. Elaine's impression of a tough talker might fail to scare a primary school outing, but Jennifer really could make her take the offer off the table, just in case Phil was even now ringing around the other publishers to see if they would offer more. And there was no guarantee that anyone else would be as desperate for it as Elaine. Kate didn't know what the publishing term for gazumping was, but she was sure it went on.

More to the point, it was inevitable that Jennifer and Elaine would find out she was involved and they would be bound to sack her. No question.

Kate pulled on her coat again and darted round to Isobel's office.

'Isobel?' she hissed.

Isobel looked up from the spreadsheet on her screen. 'There's no need to be so secretive, everyone knows where you're going. You are allowed out of class before home—'

'Isobel, you've got to help me,' said Kate, scrabbling in her handbag for her purse. 'Have you got your mobile phone with you?'

'Yes,' said Isobel, not understanding. She reached for her bag and passed the phone to Kate.

'Fantastic,' said Kate. She opened up her purse and looked hopefully in the notes section. It was full of cash withdrawal slips. She opened up the coins section and emptied it out on Isobel's desk. Ten and two pence pieces rolled everywhere. 'I'm going to make a very expensive mobile phone call,' she said. 'I hope that will cover it.'

'Don't worry. "Will pays the bills" is my motto,' said Isobel, as Kate turned to go. 'Kate! Hang on!'

Kate turned back.

Isobel selected a twenty pence piece from the pool. 'Can you get me a finger of Fudge and five penny chews?'

chapter thirty-one

'So I just told her to phone Phil back as soon as I hung up and accept the offer before Elaine withdrew it.'

'And what did she say?'

Kate sucked the last traces of unblended malt powder off the bottom of her banana and peanut butter milk shake. She was too nervy to eat anything. The Big Bubba which Harry had ordered for her (no cheese, no mayo, double salad) sat untouched and greasing on the counter next to her bag. She pulled a face at Dant. 'It might be quicker if I ran through "What didn't she say?"'

Dant sighed and did a theatrical double take at his watch. 'Well, a brief synopsis before Harry comes back from the loo would be good.'

Kate gave Dant an evil look. 'Then you promise you'll sod off?' Having him 'turn up by chance' at a theme burger bar he would normally anoint with garlic and crucifixes was pushing the boundaries of credibility – luckily, in Harry's case the boundaries of credibility were amiably flexible. But she urgently needed to brief Dant, and conjure up a contingency plan in case Cressida phoned while she was out, and this had seemed like the only way.

He looked at her as though she was the deranged and annoying one. 'You think I *want* to be seen in here? Believe me, I know too many people in Chelsea for this place to be safe.'

Kate sighed impatiently and flicked a nervous glance in the direction of the loos. 'I just told her that offers like that don't stay on the table overnight, and that if she wanted it, she had to phone Phil immediately and make him accept it on her behalf. I might have overplayed Elaine's professional brutality a little' – describing her as the most ruthless editor in London only worked over the phone – 'but if she doesn't accept now, we're all in the shit.'

'She didn't find your sudden concern fishy at all?'

Kate considered. Reception hadn't been much better than three bars throughout the call and she'd been paranoid that someone from Publicity would stroll past after a lunch at Livebait and see her. Divining the nuances of Cressida's bed-bound moodiness hadn't been uppermost in her mind, particularly compared with the blood-thickening thought of fifty thousand pounds evaporating into the thin air of the Swiss mountains.

'No, I just gave her the "This is in your best interests" spiel and tried to sound as professional as possible. Stressed that everyone *adored* the finished version. But obviously not so much that she would suspect it was all that different from the first one.' Kate shrugged. 'I think she was enjoying the attention, frankly.'

'Well, there's a novelty.' Dant picked at one of Harry's abandoned onion rings. 'Did she mention me at all?'

Kate marvelled yet again at the complete self-absorption of the Grenfell family. 'Only to speculate briefly but gleefully on how mad you'd be when you found out what a spectacular leap her career as a novelist had taken, given that you were the one who was meant to inherit all Anna's creative skills.'

'Ah!' Dant sniffed the air appreciatively. 'The sweet smell of homebaked irony!'

'Yeesss, well, as far as I know, the deal has gone ahead, since Elaine spent the next hour trying to levitate the phone by the power of positive thinking and the rest of the after-noon in the rights department sorting out the contract, and accepting shrieks of girlish congratulations from the rest of the editors.'

Apart from Cynthia. Natch.

'Which looks like home and dry to me.'

Dant and Kate looked at each other. Kate could only hold his dark stare for a couple of instants before dropping her eyes to her untouched burger. Dant had unsettlingly long eyelashes for a bloke and he did that scary 'I'm looking through you' stare of the completely self-assured. But for two newly very rich people who had just pulled off a scam worthy of Malcolm MacLaren, neither of them seemed particularly confident about it.

'Unless . . .' Kate began, staring at the poppy seeds on the burger bun.

'Unless.'

'Unless what?' said Harry, climbing back on the high chair still shaking drops of water from his hands. He *always* washed his hands after going to the loo.

Dant didn't even bother to catch Kate's eye. 'Unless you're going to finish these delicious onion rings, I'm taking them with me to my hot date. Got to keep the ladies at bay somehow.'

'Go ahead, matey,' said Harry, waving them away with a gracious hand. 'Today I sold my first proper car and I have to tell you, the commission was not unadjacent to five hundred big ones. Onion rings are go.'

Dant and Kate tried to look impressed.

'Was I hearing things or were you talking about Cress?' he said, idly twirling a sprig of coriander.

'Harry, you're getting too old for this pathetic schoolgirl stuff.' Dant turned to Kate. 'Any excuse to bring her name up. I once asked him if he was getting anything nice for Christmas and he launched into a long discussion of edible lingerie and effervescent bath salts – and that was just the stuff I didn't block out in therapy.' He slapped Harry on the shoulder; it was a playful gesture, but Kate caught a glint of sadness in Dant's usually sardonic expression. 'Get over her, Harry. She's really not the person you think she is.'

'Gosh, I don't know,' said Harry into his milk shake. To Kate's dismay, a small smile turned up the corners of his mouth and remained there as he sucked hard on the straw.

Kate's heart lurched and several unwise comments sprang to her lips. She bent her head to her milk shake and slurped up a mouthful of liquid ice-cream to stop the unwise comments coming out. It would be bad enough knowing what she knew about Cress and her literary vision of Harry, even if she didn't fancy him. She coughed on a bubble of malt powder. Fancy him. Whatever.

If she were truthful with herself, the double bind of secrecy and loyalty was driving her mad: she knew, by the laws of Cress's fictional flat at the very least, that she was entitled to a dramatic scene of revelation at some point – and in theory, the shock of discovering Cress's true personality should drive Harry to her arms faster than a greyhound in a Porsche – but then again, there was so much that could go wrong in between. Kate had read *Antony and Cleopatra*. She was well acquainted with what happened to bearers of bad Lurve news.

'Harry, there are brutal military dictators in West Africa who make more loyal and loving companions than my sister. Anyway, she's the last person I wish to discuss with ladies present and shortly after eating. I need to make a move,' said Dant. He put his hands on the stainless-steel counter and slid off the stool. 'Chicks to pick, birds to herd.'

'So, anyone I know?' Harry asked cheerfully. 'Not one of the girls from Fulham?'

'The Frontal Lobotomy Twins?' Dant stared at him as though he were recently released from a secure unit. Kate was pleased to note yet again that Dant's belief in universal stupidity wasn't confined to her. 'Harry, mate, I'm sorry to burst your bubble but the chances of meeting up with Poppy and Tizzy, or whatever they were called, are about as small as their aggregate brain cell count.'

Dant turned to Kate. 'It was not a good night, even by our standards. Poppy, a truly *intellectual* PA to some City wanker, opened the batting for the opposition with the classic conversation snowballer, "God, this is so weird for me, because, like, I only ever usually go out with really successful people!" Which was something of a chit-chat killer, you have to admit.' Dant held up his hand. 'But not to worry, because Mr Harvey here steps up almost at once to rescue the ailing situation with the classic line, "Listen, girls, I was reading the most fantastic article in *Cosmo* this month, all about the Ten Sex Aids Women Have In Their Handbags and Don't Know About!" Which, when silence fell like radioactive snow upon the table, he followed up with, "Come on! Let's have a look in your bag, then, Tizzy!"'

Dant turned back to Harry. 'Still, it was a cheap night, I suppose. Two Pimm's each and they were straight off back to Fulham in a black cab.'

'Which I paid for.'

'A true gent,' said Dant, tweaking Harry's ear. 'Later, kids.'

Kate watched him saunter out of the door and bound on to the number 19 bus which had fortuitously slowed down in the traffic outside. She felt a brief chill of awkwardness – to which she was sure Harry was completely oblivious – as the atmosphere shifted in Dant's absence, to the overt intimacy of just the two of them. It would have been a shiver she could have hoarded up and played back later, had she not been so preoccupied with the rest of the day's complications. Her mind raced to find something she could say to set the tone exactly right between them.

'What a prick,' said Harry affectionately.

Kate murmured an agreement and willed her stomach to stop sliding about. She focused on Harry's right hand, curled around his coffee mug. It had a light tracing of blond hair and two chocolate brown moles near his thumb. Her eyes and imagination wandered over the knobbly bone of his wrist, just exposed by his cuff and suddenly painfully intimate, up the sleeve of his shirt. She groaned inwardly with guilty desire.

Over the past six months, she and Harry had spent hours leaning on their elbows at this counter, talking about all sorts of rubbish, some personal, some random, some actually quite interesting. It was one of those classic ironies that when she hadn't thought of Harry as anything more than a kindly, if Sloaney, version of her brother, their conversations had been witty and free-flowing – exactly the impression she was desperate, and utterly unable, to create now. She sucked up the last of her milk shake, barely noticing the obscene amount of noise she was making, and thought for the eightieth time that day whether Cress would kill all of them when she found out about the book. Or rather, how she would kill them, given her apparent repertoire.

'Good day at work?'

'Can we not talk about work, please?' said Kate, wincing. But she seized on the one topic she knew Harry would be delighted to talk about at great length and without requiring any sort of contribution from her at all. 'I can't bear acknowledging that Eclipse exists out of office hours. Why don't you tell me about this car you sold today?'

Harry's face lit up with pleasure. 'The little Healey? Kate, you would have loved this car. Really, I could just imagine you in it. Headscarf, sunglasses, twinset, the lot.'

Interesting, thought Kate. Twinset, eh? She squirrelled away the useful fantasy material and nodded encouragingly.

Harry was drawing shapes on his napkin, illustrating the curves and undulations of the wheel arches. 'It was *adorable*. Blue and cream with cream leather interior, mint condition, been in a garage in France most of its life, but the acceleration on it! A real gem. Anyway, I knew the guy had been coming in to see it for about a month, wanted it for his wife as a present . . .'

Kate zoned out comfortably, leaving her mind free to admire Harry's blue eyes, which crinkled up round the edges with animation as he described the car. After completing a wheel arch, he moved on to illustrate the interior design for her. He was so cute. And so nice with it. Harry wouldn't have abandoned her to sink or swim in London. He would have enquired politely about whether she had a life jacket. Then maybe given her his own. Whereas Giles would have checked the label first to make sure it was the right kind of life jacket, and . . .

'. . . take it you're staying then?'

Kate's eyes snapped back to Harry as he touched her forearm to get her unfocused attention away from the specials board.

'Er, sorry?' She made herself look at him and not the hand on her arm.

'I said, can we take it you're staying then?'

Kate looked at him blankly. 'Staying . . . in what sense?'

Harry tapped her forehead gently. 'Hello? Anyone home? Didn't your six-month break clause run out at the end of last month? On the flat? Where we live?'

'Oh, right, that.' Kate considered this and wondered yet again how six months had managed to slip by without her noticing. The stress of finishing Cress's book, and doing twice as much work as normal to blot out Giles's absence, had sped her from weekend to weekend – faster even than her original plan to work her way round London via recommended second-hand record shops.

'Well, yes, I suppose I am staying,' she said thoughtfully. 'No idea when Giles is coming back.' Or even what would happen after that. And to think she'd been planning to bail out before the break clause came up . . .

'Shame,' said Harry cheerfully. 'More coffee?'

'Yes, go on,' said Kate, pushing her mug towards his. She had got over her reluctance to let Harry underwrite her dining out some time before Christmas.

'The bastard hasn't phoned me for three weeks.' Kate laced her fingers together and rested her chin on them. 'I don't think he loves me any more,' she added, without looking at him.

'Then he's even more of a prat than he was when he left you here in the first place,' said Harry stoutly. 'Filter or cappuccino?'

'Oh, God,' breathed Kate into her hands before she could stop herself.

'Sorry, didn't catch that?' Harry bent his head to look enquiringly into her half-shut eyes. She looked up and the intimate tilt of his head made her think immediately how few tiny centimetres there were between conversation and kissing. And how simple it was to destroy two, maybe three relationships in less time than it would take to fall under a Tube train.

She took a deep breath. 'I'll have a double espresso, please.'

They walked home slowly from the diner. Kate didn't want to be in when Cress phoned, if she phoned, and had begun to worry that, just as she had felt a protective rage on behalf of Harry, so he would probably go mad when he found out what she and Dant had done to Cressida. She had a funny sense that things would not be so easy between them again: that the prickling desire, so intensely pleasurable now, would either evaporate, or turn into something she would have to deal with – and despite her reputation for scenes, Kate wasn't very good at situations where she was in the wrong. Martyred women were her speciality, not lusty adultresses.

Harry had slung an arm around her shoulders as they came down the King's Road, and, prompted by some casual remark of Kate's about cricket jumpers, embarked on a long and complicated story about Dant's one and only appearance for the school cricket team. As the story wound on and on, dragging in bits of surplus information about Seth, Tosser, Tom, and their comprehensively unemployable mates, Kate thought warmly how she had become absorbed in their social life, almost without question or protest. They had come along in their strangely shaped life raft and dragged her out when she was sinking, rather than swimming. Kate was overcome with a sudden rush of emotional gratitude, which almost brought tears to her eyes. Or it could have been the coffee.

When they reached the turning for Deauville Crescent, Kate reached up and squeezed Harry's hand which hung over her shoulder. He tickled her ear, and she was tempted to miss the turning and go round the block again.

'I wish I'd taken you out in that Austin Healey before we sold it,' he said. 'You would have looked brilliant in the front seat.'

'Driving, I hope,' said Kate. 'Sorry, I hadn't realised that we'd not been talking about your sale for the last five minutes. Why not run me through it again? I might have missed something the first nine times.'

'Oi!' Harry pulled her plait playfully. 'I'll have you know that this is the beginning of my career we're talking about. No longer can Cressida say that I'm a useless salesman and a failed mechanic.'

'I don't think Cress is in a position to talk about careers,' said Kate darkly, marching up to the front steps. She jammed her key in the lock as if she were running it through Cress's eye.

'Oh, I don't know,' Harry began, following her in and sorting through the post in the pigeon-holes.

'Harry, can we not talk about her? Please?'

'Awful lot of things not to talk about today,' said Harry good-humouredly.

Kate started up the stairs so he wouldn't see her face. 'Anything for me?'

'Only this,' said Harry.

Kate turned her head slightly. 'What?'

'This!' Harry delivered a sharp slap to her arse and she bounced up three stairs at once.

'You pig!' she gasped, dragging herself upstairs as quickly as she could, as he thundered up behind her, growling. When she got to the bottom of their flight, hearing Harry building up momentum, she stepped aside and let him flounder past and stumble on the slippery carpet, where-upon she administered a ringing slap to his achingly beautiful bottom and sprinted past him.

'Come back here, you little cow!' he yelled, spluttering with laughter and sprawled like a winded horse on the stairs.

'Certainly not,' said Kate, fumbling with her keys. 'You'll have to get me first.'

'Right!' Harry pulled himself up and charged up to the next floor. Just as Kate thought it might be a good idea to let herself be caught, given that Dant was out herding birds in Chelsea, her key turned in the lock and she and Harry tumbled in at the same time.

'Oh, good,' said Dant, standing in the hall with the trans-parent phone in one hand and a Slush Puppy cup in the other. 'She's just come in. Kate, phone!'

Kate's laughter died in her throat.

Cressida. The moment had come, along with the Fedexed parcel, evidently.

She swallowed and put her bag down. Harry coughed and adjusted his dishevelled tie – like someone caught trouserless in a wardrobe, thought Kate, which gave her some little pleasure.

'God, I'm glad you're back,' said Dant, holding the receiver out at arm's length as she came over. He made no attempt to lower his voice. 'I couldn't keep up that conver-sation for longer than thirty seconds. Boring.'

'Is it Laura?' mouthed Kate hopefully. Even a conversation with Laura about divorce lawyers would be welcome at this point.

'No. Worse than that.' Dant crossed himself and raised his eyes to heaven.

Kate pulled a face at Dant and Harry and took the receiver.

'Hello, Cressida!' she said, in as neutral a tone as she could manage.

'Katie? It's Giles!'

In the closest she had ever come to an out-of-body experience, Kate watched in the hall mirror as the sudden flood in her heart showed all over her stricken face.

chapter thirty-two

'"How lovely to hear from you, Giles."'

'Er, yes, of course, it's wonderful to hear your voice – after all this time,' said Kate, gesturing furiously for Dant and Harry to piss off and leave her alone to take the call in private. She noticed, even as she was wondering whether Giles was phoning to tell her he had a green card now and was applying for US citizenship, that a faint blush was creeping up Harry's cheeks. A tiny voice in her head cheered and was promptly washed away by a tidal wave of guilt.

'What have you been up to?'

'Oh, this and that,' said Kate, jiggling her eyebrows fiercely at the boys. They jiggled their eyebrows back. Kate picked up the slack of the phone cord and swept crossly into the kitchen.

It was highly tempting to tell Giles that she had actually done something cunning and player-esque off her own bat, but she wasn't sure about his unpredictable sense of professional morals – and besides which, he was unlikely to have heard of Anna Flail, let alone remembered who all the other dramatis personae were. She was filled with a reluctance to tell him anything at all, after three weeks of silence. She suspected that the initial agreement not to disturb her equilibrium with emotional contact had slid awkwardly into something else.

It didn't register with Kate that that silence was a two-way non-conversation.

'Not too much "that", I hope?' Her insides wobbled treacherously at the confident suaveness of Giles's voice and she twisted the telephone cable round her hand.

She turned her back on the boys and fixed a wide smile on her face in the hope that it would be reflected in her voice. 'Chance would be a fine thing. Did I mention that my boyfriend is indisposed, in Chicago, indefinitely?'

'Well, what if I said he was about to return, rejoicing, within the week?'

Kate gulped and forced the smile even harder at the extractor fan. 'You're coming back to England?'

She twisted the cord more tightly around her hand, became aware of a sudden tension and heard a dramatic duet gasp behind her. She turned round to see that Dant and Harry had the cord twisted round their necks in stylish *faux* nooses and were sticking their tongues out. Dant's was bright blue after his vodka blueberry Slush Puppy. Harry had rolled his eyes skywards for better effect.

Kate gave the cord a yank and leaned her head against the fridge. This was now too much to deal with. Far too much to deal with.

'Fantastic,' she managed. The sides of her mouth were aching with the effort of smiling so hard and she still only sounded as though she'd just got a cancellation at the chiropodist's.

'*Fantasssssssstic*,' breathed Dant. She stuck two fingers up behind her back and in the reflection of the oven door saw Harry untangle himself and slope off to his room.

'Don't sound so pleased,' said Giles.

'Giles, I'm thrilled, really I am,' said Kate. 'Can you hang on one second?' She covered the mouthpiece with her hand. 'Dant, fuck off. Now.'

He pulled a face and shuffled off. The front door banged shut.

'It's just that I've tried so hard not to think about when you're coming home, so I couldn't get disappointed, you know?' said Kate. 'It's hard to adjust all of a sudden.' She pulled open her cupboard door so she could look at him while she spoke. Her eye fell on a photo of the two of them at a fancy dress cocktail party at Castle – him in James Bond black tie, her in bunny girl ears, skewed drunkenly on her unkempt hair – and something in her stomach yearned because when he came back, it wasn't going to be the same.

'Well, the project should be wrapped up by the end of the week,' he said. The highly suggestive note in his voice felt even more pronounced with Dant and Harry out of the room. Kate sank slowly on to the kitchen floor. 'I should be home in about ten days – I haven't quite got the details sorted out yet, but I thought you'd want to know as soon as possible.'

'Great,' she said weakly.

'I was really ringing to see if you wanted me to bring you anything back from the States. Clothes? Maybelline mascara? I could pop into Victoria's Secret . . .?'

'I bet you could,' said Kate, not quite sure what he was on about.

'Katie, we need to do some serious talking when I get back.' Giles dropped his voice to a more serious murmur. 'Lots of things have changed since I've been away.'

Kate's tragedy antennae twitched painfully, and the ringing in her chest intensified. For the first time in her life, she was just as scared that someone wanted to *carry on* their relationship as much as she was scared she was about to be dumped. She blinked with shock. It was not a sensation she was familiar with, and not one she could get her head round.

Instinctively she pushed the dilemma away. She would know how to react when she actually had to deal with it, and until then she wasn't going to let herself think about what Giles might mean, and what she might really want in her secret self.

Secret self. Jesus Christ. Had it really come to this?

She fiddled with the magnetic poetry on the fridge door. Black. Lover. Cloud. Streaming.

'Giles, I know things have changed, and I know we have to talk about it, but let's not do it while it's still academic? Can it not wait until you're here and I'm here and we can . . . you know.' She trailed off, disturbed by the phrases forming under her fingers.

'Of course,' said Giles smoothly. He may have a perfect back, and gorgeous eyes, and shoulders to die for, but his voice is the sexiest thing about him, thought Kate miserably. Even when he's about to dump me. Oh, *God*.

'Will you give me a call when you know exactly what flight you'll be on? I want to be there at the airport. Again.'

'As soon as I know, I'll phone,' he said. 'I can't wait to be home.'

'No, I can't wait for you to be here either,' she said. 'I can't believe it's finally happening.'

'Me neither,' said Giles.

The doorbell rang violently downstairs.

Kate felt lost for things to say. Not being able to mention the two topics that currently dominated her waking thoughts – Cress's book and Harry – tied her conversation somewhat, and she didn't want to end up swapping inanities, even if Giles *was* delivering them in the style of a chat line. For some reason, she felt almost shy talking to him, not knowing the daily details of his life to spin into chit-chat, but sensing that the mood wasn't right for Big Thoughts. She knew all the linguistics arguments for meaningless chit-chat acting as a useful social lubricant, but never really felt happy talking about nothing to someone she was meant to be close to. It felt like going through the motions.

The doorbell rang again and the intercom buzzed for good measure.

There was no sign of any movement in the house towards answering it.

Giles took in a breath prior to saying something else.

'Hang on a second, Giles,' said Kate crossly, then yelled, 'Harry! Door!' The level of manners in this flat was unbelievable. She got to her knees behind the kitchen counter and peered over the top of it. A faint rhythmic thudding came from Harry's room, which meant he was probably listening to Led Zeplin CD again.

'It's like Clapham Junction in your flat,' observed Giles.

'But without the sense of travel and urgency.' The doorbell rang again and Kate strode over the hall to Harry's room, hammered on the door, then pushed it open. Harry was lying on his bed with his back to the door, listening to the music and apparently reading a magazine. When the door was flung open, he curled himself into a defensive ball.

'Harry, there is someone at the door, please go and answer it, and don't turn round until I've left the room because I don't want to see you doing what I think you're doing,' said Kate in one breath, and shut the door again. 'Sorry, Giles, I am living with a pair of un-housetrained monkeys. We've just about got answering the phone sorted out, but the front door is more problematic when your knuckles are dragging down the stairs.'

Giles chuckled.

Fantastic, thought Kate. I can't get a man to swear he loves me but they just adore my monkey jokes. I'm turning into Dorothy Parker – but without the witty company.

'Well, that's about all I was calling to tell you,' said Giles, clearly moving back into his work persona.

Harry stumbled out of his room and down the stairs to answer the door.

'Great,' said Kate and kicked herself for not having something more meaningful to say.

'OK,' said Giles. 'You'd better find out who it was at the door, hadn't you?'

'Oh, that'll be the army of would-be suitors I've been hiding under the bed while you've been away,' said Kate lightly. Then she pulled an anguished face into the door of the microwave. What had happened to her conversation skills?

'Mmm.' She panicked at the unreadable note in Giles's voice. Sarcasm? Hope? Disapproval? 'Well, I'll phone you with the flight details as soon as I have them.' She could hear the office background noise get louder. Was he moving his phone back to his desk?

Harry appeared in the doorway, his face even redder than before. 'Er, Kate . . .' he began.

'Giles, I think one of the monkeys has got loose,' said Kate. 'I have to go.'

'Talk to you soon, sweetie,' said Giles.

Please don't get affectionate, thought Kate, then wondered why she had thought that.

'Right, yes, phone me soon,' she said and, out of habit, waited the few beats until he put the phone down. There was a pause.

'Aren't you going to hang up, Katie?' said Giles.

She stared at the phone, as if he had read her mind down the line. 'How did you know I was waiting?'

'Because I always wait for you to hang up,' he said, 'in case you have one of those famous afterthoughts of yours.'

Kate was lost for words. It flashed across her mind that she had grown two entirely different images of Giles, one for when he was in Chicago and one for when he was in London. Maybe because the busy, businesslike, not-the-man-she-slept-with image fitted in with her new arrangements here better. But underneath all her mental arrangements, he was still the Giles she had fallen in love with in Durham. Wasn't he?

'Er, Kate . . .' said Harry again, slightly louder. 'There's someone to see you.'

Kate didn't take her eyes off Harry, who was looking ominously at the door. 'Giles, let's count to three and put the phone down together.' It was a little late in the day to start this kind of thing. 'One . . . two . . .'

'I've really missed you,' said Giles unexpectedly.

Kate squeezed her eyes shut. 'And I've missed you more than you know . . . three.' And with an effort she put the phone down.

'Right,' she said. 'What the hell is going on? Please don't tell me Cress has had herself airlifted in to . . .'

Harry gestured to the front door, and Kate walked over to open it properly.

Mike was standing at the door of the flat, still in his work suit. His dark hair was sticking up in chunks, as if he'd been running his hands through it, and his cheeks were flushed redder than usual. In fact he looked as though he'd just done twenty minutes on a Stairmaster without taking his jacket off.

'Don't tell me,' said Kate. 'Some funds got unmanageable and ran you down in the office.'

Mike pushed her gently but firmly to one side and walked past her into the flat.

'Excuse me?' Kate began, following him with her hands on her hips. 'I just broke off a call to Giles to talk to you, so I think the least you could do is manage a—'

Mike turned back. 'Is she here?' His brow creased.

'Who?' asked Kate, suddenly knowing exactly who, and what. She leaned against the back of the sofa and prepared herself for the worst.

'Laura. She's not at home and her make-up bag's gone.'

Sure sign, thought Kate. Dant had dragged her and Harry to the NFT to see *Rear Window* as part of the re-education programme he was running for their joint benefit.

'Um, no, well, she's not here,' said Kate. 'Have you called her dad?'

'No,' said Mike, sinking on to the sofa next to her. 'They're on tour. Some all-woman production of *The Brothers Karamazov*.'

'Her mum?'

'Indian retreat.'

'Our mum?'

'Resits.'

Kate did a double take. 'She's failed an exam?'

Mike shook his head. 'No, she squeezed her Greek GCSE in with some resit candidates. Dad says no one's allowed to speak English in the house, let alone throw a Laura-sized wobbler.' He sank back into the cushions, removed an Aston Martin hubcap from behind him, and covered his face with his hands.

Oh, fantastic, thought Kate, checking to see Mike's shoulders weren't heaving. Here are my three impossible things before breakfast: Giles coming home, Laura taking off and Mike going humanoid on me. And that's not even counting Cress going intergalactic first thing tomorrow morning. Anything else?

Harry appeared behind them with a bottle of wine and three glasses. 'Listen, mate,' he said, 'you look like you've had a shock. Glass of wine?'

'Cheers, yeah, right,' said Mike. The relief in his voice to hear someone speaking his language was palpable.

'Shall I leave you two to it?' asked Kate. 'It's just that I've got quite a lot to do tonight . . .'

Mike's head was still in his hands.

Harry gave him a comforting but still very masculine slap on the shoulders and winked sadly up at Kate. He beckoned her down to ear level and whispered, 'Think sometimes it's easier to talk to someone you don't know, in the circs. Why don't you pop out and get some more wine, and I'll find out what the problem is.'

'I know what the problem is,' Kate whispered back. 'His wife's seen *The Omen, Part Two*, and legged it.'

Harry looked stricken. 'Run off? Oh, God, my sister's husband did that . . . Poor guy.'

They both looked at Mike, who had now raised his head from his hands and was staring blindly at Dant's biggest green scrapey painting over the fireplace. Kate couldn't believe he couldn't hear what they were saying, but he looked Mogadoned. In fact the last time she had seen him looking so spaced out was when he and three of his boring college mates had consumed fifteen grated nutmegs at the bottom of their garden in an experiment to recreate the symptoms of ME using household products. Mike had been twenty-one at the time.

'Go on.' Harry nudged her. 'I'll . . . you know.'

'OK,' said Kate, surprised and not surprised at the same time. 'If you're sure.' She got up from her squatting position at Harry's side and went to find her bag. Her purse was wedged beneath two recriminatory manuscripts, one called *Death, Schmeath* and the other called *Cover Me With Tulips*. She swept up the handful of change Harry had left on the hall table, for good measure.

When Kate got back from Victoria Wine, having taken an extra long turn around the block to be on the safe side, she found Harry and Mike deep in conversation where she had left them. Dant was lying on the floor next to the sofa, drinking wine out of the stripping girl mug and occasionally lifting his head to make a comment. Kate was stopped short at the door by the sheer maturity of the tableau, reluctant to go any nearer in case they weren't actually talking about love and commitment, but tea bagging or hot plating or some other arcanely revolting sexual practice Dant had discovered – but not actually put into practice.

She hovered.

'Kate, is that you with more wine?' said Harry without looking round.

'You took your time,' said Dant, putting his empty glass on the coffee table. 'Did you have to pick the grapes yourself?'

'No, they came ready treaded, I was just filtering them,' she said, dumping the wine on the table. Mike grabbed the bottle opener and had it uncorked before Kate had time to get a glass for herself.

'I don't understand women,' he said, taking a large mouthful. 'Or rather, I don't understand Laura. I thought it was what she wanted. It was all she ever used to go on about – marriage, babies, buying a house in a good area for schools . . .'

'Probably a sign she's taking it seriously, mate,' said Harry earnestly. 'If she wasn't thinking about it long-term, she wouldn't be so anxious about what it would mean to you. Shows she wants it all to be right.'

How could I ever have thought he was a brainless rah, thought Kate. What a diplomat! She smiled at Harry proudly, saw his concerned face and changed her expression to one of sisterly dismay.

' 'S'pose,' said Mike.

Kate sat down on the sofa next to her brother and patted his knee. Immediately he turned back to Harry, and said, 'She's been a bit twitchy recently but I thought it was just her PMT, you know.'

Harry and Dant nodded wisely and Kate resisted the impulse to rob them of this small piece of cover-all knowledge.

'You have to give her time,' said Kate, seeing that she wasn't going to be included unless she barged her way in. 'Having a baby means giving up a lot of her own freedom. And for the next twenty years. But she loves you really. She'll come back once she's sorted herself out.'

'But she knows so many divorce lawyers!' said Mike. 'I – I phoned them all up to check she wasn't there! We've just bought a new fridge, as well!' He turned back to the boys. 'I could have upgraded my car this year, but I went for the cash instead, in case . . . you know.'

'Mate!' said Harry, consolingly. 'What could you have had?'

Kate sighed and got to her feet. 'I'll leave you to it,' she said, seeing she was only going to confuse things.

She picked up her wine and went to get her manuscripts

from her bag. It was only half ten, and this evening had started so promisingly . . .

'Night,' she called out, as she passed them on the way to her room. It was disconcerting to see her brother as a husband. A possible parent like their own. Mike certainly didn't fit the secure parental mould she had stuck to resolutely as she grew up, yet chances were he would have a family like theirs, as long as Laura didn't make a break for it. She snorted to herself. Hardly the solid family unit to bring a child into. But Kate had never seen their parents fight in real bitterness, and now she wondered what lurking resentments might have come out downstairs while she and Mike had slept. The thought of her parents arguing distressed her, and it occurred to her how little she could really understand about Cress and Dant's broken childhood. Divorce, maternal exploitation, drugs, boarding school . . .

'Night.' Harry raised a vague hand in her direction, but the other two didn't bother.

'You have to understand,' Dant was saying, 'that chicks are like paper-clips . . .'

Kate didn't hang about to hear how it ended.

chapter thirty-three

'You phone,' said Kate, passing the telephone back to Harry.

'I can't phone!' He refused to take it and drained the teapot into his mug. 'Who am I meant to be? His live-in gay lover? His dad?'

'But they'll know I'm not Laura! And anyway, who am I meant to speak to? I've got no idea who he works with!'

Harry looked up at the big clock on the wall above the sink. It was half past eight. 'Kate, someone has to tell them he's not coming in. Hasn't he got any mates?'

They looked at Mike, spreadeagled on the sofa, partially covered by Harry's old Ferrari duvet and snoring like an adenoidal hippo. Kate didn't have the heart to tell Harry that that self-same duvet had nearly made a literary appearance being dragged around as a security blanket by a limp-wristed estate agent.

'Face it, he's not going to be *awake* by lunch-time, let alone doing whatever it is fund managers do.'

Kate glared at him. There was something disturbingly marital about this kind of collusion. 'Harry, if you knew what I had to get through today, you wouldn't be asking me to kick it off with—'

His eyes widened.

Kate remembered that he wasn't exactly in on what she had to do that day. 'OK, give me the bloody phone.'

He pushed it across the table at her and she looked through Mike's Filofax for a name she recognised.

She tried his work number first and on the fifth ring, just as Kate had resigned herself to going on to Voicemail, a woman's voice answered.

'Investments, Mike Craig's phone.'

'Ew, hi!' said Kate in her best Laura voice.

Harry sniggered into his tea and she swiped at him with her foot.

'This is Laura Craig here, I was just ringing in to say that Mike's had one of his tummy upsets again – I don't think he'll be making it into the office today, I'm afraid.'

'Right,' said the woman dubiously. 'Sorry, did you say you were Laura?'

'Yes,' said Kate. 'Mrs Craig. I'm sure he'll be fine by tomorrow though!'

'Laura, didn't you ring in about ten minutes ago?'

'I did?' Kate flinched. 'Gosh, silly me, I must be going a bit mad! Never mind, so long as you know! Bye now!'

She hung up and looked at Harry. 'Isn't that depressing? She knows him so well she even remembers to phone in with his sick notes in advance. Even when she's halfway through leaving him.'

'She's not leaving him,' said Harry firmly, and grabbed his keys off the table. 'Do you want a lift to work?'

Elaine was still in a party mood from the previous day, and had even gone so far as to buy a tin of organic toffee which she had left in the kitchen. By the time Kate had got in (after a half hour's delay jump-starting Harry's cold Rover from his boss Sholto's Boxster) and had dumped her bags and gone to make herself a cup of coffee, there were precisely two pieces left, and Jo was trying to decide which was the bigger of the two so she could have it. When Jo saw Kate walk into the kitchen, she put one piece in her mouth and took the other 'for Paula', her assistant, who had just come back from two weeks in Goa and, in Kate's opinion, would probably have preferred a handful of Prozac to a gobful of dairy-free toffee.

A classic Eclipse start to the day, thought Kate, picking up Elaine's post on the way over to her desk. When she opened her top drawer to get her diary out, she saw that Isobel had thoughtfully provided her with five largish toffees on a saucer, and she put one of them in her mouth as she accessed the messages from her Voicemail.

The first one was from Laura, tersely informing her that she needn't bother ringing in sick for Mike because she already had.

The second was from Personnel, reminding her to send in her holiday forms.

The third was from Cressida.

Kate clutched her mouth as the toffee attached itself to her most recent filling.

'I know you're there,' said Cressida's voice in clipped tones, 'and I will keep ringing back until you tell me why Dante has done this to me.' Click.

Dante? Dante? Where did those two get off? thought Kate crossly. All that work was hers. It was *her* idea! Then she had a frisson of fear, interrupted by Elaine strolling in, wearing her best Whistles suit and humming a rough approximation of 'La Isla Bonita'.

The phone rang again and Kate's hand hesitated over it.

Could be Giles phoning with a flight time.

Could be Harry phoning with a supper proposition.

Could be Dant phoning to tell her Cress was on her way back in a Red Cross helicopter.

Could be . . .

Kate picked the toffee off her back teeth and answered the phone.

'Well, at least you're not avoiding the telephone.'

'That would be hard, given that I work in an office and all, Cress,' said Kate. Her heart started hammering in her chest.

The sooner started, the sooner finished, as her mother used to say, before she learned all the foreign variations of the same phrase.

'Do you have any idea what you've done to me?' demanded Cress.

'*Do* you have any idea what you could have done to Harry? And to Dant?' Kate made herself go on the offensive, even though her natural reaction was to apologise comprehensively and hide in the toilet until it all went away. Rows made her feel sick. Especially with people she knew. They always seemed to turn into someone else, someone you hadn't met before. Just like Cress was doing now. This was not the girl she had drunk red wine with in bars. This was not the girl she had happily shared secrets with. Well, it was, actually. That was the whole point.

She looked around her to see if anyone was listening. The office was unusually quiet.

'Well, what would you know about creation and inspiration?' Cressida answered her own question, over the top of Kate's response – evidently following the argumentative strategy which basically ignores the other person's contribution. Still, seemed to work well enough for her normal interaction, thought Kate. Why abandon it now? 'Between you and Dant, I have suffered the most horrific rape, and I don't use that term lightly.'

'Cress, let me get this clear, what exactly do you think I – and, or, Dant – have done?' Might as well establish the boundaries straight off, she thought, drawing furious tight circles on her open diary.

'You have taken my work and satirised it!' yelled Cress down the phone. Kate flinched and thanked the benevolent God who had hospitalised Cress safely in France. 'You let me believe that you wanted to help me and then you stitched me up, making me look a complete fool in front of millions of people! I trusted you . . . I honestly thought you wanted to be involved with this. And as for Dante! Christ Almighty!

This has *destroyed* my relationship with him. As from now, I have no brother. He might as well have killed himself for all he means to me now. How can someone like you understand what this means . . . You have no *idea* how I feel right now. There *are* no words to express how I feel right now. If you had any *idea* how fucking important this book has been to me . . .' Cress was alternating her bouts of anger with worrying gasps for breath.

Kate saw her chance to get a word in, fighting down her instinct to back away from the situation and pretend it was all Dant's fault. She thought of Harry, and of all the painful confidences he had made to her about Cressida and a wave of anger surged through her. 'If you're so bothered about what you look like to other people,' she said, 'why are you using a pseudonym? And let's face it, Cressida, after what you did to Dant and Harry in that revolting parody of yours, you might as well not have had a brother in the first place. I hardly think that fraternal thoughts were going through your head when you wrote about Cameron's prolific back hair, were they?'

But Cress carried on talking over the top of her, ploughing through Kate's words like an out-of-control tank, spitting out consonants like cherry stones. Rage was making her voice wobble and break. 'All my *life* I've tried to create something of my own, something *I* was in charge of. Can you imagine what it's like to go through life with everyone knowing more about your childhood than you can remember yourself, just because your mother decided to borrow it for her own cheap profit? Can you imagine that? Can you?'

Kate went for her fall-back argumentative position, which was to allow the other person to wear themselves out and grind to a vulnerable halt. Cress had had a lot of time to rehearse all this, and there was no point trying to stem the flood. Meanwhile, she furiously jotted down notes for herself:

abuse of trust!

cash!

exploitation!
Harry!
as bad as your mother!

'. . . No, well, you couldn't, could you?' Cress raged on. 'And I thought with this novel that I would finally have the chance to take control of my own creativity – that *I* could be the filter and the observer – but no, you couldn't even allow me that, could you? What on earth do you think gives you the right to take away my identity like this? To steal my authorial control?'

'Excuse me!' interrupted Kate, before Cress got so far on to her high horse that she galloped away completely. 'No, no, no, no, no, no. Would you mind talking in proper English and not the meaningless therapy bollocks you tried to pass off as dialogue? What on *earth* did you think *you* were doing when you used our flat as some kind of home experiment in tacky spycam fiction? What did you think you were doing treating Harry like that?' Kate felt a coffee surge of energy burst through her system. 'How could you be so crass and self-serving when you've known him, and how he loves you, for all this time? All the time I thought you genuinely wanted to know how he felt about you, you were just storing it all up to hurt him in the worst possible way you could! How calculating and bitchy is that? No one's saying you haven't had a hard childhood—'

(Reserve fall-back tactic: wrong foot opponent by conceding surprise point)

'—but what you've done is exactly what your mother did to you. But it's *worse*, because you should know how it feels to be on the wrong end. And—' she went on quickly before Cress could recover from the unexpected onslaught, '—to add insult to injury, it was absolute crap! Your book was absolutely appalling! You should be bloody grateful that Dant has, by using his talent – something you wouldn't recognise if it danced naked on your head – made you a lot of money and got you a book deal that you'd never have got otherwise!'

'That's not what you said last week!'

'I was lying!' Kate felt slightly bad at this, since Elaine probably would have offered for it, but she didn't see why she should take corporate responsibility for her editor's appalling taste. 'If you think that abusing the trust of your brother, of me and of Harry, just to get some tit-for-tat revenge on your mother, was some twisted form of therapy, then you're even more fucked up than any of us thought. And, in my opinion, Cressida—'

(*Secondary reserve fall-back tactic: unsettling use of name as verbal punch*)

'—you're a pretty shitty person at that.'

Kate triumphantly ticked off *abuse of trust!*, *as bad as your mother!* and *Harry!* off her list. Her hand was shaking. Unbeknownst to her, a small crowd had gathered in Megan's office next door to listen, and Elaine had come in and let her nettle tea get cold, as her jaw dropped in direct proportion to Kate's rising voice.

'Don't tell me what is and isn't valid in terms of my personal regrowth . . .' began Cress in a warning tone.

'After what I read in that book, you have no right to tell me anything!' retorted Kate. She set her jaw. Arguing was so much easier when you didn't have to face the other person. 'And on a more basic level, you're lucky that I'm still speaking to you at all! It seems that most conversations we had must have been taped, so faithfully are they recorded. I should have been charging you! No wonder Mandy left! Did she see the draft too soon?'

'You should know that I'm consulting my lawyers . . .'

'Oh, suddenly it all becomes clear!' said Kate. She squeezed the phone between her neck and her shoulder so she could sweep her loose hair up into a pony-tail. 'I bet it wasn't a coincidence that Mandy worked for a publisher, was it? What was your little plan, then? She was going to submit the manuscript for you, get things going here, feed you with some market info so you could make sure you had the right thing at the right time . . .'

'You weren't so backward in coming forward when it came to money yourself, though, were you?'

'Shut up, I haven't finished,' snapped Kate, banging holes in the desk with her Biro. 'So that's why you were so desperate to get another girl into the flat when she walked out – to keep your plot going! And I played right into your hands by getting a job here. No wonder you were so keen to be my New Best Friend, you manipulative bitch! I should have known—'

'That I wouldn't normally be bothered with someone like you?'

Kate winced.

'I hope you realise what you have aligned yourself with in this happy little union with Dante,' said Cress, seizing the advantage. 'He is a selfish, immature, arrogant brat, who will use you for what he can get and then just trample all over you. You may think you know him, just because you've been so clever and made up this childish rubbish together, but I'd be careful if I were you. You've got no idea what you're getting into with Dant. No idea at all. He's not stable.'

'Really, Cress, you sound as though you're jealous. Would that be it? Someone else spending too much time with your brother?' In the flurry of adrenaline recklessness it was on the tip of Kate's tongue to throw out a barbed reference to Anna Flail's favourite dark implications of incest – the clinching factor in the PTA's ban on the book – but something froze her lips as the words were forming. A painful shiver through her bladder.

'Well, what is it you'd like me to do?' she said hurriedly. 'Would you like me to pop in to the editorial meeting and say that the book they've offered for isn't actually by you at all and you'd like them to withdraw the half a million pounds? Or shall I tell Phil that you're in Val d'Isere and had to get someone to finish it? Or shall I tell them who *did* write it and see if they want to give *him* the cash? I mean, Jennifer Spencer might have a good old laugh at the misunderstanding, mightn't she? Then again, she might think you're an unreliable, spoilt no-hoper who's been wasting all our time. Who can tell with these people?' Kate tried to keep her voice sarcastically light, but her head was reeling and she felt unpleasantly drunk. 'What shall I do, Cressida? Up to you, really.'

There was a long pause on the line and Kate thought she could hear Cressida drawing in a shuddering breath. She had to slap down an instinctive tug of sympathy – reminding herself that bursting into tears was Final Last Resort Only fall-back tactic. Still, Cress was a pretty pathetic case, when you stripped away the shouting and the cheekbones and the toe ring: if she honestly had so little grasp of how human beings were meant to behave towards one another, then something had gone badly wrong somewhere, and it was a shame it had gone this far without someone pointing it out to her before now.

'I just don't understand why you've done this to me,' said Cress in a very small voice. 'I don't understand why you'd want to hurt me like this. Dant, yes. He's a bastard. But I thought you were my friend, Kate.'

'Well, that's what I thought too.' Kate made herself sound cold, even though she now wanted to burst into tears as well. The tension that had been winding up in her for the past week couldn't go any tighter now. Everything around her seemed to be slipping out of her range of experience: she finally had nothing left to draw on.

'Don't think you've won, or anything as childish as that,' Cress continued, her voice still small and wounded. 'Because I don't think I'll ever recover from what you've done to me. The psychological damage is . . .'

Kate snapped. 'And the damage to Harry? And to Dant? And to me? I've just about had enough of this. I'm going to tell Elaine what's been going on, and if you want to rewrite something else then that's entirely up to you. But don't blame me if no one will touch it with a bargepole.'

'Don't!' said Cress. Then she paused as if she was struggling with herself, and said, in her more normal voice, 'My solicitor will be in touch in the next few days.' And then she hung up.

Kate slowly lowered the phone back down and tried to slow her breathing. Her entire body felt covered with a clammy film of sweat.

Her hand hesitated over the phone. Should she call Dant and let him know what had happened? Or Harry, to see if he would come and rescue her for lunch? But the complications that went with either of those options made her feel worse and she decided it would be safer to get some on-site counselling from Isobel.

And some coffee. Kate was gripped with an urgent need for an espresso.

Was this what being a drug addict felt like? she wondered, pushing her chair back from her desk with shaking legs. There was a suspicious number of people filing letters in the contracts cabinet by her office, all of whom suddenly sprang into action as she went past.

She had barely taken three steps down the corridor when Elaine headed her off by the photocopier, and beckoned her into Jennifer's office. There was not much invitation in her expression and once she had ascertained that Jennifer was not at her desk, Elaine shut the door and leaned against it ominously. She had obviously been taking lessons at the Jennifer Spencer/Dallas School of Management Stances.

'Nice suit,' said Kate. 'Are you going out for lunch?'

Elaine folded her arms. Maybe just night classes, thought Kate.

'I couldn't help overhearing your conversation just now,' Elaine began.

'I didn't see you standing behind me,' said Kate, as unused outrage spilled over into her bloodstream. 'Were you listening at the door?'

Elaine's brow darkened. 'Don't be smart with me, Kate.

What do you know about R. A. Harper? Is it you? Did you write that book?'

A weight lifted off Kate's chest. So that was all she was worried about: inadvertently giving an editorial assistant half a mill. No wonder Elaine was looking aghast – Jennifer would have gone berserk.

'No, Elaine, I am not R. A. Harper.' Well, strictly speaking. 'But it turns out that I do know her,' she added, thinking it might be wise to come clean.

'What!' shrieked Elaine. 'Her? Who is she? You've got to tell me!'

'Um, isn't that for Phil to . . .'

'Tell me now!' Elaine unfolded her skinny arms and advanced on Kate.

'She's Anna Flail's daughter, Cressida,' Kate said quickly, moving backwards on to Jennifer's filing cabinet. 'I only know her vaguely . . . I had no idea until . . .'

Elaine had stopped advancing and stood in the middle of the office, light playing on her face as though the Virgin Mary had just made herself known and asked if Elaine might be interested in this little crime thing she'd knocked off in her spare time.

'Anna Flail!' she said in reverential tones. 'Anna Flail! *Roses of* . . . That was one of the first books I ever worked on as an assistant. Do you realise what this means?' she demanded of Kate.

'Um, lots of tie-in publicity for the two of them?' suggested Kate, as yet another instrument of torture for Cress occurred to her.

'Exactly! "Like mother, like daughter!" "The Next Generation of Modern Horror!" Oh my God, I have to tell Jennifer, she'll be so—' Elaine broke off and looked at Kate with new annoyance.

'What?' said Kate, reverting at last to her full pre-office-job university belligerence.

Elaine narrowed her eyes. 'You told me you didn't have

any friends with an unpublished manuscript.'

'I don't. Didn't. She's not my—'

'You could have scooped this weeks ago. We could have had this for peanuts . . .'

Before Elaine could get herself going, the door swung open and Jennifer walked in with an armful of red-black roses and a green bicycle pump.

'What's going on in here?' she asked, picking up the phone. 'Isobel, can we get a bike as soon as possible to go to Pearl Whiteside Associates?' She clunked the receiver down and looked at Kate. 'Hmm? What?'

'Kate has just told me that R. A. Harper is Anna Flail's daughter, Cressida!' Elaine gave Kate a quick 'I'll deal with you later' glare out of the corner of her eye.

'What? The fat pyromaniac?' Jennifer's expression lit up. 'And you know her?'

What is this, Top Trumps? thought Kate. 'Sort of,' she mumbled.

'Excellent! Excellent news!' said Jennifer. 'Elaine, we are having lunch today, aren't we?'

'Yes, with Phil Hill.' Elaine tugged at the hem of her skirt. Oooh, big date.

'Well, why don't we go now? Have a pre-lunch meeting so we can sort our strategy out. Hmm?'

'Um, it is only . . . Fine, yes, let's!' said Elaine.

'That's all, thank you, Kate.' Jennifer gave her a brief smile and sat down at her desk. She flipped through her Rolodex as Elaine sank on to the comfortable chair. 'Now, Elaine, where do you fancy . . .? Le Gavroche? The Orrery?'

Kate backed out of the office, and went straight to Elaine's desk, where she ingested half a bottle of Rescue Remedy, and then went off to find Isobel.

chapter thirty-four

Kate threw her bag on the kitchen table and from a great height dropped the manuscript on to a pile of Harry's socks, which he had left helpfully next to the washing machine. She had long ago formed the theory that Harry and Dant believed that such appliances worked by osmosis – as long as they left dirty stuff near enough, it would somehow become cleaner. In this case, the manuscript stank almost as much as the socks did. Goblins and their feudal wars were never a good road to go down in the first place, and she'd lost about nine pages under her seat when the bus had stopped without warning outside High Street Kensington. In an epic that promised 250,000 words, 15,000 of which were freshly invented by the author, she didn't really think anyone would notice nine missing pages.

Kate filled the coffee machine and began composing the rejection letter in her head. It was beyond sarcasm. She switched off the espresso maker and opened the fridge to see if there was any cold beer.

A pleasant smell was coming from the oven and when she looked closer, Kate was surprised to see it wasn't a pizza.

The door slammed in the hall.

'Any plans for eating out tonight? Fnar, fnar,' said Harry, strolling in with a clinking Oddbins bag.

'Nope. I have Gandolph the Warmongering Overlord and

all his kingdom of sprites to reject, and when I've done that there's an Irish romance about a lovelorn astrologer from Limerick to assess and despatch.'

'How do you know you're going to despatch it if you haven't read it yet?' Harry opened up a pack of butter, and Kate noticed the bag of garlic, the chicken and the bundle of herbs on the work surface.

'Because if they were any good, I wouldn't be reading them in the first place, would I?' she said. 'I mean, if you had the most fabulous Aston Martin come into the garage, would Sholto let you take it out for a first spin round the block?'

'Guess not.' Harry pulled off a sprig of parsley and chewed it. 'But then we both know I'd probably prang it.'

'Well, Jennifer Spencer goes on the same principle. 'Cept at this rate, I don't think I'd be able to *recognise* an Aston Martin novel if someone put the keys in my coffee.' Kate flipped through the unread pages of *Dragonscale Vark II*. The whole manuscript was typed in a font that looked like handwriting – which sort of defeated the purpose of typing. 'But I think it's safe to say that these two are pretty much your clapped-out Fiat Pandas.'

Harry sliced up the butter and took two wineglasses out of the dishwasher. He glanced over at the manuscript. 'Not so long ago you were crossing off the days before you could tell Jennifer Spencer where to stick *Dragonscale Vark* and all its little goblin friends. But now, hey – anyone would think you wanted to stay.'

'Yeah, well, as they say on *Top Gear*, that was then, this is now.' A flicker of guilt ran through Kate as she caught the deep blue glint in Harry's eye. It was hard to distinguish between guilt and desire these days – they tended to come as a party pack. She concentrated on opening the bottle of wine he had pushed towards her.

'Glad you stayed?'

She shrugged. At least three more salacious replies ran through her mind, but she kept them to herself.

'I am.'

Kate's head shot up. Harry was stuffing slices of butter under the skin of the chicken, the sleeves of his smart work shirt rolled up untidily. A blond hank of hair hung over his eyes. The chicken, with enough butter inside it to make a bypass surgeon weep, looked like a badly plated tortoise.

When she didn't respond he looked up too. 'You're the first person who has ever lived with me and Dant for longer than six months, for a start. And the only person ever to work out how to use the dishwasher. And—' He stopped and fiddled with the pepper grinder.

With half a bottle of wine inside her, Kate knew she would have lowered her eyelashes and said, 'Go on.' But she hadn't and she couldn't. Besides, she didn't want to hear about how much she'd helped him work out his feelings for Cress. It might lead her to tell him what Cress had done with those feelings, and she had promised herself that Harry would never know from her. Instead she poured him a glass of Merlot and slid it along the work surface.

'Ah, yerp, cheers,' he said, raising his glass.

'Cheers!' Kate took a sip of wine and said, 'Well, I'm glad I stayed too. For all sorts of reasons.' She looked at him again but he was intent on inserting an entire lemon up the chicken. 'Can I help?'

'Well, you could chop some garlic. I don't know how much you're meant to put in this when you're cooking it properly. When I've made it for the lads we do go rather overboard with the old garlic.' He frowned. 'Would one bulb be enough?'

'More than enough,' said Kate, reaching for a chopping board. 'Is this a special occasion? Or are you trying to seduce me and Dant with your culinary skill?' She tried to be light, but was not surprised by the sudden plummet in her stomach. There was no excuse. Flirting with a man you knew was in love with someone else was pure masochism.

Harry shook his head. 'No, I just fancied making something a bit different, you know, had a bit of a Jamie Oliver attack in Sainsbury's. Got a garlic urge in the vegetable section.'

'So not a romantic dinner then?' Kate finished dicing up the garlic and took another hopeful swallow of her wine.

'Cheers. Er, no. Not really.' He scattered the chopped garlic over the chicken and put it in the oven. 'Though it might just be you and me. Don't know where Dant's got to. He's been a bit funny recently.'

Kate wondered privately how Harry could tell since Dant was a bit funny at the best of times, and took her wine over to the table, where she flipped halfheartedly through her Irish frothbuster. Harry carried on sticking small potatoes on to skewers.

She couldn't concentrate on the close type and her eyes wandered round the flat. When they fell on the sofa bed, still with the spare duvet on it, she remembered Mike and was struck with remorse that she hadn't thought of him before. It was a bad sign for her life if marital breakdown was being edged off the top spot of her attention.

'Was Mike here when you got back?'

Harry looked up from the chicken and slapped his head. 'God, I'm so dumb. No, here, he left you this. Sorry, I meant to say.' He passed her a note written on the back of a discarded British Gas reminder across the counter. 'I haven't read it, honestly.'

Kate unfolded it. 'I wouldn't worry, Mike doesn't normally go in for the personal touch.' As she had expected, the note was short and to the point.

'*Cheers for putting me up. Have gone home to sort things out. Will call soon. DON'T TELL MUM.*'

Kate folded it up and put it in the side pocket of her bag. She wasn't sure if Laura would have gone home quite yet. There had been an almost tangible desperation about her in the park, as though hundreds of wheels and cogs were spinning wildly just beneath the surface. As far as Kate knew, Laura's marriage to Mike was the central point of her life, so bailing out, even temporarily, wasn't something she'd decide to do on the way back from the shops.

Another reference point collapsing in her hands. Kate told herself there was nothing she could do, one way or the other, but she had a sour taste of panic at the back of her mouth.

'Bad news?'

'Um, I don't know. I thought Mike's marriage was made of concrete, but maybe I was making the mistake of thinking Laura was as stupid as he is.' Kate bit her tongue as she said it. It wasn't what she thought, it sounded brittle and careless, Harry would think she was a real cow. Why couldn't she rein in her sarcasm? Where had this overwhelming desire to be funny come from?

She pulled the manuscript back towards her. Yet another example of the malign London influence on her personality.

'Is it a good thing, or a bad thing, in your opinion, if a heroine is called something you can't pronounce?' she asked Harry, before her previous comment had time to solidify in the air.

'Like what?'

'Can't say it, it's one of those stupid Irish names – too many consonants. Tdge? Trge?'

'Here's the thing,' said Harry, pointing a skewer at her like a baton. 'When I was reading *Catch-22*, I couldn't pronounce the hero chap's name, so I just called him John in my head all the way through. Dare say it wasn't quite as atmospheric as the original, but worked fine for me.' He put his skewers in the oven. 'Worked for girls too.'

'Sorry?' Kate noticed to her surprise that she'd finished her wine and poured herself some more. Harry had barely touched his.

'Oh, you know,' said Harry, blushing. 'You go out with one girl, but in your head, you're calling her something else. Someone else.'

Kate huffed. 'You and Dant are shocking. You're lucky anyone wants to go out with you, never mind your first choice. Are you not drinking this? It's very . . . what would Dant call it?'

'Quaffable.'

'It's very quaffable. I *don't* think I'm going to take this one on,' she said, skimming through the final page. 'There are three names on the last page I can't pronounce and they're apparently sitting in a field in Fethard talking about lunar alignment.'

'Is that a good reason for rejecting something?'

'No, you reject them all for the same basic reason, which is that you "can't see how you could do justice to such a promising manuscript within the current list in the crowded UK marketplace". Obviously, when Eclipse sets up its specialist goblin warfare imprint, we'll all have to think of something different to say.'

'Would that work with girls too, do you think?'

'What?' Kate gave him a hard look. 'You dump them because you can't do them justice in the hard and competitive marketplace that is yours and Dant's whirling love lives?' She scribbled some vague notes about crowded marketplaces on the agent's covering letter. 'You could give it a go. Can't guarantee the results. But then you two can't guarantee the dumpees, can you?'

'Yerp, well, you might just be wrong there,' said Harry. He set the Bart Simpson oven-timer to one hour. 'I'm having a bit of a spring clean in the old romance department. I'm going to be twenty-eight next month and it's about time I sorted myself out.'

'Don't wipe your hands on your trousers,' said Kate automatically. 'You're very confessional tonight.'

'Age,' said Harry. 'You wouldn't understand.' He took a sip of wine.

'I'm very mature for my years,' said Kate, thinking of Mike who was older than Harry, married and still unable to pass a traffic cone without picking it up and trying to conceal it about his person. Well, still just about married. She sighed. 'What time do you expect that chicken to have reached optimum garlic saturation?'

'About eight-ish. Just enough time for a spot of Gran Turismo.' Harry rubbed his hands together. 'I'll give you a head start for being a girl?'

Eight o'clock came and went. There was no sign of Dant. Kate finished off the wine and opened another bottle. Harry took the chicken out of the oven with some sadness.

'Look at that,' he said, picking some crispy skin off a leg and crunching it. 'That is the most perfect bird I have ever cooked.'

Kate giggled suggestively because she had reached the giggling stage of being completely pissed on an empty stomach.

'Just falling apart,' he continued. 'Well, Dant's had his chance. Bastard. Get some plates, Kate.'

Kate took two plates out of the dishwasher, put them on the table and went back to the sitting room to change the music. Harry, unlike Dant, preferred to play Gran Turismo with the soundtrack off, so he could listen to the engine note better, which struck Kate as being rather pointless on a computer game, albeit one that Harry took very seriously. So they had been listening to *Nevermind*, too loudly; Kate changed the CD to *Revolver*.

'Leg or breast?' shouted Harry from the kitchen.

Kate walked into the arm of a chair and sat down on it with a bump. Now she would really have to watch herself. She was all too aware of what she was like when she was drunk; the synapse which prevented thoughts being directly translated into actual speech was broken down by alcohol, closely followed by the one which connected thoughts and actions. So it was no good *thinking* about fancying Harry, because that could lead to all sorts of trouble. And there was no point pretending that she was thinking Harry and meaning Giles, because she knew now she wasn't.

Kate stood up and had to steady herself on the bookshelf. No more wine. Lots of food to soak up the alcohol. That would sort things out. She hadn't noticed the gradual effect of topping up her glass as she went along; in fact, it had improved her car control no end. What had really distracted her was how smooth Harry's neck was as he lay on the floor next to her, and how he had undone the second button on his shirt to make himself more comfortable. At the point when she breathed in and could smell him, she had driven her car into a crowd of spectators. She wondered if she had a red wine moustache.

In the kitchen Harry was deftly carving up the chicken. Kate realised with a jolt that he was completely sober. He'd lit the candles on the table and for the first time, now the piles of dirty washing were obscured in shadow, the place looked almost passable.

'There you go,' he said handing her a plate. 'Chicken, baked potatoes, and some broccoli.' The chicken was fragrant and swimming in pools of molten yellow butter. Kate thought that Giles would have a heart attack if he could see it – probably literally.

'How much butter did you lard on to that poor bird?'

'Ah, you need to be generous with these supermarket hens,' said Harry. 'Got to make it taste of something.' He piled up his plate and sat down at the table.

'I've put on pounds since I moved in here.' Kate ground salt over her potatoes with abandon. 'First comfort eating and now Bloke Cuisine.'

'And you look much better for it. Don't like skinny girls. Don't understand them. They nag you to take them out for supper somewhere bloody expensive then either don't eat anything, or eat loads and then disappear to the Ladies' after coffee and come back smelling of breath freshener.' Harry wagged a forkful of chicken and broccoli at Kate. 'I've got two sisters, I read *Cosmo* in the loo at home, I know these things.'

Kate munched appreciatively for a few minutes, listening to the Beatles and enjoying the powerful taste sensation of garlic butter strong enough to cure flu.

'Do you like the Beatles?' she asked, as it went through her head. And that was a stupid question, she thought, because if he says no, you know you're going to be unreasonably disappointed.

'Yerp. Though probably not as much as you do.'

'Oh, I love them,' said Kate. 'Each album means something different to me, but *Revolver* is like an anul . . . an analjeez . . .' Her tongue stumbled drunkenly over the word and she blushed, hating herself for how stupid she must sound. 'A painkiller. You know, every time I get dumped, every time I'm lonely or sad or whatever, I play this and it reminds me of when I first heard it at home, when I was eight. All the songs were fresh and gave me a sort of thrill of anticipation – of being grown up. When I heard this—' she waved her hand towards the music coming from the sitting room, '"Here, There and Everywhere", for the first time, I thought, wow, that's what falling in love must be like. The melody as much as the words. 'Course, it's never been as good as that.' Kate was conscious of speaking as she was thinking again and stopped. 'Maybe because I've never had the twenty-four-year-old Paul McCartney singing to me.'

'Not even with Giles?' Harry's eyes were fixed on her chin.

Kate passed a discreet hand over it to wipe away whatever he was staring at. 'No,' she said, honestly. 'But I still think, one day . . .'

'Yeah,' he said. 'Right.'

Kate couldn't tell whether that was a 'Yeah, right' or just a 'Yeah. Right.' She hated being too drunk to interpret properly. 'But the best thing is,' she went on, 'that it doesn't have any associations to spoil it. It's all mine. So when I get dumped, I can go back to this wonderful music that reminds me of a time before I knew the boring reality of being grown up, when it was all still magical, Christmas Eve stuff.' She looked up and was disconcerted to see Harry looking at her with a soft expression on his face. Was she talking gibberish? 'Don't you have an album like that?'

'Only "Appetite for Destruction". It was the first record I bought for myself at school and I loved it because it was the first time I heard anyone say fuck in a song.'

'I must reek of garlic,' said Kate.

Harry moved a little nearer and her heart started thumping. 'Well, if we've both had it . . .'

He was looking at her in a curious way, and Kate rubbed a finger up the side of her mouth in case she really did have a red wine moustache. Giles usually removed them for her with a corner of his napkin. Harry opened his mouth hesitantly to say something, but before he could start, the first line of 'Yellow Submarine' crashed through the delicately balanced mood.

Kate didn't think she had ever hated Ringo Starr as savagely as at that moment.

'And there you have the only advantage of CDs,' she said with a wry smile.

Harry tilted his head in enquiry.

'Track listings,' she said, dipping her nose in her wine glass. 'You can rearrange them for a reason.'

Harry laughed and Kate realised the implications of what she had said. She bit her lip in embarrassment. But then he hadn't disagreed or protested . . .

She put her glass down and forbade herself to have any more to drink.

'You're nearly empty there,' said Harry, reaching for the bottle. 'Can I top you up?'

'Yes, thanks,' she said, without thinking.

He caught her eye and smiled, as though he had read her thoughts, and Kate felt herself slip even faster and deeper into warm moral quicksand.

They talked their way through three candles, Elvis Costello's

Greatest Hits and 'March' by Michael Penn, and inevitably the conversation came round to cars.

'So, what would you drive if won the Lottery?' said Harry, dangling a small coffee cup from his finger.

'Jaguar XK120,' said Kate, enunciating the syllables carefully. Oh, for God's sake, she thought crossly, he's seen you far drunker than this. You've vomited on his shoes.

'Why's that then?'

'Because they look like Jayne Mansfield on wheels,' said Kate earnestly. No one had ever asked her this question and she'd been waiting all her life to give the answer. 'All creamy curves and red leather inside. Very sexy car.' She nodded wisely.

'Have you never been in an Aston Martin?'

'When do you imagine that I would have been in one of those?' asked Kate, dangling her wineglass from two fingers. 'You think I have one round the back to do the shopping run in?'

Harry pushed his chair away from the table and picked up his suit jacket from where he'd thrown it over the back of the kitchen door. 'Well, what better time to start?'

'But we've been drinking! You can't drive,' slurred Kate.

'No, Kate, you've been drinking. I've had one glass all evening and you've had the best part of two bottles, so I'd be grateful if you don't honk on the upholstery.' Harry grinned from the doorway. 'Come on, get your coat.'

'But it's nearly two o'clock!'

'Don't go soft on me now.' He threw her a cardigan from the coatstand, and Kate added, 'Fnar, fnar,' out of habit, pulling her fleece on top of it.

'Keys?'

'Yup,' said Harry and locked the door behind them.

Kate stood on the front step of the flats and shivered.

'Stay there,' said Harry, 'and I'll be with you in a minute.' He trotted off round the corner. Kate pulled her fleece tighter round herself and decided that she was sobering up. It was late, but she didn't feel tired at all; there was something dreamlike about this evening, which she hoped would be an adequate excuse should anything go horribly wrong. After a day like today, plenty could go wrong and upsetting the fine balance of her relationship with Harry would be the final straw.

She was walking a tightrope, dreading saying the wrong word which would break the mood between them, make her feelings obvious, putting them beyond the flexible interpretation of flirting. Dreading bringing up the topic that would make him mention Cress, that would make her feel obliged by conscience to mention Giles – and acknowledge to herself that she was being unfaithful in thought, if not deed. Yet so far, Cress and Giles seemed an equal number of million miles away.

There was a subdued roar of a big engine being started and a dark green sports car nosed round the corner into the Crescent. Harry opened the passenger side door for her from the inside and beckoned her in.

From her vantage point beneath the porch security light, Kate admired the almost feminine line and curve of the car, and how confident Harry looked behind the wheel. Like he knew what he was doing. It was a transformation of the usual slightly bumbling boyish persona. She walked over and got in. Harry was fiddling with the stereo which was stuck on Radio Four. Kate pretended not to know that the radio in the Rover was permanently tuned to it.

'Don't know who can have had this last. I can never get these things to work,' he said. 'It's the most technical part of the whole bloody car. Can you sort it out?'

Kate located something with guitars and Harry pulled the car smoothly out on to the main road, as 'Alison' finished and 'Sympathy for the Devil' started.

'Oh, perfect,' said Kate. The car picked up speed and the stray strands of hair that had slipped from her plait began to lift up and float out behind her.

'Why don't you let your hair loose, Kate,' said Harry. 'That's what cars like these are for.'

'Is that why so many hairdressers drive them?'

'You poor ignorant woman,' he replied, pretending to be offended. 'I'll have you know we have people fighting over this car. I've only got it because Sholto wants me to take it for a test drive tomorrow morning.'

'Where are we going?' she asked, shaking her long coppery hair out of the loosened plait. The night air was brisk in the open car and she could feel the breeze tingling on her scalp.

'Wherever you want.'

'But I don't really know anywhere except the office and our road. You're forgetting I'm not a big London fan.'

'I know. I thought it was about time you saw it properly.' Harry turned down towards the centre of town. 'The way I see it. Just shut up and look around you.'

Kate slid back in the big leather bucket seat and watched the black taxis Harry was leaving behind in the bus lane. Each was carrying someone to another place in the city, some couples, some businessmen, some too far back in the seat to be seen. Each one a little life, a separate evening over, or beginning, their white faces like stars appearing and then vanishing in the wing mirror.

Harry caught her looking into the cab windows. 'Where are they going, eh? Or rather, where've they been?'

'Don't you find that chilling? A city full of all these anonymous people?'

'Never really thought of it like that.' Harry took Hyde Park Corner at high speed – or Kate saw it was high speed from the speedo despite feeling cradled and safe in the low seat. 'I like the freedom of being able to do anything you want, that there will always be people on the streets doing something, going somewhere, even at this time of night. That feeling that the day never really ends in London. Know what I mean?'

'Sort of.' The streets weren't as empty as Kate had supposed, the lights still on in the shop windows of Knightsbridge. She noticed with a rush of pride when a couple wandering slowly home, window shopping in Harvey Nichols, turned and looked up at the car as they drove by, probably imagining a romantic story for her and Harry just as she was imagining one for them.

They drove on in silence, listening to the music on the radio. Kate watched out for plate-glass shop windows so she could see their reflection driving past, feeling as though they were in a pop video. The boiled-sweet lights of Oxford Street, one area she could recognise, were still flashing on and off and she had an odd moment of affection for it, stripped of the jostling litter of Saturday shoppers.

'I asked you where we were going and you didn't give me an answer.'

'I thought I'd drive you down to the old part of the city, where it really is quiet at this time of night.' Harry overtook a Marks and Spencer refrigerator van with a sudden surge of effortless acceleration, and slotted back into the right side of the road. Kate released a sigh of pleasure at the burst of speed. 'It's my favourite place, all higgledy-piggledy architecture and back alleys. You should like it, with your English degree. Very Dickensian.'

'OK.' Kate drummed casually on her knees to the driving beat of the song, then stopped when it faded out and the music changed to something slow and romantic, not wanting to draw attention to the shift in mood.

The silence fell again, but it was companionable. So companionable that Kate was gripped by a reckless impulse to talk rubbish, to dissipate the intimacy that was spreading between them. They were close enough for her to be aware of the warmth of his arm as he changed gear. Soon he would probably smell the sweat that was pooling nervously under her arms. Wasn't this what she had been longing for all these months? Well, not the sweaty pits, obviously. So much for Mitchum.

She chanced a quick look at him in the rear-view mirror. Harry's long-lashed eyes were intent on the road ahead, his cheekbones sharp with the shadows falling from the street lights above. A shiver of desire ran up her neck and she had to acknowledge this was the dream scenario she hadn't even admitted to wanting.

Kate saw from the street signs that they were heading through Clerkenwell now and the bright lights were thinning out. Yellow street lamps illuminated all-night photo labs and kebab houses, unreal phosphorescent light glowed from behind the opaque fronts of trendy restaurants. In the quieter roads, the throaty rumble of the engine seemed even louder; Harry was weaving through short cuts behind tall Victorian office blocks, whose looming storeys, all windows darkened, seemed to hover over the open top of the car.

'Lean your head back and look at the sky,' he said. 'It's a gorgeous night.'

Kate bit back a retort about seeing proper stars in the countryside, leaned her head on the leather headrest and looked up. Houses and offices formed margins on each side of her field of vision, fluctuating in height and colour as they drove through the narrow streets. The odd tree, mazey outlined after the solid houses, filled in the gaps, moonlight and street light shining through its branches like the delicate tracery of veins inside a lung. Kate felt as though she were floating on the cushion of red wine she'd drunk.

'Beautiful, aren't they, the buildings?' he said. 'I know you'll think it's a bit silly, but when I drive through here, I think of them as bookmarks in history, fixing points of time and style in the city for ever. As long as they're there you can see when people rode up to the doors on horses, not on courier bikes, or when ladies had to have doors widened for crinolines, and so on.'

Kate turned her head on the headrest in surprise. Harry had always struck her as being sensitive underneath all the incompetent laddish banter, and his handling of Mike had amazed her, but she'd never experienced such a sustained display of articulate thought from him. He might have been blushing – she couldn't see in the monochrome light – and she suddenly realised exactly how personal this drive was for him. He was showing her the city he loved, because she had been so impervious to it for all the months she had lived in the flat, sitting on her misery like a hen on eggs. She had been determined not to like London, first because it was an unknown force so much bigger than her, and then because it was her punishment for Giles not loving her enough.

But Harry had gradually shown her something else. Kate looked up at the skies and watched the red and white flashing lights of a police helicopter move across the deep blue of the sky, disappearing behind one building and reappearing above another like a giant dragonfly. She saw flecks of stars, clean and glittering, and felt the night air rush on her face. For the first time, she saw a city beauty in the night sky.

She'd never been out this late, entering the secret sleeping side of London, flushed clean of people and noise. She wondered now if Harry had seen her loneliness from the start, all the rejection of being lost in a city she was scared of, and had been sorry for her – and whether the burgers out and walks around town had been his way of making her like the place, so she would feel less alone.

'You're right, this is beautiful,' she murmured.

Harry didn't reply.

Or maybe, in his painful crush on Cress, he had sensed another bleeding heart, watching her as she moped around the flat, with her photos of Giles Sellotaped on the inside of her kitchen cupboard. Kate felt the pressure of her stomach against the waistband of her jeans and thought that that little mental incentive to stay off the chocolate had been a waste of time. Two dumpees together. Maybe he had needed to fall back in love with the city too.

She turned her head towards him on the cool leather of

the headrest, feeling pleasantly vulnerable. Kate could understand why he was able to be so much more eloquent in the darkness of the car, partly muffled by the engine noise; there was something easy about darkness. There was something undeniably sexy about the car – OK, OK, so the lads had been right about TOCA 2. She saw an orange traffic light up in the distance and hoped it would turn to red so he could stop and see the paleness of her neck in the street light and maybe kiss it.

Her heart thumped as her conscience caught up with her thoughts.

Travelling at high speed. over the crossing, Kate saw the light turn red as Harry accelerated to drive through, and her stomach contracted at the missed chance.

'Which bridge would you like to go over?'

'Don't mind. Whatever one's nearest.'

'This one OK?'

Kate sat up and drew in her breath as they crossed the river. Strings of white lights looped along the Embankment, reflecting in the water, and in the background were layers and layers of familiar towers and spires, like a collage of postcards: the fluctuating colours on the Hayward Gallery wind sculpture, the red lights of the Oxo Tower, the surreal green illumination of St Paul's Cathedral. It was beautiful. She laughed aloud at the prettiness of it all, then laughed at herself.

'Thank you for showing me this,' she said, putting an unconscious hand on Harry's knee. 'And in such a glamorous way.'

'My pleasure.' He covered her hand with his own until they came to the Waterloo roundabout and he needed to change gear. It felt cold when he moved his hand away.

Kate combed her hair through her fingers, which were tingling from the contact, and piled the messy curls on top of her head. 'I feel . . .' She searched for the right words.

Harry pulled up at the lights. He turned to her and put a

finger on her lips. 'Don't. Just enjoy travelling and stop feeling you have to *describe* everything?'

The news bulletin on the radio finished and the first plangent piano chords of 'Take Another Piece of My Heart' rang out, very loud in the night air; it was a song that gave Kate a Pavlovian melting reaction in the pit of her stomach: her all-time favourite school disco slow dance.

Kate felt giddy. None of this was real any more. It was turning out like one of her wish-fulfilment dreams, too easily. In a moment he would . . .

He would . . .

The lights were still red. There was no traffic behind them, and no cars on the roundabout. Harry fixed his eyes on hers and bent his head very slightly, a tiny unambiguous motion. Kate instinctively tilted her head the other way, watching how his lips were parting, how slight the golden stubble on his jaw was, how she was almost horizontal in her seat already. She could smell his closeness, a heady mixture of Armani and male hormone and realised her eyes were closing in an automatic school disco reaction.

Then, just as quickly, she knew that she couldn't let herself kiss Harry. Much as she desperately wanted to. Kate had never been able to hear a song without listening to the words and now, hearing the familiar lyrics of the song as if for the first time, Kate suddenly realised what had sparked off her crush: her own frustrated longing for Giles reflected in Harry's unrequited love for Cress. The shock of it made her catch her breath. Here was someone in even bigger trouble than she was, prepared to carve up his heart time after time, just as she had become addicted to offering her own inferiority up to Giles. Pretending to be someone she wasn't. Allowing him to change her into someone she didn't want to be.

And she had to sort herself out, not just cover it up by pretending to be the person Harry wanted Cress to be, even though he knew in his heart that she was far nicer in his head than in reality. There wasn't any point until he saw that himself anyway. She had been so determined to be faithful to Giles; giving that up now, to be an Elastoplast for someone else's broken heart, made the sheer fact of her staying in London to wait for him meaningless. She had to put her money where her conscience was, for once in her life.

Kate's eyes snapped open and it was a wrench not to touch Harry's face. God, it was agonising. This was a moment straight out of her teenage 'Sweet Valley High' fantasies. His eyes were shut and she could see his lashes, longer and sootier than any mascara could make hers, on his strong cheekbone. Not as classically handsome as Giles, but more real. When his lips didn't make contact where they should have done, Harry opened his eyes and looked, confused, into hers.

'You can't say Kate and be thinking Cressida,' she whispered sadly. She hoped he could read her face better than she could express herself.

Harry blinked once and sighed. 'But I'm not.'

They looked at each other, aghast. Then the lights changed and a black Golf came racing up behind, hooting at them to move. Harry slumped back in his seat and put the car into first gear. The Aston purred away from the junction and into Waterloo.

chapter thirty-five

Kate went straight back to her room, shut the door behind her until the catch clicked, and set her alarm clock for seven. Early enough to be out of the house and into some gallery or park where she could stay for the rest of the day. The rest of the weekend if necessary.

She stood, looking at the clock in her hands, for about five minutes, seeing only the figures and the twitching second hand, trying to avoid the images bubbling up like tar through the gaps in her concentration. She had never wanted to whitewash over her mind as much as now, and she couldn't. Her pulse was racing and despite the chill in the night air she felt sweaty. She repeated the same thoughts over and over again, stroking her conscience as she would stroke Ratcat, if he deigned to let her: as long as she stayed in the safety of the mundane, setting her alarm, standing in her room, she would be fine. The moment would go away, and she would be untouched by it.

Kate could hear Harry moving around in the kitchen, noisily filling the kettle to make coffee, opening and shutting cupboards – each obvious noise an invitation to join him – but she was frozen like a statue, her hands cradling the Minnie Mouse alarm clock. The night air had sobered her up a little, but residual alcohol still disjointed her thoughts as they ran into one another: Why are you running away? Why do you fall in love after the event? What are you scared of? Why do you think the world will stop for you?

She imagined Harry on the other side of the thin door, waiting for her to reappear, wondering what she was doing, why she'd unbuckled her seatbelt as if the car were on fire and legged it up the stairs. How could she explain that it was because she wanted him so much that she felt the overwhelming impulse to hide, rather than the other way round? His courage could be slipping away as fast as hers and the fragile bubble of opportunity could be lost for ever. What were the chances of two people wanting each other with exactly the same intensity, at exactly same time? He won't ask again now he thinks he's embarrassed you. Kate groaned with frustration.

You have to go out there and talk to him, she thought angrily. Tell him how you feel. The school prefect in her head joined forces with the Voice of Laura. It was a powerful combination. Kate was usually very strong on conscience theory, especially for other people, less good at carrying it out herself. She could make up endless withering reviews of her own character, but often wondered how seriously she took them, deep down.

He's hardly going to give you the knock back, is he? the voice went on persuasively. And Giles is coming home soon. Not to mention Harry finding out what you did to Cress's *Meisterwerk*. Could be a bit of a passion killer. Time is running out. This might be your only chance.

But how *do* I feel? Kate sank on to the bed still holding the clock. Her eye fell on the Ball photo of her and Giles and she turned it face down on her bedside table, the first time she had ever experienced anyone turning a picture face down in real life. I don't *know* how I feel. I know I don't want to be a cheating girlfriend, even if I'm not . . . She shoved that thought to the back of her head. Too complicated.

And I know I don't want to be second best to Cressida.

And I know I really did want him to kiss me.

Your trouble is that you just don't take control of your own destiny, parried the Laura Voice.

Kate squirmed. This was not unlike a scene in *Roses of Death* – one which ended with the Cress character setting fire to her parents' house because the voices told her it would be a good thing to destroy the bad spirits.

You just let things happen to you and then whine about the consequences, it went on relentlessly. If you choose to take the wrong path, then at least the choice was yours and not a passive affliction. Why are you in London? Because Giles made the decision for you. Why are you at Eclipse? Because Laura made the decision for you. Why are you . . .

I *chose* to be here, she reminded herself. I *chose* this house, I *chose* to sort out Cressida, and maybe that means I can *choose* to have Harry.

Before Kate was aware what she was doing, she found she had her hand on the doorknob. What she intended to do after that, she had absolutely no idea, but as she was extending her arm to swing the door open and offer to warm Harry's cafetiere for him, she heard a familiar knocking on the front door.

Dant was back and he was too pissed to negotiate the lock. Either that or he simply couldn't be bothered locating his keys.

'Oh, fuck,' breathed Kate, leaning her forehead against the door.

She heard Harry put something down on the counter (the coffee jar? The pen with which he was writing her an impassioned note? His clay-pigeon shooting pistols?) and walk over to the door, where he undid various deadbolts and let Dant stagger in.

'Mate!' said Harry, in the kitchen. She couldn't hear his intonation very clearly, and didn't want to read too much into it, but it didn't sound like an opener to a long conversation.

Oh, for God's sake, please don't embarrass me now,

thought Kate. Please don't come out with any Sloaney inanities you wouldn't want me to hear if you knew I was listening. Which you surely must.

'Mate!' said Dant.

There was a pause, in which they would either be doing a school handshake, or head-butting each other's chests, or perhaps opening another bottle of wine.

Suddenly attacked by paranoia, Kate pressed her ear against the door and listened harder in case they'd broken with tradition and begun a Jacobean-tragedy-style *sotto voce* conversation about her behind their hands.

She was rewarded by a melodic series of burps from Dant, followed by a burst of admiring applause from Harry. The build-up had evidently been critical.

The usual eavesdropper's dilemma now seized her: should she brave the difficult social situation outside or should she risk hearing Harry say something potentially embarrassing about where they had been/how he felt/what kind of a silly cow she was? The thought of Dant being privy to any of the night's events made up her mind for her and she pushed open the door and made herself walk into the kitchen before she had time to think about what she was doing.

'Oh, hello,' said Harry, blushing.

'Um, hi.' Kate walked to the counter and clung on to it.

'Would you like some coffee?'

Dant looked between one and the other like a tennis umpire.

'Yes, please,' said Kate, fixing her eyes on the espresso machine and keeping the word 'pleasant' uppermost in her mind. 'That would be nice.'

'You can speak more complicated English if you want,' said Dant sarcastically. 'It *is* my first language. Or are we being simultaneously translated into Bulgarian by the World Service?'

Kate didn't think she had ever been so grateful to hear

Dant being snide. It broke the mood perfectly. She glared at his smugly raised eyebrow.

'The great paradox about alcohol for most people is that the more they drink, the wittier they think they are, and yet the less they can articulate their fabulous one-liners,' she said. 'With you, it seems, the more you drink, the less witty you get, but, tragically *more* able to talk.'

Harry looked confused.

'Don't worry, Kate.' Dant walked over to the fridge and poured the contents of her carefully hoarded, very expensive and freshly squeezed orange juice into a pint glass. 'My comment was just a mordant observation. I'll let you know when I start with the wit.' He swigged most of the juice back in one and fixed her with his scary Rufus Sewell black eyes. 'Not my fault you can't tell the difference – I suppose it's lack of exposure to quality conversation.'

'Only since I came here.' Kate remembered too late that she was meant to be presenting a vision of snoggable womanhood for Harry's benefit, not a Camille Paglia figure of witchery.

Harry's kettle boiled and they all turned to look at it.

Apologetically, Harry made an unnecessary gesture towards it, and, collecting himself, took two coffee mugs out of the dishwasher and put two teaspoons of coffee granules into each.

'Harry makes the coffee,' said Dant in a monotone. 'See how he stirs the coffee, Janet! Mind that hot water, John!'

'What's your problem, Dant?' said Kate. 'If you can narrow it down for us.'

'I have no problems,' said Dant, raising his empty hands like a magician. His eyes glittered and Kate's skin crawled, as she sensed a fresh pain about him tonight. When he was drunk he always seemed more dangerous. Sober, his savagery was channelled into wit and attitude; when he was drunk, she felt that the safety-catch could come off at any minute. Kate couldn't put her finger on why – whether it was because Dant himself was scared of revealing some hidden vulnerability when he wasn't quite in control, or whether a childhood of doing whatever he wanted, to fulfil everyone's worst expectations, had left him with little inhibition for bad behaviour, she didn't know.

But it was now obvious in her head that the sexy pictures of Cress weren't taken by Harry, and that, combined with the growing worry that in changing Cress's manuscript she might have done something seriously damaging, was throwing a dark shadow over Kate's conscience. Dant *was* scary. Not the textbook villainery of Cameron, but in a very authentic, completely plausible, perhaps slightly sociopathic way. However, much as she hated to agree with Cress, she was beginning to see that that could be an interesting, if not ultimately desirable, quality in a man.

Harry sloshed milk in the coffee and handed one of the mugs to Kate. 'Um,' he began uncertainly, 'it's pretty late and I really need to . . . um, go to bed, so I'll, er . . . see you both in the morning.'

'Night,' said Kate, holding his nervous gaze and hoping that he could infer more than she could say.

He shrugged in an ambiguous fashion and shuffled off to bed.

Kate felt disappointment crash over her like a cold shower.

'Oh, bad luck,' said Dant, seeing her face fall. 'Put those pants straight in the wash, why don't you.'

'Shut up, Dant, I'm not in the mood,' snapped Kate, walking towards her room.

'Neither's Harry by the looks of things.'

Kate turned round slowly and pushed her hair off her forehead. The night wind had blown the loosened plait into a tangled mass of ginger coils, and it stood out around her head like a wild halo. Her eyes were shining and bright green through gathering tears of frustration. Despite the aching inside, on the outside she looked like a fierce angel. Balling her hands up into fists, she leaned on the scratched marble surface of the kitchen counter. There was a sour stale wine taste in her mouth.

'I have had a long and arduous day,' she said carefully. Her heart was stinging, not just from anticlimax, but from Dant's casual cruelty. Tonight it wasn't sliding off her back. 'And putting up with your one-man humanity police is exactly what I do *not* need to round it off. You really don't know when to stop, do you? I'm not Cress, you don't have to score points off me. Harry's not one of your trendy friends, you don't have to make him look small. Why don't you listen to yourself some time? We're real people here. It's not all dialogue.' She corrected herself. 'Or mordant observation.'

Dant threw up his hands in an unconvincing impersonation of a sorry person. They both knew how unconvincing it was.

Kate opened her mouth to say something else, but at the last moment couldn't be bothered.

'Goodnight,' she said instead and swept towards her room.

'Aren't you going to ask me where I've been?'

She stopped and considered. How much did she care where Dant had been? It was two o'clock in the morning. She had things to do this weekend. On the other hand, it sounded ominously as though she ought to know. He might have been consulting a solicitor about their verbal and not even vaguely watertight contract with Cress.

Kate sighed and said, without turning round, 'No, where have you been this evening?'

'Round at Cress's flat. Someone from her hospital phoned me this afternoon.' Dant paused for dramatic effect, but Kate resisted the impulse to turn, as he clearly wanted her to do. 'Apparently she's had some kind of a breakdown.'

Kate spun to face him, her mouth and eyes a classic 'O' of horror. 'Oh, my God! Dant, no! Is she OK? What happened?' She clutched herself, spilling hot coffee all down her front, but barely noticed the scalding. Catholic family packs of guilty images flashed before her eyes and she felt the tears that had been building up for so long begin to slide down her face. Even as they were dropping hotly on to her cheeks, she knew that they weren't really for Cress – they were for herself, for Harry, who would no doubt be stricken with horror when he found out, for Dant who would have to cope with it all. Tears for anyone except Cress – and that only doubled the flood.

Dant gently took the cup off her and pushed her down on the sofa. 'She's . . . well, she's not OK, I won't pretend she is.' He let out a harsh breath. It smelled of whisky. 'Her consultant told me that she had some kind of hysterical fit after . . .' He paused and smiled ruefully to himself, and then the smile disappeared as though it had never been there. 'After some bad news from England, as he put it, and they had to sedate her. Which is probably what she wanted when you think about it, some kind of chemical assistance. Anyway, she wouldn't talk or eat or take her medicine, so they put her under suicide watch, and eventually they made her call her next of kin. Which in these circumstances was, unfortunately enough, me.'

Kate covered her mouth. 'Shit,' she breathed.

Dant mimicked her widening eyes. 'Indeed. "My life is shit." "You are a shit." "You have shat on my dreams." "You and Kate have taken what was precious to me, eaten it up and shat it out." We ran through most scatological variants on that theme. Some of them very inventive. But Cress is really miserable this time – it wasn't just her normal paranoid rage. I think this time it's pretty life-changing. The cleansing force of rage. If you'll excuse the therapy-speak.'

Kate buried her head in her hands to stop the ringing in her ears. She was responsible for this. Solely responsible. So much in her own life just happened, as she let herself be swept along in the relentless, easy flow of events. But she had done this to someone else, caused them to lose their grip on their own life because of something she had done on the spur of the moment. She wanted to cry with the shame and fear of it.

Dant slipped down on to the sofa next to her. He didn't put an arm round her as Harry would have done, but his presence was reassuring. It wasn't just her. She knew that even with his slippery personality, he wasn't going to pretend innocence of this. She lifted her stricken face silently, unable to say more than her expression would convey on its own.

They looked at each other for a moment.

'Kate, it's not the first breakdown she's had,' said Dant.

'You make her sound like the RAC.' She winced at her inability to pass up a feed line. And she said Dant was callous.

He was good enough to ignore it. 'I know this sounds tragic, but . . .' Dant picked at his nails. 'I do honestly think that this might be the only way for her to move on. I mean,' he looked straight ahead, out of the window, where the orange city lights on the horizon were shimmering in the night smog, 'I knew this would come eventually. I suspect the reason is because she's learned a few truths about herself, and about me and about Mom and about the people around her. That she can't keep reinventing things to suit herself. That she has to sort her life out with what she's got.'

'But Dant, what we did was . . . cruel.'

'Yes. No. It wasn't any more or less cruel than what she'd done in the first place. And I think she saw that, which was why she flipped. Cress doesn't go a bundle on personal responsibility. Well, neither of us do. She doesn't see how her actions affect other people, because she's always blamed the way she is, and what she does, on what people have done to her. All our lives we've been angry with each other for not being better, for not realising our full potential, but at the same time conveniently ignoring the sad fact that our own shortcomings are pretty much mirrored in each other.'

'Twins,' said Kate.

'Yeah, well, you'd think we'd have noticed.'

There was a pause.

'Is she going to be all right?' A small part of Kate was praying that Dant wouldn't say Cress was coming back to live in the flat with them.

'She'll be fine. Once she's milked this for all she can get, obviously. She wants me to go over to see her in the hospital with a selection of more glamorous bedwear.' Dant snorted. 'I hope that's a thinly veiled desire to see me and have a proper talk, but I suspect it really might be just to get her Agent Provocateur bedjacket brought over.' He turned to Kate. 'I meant to say, can you drive me to Heathrow tomorrow morning? I would ask Harry, but that would mean telling him about Cress's breakdown, and that would mean telling him about the book, and that would mean telling him about David, and that would mean telling him about men who love other men and that would—'

'OK, OK. I'll take you.' Kate's brow furrowed. 'But in what? I suppose that means I can't borrow Harry's Rover?'

Dant held up a set of keys. 'I picked these up from her flat this afternoon.'

'Did she say you could borrow her car?' asked Kate sternly. Cress had a Mini Cooper which Kate had never been in, since it was always in the garage being repaired, or in the garage to protect it from prying eyes. Cress loved it so much she almost never drove it.

'Yes.'

'But she knows you can't drive.'

'Mmm-hmm.'

Their eyes met in a duet of disbelief. 'So she knew that either Harry or I would have to take you to the airport.'

'That's what I mean about Cressida,' said Dant. 'Maximum audience for everything. Don't break your heart too much.'

When her alarm went off the next morning, Kate lay for a

few minutes arranging the events of the previous night into some kind of order and then rolled on to her side and switched on the radio. Elation and panic were see-sawing up and down inside her, and for the moment, she couldn't quite define what emotion went with what event.

After six months of research, Kate had drawn the conclusion that she could switch on Virgin Radio at any given time and hear three songs she loved and then one which she hated so much she had to get out of bed. The delay varied from station to station, but she hadn't found one yet she could lie there all morning and listen to. For that she needed to get up sufficiently to find a CD or tape, and by then she usually felt obliged to get up properly anyway.

This morning an old Big Country ballad and an Aretha Franklin song slipped by peaceably while she probed away at her conscience, but she was out of bed and scrabbling for a tape within the first five seconds of 'Wonderwall' 's introduction.

Dant was already dressed and eating two boiled eggs in the kitchen.

'Very healthy,' observed Kate, tying her dressing gown cord a bit tighter and searching in Harry's cupboard for his stash of Ready Brek. She had a terrible craving for some stodge. 'Bit antisocial for a plane journey though?'

'Depends what you mean by antisocial.' He finished off his last soldier. 'Farting in a confined space kind of pales into insignificance compared with wholesale character hijacking and dragging your brother across Europe to furnish you with tart's knickers.'

'Dant, you don't mean that.'

'Don't I?'

She looked at him, sitting there glowering in a smartish black polo neck and jeans, and realised that he had taken refuge in rudeness again. It was, after all, at least three hours before he normally showed his face in civilised society.

'You don't.'

Kate poured the last of the milk into the bowl of desiccated oatmeal and put it in the microwave. An old memory of her mother making Ready Brek for her before school came unexpectedly into her mind: Mum wearing some lairy dirndl skirt, heating up milk in a saucepan and dropping lumps of molasses in the middle of the porridge to make her eat it. The blue and white dirndl gypsy skirt. She took the Ready Brek out of the microwave and stirred it thoughtfully. It had embarrassed her that her mother still bought clothes from Chelsea Girl and Dorothy Perkins while the other mums wore Country Casuals box-pleat suits, but simple arithmetic, which had evaded her at the time, now revealed that her mother was only thirty or so and still perfectly entitled to show her lower legs. What a bunch of fascists children are, she thought.

'What time's the flight?'

'Eleven o'clock.'

'And what time is it now?' She lifted a heaped spoonful to her mouth.

'About nine-ish.'

Kate gasped as the nuclear-heat porridge burned her tongue. The rest had already developed a skin around the sugar she had sprinkled on with a lavish hand. 'Why didn't you tell me last night?' she demanded, fanning her mouth with her hand. 'Presumably we have to go and get Cress's car? You have to be there early to check in. For God's sake, Dant.'

'Calm down, Goldilocks. If we leave in the next quarter of an hour . . .'

She swept a sarcastic hand down her dressing gown, taking in her hair (in need of a wash), her face (in need of make-up) and her glasses (in need of immediate replacement with contact lenses).

'Or we could wait for Harry,' said Dant.

Kate scowled at him and dumped her dish of porridge on the table. 'You can finish that, Grandma.' She licked an oaty finger. 'Tell me why I'm not just letting you go in a minicab like a normal person.'

Dant put a finger to his chin. 'Because . . . you *are* the Heathrow minicab?'

'Er . . . no.'

'Because . . . you want to support me in my moment of family trauma?'

'Very good. Now keep repeating that at least once every ten minutes until we're at Heathrow, OK?'

Kate stomped off to the bathroom and stood under the shower for as long as it took her to wash both armpits. She allowed herself an additional thirty seconds to soap her rounded stomach fondly. It seemed appropriate to have a little Pooh Bear belly in the depths of miserable winter.

She dressed quickly since it was cold, tugging on her long jersey trousers and a tight silk rib top Isobel had forced her to buy in the January sales. For once she managed not to get white streaks of deodorant on them. Then she pulled a big jumper over the top for good measure. I look like a big black bat, Kate thought. Excellent. She pulled her hair out of the funnel neck and examined the effect in the mirror.

'Hurry up,' said Dant, passing her room on the way to the bathroom and banging on the door as he went.

'Dant!' she shouted as a thought occurred to her. 'We're not going to have time to get to Cress's on the Tube, so call a cab, OK? There are cards on the fridge.'

There was a grunt of assent.

She ran through her morning checklist as quickly as she could – dry hair, tame hair, brush hair. Dress. Find shoes. Kate looked at her face in the mirror over the back of the door and wondered whether to bother with make-up. Her skin was probably the only bit of herself that she was completely happy with: clear, bright, very pale, which made her lips and eyes stand out undeservedly with minimal make-up. She dusted a bit of brown shadow over her lids and curled her eyelashes, then remembered she was only taking Dant to the airport and back. Her hand holding the mascara wand hovered at cheek level.

'Oh, my God,' she said aloud to her stunned reflection. 'Working in an office has made me make-up dependent!'

Determinedly she shoved the mascara back in her bag and put on her glasses, as a show of defiance to her vanity.

'What are you doing in there?' demanded Dant at the door.

Kate flung it open. He had his overnight bag over one shoulder and a matt black holdall, presumably belonging to Cressida, over the other.

'Let me amend that to, "What are you doing in there, Ronnie Barker?"'

'Waiting for you to do one of your dull monologues, unfunny one. OK, I'm ready to go.' She looked at her watch. 'Did you call a cab to get to Cress's?'

Dant dumped his bags on the ground and turned his eyes skywards. 'Of course I did. They were sending one straight away.'

'And is it here yet?'

'Yes, it's parked in the kitchen.'

'Well, why don't you phone them back and . . . No.' Kate pushed past him into the hall. 'No, let me, I don't trust you to tell it to come to the right place.' She strode into the kitchen and picked up the phone from its last resting place on the ironing board. The dial tone was making the syncopated burping noise which indicated that there were messages on the answering service.

Ignoring that for the moment, she called the cab firm and speeded their cab up by ten minutes, using her best Jennifer Spencer techniques of persuasion, then dialled up Call Minder.

'You. Have. One. Message,' it said. 'To. Hear . . .'

Kate pressed one immediately.

'First message.'

His voice was unmistakable, and so was the excitement in

it. 'Katie, this is Giles calling at about six o'clock your time. Guess you're not back from work quite yet, but this is just to say that I'm getting on a plane tonight that will get me into Heathrow at about midday Saturday, so that's when I'll be back, if you want to come and meet me off the plane. Um, I know it's short notice, but it was meant to be a surprise, so if you can't come then I'll be back in town in the afternoon . . .' His voice trailed off. It was obvious that he hadn't expected to have to deliver such fabulous news to an answering machine. 'So, I'll see you then. Um, I just thought that if you could come out then we could have some time together before my family demand my undivided presence for a while and we could . . . have a talk.' Kate held her breath without realising at the pause. There was a world of chaos hiding in that fractional silence. 'Anyway, I'll try you later. But I hope I'll see you tomorrow. OK. Right. See you soon.'

She put the phone down very slowly, then looked at the clock. Even as she was standing there, with every twitch of the second hand, the plane bringing Giles back to London was speeding nearer and nearer. She tried to stoke up some reaction in her stomach, but none came. So this is the flip-side of all the nights I lay in bed trying to will away the pain by pretending he didn't exist, Kate thought. An ironic smile came to her lips, although she was not smiling inside.

She looked around the messy kitchen which now seemed permanently familiar to her. Each random pile of washing, or stack of books, which to the untrained eye looked like squalor, was there for some reason. Giles had never been here, in this place which had been so loathsome and alien to her when he left, and which was now a home. Of sorts, she corrected herself. Let's not get too Waltons here. Seeing Giles sitting on the grubby sofa would be like seeing someone from *EastEnders* pop in for coffee: familiar and yet definitely not part of the real-life setting.

A car honked its horn outside.

'Hello?' said Dant in her ear. 'Can you come back from whichever planet you're on and go out to the cab, please?'

Kate shook herself. 'Why didn't you check the answering machine last night?'

He stared at her. 'Sorry, have you been listening? Because I was round at Cressida's, sorting her things out all evening. You were the one playing Happy Families back here with Harry.'

'How did you . . .?' Kate stopped herself before she revealed too much.

'I saw the washing up you didn't bother to put in the machine.' Dant rolled his eyes. 'Garlic and lemon chicken, eh? The Harvey *pièce de résistance*.'

Kate opened her mouth to ask at least three immediate questions and then shut it again. For a second. 'Giles is on his way back. His flight gets in an hour after yours leaves.' She clapped her hands to her cheeks. 'Oh, my God! I can't meet him like this!' She thrust her bag into Dant's hands. 'Go down and get the cab and I'll be there as soon as I've got some better clothes on!'

'We can't wait for you to go through your entire wardrobe,' said Dant in a tone of high annoyance. 'Even though it would take about three minutes. Just get some clothes and get changed there. You've got time.'

'OK,' said Kate. 'OK.'

She ran into her room and flung open her wardrobe door. What would Giles want her to be wearing? She rifled through her hangers. The green dress.

She pulled it out and held it to the light. Sexy, if of course she could get it over her head these days, but not the thing to wear for a Saturday lunch-time at Heathrow. Reluctantly, since she knew it was his favourite, she pushed it back in.

Kate racked rapidly through a selection of work-type clothes. All the nice things she had were summery dresses and it was freezing outside. Added to which she hadn't bought any nice clothes for non-work situations since she came to London – mainly because her non-work situations involved either bowling, going to the pub or aqua aerobics.

Grey Nicole Farhi sale suit Cress had made her buy from Amazon.

She had it halfway out of the wardrobe before she was struck by the absurdity of meeting your boyfriend after eight months' separation in a grey suit.

'What's *happened* to me?' she wailed at the shoe rack Mandy had left behind.

Outside the car honked again.

Kate threw the suit on the bed and stared at the pile of clean but unironed clothes in the corner. What had she been wearing when she came down to London in July?

Her jeans.

Kate scrabbled in the back of the wardrobe for the blue jeans. Things had been stressful at work, maybe she had lost some weight without being aware of it. She held up the jeans to the light to check for chocolate stains, then realised she had probably answered her own question.

'Bugger,' she said and pulled open her underwear drawer, turning it upside down on the bed. This would have to do. Pain came second to presentation on this one-off occasion. Laura had given her a pair of 'Instant Liposuction' knickers for Christmas and if she wore her Wonderbra with this tight top, maybe Giles wouldn't notice the flap of Pooh Bear belly hanging over the top of, and perhaps through the flies of her jeans.

Bingo! She dragged out the M&S knickers, with the label still attached, fished about for her Wonderbra, grabbed a can of deodorant from the dresser and shoved everything back into her make-up bag. When she was halfway out of the room she remembered her high-heeled mules and went back for them.

The honking horn was now accompanied by a revving engine.

Kate staggered down the stairs with her armfuls of stuff,

having grabbed a Tesco bag from behind the door. Dant was sitting in the back of the Nissan Bluebird looking bleak.

She pulled open the back door and crawled in. Bob Marley's Greatest Hits were playing very loudly. In as much as she could tell the difference between one Greatest Hit and another. She winced. Kate loved all kinds of music, apart from reggae. In direct contrast to its effect on everyone else, reggae music triggered some violent instinct within Kate to wipe out large tracts of innocent bystanders with grenades. They set off at TOCA 2 high speed.

This can't get any worse, thought Kate.

Then they hit roadworks on the Cromwell Road.

chapter thirty-six

'There must be something about my innocent schoolgirl appearance that people give me these cars to drive,' said Kate, pulling Cress's green Mini out into the fast lane and putting her foot to the floor. 'I mean, do I look reliable? Do I look like I'm not going to take them out to the nearest piece of motorway and floor them?' She shook her head and turned up the radio. It was the Black Crowes and she drummed her fingers on the wooden steering wheel to the rhythm section as they whizzed past family cars and motorbikes. She was following the bass line with a concentration that happily shut out all other peripheral thought.

'You look like your dad is a policeman,' Dant replied. He was folded up in the passenger seat like a deckchair with his bag on his knee, looking darkly incongruous.

'How are we doing for time?'

'We're OK now you've broken the sound barrier, and we're actually heading backwards in a parallel sonic zone. Could you slow down a bit, please? We passed the Tardis at the Chiswick roundabout.'

Kate slowed down by five miles an hour. 'No, we don't want to get pulled over by the police now, do we?'

'I don't know why we're in such a rush anyway,' said Dant. He fished about in Cress's glove compartment and inexplicably came up with some sour cherry travel sweets. 'It's not as though I'm desperate to get to Val d'Isère, and I don't think you're all that keen to meet the International Financial Wizard, are you? Sour cherry sucky sweet?'

'What do you mean?' said Kate hotly, trying to control the car and her suddenly rising temper at the same time. 'Of course I can't wait to see Giles. He's the one with the "Get Out Of Deauville Crescent Free" card. And lest we forget, he's my boyfriend.'

Dant made sarcastic sucking noises with his sweet. 'If you say so.'

'What's your point, pyro boy?'

'Just that your options are a little more advanced than they were this time six months ago. You've got a tidy little sum coming your way for one thing, and you might just be on the verge of discovering a cure for Cressida Grenfell Syndrome, previously thought terminal.'

Kate checked in her mirror, saw a police car and slowed down to a more sedate seventy-five. 'I still feel really bad about Cress, so don't rub it in. If I could think of anything to do to help her – within reason – you know I would offer.'

'I wasn't talking about Cress.'

Kate shut up.

They drove past the Short-Term/Long-Term dilemma point and Kate elected to go Short Term again, since she was making Dant pay for her parking.

'Give me a twenty and I'll go to the pictures,' she said, tucking the car in next to a pillar.

Dant grumbled but took a twenty-pound note out of his wallet and handed it over as they walked to the European flights terminal. She carried his overnight bag to the check-in desk, noting how depressingly familiar all the shops were. Predictably, her gastric juices perked up at the thought of a blueberry muffin.

'Why don't you try boarding the plane naked and see if you can get onto *Airport Watch*?' she suggested as they browsed through the glossy mags at W. H. Smiths.

'No, I don't have your innate sense of drama.' Dant flicked a dismissive hand towards the selection of shiny, breast-fixated titles. 'I can't be bothered. I'm going to sleep on the plane. God knows I'm going to need some rest.'

'When are you coming back?' Kate asked. She was mentally calculating how much time she would have to transform herself before Giles's flight got in. Did that branch of Boots do mini-makeovers?

'Soon.' Dant picked up a couple of newspapers and the *Literary Review*. 'Sunday night? How soon is soon? Depends on whether she manages to have me checked into the bed next to her with matching fractures.'

They walked over to the departure gates. Kate checked Giles's arrivals board, and the plane seemed to be on schedule. At least she knew which gates to go to this time.

'Well, I suppose I'll see you on Sunday then,' she said.

'No, you won't.'

'Won't I?'

Dant twitched his eyebrows at her. 'Won't you be holed up in Chelsea for the rest of the week? I can't imagine that you'll be queueing up for your go on "Silent Hill" now that the Great Gatsby's back in town.'

'Dant, will you stop it?' Kate snapped. 'You're really spoiling this for me. You've got no idea how long I've waited for this, and you're just . . .' She ran out of words. 'You've never even met him.'

'Indeedy,' said Dant irritatingly, and then switched direction almost visibly. 'Any last messages for Cressida?'

Kate flushed. 'Just hello? I'm really, really sorry she's had this breakdown thing, but I still feel what she did to you and Harry was vile and—' She blushed deeper and looked at her feet. 'It would be hypocritical of me to pretend that what she did didn't matter, just because she's ill and you're not. So just say that I hope she feels better soon.'

'OK,' said Dant. 'Then you can deck her and not feel so guilty.' He patted her shoulder and took the overnight bag off it. 'Right then, I'd better go. I'll phone Harry to come and get me, but don't tell him where I've gone until I know how bad things are with Lucrezia Borgia.'

'Or you could just pay for a cab.'

'Er . . . no.'

'See you,' said Kate, raising a hand. Dant gave her a quick unshaven smile. Then she hared off to the loos. A phone box would have been more Wonder Woman, but Kate needed to do make-up as well.

Once safely locked inside the nearest disabled toilet (and she did feel a bit bad about that, but intended to be as quick as possible) Kate pulled the jeans out of the carrier bag and held them up in front of her.

God, they looked small.

Heroically, she stripped off her layers, trying not to look in the mirror as she did so, and replaced her underwear with the holding-in/pushing-out combo. Then she put on the skinny-rib top, which now looked distinctly Sophia Loren in conjunction with the waist-high pants. Thank God for pale body hair, thought Kate, trying to remember the last time she had deforested herself.

That was the easy bit. The jeans lay on the loo seat next to her.

Kate tried to think of Giles and all the sexy things he had said about her legs in the past. Her lovely skinny shoulders. Her creamy white stomach.

The same creamy white stomach now curving voluptuously over the top of her granny pants.

Mind over matter, she thought, picking up the jeans. I haven't put on that much weight. I mean, I don't feel fat. I don't feel *hungry* either, but that has to be an improvement on eating exactly half of everything on my plate and denying that chocolate is an essential part of life's rich tapestry.

She sat on the loo and slipped her feet into the jeans.

They felt ominously tight around the calves. Kate stood up quickly and yanked as hard as she could.

The jeans stuck around her thighs and wouldn't move.

Tears began to prickle at the back of her eyes.

Kate pushed aside her pride and lay down on the puddly floor of the cubicle, and sucked in her stomach, wriggling her bottom down into the jeans like a worm samba-ing for Cuba. She could feel the rough material grinding against the tender skin of her soft upper thighs and felt very bad for them. For the past six months they had been encased in flexible warm jersey or 90-denier opaque tights. This was as much of a shock to her thighs as it was to her. She squeezed and strained until it felt as though her stomach was touching the base of her spine.

The jeans weren't going anywhere.

Kate relaxed her efforts for a moment and wondered desperately whether going to the loo might make a difference.

Maybe she shouldn't have had that porridge.

She thanked God that the mirror was too high for her to see herself grovelling on the floor with a pair of jeans, much like the bad seventies advert for skin-tight jeans that used to adorn the changing rooms of the boutique in the village. For years she had believed that was the only way to put her jeans on.

No *material* is going to tell me I'm fat, she thought wildly. Why should I be made to feel a failure by some fascist pattern-cutter in Hicksville, Minnesota? I will get these jeans on if it's the last thing I do and they have to winch me out of this toilet.

She gritted her teeth and hauled the jeans up by the belt loops until the skin on her fingers was raw and white. By some divine intervention, and with some help from M&S lycra tummy-control panelling, she got the jeans over her hips.

Then she had a pause to get her breath back.

Then, with her fingers singing out with pain, she managed to get the buttons done up. One by one.

Little folds of pink skin kept getting caught between her finger and the button hole, but throughout all this, Kate could not be mad at her stomach for expanding beyond the jeans's permission. It felt warm and soft beneath her hands, comforting and ripe. She felt like apologising to it, rather than berating it. For ages she had hated her body for defying her mental image of what it should look like, but recently she had felt more benevolent towards it as she lay in the bath and stroked the curves of her legs and soaped her softer shoulders. With no one commenting on it but her, Kate felt she and her body had entered into a complicity they hadn't had before. London had made her more adaptable, and so her body had adapted too.

She lay there getting her breath back – or at least as much as she could get while her lungs and stomach were corseted in denim. It dawned on her that there could be a queue of people in wheelchairs, desperate for the loo and waiting patiently outside: struck with guilt she began the careful process of winching herself to her feet, using the helpfully provided guide rails.

Upright, she examined herself in the mirror. For all the struggle to get the jeans done up, she didn't look fat. She looked like a healthy, if a bit pallid, woman. Wearing a pair of jeans a size too small.

Kate ignored the jeans issue for the moment and emptied her make-up bag into the sink. What had Giles gone so mad for when she had that makeover?

The fact that it wasn't really her?

She pushed the Voice of Laura away. The red lips. He'd stared at her mouth all the way through that bloody chocolate cake he had eaten and not offered to share.

Kate smoothed a thin layer of foundation over her face and drew a careful red cupid's bow round her lips with a lip brush, then filled the heart-shape in with quick strokes, loading the brush each time with rich colour. Her mouth disappeared beneath the explosion of red pigment on her pale skin.

She blew a kiss to herself in the mirror. That did look sexy. She smiled to make sure she didn't have an attractive tideline of lippie on her teeth. It would all come off as soon as they kissed though. She blotted it on some loo paper, leaving a perfect Marilyn Monroe print, and thought guiltily that it wasn't a very good sign that her first thought was for her lipstick, rather than the kiss.

Kate remembered the make-up artist telling her that deep lips meant bare eyes, so she junked all the eye make-up back into the bag and scrabbled around in her handbag for her lenses.

The lenses weren't in her bag. She turned it upside down so the contents joined the jumble of make-up in the sink, and scrabbled around in the mess.

Kate suddenly stopped, wrist deep in powder compacts and free postcards. Had she actually put the lenses in her bag at all?

She stared at her reflection in the mirror above the sink as the events of the morning action-replayed in her head.

No, she hadn't put them in her bag. She had been teaching herself a lesson.

She shut her eyes so that she wouldn't see the heavy-rimmed spectacles looking back at her, and sank her elbows on to the rim of the basin.

There was a banging at the door, like a wheelchair being rammed crossly against the frame.

'Coming, coming!' yelled Kate, hating herself even more.

She took a deep breath and looked objectively at her reflection, as if she were criticising someone on television with Dant and Harry.

The jeans and the glasses belonged to two different people. To carry off the ridiculously tight jeans, she would need the wide-eyed little girl look provided by her lenses, and possibly something 'fun' doing to her hair.

On the other hand, the glasses would look fine with the jersey trousers, and her hair smoothed down with some serum she had forgotten she'd bought but had rediscovered one and a half minutes ago in her bag. She knew this for a fact since she had been wearing the glasses when she bought the trousers and the serum.

It wasn't what Giles would be expecting.

Kate gripped the basin and gave herself a beady look. 'It's what you *are* now, though,' she said fiercely. 'You silly cow.'

She jerked back, unnerved by the note in her voice. Really, all this hanging out with the pyromaniac sisterfucker had to stop. Next thing she knew she'd be setting fire to the sanitary bin.

With some effort she prised the jeans off and slipped the trousers back on. Her legs tingled with relief. The wide-leg trousers matched the top exactly and the high heeled mules, which she hadn't worn for five months, gave her a bit of a twinge around the instep but, more importantly, bonus height.

Fabulous, thought Kate, doing a quick reverse view in the big mirror. Very Late Thirties/Early Forties.

There was a new banging on the door. 'Hello, are you all right in there?' The voice was concerned and speaking very slowly and clearly. 'If you're in trouble, just press the alarm button by the toilet unit and we can have a qualified aider with you very shortly.'

Kate froze. This was all she needed – a repeat appearance on *Heathrow Tonight* or whatever the stupid programme was called. She shoved everything into the one bag and grabbed the Ray-bans that had been in her handbag since September. Cheap shot, but short of doing a Long John Silver, there wasn't a quick disability she could think of faking on the spur of the moment. She'd just have to brazen it out. Or double bluff the camera crew and pretend she was doing a survey on disabled facilities for *Watchdog*.

With a final baleful look in the mirror, she swapped her glasses for her Ray-bans and undid the lock on the door. It was actually natural clumsiness and suddenly being elevated three inches above her normal centre of gravity that made her walk into the side of the door as she came out, but it did make the two assembled stewards and two wheelchair-bound queuers move out of her way so she could stumble out of sight as quickly as possible.

Kate marched right out of sight to the Coffee Republic stand she knew so well, and got herself a coffee and a low-fat blueberry muffin. Then she found a table and settled down to wait for the flight to come in. All her exertions meant that she only had about twenty minutes to waste and that was just enough time to down a shot of espresso, eat the muffin and get another espresso to take away. She needed at least one espresso to deal with this. At the moment she was feeling disturbingly disconnected from anything.

Kate brushed the muffin crumbs off her trousers and thought happily how much more accommodating jersey was.

Then she set her jaw and walked down to the arrivals hall.

chapter thirty-seven

It was only when the first passengers began to filter through the customs barrier that Kate saw the full reality of what was happening. She had got very good at not dealing with problems until the last possible second, and the last possible second was now hurtling towards her at some speed.

She poked at her heart to get some Welcome Home butterflies going. Giles is coming back! Any minute now!

No response.

No, really, he is this time! He'll be walking round that corner any minute and he's back for good!

Mild panic set in.

Kate's eye was caught by someone who looked as though he might be Giles from a distance, but within three steps she knew it wasn't him. The adrenaline reaction surged round her body.

The wife and small child waiting for the Giles lookalike descended on him with squeals of delight.

Kate felt even more guilty.

Come on! she cajoled her heart. Giles! Back! Sex!

A terrible numbness settled in her chest.

Then Giles appeared.

He was carrying one piece of discreetly logo'd hand luggage and wheeling one suitcase. His eyes skated round the crowd of meeters and greeters, until he found Kate and then he was coming towards her.

He's so handsome, thought Kate, noticing that he'd had his hair cut much shorter. It suited him. Very Wall Street. So smart. So successful looking. And I know exactly what the first thing he'll say to me will be . . .

'Katie! I almost didn't recognise you!'

Exactly, thought Kate, coming towards him with a smile. Exactly.

She opened her arms and folded him in a big hug, burying her head in his shirt. Safe from any kisses. Kisses seemed to be a problem at the moment. Not that it had ever been a problem before, she thought.

Giles seemed surprised that she hadn't met the kiss he'd been intending to plant on her, but hugged her anyway.

'It's so good to be back,' he said into her hair.

'And it's fantastic to see you,' she mumbled into his chest, playing for time while she desperately tried to sort through the mixed messages in her heart. To get this wrong now would be a disaster, but the light-bulb in her heart, which she had tried to switch off while he was away, to stop the constant pain of missing him, wouldn't go back on again. It wouldn't. She had tried so hard not to drive herself mad with missing him – and had obviously succeeded too well. She flicked and flicked the switch, reminding herself of all the things they had done and all the things they would do now he was back, but nothing was happening.

Yes, she was pleased to see him back, but not the same way she had been at Christmas. That had been like a flame flaring into life, enhancing all the colours around them. London had seemed dull before, but that day they walked through the narrow streets, the light had bounced and played on almost every surface. Today, Heathrow seemed stark. And their reunion so much less lifelike than those going on around them.

Giles drew her back to arm's length to see her properly.

'You look like a fashion editor,' he said.

'Get away.'

He took her glasses off and bent his face down to hers and kissed her gently. Kate responded, but felt for the first time that she was feigning her enthusiasm. It felt wrong, and she felt more wrong for going along with it.

She broke off and tried to smile. 'You must be desperate to get out of here. Let me take your suitcase.'

'Not so desperate.' He held her glasses out of her reach and kissed her again.

While her lips were moving on his, Kate kept seeing a picture of them in her head, as though they were on film and she was watching. It didn't feel real. Little things were screaming out at her that had never been a problem before – why did he assume she would drop everything and trek out here at a minute's notice? Wasn't that signet ring a bit pretentious? What did he mean by 'You look like a fashion editor'? Why was the Giles she had had in her head slightly taller than the real one? Had she been mentally air-brushing him for the past eight months?

He must have sensed the resistance in her kiss, because he stopped and looked at her quizzically. As though he wanted her to start the conversation she didn't want to hear from him, or initiate herself.

'Come on, I've got the car,' she said, taking his hand. Their hands slipped together naturally and she felt secure and warm holding his as they walked to the car park. It wasn't that she didn't feel something for him; she did, but it wasn't enough. It was the *fondness* that she had always been so scared of men feeling for her, the embarrassed short change for her passion. It was genuine, but it wasn't enough. And compared to what had gone before, it was painfully inadequate.

Kate found Cress's Mini easily enough and realised that there might not even be enough room in it for Giles's bags. She opened the boot and squeezed his hand luggage in.

'Nice car,' he said, approvingly. 'What happened to the Rover?'

'Oh, that belonged to my flatmate. This belongs to the sister of my other flatmate.'

'They run a car hire business?'

'No, it's protection rackets, mainly.' Kate put her seat forward and pushed Giles's suitcase on to the back seat. 'Can you squeeze in?'

Giles folded himself into the passenger side.

'You're travelling very light,' said Kate, fastening her seatbelt. 'Are you sure you're really staying?' Her heart leapt at this possible get-out clause and she felt very sad.

'Yep, I'm having a whole heap of stuff crated back,' said Giles. 'There was too much to carry and I wanted to get through customs as quickly as possible.'

This awful polite conversation, thought Kate. How long can we do this for?

They drove out into the Heathrow slip-roads and were soon heading back for London. The polite conversation sputtered once or twice and then Giles switched on the radio.

Kate tried to catch glimpses of his expression in her mirrors. It's not just me, she thought. I can sense something's up with him too. *He* had flatmates in Chicago, maybe he wasn't so scrupulous about me. She pushed the thought away. It was hardly the point.

She struggled to put into words the instinct she was feeling. That was the least she could do.

There was her life here, with Dant and Harry, and Eclipse and Isobel, and London, and there was her life with Giles – which was based in Durham. Kate swallowed. Durham was over. Did she have a life in *London* with Giles? They'd have to start from scratch. Where would they begin?

Could she really be part of his world of glass-fronted offices and international figures, of coming home late and working over weekends? Would he want a girlfriend who didn't honestly understand the work that was the pivot of his life? More to the point, could she imagine Giles at the pub quiz with Harry, Dant, Seth and the lads, or helping her with some saga jacket copy?

Giles didn't keep non-textbooks, she remembered unhappily. He put all his paperbacks into a box at the end of each term and gave them to Oxfam, so they wouldn't clutter up his shelves.

He'd never come and pick her up from work, or share a picnic at lunch-time, because he'd always be finishing work four hours later than she did, and then he'd probably be off to the company squash court, bounding up the corporate ladder with his usual effortless inevitability.

Kate wondered if she had just made the squash court thing up out of martyrdom, but remembered that she had read it in one of his letters. He had won the post-work squash ladder for the Chicago office.

Pragmatically, time would always be a problem. She knew instinctively that it would always be the same: she would have to fit in with Giles. She'd always had to fit in with Giles, and now it would be even worse, now his career really would have the upper hand. His life was packed so tightly with ambition and drive that he just wouldn't make time to spend an evening doing nothing more important than arguing about the Nolan Sisters, and she wouldn't want to make him. *Forcing* him to share her new life would hurt even more than not being part of his.

But this is just finessing, she argued to herself. You know what the real problem is. Don't tell me *work* is now the centre of your priorities. Please!

Kate bit her lip and signalled back into the middle lane.

He doesn't like books, her inner voice went on, he doesn't have a favourite group, he doesn't like endless meandering conversation, he argues with waiters in restaurants, he has no idea what it's like to be turned down for every credit card going, he reads the pink bit of the newspaper and ignores the rest . . . None of these things mattered at college, but in the cold light of day – and you're not justifying yourself to Dant here – what have you got in common apart from the shared history of your relationship? He's a lovely man, but.

But.

Kate blanched and almost shot a red light. She made herself breathe hard and focus on the road. The traffic was full of Saturday drivers. Like her, in fact.

Her conscience tried a new tack.

If you met him in a bar now, would you want to take him home?

She flicked a glance at Giles in the mirror. Of course she would. He was gorgeous. Gorgeous in a heart-stoppingly casual sort of way. Short hair suited him and he was still tanned-looking at the end of February. And he was wearing a *suit*. Kate felt a twinge of lust in her lower stomach. It had been a deeply frustrating couple of days, what with one thing or another.

But would you want to start a relationship with him?

The answer came into her mind before she had time to think about it, or put up reflex explanations.

No.

Kate felt sick and her hands, damp with sweat, slipped on the wheel. She knew now that this painful lump of truthfulness had been lurking at the back of her mind for weeks. It had been there for a long time, but she had managed to cover it up with other things. Her desire to write him letters had faded with each trivial work matter, so important to her, that she knew he wouldn't be interested in, and so hadn't bothered to tell him. Yes, she knew he'd *try* to be interested, in the same way she *tried* to get her head round the incomprehensible things he did at work, but it wasn't enough. Kate found it hard to waffle in letters when she had nothing to say, and impossible to conduct a phone conversation with someone she loved where the silences began to outnumber the words – it made her cringe inside. And that was why the communication between them had tailed off – not because they were busy at work, or rushed off their feet with social life. Because they were running out of things to say to each other.

The realisation stung Kate like personal criticism, but she knew it was true. And it was as much down to the changes in *her* personality as his. She wasn't prepared to make as many allowances as she used to. Giles hadn't really changed, she didn't think. Well, she corrected herself, how would I know? I haven't exactly asked him, have I? I've been too busy examining my own navel to ask about his.

But she *had* changed. She felt as though all the time she had been in London she had been running two parallel realities at once: the undeniable struggle she had had to settle in, to learn how to work and make friends in an unfamiliar, unfriendly city, and over the top of that, like a layer of tissue paper, the borrowed reality of her and Giles, fragile and glamorous. Fragile, she realised now, because it wasn't growing. It had gradually faded, until what they both thought was reality was actually a ghost from the recent past, still bright enough to convince them it was alive, but starved of the idealistic, pressureless atmosphere of the university life it was part of. Both of them had wanted to keep it alive while their new lives were difficult and cold, but their need had been reflected on to it like borrowed light, making it seem more solid than it was.

Without even knowing it, the moment Kate had resigned herself to being in London for good, she realised, she had transferred her energy from one existence to the next, and now she couldn't make the step backwards into a world that didn't exist any longer. The wardrobe had shut behind her.

And most importantly, she had changed.

She looked at herself in the rear-view mirror to see if any of the churning she was experiencing inside was showing on her face. Outwardly she looked calm, if a bit pale, her eyes very green inside the black frames of her glasses. Giles too was staring out straight ahead of him. She wondered if he was struggling with the same kind of difficult thoughts. Kate hoped in a miserable way that he was. That it wasn't just her who could switch off like a light-bulb without fair notice.

There were only so many ways to drive from Heathrow to Chelsea, and eventually Kate turned into Redcliffe Square. It dawned on her for the first time as she passed signs to Brompton Cemetery that she had been virtually living round the corner from Selina.

'Pull up here,' said Giles suddenly, before they got to his parents' house. Kate did a creditable emergency stop behind a Mercedes estate. Cress's Mini Cooper had big wheels and big brakes. Mmm, she thought, distractedly, maybe I should get one of these with the fifty grand.

'Kate.' Giles put his hand on her knee and there was a long pause in which they both stared at each other, mentally sifting through clichés.

I have to do this, thought Kate, with a fierceness that surprised her. The whole point is that I know what I want for myself now, and that's why we have to split up, so if I can't do the splitting up then it's all meaningless, and I might as well just have snogged Harry.

'Giles,' she said.

Once the words were out, there would be no going back. But there was no going back anyway.

'Giles, the thought of you coming home has kept me going through some horrible times here, and I'm grateful for that. But I think we both know it's not going to be the same in London as it was in Durham. And that was such a happy time in my life that I don't want to spoil it now, by seeing you once a week, and not being able to share things properly. I'd rather draw a line under that part of our relationship, and leave it as it was.'

Kate felt tears climbing up her throat and she swallowed hard. Giles, she noticed, did not help her out by taking over the baton of guilt.

'I didn't realise how much being here could change me in so short a time. You were right. I mean, I thought I could just stay here for four months and then run away, without being affected by anything. I thought . . .' she hesitated, unsure of how pretentious her thoughts would sound to him. Not a good sign, said her conscience. 'I thought I had this shell around me . . .' Kate stopped. 'I think I've changed a lot since I've been moved to London. For the better. I think. I don't know.'

'You have,' agreed Giles quietly.

'Do you think so?'

For God's sake! How insecure are you?

He smiled sadly. 'I knew you'd changed when you drove to the airport to pick me up at Christmas. When I left, you didn't even know how to use the Underground, did you? And there you were, in that big car. Admittedly, you didn't know how to work the car parking system . . .' He raised his hands in pretend despair.

He's trying to make this easier for me, thought Kate. Now I really am going to cry.

'You're not the scared little girl I left here. You're much more confident and determined and . . . I don't know, aware of yourself. You even look like a different person.'

Kate's hand flew instinctively to her glasses, but Giles caught it in his own.

'No, don't. You suit them. You wear them if you want to.'

Kate looked away. 'It's not that I don't love you because I do' (how true was that? She honestly didn't know), 'but I don't want our relationship to be any less than it was, and I just feel it will be.' Her mind raced off into metaphor, to disguise for both of them the unpalatability of what she had to say. 'We would be like two people who've been set up by good mutual friends. We'd sort of know each other, but have to find out all the little things, all over again, and start with that, rather than take in and adjust our old relationship to fit the two new people wearing it.'

Kate's eyes filled up and she took off her glasses to rub away the tears. What a load of bollocks. Why couldn't Dant be doing her dialogue now? At least he could make it witty.

Giles pulled her hands away from her face and wiped up the tears with a handkerchief. 'I know exactly what you mean,' he said gently. 'I was going to try to say it myself, but I don't think I'd have done it so imaginatively.'

Oh, please don't say I'm dumped, thought Kate wildly, hating her irrational instinct to protect herself from dump-dom, even at the last moment.

'I think we should give ourselves some time,' he went on. Kate searched his voice for signs of distress, but it was calm and reasonable, with faint shades of Jerry Springer. 'I need some time to sort myself out here, move into the flatshare I've agreed with some people from work, see where my internship is going. I won't have much free time anyway, and that wouldn't be fair on you. You deserve far more than I'll be able to give you.'

Kate fixed her gaze on the tiny white button-down buttons on his shirt. She couldn't meet his eyes for fear of sobbing out loud, but she didn't want to seem to be looking away. Bloody hell, we're racing through the clichés now, she thought. But that's the thing about splitting up – no one wants to think about it enough to make up new ones. It's easier just to slide down the old lines and be done with it as soon as possible.

'Can I ask you something?' said Giles.

Kate looked up and something at the back of her mind was pleased to see a shadow of unhappiness in his eyes. She nodded.

'How long have you been thinking about this? Have you wanted to . . .'

'No,' she said firmly. 'There hasn't been anyone else, and there isn't anyone else now.'

She realised that she hadn't asked him the same and, too late, felt it would be churlish if she did. Much as she now desperately, masochistically, wanted to know. It might make it better, or it might break her heart.

'Please believe me when I say that I didn't want this to happen at all,' she said. 'For the past eight months I've been kidding myself that once you were back things would go on as normal, but I just knew, when you came through the arrivals gate, that they just couldn't, you know, that it would be impossible to pick up where we left off, and I had a horrible British feeling that this would be the best thing to do. I can't tell you how much this is physically hurting me, but I think if our relationship petered out and we could only talk on the office phone and I tried to be the person I was when you left, to make it easier . . .'

She was speaking faster and faster to stem the tide of images filling up her mind, but it was impossible. Her voice cracked and suddenly Giles's arms were round her and her face was buried in his shirt, which smelled painfully familiar: of nights when she would prop herself on her elbow in bed and just look at him, breathing the secret scent of his sleeping body. Kate could feel the warmth of his chest through the material and the thought that, though she could hang around Boots counters squirting herself with Chanel Egoiste, she would never ever smell the intimate muskiness again almost made her retch with sorrow.

'You're right,' he said sadly. 'This is the right thing to do.'

She lifted her face to his and he kissed her, sad open-mouthed kisses, fitted around Kate's gasping sobs. Giles kissed the trails of tears down her cheeks and laid his lips over her eyelids. He stroked her hair and buried his nose in the soft curls, until she had cried all the water from her tear-ducts. She had never known him to be so tender, and it wrenched her stomach even more. Then they sat holding each other silently, not wanting to be the one to break the finality of the moment.

'You were like a life raft,' said Kate eventually, into his shirt. She didn't trust herself to raise her head. 'When you left me here in London, I thought I was drowning. But knowing you were coming home gave me something to look forward to. And I hung on to that when my job was hard and when I hated my flatmates and when I hated everything about London, and gradually, I learned how to cope. And then I . . .'

She stopped abruptly, aware of what the next sentence was going to be.

'Didn't need that life raft any more?' Giles finished for her.

'I don't mean that I didn't—'

He stopped her. 'I know what you mean, it's OK. All I ever wanted was for you to be happy here. And I think I always knew this would happen – that once you stopped railing against everything, you'd see how amazing you are. Now I guess everyone knows how amazing you are, not just me.' He gave her a sad smile and traced his finger down the bump of her nose as if he were trying to memorise it. 'It was a risk, but you had to do it. I had to do it. Thing is, I should have known that caterpillars turn into butterflies and butterflies have wings.'

'Are you saying I was a caterpillar?' protested Kate, to defuse the cheese potential of what he had just said. He didn't have to try to do metaphors just because she was.

'No, I'm saying that you're a butterfly.'

He's so rational, thought Kate! It was a risk! He'd balanced everything up and . . . And what?

Another minute or so passed while they stared at each other, trying to imprint every detail of the other's face before Giles opened the car door and they were demoted back into friends.

'Kate, I'm going to go now,' he said. 'Otherwise we will stay here for hours, and you were brave enough to start this conversation, so I think it's up to me to end it, don't you?'

Kate nodded. Suddenly she didn't trust herself to speak. Up to now, the finality of what she had done hadn't quite sunk in. But now it did. She had to fight a powerful impulse to grab his arm.

'I had a wonderful time being with you,' he said. 'And I hope that in the future, when our lives are a bit more coherent than they are now, we might find that we've got more in common than we thought. Yes?'

Kate nodded.

'Thank you,' he said and leaned over and kissed her cheek.

The first kiss as just his friend, thought Kate, stricken.

'Giles,' she said suddenly. 'Please don't call me for a while. Um, I need time to get used to not being your girlfriend when I talk to you.' Oh, the irony!

'Sure.' Giles opened the car door without taking his eyes off her face. 'Of course.'

Kate gripped the steering wheel so tightly her knuckles stood out white on her hands. It stopped her crying though.

Giles was getting his bags out of the back of the car. The time that's racing past now will race through all this hurt too, she thought. It goes the same speed for good things and bad things.

Go away, Rose Ann!

And now he was leaning in through the passenger door window to say goodbye.

'You never look so gorgeous as when you're saying goodbye,' Kate said before she could stop herself. But it was true and she wouldn't get another chance to tell him, would she?

Giles's eyes crinkled up in a smile. 'And you've never looked so gorgeous, full stop,' he said. 'Ever.'

He bent his head towards her and kissed her again.

'Call me when you're ready and I'll take you out for dinner. I believe I owe you a dinner out.'

Kate smiled a wobbly smile. 'OK.'

He stood up, her signal to leave. She started the engine, which made a pleasant roaring noise, and switched on the radio. I will do this without looking back, she thought. Think Emma Peel.

Kate crunched the Mini into gear and drove round

Redcliffe Square on autopilot. She allowed herself a quick glimpse back as she came to the junction with the main road. Giles was a tall figure in the distance, walking very slowly and carrying his bag over his shoulder like a tennis player. The traffic behind her forced her on. By the time she was on Redcliffe Gardens, a curious sensation of lightness was coursing through her body, as though she might float away, unanchored, through the roof of the car and up and up and up.

She drove the few hundred yards back to Deauville Crescent and pulled up outside the flat. Ratcat was sitting on the front steps with a furry inanimate object in his mouth. She turned off the engine and a dead silence fell in the car. But something other than Ratcat stopped her from getting out.

Kate listened to herself breathing. She didn't want to see Harry, or Dant, or anything that would make her feel she had swapped Giles for anything less than herself.

Cress had a big *A–Z* in the passenger side door pocket and Kate dragged it out. Where could she go? She flipped over pages of streets and main roads until she came to outer London. Richmond Park, a friendly mass of green, looked big enough to lose herself in.

Kate started the engine again and drove off.

chapter thirty-eight

'Sorry?' said Isobel, whose characteristic adeptness at concealing her feelings also seemed to have temporarily deserted her.

Kate laced her fingers through the spiral edge of her notepad and raised an eyebrow in polite enquiry. Not the most eloquent response to Jennifer Spencer's bombshell but marginally better than going 'Whaaaat?', which had been her first impulse.

'It's a working concept we've decided to bring over from the American imprints,' said Jennifer. 'I must stress that it's entirely a trial situation and contained within the limited period I've outlined. And since Megan and Cynthia have decided to leave us anyway, it seemed like a good time to reorganise and refresh the department.'

They all adopted expressions of nasal affront at the mention of Megan.

Megan's notice had landed on Jennifer's desk the day Elaine finalised Cress's (or R. A. as she was still referred to, pre-embargo) contract. Her notice period was, by mutual agreement, minimal. She had put it about in the kitchen that she had been head-hunted but Isobel had made some discreet enquiries and discovered that Megan had been on the list of a recruitment agency for some time. She also discovered that Megan's new job had a turnover rate faster than a McDonald's grill plate but Kate and Isobel decided it would be kinder to keep that snippet to themselves.

'Since we now have a substantial array of young talent on the list, it does make sense to devote a think-tank arrangement to producing more of the same, and, concomitantly, since Elaine will be concentrating more and more on the Rose Ann Barton brand image, I do think it's a window of opportunity for you to take on some of her responsibilities, Isobel.' Jennifer peered over the top of her steepled hands. 'With the appropriate supervision, naturally.'

Isobel nodded obediently.

Jennifer turned her steeples in Kate's direction. 'Kate, you will experience some of Isobel's responsibilities in a waterfall arrangement, if you will.'

Jennifer's hands made waterfall motions in the air.

'Wonderful,' said Kate, resisting the hypnotic impulse to copy her.

'I will be keeping a close eye on the project as a whole, and I don't feel that it should impinge on your general editorial responsibilities within the department.'

Except that I won't be trotting off to Boots the Chemist for Elaine half the time, thought Kate, gleefully. Better get myself stocked up on Rescue Remedy before my desk gets moved too far from the source.

'It's a project I've been under some pressure from Eclipse's parent company to implement for a while now, but I haven't been entirely confident of its chances of success.' Jennifer's tone made it clear that she still wasn't convinced about the Isobel/Kate talent show but was determined to make the best of a potentially disastrous job. 'We will be reviewing this on a weekly basis at first,' Jennifer went on. 'And I'm sure great things will come from this kind of free management thinking.'

Isobel and Kate smiled on cue.

'So don't let me down.' Jennifer glared savagely and then gave them her best Joanna Lumley smile. 'Isobel, don't you have a plane to catch?'

'Er, yes,' said Isobel, wondering how Jennifer could possibly have extracted that information from a two-day holiday form. Her hand dithered nervously around her plait.

Kate could see that Isobel was torn between dislike of volunteering information to Jennifer about her personal life and her general euphoria about the fact that Will was taking her off on a minibreak to hammer out their unofficial prenuptial agreement. God help them both, she thought, if Jennifer had caught up with Isobel in the office espionage stakes.

'I'm going to Dublin for a day or two,' Isobel said and clamped her mouth shut. Maybe it was the new pink twinset that had given it away. She did look unnecessarily smart for a Monday.

'Lovely,' said Jennifer, shuffling together the briefing hand-outs she had had prepared for them. 'Always nice not to have to go too far on these short breaks, isn't it?'

She passed the paper over the desk and sent out her usual radar signals that the conversation had left the building. Kate and Isobel rose to their feet.

'Um, thanks, Jennifer,' said Kate, feeling some small tribute was now expected. 'I think this will be a really exciting project, and I promise you your confidence in us won't be misplaced.' This sounded as though she had read it straight out of the Girl Guides' Book of Public Speaking, so she smiled sincerely and left it at that. The truth was that the news was so unexpected that she hadn't even worked out whether it was the most fantastic career opportunity she could ever wish for, or a cunningly concealed move to eject her and Isobel from the bosom of Eclipse quicker than a dose of salmonella vindaloo.

'Can't *wait* to get started!' said Isobel, very Scottishly.

Kate looked at her and wondered if she was going to slap her thigh too, just to emphasise her point.

Jennifer smiled tightly at them both and said, 'Well, read through that and we'll discuss the bigger picture in the meeting I've outlined for Friday. Isobel, can you book me a table at the Savoy for breakfast tomorrow, please?'

'Only another three weeks of that,' muttered Isobel as they sloped off to the kitchen.

'She's getting a new you?'

'Absolutely.' Isobel started steaming some milk. 'After three years of hard labour. That's what happens when you become an editor. Unless your name is Kate "Who Ate All The Jam?" Craig, in which case you abandon your previous slave driver and just . . . "float".' Isobel put the word in quotation marks.

Kate opened the fridge door in case the Production Department had received any edible bribes from the printing houses recently. There was a much depleted box of Belgian seashells, half a mango and a bottle of champagne with a spoon stuck in the neck. Kate extracted the pralines.

'Hadn't you better get a move on?' she asked through a mouthful of chocolate snail. 'You'll need to get a cab.'

Isobel looked at her watch and did a double take. 'Oooh, better had.' She accepted a snail and ate it in one.

They stood chewing a second round of seahorses appreciatively until Isobel smacked her hands to her cheeks and gasped, 'God, the post! It still hasn't come and I really have to go. Can you do Jennifer's post for me? Open everything and don't bother letting her see the weird author letters. Just upsets her.'

'No problem,' said Kate. 'I like post. Elaine never gets much. Shame you no longer have your old influence with Mark in the post room. Post never used to be this late in the old days.'

Isobel slapped her arm playfully. 'We don't talk about the old days. I'm a One Man Gal now.'

As Isobel said it, Kate realised that she had managed to keep Giles out of her head for a whole twenty minutes, but now he slid back in like a slide in a projector. Ker-chunk. Giles in a fisherman's sweater. Ker-chunk. Giles knowledge-

ably ordering the wine in a nice restaurant. A veritable animated lecture had been playing non-stop in the back of her
mind for nearly forty-eight hours now. Just pictures though,
no accompaniment. Ker-chunk. This time it was the image
of them walking silently through the City in the December
twilight, wondering how they could contain their longing
for one another for another few months. Where had that
gone? Kate had thought she had cried herself out, walking
round Richmond Park in circles until it got too dark to be
safe, and still all Sunday the tears had flowed soundlessly
down her cheeks. That had been replaced now by a martyred
numbness, born, she suspected, of reading too much late-
Victorian fiction at college. And she wasn't even the one
who had been dumped, for God's sake.

She bit her lip and decided not to tell Isobel about Giles
until she got back from Dublin. It wasn't fair to spoil her
romantic trip.

'Have a wonderful time,' she said, giving Isobel a sad kiss
on the cheek. 'Do everything I would do.'

'Oh, I will.' Isobel grinned devilishly. 'Well, I'll get my
bag and be off. I've made you some coffee,' she added, as
Kate appeared to be somewhere else.

'Oh, right, thanks.' Kate took the cup, even though she
really didn't feel like it. Even coffee reminded her of Giles.

Not of *Giles*, she corrected herself. Of the times you *had*
with Giles when you were both happy. That's what you're
missing. Not Giles himself now, whom you've accepted isn't
right for you.

Yesyesyes. Kate walked through the office to her desk
and started to make a list of her overdue chores.

At three, an enormous bunch of roses walked up to her
chair.

'Put them in Elaine's office,' said Kate automatically.
Roses. Her heart dropped another notch as the slide of Giles
screeching to a halt by the phone box in North London

slotted into her mind. Those amazing orange roses he'd given her. It was clear to her now that he probably hadn't chosen them himself, but the faint taste of the excitement she'd felt was still painful.

'They're for you,' said Mark from the post room through the cellophane wrapping. 'Where do you want them?'

Kate swivelled in her chair. 'Are you sure?'

The roses nodded.

'Oh, um, just here, I suppose.' Heads were beginning to pop out of office doors. 'In the bin so they don't fall over?'

Mark deposited them as carefully as he could and winked his good eye knowingly at her.

Kate blushed and waved him off. Isobel, she thought, what were you thinking of?

She felt quite self-conscious looking for the card, knowing that most of Editorial and the bits of Marketing next door were unashamedly waiting to find out who they were from.

She raced through a couple of choice possibilities.

Harry? Her heart speeded up.

Giles . . . to try to get her back? A wave of sickness washed up her throat, so physical she was shocked by it.

Dant? She pushed that one away. Dant?

Cressida as peace offering?

Kate fumbled for the card, hidden in the heart of the arrangement, and slit open the envelope.

'A bunch of Peace roses with love and grateful thanks from Mike and Laura xoxoxo'

Oh.

Kate looked at it again: a simple sentence which meant that three hearts – Mike's, Laura's and her mother's – wouldn't be broken after all, condensed into a rounded junior florist's hand, with lollipop i's and no punctuation. It looked simple, but she suspected it wasn't.

'It's OK,' she said to Jo, whose fashionably black roots were hovering out of the nearest door. It seemed a bit un-

English to address all the heads as if they were a West End chorus line. 'My brother and his estranged wife have got back together.'

'How lovely,' said Jo, managing to imply that she didn't think the flowers were from them at all, and disappeared back into her office. Doors shut discreetly all the way down the corridor, as if choreographed by Busby Berkeley.

At four o'clock, Kate went to the sweetie shop from force of habit, even though Isobel wasn't there to go with her. When she got back to her desk there was another bunch of roses on her seat, this time orange and tigerish and bearing a card envelope from Veevers Carter.

Kate felt really sick this time. There was no mistaking who these were from. She felt as though there were an invisible barrier of magnetic energy around her desk, repelling her, but she made herself walk over and open the card, already trembling with the embarrassment it would surely contain.

'Can't wait to see you soon – hope I see you before these flowers do. All my love, Giles.'

Kate pushed the roses under her desk where no one would see them and make the wrong comment. She didn't think she could bear any remarks about how lucky she was. He must have phoned London and arranged for them to be sent before he got on the plane, in case she didn't get his message.

'All my love.' Kate had always hated the empty 'Forever Friends' sentiment of that phrase – how could it be all your love? What about your parents? Your sense of self-preservation? – and it rang particularly hollow now. She wished she could join the roses beneath her desk and cry. It was all very well knowing she was doing the right thing, but how could it be so hard to let go of the man and the memories of the way things had been between them? Even the flowers were reaching in from the past, paid for by credit card before Giles rejoined her life in England, and sent to the woman he had in mind when he thought of her miles away in Chicago.

Not quite the same woman as the one receiving them. But how was he to know that?

Kate drew a breath and was surprised to find it shuddered. The misery hangover wasn't going to go away that quickly. Sending the flowers was the proper thing to do, of course, but it didn't quite feel like Giles, and Kate didn't know why. It felt a bit . . . scripted. She pushed the card back into the envelope so that she wouldn't have to look at the words – even disguised in someone else's handwriting, it didn't sound like him – and tucked the card down into the bottom of her bag. Her desk now smelled like a maternity ward.

Elaine walked past Kate's desk, ostentatiously reading a letter.

'The post is still in the pigeon-holes,' she pointed out.

So why didn't you bring it with you, Kate fumed internally. 'Two seconds,' she said, making random busy-busy typing noises on her keyboard. Elaine didn't ask about her roses and sailed into her office.

For a person apparently operating without use of arms or legs Elaine certainly copes well around the office, thought Kate, pushing her chair back. Giles's roses glowed brightly up at her from under the desk and with a rush of shame she hid them with her chair.

There wasn't even that much post when she got to the pigeon-holes. Elaine had been through it and removed what was probably the only non-insulting or undemanding communication. The rest was fan mail, mainly for Rose Ann, chasing letters from agencies, or corrected proofs.

Kate balanced it all on one arm and pulled out Jennifer's selection of mail, which was twice as thick and seemed largely made up of manuscripts, personal invitations and postcards. Jennifer still hadn't made it back from lunch, so wouldn't notice what time the post landed on her desk. Even so, it looked substantially more interesting than Elaine's and Kate carted it off to Isobel's desk to go through it.

It was easy to see where Isobel got her information from, thought Kate, as she skimmed through a gushing letter from an author currently published by one of Eclipse's rivals, thanking Jennifer for a fabulous lunch at Gordon Ramsay the previous week. There was a manuscript from a major television presenter and the first two chapters of a new novel by a celebrity chef – both of which seemed to be about male pregnancy – some internal sales figures for Rose Ann's main rivals (all reaching a quarter of her sales, according to the report by Chris, the key accounts manager), some invitations to launches and a big brown envelope marked 'Private'.

Kate hesitated. Isobel had told her to go ahead and open anything marked 'Private': many packages came in, sternly decorated with stickers and dire warnings, and turned out to be faintly spicy unsolicited manuscripts about Italian immigrant families in the Gorbals, rather than letter bombs or fuzzy pornographic long-lens photos of editors in compromising positions with booksellers and supermarket buyers. Kate's thumbnail picked at the flap. If she threw away the envelope, Jennifer wouldn't even know. Besides, she was naturally nosy like that.

Kate slit the flap with Isobel's potentially lethal letter opener, and shook out the contents.

A Kodak packet fell out, too thin to contain a whole roll of pictures, and a card in an unsealed envelope. Kate's conscience made her ignore the card but instead she opened the packet of photographs and was disappointed to see that they seemed to be of Rose Ann, surrounded by her many fans in the old people's ward of a hospital, all smiling gummily up at her as she dispensed large-print copies of *Born in a Barn* amongst them. The books were roughly the same size as pizza boxes, on account of the large print having to cope with the verbose nature of Rose Ann's style.

'She may be rich now, but she's never lost 'er accent, nor forgot 'er roots,' Kate could hear them saying, in unwitting imitations of Rose Ann's less convincing characters. 'Rooooose Ann, she's the salt o' the earth, with 'er down-home wisdom and 'er famous turnip recipes.' She knew for a fact that they said things like this, since the Marketing Department had made tapes of her fans singing the praises of her simple style and her broad accent, and used them in a radio advert for her last hardback. Well, alleged fans. Diane could just as easily have rounded up the three or four people in the office who could do a reasonably authentic Northern accent and made them read into a tape recorder, Kate thought, then shook herself. Had publishing made her so cynical so soon?

They're probably for the Mother's Day flier, she thought with a sense of disappointment. Mother's Day accounted for Rose Ann's biggest sales, as every publishing house in the country rushed to fill the shops with tales of abandoned children and North Country wife-beating as the low-cal alternative to a box of Black Magic.

Well, I say Rose Ann, Kate corrected herself again. Whoever 'Rose Ann's' gender-specific representative on earth is. She flicked through the rest in case the Real Rose Ann was featured stroking the walls or eating glass, but the other photos were of 'Rose Ann' with some reconditioned donkeys from Morecambe Sands, 'Rose Ann' sitting in a spacious garden pretending to write on an old-fashioned typewriter, 'Rose Ann' looking wistful in a dark two-up, two-down kitchen, leaning on a mangle, and 'Rose Ann' surrounded by some far from urchin-type children dressed in Baby Gap clothes. And Jennifer.

Jennifer? Kate looked more closely. God, even Jennifer was getting in on the act, lending her children to the Eclipse Marketing Department. And they *were* Jennifer's children – she could tell from the Afghan hound noses on them.

Kate put the photos back in the packet. Her hand hovered over the notelet. It wasn't sealed, no one would know, Isobel would go mad if she found out she hadn't gone the extra mile . . .

She slipped the card out of the envelope. It was a folding-up notelet, of the type much beloved of her grandmother, depicting, in a bizarre interpretation of natural law, a benign-looking fox with its paw resting on the head of a baby badger. Kate glanced nervously up to check that no one was about to walk into Isobel's office. She was almost surprised Isobel hadn't trip-wired it.

Dear Jen, the note read. *Here are the 'snaps' as requested! The ones of the kiddies are especially nice, Marmaduke gets more like his granddad every day, although Aphra has 'a look of' me, they all say here! It'll be nice to see you again soon, next time you're up in this 'neck of the woods', though I suppose it won't be long before I'll be in 'the big Smoke' for the Mother's Day signings! Will you be booking 'the usual place'? It's a lovely hotel, though it is a 'bit of a trek' to go from Knightsbridge to the big M&S on these old legs! Give me a call soon, won't you pigeon, much love to you all, from Mam xx*

Kate read it again to make sure she'd got Jennifer's children's names right.

Then she read it again to make sure generally.

When she began it for the fourth time, having failed to dispel her sense of complete amazement, her nerve failed her and she shoved the whole lot back into the envelope with trembling fingers.

Rose Ann Barton was Jennifer Spencer's mother. It was a double life worthy of *Corkickle Urchins*, apart from the fact that she was actually a fake Rose Ann, but even so . . . Matching the old lady who shared her own gran's diffident habit of putting any phrase longer than two words in quotation marks with the coiffeured and bespoke-shod powerbroker required a plot twist beyond even Rose Ann's loose grasp on reality.

'By, there's nowt so queer as folk,' breathed Kate.

As she was trying to work out where they had got the mangle from, Jennifer breezed in from lunch, carrying a gigantic blue Tiffany's bag and a Tefal pressure cooker. Once she was safely past, Kate bundled all her post together and stood up to take it through to Jennifer's office. She considered sticking the envelope back up again with some tape (her mother could quite easily have done that herself, to add another photo, maybe) but the sound of Jennifer ripping into some unfortunate individual in the Rights Department over the phone like a velociraptor after elocution lessons gave her an unexpected burst of Isobel-ness, and she put the envelope in the middle of the pile, where Jennifer would know she'd seen it.

It's not that I'm getting hard-faced, Kate reasoned, I'm just getting . . . aware of the rules.

She took the whole lot through and put it carefully in Jennifer's in-tray.

'Thanks *soooo* much,' mouthed Jennifer, although she diminished the effect of her smile immediately by bellowing, 'I've had people sacked for exactly this kind of sloppiness, you know, Tamsin!' down the phone.

Kate smiled back and went off to deal with Elaine's post.

Improbably enough, there was yet another bunch of flowers on her chair when she got back. A modest tied bunch of five blue hyacinths floating in purple tissue and gold ribbon, with no card, or label. Kate picked it up and breathed in the gentle scent. The smell reminded her of Easter eggs, but she had no idea who'd sent them.

'Are you up the duff?' asked Sarah from Production, going past with a sheaf of forms.

'No!' said Kate, thinking at once of her stomach. Was it that bad? 'Why?'

'All those flowers arriving for you. I've been down in the post room, there's a sweepstake on.' Sarah stopped. 'Or are you getting married?'

'No, I am not.'

Sarah tipped her head on one side. 'Awww,' she wheedled. 'You couldn't just hint to the post room lads that you've got engaged, could you? I've got a couple of pints riding on it.'

'What are the other options? That I've just had a life-saving operation? Or I've won Miss West London?'

'Well,' said Sarah shiftily, 'there was some mention of you and R. A. Harper being a bit of an item . . .'

Kate glared at Sarah. 'Megan?'

Sarah drew a finger across her lips. 'I am not at liberty to reveal my sources.'

'Well, it's all rubbish. I'm just . . . a very popular girl.'

'Yearight,' said Sarah and carried on down the corridor. Kate heard her call, 'It's a girl!' into Jo's office as she passed it.

Jennifer came by her desk at going home time to offer her a lift back to Kensington. She was wearing the same expression as the wolf would have done, had he been able to offer Little Red Riding Hood a lift to Grandma's on the back of his Vespa.

'Oh, thanks, Jennifer, but I'm meeting someone for dinner,' lied Kate, brightly. *How does she know where you live?* the voice in her head pointed out. Kate increased the wattage on her smile.

'It's not out of my way,' Jennifer assured her, although Kate knew this to be rather a flexible version of the truth, since Jennifer lived in St John's Wood.

'No, really, I do have a date for dinner,' Kate insisted.

'Shame, I had hoped to have a chat about this new brain-storming project,' sighed Jennifer. 'I think you're going to be very pleased—' she added a significant look at this point, '—with the new salary package we've worked out for you and Isobel. It's going to be a very challenging experience for you, and I need to know that you can both be trusted on some pretty confidential information, company-wise.'

Kate nodded, not trusting herself to come up with

something that would suggest complicity and innocence well enough.

'As long as we're clear on where we stand,' said Jennifer, with another significant look.

'Yes, I think I'm pretty clear,' said Kate. 'I know when to keep mum on most things.'

Jennifer's throat clenched, but she dredged another smile out of somewhere. 'Well, have a good dinner.' She turned to go, then swivelled on her kitten heel and added, 'If you could get that pressure cooker over to IAA first thing tomorrow, with some suitably punning note? It's a detective sous-chef.'

Kate did a thumbs up, because she knew it would annoy Jennifer and, besides, it added a certain 'last cheesy freeze frame in *Moonlighting*' feel to their conversation.

'Goodnight!' said Jennifer tightly. 'Night, Elaine!' she called towards Elaine's office, although Elaine had left three-quarters of an hour ago to get her chakras rebalanced. By prior arrangement, Kate switched off her computer and removed her spare hat and coat from the pegs at about six.

Kate was in no hurry to go home. The flat prompted all sorts of unwelcome thoughts about Giles, guilt and anger about Cress, and she simply didn't know what to say to Harry.

Maybe that was half the problem, she thought, feeding more paper into the printer, as she caught up on Elaine's overdue rejection letters. Maybe you need to ditch the words and just get on with it. Or maybe you have to give up Harry as your penalty for ending things with Giles. She stared out of the window at the tail lights of passing cars, strung like red rosary beads up the road as they drove away from the city.

Maybe you think about things too much, she countered crossly. The final letter came out and she put them all in Elaine's tray for her to sign in the morning. The scent of the hyacinths, in a small vase on her desk, was developing in the evening and hung around her office like a cloud, overpowering even the roses. Kate didn't know who had sent them, but didn't want to think about it. If they wanted to remain anonymous, who was she to spoil the gesture?

As she reached under her desk for her bag, Giles's fiery orange roses loomed out at her reproachfully. Mike and Laura's bouquet was sitting in one of Jennifer's massive vases on the filing cabinets, for communal enjoyment, but these she had kept hidden.

Kate took a deep breath, as though she were grasping a bunch of nettles, and lifted them out of the bucket she had plunged them in. An inseparable collage of all the things she had done with Giles flashed before her closed eyes, followed by a wave of loneliness as strong as gas, and she burst into tears, dipping her head into the soft petals and weeping tears of shame and relief and regret into their thornless depths. *Again*, she thought, desperately. When am I going to stop *doing* this?

Underneath all the pain, something in the smell of the roses told her she was right to do what she had done. Soothing thoughts seeping into her head from nowhere: being at the end of one chapter meant being at the start of the next. These weren't the same roses Giles had given her in July, they were just the same *kind*. There would be new orange roses every day, day after day after day, if she wanted them. She didn't have to wait to be sent them by Giles, or anybody else. She could fill her room with bloody roses for the same price as a monthly travel card. Any flower she wanted. And so there would be new roses and new people to discover and new parts of herself that she didn't know about yet. London and all the secret things in it was open to her. She didn't ever again have to limit her own possibilities the way she had before. And if it all went wrong, then she would cope. As she had done for the past eight months.

Kate squeezed her eyes tightly shut as they filled up again with fresh tears.

*

Gradually her breathing returned to normal and she carried the flowers and her bag into the kitchen to splash her face. The Production Department had left a crate of dried figs they'd been sent, with a sarcastic note pinned over the top. Unusually, the box hadn't been decimated. There were two missing, and half of one had been abandoned on the water filter. Kate managed a wry laugh, and smiled at the fact that she'd laughed.

She got off the Tube a stop early at Earl's Court, wanting to spin out the journey as long as possible. She carried Giles's roses by her side with a vague feeling of revulsion. A month ago, the idea of Giles sending roses to her office would have filled her with hysterical joy. Now it was all over – and technically all her fault – they made her feel uncomfortable.

It had occurred to her that she could get the flowers couriered round to Laura's office – without the card, natch – and pretend they were from Mike. But that would involve explaining the situation to Mike, and even though Laura would love them, he was bound to get something wrong and spoil the effect, and the last thing Kate wanted to do was to set off another row.

The smell of spit-roasted chicken caught her nose as she walked past a late-night grocer's and she was about to walk in and buy some when she caught sight of herself in the shop window. She looked like a plain-clothes bride. She couldn't go home like this. Kate was tempted for a moment to dump the roses in the buckets of wilted chrysanthemums outside and walk away, leaving them shimmering like an expensive floral changeling in the neon light from the sign above, but at the last minute something stopped her. It would be a cheap thing to do. And whatever she and Giles had been to each other, their relationship had never been cheap.

Suddenly she didn't feel like chicken any longer.

Kate turned away from the grocer's and walked the other way down the street, past the Exhibition Building to the

Brompton Road. She had walked around here in the empty time after Christmas, counting the Christmas trees in the windows. She crossed the road self-consciously and let herself into the cemetery.

Graveyards had never bothered Kate, being just too young to have missed *Thriller*. She wandered through the plots until she came to the first grave with no flowers beneath it and, tugging off the ribbon, scattered the bouquet on the scrubby earth, turning her head before she could read the name on the stone. Then she walked briskly away.

Harry and Dant were sitting round the kitchen table looking shocked and serious respectively when she let herself into the flat.

'Evening.' Kate unwound her scarf from her glowing cheeks. 'Or should I say "Welcome Back to London"?'

'Fabulous to be back,' said Dant. 'In a fat/frying pan relocation sense.'

Harry turned his big brown Labrador eyes up to Kate. They were very sad but, Kate was relieved to note, not overtly angry. 'Kate, Dant's told me everything.'

'Has he?' said Kate, shifting her gaze to Dant. How much was everything? Was Harry about to throttle her in defence of Cress's literary honour? Or was he about to shoot himself in an attack of the E. M. Forsters?

'Cress will be coming back to England when she is out of plaster,' said Dant flatly. 'She has announced that she will be giving up the demanding task of running a wine bar and taking up residence here, to concentrate on her writing career.'

'Well, she'll *need* to concentrate, won't she?' said Kate automatically, then saw the tortured expression on Harry's face and bit her lip. 'But what about her own flat?' She forced herself to ask the obvious question, just in case the obvious answer had been overlooked.

'Selling it. Out of spite, I reckon.'

'But . . .' Kate began, 'if Cress is living here, then . . .' She faltered, unsure of how to go on without sounding deeply selfish.

'Yes, well, she's getting very good at twists is our Cressida,' said Dant. 'I think it rather goes without saying that you and I aren't really going to want to share bathroom cabinet space with the new unimproved R. A., now we know the kinds of things she can do to your moisturiser. But she isn't going to be the one who kicks us out.'

'Cress wants me to stay,' said Harry. 'Well, she didn't say she wanted you and Dant to *go*, but it sort of looks as though . . .' Kate looked at him closely. In her opinion, he didn't seem as happy as he should have done, given that he had just been given a house-share with the woman he had fantasised about since he had started *having* fantasies. Maybe Dant *had* told him everything. Even the bits *she* didn't know about.

'You don't have to stay,' said Kate. 'Come with us. At least you know what we're like first thing in the morning. Cress might turn out to be a troll without her slap. Sorry,' she added, seeing Harry's face. Tact wasn't getting any better.

'No, she asked for me, and, you know, I think she needs some support just at the moment.' Harry fiddled with the penknife lying on the table in front of him, next to assorted parts from the washing machine, which was evidently out of commission again.

Oh, God, thought Kate, with a pang of guilty desire, he's like something from a First World War film. And I can't stop him. She saw immediately the bind Harry's conscience would have him in. Loyalty to Cress would override any fresh feelings he might be harbouring for her, and the more she tried to divert him from the true and noble way, the more it would reinforce his instinct to protect Cressida.

So Dant can't have told him everything, she thought bitterly. It crossed her mind that now would be a good time to reveal the full extent of Cress's treacherous behaviour – after all, she very obviously didn't deserve loyalty like this, hour of need or not.

'And now Giles is back . . .' Harry began to mumble, but Kate had risen to her feet and was leaning on the table, like Jennifer doing her Sue Ellen impression.

'You know, Harry, the one thing I've learned from the whole miserable business of splitting up with Giles is that you have to think about yourself. Now I realise that Cress has taken that to ridiculous extremes, because she seems clinically unable to think about anyone else, but the last thing I want is for you to end up being used and tossed aside.'

'Well, I don't know about the tossing bit,' murmured Dant.

'You've . . .?' began Harry.

'Shut up, Dant,' Kate threw over her shoulder. 'Now if you really love Cressida,' she continued to Harry, 'and you want to help her through this then there are various things you need to know about her. Things I suspect Dante hasn't told you.'

She turned to Dant, who shrugged his shoulders.

'The reason Dant and I had to rewrite that filth of Cressida's was because she had—'

'Don't.' Harry got to his feet. 'Don't. Don't tell me any more. I know she's been a bitch, but I still believe that—' He turned to Dant. 'Can you go away for a minute, please?'

'Certainly not. This is my sister you're talking about. Besides, how will I find out what's been going on?'

Kate glared at Dant, but it was clear he wasn't going to move. He had his irritating obtuse expression on. Kate could understand why his mother might have wanted to set fire to him.

Harry turned back to Kate. His face was a mess of emotions. 'When we talked about . . . how I feel about Cress . . . I told you that I thought I could make her happy. And now she's more or less asked me to . . . I don't think I can say no.

Not without closing the door on her ever trying to be a nicer person again.'

'Harry, you don't have to be . . .' Kate searched wildly through her stock of sacrificial women types but couldn't find an appropriate one. Who was the Greek girl who'd agreed to marry the monster? 'The woman out of Beauty and the Beast,' she finished lamely. Grow up! she wanted to yell. She doesn't have some kind of licence for you!

'Pasiphaë,' supplied Dant, dryly.

'I know. I know that.' Harry looked thoroughly miserable. 'And I wish you hadn't said about you and Giles, because that just makes it worse, shut up, Dant,' he warned, before Dant could follow through with what he was about to say. 'Oh, fuck. What a pile of shiteing shite.'

Kate stretched out her hand to Harry, but he had already turned on his heel. He picked up the phone on his way past and took it into his bedroom. The door clicked shut.

She and Dant stared after him.

Kate half rose from her seat, and sank down again. Should she go to him? Was there any point in trying to change his mind? If Cress really was determined to start again and put herself back together, at least Harry was strong enough to help her. It might stop her breaking Dant any further. Kate pushed away the thought of what it might do to Harry. But he wanted it so much. So badly. Cress had probably shaped his life more than her own.

'Poor Harry,' whispered Kate.

'Poor Harry my arse,' said Dant. 'Well, actually, yes, poor Harry.'

They had half a minute's silence for Harry.

'Oh, yeah, I've got something for you,' said Dant, reaching into his back pocket. He pulled out an envelope and handed it to her. 'Actually I've got something else too. Never say I don't think about you.' His curly head disappeared beneath the table while he rummaged in his rucksack and emerged again with a large Toblerone, which he banged on the table in front of her.

Kate was trying to get the envelope open. Her nails, which she'd been chewing down to painful crops all weekend, were too short to pick the flap and in the end she had to use the butter knife from breakfast.

A cheque for £50,000 slid on to the table. Kate shook the envelope to see if there was a short and savage note with it, but there wasn't. Just the cheque, drawn on the account of the Hon. Cressida Grenfell. Made out to her. For fifty thousand pounds.

Kate said nothing. After a few moments she put it down, opened the Toblerone and ate two chunks at once, still looking at the cheque.

'Is it real?' she asked eventually.

'Of course. One thing you have to say about my sister is that she never bounces cheques.'

'But she hasn't got her signature advance yet.'

Dant gave her a pitying look. 'Shaking cocktails evidently pays better than we thought.'

'God.' Kate picked it up and looked at it again.

'You didn't say that you and the Boy Wonder had split up,' said Dant conversationally.

'Yes, at the weekend. I decided that he might have been the man for me when he left me in a quivering heap at Heathrow, but probably wasn't now I was less quivery and more shouty.' And he'll never know how much control that took, thought Kate, as her stomach raged at her again and the tragic slide projector threw up an image of her and Giles having their Happy Meal in the City.

But *that* wasn't much fun, actually, she remembered suddenly.

'Good.'

She looked up at Dant.

'I mean, I'm sorry, and all that, but pleased you've realised that you weren't getting what you deserved from it.' Dant held her gaze quite boldly, but he was blushing.

Dant Grenfell, relationship counsellor? Moving swiftly on . . . 'How do you want to do this?' she asked.

'What?'

'The money. I said we'd split it and I think that's only fair.'

'Um, what were you thinking of doing with your half?'

Kate considered. 'What, after I've got completely pissed on champagne in Kensington Gardens, bought myself a fabulous new stereo to replace the one I'll have to give back and spent a fortune on new shoes?'

'Obviously. And the ridiculously expensive dinner at Petrus.'

Isobel, the soon-to-be houseowner had made her thoughts very clear on what Kate should do with her money, and although Kate had scoffed at the time, unfortunately now it made a lot of sense. 'Um, I suppose I should put it down as a deposit on a flat, if Cress is kicking us out. I won't get much of a mortgage on my salary, so I suppose I should make the most of such a big lump sum. God, isn't that boring? What are you smiling about?'

'The fact that you've gone from "I'm moving out in four months' time" to "I'm buying a flat now because house prices are going mad in London".'

'Happens to us all,' said Kate, grimly. 'The aging process.'

Dant broke off a bit of Toblerone and chewed it. 'Well,' he began, rather more hesitantly than normal, 'we don't *have* to split it. We could . . . get a place together. Since we both have to move out. And we might as well double the cash we can spend. We can get a lawyer on to it. And you don't have to marry me.'

Kate looked at him. It did make perfect sense. Except for the fact that it would probably result in a tragic carving knife double death shocker before they'd got unpacked.

'And how are you planning to fill up your days?' she enquired. 'Keeping the place nice for when the breadwinner comes home? Bit of light Hoovering? Some dusting? Will I have to give you housekeeping money?'

'No,' said Dant defensively. 'I've decided to write. I don`t` see why Cress should have all the glory when I'm the one with the talent. And we can be in those sick-making "Me and My Sibling" articles in the Sunday supplements. Anna can write about us.'

He looked really cross, but strangely like a normal person. Kate wondered what it was that was making him look so normal and then realised it was the fact that he appeared to have some energy going on somewhere inside. It suited him. He was never going to be driven like Giles, but at least he seemed to have engaged first gear.

'Wow!' she said. 'You go, girlfriend!' She leaned across the table to give him a high five, but Dant caught her hand and, with surprising strength, pulled her towards him. Kate had a millisecond to recognise what was going on – and register the fact that her jumper had trailed all the way through the butter dish – before her mouth made contact with his.

Dant tasted of Toblerone and red wine and tobacco, and the pricklings of stubble – that only minutes before she had been thinking looked Mr Darcy-esque but could do with a shave – scratched her cheek in a not unpleasant way. To her surprise, Kate felt her own hand reaching up urgently and tangling in his hair, pulling him closer, while the other hand reached round his shoulders. She could feel the soft down on the back of his neck and shuddered at the thought of how hairy he must be. He did not attempt to ram his tongue down her throat, but kissed her with the kind of passion that made her realise how much more he could be reining in.

Dant broke off suddenly and Kate was left gasping, halfway across the kitchen table and completely lost inside.

They looked at each other without speaking. Kate saw Dant's dark eyes moving in a rapid triangle of desire round her face, flickering from her eyes to her mouth and back to her eyes. It was as though a screen had gone back, and there

...ont of her. Obvious and surprising at the same
... y Mary, she thought.

..., that was probably a bit insensitive,' he said eventu-
... 'So soon after ditching your man and all.'

'Dante, you don't have to pretend you've had a personality transplant,' said Kate, wiping her mouth discreetly.
Damn, did that mean she wouldn't be able to try it again
without looking like a complete slut? The blood scorching
round her body stopped and screamed in protest at the idea
of never feeling that rush of sensation again. Maybe she *was*
a complete slut. Because thoughts of Giles and even poor
Harry seemed to have evaporated from her mind as though
they'd never been there. Like rain off marble. 'You forget
that I know what you're like.'

'This flat,' he said, looking directly at her. 'We'll move in
as flatmates, yeah?'

'Of course.' Kate stared straight back boldly. So what if he
could look straight inside her? 'Anything else would be
asking for trouble.'

'Of course.'

There was a polite pause.

'Flat-on-your-back mates,' said Dant under his breath.

Kate widened her eyes in horror, but couldn't stop a very
dirty laugh sneaking out. She wanted to laugh and laugh and
laugh.

'Kate Craig! You filthy slapper!'

She held up her hands as he gave her a look of moral outrage. 'It's just a backlash to my immense sense of personal
loss. I'm laughing through the pain. Don't read anything
into it.'

'Yearight,' said Dant.

'Yeah. Right,' said Kate.

'Yearight.'

'Yeah. Right.'

'Yearight.'

They were edging closer and closer over the table, and the

distance between their faces was diminishing rapidly. Kate felt as though she was being dragged by a magnet: she was barely aware of anything except Dant's half-satirical, half-hungry mouth. With a sweep of his arm, he cleared the surface of dirty washing and teacups, which clattered noisily on to the floor.

'You've seen too many films,' observed Kate sarcastically. But she couldn't stop edging closer to Dant's parted lips.

'And you talk in song lyrics.'

'Yearight.'

'Yeah. Right.'

'Yearight.' Kate noticed Dant's teeth for the first time; shiny and sharp. The warm smell of his breath so close to hers made her miss a sudden breath and she closed her eyes.

'Yeah. Right.'

'Yeah . . .'

Kate heard Harry's door being opened and jerked back rapidly. Dant, with his back to the door, didn't hear, and the shock ricocheting across his face was painful when Harry said, 'Can we dial out for a Chinese? I feel like getting wrecked on MSG and Stella.'

Good, thought Kate, straightening her hair self-consciously as Dant bounced back on his heels. About time he started finding out about nerves.

She flicked a look from underneath her lashes at him, but his face was impassive again, if shell-shocked. Well, that's three of us then, she thought.

Kate picked up Cress's car keys which were still on the table. Might as well make the most of the Mini before the wicked witch blew back into town. She slung her bag over her shoulder and went to put her arm around Harry. He felt very like Mike, to hug. And, as with Mike, she knew instinctively not to offer too much sympathy. Instead she hugged him hard.

He squeezed her arm miserably but said nothing.

'Why don't we take Cress's car back and have supper in Chinatown? On me,' she said.

Harry, 'you've had a terrible weekend with Giles
at. On me.'

said Dant, grabbing his coat. 'Looks like I'm the only
with anything to celebrate round here, so supper's on
me.'

'Yeah,' said Harry, sarcastically. 'Right.'

'No, really,' said Kate. She gave Harry's arm an affectionate
squeeze and looked up secretly at Dant. For the first time,
there was no hostility in his eyes. Just confusion. Very Rose
Ann. 'It's on me.'